PHILIP ROTH

PHILIP ROTH

NOVELS 1967–1972

When She Was Good
Portnoy's Complaint
Our Gang
The Breast

THE LIBRARY OF AMERICA

When She Was Good copyright © 1967 by Philip Roth. *Portnoy's
Complaint* copyright © 1967, 1968, 1969 by Philip Roth. Published
by arrangement with Random House Trade Publishing, a
division of Random House, Inc.

Our Gang copyright © 1971 by Philip Roth. Published by
arrangement with the author, c/o The Wylie Agency, Inc. Prefaces
to *Our Gang* copyright © 1973, 1974 by Philip Roth and reprinted
by permission of the author.

The Breast copyright © 1972 by Philip Roth. Reprinted by
arrangement with Farrar, Straus & Giroux.

The paper used in this publication meets the
minimum requirements of the American National Standard for
Information Sciences—Permanence of Paper for Printed
Library Materials, ANSI Z39.48—1984.

Distributed to the trade
in the United States by Penguin Putnam Inc.
and in Canada by Penguin Books Canada Ltd.

Library of Congress Catalog Number: 2005040917
For cataloging information, see end of Notes.
ISBN 1–931082–80–4

―――――

First Printing
The Library of America—158

Ross Miller
wrote the Chronology and Notes
for this volume

Contents

When She Was Good   I

Portnoy's Complaint 227

Our Gang 469

The Breast 601

Chronology 645

Note on the Texts 656

Notes 658

WHEN SHE WAS GOOD

To my brother Sandy;

to my friends Alison Bishop, Bob Brustein, George Elliott, Mary Emma Elliott, Howard Stein, and Mel Tumin;

and to Ann Mudge:

For words spoken and deeds done

I

Nοτ to be rich, not to be famous, not to be mighty, not even to be happy, but to be civilized—that was the dream of his life. What the qualities of such a life were he could not have articulated when he left his father's house, or shack, in the northern woods of the state; his plan was to travel all the way down to Chicago to find out. He knew for sure what he didn't want, and that was to live like a savage. His own father was a fierce and ignorant man—a trapper, then a lumberman, and at the end of his life, a watchman at the iron mines. His mother was a hard-working woman with a slavish nature who could never conceive of wanting anything other than what she had; or if she did, if she was really other than she seemed, she felt it was not prudent to speak of her desires in front of her husband.

One of Willard's strongest boyhood recollections is of the time a full-blooded Chippewa squaw came to their cabin with a root for his sister to chew when Ginny was incandescent with scarlet fever. Willard was seven and Ginny was one and the squaw, as Willard tells it today, was over a hundred. The delirious little girl did not die of the disease, though Willard was later to understand his father to believe it would have been better if she had. In only a few years they were to discover that poor little Ginny could not learn to add two and two, or to recite in their order the days of the week. Whether this was a consequence of the fever or she had been born that way, nobody was ever to know.

Willard never forgot the brutality of that occurrence, which for him lay in the fact that nothing was to be done, for all that what was happening was happening to a one-year-old child.

What was happening—this was more his sense of it at the time —was even deeper than his eyes . . . In the process of discovering his personal attractiveness, the seven-year-old had lately discovered that what someone had at first denied him would sometimes be conceded if only he looked into the other's eyes long enough for the honesty and intensity of his desire to be appreciated—for it to be understood that it wasn't just something he wanted but something he *needed.* His success, though meager at home, was considerable at the school in Iron City, where the young lady teacher had taken a great liking to the effervescent, good-humored and bright little boy. The night Ginny lay moaning in her crib Willard did everything he could to catch his father's attention, but the man only continued spooning down his dinner. And when finally he spoke, it was to tell the child to stop shuffling and gaping and to eat his food. But Willard could not swallow a single mouthful. Again he concentrated, again he brought all his emotion up into his eyes, wished with all his heart—and a pure selfless wish too, nothing for himself; never would he wish anything for himself again—and fixed his plea on his mother. But all she did was to turn away and cry.

Later, when his father stepped out of the shack and his mother took the dishes to the tub, he moved across the darkened room to the corner where Ginny lay. He put his hand into the crib. The cheek he touched felt like a sack of hot water. Down by the baby's burning toes he found the root the Indian woman had brought to them that morning. Carefully he wrapped Ginny's fingers around it, but they unbent the moment he let go. He picked up the root and pressed it to her lips. "Here," he said, as though beckoning to an animal to eat from his hand. He was forcing it between her gums when the door opened. "You—let her be, get away," and so, helpless, he went off to his bed, and had, at seven, his first terrifying inkling that there were in the universe forces even more immune to his charm, even more remote from his desires, even more estranged from human need and feeling, than his own father.

—

Ginny lived with her parents until the end of her mother's life. Then Willard's father, an old hulk of a thing by this time, moved into a room in Iron City, and Ginny was taken to

Beckstown, off in the northwestern corner of the state, where the home for the feeble-minded used to be. It was nearly a month before the news of what his father had done reached Willard. Over his own wife's objections, he got into the car that very evening and drove most of the night. At noon the following day he returned home with Ginny—not to Chicago, but to the town of Liberty Center, which is a hundred and fifty miles down the river from Iron City, and as far south as Willard had gotten when at the age of eighteen he had decided to journey out into the civilized world.

Since the war the country town that Liberty Center used to be has given way more and more to the suburb of Winnisaw it will eventually become. But when Willard first came to settle, there was not even a bridge across the Slade River connecting Liberty Center on the east shore to the county seat on the west; to get to Winnisaw, you had to take a ferry ride from the landing, or in deep winter, walk across the ice. Liberty Center was a town of small white houses shaded by big elms and maples, with a bandstand in the middle of Broadway, its main street. Bounded on the west by the pale flow of river, it opens out on the east to dairy country, which in the summer of 1903, when Willard arrived, was so deeply green it reminded him—a joke for the amusement of the young—of a fellow he once saw at a picnic who had eaten a pound of bad potato salad.

Until he came down from the north, "outside of town" had always meant to him the towering woods rolling up to Canada, and the weather roaring down, waves of wind, of hail, of rain and snow. And "town" meant Iron City, where the logs were brought to be milled and the ore to be dumped into boxcars, the clanging, buzzing, swarming, dusty frontier town to which he walked each schoolday—or in winter, when he went off in a raw morning dimness, ran—through the woods aswarm with bear and wolf. So at the sight of Liberty Center, its quiet beauty, its serene order, its gentle summery calm, all that had been held in check in him, all that tenderness of heart that had been for eighteen years his secret burden, even at times his shame, came streaming forth. If ever there was a place where life could be less bleak and harsh and cruel than the life he had known as a boy, if ever there was a place where a man did not have to live like a brute, where he did not have to be reminded at every turn that something in the world either did not like mankind, or did not even know of its existence, it was here. Liberty Center! Oh, sweet name! At least for him, for he was indeed free at last of that terrible tyranny of cruel men and cruel nature.

He found a room; then he found a job—he took an examination and scored high enough to become postal clerk; then he found a wife, a strong-minded and respectable girl from a proper family; and then he had a child; and then one day—the fulfillment, he discovered, of a very deep desire—he bought a house of his own, with a front porch and a backyard: downstairs a parlor, a dining room, a kitchen and a bedroom; upstairs two bedrooms more and the bath. A back bathroom was built downstairs in 1915, six years after the birth of his daughter, and following his promotion to assistant postmaster of the town. In 1962 the sidewalk out front had to be replaced, a whacking expense for a man now on a government pension, but one that had to be, for the pavement had buckled in half a dozen places and become a hazard to passers-by. Indeed, to this very day, when his famous agility, or jumpiness, has all but disappeared; when several times in an afternoon he finds himself in a chair which he cannot remember having settled into, awakening from a sleep he cannot remember needing; when at night to undo his laces produces a groan he does not even hear; when in his bed he tries for minutes on end to roll his fingers into a fist, and sometimes must go off to sleep having failed in the attempt; when at the end of each month he looks at the fresh new calendar page and understands that there on the pantry door is the month and the year in which he will most assuredly die, that one of those big black numerals over which his eye is slowly moving is the date upon which he is to disappear forever from the world—he nevertheless continues to attend as quickly as he is able to a weak porch rail, or the dripping of a spigot in the bathroom, or a tack come loose from the runner in the hall—and all this to maintain not only the comfort of those who live with him yet, but the dignity of all too, such as it is.

—

One afternoon in November of 1954, a week before Thanksgiving, and just at dusk, Willard Carroll drove out to Clark's

Hill, parked down by the fence, and on foot climbed the path until he reached the family plot. The wind was growing colder and stronger by the minute, so that by the time he had reached the top of the hill, the bare trees whose limbs had only been clicking together when he left the car were now giving off a deep groaning sound. The sky swirling overhead had a strange light to it, though below, it already appeared to be night. Of the town he was able to discern little more than the black line of the river, and the head lamps of the cars as they moved along Water Street toward the Winnisaw Bridge.

As though this of all places had been his destination, Willard sank down onto the cold block of bench that faced the two stones, raised the collar of his red hunting jacket, pulled on the flaps of his cap, and there, before the graves of his sister Ginny and his granddaughter Lucy, and the rectangles reserved for the rest of them, he waited. It began to snow.

Waiting for what? The stupidity of his behavior dawned quickly. The bus he had left the house to meet would be pulling up back of Van Harn's store in a few minutes; from it Whitey was going to disembark, suitcase in hand, whether his father-in-law sat here in a freezing cemetery or not. Everything was in readiness for the homecoming, which Willard had himself helped to bring about. So what now? Back out? Change his mind? Let Whitey find himself another sponsor—or sucker? That's right, oh, that's it exactly—let it get dark, let it get cold, and just sit it out in the falling snow . . . And the bus will pull in and the fellow will get off and head into the waiting room, all brimming over with how he has taken someone in once again—only to find that this time no sucker named Willard is waiting in the waiting room.

But at home Berta was preparing a dinner for four; on the way out of the kitchen door to the garage, Willard had kissed her on the cheek—"It's going to be all right, Mrs. Carroll," but he might have been talking to himself for all the response he received. As a matter of fact, that's who he *was* talking to. He had backed the car down the driveway and looked up to the second floor, where his daughter Myra was rushing around her room so as to be bathed and dressed when her father and her husband came through the door. But saddest of all, most confusing of all, a little light was on in Lucy's room. Only the week before, Myra had pushed the bed from one end of the room to the other, and taken down the curtains that had hung there all those years, and then gone out and bought a new bedspread, so that at least it no longer looked like the room in which Lucy had slept, or tried to sleep, the last night she had ever spent in the house. Of course, on the subject of how and where Whitey was to spend his nights, what could Willard do but be silent? Secretly it was a relief that Whitey was to be "on trial" in this way—if only it could have been in a bed other than that one.

And over in Winnisaw, Willard's old friend and lodge brother Bud Doremus was expecting Whitey to show up for work at his hardware supply house first thing Monday morning. The arrangements with Bud dated back to the summer, when Willard had agreed to accept his son-in-law once again into his house, if only for a while. "Only for a while" was the guarantee he had made to Berta; because she was right, this just could not be a repetition of 1934, with someone in need coming for a short stay and managing somehow to stretch it out to sixteen years of living off the fat of another fellow's land, which wasn't so fat either. But of course, said Willard, that other fellow did happen to be the father of the man's wife— And just what does that mean, Berta asked, that it is going to be sixteen years again this time too? Because you are certainly still father to his wife; that hasn't changed any. Berta, I don't imagine for one thing that I have got sixteen years left to me, first of all. Well, said she, neither do I, which might be just another reason not even to begin. You mean just let them go off on their own? Before I even know whether the man really is changed over or not? asked Willard. And what if he really has reformed, once and for all? Oh sure, said Berta. Well, sneering at the idea may be your answer, Berta, but it just does not happen to be mine. You mean it does not happen to be Myra's, she said. I am open to opinion from all sides, he said, I will not deny that, why should I? Well then, maybe you ought to be open to mine, Berta said, till before we start this tragedy one more time. Berta, he said, till January the first I am giving the man a place to get his bearings in. January the first, she said, but which year? The year two thousand?

—

Seated alone up in the cemetery, the tree limbs rising in the wind, and the dark of the town seemingly being drawn up into the sky as the first snow descended, Willard was remembering the days of the Depression, and those nights too, when sometimes he awoke in the pitch-black and did not know whether to tremble or be glad that someone in need of him was asleep in every bed of the house. It had been only six months after going off to Beckstown to rescue Ginny from her life among the feeble-minded that he had opened the door to Myra and Whitey and their little three-year-old daughter, Lucy. Oh, he can still remember the tiny, spirited, golden-haired child that Lucy had been—how lively and bright and sweet. He can remember when she was first learning to care for herself, how she used to try to pass what she knew on to her Aunt Ginny, but how Ginny, the poor creature, was barely able to learn to perform the simplest body functions, let alone mastering the niceties of tea parties, or the mystery of rolling two little white socks together to make a ball.

Oh, yes, he can remember it all. Ginny, a fully grown, fully developed woman, looking down with that pale dopey face for Lucy to tell her what to do next—and little Lucy, who was then no bigger than a bird. Behind the happy child, Ginny would go running across the lawn, the toes of her high shoes pointing out, and taking quick little steps to keep up—a strangely beautiful scene, but a melancholy one, too, for it was proof not only of their love for each other, but of the fact that in Ginny's brain so many things were melted together that in real life are separate and distinct. She seemed always to think that Lucy was somehow herself—that is, more Ginny, or the rest of Ginny, or the Ginny people called Lucy. When Lucy ate an ice cream, Ginny's eyes would get all happy and content, as though she were eating it herself. Or if as a punishment Lucy was put to bed early, Ginny, too, would sob and go off to sleep like one doomed . . . a different kind of scene, which would leave the rest of the family subdued and unhappy.

When it was time for Lucy to start school, Ginny started too, only she wasn't supposed to. She would follow Lucy all the way there, and then stand outside the first floor where the kindergarten was and call for the child. At first the teacher changed Lucy's desk in the hope that if Ginny didn't see her she would grow tired, or bored, and go home. But Ginny's voice only grew louder, and as a result Willard had to give her a special talking-to, saying that if she didn't let Lucy alone he was going to have to lock a bad girl whose name was Virginia in her room for the whole day. But the punishment proved toothless, both in the threat and the execution: the moment they let her out of her room to go to the toilet, she was running in her funny ducklike way down the stairs and off to the school. And he couldn't keep her locked up anyway. It wasn't to tie her to a tree in the backyard that he had brought his sister home to live in his house. She was his closest living relative, he told Berta, when she suggested some long kind of leash as a possible solution; she was his baby sister to whom something terrible had happened when she was only a one-year-old child. But Lucy, he was reminded—as if he had to be—was Myra's daughter and his grandchild, and how could she ever learn anything in school if Ginny was going to stand outside the classroom all day long, singing out in her flat foghorn of a voice, "*Loo*—cy . . . *Loo*–cy . . . ?"

Finally the day came which made no sense whatsoever. Because Ginny wouldn't stop standing outside a grade-school classroom calling out a harmless name, Willard was driving her back to the state home in Beckstown. The night before, the principal had telephoned the house again, and for all his politeness, indicated that things had gone about as far as they could. It was Willard's contention that it was probably only a matter of a few weeks more before Ginny got the idea, but the principal made it clear to Mr. Carroll, as he had a moment earlier to the little girl's parents, that either Ginny had to be restrained once and for all, or Lucy would have to be kept away from the school, which of course would be in violation of state law.

On the long drive to Beckstown, Willard tried over and over again to somehow make Ginny understand the situation, but no matter how he explained, no matter how many examples he used—look, there's a cow, Ginny, and there's another cow; and there's a tree, and there's another tree—he could not get her to see that Ginny was one person and Lucy was someone else. Around dinnertime they arrived. Taking her by the hand, he led her up the overgrown path to the long one-story wooden building where she was to spend the rest of her days. And why? Because she could not understand the most basic fact of human life, the fact that I am me and you are you.

In the office the director welcomed Ginny back to the Beckstown Vocational School. An attendant piled a towel, a washrag and a blanket into her outstretched arms and steered her to the women's wing. Following the attendant's instructions, she unrolled the mattress and began to make the bed. "But this is what my father did!" thought Willard. "Sent her away!" . . . even as the director was saying to him, "That's the way it is, Mr. Carroll. People thinking they can take 'em home, and then coming to bring 'em back. Don't feel bad, sir, it's just what happens."

Among her own kind Ginny lived without incident for three years more; then an epidemic of influenza swept through the home one winter, and before her brother could even be notified of her illness, she was dead.

When Willard drove up to Iron City to tell his father the news, the old man listened, and received what he heard without so much as a sigh; not a single human thing to say; not a tear for this creature of his own flesh and blood, who had lived and died beyond the reaches of human society. To die alone, said Willard, without family, without friends, without a home . . . The old man only nodded, as though his heartsick son were reporting an everyday occurrence.

Within the year the old man himself fell over dead with a brain hemorrhage. At the small funeral he arranged for his father up in Iron City, Willard found himself at the graveside suddenly and inexplicably stricken with that sense of things that can descend upon the tender-hearted, even at the death of an enemy—that surely the spirit had been deeper, and the life more tragic, than he had ever imagined.

—

He brushed the snow off the shoulder of his jacket and stamped away a tingling that was beginning in his right foot. He looked at his watch. "Well, maybe the bus will be late. And if it's not, he can wait. It won't kill him."

He was remembering again: of all things, the Independence Day Fair held in Iron City—the Fourth of July almost sixty years back when he had won eight of the twelve track events

and so set a record that stands till today. Willard knows this because he always manages to get hold of an Iron City paper
every fifth of July just so as to take a look and see. He can still
remember running home through the woods when that glorious day was over, rushing up the dirt road and into the cabin,
dropping onto the table all the medals he had been awarded;
he remembers how his father hefted each one in his hand, then
led him back outside to where some of the neighbors were
gathered, and told Willard's mother to give them an "on your
mark." In the race that followed, some two hundred yards, the
father outdistanced the son by a good twenty feet. "But I've
been running all day," thought Willard. "I ran the whole way
home—"

"Well, who's the fastest?" one of the bystanders teased the
boy as he started back to the cabin.

Inside, his father said, "Next time don't forget."

"I won't," said the child . . .

Well, there was the story. And the moral? What exactly were
his memories trying to tell him?

Well, the moral, if there is one, came later, years later. He
was sitting in the parlor one evening, across from his young
son-in-law, who had stretched himself out with the paper and
was about to munch down on an apple and so let the comfortable evening begin, when suddenly Willard couldn't bear the
sight of him. Four years of free room and board! Four years of
floundering and getting on his feet again! And there he was,
on his back, in Willard's parlor, eating Willard's food! Suddenly Willard wanted to pull the apple out of Whitey's hand
and tell him to pick up and get out. "The holiday is over! Scat!
Go! Where, I don't care!" Instead he decided that it was a
good night to give his mementos a look-through.

In the kitchen pantry he found a piece of soft cloth and
Berta's silver polish. Then from beneath the wool shirts in his
bureau he removed the cigar box full of keepsakes. Settling
onto the bed, he opened the box and sorted through. He
pushed everything first to one side, then to the other; in the
end he laid each item out on the bedspread: photos, newspaper clippings . . . The medals were gone.

When he came back into the living room, Whitey had fallen
off to sleep. The snow drifts, Willard saw, were floating up to

obscure the glass; across the street the houses looked to be going down into the rising white waves. "But it can't be," thought Willard. "It just can't. I am jumping to a rash conclusion. I am—"

During his lunch hour the next day, he decided to take a walk down to the river and back, stopping on the way at Rankin's pawnshop. Ha-haa-ing all the while, as though the whole affair had been a family prank, he recovered the medals.

After dinner that night he invited Whitey to come with him for a brisk walk downtown. What he said to the young fellow, once they were out of sight of the house, was that it was absolutely and positively beyond his understanding how a man could take the belongings of another man, go into a person's private belongings and just *take* something, particularly something of sentimental value; nevertheless, if he could receive from Whitey certain assurances about the future, he would be willing to chalk up this unfortunate incident to a combination of hard times and immature judgment. Pretty damn immature judgment too. But then, no one deserved to be discarded from the human race on the basis of one stupid act—a stupid act you might expect of a ten-year-old, by the way, and not a fellow who was twenty-eight, going to be twenty-nine. However, the medals were back where they belonged, and if he were given an ironclad promise that nothing like this would ever happen again, and furthermore, if Whitey promised to cut out immediately this new business of whiskey drinking, then he would consider the matter closed. Here he was, after all, a fellow who for three years running had been third baseman on the Selkirk High School baseball team; a young man with the build of a prizefighter, good-looking too—Willard said all this right out—and what was his intention, to wreck the healthy body the good Lord had blessed him with? Respect for his body alone ought to make him stop; but if that didn't work, then there was respect for his family, and for his own human soul, damn it. It was up to Whitey entirely: all he had to do was turn over a new leaf, and as far as Willard was concerned, the incident, stupid, mean and silly as it was, beyond human comprehension as it was, would be completely forgotten. Otherwise, there were no two ways about it, something drastic was going to have to be done.

So overcome was he with shame and gratitude that first all the young man could do was take hold of Willard's hand and pump it up and down, all the while with tears glistening in his eyes. Then he set out to explain. It had happened in the fall, when the circus had come to the armory down in Fort Kean. Right off Lucy had started talking a mile a minute about the elephants and the clowns, but when Whitey looked in his pocket he found only pennies, and not too many of them either. So he thought if he borrowed the medals, and then returned them a few weeks later . . . But here Willard remembered just who it was that had taken Lucy down to the circus, and Myra and Whitey and Berta too. None other than himself. When he pointed out this fact, Whitey said yes, yes, he was coming to that; he was, he admitted, saving the most shameful for the last. "I suppose I am just a coward, Willard, but it's just hard to say the worst first." "Say it anyway, boy. Make a clean breast of the whole thing."

Well, confessed Whitey, as they turned off Broadway and started back home, after having borrowed the medals he was so appalled and shocked with himself that instead of using the money as he had intended, he had gone straight over to Earl's Dugout and made himself numb on whiskey, hoping thereby to obliterate the memory of the stupid, vicious thing he had just done. He knew he was confessing to terrible selfishness, followed by plain idiocy, but that was exactly how it had happened; and to tell the truth, it was all as mysterious to him as it was to anyone else. It had been the last week of September, just after old man Tucker had had to lay off half the shop . . . No, no—removing a calendar from his wallet, studying it under the front-porch light as they both stood stamping the snow off their boots—as a matter of fact it was the first week of October, he told Willard, who earlier in the day had had the date fixed for him by the clerk at Rankin's as just two weeks back.

But by this time they were already inside the door. Knitting by the fire was Berta; sitting on the couch, holding Lucy in her lap, was Myra—reading to the child from her poem book before sending her off to sleep. No sooner did Lucy see her Daddy than she slid from her mother's lap and came running to drag him off to the dining room, to play their nightly "yump" game. It had been going on for a year, ever since Whitey's old father had seen the tiny child go leaping from the dining-room window seat down to the rug. "Hey," the big farmer had called out to the others, "Lucy yumped!" That was how he pronounced it, for all that he had been a citizen of this country for forty years. After the old man's death it became Whitey's task to stand admiringly before his daughter, and after each leap, sing out those words she just adored to hear. "Hey, Lucy yumped! Yump again, Lucy-Goosie. Two more yumps and off to bed." "No! Three!" "Three yumps and off to bed!" "No, four!" "Come on, yump, yump, and stop complaining, you little yumping goose! Hey, Lucy is about to yump—Lucy is ready to yump—ladies and gentlemen, Lucy has just yumped once again!"

So what could he do? In the face of that scene, what on earth could he possibly do? If after the long deliberation of that afternoon he had decided to consider Whitey's theft forgivable, was he now going to bother to catch his son-in-law in a petty face-saving lie? Only why, why if Whitey felt so depraved after taking the medals, why in hell didn't he put them back? Wasn't that just about the easiest thing for him to do? Now why hadn't he thought to ask him that? Oh, but he was so busy trying to be rough and tough and talking no-nonsense and letting there be no two ways about it, and so on, that the question hadn't even passed through his mind. Hey, you, why didn't you put my medals back if you felt so awful about it?

But by this time Whitey was carrying Lucy up the stairs on his shoulders—"Yump, two, three, four"—and he himself was smiling at Myra, saying yes, yes, the men had had a good bracing walk.

—

Myra. Myra. Without a doubt she had been the most adorable child a parent could dream of having. Mention a thing girls do, and Myra was doing it while the other little girls were still taking from the bottle. Always she was practicing something feminine: crocheting, music, poetry . . . Once at a school program she recited a patriotic poem she had written all by herself, and when it was finished some of the men in the audience had stood up and applauded. And so beautifully behaved was she that when the ladies came to the house for a meeting of the Eastern Star—back when they were still a family of three and Berta had the time to be active—they used to say it was perfectly all right with them if little Myra sat in a chair and watched.

Oh, Myra! A pure delight to behold—always tall and slender, with her soft brown hair, and her skin like silk, and with Willard's gray eyes, which on her were really something; sometimes he imagined that his sister Ginny might have been much like Myra in appearance—fragile, soft-spoken, shy, with the bearing of a princess—if only it hadn't been for the scarlet fever. Back when she was a child the very frailty of his daughter's bones could bring Willard almost to tears with awe, especially in the evening when he sat looking over the top of his paper at her as she practiced her piano lesson. There were times when it seemed to him as though nothing in the world could so make a man want to do good in life as the sight of a daughter's thin little wrists and ankles.

—

Earl's Dugout of Buddies. If only they had knocked that place down years and years ago! If only it had never even been . . . At Willard's request they had agreed to stop letting Whitey drink himself into a stupor at the Elks, and at Stanley's Tavern too (now under new management—the thought occurred to him as the streetlights went on down in town), but for every human or even semi-human bartender, another (named Earl) was actually *amused* to take the pay check of a husband and a father and cash it for him. And the ironic part was that in that whole so-called Dugout of Buddies there was probably never a man who was one-tenth the worker, or the husband, or the father that Whitey was—that is, when things weren't overwhelming him. Unfortunately, however, circumstances seemed always to conspire against him at just those times, rarely more than a month at a stretch, when he was suffering through a bad siege of what you finally had to call by its rightful name—lack of character. Probably that Friday night he would at worst have weaved up the walk, thrown open the door, made some insane declaration, and dropped into bed with his clothes on—that and no more if circumstances, or fate, or whatever you wanted to call it, hadn't arranged for his first vision upon entering the house to be his wife Myra, soaking those fragile little feet of hers in a pan of water. Then he must have seen Lucy bent over the dining table, and understood (as he could understand, down in that alcoholic fog, if he believed an insult was involved) that she had pushed back the lace luncheon cloth and was doing her homework downstairs so that her mother wouldn't have to face the dragon alone when he returned.

Willard and Berta had gone off to play their Friday rummy. Driving to the Erwins' that night, he agreed that this time they were staying clear through to coffee and cake, like normal people, no matter what. If Willard wanted to go home early, said Berta, that was his business. She herself worked hard all week, and had few pleasures, and she simply would not cut short her night out because her son-in-law had come to prefer drinking whiskey in a musty bar at the end of the day to eating a home-cooked dinner with his family. There was a solution to the problem, and Willard knew very well what it was. But she would tell him one thing—it wasn't giving up the Friday night rummy game and the company of her old friends.

But Myra soaking her feet . . . Something told him he shouldn't go off leaving her that way. Not that she was suffering so from the pain, not as she did in later years with her migraines. It was just the *picture* that he didn't like somehow. "You should sit down, Myra. I don't see why you have to stand so much." "I do sit, Daddy. Of course I sit." "Then how come you're having this feet trouble." "It's not trouble." "It's from giving them lessons all afternoon long, Myra, standing over that piano." "Daddy, no one stands over a piano." "Then where did this feet business come from . . . ?" "Daddy, please." What more could he do? He called into the dining room, "Good night, Lucy." When she failed to respond, he walked over to where she sat writing in her notebook and touched her hair. "What's got your tongue, young lady? No good night?" "Good night," she mumbled, without bothering to look up.

Oh, he knew he ought not to leave. But Berta was already sitting out in the car. No, he just did not like the look of this scene. "You don't want to soak them too long, Myra." "Oh,

Daddy, have a nice time," she said, and so at last he went out the door and down to the car to be told that it had taken him five full minutes to say a simple thing like good night.

Well, it was just as he had expected: when Whitey got home, he didn't like the scene either. The first suggestion he had for Myra was that she might at least pull the shades down so that everybody who walked by didn't have to see what a suffering martyr she was. When in her panic she didn't move, he pulled on one to show her how and it came clear off the fixture. She had only taken on all those piano students (seven years earlier, he neglected to add) so as to turn herself into a hag anyway, to cause him, if she could manage it—this, waving the shade in his hand—to start running around with other women, and then have that to cry over as well as her poor crippled toesies. Why she taught piano was the same damn reason she wouldn't go down with him to Florida and let him start a brand-new life down there. Out of disrespect for what he was!

She tried to tell him what she had told her father—that she believed there was no essential connection between her feet and her job—but he would not hear of it. No, she would rather sit up here with her poor toesies, and listen while everybody told her what a no-good rotten s.o.b. she had for a husband, just because he liked to have a drink once in a while.

There was apparently nothing that a man shouldn't say to a woman—even to one he hates, and the fact was that Whitey loved her, adored her, worshipped her—that he didn't say to Myra. Then, as if a torn shade and a broken fixture and all those garbled insults weren't enough for one night, he picked up the dishpan full of warm water and Epsom salts, and for no rational reason in the world, poured it out on the rug.

Most of what happened subsequently Willard learned from a sympathetic lodge brother who was on duty in the squad car that night. Apparently the police tried as best they could to make it look friendly and not like an out-and-out arrest: they drove up without the siren blowing, parked out of the glow of the street lamp, and stood patiently in the hallway while Whitey worked at buttoning up his jacket. Then they led him down the front steps and along the path to the patrol car so that to the neighbors in the windows it might appear that the three men were just off for one of those bracing strolls, two of them wearing pistols and cartridge belts. They were not so much holding him down as up, and trying to joke him along some too, when Whitey, using all his physical strength, broke from between them. In the first moment no one watching could figure out what he was doing. His body folded once in half, so that for a moment he seemed to be eating the snow; then with a jerk he straightened up, and swaying as if in a wind, heaved an armful of snow toward the house.

The powder fell upon her hair and her face and the shoulders of her sweater; but for all that she was only fifteen, and with her upturned nose and her straight blond hair looked to be no more than ten, she did not so much as flinch; she stood as she was, one loafer on the bottom step and one on the walk, and a finger in her schoolbook—all ready, it seemed, to return to her studies which she had interrupted only to dial the station house. "Stone!" Whitey shouted. "Pure stone!" And here he made his lunge. Willard's lodge brother, frozen till then by the scene—by Lucy, he said, more than by Whitey, whose kind he'd seen before—leaped to his duty. "Nelson, it's your own kid!" Whereupon the drunk, either remembering that he was father to the girl, or hoping to forget that connection for good, evaded the policeman's grasp and went ahead and did apparently all it was he had intended to do in the first place: he pitched himself face-down into the snow.

The following morning Willard sat Lucy down first thing and gave her a talking-to.

"Honey, I know you have been through a lot in the last twenty-four hours. I know you have been through a lot in your whole life that would have been better for you never to have seen. But, Lucy, I have got to ask you something. I have got to make something very clear. Now, I want to ask why, when you saw what was happening here last night—Lucy, look at me—why didn't you phone me out at the Erwins'?"

She shook her head.

"Well, you knew we were out there, didn't you?"

To the floor she nodded.

"And the number is right there in the book. Well, isn't that so, Lucy?"

"I didn't think of it."

"But what you did think of, young lady—*look at me!*"

"I wanted him to *stop*!"

"But calling the jail, Lucy—"

"I called for somebody to make him stop!"

"But why didn't you call *me*? I want you to answer that question."

"Because."

"Because why?"

"Because you can't."

"I *what*?"

"Well," she said, backing away, "you don't . . ."

"Now sit down, now come back here, and listen to me. First thing—that's it, sit!—whether you know it or not, I am not God. I am just me, that's the first thing."

"You don't have to be God."

"No backtalk, you hear me? You are just a schoolchild, and maybe, just maybe, you know, you don't know the whole story of life yet. You may think you do, but I happen to think different, and who I am is your grandfather whose house this is."

"I didn't ask to live here."

"But you do, you see! So quiet! You are never to call the jail again. They are not needed here! Is that clear?"

"The police," she whispered.

"Or the police! Is that clear or not?"

She did not answer.

"We are civilized people in this house and there are some things we do not do, and that is number one. We are not riff-raff, and you remember that. We are able to settle our own arguments, and conduct our own affairs, and we don't require the police to do it for us. I happen to be the assistant post-master of this town, young lady, in case you've forgotten. I happen to be a member in good standing of this community— and so are you."

"And what about my father? Is he in good standing too, whatever that even *means*?"

"I am not talking about him right this minute! I will get to him, all right, and without your help too. Right now I am talking about you and a few things you may not know at fifteen years of age. The way we do it in this house, Lucy, is we talk to a person. We show him the right."

"And if he doesn't know it?"

"Lucy, we do not send him to jail! That's the only point. Is it clear?"

"No!"

"Lucy, I ain't the one who is married to him, Lucy. I don't live in the same room with him, Lucy."

"So *what*?"

"So what I am saying to you is that a lot of things, a great many things, you do not know the slightest thing about."

"I know it's your house. I know you give him a home, no matter what he does to her, or says to her—"

"I give my daughter a home, that's what I do. I give you a home. I am in a situation, Lucy, and I do what I can for the people I happen to love around here."

"Well," she said, beginning to cry, "you're not the only one who does, maybe, you know."

"Oh, I know that, I know that, sweetheart. But, honey, don't you see, they're your parents."

"Then why don't they act like parents!" she cried, rushing out of the room.

Then Berta started in.

"I heard what she said to you, Willard. I heard that tone. It's what *I* get all the time."

"Well, I get it too, Berta. We all get it."

"Then what are you going to do about it? Where will it stop with her? I thought becoming a Catholic at the age of fifteen was going to be the last thing up her sleeve. Running off to a Catholic church, going up to visit nuns for a whole weekend. And now this."

"Berta, I can only say what I can say. I only got so many words, and so many different ways to say them, and after that—"

"After that," said Berta, "a good swat! Whoever in their life heard of such a thing? Making a whole household into a public scandal—"

"Berta, she lost her head. She got scared. *He* made the scandal, the damn idiot, doing what he did."

"Well, any fool could have seen it coming a mile away. Any fool can see the next thing coming too—probably involving the Federal Bureau of Investigation."

"Berta, I'll take care of it. Exaggerating don't help things at all."

"How are you going to start taking care of it, Willard? By going down to the jail and letting him out?"

"I am deciding about that right now, what I'm going to do."

"I want to remind you, Willard, while you are deciding, that Higgles were among the founders of this town. Higgles were amongst the first settlers who built this town from the ground. My grandfather Higgle built the jail, Willard—I am glad he is not alive to see who it was he built it for."

"Oh, I know all that, Berta. I appreciate all that."

"Don't you make light of my pride, Mr. Carroll. I am a person too!"

"Berta, she won't do it again."

"Won't she? Beads and saints and every kind of Catholic gimcrack she has got up in that room of hers. And now this! She's taking over here, as far as I can see."

"Berta, I have explained to you: *she got frightened.*"

"And who isn't when that barbarian goes on the warpath? In the olden days a man like that, they would put him on a rail and run him out of town."

"Well, maybe this ain't the olden days any more," he said.

"Well, more's the pity!"

Lastly Myra. His Myra.

"Myra, I am sitting here debating what to do. And I am really of two minds, I'll tell you that. What has happened here, I never thought I would ever live to see. I have spoken to Lucy. I have gotten her to promise that nothing like this is ever going to happen again."

"She promised?"

"More or less, I would say, yes. And I have just finished talking with your mother. She is at the end of her tether, Myra. I can't say that I blame her. But I believe I have made her see the light. Because her feeling, to put it blunt, is to let him sit in that jail and rot."

Myra closed her eyes, so deep, so deep in purple rings from all her secret weeping.

"But I have calmed her down," he said.

"Yes?"

"More or less, I think so. She is going to accept my judgment of the thing. Myra," he said, "it has been a long twelve-year haul. For everybody living here it has been a long struggle."

"Daddy, we're going to move, so it's over. The struggle is over."

"*What?*"

"We're going to Florida."

"Florida!"

"Where Duane can start fresh—"

"Myra, there ain't a morning of his life he can't start fresh, and right here."

"But here someone else's roof, Daddy, is over his head."

"And how come? Well, what's the answer, Myra? Where is it he is going to get the stick-to-it-iveness in Florida that he is not able to have up here? I'd like to know."

"He has relatives in Florida."

"You mean now he's going to go down and live off them?"

"Not live *off* them—"

"And suppose last night had happened in Florida. Or Oklahoma. Or wherever!"

"But it wouldn't!"

"And why not? The nice climate? The beautiful color of the sky?"

"Because he could be on his own. That's all he wants."

"Honey, it's all I want too. It's what we all want. But where is the evidence, Myra, that on his own, with a daughter, with a wife, with all the thousand responsibilities—"

"But he's such a good man." Here she began to sob. "I wake up in the night—oh, Daddy, I wake up, and 'Myra,' he says to me, 'you are the best thing I have, Myra—Myra, don't hate me.' Oh, if only we could *go*—"

—

In the middle of her very first semester, when Lucy came home at Thanksgiving time to say that she was getting married, Whitey sat himself down on the edge of the sofa in the parlor and just caved in. "But I wanted her to be a college graduate," he said, lowering his head into his hands, and the sounds that emerged from his mouth might have softened in you everything that had hardened against him, if you didn't have to wonder if that wasn't why he was making the sounds in the first place. For the first hour he wept steadily like a woman, then gaspingly like a child for another, until even though he wanted you to forgive him, you almost had to anyway, watching him have to perform that way within plain view of his own family.

And then the miracle happened. At first he looked to be sick, or maybe even about to do something to himself. It was actually frightening to see. For days on end he hardly ate, though he was there at every dinner hour; in the evening he would sit out on the front porch, refusing to speak or to come in out of the cold. Once in the middle of the night Willard heard moving in the house and came into the kitchen in his robe to see Whitey looming over a cup of coffee. "What's the trouble, Whitey, can't you sleep?" ". . . don't want to sleep." "What is it, Whitey? Why are you all dressed?" Here Whitey turned to the wall, so that all Willard could see, as his son-in-law's whole big body began to tremble, was the back of his broad shoulders and his wide powerful neck. "What is it, Whitey, what is it you are thinking of doing? Now tell me."

The day after Lucy's wedding Whitey came down to breakfast wearing a tie with his workshirt, and went off to the shop that way; at home in the evening he took out the box of brushes, rags and polish and gave his shoes a shine that looked to be professional. To Willard he said, "Want one, while I'm at it?" And so Willard handed over his shoes and sat there in his stockinged feet while the incredible happened before his very eyes.

When the weekend came Whitey whitewashed the basement and chopped practically a whole cord of wood; Willard stood at the kitchen window watching him bring down the ax in violent, regular whacks.

So that month passed, and the next, and though eventually he came out of the silent morbid mood and took up a little more his old teasing and kidding ways, there could no longer be any doubt that at long last something had happened to penetrate his heart.

That winter he grew his mustache. Apparently in the first weeks he got the usual jokes from the boys at the shop, but he just kept on with it, and by March you actually forgot how he used to look, and began to believe that the big strapping healthy misdirected boy had, at the age of forty-two, decided to become a man. More and more Willard heard himself calling him, as Berta and Myra always had, by his given name, Duane.

He actually began to behave now as Willard had had every reason to expect he would, given the eager young fellow he had been back in 1930. At that time he was already a first-rate electrician, and a pretty good carpenter too, and he had plans, ambitions, dreams. One of them was to build a house for himself and Myra, if only she would be his bride: a Cape Cod–style house with a fenced-in yard, to be built with his own hands . . . And that wasn't so far-fetched a dream either. At the age of twenty-two he seemed to have the strength and the vigor for it, and the know-how too. The way he figured it, with the exception of the plumbing (and a friend over in Winnisaw had already agreed to install the piping at cost), he could put up a whole two-story house in six months of nights and weekends. He even went ahead and plunked down a one-hundred-dollar deposit on a tract of land up at the north end, a wise move too, for what was only woods then was now Liberty Grove, the fanciest section of the town. He had plunked down a deposit, he had begun to draw up his own building plans, he was halfway into his first year of marriage, when along came national calamity—followed quickly by the birth of a daughter.

As it turned out, Whitey took the Great Depression very personally. It was as though a little baby, ready to try its first step, stands up, smiles, puts out one foot, and one of those huge iron balls such as they used to knock down whole buildings comes swinging out of nowhere and wallops him right between the eyes. In Whitey's case it took nearly ten years for him to get the nerve to stand up and even try walking again. On Monday, December 8, 1941, he took the bus down to Fort Kean to enlist in the United States Coast Guard, and was rejected for heart murmur. The following week he tried the Navy, and then his last choice, the Army. He told them how he had played three years of ball up at the old Selkirk High, but to no avail. He wound up working over in the fire-extinguisher plant in Winnisaw for the duration, and in the evenings was less and less at home and more and more at Earl's Dugout.

But now, here he was on his feet again, informing Myra that

when the school year was over she was to call the parents of her students and tell them that she was going out of the piano business. She knew as well as he did that when she had started giving lessons it was only supposed to be temporary anyway. He should never have allowed her to keep it up, even if it did mean extra dollars coming in every week. And he didn't *care* whether she didn't mind occupying herself that way or not. That wasn't the issue. The issue was, he did not require a cushion behind him to catch him if he fell. Because he wasn't falling any longer. That was the whole trouble to begin with: he had gotten himself all those props and cushions to give him a start back into the world, and all they had done was impede his progress by reminding him of the failure he had been, right off the bat. Somehow you start thinking you're a failure, and that there's nothing to do about it, and so the next thing you know there is nothing you *are* doing about it, except failing some more. Drinking, and losing jobs, and getting jobs, and drinking, and losing them . . . It's a vicious cycle, Myra.

Maybe, he said, if he had gone into the Army he would have come out of that experience a different person, with some of his confidence back. But instead he had to walk the streets of Liberty Center all those years while other men were risking their lives—and while people in town wondered how a big bruiser like Whitey Nelson had got out of the fighting and dying, and pointed a finger at him under their breath for living off his father-in-law. No, no, Myra, I know what people gossip, I know what they say—and the worst of it is, they are probably right. No, heart murmur isn't a person's fault, I know that; no, the Depression isn't a person's fault either, but this isn't the Depression any more, you know. Take a look around. This is booming prosperity. This is a new age, and this time he was not going to be left behind, not when every Tom, Dick and Harry you could think of was getting rich and making the money that was just out there for the asking. So the first thing, she was to inform those parents that she was out of the music business as of the end of the school year. And the next thing was to think about moving out of her father's house. No, not to Florida. Willard was probably right about that being so much running away from the truth. What he had begun to think about—and he wasn't going to promise right off and be made a fool of a second time—but what he had begun to think about was maybe looking into one of these prefab jobs like the kind the fellow had put up out near Clark's Hill . . .

And here Myra, who had been recounting to her father all that Duane had said, became teary-eyed, and Willard patted her back and got all filled up too, and thought to himself, "Then it has not been in vain," and the only thing that made him feel unhappy was that it all seemed to be coming about because little Lucy had gone ahead and married the wrong person for the wrong reason.

Spring. Each evening Duane would get up from the dinner table—slapping at his knees, as though just to rise to his feet was a strengthening experience in itself—and pitting the new self against the old temptations, take a walk all the way down Broadway to the river. At eight on the nose he would be back shining his shoes. Night after night Willard sat across from him in a kitchen chair, watching as though hypnotized, as though his son-in-law was not just another man cleaning his shoes at the end of a hard day, but before Willard's eyes inventing the very idea of the shoe brush and polish. He actually began to think that instead of encouraging the fellow to move out of the house, he ought now to encourage him to stay. It was becoming a genuine pleasure to have him around.

One night in May the two men got to talking seriously together before bedtime; the subject was the future. When dawn rose neither could remember who had first suggested that maybe it was really time for Duane to go back to the original plan of his life, which was to be out contracting on his own. With new housing developments going up everywhere, a fellow with his electrical know-how would be swamped with work within a matter of weeks. It was a matter of the necessary capital to begin, and the rest would take care of itself.

Several hours later, a sunny Saturday morning, shaved and in suits, they drove to the bank to inquire about a loan. At seven that evening, after a nap and a good dinner, Duane went off for his constitutional. Meanwhile Willard sat down with a pencil and pad and began to figure up the available money, what the bank said they would loan, plus certain savings of his own . . . By eleven he was filling the paper with circles and

X's; at midnight he got into the car to make, once again, the old rounds.

He found Whitey in the alleyway back of Chick's Barber-shop, along with a strange Negro and a white-wall automobile tire. Whitey had his arms wrapped around the tire; the colored fellow was out cold on the cement. He did all he could to pry Whitey loose from his tire, short of kicking him in the ribs, but it appeared he was having some kind of romance with it. "Now damn it," Willard said, dragging him toward the car, "let go of that thing!" But Whitey staged a sit-down strike on the curb rather than submit to him and his tire being parted. He said he and Cloyd here had run great risks in procuring it, and be-sides, couldn't Willard see? It was brand-new.

He carried fifty pounds more than Willard, and twenty years less, and so, drunk as he was, it was still nearly half an hour back in Chick's alleyway before Whitey could be detached from what he and his new friend had "borrowed" from God only knew where.

The next morning, for all that he was the color of oatmeal, he came down to breakfast right on time. Wearing a tie. Never-theless, two weeks passed before mention was made again of bank loans, or personal loans, or the electrical contracting business, and then it was not Willard who brought the matter up. The two were sitting alone in the parlor listening to the White Sox game one Saturday afternoon, when Whitey stood, and glaring at his father-in-law, made his indictment. "So that's the way it is, Willard. One lapse, and a man's whole new life—right down the drain!"

Then in June, while they were all getting ready for bed one night, Myra made a remark to Whitey that did not set very well with him, as it was on the subject of his new life, and hers. Adolph Mertz, who had picked up Gertrude after her lesson that afternoon, had asked if Whitey was still interested in going into electrical contracting; a fellow up in Driscoll Falls was retiring, selling everything he owned at a good price, equip-ment, truck . . . Here Whitey swung at her with his trousers and nearly took her eye out with the buckle of his belt. But he hadn't meant to—he was only warning her not to tease him again about something that wasn't his fault! Why did she go shooting her mouth off about plans that weren't finalized?

Didn't she know what the business world was all about? At this stage of the game it was nobody's concern but his—and Willard's, no matter how much her father wanted now to sneak out of the whole thing. As a matter of fact, if it was up to Whitey, he would go back to that bank any day of the week. It was Willard who had withdrawn his support and knocked the confidence out of him about the whole idea, after having encouraged him into it to begin with. Actually, it was living in Willard's house that had undermined his confidence all along, right from the beginning. A grown man being treated like a charity case! Sure, blame it on him—blame it all on him. But who was it who had cried for her Daddy, years back, just because it was a depression and he was out of work, like half the country was, damn it! Who was it that had led them back to her Daddy with his cushy no risk government job? Who was it that wouldn't leave for the South with her own husband so as to start a new life? Who? *Him?* Sure, always *him!* Only *him!* Nobody but *him!*

And as for striking her—this he said when he came back from the kitchen with an ice pack for her eye—had he ever struck directly at her with the intention of doing her harm? "Never!" he cried, getting back into his clothes. "Never *once!*"

Willard rushed into the hallway as the outraged Whitey started for a second time down the stairs. "Now all of you can just stand around day and night," said Whitey, buttoning his coat, "and talk and laugh and tell stories about what kind of failure I am—because I'm going!" There were tears rolling down his face, and he was clearly so miserable and broken-hearted that for a moment Willard became totally confused, or enlightened. At any rate he saw the truth more clearly than he ever had before in all these fifteen years: *There is nothing the man can do. He is afflicted with himself. Like Ginny.*

But when Whitey passed him the second time—having gone back to the kitchen for one last glass of their precious water, if they didn't mind—he nonetheless let the afflicted fellow proceed out the door, and for good measure, bolted it—and shouted after him, "I don't care what you are! Nobody strikes my daughter! Not in this house! Or outside either!"

Whitey began knocking around two A.M. Willard appeared in the hallway in his robe and slippers and found Myra at the top of the stairs in her nightdress. "I think it's raining," she said.

"Isn't bad feet enough?" Willard shouted up the stairs at her. "Do you want to be blind too?"

Whitey began ringing the bell.

"But what help is it to anything," she said, "for someone to stand out in the rain? And the bad feet have nothing to *do* with him."

"I ain't his father, Myra—I am yours! Let him feel a little rain on him! I just can't worry no more about what help things are doing him or not!"

"But I shouldn't have brought it up. I knew it."

"Myra, will you please stop taking the blame? Do you hear me? Because it is not your doing. It is his!"

Berta came into the hall. "If it is your fault, then you go out and stand in the rain too, young lady."

"Now, Berta—" said Willard.

"That is the solution, Mr. Carroll, whether you like it or not!"

She left her husband and her daughter alone in the hallway. Whitey began to kick against the door.

"Well, that sure takes brains, Myra, doesn't it? To kick a door, that really takes brains, all right."

The two of them stood in the hallway while Whitey continued kicking the door and ringing the bell.

"Sixteen years," said Willard. "Sixteen years of solid this. And listen to him, making an idiot of himself still."

After five minutes more, Whitey stopped.

"Okay," said Willard. "That's more like it. I am not giving in to that kind of behavior, Myra, not now, and not ever either. Now that it is calm I am going to open the door. And us three are going to sit down in the parlor right now, and I don't care if it takes till morning, we are going to get to the bottom of this. Because he will not hit you—or anyone!"

So he opened the door, but Whitey was no longer there.

That was a Wednesday night. On Sunday Lucy came to town. She wore a dark brown maternity dress of some thick material, from which her face emerged like a smooth little light bulb. Everything about her looked so small, as indeed everything was, except for the belly.

"Well," said Willard cheerfully, "what's on Lucy's mind?"

"Roy's mother told Roy all about it," she replied, standing in the middle of the parlor.

Willard spoke again. "About what, honey?"

"Daddy Will, don't think you're sparing me. You're not."

No one knew what to say.

Finally, Myra: "How is Roy's schooling going now?"

"Mother, look at your eye."

"Lucy," said Willard, and took her by the arm, "maybe your mother doesn't want to talk about it." He sat her down beside him on the sofa. "How about you tell us about you? You're the one with the brand-new life. How's Roy? Is he coming over?"

"Daddy Will," she said, standing up again, "he *blackened* her *eye*!"

"Lucy, we don't feel any better about it than you do. It is not a pleasant thing to look at, and burns me every time I see it—but fortunately, there was no real physical harm."

"Oh, wonderful."

"Lucy, I am plenty angry, believe me. And he knows it. Word has gotten around to him, all right. He has stayed away three whole days already. Four including now. And from all I understand he is carrying his tail between his legs and is one very ashamed person—"

"But what," said Lucy, "will be the upshot of all this, Daddy Will? What *now*?"

Well, the truth was, he had not quite made up his mind yet on that score. Of course, Berta had made up hers, and told him so every night when they got into their bed. With the lights out he would turn one way, then the other, till his wife, who he had thought was asleep beside him, said, "It does not require squirming, Willard, or thrashing around. He goes, and if she wants to, she goes with him. I believe she is now thirty-nine years old." "Age isn't the question, Berta, and you know it." "Not to you it isn't. You baby her. You watch over her like she was solid gold." "I am not babying anybody. I am trying to use my head. It is *complicated*, Berta." "It is simple, Willard." "Well, it certainly is not, and never was, not by any stretch of imagination. Not with a teen-age high school girl involved, it wasn't. Not when it was a matter of uprooting a whole family—" "But Lucy doesn't live here any longer." "And just suppose they had gone? Then what? You tell me." "I don't know, Willard, what would happen to them then or what will now either. But we two will live a human life for the last years we are on this earth. Without tragedy popping up every other minute." "Well, there are others to consider, Berta." "I wonder when it will be my chance to be one of those others. When I am in the grave, I suppose, if I last that long. The solution, Willard, is simple." "Well, it's not, and it doesn't get that way, either, just by your telling me so fifty times a night. People are just more fragile than you give them credit for sometimes!" "Well, that is their lookout." "I am talking about our own daughter, Berta!" "She is thirty-nine years old, Willard. I believe her husband is over forty, or is supposed to be. They are their own lookout, not mine, and not yours." "Well," he said after a minute, "suppose everybody thought like that. That would sure be some fine world to live in, all right. Everybody saying the other person is not their lookout, even your own child." She did not answer. "Suppose Abraham Lincoln thought that way, Berta." No answer. "Or Jesus Christ. There would never even have *been* a Jesus Christ, if everybody thought that way." "You are not Abraham Lincoln. You are the assistant postmaster in Liberty Center. As for Jesus Christ—" "I didn't say I was comparing myself. I am only making a point to you." "I married Willard Carroll, as I remember it, I did not marry Jesus Christ." "Oh, *I* know that, Berta—" "Let me tell you, if I had known beforehand that I was agreeing to be Mrs. Jesus Christ—"

So to Lucy's question as to what the upshot would be— "The upshot?" Willard repeated.

To gather his thoughts, he looked away from Lucy's demanding eyes and out the window. And guess who just then came strolling up the front walk? With his hair wet and combed, and his shoes shined, wearing his big man's mustache?

"Well," said Berta, "Mr. Upshot himself."

The doorbell rang. Once.

Willard turned to Myra. "Did you tell him to come? Myra, did you know he was coming?"

"No. No. I swear it."

Whitey rang once again.

". . . It's Sunday," explained Myra when no one moved to open the door.

"And?" demanded Willard.

"Maybe he has something to tell us. Something to say. It's Sunday. He's all alone."

"Mother," cried Lucy, "he hit you. With a belt!"

Now Whitey began to rap on the glass of the front door.

Myra, flustered, said to her daughter, "And is that what Alice Bassart is going around telling people?"

"Isn't that what *happened*?"

"No!" said Myra, covering her blackened eye. "It was an accident—that he didn't even mean. I don't *know* what happened. But it's over!"

"Once, Mother, just once, protect yourself!"

"—All I know," Berta was saying, "are you listening to me, Willard? All I know is that it sounds to me as if he is planning to put his fist through that fifteen dollar glass."

But Willard was saying, "Now first off, I want everyone here to calm down. The fellow has been away three whole days, something that has never happened before—"

"Oh, but I'll bet he's found a warm corner somewhere, Daddy Will—with a barstool in it."

"I know he hasn't!" said Myra.

"Where was he then, Mother, the Salvation Army?"

"Now, Lucy, now wait a minute," said Willard. "This is nothing to shout about. As far as we know he has not missed a day of work. As for his nights, he has been sleeping at the Bill Bryants', on their sofa—"

"Oh, you *people*!" Lucy cried, and was out of the room and into the front hallway. The rapping at the glass stopped. For a moment there was not a sound; but then the bolt snapped shut, and Lucy shouted, "Never! Do you understand that? Never!"

"No," moaned Myra. "No."

Lucy came back into the room.

Myra said, ". . . What—what did you do?"

"Mother, the man is beyond hope! Beyond everything!"

"A-men," said Berta.

"Oh, you!" said Lucy, turning on her grandmother. "You don't even know what I'm saying."

"Willard!" said Berta sharply.

"Lucy!" said Willard.

"Oh *no*," cried Myra, for in the meantime she had rushed past them into the hallway. "Duane!"

But he was already running down the street. By the time Myra had unlocked the door and rushed out on the porch, he had turned a corner and was out of sight. Gone.

—

Till now. Lucy had locked him out, and Whitey had watched her do it to him; through the glass he had seen his pregnant eighteen-year-old daughter driving shut the bolt against his entering. And had never dared return after that. Until now, with nearly five years gone and Lucy dead . . . He must be waiting down in that station twenty minutes already. Unless he had become impatient, and decided to go back where he came from; unless he had decided that maybe this time he ought to disappear for good.

—The pain shot down Willard's right leg, from the hip to the toe, that sharp sizzling line of pain. Cancer! Bone cancer! There—again! Yesterday too he had felt it, searing down his calf and into his foot. And the day before. Yes, they would take him to the doctor, X-ray him, put him to bed, tell him lies, give him painkillers, and one day when it got too excruciating, ship him off to the hospital and watch him waste away . . . But the pain settled in now, like something bubbling over a low flame. No, it was not cancer of the bone. It was only his sciatica.

But what did he expect sitting outside like this? The shoulders of his jacket were covered with snow; so were the toes of his boots. The first sheen of winter glowed on the paths and stones of the cemetery. The wind was down now. It was a cold, black night . . . and he was thinking, yes sir, he would have to pay attention to that sciatica, no more treating it like a joke. The smart thing was probably to take to a wheelchair for a month or so, so as to get the pressure off the sciatic nerve itself. That was Dr. Eglund's advice two years ago, and maybe it wasn't such a silly idea as it had seemed. A nice long rest. Throw an afghan over his knees, settle down into a nice sunny corner with the paper and the radio and his pipe, and whatever happened in the house, let it just roll right by him. Just concentrate on getting that sciatic nerve licked once and for all. Surely that is a right you have at seventy years of age, to wheel yourself off into another room . . .

Or he could pretend not to hear everything; let on that he was getting a little deaf. Who'd know the difference? Yes, that might well be a way of solving the whole thing, without bringing a wheelchair into the bargain. Just look blank, shrug your shoulders and walk away. In the months to come he could pretend every once in a while to be slipping some with his faculties. Yes sir, just have to make their way without him. Welcome to use his house for a while, that was fine with him, but beyond that—well, he just wasn't all there in the head, you know. Maybe to make his point so that it stuck, he ought to, on purpose to be sure, and knowing exactly what he was doing all the while, and not in Berta's direction of course, do as his sad old friend John Erwin had begun unfortunately to do, and wet the bed.

"But why? Why should I be senile? Why be off my head when that is not the case!" He jumped to his feet. "Why be getting pneumonia and worrying myself sick—when all I did was good!" The fear of death, horrible, hateful death, caused him to bring his lids tight down over his eyes. "Good!" he cried. "Unto others!" And down the hill he went, shedding snow from his jacket and his cap, while his old, aching legs carried him as fast as they could out of the graveyard.

—

Not until he was past the cemetery road and under the street lamps of South Water Street did Willard's heartbeat begin to resume something resembling a natural rhythm. Just because winter was beginning again did not mean that he was never going to see the spring. He was not only going to live till then, he was alive *right now*. And so was everybody shopping and driving in cars; problems or not, they are alive! Alive! We are all alive! Oh, what had he been doing in a cemetery? At this hour, in this weather! Come on, enough gloomy, morbid, unnecessary, last-minute thinking. There was plenty more to think about, and not all of it bad either. Just think how Whitey will laugh when he hears how in the middle of the night, as though in judgment of itself, the building that used to house Earl's Dugout caved right in, roof first, and had to be

demolished. And so what if Stanley's is under new management? Whitey had as much disdain of a low-down saloon as
anybody when he was being himself—and that was a good deal
more often than it might appear, too, when you were purposely setting out to remember the low points in his life. You
could do that with anybody, think only about their low points
. . . And wait till he sees the new shopping center, wait till he
takes his first walk down Broadway—sure, they could do that
together, and Willard could point out to him how the Elks had
been remodeled—

"Oh hell, the fellow is nearly fifty—what else can I even *do*?"
He was speaking aloud now, as he drove on into town. "There
is a job waiting for him over in Winnisaw. That has all been
arranged, and with his say-so, with his wanting it, with his
asking for it. As for the moving in, that is absolutely temporary. Believe me, I am too old for that other stuff. What we
are planning is January the first . . . Oh, look," he cried to
the dead, "I am not God in heaven! I did not make the
world! I cannot predict the future! Damn it anyway, he is her
husband—that she loves, whether we like it or not!"

Instead of parking at the back of Van Harn's, he pulled up in
front so as to take the long way to the waiting room, so as to
have just another thirty seconds of reflection. He entered the
store, slamming his wet cap against his knee. "And most
likely," he thought, "most likely won't be there anyway."
Without coming into the waiting room, he set himself to peer
inside. "Most likely I have sat up there for no good reason at
all. In the end he probably did not even have it in him to come
back."

And there was Whitey, sitting on a bench, looking down at
his shoes. His hair was now quite gray; so was the mustache.
He crossed and recrossed his legs, so that Willard saw the
undersides of his shoes, pale and smooth. A little suitcase, also
new, sat beside him on the floor.

"So," said Willard to himself, "he did it. Actually got on a
bus and came. After all that has happened, after all the misery
he had caused, he has had the nerve to get on a bus and then
get off it and to wait here half an hour, expecting to be picked
up . . . Oh, you idiot!" he thought, and unseen yet, glared at
his middle-aged son-in-law, his new shoes, his new suitcase—

oh, sure, new man too! "You dumb cluck! You scheming, lying, thieving ignoramus! You weak, washed-out lushhead, sucking the life's blood from every human heart there is! You no-good low-life weakling! So what if you can't help it! So what if you don't mean it—"

"—Duane," said Willard, stepping forward, "How you doing, Duane?"

II

WHEN young Roy Bassart came out of the service in the summer of 1948, he didn't know what to do with his future, so he sat around for six months listening to people talk about it. He would drop his long skinny frame into the big club chair in his uncle's living room and instantly slide half out of it, so that his Army shoes and Army socks and khaki trousers were all obstacles to cross over if you wanted to go by, as his cousin Eleanor and her friend Lucy often did when he was visiting. He would sit there absolutely motionless, his thumbs hooked around the beltless loops of his trousers and his chin tipped down onto his long tubular chest, and when asked if he was listening to what was being said to him, he would nod his head without even raising his glance from his shirt buttons. Or sometimes, with his bright, fair face, with those blue eyes as clear as day, he would look up at whoever was advising him or questioning him, and see them through a frame that he made with his fingers.

In the Army, Roy had developed an interest in drawing, and profiles were his specialty. He was excellent on noses (the bigger the better), good on ears, good on hair, good on certain kinds of chins, and had bought a manual to teach himself the secret of drawing a mouth, which was his weak point. He had even begun to think that he ought to go ahead and try to become a professional artist. He realized it was no easy row to hoe, but maybe the time had come in life for him to tackle something hard instead of settling for the easiest thing at hand.

It was his plan to become a professional artist that he had announced upon his return to Liberty Center late in August; he had barely set down his duffel bag in the living room when the first argument began.

You would have thought he was a kid returning home from Camp Gitche Gumee instead of the Aleutian Islands. If he had forgotten in the time away what life had been like for him during his last year of high school, it did not take Lloyd and Alice Bassart more than half an hour to refresh his recollection. The argument, which went on for days, consisted for the most part of his parents saying they had had experiences he hadn't, and Roy saying that now he had had experiences they hadn't. After all, it just might be, he said, that his opinion counted for something—particularly since what they were discussing was his career.

To make a point, in fact, he spent the whole of his third day home copying a girl's profile off a matchbook cover. He worked it over and over and over, taking just a quick break for lunch, and only after an entire afternoon behind the locked door of his bedroom did he believe he had gotten it right. He addressed three different envelopes after dinner, until he was satisfied with the lettering, and then sent the picture off to the art school, which was in Kansas City, Missouri—walking all the way downtown to the post office to be sure that it made the evening mail. When a return letter announced that Mr. Roy Basket had won a five-hundred-dollar correspondence course for only forty-nine fifty, he tended to agree with his Uncle Julian that it was some kind of clip joint, and did not pursue the matter any further.

Just the same, he had proved the point he had set out to prove, and right off. When he had been called up by the draft board for his two years' service, his father had said that he hoped a little military discipline would do something toward maturing his son. He himself seemed willing to admit bungling the job. Well, the way things turned out, Roy had matured, and plenty, too. But it wasn't discipline that had done it; it was, to put it bluntly, being away from them. In high school he may have been willing to slide through with C's and C-minuses, when with a little application of his intelligence (*Alice Bassart:* Which you have, Roy, in abundance), he could easily have had straight B's—probably even A's, if he had wanted them. But the point he wished to make was that he was no longer that C student, and no longer would be treated like him either. If he put his mind to a job he could do it, and do it well. The only problem now was which job it was going to be. At the age of twenty, nobody had to tell him that it was high time to begin thinking about becoming a man. Because he was thinking about it, and plenty, don't worry.

He continued to work on his own out of the art manual, in exasperation moving on to the neck and the shoulders, after four days of going from bad to worse with the mouth. Though he by no means relinquished his first choice of being a professional artist, he was willing to meet his family halfway and at least listen to whatever suggestions they might have. He had to admit being tempted by Uncle Julian's suggestion that he come to work for him and learn the laundromat business from the ground up. What was particularly appealing about the idea was that the people in the towns along the river would see him driving around in Julian's pickup truck and think of him as some punk kid; and the ladies who managed the laundromats would think of him as the boss's nephew, and suppose his life was just a bed of roses—when in actuality his real work would only begin at night, after everyone was asleep, and behind his bedroom door he stayed awake till dawn, perfecting his talent.

What wasn't too appealing was the idea of using family as a crutch, and right at the outset. He couldn't bear the thought of hearing for the rest of his life, "Of course, it was Julian gave him his start . . ." But of more significance was the damage that accepting something like this could do to his individuality. Not only would he never really respect himself if he just stepped into a job and rose solely on the basis of personal privilege, but how would he ever realize his own potential if he was going to be treated like one of those rich kids who were just coddled up the ladder of success their whole life long?

And there was Julian to consider. He said he was altogether serious about the offer, provided Roy really wanted to work the long hard hours he would demand of him. Well, the long hard hours didn't bother him. A really vicious mess sergeant had once, just out of meanness, kept him on KP for seventeen consecutive hours scrubbing pots and pans, and after that experience Roy realized he could do just about anything. So once he had made up his mind about the direction his life was going to take, he had every intention—to throw Julian's language right back at him—of working his balls into the ground.

But what if he went in with Julian, started taking a salary, and then decided to go off in September to the Art Institute in Chicago; or even to art school in New York, which was by no means impossible? He was giving his parents' objection every consideration (whether they appreciated that or not), but if he finally did decide in favor of professional artist as a career, wouldn't he have wasted not only his time, but Julian's as well? Probably to his uncle, whose affection he valued, he would wind up seeming ungrateful—and maybe that would even be sort of true. Ingratitude was something he had to guard against in himself. Though he was sure his classmates at school and his buddies in the service thought of him as easy-going and generous—his first sergeant used to sometimes call him Steppin' Fetchit—he had been told he had a tendency to be selfish. Not that everybody didn't have one, of course, but certain people had a way of exaggerating things all out of proportion, and he just didn't feel like giving an ounce of support to a suspicion about him which it was actually unfair for anybody (particularly a person's own father) to hold in the first place.

Moreover, what he had a real taste for, following the monotony and tedium of the preceding months, was adventure, and you couldn't really expect that the laundromat business would be packed with thrills, or even particularly interesting, to be frank about it. As for the security angle, money really didn't matter that much to him. He now had two thousand dollars in savings and separation pay, plus the G.I. Bill, and anyway he had no ambition to be a millionaire. That's why, when his father told him that artists wind up living in garrets, Roy was able to say, "What's so wrong with that? What do you think a garret is? It's an attic. My own room used to be the attic, you know," a fact Mr. Bassart couldn't easily dispute.

What he had a taste for was adventure, something to test himself against, some way to discover just how much of an individual he really was. And if it wasn't the life of an artist, maybe it was some kind of a job in a foreign country, where to the natives he would be a stranger to be judged only by what he did and said, and not by what they knew about him from before . . . But saying such things was often only another way of saying you wanted to be a child again. Aunt Irene made that point, and he was willing to admit to himself that she could be right. He was always willing to listen to what ideas his Aunt Irene had, because (1) she usually said what she had to say in private and wasn't just talking to impress people (a tendency of Uncle Julian's); (2) she didn't butt in, or raise her voice, when you argued back or disagreed (his father's courteous approach); and (3) she didn't ever respond with sheer hysterics to some idea or other he had most likely thrown out just to hear how it sounded (as his mother had a habit of doing).

His mother and his Aunt Irene were sisters, but two people couldn't have been more different in terms of calmness. For example, when he said that maybe what he ought to do was leave Liberty Center with a pack on his back and see what the rest of the country had to offer, before making any major choice he would later be stuck with, Aunt Irene registered some interest in the idea. All his mother could do was push the old panic button, as they used to say in the service. Instantly she started to tell him that he had just returned from two years away (which of course he didn't know), and to tell him that he ought to make up his mind to go to the state university (and use that intelligence of his "as God meant you to use it, Roy") and then finally to accuse him of not listening to a word she said.

But he was listening, all right; even sunk down in that big chair, he took in all her objections, more or less. Those she had raised previously a hundred times or more he felt he had the right to tune out on, but he got the drift of her remarks, more or less. She wanted him to be a good little boy and do what he was told; she wanted him to be just like everybody else. And really, right there—in his mother's words and tone—was reason enough for him to be out of town by nightfall. Maybe that's what he ought to do, just shove off and not look back— once he had made up his mind what part of the country he ought to see first. There was always a sack for him in Seattle, Washington, where his best Army buddy, Willoughby, lived (and Willoughby's kid sister, whom Roy was supposed to be fixed up with). Another good buddy, Hendricks, lived in Texas; his father owned a ranch, where Roy could probably work for his grub if he ever ran short of loot. And then there was Boston. It was supposed to be beautiful in Boston. It was the most historic city in America. "I might just try Boston," he thought, even as his mother went gaily on losing her senses. "Yes sir, I might just pick up and head East."

But to be honest, he could use a few more months of easy living before starting in roughing it again, if that's what he finally decided it was best for him to do. He had spent sixteen months in that black hole in Calcutta (as they called it), eight to five every day in that scintillating motor-pool office—and then those nights. If he ever saw another ping-pong ball in his *life* . . . and the weather! It made Liberty Center seem like a jungle in South America. Wind and snow and that big gray sky that was about as inspiring to look at as a washed blackboard. And that mud. And that chow! And that narrow, soggy, under-sized son-of-a-bitching (really) excuse for a bed! Actually he *owed* it to himself not to go anywhere until he had caught up on all the rest he had probably lost on that g.d. bed—and gotten one or two of his taste buds back to functioning too. After an experience like that he surely couldn't say he minded having breakfast served to him in a nice bright kitchen every morning, and having a room of his own again where everything didn't have to be squared away with a plumb bob, or taking as long as he wanted (or just *needed*) in the john, with the door closed and nobody else doing his business at either elbow. It felt *all* right, he could tell you, to eat a breakfast that wasn't all dishwater and cardboard, and then to settle down in the living room with the *Leader*, and read it at your leisure, without somebody pulling the sports page right up out of your hands.

As for his mother chattering away at him nonstop from the kitchen, he wasn't so stupid that he couldn't understand that why she was concerned for him was because he happened to be her son. She loved him. Simple. Sometimes when he finished with the paper he would come into the kitchen where she was working, and no matter what silly thing she was saying, put his arms around her and tell her what a good kid she was. Sometimes he'd even dance a few steps with her, singing some popular song into her ear. It didn't cost him anything, and as far as she was concerned, it was seventh heaven.

She really meant well, his mother, even if some of her pampering ways were a little embarrassing at this stage of the game. Like sending him that package of toilet-seat liners. That's what he had received at mail call one day: a hundred large white tissues, each in the shape of a doughnut, which she had seen advertised in a medical magazine at the doctor's office, and which he was supposed to sit on—in the Army. At first he actually thought of showing them to his first sergeant, who had been wounded in the back at Anzio during World War II. But thinking that Sergeant Hickey might misunderstand, and instead of making fun of his mother, make fun of him, he had strolled around back of the mess hall late that night and furtively dumped them into a can of frozen garbage, careful first to remove and destroy the card she had enclosed. It read, "Roy, please use these. Not everyone is from a clean home."

Which was a perfect case of her meaning well, but not having the slightest idea that he was a grownup whom you couldn't *do* things like that to any more. Nevertheless, there had been times up in Adak when he missed her, and even missed his father, and felt about them as he had in those years before they had started misunderstanding every word that came out of his mouth. He would forget about all the things they said he did wrong, and all the things he said they did wrong, and think that actually he was a pretty lucky guy to have behind him a family so concerned for his well-being. There was a guy in his barracks who had been brought up in Boys Town, Nebraska, and though Roy had a lot of respect for him, he always had to feel sorry for all that he had missed, not having a family of his own. His name was Kurtz, and even though he had the kind of bad skin Roy didn't exactly like to have to look at at mealtime, he often found himself inviting him to come to visit in Liberty Center (after they all got sprung from this prison) and taste his Mom's cooking. Kurtz said he sure wouldn't mind. Nor would any of them have minded, for that matter: one of the big events in the barracks was the arrival of what came to be known as "Mother Bassart's goodies." When Roy wrote and told his mother that she was the second most popular pinup girl in the barracks, after Jane Russell, she began to send two boxes of cookies in each package, one for Roy to keep for himself, and another for the boys who were his friends.

As for Miss Jane Russell, her latest film had been banned by a court order from the movie house in Winnisaw, a fact which

Alice Bassart hoped Roy would take to heart. *That* Roy read to Sergeant Hickey, and they both got a good laugh out of it.

In the months, then, after his discharge, Roy made it his business first to catch up on his sleep, and second to catch up on his food. Every morning about quarter to ten—well after his father had disappeared for the day—he would come down in khakis and a T-shirt to a breakfast of two kinds of juice, two eggs, four slices of bacon, four slices of toast, a mound of Bing cherry preserves, a mound of marmalade, and coffee—which, just to shock his mother, who never had seen him take anything at breakfast but milk, he called "hot joe" or "hot java." Some mornings he downed a whole pot of hot joe, and he could see that actually she didn't know whether to be scandalized by what he was drinking or thrilled by the amount. She liked to do her duty by him when it came to food, and since it didn't cost him anything, he let her.

"And you know what else I drink, Alice?" he'd say, smacking his gut with his palm as he rose from the table. It didn't make the same noise as when Sergeant Hickey, who weighed two twenty-five, did it, but it was a good sound just the same.

"Roy," she'd say, "don't be smart. Are you drinking whiskey?"

"Oh, just a few snorts now and then, Alice."

"*Roy*—"

Which was where—if he saw she was really taking it all in—he might come up, put his arms around her and say, "You're a good kid, Alice, but don't believe everything you hear." And then he'd give her a big, loud kiss on the forehead, sure it would instantly brighten not only her mood, but the whole morning of housework and shopping. And he was right—it usually did. After all was said and done, he and Alice had a good relationship.

Then a look at the paper from cover to cover; then back into the kitchen for a quick glass of milk. Standing beside the refrigerator, he would drink it down in two long gulps, then close his eyes while the steely sensation of the cold cut him right through the bridge of the nose; then from the breadbox a handful of Hydrox cookies, one of his oldest passions; then "I'm going, Mom!" over the noise of the vacuum cleaner . . .

In his first months back he took long walks all over town,

and almost always wound up by the high school. It was hard to
believe that only two years before, he had been one of those
kids whose heads he would see turned down over their books,
suffering. But it was almost as hard to believe that he wasn't
one of them too. One morning, just for the heck of it, he
walked all the way up to the main door, right there by the flagpole, and listened to the voice of his old math teacher "Criss"
Cross, that sweetheart, droning through the open window of
104. Never again in Roy's entire life—*never*—would he have
to walk up to the board and stand there with the chalk in his
hand while old "Criss" gave him a problem to do in front of
the entire class. To his surprise, the revelation made him very
sad. And he had hated algebra. He had barely passed. When
he had come home with a D his father had practically hit the
ceiling . . . Boy, the things you can miss, he thought, if
you're a little crazy in the head, and strolled on, down through
the ravine and out to the river, where he sat in the sun by the
landing, separating Hydrox cookies, eating first the bare half,
then the half to which the filling had adhered, and thinking,
"Twenty. Twenty years old. Twenty-year-old Roy Bassart." He
watched the flow of the river and thought that the water was
like time itself. Somebody ought to write a poem about that,
he thought, and then he thought, "Why not me?"

> The water is like time itself,
> Running . . . running . . .
> The water is like time itself,
> Flowing . . . flowing . . .

Sometimes even before noon he was overtaken with hunger,
and he would stop off downtown at Dale's Dairy Bar for a
grilled cheese and bacon and tomato, and a glass of milk. At
the PX in Adak they wouldn't make a grilled cheese and bacon
and tomato sandwich. Don't ask why, he once said to Uncle
Julian. They just wouldn't do it. They had the cheese and the
bacon and the tomato and the bread, but they just wouldn't
put it all together on the grill, even if you told them how. You
could talk yourself red in the face to the guy behind the
counter, but he simply wouldn't *do* it. Well, that's the old
chicken s—t Army, as he told Julian.

Afternoons he would often drop by the public library, where

his old steady, Bev Collison, used to work after school. With his drawing pad in his lap, he would look through magazines for scenes to copy out. He had lost interest in the human head, and decided that rather than drive himself crazy trying to get a mouth to look like something that opened and closed, he would specialize in landscapes. He looked through hundreds of *Holiday* magazines—without much inspiration—though he did get to read about a lot of places and national customs of which he was totally ignorant, so it wasn't time wasted—except when he fell asleep because the library as usual was so damn stuffy, and you actually had to make a requisition to get them to open a window and let some air in the place. Just like the Army. The most simple-minded thing, and you had to go around all day getting somebody's permission to do it. Oh, brother, was it good to be free. With a whole life ahead of him. A whole future, in which he could be and do anything he wanted.

During the fall he would usually walk back out to the high school late in the afternoon to watch the football team practice, and stay on until it was practically dark, moving up and down the sidelines with the plays. Close in like that he could hear the rough canvasy *slap!* as the linemen came together—a sound he especially liked—and actually see those amazing granite legs of Tug Sigerson, which were said never to stop churning, even at the bottom of a pile-up. They would pull ten guys off him and there would be old Tug, still going for the extra inch, the inch that by the end of a game really could be the difference between victory and defeat. Or suddenly he would have to go scattering back with the little crowd of spectators, as one of the halfbacks came galloping straight at them, spraying chunks of dirt so high and so far that on his way home Roy sometimes found a little clump of the playing field in his hair. "Boy," he'd think, breaking the earth in his fingers, "that kid was *movin'*."

The guy you especially wanted to watch up close, just for the beauty of it, was the big left end, Wild Bill Elliott. Wild Bill had spent three years faking the opposition out of their pants, and was the highest-scoring end at Liberty Center since the days of Bud Brunn himself. In about one second flat he would fake the defense right, left, then *cut* left, buttonhook, take a

Bobby Rackstraw bullet right in the belly, then—with just a *shoulder*—fake right again, only to turn and zoom straight down the center of the field—until Gardner Dorsey, the head coach, blew his whistle, and Bill came loping on back in that pigeon-toed way he had, tossing a long underhand spiral toward the line of scrimmage, and calling out, "Heads up, baby." Whereupon one of the onlookers beside Roy would say, "Ol' Bill would have gone all the way that time," or Roy might even say it himself.

From over on the baseball field he would hear the band being put through their paces for Saturday's game. "Attention, please, band. *Ba-and!*" he could hear Mr. Valerio calling through his megaphone . . . and really, it is about as good a feeling as he can ever remember having, hearing the band start up with the alma mater—

> We're driving *hard*
> For Li-ber-*ty*,
> We're going to *win*,
> A vic-to-*ry*

—and seeing the first team (three consecutive years unde-feated—twenty-four straight) rise up out of the huddle, clap-ping their hands, and the second team digging in, and Bobby Rackstraw, the spidery quarterback, up on his toes piping out the signals—"Hut *one* hut *two*"—and then, just as the ball is snapped, looking up to see a faint white moon in the deep-ening sky over the high school.

For the hour of the day, for the time of his life, for this America where it is all peacefully and naturally happening, he feels an emotion at once so piercing and so buoyant it can only be described as love.

—

One of the stars of the football team in the fall following Roy's discharge from the Army was Joe "The Toe" Whet-stone. He was a fleet-footed halfback (he'd done the hundred in 9.9) and the greatest place-kicker in the history of the high school—some said, the history of the state. Since the summer Joe had been dating Roy's kid cousin Ellie, and on Saturday nights, while Julian and Roy were having a talk together, or a beer, Joe would come around to pick up Ellie and take her to what had become a weekly event for the Liberty Center Stallions, the victory party. He would sit with the two of them in the TV room while "The Princess Sowerby," as Julian called her, decided what dress to wear. At first Roy didn't have too much to say to Joe. He had never really traveled with the athletes in high school, or with any gang, if he could help it; you lost your identity in a gang, and Roy considered himself a little too much of an individualist for that. Not a loner, but an individualist, and there's a big difference.

But Joe Whetstone turned out to be nothing like Roy had imagined. You might have thought that with his reputation, and being so good-looking, he would turn out to be another one of those swell-headed wise guys (like Wild Bill Elliott, who was big for spitting through his teeth into the aisle at the movies in Winnisaw, or so Roy had heard). But Joe was respectful and polite to the Sowerbys—and to Roy too. It took a while, but slowly Roy began to understand that the reason Joe sat there in his coat, nodding his head at whatever Roy might say, and himself saying hardly anything at all, was not because he was looking down his nose at him, but because he was actually looking up. Joe might be the greatest high school place-kicker in the history of the state, but Roy had just come back from sixteen months in the Aleutian Islands, across the Bering Sea from Russia itself. And Joe knew it. One Saturday night when Ellie came bounding down the stairs, Joe jumped to his feet, and Roy realized that the famous Joe "The Toe," with six different scholarship offers already in his hip pocket, was really nothing more than what Ellie was—a seventeen-year-old kid. And Roy was twenty, Roy was an ex-G.I. . . . .

Very shortly Roy began to hear himself on Saturday nights saying things like "They sure gave you the rush act today, Joe," or "How's Bart's ankle?" or "How bad's the rib going to be on the Guardello kid?" Some nights now it was Ellie who had to do the waiting while the three men finished up discussing whether Dorsey ought to have converted Sigerson from a tackle in the first place; or whether Bobby (Rackstraw) was going to be too slight for college ball, bullet arm or no bullet arm; or whether Wild Bill ought to go to Michigan (which had the big name) or to Kansas State, where at least he could be sure he was going to be with a coach who liked to move the old ball in the air.

Those afternoons Roy went over to watch football practice he would almost always end up moseying over to the wooden bleachers back of the goal post so as to watch head-on as Joe placed his fifty through the uprights.

"How you doin', Joe?"

"Oh, hi, Roy."

"How's the old toe?"

"Oh, holding up, I guess."

"That a boy."

It was also down at this end of the field that the cheerleaders practiced. After Joe had finished up—"So long, Roy"; "See you, kiddo"—Roy would button his field jacket, turn up the collar, lean back on his elbows, stretch his legs down across three rows of wooden stands, and with a little smile on his face, hang around a few minutes more watching the cheerleaders go through their oh-so-important repertoire of tricks.

> "Give me an L—"

"L," Roy would say, in a soft mocking voice, not caring whether they heard or not.

> "Give me an I—
> Give me a B—"

Throughout his four years of high school Roy had had a secret crush on Ginger Donnelly, who had become head cheerleader when they were juniors. Whenever he saw her in the hall he would begin to perspire along his upper lip, just as he did in class when suddenly he found himself called upon to answer a question he hadn't even heard the teacher ask. And the fact was that he and Ginger had never exchanged a word, and probably never would. However, she was built, as the saying goes, like a brick s. house, a fact Roy couldn't seem to ignore, not that he always tried. In bed at night he would begin to think about the way she had of leaning back from the waist to do the Liberty Center locomotive, and he would get an erection; at the games themselves, after a touchdown, Ginger would do cartwheels the length of the field, and everybody would be screaming and cheering, and Roy would be sitting there with an erection. And it was ridiculous, because she wasn't that kind of girl at all. Nobody had ever even kissed her, supposedly, and besides, she was a Catholic, and Catholic girls wouldn't even let you put your arm around them in the movies until you were married, or at least engaged. Or so went one story. Another was that all you had to do was *tell* them you were going to marry them, right after graduation, and they "spread," as the saying goes, on the very first date.

Even where Ginger was concerned there had been stories. Almost every guy in Liberty Center would tell you that you couldn't get near her with a ten-foot pole, and a lot of the girls said she was actually thinking about becoming a nun. But then this fellow named Mufflin, who was about twenty-five and used to hang around the high school smoking with kids, said that his friends over in Winnisaw told him that at a party across the river one night, back in Ginger's freshman year (before she'd gotten so snooty), she had practically taken on the whole Winnisaw football team. The reason nobody knew about it was because the truth was immediately suppressed by the Catholic priest, who threatened to have all those involved thrown in jail for rape if even one of them opened his mouth.

It was a typical Mufflin story, and yet some guys actually believed it—though Roy wasn't one.

Roy's usual taste in girls ran to the ones who were a little more serious and sedate about things—Bev Collison, for instance, who had more or less been his private property during senior year, and was now a junior in elementary ed at the University of Minnesota (where Roy thought he might decide to go at the last minute, if everything else fell through). Bev was one of the few girls around who didn't live her life as though she were in a perpetual popularity contest; she would just as soon leave the showing off to the show-offs, and didn't go in for giggling and whispering and wasting whole evenings on the phone. She'd had a straight B average, worked after school at the library, and still had time for extracurricular activities (Spanish Club, Citizenship Club, *The Liberty Bell* advertising manager) and a social life. She had her two feet on the ground (even his parents agreed—bravo!) and he had always respected her a lot. Actually, it was because of this respect that he had never tried to make her go all the way.

Still, it was the hottest and heaviest he had ever gone at it with anyone. In the beginning they used to kiss standing up in her front hallway (for as long as an hour at a stretch, but all the time in their coats). Then one Saturday after a school dance Bev agreed to let him into the living room; she took off her own coat and hung it up, but refused to let Roy remove his, saying he had to go in two minutes because her parents' bedroom was directly over the sofa, toward which Roy was to stop trying to push her. It was several weeks more before he was finally able to convince her that he ought really to be allowed out of his coat, if only as a health measure; and even then she didn't consent, so much as give up the fight, after Roy had already sort of slipped it half onto the floor, necking with her all the while so she wouldn't know. And then one night after a long bitter struggle, she suddenly began sobbing. Roy's first thought was that he ought to get up and go home before Mr. Collison came down the stairs; but he patted her a lot on the back and said everything was all right, and that he was really sorry, he hadn't actually meant it; and so Bev asked, sounding relieved, hadn't he really? and though he didn't know exactly what they were talking about, he said, "Of course not, never, no," and so from then on, to his immense surprise, she was willing to let him put his hand wherever he wanted above the belt so long as it was outside her clothes. There followed a bad month during which Bev got so angry with him that they very nearly broke up; meanwhile Roy was pushing and pulling and pleading and apologizing, all to no avail—until one night, fighting him off, Bev (inadvertently, she tearfully contended later) sank a fingernail so deep into his wrist that she drew blood. Afterward she felt so rotten about it that she let him put his hand in her blouse, though not inside her slip. It so excited Roy that Bev had to whisper, "Roy! My family— stop snorting like that!" Then one night in Bev's dark living room they turned on the radio, very, very low, and of all things, on "Rendezvous Highlights" they were playing the music from the movie *State Fair*, which had recently been revived over in Winnisaw. It was their movie, and "It Might as Well Be Spring" was their song—Roy had gotten Bev to agree. In fact, Roy's mother said that he looked a little like Dick Haymes, though, as Bev commented, least of all when he tried to sing like him. Nevertheless, in the middle of "It's A Grand Night For Singing" Bev just fell backward on the sofa with her eyes closed *and her arms behind her neck*. He wondered for a moment if it was really what she wanted, decided it must be, decided it *had* to be, and so, taking the chance of his life, drove his hand down between her slip and her brassiere. Unfortunately, in the newness and excitement of what she was letting him do, he caught the buckle of his watchband on the ribbing of her best sweater. When Bev saw what had happened she was heartsick, and then scared, and so they had to stop everything while she worked to pick up the stitch with a bobby pin, before her mother saw it in the morning and wanted an explanation. Then on the Saturday before graduation it happened; in the pitch-black living room he got two fingers down onto her nipple. Bare. And the next thing he knew she was off visiting her married sister in Superior, and he was in the Army.

As soon as he was shipped to the Aleutians—even before the first shock of the place had worn off—he had written Bev asking her to get the University of Minnesota to send him an application form. When it arrived, he began to spend a little time each evening filling it out, but shortly thereafter it became evident to him that letters from Bev herself had just stopped coming. Fortunately by this time he was more adjusted to the bleakness of his surroundings than he had been on that first terrible night, and so was able to admit to himself that it had been pretty stupid to think of choosing a university because a girl he once knew happened to be a student there. And absolutely idiotic is what it would have been if after being discharged he had gone ahead and showed up in Minneapolis, to find that this girl had picked up with somebody new, neglecting however to tell him anything about it.

So the application remained only partially completed, though it was still somewhere among "his papers," all of which he planned to go through as soon as he could have two or three uninterrupted days so as to do the job right.

—

The cheerleader Roy was sort of interested in was named Mary Littlefield, though everybody called her "Monkey," he soon discovered. She was small and had dark bangs, and for a short girl she had a terrific figure (which you really couldn't say was the case with Beverly Collison, whom in his bitterness

Roy had come to characterize, and not unjustly, as "flat as a board"). Monkey Littlefield was only a junior, which Roy figured was probably too young for him now; and if it turned out that she didn't have a brain in her head, then it was just going to be curtains for little Monkey, even before the first date. What he was in the market for this time was somebody with a little maturity in her attitudes. But Monkey Littlefield did have this terrific figure, with these really terrifically developed muscles in her legs, and that she was a big-shot cheerleader didn't faze him as it had with Ginger Donnelly two years before. What was a cheerleader, anyway, but a girl who was an extrovert? Moreover, Monkey lived up in The Grove, and so she knew who Roy was: Ellie Sowerby's cousin and a good friend of Joe Whetstone's. He imagined that she knew he was an ex-G.I. simply because of his clothes.

When she and her cohorts started in practicing their cartwheels, Roy would lace his fingers together behind his neck, cross one ankle over the other, and just have to shake his head; "Oh, brother," he would think, "they ought to know what it's like up in the Aleutians."

By then it would be nearly dark. The team would begin drifting off the field, their silver helmets swinging at their sides as they headed for the locker room. The cheerleaders would pick up their coats and schoolbooks from where they lay in piles on the first row of bleachers, and Roy would raise himself up to his full six feet three inches, stretch his arms way out and yawn so that anybody watching would just think of him as being more or less easygoing and unruffled. Then, taking one long leap to the ground, he'd plunge his hands down into his pockets and start off toward home, maybe kicking high out with one foot, as though practicing his punt . . . and thinking that if he had a car of his own there would probably be nothing at all to saying to Monkey Littlefield, "I'm going up to my cousin's, if you want a lift."

Buying a car was something he had begun to give a lot of thought to recently, and not as a luxury item either. His father might not like the idea now any more than he had in high school, but the money Roy had saved in the service was his own, and he could spend it just as he liked. The family car had to be asked for days in advance and had to be back in the garage at a specific time every night; only with a car of his own would he ever be truly independent. With a car of his own he might just give this Littlefield a run for her money—once he had made sure that she wasn't just an extrovert and nothing else . . . And if she was? Should that stop him? Something about the muscles in her legs told Roy that Monkey Littlefield either had gone all the way already, or would, for an older guy who knew how to play his cards right.

. . . Up in the Aleutians it seemed that almost every guy in the barracks had gotten some girl to go all the way, except Roy. Since it didn't hurt anyone, and wasn't so much a lie as an exaggeration, he had intimated that he himself had gone all the way pretty regularly with this girl from the University of Minnesota. One night after lights out, Lingelbach, who really had the gift of gab, was saying that the trouble with most girls in the U.S.A. was that they thought sex was something obscene, when it was probably the most beautiful experience, physical or spiritual, that a person could ever have. And because it was dark, and he was lonely—and angry too—Roy had said yeah, that was why he had finally dumped this girl from the University of Minnesota, she thought sex was something to be ashamed of.

"And you know something," came a southern voice from the end of the barracks, "in later life those are the ones wind up being the worst whores."

Then Cuzka, from Los Angeles, whom Roy couldn't stand, began to shoot his fat mouth off. To hear him talk, he knew every sex secret there ever was. All you have to do to make a girl spread her chops, said Cuzka, is to tell her you love her. You just keep saying it over and over and finally ("I don't care who they are, I don't care if they're Maria Montez") they can't resist. Tell them you love them and tell them to trust you. How do you think Errol Flynn does it? asked Cuzka, who acted most of the time as though he had a direct pipeline to Hollywood. Just keep saying, "Trust me, baby, trust me," and meanwhile start unzipping the old fly. Then Cuzka began to tell how his brother, a mechanic in San Diego, had once banged this fifty-year-old whore with no teeth, and soon Roy felt pretty lousy about saying what he had out loud. Skinny and scared as Bev had been, she was really a good kid. How could she help it if her parents were strict? The next day he was able partially to console himself over his betrayal by remembering that he hadn't actually mentioned her name.

—

Lloyd Bassart had come to the conclusion that Roy ought to apprentice himself to a printer over in Winnisaw. His father liked to say the word "apprentice" just about as much as Roy hated to hear him say it. The knowledge of this aversion in his son didn't stop him, however: Roy ought to apprentice himself to a printer over in Winnisaw; he knew his way around a print shop, and it was an honorable trade in which a man could make a decent living. He was sure that the Bigelow brothers could find a place for Roy—and not because he was Lloyd Bassart's boy but because of the skills the young man actually possessed. Artists starve, as anyone knows, unless they happen to be Rembrandt, which he didn't think Roy was. As for enrolling in college, given Roy's grades in high school, his father could not imagine him suddenly distinguishing himself at an institution of higher learning by his scholarly or intellectual abilities. Though Alice Bassart pointed out that stranger things had happened, her husband did not seem to believe they would in this instance.

Lloyd Bassart was the printing teacher at the high school—not to mention the right arm of the principal, Donald "Bud" Brunn, the one-time all-American end from the University of Wisconsin. When the new consolidated high school had been built in Liberty Center in 1930, people still had a picture in their minds of Don Brunn making those sensational end-zone catches over his shoulder during his four years in the Big Ten. What catching a football over your shoulder had to do with organizing a curriculum or estimating a budget was something that would remain incomprehensible to Alice Bassart until the day she died, but nevertheless, on the basis of that skill, Don, who had been teaching civics and coaching athletics down in a high school in Fort Kean, was offered the position in his old hometown. Being no fool, at least where his own interests were involved, he accepted. And so for eighteen years— eighteen solid years of midstream, as Alice expressed it whenever her anger caused her to become slightly incoherent—Don had been the principal (at least he sat in the principal's office) and Lloyd had been what Alice Bassart called "the unofficial unsung hero." Don wouldn't so much as hire a new janitor without letting Lloyd take a look at him first, and yet Don got the salary of a principal, and was some kind of household god to parents in the community, while Lloyd, as far as the general public was concerned, was nobody.

When Alice got off on this subject, Lloyd often found it necessary to quote what he said were the words of a man far wiser than either of them, the poet Bobbie Burns:

> "My worthy friend, ne'er grudge an' carp,
> Tho' Fortune use you hard an' sharp."

He agreed that Don was a grinning nincompoop, but that was one of the facts of life he had learned to accept long ago. After this much time you certainly couldn't go around all day hoping and praying that the fellow might see the light and resign; if he could see that much light there might not be any cause for him to resign. Nor could you wait for him to slip on a banana peel; for one thing, Don was a healthy ox, destined to outlive them all, and for another, such an idea was beneath Alice even to think, let alone to say aloud. Either you could make your way through life with the bitter taste of envy always in your mouth, or you could remember that there are people in this world far worse off than yourself, and be thankful that you are who you are, and have what you have, and so on.

Could Roy help it if he felt more like spending his evenings at Uncle Julian's than at home? Not that he considered Julian perfect by any means, but at least his uncle believed in having something of a good time in life, and all his ideas weren't about two centuries old. "Wake up!" Roy wanted to shout into his father's ear. "It's 1948!" But that Julian knew what year it was you could see right off, even in something like his clothes. Whereas the big magazine in Roy's house was *Hygeia*, Julian took *Esquire* every month, and followed their clothing tips from top to toe. He was maybe a little too loud with his color combinations, at least for Roy's taste, but you had to admit he was right in the current style, whatever it happened to be. Even his opinion of Mr. Harry S Truman ("half asshole and half Red") didn't keep him from having a collection of Harry Truman sport shirts that could knock your eye out

. . . At any rate, to appear in a public place without a tie wasn't something Julian considered a scandal, nor did he act as though life on this planet was coming to an end if Roy showed up at the house with his shirttail accidentally hanging out. That Roy wasn't going to get all worked up over things that were only "externals" was something Uncle Julian seemed capable of understanding. "Well," he'd say, opening the door to his nephew in the evenings, "look who's here, Irene—Joe Slob." But smiling; not like Roy's father, whom all through the Army his son had remembered most vividly as he used to see him coming out of Mr. Brunn's office—gray hair combed slick, mouth shut, tall and straight as an arrow—and wearing that damn gray denim apron, like the town cobbler.

After he had come home from World War II, Julian had sat down to figure out what people needed that would be cheap and helpful to them and profitable to himself: he had come up with the idea of the laundromat. So simple, and yet within a year the quarters and half dollars that the ladies in the towns along the river dropped into the washers and driers of the El-ene Laundromatic Company left Julian twenty thousand dollars to himself.

Now, Roy had no particular desire to follow in the footsteps of a businessman; it was not only personal consideration that caused him to hesitate before Julian's offer to teach him the business; there was a matter of principle involved. Roy didn't know if he still believed the way he used to in free enterprise, at least as practiced in this country.

During his last few months up in the Aleutians, Roy had listened from his sack when some of the college graduates in his barracks had their serious discussions at night about world affairs. He himself didn't say much then and there, but often on the following day he would find occasion, while sitting around the motor-pool office where he was supply clerk, to talk over some of the things he had heard with Sergeant Hickey. To be sure, he didn't swallow everything this Lingelbach said that was critical of America. Sergeant Hickey was perfectly right: anybody could make destructive criticisms, anybody could just go ahead and start knocking things left and right all day long; to Sergeant Hickey's way of thinking, if you didn't have something constructive to say, then maybe you shouldn't say anything at all, especially if you happened to be wearing the uniform and eating the chow and drawing the pay check of the country you thought was so terrible and awful. Roy agreed that Sergeant Hickey was perfectly right: there were some guys in the world who would never be satisfied, even if you fed them all day long with a silver spoon, but still you had to give this guy from Boston (not Lingelbach, who was an outright loner and odd-ball, but Bellwood) a lot of credit for his arguments about the way they did things in Sweden. Roy agreed right down the line with Sergeant Hickey and his Uncle Julian about Communism, but as Bellwood said, Socialism was as different from Communism as day from night. And Sweden wasn't even *that* socialistic.

What had made Roy begin to wonder if after his discharge a person like himself might not be happy living in a place like Sweden was (1) they had a high standard of living, and it was a real democracy with the Four Freedoms; but (2) they weren't money-mad, Bellwood said, the way people in America were (which wasn't a criticism, it was a fact); and (3) they didn't believe in war, which Roy didn't believe in either.

Actually, if he hadn't just returned from sixteen months in the Aleutians, he might have gone off and gotten himself a job as a deckhand aboard a freighter bound for Sweden, and once there, found some kind of good, honest work, and not in Stockholm either, but in some fishing village such as he had seen photographs of in *Holiday*. He might even have settled down there and married a Swedish girl, and had Swedish children, and never have returned to the United States again. Wouldn't that be something? To think, if that was what he wanted, he could pick up and do it, and without explaining himself to anyone . . . However, for the time being he'd really had his fill of the sun coming up at ten A.M. and going down practically at noon, and the rest of what should be day being night. Probably that's what got to the Swedes themselves— because something did. Sergeant Hickey, who saw all the magazines before they were put in the day room, came into the office one morning and announced that in the new issue of *Look* it said that more people jump off of buildings in Sweden than in any out-and-out capitalistic country in the world. When Roy later brought this up with Bellwood, he didn't really have much to say in Sweden's defense, except to start quibbling over percentages. Apparently there was a heck of a lot of gloom over there that Bellwood hadn't mentioned, and very frankly, for all Roy's willingness to sympathize with their form of government so long as it was a democracy with free elections, by and large he would prefer at the end of a day's work to spend his leisure time with people who knew how to relax and take it easy. Moderation in all things, that was his motto.

Consequently, he found that he would just as soon spend his evenings at the Sowerbys' as hang around at home, where he either had to keep the radio at a whisper because his father was upstairs writing some report for Mr. Brunn, or else his father was downstairs and they were discussing something called Roy's Future as though it were a body he had found on the front lawn: now look here, Roy, what do you intend to do with it?

As for Lloyd Bassart's disapproval of Roy's nightly social call over to the Sowerbys' (and of his brother-in-law Julian as an influence and confidant), he disguised his real objections by saying that he didn't feel Roy should make himself a permanent fixture in another family's house simply because they had a television set. Roy said why should his father mind if the Sowerbys themselves didn't? Uncle Julian was interested in what the postwar Army was like, and in what the younger generation was thinking, and so he liked to talk to Roy. What was so wrong with that?

However, the "talks" between Julian and Roy consisted, as frequently as not, of Julian's pulling Roy's leg. Julian got a kick out of kidding Roy, and Roy got sort of a kick out of being kidded, since it really put them on a buddy relationship. Of course, sometimes Julian went too far with his kidding, particularly the night Roy had said he really didn't think he could ever be satisfied as a human being unless he was doing something creative. As it happened, he was only repeating something he had once heard Bellwood say, but it applied equally as well to him, even though he hadn't thought it up personally. Uncle Julian, however, chose deliberately to miss the point, and said it sounded to him as though what Roy needed was a good piece. Roy had laughed it off and tried to act nonchalant, even though his Aunt Irene was in the dining room, where she could hear every word they said.

Julian's sense of humor wasn't always up Roy's alley. It was one thing if you were in the barracks, or the motor-pool office, to say f. this and f. that, and another when there were women around. Where Uncle Julian's language was concerned, Roy felt his father had his strongest case. And then sometimes Julian got his goat with his opinions on art, which were totally uninformed. It wasn't the security angle he wanted Roy to think about before going off to some la-dee-da art school; it was the sissy angle. "Since when did you become a lollipop, Roy? Is that what you were doing up there in the North Pole, turning pansy on the taxpayers' money?"

But by and large the kidding was good-natured, and the arguments they had didn't last very long. Though Uncle Julian was just a couple of inches over five feet, he had been an infantry officer during the war, and had nearly had his left ball shot off more times than he could count. And even though he said it just that way, regardless of the age or sex of anyone listening, you had to admire him, because it was the pure truth. The guy who had called out "Nuts!" to the enemy had gotten all the publicity at the time, but apparently Julian had been known throughout the 36th Division as "Up Yours" Sowerby; more than once that was the message he had shouted back to the Germans, when another man would have withdrawn or even surrendered. He had risen to the rank of major and been awarded a Silver Star; even Lloyd Bassart took his hat off to him on that score, and had invited him to address the student body of the high school when he returned from the war. Roy remembered it yet: Uncle Julian had used hell and damn twelve times in the first five minutes (according to a count kept by Lloyd Bassart), but fortunately thereafter simmered down, and when he was finished, the students had risen to their feet and sung "As the Caissons Go Rolling Along" in his honor.

Julian called Roy "you long drink of water," and "you big lug," and "Slats," and "Joe Slob," and hardly ever just Roy. Sometimes his nephew had no sooner stepped into the foyer than Julian had his fists up and was dancing back into the living room, saying, "Come on, come on, Slugger—try and land one." Roy, who had learned in gym class how to throw a one-two punch (though he had not yet had occasion to use it in the outside world), would come after Julian, open-handed, leading with his right, while Uncle Julian would bob and weave, cuffing aside the *one* before Roy could deliver the *two.* Roy would circle and circle, looking in vain for his opening, and then—it never failed to happen—Julian would cock back his right arm, cry "Ya!" and even as Roy was ducking his chin behind his fists and hiding his belly back of his elbows (just as he had been taught in high school), Julian would already be swinging one leg around sideways to give his nephew a quick soft boot in the behind with the toe of his bedroom slipper. "Okay, Slim," he'd say, "sit down, take a load off your mind."

But the best thing about Julian wasn't his happy-go-lucky manner: it was that his experience in the Army made him appreciate how hard it was for an ex-G.I. to adjust back to civilian life at the drop of a hat. Roy's father had been too young for World War I and too old for World War II, and so the whole business of being a veteran was just one more aspect of modern life that he couldn't get into his head. That a person's values might have changed after two years of military service didn't seem to mean anything to him. That a person might actually *benefit* from a breather in which he got a chance to talk over some of what he had learned, to digest it, didn't strike him as anything but a waste of precious time. He really made Roy's blood boil.

Julian, on the other hand, was willing to listen. Oh, he made plenty of suggestions too, but there was a little difference between somebody making a *suggestion* and somebody giving you an *order.* So all through that fall and into the winter, Julian listened, and then one evening in March, while he and Roy were smoking cigars and watching the Milton Berle show, Roy suddenly began during the commercial to say that he was starting to think that maybe his father was right, that all this valuable time was just slipping through his fingers, like water itself.

"For crying out loud," Julian said, "what are you, a hundred?"

"But that isn't the point, Uncle Julian."

"Come on, get off your own back, will you?"

"But my life—"

"Life? You're twenty years old. You're a twenty-year-old kid.

Twenty, Long John—and it won't last forever. For Christ's sake, live it up a little, have a good time, get off your own back. I can't stand hearing it any more."

And so the next day Roy finally did it; he hitched over to Winnisaw and bought a two-tone, second-hand 1946 Hudson.

2

From between the curtains in her bedroom, Ellie Sowerby and her friend Lucy watched him begin to take it apart and put it together again. Every once in a while he would stop and sit up on the fender, with his knees to his chest, swinging a Coke bottle back and forth in front of his eyes. "The war hero is thinking about his future," Eleanor would say, and the very idea caused her to snort out loud. Roy, however, appeared to pay no attention to either of them, even when Eleanor rapped on the window and ducked away. As the weather grew warmer, he would sometimes be seen slouched down in the back of the Hudson, his legs thrown up over the front seat, reading a book he had taken out of the library. Ellie would call out the window, "Roy, where in Sweden are you going to live?" To which his answer would generally be a loud slam of the rear door of the car. "Roy's reading all about Sweden. Half the farmers around here came running from there. He wants to *go* there."

"Really?" asked Lucy. She did not take offense, because her own grandfather who had been a farmer had come from Norway.

"Well, I hope he goes somewhere," Ellie said. "My father's worried he's liable to decide to move in with us. He practically lives here as it is." Then, out the window, "Roy, your mother phoned to say she's selling your bed."

But by this time he was under the car, the soles of his shoes all that was visible from the second floor. The only time that he appeared to experience the girls as alive was down in the living room, when he wouldn't move his legs so much as half an inch, and the two had to step over him to get out through the French doors to the back lawn. Generally he acted as though teams had been chosen, himself and his Uncle Julian on one, and the two girls and Mrs. Sowerby on the other.

But if there were such sides, Lucy Nelson had no sense that

Irene Sowerby was on hers. Though Mrs. Sowerby was polite and hospitable to her face, Lucy was almost certain that behind her back the woman disapproved of who and what she was. The very first time Ellie had brought her home, Mrs. Sowerby had called Lucy "dear" right off the bat; and a week later Ellie was no longer her friend. She disappeared from her life as unexpectedly as she had come into it, and the person responsible was Irene Sowerby, Lucy was sure. Because of what she knew about Lucy's family, or because of whatever she heard about Lucy herself, Mrs. Sowerby had decided that she was not the kind of girl she wanted Ellie bringing home in the afternoons.

That was in September of senior year. In February (as if four months of conduct not quite becoming so refined a young lady hadn't intervened) Ellie slid a note, all cheery and intimate, into Lucy's locker, and after school they were walking together up to The Grove. Of course Lucy should have left her own note in return: "No, thank you. You may be insensitive to the feelings of others but you are not going to be insensitive to mine and get away with it. I am not nothing, Ellie, whether your mother thinks so or not." Or perhaps she should not have given Ellie the courtesy of any reply, and just let her show up at the flagpole at three-thirty to find no Lucy waiting breathlessly to be her idea of a "friend."

She felt bitter toward Eleanor, not only because she had picked her up so enthusiastically and dropped her so suddenly, but because Ellie's instantaneous display of affection had caused Lucy to make a decision she wouldn't otherwise have made, and which later she was to regret. But that was not really Eleanor's fault as much as it was her own (or so she seemed willing to believe as she reread the note scrawled across the blue stationery monogrammed EES at the top). The reason she should have nothing to do with Ellie Sowerby was because she was Ellie's superior in every way imaginable, except for looks, which she didn't care that much about; and money, which meant nothing; and clothes; and boys. But just as she had known Ellie to be her inferior, and had gone off with her when invited back for a second afternoon in September, so in the last week of February she followed along once again.

Where else was there to go? Home? As of February 28 she

had only two hundred more days to live in that house with those people (times twenty-four is four thousand eight hundred hours—sixteen hundred of them in bed, however) and then she would be down in the new Fort Kean branch of the women's state college. She had applied for one of the fifteen full honors scholarships available to in-state students, and though Daddy Will said that to have received anything at all was an honor, she had been awarded only what the letter of congratulation called "A Living Aid Scholarship," covering the yearly dorm bill of one hundred and eighty dollars. She would be graduating twenty-ninth in a class of one hundred and seventeen, and now she wished that she had worked and slaved for A's in those courses like Latin and physics, where she had felt it a real victory to get even a B-minus. Not that financial difficulties were going to prevent her going off to school. Over the years her mother had somehow managed to save two thousand dollars for Lucy's education; this, plus Lucy's own eleven hundred dollars in savings, plus the Living Aid Scholar ship, would see her through four years, provided she continued to work full time at the Dairy Bar in the summers and was careful about spending on extras. What disappointed her was that she had wanted to go off completely independent of them; as of September, 1949, she had hoped to have to rely upon them for nothing more for the rest of her life. The previous summer she had settled upon Fort Kean State College because it was the least expensive good school she could find, and the one where she had her strongest chance to get financial assistance; she had declined to apply anywhere else, even after her mother had revealed the existence of her secret "college fund."

Why Lucy detested taking the money was not only because it would continue to bind her to home, but because she knew how it had been paid out to her mother, and she knew why too. Almost into the fifth grade she had thought it made her rather special to be the daughter of Mrs. Nelson, the piano teacher; then, all at once, the kids waiting on the porch in warm weather or sitting on their coats in the hallway in winter, were her own classmates—and that fact caused her to be filled with a kind of dread. No matter how fast she ran home from school, no matter how silently she tried to make it into the house, there would always be some child already at the piano, invariably a boy, who invariably would turn his head away from his lesson in time to catch sight of his classmate, Lucy Nelson, scooting up the stairs to her room.

At school she came to be known not as the kid whose mother gives the piano lessons but the kid whose father hangs around Earl's Dugout—of that she was sure, though the division she now sensed between herself and her schoolmates was such that it did not permit her to ask what they actually thought, or to learn what it was they really did say behind her back. She pretended, of course, that hers was a normal household, even after she had begun to realize it was not—even after her mother's pupils went back out into town to spread the story of what Lucy Nelson's family was really like.

Of course, when she was small, she was nearly able to believe it when she told her friends that it was actually her grandparents who lived with them in their house, and not the other way around. Right off she told new friends that why she couldn't bring anyone home in the afternoon was because her grandmother, whom she loved dearly, had to take her nap then. And she had new friends often. There was a period when every girl her age who moved to town heard from Lucy about her grandmother's nap. But then a new girl named Mary Beckley (whose family moved on again the following year) began to giggle at the story, and Lucy knew that somebody had already cornered Mary Beckley and told her Lucy's secrets. This so angered Lucy that tears came popping out of her eyes, and that so frightened Mary that she swore on her life that she'd giggled only because her baby sister took naps too . . .

Only, Lucy didn't believe her. And from then on she refused ever to tell a lie again, to anyone about anything; from then on she brought no one to her home, and did not offer explanations for her behavior either. So, from the age of ten, though she had no friend who was her confidante, nobody she cared about ever saw her mother taking from her students the little envelopes of money (and saying, "Thank you very much," so very, very sweetly), or what was far worse, the dread of dreads, saw her father coming through the front door and falling down drunk in the hall.

Not even Kitty Egan, whom she discovered in her second year of high school, and who for four months was as intimate a companion as Lucy had ever had. Kitty didn't go to Liberty Center High, but to the parish school of St. Mary's. Lucy had just started working four nights a week at the Dairy Bar, and she met Kitty because of the scandal: Kitty's older sister, Babs, who was only seventeen, had run away from home. She hadn't even waited until Friday, when the girls at the Dairy Bar were paid, but had taken flight after work on a rainy Tuesday night, probably still in her waitress uniform. Her accomplice was an eighteen-year-old boy who swept up at the packing company and came from Selkirk. A post card addressed to "The Slaves at Dale's Dairy Bar" and mailed from Aurora, Illinois, had arrived in town at the end of the week. "Headed for West Virginia. Keep up the good work, KIDS." And signed, "Mrs. Homer 'Babs' Cook."

Kitty was sent around to the Dairy Bar by her father to pick up Babs' wages for Monday and Tuesday. She was a tall, skinny girl whose most striking feature was the absence of any complexion; she had no more coloring than the inside of a potato, even when she came in out of the cold. At first she seemed as unlike Babs as she could be, until Lucy learned that Babs had dyed her hair black so as to look like Linda Darnell (it had originally been orange like Kitty's); as for her skin, Babs caked it in so much mud, Kitty said, you would never know that actually she was part anemic.

The family had always had their troubles with Babs. The only satisfaction she gave them was to wear crucifix earrings in her pierced ears and a cross around her neck, and *that*, Kitty said, was only to draw attention to the space between her breasts—which was the only real thing there anyway, the space. The breasts were things like toilet paper or her brother Francis' socks that she stuffed into her brassiere. Babs wasn't five minutes away from St. Mary's—a dark brick building just by the Winnisaw Bridge—when she would duck into some alleyway to cover herself with pancake make-up, from the roots of her dyed hair to the tops of her homemade breasts, all the while puffing a Lucky Strike cigarette. Kitty told Lucy about the terrible thing she had once found in her sister's purse—"Then I found this terrible thing once in her purse"—and when Babs discovered that Kitty had flushed it down the toilet, she screamed and yelled and struck her in the face. Kitty never told anyone—except the priest—for fear that her parents would severely punish her older sister, who, she said, needed mercy and forgiveness and love. Babs was a sinner and knew not what she was doing, and Kitty loved her, and every morning and every night she prayed for her sister living down there in West Virginia with a boy who Kitty believed was not even her husband.

There were three more children at home, all younger than Kitty, and she prayed for them too, especially for Francis Jr., who was soon to have an operation for his "mastoidistis." The Egans lived out near the Maurer Dairy Farm, where Mr. Egan worked, in a house that was nothing more than a dilapidated old shack. There were nails poking out of the timbers, and fly-paper dangling, though it was already fall, and every unpainted two-by-four seemed to have its decoration of exposed wire. Lucy, upon entering, was afraid to move for fear of brushing up against something that would cause her to feel even more nausea and more despair than came from simply seeing the place where Kitty had to eat and sleep and do her homework.

And when Kitty said that in the afternoons her mother had to take a nap, Lucy was afraid to ask why, knowing that behind such a lie there could only be some dreadful truth she did not want to hear; she wanted only to get outside into the air, and so, thinking that the door nearest her led to the yard, she pushed against it. In a tiny room, asleep on a double bed, lay a pale woman in a long gray cotton slip, wearing on her left foot—in bed!—a crippled person's shoe. Then she was introduced to Francis Jr., who instantly showed her the spot where he appeared to have been whacked with a stick behind the ear. And Joseph, aged eight, whom Kitty had to take into the house to change out of his overalls, which were—"as usual," Kitty said—soaking wet. And tiny Bing—named for the singer —who just dragged his sleeping blanket around and around the backyard, crying for someone named Fay, who Kitty said didn't even exist. And then Mr. Egan appeared, whom Lucy might even have liked for his big lumbering stride and his blazing green eyes had not Kitty earlier pointed to something hanging from a nail in the rear of an open shed, which she whispered was a cat-o'-nine-tails. In all, it was the most wretched and unhappy family Lucy had ever seen, heard of, or imagined; if possible, it was worse even that her own.

She and Kitty began to meet regularly after school. Lucy, standing in the park across the street from St. Mary's, would watch the Catholic kids rushing out the side doors and imagine them all going back to houses just like Kitty Egan's, even though the old Snyders, who were Catholics and lived three doors down on Franklin Street, owned a house almost exactly like her Daddy Will's.

Lucy told Kitty her secret. They walked down to the south end of Water Street, and from a safe distance she pointed out the door to Earl's Dugout of Buddies. Kitty whispered, "Is he there now?"

"No. He's working. At least he is supposed to be. He goes there at night."

"Every single night?"

"Almost."

"Are there women?"

"No. Whiskey."

"Are you sure there are no women?"

"Well, no," Lucy said. "Oh, it's awful. It's horrible. I hate it!"

It didn't take very long for Kitty to tell Lucy about Saint Teresa of Lisieux, the Little Flower—Saint Teresa, who once said, "It is for us to console Our Lord, not for him to be consoling us . . ." Kitty had a little book with a blue cover called *The Story of a Soul*, in which Saint Teresa herself had written down all the wonderful things she had ever thought or said. Even though the weather had begun to turn and the days to grow dim by late afternoon, the two girls would sit on a bench in the little park across from St. Mary's, huddled close together in their coats, while Kitty read to Lucy passages that she said would change her whole life, and get her into heaven for all eternity.

In the beginning Lucy could not seem to get the hang of it. She listened attentively, sometimes with her eyes closed so as to concentrate better, but soon it began to seem that not being a Catholic, she was fated never to understand whatever it was that so inspired Kitty. She herself was Lutheran on one side and Presbyterian on the other, and the latter had been her church, back when her mother had been able to get her to go. A kind of melancholy about her spiritual stupidity slowly settled upon her, until one day, despising both herself and her narrow Protestant background, she looked over Kitty's shoulder at a page of the mysterious book, and discovered that it wasn't hard to understand at all. It was only that in reading aloud, Kitty—who suddenly seemed to her so hopelessly, so disgustingly, ignorant—substituted "a" for "the" and "he" for "she" and "what" for "when," and left out entirely those words she couldn't pronounce, or changed them into others.

Still, Kitty loved Saint Teresa as Lucy had never loved anything, at least that she could remember; and so, gradually, when she began to get the drift of Saint Teresa's meaning, and saw again and again how it flooded Kitty with joy to pronounce aloud those very words, nearly all of which Saint Teresa herself had written, she began to wonder if perhaps she shouldn't forgive Kitty Egan her reading problem and try to love Saint Teresa too.

It was Kitty who brought her to meet Father Damrosch. She began to take instruction from him for an hour after school two days a week, and to spend still other hours in the church, lighting endless candles to Saint Teresa, after whose life she and Kitty were going to model their own. At her first retreat she was given a black veil to keep by Sister Angelica of the Passion, a dark little woman with shiny skin and rimless spectacles and hair beneath her nose that so resembled a man's mustache that Lucy said nothing of it for fear of offending Kitty, who adored Sister Angelica and didn't even seem to notice the long black hairs. Kitty had told Sister Angelica about Lucy in a letter, and so the sister knew all about Lucy's father, for whom she had already prayed at Kitty's request. Sister Angelica was also praying for Babs in West Virginia. In vain, however, did they all wait for news from the vanished sinner. It was as though she had stepped directly from that restaurant in Aurora, Illinois, into Hell itself.

Kitty and Lucy would read aloud to each other their favorite passages from Saint Teresa, who had left this fallen world at twenty-four, a gruesome death of weakness, cold, coughing and blood. "'. . . to become a saint one must suffer the great deal,'" Kitty read, "'always seek when is best, and forgot one-selfish . . .'"

They both chose what Sister Angelica called "Saint Teresa's little way of spiritual childhood." Teresa's only care, said Sister Angelica to Lucy, was that no person should ever be distressed or even inconvenienced by what she was enduring; "daily she sought opportunities for humiliating herself" (Sister Angelica read this to Lucy from a book, so it was not just something she was making up)—"for instance, by allowing herself to be un-justly rebuked. She forced herself to appear serene, and always courteous, and to let no word of complaint escape her, to ex-ercise charity in secret, and to make self-denial the rule of her life." The doctor who attended Teresa in her final illness had said, "Never have I seen anybody suffer so intensely with such an expression of supernatural joy." And her last words, in the slow agony of her dying, were, "My God, I love Thee."

So Lucy dedicated herself to a life of submission, humility, silence and suffering; until the night her father pulled down the shade and up-ended the pan of water in which her mother was soaking her beautiful, frail feet. After calling upon Saint Teresa of Lisieux and Our Lord—and getting no reply—she called the police.

———

Father Damrosch did not choose to call upon her himself when she (who usually attended at least two) failed to show up at a single Mass that Sunday, nor when she did not appear the following week for her instruction. Instead he apparently arranged for Kitty to be excused early from school one day so as to meet Lucy outside the high school, which recessed each afternoon thirty minutes before St. Mary's. Kitty said that Father Damrosch knew about Lucy's father spending the night in jail. Kitty said that this was only another reason for her to hurry and be converted. She was sure that if Lucy asked, Father Damrosch would see her an extra hour a week, and rush the conversion along so that she could be taking her first Communion within a month. "Jesus will forgive you, Lucy," Kitty said, whereupon Lucy turned in anger and said that she did not see that she had anything for which to be forgiven. Kitty begged and begged, and finally when Lucy told her,

"Stop following me! You don't know anything!" Kitty began to weep and said she was going to write Sister Angelica so that she too would pray for Lucy to embrace the teachings of the Church before it was too late.

She feared for a while that she would run into Father Damrosch downtown. He was a big burly man, with a mop of black hair, who liked to kick the soccer ball around with the Catholic boys after school. His voice and his looks made girls who were even Protestant swoon openly in the street. He and Lucy had had such serious discussions, during which she had tried so hard to believe the things he said. "This life is not our real life," and she had tried with all her might to believe him . . . How had he found out so quickly what had happened? How did everybody know? At school, kids she hardly recognized had begun to say, "Hi," as though it had been discovered she were dying of some dread disease and everybody had been told to be nice in the few weeks remaining to her. And after school a group of hideous boys who hung out smoking back of the billboard shouted after her, "Hey, Gang Busters!" and then imitated a machine gun firing. After they had kept at it for a whole week, she picked up a stone one afternoon, turned suddenly around, and threw it so hard that it left a dark mark where it struck against the billboard. But the boys only continued to jeer at her from where they had fled into a vacant lot.

At home she continued to insist upon eating by herself in the kitchen, rather than with *him*, whom her grandfather had gone down and taken out of jail the very next morning. If the phone beside the table rang while she sat looking angrily at her food, she prayed that it would be Father Damrosch. What would her grandmother do when the priest announced himself? But he never did. She even thought of going directly to him—not to ask his help or his advice, but because she recognized one of the boys who called her "Gang Busters" from seeing him at nine o'clock Mass with his family every Sunday. However, she would let Father Damrosch know right off, she had nothing to be forgiven for and nothing to confess. Who was Kitty Egan even to suggest such a thing? A homely, backward girl from an illiterate family, whose clothes smelled like fried potatoes and who couldn't read a sentence from a book without getting it all balled up! Who was she to tell Lucy *anything*? And as for Saint Teresa, that Little Flower, the truth was, Lucy couldn't stand her suffering little guts.

She gathered together her black veil, her rosary, her catechism, her copy of *Story of a Soul* and all the pamphlets she had accumulated at the retreat and from the vestibule at St. Mary's, and put them into a brown paper bag. What prevented her from simply dropping the items separately into the bottom of her wastebasket was the knowledge that her grandmother would see them there, and think that it was because of her objections to "all that Catholic hocus-pocus" that Lucy was giving up going into the Church. She did not wish her to have the satisfaction. What she decided to do about her religion, or about anything relating to her personal life, was the business of nobody in that house, least of all that snoop.

She carried the paper bag with her to work that night, intending to drop it into a garbage can along the way, or toss it into a lot. But a rosary? a veil? a crucifix? Suppose the bag was found and brought to Father Damrosch? What would he think then? Perhaps the only reason he had refrained from calling her so far was because he felt it improper to interfere in a family already so strongly opposed to conversion; or perhaps he believed it improper to meddle in a private matter before his assistance had been asked for; or perhaps he had sensed all along that Lucy only half believed the things he told her and so would be immune to anything further he might have to say; or perhaps he had never really been that interested in her to begin with, thought of her as just another kid, and if she came to him, would only resume stuffing her full of catechism so as finally to stuff her into the confessional, where, like stupid Kitty Egan, she could ask forgiveness for sins that were not really her own and say prayers for people that did them absolutely no good. He would try to teach her to learn to love to suffer. But she hated suffering as much as she hated those who made her suffer, and she always would.

After work she hurried out Broadway toward the river. At St. Mary's she entered without genuflecting, placed the bag on the last bench, and ran. Outside, there was only one light on in the rectory . . . Was Father Damrosch standing behind one of the desk windows, looking down at her? She gave him a moment to call for her to come inside. And tell her what? This life is a prelude to the next? She didn't believe it. There is no next life. This is what there is, Father Damrosch. This! Now! And they are not going to ruin it for me! I will not let them! I am their superior in every single way! People can call me all the names they want—I don't care! I have nothing to confess, because I am right and they are wrong and I will not be destroyed!

One night two weeks later Father Damrosch came into Dale's Dairy Bar for a black and white ice cream soda. Dale popped immediately out from the back to say hello, and to serve the priest personally, saying all the while what a great honor it was. He refused to take Father Damrosch's money, but the father insisted, and when he left, one of the waitresses said to Lucy, "He's absolutely *gorgeous.*" But Lucy only continued carefully refilling the sugar bowls.

—

The very next term Lucy took the music appreciation course, where she was prevailed upon by the teacher, Mr. Valerio, to become interested in the snare drum; so for the next year and a half the problem of what to do after school was solved by band. Either they were practicing in the auditorium, or on the field, or on Saturdays were off and away to a football game. There were always kids dashing in and out of bandroom, or shoving from behind onto the bus, or jamming together, epaulet to epaulet, in the band section, to stay warm while the game itself—which Lucy hated—wore interminably on. As a result, she was hardly ever alone around school to be pointed out as the kid who had done this or that terrible thing. Sometimes as she was rushing up out of the school basement with her drum, she would see Arthur Mifflin slinking around the basketball courts, or perched on his motorcycle, smoking. He had been thrown out of Winnisaw High years ago, and was some kind of hero to the boys who used to call her "Gang Busters" and "J. Edgar Hoover." But if he himself had any smart remarks to make she didn't wait to hear them. She would just start in practicing the marching cadence and continue all the way to the field, beating it out so loud that whether he called to her or not, she didn't even know.

But then, altogether unexpectedly, at the very start of her

senior year, band was over. She had cut practice twice in two
weeks to go up with Ellie Sowerby to The Grove; to Mr. Valerio she explained (her first lie in years) that her grandmother
was ill and needed her—and he had swallowed it. So there was
no tension between them at all; she was still his "dream girl."
Nor had the thrill gone out of marching up the field at the
start of the afternoon, guiding her line, "Left . . . left . . .
left, right, left," and drumming out the muffled cadence till
they reached the midfield stripe and launched into the National Anthem. It was the moment of the week she had come
to live for, but not because of anything so ridiculous as school
spirit—or even love of country, which she supposed she had,
though no more than an ordinary person. It wasn't the flag,
snapping in the breeze, that gave her the gooseflesh so much
as the sight of everybody in the stands rising as it moved down
the field. She saw from the corner of her eye the arms sweep
up, the hats swept off, and felt the drum thump-thumping
softly against the guard on her leg, and the warmth of the sun
fell on her hair where it poked out from under her black and
silver hat with the yellow plume and oh, it was truly glorious—
until that third Saturday in September, when they turned at
the midfield stripe to face the stands (where everyone was
silently standing facing them) and she tightened her hold on
the smooth sticks, and Mr. Valerio climbed onto the folding
chair that had been brought out to the field for him, and he
looked down at them—"Band," he whispered, smiling, "good
afternoon"—and then in the moment before he raised his baton, she realized (for no good reason at all) that in the entire
Liberty Center Consolidated High School Marching Band,
there were only four girls: Eva Petersen, who played the clarinet and had a wall-eye; the harp-bell player, Marilynne Elliott,
whose brother was a big hero, but who herself stammered;
and the new French-horn player of whom Mr. Valerio was
so proud, poor Leola Krapp, who had that name and was
only fourteen and already weighed two hundred pounds—
"stripped," the boys said. And Lucy.

On Monday she told Mr. Valerio that working in Dale's
Dairy Bar at night and having band practice in the afternoons
wasn't giving her time enough to study. "But we finish by
four-thirty." "Still," she said, looking away. "But you managed

last year, Lucy. And on the honor roll." "I know. I'm really sorry, Mr. Valerio." "Well, Lucy," he said, "you and Bobby Witty are my mainstays. I don't really know what to say. The big games are just coming up." "I know, Mr. Valerio, but I think I have to. I think I better. College is coming up too, you know. And so I really have to knuckle down and make an all-out effort—for my scholarship. And I have to make the money at the Dairy Bar. If I could quit that, of course, then I could have this . . . but I just can't." "Well," he said, lowering the lids of his big black eyes, "I don't know what's going to happen to the rhythm in that drum section. I hate even to think about it." "I think Bobby can carry them, Mr. Valerio," she said, feebly. "Well," he sighed, "I'm not Fritz Reiner. I suppose this is what they mean by a high school band." "I'm really sorry, Mr. Valerio." "It's just I don't often get a person, boy or girl, who is serious about the snare drum the way you are. Most of them, if you'll pardon my language, just beat the damn thing to death. You *listen*. You've been my dream girl, Lucy." "Thank you, Mr. Valerio. I really appreciate that. That means a lot to me. I sincerely mean that." Then she laid on his desk the box in which she had folded up her uniform. The silver hat with the black peak and the gold plume she carried in her hand. "I'm really sorry, Mr. Valerio." He took the hat and put it on his desk. "My drums," she said, weakening by the moment, "are in bandroom."

Mr. Valerio sat there flicking the plume on her hat with one finger. Oh, he was such a nice man. He was a bachelor with a slight limp who had come to them all the way from a music school in Indianapolis, Indiana, and his whole life was band. He was so patient, and so dedicated; he was either smiling or sad, but never angry, never mean, and now she was letting him down, for a selfish, stupid, unimportant reason. "Well, so long, Mr. Valerio. Oh, I'll stop by and say hello, and see how things are going—don't worry about that."

Suddenly he took a very deep breath and stood up. He seemed to have collected himself. He took one of her hands in his two and shook it, trying to look happy. "Well, it was good having you aboard, Dream Girl."

The tears rolled down her cheeks; she wanted to kiss him.

Why was she doing this? Band was her second home. Her first home.

"But," Mr. Valerio was saying, "I suppose we are all going to survive." He clapped her on the shoulder. "You take care now, Lucy."

"Oh, you take care, Mr. Valerio!"

A little girl with braids was sitting in the swing on the porch when Lucy came running up the front stairs. "Hi!" the child said. Whoever was already at the piano stopped in the middle of a bar as she slammed the door and took the stairs, two at a time.

As she turned the key in the bedroom door she heard the piano start up again downstairs. Instantly she pulled out her desk chair, stood up on it, and looked at her legs in the mirror over the dresser. They had hardly any shape; she was just too short and too skinny. But what could she do about that? She had been five one and a half now for two years, and as for weight, she didn't like to eat, at least not at home. Besides, if she got any heavier her legs would just get round, like sausages —that's what happened to short girls.

She climbed down off the chair. She looked at herself straight on in the mirror. Her face was so square—and boring. The word "pug" had been invented to describe her nose. Eva Petersen had tried to give her that as a nickname in the band, but Lucy had told her to cut it out, which she did instantly, what with her own wall-eye. A pug nose wasn't that bad, actually, except that where hers turned up at the end it was too thick. And so was her jaw, for a girl at any rate. Her hair was a kind of yellowish-white, and she knew that bangs didn't help all that squareness any, but when she lifted them up (as she did now), her forehead was so bony. Well, at least her eyes were nice—or would have been had they belonged to someone else, though that was the trouble: they *did* belong to someone else. Sometimes she used to look at the mirror in the band-room, and with her hat on she would be terrified by the resemblance she bore to her father—particularly those two round blue stains beneath the steep pale brow.

She had freckles too, but no pimples—her only physical blessing.

She stepped backward so as to see all of herself again. All she ever wore was that plaid skirt with the big safety pin in front, and her gray sweater with the sleeves pushed up, and her ratty loafers. She had three other skirts, but they were even older. And she didn't care about clothes. Why should she? Oh, why had she quit band?

She clutched at the back of her blouse so that it pulled tight across her front. Her breasts had started growing when she was eleven; then to her relief, a year later, they had just stopped. But weren't they going to start again? She did know an exercise that supposedly could enlarge them. The health teacher, Miss Fichter, had demonstrated it to them in class. It was out of *American Posture Monthly*, a magazine with a picture on the cover of little twin boys in white briefs, standing on their heads and smiling. There was nothing there to cause giggling, as far as Miss Fichter could see, and that went for the exercise as well, whose purpose was all-around health and attractiveness. If only they got into the habit of exercising their muscles when they were young, they would always be proud of themselves physically. Too many teen-age girls in this school *slouch*, said Miss Fichter, and she said it was as though she really meant *lie* or *steal*.

You did the exercise with your hands out in front of your chest: first you pushed the right fist into the open left palm, and then the left fist into the open right palm. You did this twenty-five times, each time chanting in rhythm, as Miss Fichter did, "I must, I must, I must respect my bust."

In front of the mirror, behind the locked door, and without the words, Lucy gave it a try. How long before it began to work? "Da *dum*," she said, "da *dum* . . . da-*dum*, da-*dum*, da-*dum*."

Oh, how she would miss band! How she would miss Mr. Valerio! But she simply couldn't march any more with those girls—they were freaks. And she wasn't! And nobody was going to say she was either! From now on it would just be her and Eleanor Sowerby together. In Ellie's room was a bed with a white organdy canopy and a dressing table with a mirror top, where they would do their homework on the afternoons when it rained; on nice afternoons they would sit out in the back, reading together in the sun, or just walk around The Grove, doing nothing except looking at lawns and gabbing. If by the time they got back it was dark, most likely the Sowerbys would invite her to join them for supper. On Sundays they would ask her to come with them to church, and stay on afterward for dinner. Mrs. Sowerby was so soft-spoken and attentive, she had called her "dear" the very afternoon they were introduced—to which Lucy had nearly, idiotically, responded with a curtsy. And Mr. Sowerby had come noisily into the house at five—"Pappy Yokum's home!" he'd called, and then had given his wife a loud wet kiss right on the mouth, even though she was a plump woman with gray hair who, Ellie said, had to wear rubber stockings to keep her veins in. It was Ellie's current joke to call him Pappy Yokum, and his to call her Daisy Mae, and silly as this struck her, Lucy had nonetheless found herself very much in awe of what appeared at last to be a happy family.

So she quit band. And Ellie dumped her. "Oh, hi there," Ellie would say as they passed in the corridors, and then just keep walking. For a week Lucy was able to tell herself that Ellie was only waiting for her to return the invitation. But how could she invite her home if she didn't even get a chance to talk to her? And even if she was able to, did she want to? One day, after two solid weeks of being ignored, she saw Ellie sitting in the cafeteria at the same table with some of the shallowest and silliest girls in the entire school, and so she thought to herself, well, if *those* are the kind of girls she really prefers, et cetera, et cetera.

Then in late February she found the note slipped down through the air vents into her locker.

Hi, Stranger!
I've been accepted at Northwestern (big deal) so the pressure is off, and I can relax now. Meet me at the flagpole at three-thirty (please please).

Your fellow suffering senior,
Ellie
LCCHS, Class of '49
Northwestern '53 (!)

This time Lucy was far less impressionable. Thinking back to September, to the sheer idiocy of quitting band so as to be

Ellie Sowerby's friend—well, it was as though she had been
ten years old. She had really gone against every principle she
had. It had been weak and stupid and childish, and though in
the interim she had despised Ellie, and plenty, she had despised
herself no less. For one thing, it was a matter of absolute indifference to her who lived in The Grove—that was the truth.
Nothing used to infuriate her more than to take a drive with
her family on Sunday (back when she was young enough to
have to go where they wanted her to) and have her mother
point out the house up in The Grove that her father had once
almost bought. As if where you lived or how much money
you had was what was important, and not the kind of human
being you were. The Sowerbys had a full-time maid, and a
$30,000 house, and enough money to send a daughter off to a
place like Northwestern for four years, but the fact remained
that Lucy Nelson was still more of a person than their own
daughter would ever be.

To Ellie the biggest thing in life was clothes. Outside Mar-
shall's store in Winnisaw, Lucy had never seen so many skirts
in one place as Ellie had hanging in her big wall-length closet
with the sliding doors. Some afternoons, when it rained and
they studied together in Ellie's room (exactly as she had imagined they would), she looked up to discover the closet doors
ajar; whole minutes often passed before she was looking down
into her book again, trying to find her place. When the
weather began to turn warm and by three o'clock it was suddenly too hot for the coat that Lucy had worn to school that
morning, Ellie would tell her just to pull any old sweater out
of the bureau drawer and wear it for the rest of the afternoon.
Only there weren't any old sweaters in there.

One afternoon the sweater she put on turned out to be one
hundred percent cashmere. She didn't realize this until out
on the lawn, she took a quick look at the label and went
breathless at what she had done. By this time, however, Ellie
was calling for her to help pound in the croquet wickets, and
Mrs. Sowerby had already seen her pass through the living
room. And she had already seen the look of disapproval move
across Mrs. Sowerby's face, at the first glimpse of the sagging
plaid skirt coming down the stairs topped by Ellie's lemon-
colored sweater. "Have a good game," Mrs. Sowerby had said,

but that, Lucy realized too late, wasn't at all what she had been thinking. To go back upstairs, however, to change the cashmere for cotton, or even lamb's wool, would be to admit that she was indeed guilty of choosing it deliberately, when in actuality she had taken it in all innocence. Upon lifting it from the overstuffed drawer she had not thought *cashmere*, she had only thought *how soft*. It had nothing to do with being covetous and she would not give credence to any such suspicion by traipsing all the way past Mrs. Sowerby a second time. She had no intention of ever being made to feel inferior again, not by Ellie, and not by any member of her family . . . and that was the reason she gave herself for keeping the soft lemon-colored sweater on her back until the very minute that she changed back into her heavy winter coat and left for home.

Shortly thereafter Ellie trimmed her bangs for her. Lucy kept saying, "Not too much. Really. My forehead, Ellie."

"What a difference!" Ellie said when they looked at the results in the bathroom mirror. "I can *see* you now."

"You took too much off."

"I didn't. Look at your eyes."

"What's wrong with them?"

"They look great. They're really a great color if you could ever see them."

"Yes?"

"Hey, what about wearing it up? Let's see what it looks like up."

"My head's too square."

"Let's just see, Lucy."

"Don't cut anything."

"I won't, jerk. I just want to *see*."

So, too, Ellie just wanted to see what Lucy's plaid skirt would look like if they let down the hem three inches to give it "The New Look."

It seemed so silly to be allowing this to happen to her, so incredible that it *was* happening. She didn't even respect Ellie, so where did she get off treating Lucy like her stooge? And she didn't respect Ellie's parents that much any more either. What was Mrs. Sowerby but a social snob? As for Mr. Sowerby— well, she hadn't figured him out yet. Daddy Will liked to crack corny jokes, and her father used to think he was being funny

when she was small and he called her "Goosie," but Mr.
Sowerby was almost always joking, and was almost always
loud. Whenever he was down in the living room, Lucy took
her time going between Ellie's bedroom and the bathroom
at the end of the hall. "Pike this," he'd call to his wife in the
kitchen. "Just pike this!" And then at the top of his voice he
would read from the newspaper something that Harry Truman
had done which just infuriated him. Once he called, "Irene,
come here, Irene," and when she came into the living room, he
put a hand on her behind and said (softly now, but Lucy,
frozen in the upper hallway, could hear by holding her breath),
"How's the health, tootsie?" How could she approve of the
way he talked to Mrs. Sowerby, or the kind of language he
used? She certainly didn't believe that Mrs. Sowerby did,
what with all her airs. She had the distinct feeling that all this
hugging and kissing was something Mrs. Sowerby simply had
to endure. It almost made Lucy feel sorry for her.

On the other hand, Mr. Sowerby *was* Liberty Center's outstanding war hero. On his return to town the Mayor had actually led a motorcade down to the train station to meet him.
Lucy had only been a freshman when he came to the high
school to talk, but she remembered that his speech had left a
sobering impression on the people in the community who
had thought the worst was now over. His topic had been,
"How to Make This World a Better Place to Live In"—or, as
some of the boys referred to it afterward, "How the Hell to
Make This God Damn World a Helluva Better Place to Live
In—Damn It!" It was mostly about remaining vigilant in the
coming years against what Mr. Sowerby called the threat of
atheistical Communism. The very next day there had been an
editorial on the front page of the Winnisaw *Leader* calling
upon Major Sowerby to run for Congress in the 1946 elections. Ellie said that he had decided not to only because her
mother didn't feel it would have been right to take Ellie out of
her school once again, if they had had to move to Washington,
D.C. Because of the war she had already had to attend
schools in North Carolina and Georgia (which, said Ellie, accounted for her sometimes falling into a southern accent without even realizing it). Ellie loved to tell how the Governor had
spoken to her father on the phone, and how her father had

said he didn't want the Governor to think he was putting responsibility to family above responsibility to country, and so on and so forth. The conversation came out different each time Ellie reported it; once it even occurred at the Governor's "mansion." Only the tone in which the story was told remained the same: smug.

Of course Lucy appreciated Ellie's generosity with her possessions, and it was hard to say she wasn't good-natured, but one thing that was unforgivable was being condescended to. The day that Ellie began to fuss with her clothes she got so furious that she wanted to leave right then and there; and she would have too, were it not that Ellie had already unstitched the hem and was busy pinning up a new one, and she herself was in her slip and blouse, sitting at Ellie's dressing table and looking out between the curtains at Ellie's cousin, the Army veteran, working on his Hudson.

Roy. She had never called him that, or anything. And he did not appear even to *know* her name, or even to associate her with the girl who worked behind the counter at Dale's Dairy Bar. Between September, when she had caught her first glimpse of him at Eleanor's, and February, when grace had fallen upon her a second time, she had observed him many times as he sat at the counter of the Dairy Bar; sometimes she had seen him headed down Broadway carrying his sketch pad. During those months without band and without Ellie, when she used to hole herself up every afternoon in the public library, there was a period of a few weeks when he always seemed to be coming out of the library just as she was going in. He was friendly with Dale, and once she'd seen him talking seriously with Miss Bruckner, the librarian. So it wasn't shyness that explained his solitude; he just seemed to prefer to be alone—which was one of the things that had begun to make her think that he might be an interesting person. Also she knew who his father was—Mr. Bassart, who introduced the speakers at assembly programs, and was known to be one of the strictest though one of the fairest teachers in the entire school. And she knew he had recently returned from serving two years in the Army, overseas.

Ellie always made fun of him. "He thinks he looks like Dick Haymes. Do you think he does?"

"I don't know."

"If he wasn't my cousin I suppose I'd think he was cute. But I *know* him," she would add ominously. Then, out the window: "Roy, sing like Dick Haymes. Come on, Lucy never heard your imitations. Do Vaughan Monroe, Roy. You really look more like him anyway, now that you're so *mature*. Sing 'Ballerina,' Roy. Sing, 'There, I've Said It Again.' Oh, please, Roy, please, we beg of you on bended knee."

Lucy would go scarlet, and Roy would make a sour face, or say something like, "Act your age, will you?" or "Really, Ellie, when are you going to grow up?"

Roy was going to be twenty-one. What he was doing the times she saw him meandering slowly down Broadway, whacking his sketch pad against his thigh, or on the evenings he sat at the Dairy Bar counter, rattling the ice round and round at the bottom of his Coke, or on the weekends he spent sunk down into the club chair talking with his Uncle Julian, was trying to decide just what to do with his life. He was at a genuine turning point: that was the expression she had heard him using one Saturday. And it had stayed with her.

What was Roy going to become? An artist? A businessman? Or was he going to ship out, and really give Sweden a chance? Or would he do something completely bizarre and unpredictable? Once she heard him remind his uncle that he didn't only have the G.I. Bill, he had a G.I. home loan too. If he wanted to, he could actually go off and buy a house of his own, and then live in it. His Uncle Julian laughed, but Roy said, "Poo-poo my ideas all you want, kiddo, but it's true. I don't have to be anybody's slave, not if I don't want to be."

From the bed where she was sitting hemming Lucy's skirt, Ellie said, "What are you looking at?"

Lucy dropped the edge of the curtain.

"Not Roy, I hope," Ellie said.

"I was just looking outside, Ellie," she said coldly.

"Because don't waste your breath on that one," said Ellie, biting the thread. "You know who he likes?"

"Who?"

"Monkey Littlefield."

To Lucy's astonishment her heart made some sort of erratic movement.

"Roy's major interest these days is s-e-x. Well, he's picked the right girl, all right."

"Who?"

"Littlefield."

". . . Does he take her out?"

"He's still deciding whether to lower himself or not. Or so he says. He said to me, 'Is she a kid, or has she got a brain in her head? Otherwise I don't want to waste my time.' I said, 'Don't worry, Roy. She's no kid.' So he said, 'What is that supposed to mean?' And I said, 'I know why you like her, Roy.' And he got all red in the face. I mean, everybody knows her reputation. But Roy pretended he didn't."

Lucy pretended by her expression that she did.

Ellie went on, "I said, 'It isn't her personality that makes her popular, Roy.' So he said, 'Well, that's all I asked, Ellie, whether she even had a personality or not.' 'Well, ask Bill Elliott about her personality, Roy, if you haven't already.' So he said, 'I didn't even know she went out with him.' 'Not any more, Roy. Even *he* doesn't respect her any more. I'll leave the rest to your imagination,' I said, and then you know what he said? 'Go play with your jacks, Ellie.' He tells my father all his big sex exploits in the Army, and Daddy lets him, which he shouldn't, either. You know when they start laughing down there together?"

"No. I don't think so."

"Well, they do. And what do you think they're laughing about?"

"Sex?"

"He's got it on the brain. Roy, I mean," Ellie added.

By April the elastic at the top of Roy's Army socks had begun to unravel. Every time the two girls stepped over him— "Excuse us, cousin, will you, *please*?" said Eleanor—Lucy saw, between the shrunken, fading khaki trousers and the drooping socks, the white and slender part of his leg. At the beginning of the month, a week of hot, wonderful, summery weather swept across the Middle West, pushing into bloom almost overnight the forsythia in the Sowerby garden; one afternoon, just as she stepped to Ellie's bedroom window to take a quick look outside—at the new flowers—Roy began pulling his T-shirt off over his head. In only a matter of seconds she had turned back to Ellie, who was searching a drawer for an old pair of shorts for Lucy to wear, but the sight of his long smooth cylindrical upper half stretching down over the open hood of his car remained in her mind all afternoon.

Near the end of the month, when Roy bought the camera and began to get the photography magazines, he came to Eleanor and said that he wanted to do some studies in black and white down by the landing. He needed a girl to sit under the tree he'd picked out. It might just as well be Ellie.

Ellie's color rose; she had auburn hair that shone, and hazel eyes that changed sometimes to cat-gray, and in repose she was not only one of the prettiest girls Lucy had ever seen, but also looked altogether poised and intelligent. She could easily have passed for nineteen or twenty, and she knew it.

"Look, Roy," she said, dropping into her southern accent, "why don't you-all get Monkey Littlefield? Probably she'll even do cheesecake fo' ya'. A la Jane Russell—yo' favorite actress."

"Look," he said, making his sour face, "I don't even know that Littlefield kid. And I've never even seen a Jane Russell movie in my life, actually."

"Oh, I'm *shoo*-wa of that. You only had her little ol' pinup all over your walls in the Army, but you never *seen* her in a movie."

"Look, Ellie, who are you supposed to be, *Gone With the Wind*? I want to do this study. So say either yes or no. I haven't got all day."

Ellie said she'd think about it, and then went up and changed into her new white linen dress, all the while telling Lucy about the kind of letters her Aunt Alice had gotten while Roy was in the Army. S-e-x, to his own family.

They drove off to the river. Lucy came along for the ride. That was how Roy had extended the invitation, when she said that she'd better go home. "You can come for the ride, if you want. I don't charge anything"—all the while using a little pressure gauge he had bought to check the air in a front tire that he said looked to him to be low.

He posed his subject (because that's all she was, and he hoped she could understand what that meant) by the big oak near the old pier. Ellie kept wanting to look off in profile toward Winnisaw, but Roy wanted her looking straight up into the tree. Every few shots or so he came over and yanked on one of the branches so as to get the shadows to fall in the right places.

Ellie said she would like to know what he meant by "the right places."

"I'm talking technically, Eleanor. Will you shut up?"

"Well, it's hard to know these days, Roy, when you say 'the right places.' Considering where your mind is."

"Oh, look at the branches, *please*? The whole idea, Ellie, is The Marvel of Spring. So look up, and not at me."

"I hear you at night, Roy."

"Hear me *what*?"

"Laughing. And I know what you're laughing about too."

"Okay, what?"

"Guess."

At the end of the afternoon Ellie said, "Why don't you take some of my friend?"

He sighed deeply. "Oh—okay. One." He turned all around. "Well, where'd she disappear to? I haven't got all day."

Ellie pointed to the bank of the river where the black pilings jutted out into the water.

"Hey," Roy called, "want your picture taken? I've got to leave, so if you want it, let's go."

Lucy looked up. "No," she said.

"Lucy, come on," Eleanor called. "He needs one of a blonde."

Roy had to slap his own forehead. "Who said that?" he wanted to know.

"She *likes* you," Ellie whispered.

"Now who told you that, Eleanor? Who told you something like that?"

Lucy stood at attention under the tree, looking straight at the hole in the camera, and he took a picture. One. She noticed that he did not refer to the light meter first.

When the picture was developed, he showed it to her. She was heading down the Sowerby drive for home when he came out of the house behind her. "Hey."

Despite herself, she turned. He trotted down the drive in a kind of loping, pigeon-toed run.

"Here," he said. "You want it?"

She had hardly taken the picture from his hand when he added, "Otherwise I'm going to throw it away. It's not too hot."

Glaring at him she said, "Just who do you think you're talking to, you!" and thrust the photograph at his chest and walked angrily home.

That evening he appeared at Dale's Dairy Bar, where she worked on Mondays, Tuesdays and Wednesdays from seven to ten, and on Fridays and Saturdays from seven to eleven-thirty. He sat where she had to take his order: a grilled cheese with bacon and tomato.

When she put down the sandwich in front of him, he said, "Hey, about this afternoon"—he took a bite out of the sandwich—"I'm sorry." She went on about her business.

When finally she came back to ask if he would care for anything more, he said it again, as sincerely as he could, and this time without a mouthful of food.

"Pay the cashier," she answered, giving him his check.

"*I* know that."

She had been watching him, however, for months; he was always so busy thinking about himself that he usually left the money on the counter. "You never *do* it," she answered sharply, and started away, realizing that she had said the wrong thing.

Sure enough, he followed her down the counter. What a smile. From ear to ear. "Don't I?"

"Pay the cashier, please."

"What time do you get off work?"

"Never."

"Look, I really am sorry. I meant the picture was no good. Technically."

"Pay the cashier, please."

"Look, I'm really genuinely sorry. Look . . . I don't lie," he said when she did not respond. "I don't have to," he said, hitching up his trousers.

He was parked outside at closing time. She refused to accept a lift home. She did not even acknowledge the offer.

"Hey," he said, driving slowly along beside her, "I'm only trying to be nice." She turned off Broadway, up Franklin, and the car turned with her.

After proceeding in this way for another block, he said, "Well, no kidding, what's wrong with trying to be nice?"

"Look, you," she said, and her heart was beating as though

some terrible catastrophe had just occurred, "look, you," she said again, "leave me alone!" And from then on, he was unable to.

—

He took hundreds of pictures of her. Once they spent a whole afternoon driving around the countryside in search of the right barn for her to stand in front of. He wanted one with a falling roof and a gloomy air, and all they could find were big red ones freshly painted. Once he made her stand in front of a white cement wall by the high school, in the full noon light, so that her bangs looked like white straw, and her blue eyes like the eyes in a statue, and the bones of her square serious face appeared to be stone beneath her skin. He entitled the photograph "Angel."

He began a whole series of black and white studies of Lucy's head, which he called "Aspects of an Angel." At first he had to tell her to stop frowning, or glaring, or fidgeting, and to stop saying "This is ridiculous" every two minutes; but after a while, as her embarrassment diminished, he did not have to tell her to stop doing anything. He told her practically every day that she had fantastic planes in her face, and that she was a far better subject than someone like Ellie, who was all glamour and no substance. He said girls like Ellie were a dime a dozen —just look at the magazines. *Her* face had character in it. Every afternoon he picked her up at school at three-thirty, and they went off on one of their photographic expeditions. And at night he was parked outside the Dairy Bar, waiting to drive her home.

At least that was where he drove her the first week. When he asked one night about coming inside awhile, she said absolutely no. To her relief, he did not ask again, once she had consented to drive with him out beyond The Grove to the wooded bluff that overlooked the river, which was called Picnic Paradise by the Winnisaw County Park Commission and Passion Paradise by the high school kids. There Roy would turn off the lights, flip on the radio, and try with all his might to get her to go all the way.

"Roy, I want to leave now. Really."

"Why?"

"I want to go home, please."

"I sort of love you, you know that."

"Don't say that. You don't."

"Angel," he said, touching her face.

"Stop. You almost put your finger in my eye."

"'You sigh, the song begins,'" he sang along with the radio, "'you speak and I hear violins, it's maaaa-gic.'"

"Roy, I'm not going to do anything. So let's go now."

"I'm not asking you to do anything. I'm only asking you to trust me. Just trust me," he said, trying once again to put his fingers between the buttons of her uniform.

"Roy, you're going to tear something."

"I'm not. Not if you don't fight. Just trust me."

"I don't know what that means. You say that, and when I do, then you only start going further. I don't want that, Roy."

But he was singing into her ear.

> "Without a golden wand,
> Or mystic charms,
> Fantastic things begin,
> When I am in your . . . *arms!*

"Oh, Lucy," he said.

"Not there," she cried, for on *arms* he had sunk an elbow into her lap, as though by accident.

"Oh, don't fight me, don't fight me, Lucy," he whispered, digging round and round, "trust me!"

"Oh, stop! No!"

"But I'm outside your clothes—it's only an elbow!"

"Take me home!"

Three weeks passed. She said that if that was all he was interested in each and every night, she did not think they should see each other ever again. He said that it wasn't all he was interested in, but he was a grown man and he hadn't thought she was going to turn out to be just another kid who didn't know what life was all about. He hadn't thought she was going to turn out to be like Ellie, a professional virgin—a c.t., if she knew what that was. She didn't, and he said he had too much respect for her to tell her. The whole point was that he wouldn't even have started up in the first place with a girl he couldn't respect; nor would he have invited her out in the car if he didn't think she was mature enough to handle some ordinary premarital petting. She said petting was one thing and what he wanted was something else. He said he would even settle for petting if she would just relax; she said that as soon as she started to relax, he stopped settling. She said she wasn't Monkey Littlefield; he said well then, maybe that was just too bad for her; and she said well then, go back to her if that's what you're really after; and he said maybe I will. And so the next afternoon when she came out of school the car wasn't there. Ellie wasn't waiting for her either; she had stopped weeks ago, once Roy got involved with Lucy on his "Aspects of an Angel" series. Lucy didn't know what to do with herself. Again, nowhere to go.

That night she was walking home from the Dairy Bar when a car pulled up alongside her. "Hey, girlie, want a lift?"

She did not look around.

"Hey, Lucy." He blew the horn and pulled over to the curb. "Hey, it's me. Hop in," he said, throwing open the door. "Hi, Angel."

She glared at him. "Where were you this afternoon, Roy?"

"Around."

"I'm asking a question, Roy. I waited for you."

"Oh, come on, forget it—get in."

"Don't tell me what to do, Roy," she said. "I'm not Monkey Littlefield."

"Gee, I thought you were."

"And just what is that supposed to mean?"

"Nothing, nothing. It's a joke!"

"Is that where you were this afternoon? With her?"

"I was pining for you. Well, come on, I'll drive you home."

"Not until you apologize for this afternoon."

"But what did I do?"

"You broke an engagement, that's all."

"But we had a fight," he said. "Remember?"

"Well, if we had a fight, why are you here now? Roy, I won't be treated—"

"Okay, okay, I'm sorry."

"Are you? Or are you just saying it?"

"Yes! No! Oh, get in the car, will you?"

"But you do apologize then," she said.

"*Yes!*"

She got into the car . . . "Where do you think you're driving, Roy?"

"I'm just driving. It's early."

"I want to go directly home."

"You'll get home. Did you ever *not* get home?"

"Turn around, Roy. Please, let's not start this again."

"Maybe I want to talk to you. Maybe I have some more apologizing to do."

"Roy, you're not funny. I want to go home. Now stop this."

Just past The Grove he pulled onto the dirt road, instantly turning down his headlights (the unwritten code of Passion Paradise) until he came to a clearing where no other car was parked.

He flipped the parking lights off now, and the radio on, and tuned in "Rendezvous Highlights." Doris Day was singing "It's Magic."

"Boy, either it's coincidence or it's just our song," he said, trying to pull her head toward him. "'Without a golden wand, or mystic charms'—" he sang. She resisted his gentle tug on the back of the neck, so he bent his face toward her closed mouth and wide-open eyes. "Angel," he said.

"You sound like a movie when you say that. Don't."

"Oh, brother," he said, "you can really destroy a mood."

"Well, I'm sorry. I expected to be driven home."

"I'll take you home! You can at least move over for the time being," he said. "Well, will you move over, *please*? So I don't get a steering wheel in my chest, *do you mind*?"

She began to shift to her right, but before she knew it he had her pinned up against the door and was kissing her face. "Angel," he whispered. "Oh, Angel. You smell like the Dairy Bar."

"Well, I happen to work there. I'm sorry."

"But I *like* it," and then before she could speak again, he pressed his mouth on hers. He did not fall away until the record was over, then with a sigh. He waited to hear what the next song would be.

"Don't fight me, Lucy," he whispered, stroking her hair. "Don't; it's not worth it," and along with Margaret Whiting he began to sing "'There's a tree in the meadow, with a stream drifting by'—" and to move his hand up under her slip.

"Don't," he said, when she began to struggle. "Trust me. I just want to touch your knee."

"I don't believe that, Roy. That's ridiculous."

"I swear. I won't go any higher. Come on, Lucy. What's a knee?"

> I will always remember
> The love in your eye—
> The day you carved upon that tree,
> I love you till I die.

They continued kissing. "See?" he said, after several minutes had passed. "Did I move it? Well, did I?"

"No."

"Didn't I say you could trust me?"

"Yes," she said, "but don't put your tongue on my teeth, please."

"Why not? What's it hurting?"

"Roy, you're just licking my teeth, what's the sense to it?"

"There's a lot of sense to it! It's passion!"

"Well, I don't *want* any."

"*Okay*," he said, "okay. Calm down. I'm sorry. I thought you liked it."

"There's nothing even to like, Roy—"

"*Okay!*"

> There was a boy,
> A very strange, enchanted boy.
> They say he wandered very far,
> Very far, over land and sea.

"I love this," Roy said. "It's just out. They guy who wrote it is supposed to live just like that."

"What is it?"

"'Nature Boy.' Just what the guy wrote it actually is. It's really got a great message. Listen to the words."

> This he said to me:
> "The greatest thing you'll ever learn,
> Is just to love, and be loved in return."

"Lucy," Roy whispered, "let's sit in the back."

"No. Positively no."

"Oh, hell, you don't have any respect for a mood—do you know that?"

"But we don't *sit* in the back, Roy. We tried to, but you really want to lie *down* in the back."

"Because the back doesn't have a steering wheel, Lucy, and it's more comfortable—and it's plenty clean too, because I cleaned it out myself this afternoon."

"Well, I'm not going back there—"

"Well, I am! And if you want to sit up here alone, go right ahead!"

"Oh, Roy—"

But he was out of the car and into the back seat, where he promptly stretched out, his head against one door and his feet through the open window opposite. "That's right, I'm lying down. Why shouldn't I? It's my car."

"I want to go home. You said you'd take me home. This is ridiculous."

"To you, sure. Boy, no wonder you and Ellie are friends. You're a real team." He mumbled something she couldn't understand.

"I'd like to know what you said just then, Roy."

"I said two c.t.'s, that's what."

"And what are they?"

"Oh," he moaned, "forget it."

"Roy," she said, turning on her knees, now in real anger, "we went through this last week."

"Right! Right! We sat in the back. And did anything terrible happen?"

"Because I wouldn't let it," she said.

"So then don't let it this time," he said. "Look, Lucy," and he sat up and tried to take hold of her head, which she pulled away. "I respect what you want, you know that. But all you want to do," he said, slumping backward, "is to get your picture taken, and get driven home at night, and what the other person feels . . . well, I happen to *feel* something! Oh, forget the whole mess, really."

"Oh, Roy," and she opened the front door and got out of the car, as she had on that awful night the week before. Roy threw open the back door so violently that it careened on its hinges.

"Get in," he whispered.

In the back he told her how much he could love her. He was pulling at her uniform buttons.

"Everybody says things like that when they want what you want, Roy. Stop. Please stop. I don't want to do this. Honestly. Please."

"But it's the *truth*," he said, and his hand, which had touched down familiarly on her knee, went like a shot up her leg.

"No, *no*—"

"Yes!" he cried triumphantly. "*Please!*"

And then he began to say trust me to her, over and over, and please, please, and she did not see how she could stop him from doing what he was doing to her without reaching up and sinking her teeth into his throat, which was directly over her face. He kept saying please and she kept saying please, and she could hardly breathe or move, he was over her with all his weight, and saying now don't fight me, I could love you, Angel, Angel, trust me, and suddenly into her mind came the name, Babs Egan.

"Roy—!"

"But I love you. Actually now I do."

"But what are you doing!"

"I'm not doing anything, oh, my Angel, my Angel—"

"But you will."

"No, no, my Angel, I won't."

"But you're doing it *now*! Stop! Roy, *stop* that!" she screamed.

"Oh, damn it," he said, and sat up, and allowed her to pull her legs out from under him.

She looked out the window at her side; the glass had fogged over. She was afraid to look over at him. She didn't know whether his trousers were just down, or completely off. She could hardly speak. "Are you crazy?"

"What do you mean, crazy? I'm a human being! I'm a man!"

"You can't do something like that—by force! That's what I mean! And I don't want to do it anyway. Roy, get back in front. Dress yourself. Take me home. Now!"

"But you just wanted to. You were all ready to."

"You had my arms pinned. You had me trapped! I didn't want anything! And you weren't even going to—to be careful! Are you absolutely *insane*? I'm not doing that!"

"But I would use something!"

She was astonished. "You would?"

"I tried to get some today."

"You *did*? You mean you were planning this all day long?"

"No! No! Well, I didn't get them—did I? Well, did I?"

"But you tried. You were thinking about it and planning it all day—"

"But it didn't *work*!"

"Please, I don't understand you—and I don't want to. Take me home. Put your trousers on, *please*."

"They're on. They were always on. Darn it, you don't even know what I went through today. All you know is your own way, that's all. Boy, you are another Ellie—another c.t.!"

"Which is *what*!"

"I don't use that kind of language in front of girls, Lucy! I respect you! Doesn't that mean anything to you at all? You know where I was this afternoon? I'll tell you where, and I'm not ashamed either—because it happened to involve respect for you. Whether you know it or not."

And then, while she pulled her slip down and rearranged her skirt, he told her his story. For almost an hour he had waited outside Forester's for Mrs. Forester to go upstairs and leave her goofy old husband alone at the counter. But once Roy got inside, it turned out that Mrs. Forester had only gone back into the storeroom, and she was up by the register ready to wait on him before he could even turn around and walk out.

"So what could I do? I bought a pack of Blackjack Gum. And a tin of Anacin. Well, what else was I supposed to do? In every store in town my father's name is a household word. Every place I go it's 'Hi, Roy, how's G.I. Joe?' And people see me with *you*, Lucy. I mean, they know we're going together, you know. So who would they think it was for? Don't you think I think about that? There's your reputation to consider too, don't you think? There are a lot of things I happen to think about, Lucy, that maybe don't cross your mind, sitting in school all day."

Somehow he had confused her. What really did she want

him to do? To have bought one of those things? He certainly wasn't going to use it on her. She wasn't going to let him *plan* what he was going to do to her hours in advance, and then act as though the whole thing was the passion of the moment. She wasn't going to be used or tricked, or be treated like some street tramp either.

"But you were overseas," she was saying.

"The Aleutians! The Aleutian Islands, Lucy—across the Bering Sea from the U.S.S.R.! Do you know what the motto is up there? 'A woman behind every tree'—*but there are no trees.* Get it? What do you think I did up there? I made out order forms all day. I played eighteen thousand ping-pong games. What's the *matter* with you!" he said, sinking in disgust into the seat. "Overseas," he said sourly. "*You* think I was up in some harem."

". . . But what about with someone else?"

"I never did it with anyone else! I've never done it in my entire life, all the way!"

"Well," she said softly, "I didn't know that."

"Well, it's the awful truth. I'm twenty years old, almost twenty-one, but that doesn't mean I go around doing it with every girl I see. I have to *like* the person, first of all. You listen to stupid Ellie, but Ellie doesn't know what she's talking about. The reason, Lucy, I don't take Monkey Littlefield out is because I don't happen to respect her. If you want the truth. And I don't like her. And I don't even know her! Oh, forget it. Let's just go, let's just call it quits. If you're going to listen to every story about me you hear, if you can't see the kind of person I am, Lucy, then pardon my language, but the hell with it."

He liked her. He actually did like her. He said people knew that they were going together. She hadn't realized. She was going with Roy Bassart, who was twenty and had been in the service. And people knew it.

"—over in Winnisaw," she was saying. Oh, why was she going on and on with this subject?

"Sure, I suppose they have them over in Winnisaw, they probably give them out on the streets in Winnisaw."

"Well, you could have driven over, that's all I mean."

"But why should I? Even going into Forester's on Broadway is going too far, as far as you're concerned. So what's the sense? Who am I kidding? Myself? I spent a whole afternoon hanging around outside waiting for that old hag to disappear, and it wouldn't have made any difference anyway. You'd only hate me worse. Right? So where does that leave me? Well, what is it you want to say, Lucy? That you'd say yes, if I had something?"

"No!"

"Okay, now we know where we stand! Fine!" He threw open the back door on his side. "Let's go home! I can't take any more of this, really. I happen to be a man and I happen to have certain physical needs, as well as emotional needs, you know, and I don't have to take this from any high school kid. All we do is discuss every move I make, step by step. Is that romantic to you? Is that your idea of a man-woman relationship? Well, it's not mine. Sex is one of the highest experiences anybody can have, man or woman, physical or mental. But you're just another one of those typical American girls who thinks it's obscene. Well, let's go, Typical American Girl. I'm really a good-natured, easygoing guy, Lucy, so it really takes something to get me in a state like this—but I'm in it, all right, so let's go!"

She didn't move. He was really and truly angry, not like somebody who was trying to deceive you or trick.

"Well, what's the matter now?" he asked. "Well, what did I do wrong now?"

"I just want you to know, Roy," she said, "that it isn't that I don't like you."

He made the sour face. "No?"

"No."

"Well, you sure do hide it."

"I don't," she said.

"You do!"

". . . But what if you don't like me? Really? How can I know you're telling the truth?"

"I told you, *I don't lie*!"

When she didn't respond, he came closer to her.

"You say love," Lucy said. "But you don't mean love."

"I get carried away, Lucy. That's not a lie. I get carried away, by the mood. I like music, so it affects me. So that's not a 'lie.'"

What had he just said? She couldn't even understand . . .

He climbed back into the car. He put his hand on her hair. "And what's wrong with getting carried away by the mood anyway?"

"But when the mood leaves you?" she asked. She felt as though she weren't there, as though this were all happening a long time ago. "Tomorrow, Roy?"

"Oh, Lucy," he said, and began kissing her again. "Oh, Angel."

"And what about Monkey Littlefield?"

"I told you, I told you, I don't even know her—oh, Angel, *please*," he said, sliding her down against the new slipcovers he himself had installed. "It's you, it's you, it's you and only you—"

"But tomorrow—"

"I'll see you tomorrow, I promise, and the next day, and the next—"

"Roy, I *can't*—oh stop "

"But I'm not."

"But you are!"

"Angel," he moaned into her ear.

"Roy, no, please."

"It's okay," he whispered, "it's all right—"

"Oh, it's not!"

"But it is, oh, it is, I swear," he said, and then he assured her that he would use a technique he had heard about up in the Aleutians, called interruption. "Just trust me," he pleaded, "trust me, trust me," and, alas, she wanted to so badly, she did.

—

A week before Lucy's graduation the news arrived: Roy had been accepted at the Britannia School of Photography and Design, which had been established, according to the catalogue and brochure, in 1910. They were delighted to enroll him for the September session, they said, and returned with the letter of acceptance the dozen studies of Lucy he had enclosed with his application.

At the little impromptu party he gave that evening in Roy's honor—Ellie and Joe, Roy and Lucy, Mr. and Mrs. Bassart—Uncle Julian said they all owed a debt of gratitude to Lucy Nelson for being so photogenic. She deserved a prize too, so he gave her a kiss. He was still somebody whom she hadn't made up her mind she actually approved of, and when she saw his lips coming her way she had a bad moment in which she almost pulled away. It wasn't just Mr. Sowerby's behavior with his wife, or his language, that caused her to be slightly repulsed; nor the fact that someone five foot five and smelling of cigars wasn't particularly her idea of attractive. It was that during the last month there had been several occasions when she thought she had caught him looking too long at her legs. Could Roy be telling his uncle what they were doing? She just couldn't believe it; he might know they parked up at Passion Paradise, but so did Ellie and Joe Whetstone, and all they did was neck. At least that's what Ellie *said*—and surely what her parents believed. No, nobody knew anything at all, and Mr. Sowerby was probably only looking at the floor, or at nothing, those times she thought he was looking at her legs. After all she was just eighteen, and he was Eleanor's father, and her legs had no shape, or so she thought, and it was ridiculous to imagine, as she had when she had found herself alone with him in the house one Saturday afternoon, that he was going to follow her up to Ellie's room and try to do something to her. She was getting sex on the brain, too. She and Roy really had to stop what they had begun, she just knew it. He liked it so much he was dragging her up there every night, and maybe she liked it too, but liking it wasn't the issue . . . What was, then? That's what Roy asked, whenever she started saying, "No, no, not tonight." But why not tonight, if last night?

Anyway, when Mr. Sowerby kissed her it was loud and on the cheek, and everyone was laughing, and Mrs. Sowerby was right there watching, trying to laugh too. It was as unlike Lucy as anything could be—in a way it was one of the strangest things she had ever done—but in the confusion that came of being told in public that she was attractive, in the excitement that came of being so much a part of this celebration, of this family, of this house, she shrugged her shoulders, turned bright red and kissed Uncle Julian back. Roy applauded. "Bravo!" he cried, and Mrs. Sowerby stopped trying to laugh.

Well, too bad for her. There really was very little Lucy could do that met with Mrs. Sowerby's approval. She was a dowdy, snobbish woman who even seemed to hold against Lucy the fact that it was she who had finally had the strongest influence in deciding what Roy should become. Which was certainly none of Mrs. Sowerby's business—even though that did appear to be the case: why Roy had decided to go to photography school in Fort Kean, where Britannia was located, seemed to have less to do with the quality of the training he would receive there—or with whatever natural talent he had for taking pictures, to be frank—than with the fact that Lucy happened to be going down to school in Fort Kean too.

That Roy had been guided in his decision by such a consideration was hardly a fact that displeased Lucy. On the other hand, it was one more refutation of that idea she had formed of him before they had met: that he was a serious young man who had choices before him of real magnitude and gravity. No, he wasn't exactly turning out to be entirely as she had imagined him back then—not that that was all to his discredit, however. For one thing, he really wasn't as rude and ill-mannered as he had first appeared. And he wasn't indifferent to others' feelings; least of all to hers. Once the showing off had stopped, once he was no longer as frightened of her (she realized) as she had been of him, he was altogether sweet and considerate. In his amiability he even reminded her a little of Mr. Valerio, which was certainly a compliment.

Nor was he superior in his attitudes, which was something she had just assumed would be the case, given his age and experience. He never tried to boss her around—except for sex; and even there she knew that when she decided enough was enough (probably that very night), there was nothing he would be able to do to force her to resume. There was nothing he could have done to force her to start, either, only why hadn't she realized that at the time? The worst that could have happened was that he would never have seen her again. And would that have been a tragedy? Truthfully, there were a lot of important ways in which she was discovering that she didn't like Roy that much. At times it even seemed as though it were she who was two and a half years older than Roy, not the other way around. She simply couldn't bear him when he sang those songs into her ear, first of all. He was so childish sometimes, even if he was now twenty-one and old enough to vote, as he kept saying to everyone. Sometimes the things he said were nothing less than stupid. In the car, for instance, he kept telling her that he loved her . . . But was that stupid? What if it was true? Or what if he was only saying it for fear that if he didn't she wouldn't let him go all the way any more? Oh, she knew, she knew, she knew—they should never have started up in the car. It wasn't right if you weren't married, and it was even worse with someone you never could marry, either. *We must stop!* But somehow it made no more sense to stop now that they had begun than it had made to start in the first place. What she should really stop was the whole stupid thing!

Yes, she was very, very confused—even on that wonderful, cheery night at the Sowerbys', which began with Uncle Julian (as Roy had encouraged her to call him) kissing her as though she were another member of the family, and ended with his bringing out of the refrigerator a real bottle of French champagne, exploding cork and all . . . Oh, how could she possibly believe the suspicion, growing larger in her every day, that he probably wasn't going to have one of any consequence at all, when they all stood around him with glasses raised, and said in unison, "To Roy's future!"

—

After graduation she began her summer schedule at the Dairy Bar: from ten to six, every day but Wednesday and Sunday. Midway through July she and Roy drove down to Fort Kean one Wednesday to look for a place for him to live in September. After inspecting each rooming house he came back to where Lucy sat in the parked car, and said he didn't think the place was right, at least for him; either the room smelled funny, or the landlady looked suspicious, or the bed was too short, something he had had enough of for sixteen months in the Aleutians. In the one place that was ideal—one huge room with a bed in it that used to be the landlady's husband's (who'd been six foot *five*), where the toilet was spotless, and the roomer guaranteed a shelf of his own in the refrigerator—there was no private entrance.

Well, said Lucy, there had to be.

At four that afternoon they had the worst argument they had ever had with each other, and far and away the worst Roy had ever had with anyone, his father included. To what was still the best all-around deal, all she could do was vehemently shake her head and say no, there had to be a private entrance if he expected ever to see her again. Suddenly, crying out, "Well, I don't care—it's me who has to live here!" he wheeled the Hudson around and drove back to the house with the long bed.

When he got back to the car he took a road map from the glove compartment and on its face carefully drew a rectangle. "This is my room," he said, managing not to look at her. It was on the first floor, a corner room with two tall windows on either side; all four let out onto a wide porch surrounded by shrubs. They were as good as four private entrances. At night a person could just step in and out of the windows exactly as though they were doors . . . Well, what did she want to say? Was she really planning on never speaking to him again, or did she have an opinion to express?

"I expressed my opinion," she said. "It didn't mean anything to you."

"It did."

"But you went ahead and rented the room anyway."

"Because I wanted to, yes!"

"I have nothing further to say, Roy."

"Lucy, it's a room! It's only a room! Why are you doing this?"

"You did it, Roy. Not me."

"*Did what?*"

"Acted like a child, again."

Before starting back to Liberty Center, Roy drove around to the Fort Kean College for Women. He pulled the car to the curb so Lucy could take another look at her new home. The college was across Pendleton Park from the main business section of Fort Kean. It had been built as a boys' preparatory school in the 1890's; in the thirties the school went under, and the property had been unused until the war, when it was occupied by the Army Signal Corps. After V-J Day the site had been purchased by the state, barracks and all, for its expanding educational program. It was certainly not the ivy-covered college campus one saw in the movies, or read about in books; the barracks that the Army had thrown up, long faded yellow buildings, were used as classrooms, and the administration building and dormitory was an old square fortress-like structure of gray stone that stood almost directly onto the street and resembled the County Courthouse in Winnisaw. At the sight of it, however, Lucy thought, "Only fifty-nine days more."

"Which is your room?" asked Roy, looking out the car window.

She did not answer.

The school was across from a row of stores, one of which was called "The Old Campus Coffee Shop." Roy said, "Hey, want a Coke in The Old Campus Coffee Shop?"

No answer.

"Oh, Angel, I do care what you think. You know that. What you think is important to me. But I have to live somewhere, don't I? Well, Lucy, just be reasonable—don't I? That's not being a kid, or a child, or whatever you said."

"Yes, Roy," she finally said, "you have to live somewhere."

"Don't be sarcastic, Lucy, really. Sometimes you're just too sarcastic, when I'm only asking for a simple answer. I've got to get my eight hours' sleep if I expect to get the most out of classes. Well, *don't* I? So I *need* the long bed. Well, is that a stupid statement too?"

She thought, *Everything you say is a stupid statement!* "No," she said, for he had taken her hand, and really seemed to be in pain.

"So then how can you be angry? Lucy, come on, what's the sense of fighting? Let's have a Coke, okay? Then we'll start home. Come on, say the fight is over. Why ruin the day? Look, am I forgiven for my terrible sin, or are you going to keep this silly thing up forever?"

He actually appeared to be near tears. She saw that there was no point in arguing with him any further. For in that instant she made up her mind—if only she had made it up earlier in the day, she could have saved them both the misery of a fight: she would never set foot in that room of his so long as she lived, no matter how many windows it had, or even doors. It was really as simple as that.

"Okay," she said, "let's have a Coke."

"That's my girl," said Roy, kissing her on the nose, "that's my old angel girl."

From that afternoon on she knew for sure that Roy wasn't for her. That very night she would not drive up with him to Passion Paradise. When instantly he grew sulky and morose, and seemed about ready to break into tears again, she told him it was because she was not well. It happened to be the truth, but then at home with a thick black crayon she circled on her calendar the day she would make it altogether clear their romance was over (at the same time x-ing out another day of her life in Liberty Center: fifty-eight to go).

It looked as though the bad news could not be broken to Roy until Sunday: the following night there were already plans to drive up to the Selkirk Fair with Ellie and Joe, with whom they doubled at least once a week now that Lucy was working only during the day; and on Friday evening Roy expected her to go to Winnisaw with him to see *A Date with Judy*; then on Saturday there was the barbecue at the Sowerbys'. It was a barbecue for the Sowerbys' adult friends, and when Roy's uncle had invited "the long drink of water" to come and to bring "Blondie" with him, it had delighted Lucy (secretly) no less than Roy. She was coming to like Mr. Sowerby more all the time, and to admire certain of his qualities. As Roy said, he really didn't give a hoot about people's opinions; he did and said whatever he wanted, whenever he wanted. She still thought he was a little coarse with his language, but she didn't object, corny though it was, when he called her "Blondie," which seemed to have become his nickname for her, or even when he put his arm around her waist one evening and said (in a joshing way, of course, and winking at Roy), "You just tell me, Blondie, when you get tired of looking up at this big lug and want to look down at a little one."

She would have circled Friday then instead of Sunday, had it not been for the Sowerbys' Saturday night barbecue, at which her presence had specifically been requested by the host himself. That was awfully hard to turn down. She supposed she could wait until Sunday without losing anything—gaining three nights more away from home, in fact. Surely any diversion, even if it involved Roy, was better than sitting up in her hot room, listening to her family rocking downstairs on the porch; or lying awake in the dark bedroom, unable to sleep until she heard her father's footsteps coming up the stairs and she had determined (solely for the record) whether he was actually going off to bed sober.

What had always made summer particularly awful was that with all the doors and windows open, her sense of the presence of those whom she could hardly abide was painfully, horribly acute. Just to hear someone she hated *yawn* could drive her to distraction if she happened to be in an angry mood. Now, however, she was out every night until twelve-thirty, by which time they were usually asleep (not that it was any pleasure hearing someone you hated snore, if it made you start thinking about them). On the hottest nights, rather than being locked up with her family, she and Roy would sit on one of the benches down by the river, catching what breeze there was and staring off into the black stillness of water under the Winnisaw Bridge. She would think about college and Fort Kean—*away, away*—and often Roy would begin to sing to her, in a voice that really wasn't that bad, or so she was willing to admit in the pleasure of contemplating the future that would soon be hers. He sang like Vaughan Monroe, and like Dick Haymes; he could do Nat "King" Cole singing "Nature Boy," and Mel Blanc doing "Woody Woodpecker," and Ray Bolger (whom he thought he resembled in build) doing "Once in Love with Amy." After they saw *The Jolson Story* he did for her his imitation of the incomparable Al Jolson. That was how Roy introduced himself as hand in hand they sat down by the river on those close nights during what was to be the last summer of Lucy's arduous and unhappy youth. "Ladies and gentlemen, if you will, the incomparable, the one and only, Al Jolson.

> "Oh, how we danced,
>   On the night we were wed,
>   We danced and we danced—"

Fifty-eight days. Fifty-seven. Fifty-six.

At the Sowerby barbecue on Saturday night she got into a long, serious discussion with Roy's father—their first real talk—in which she heard herself assuring Mr. Bassart that he really shouldn't have anxiety or doubt any longer about Roy's future. Mr. Bassart said that he still could not figure where the interest in photography had suddenly come from. His experience with young people had long ago convinced him not to bank too heavily on sudden enthusiasms, since they had a habit of disappearing under strain. He was, he admitted, relieved that the months wasted wading around in what he called "a swamp of half-baked ideas" had come to an end, but now what concerned him was whether Roy had really chosen something he was going to be able to stick with when the going got rough. What did Lucy think? Oh, said Lucy, his heart was really in photography, she was sure of it.

"What makes you so sure?" asked Mr. Bassart in his flat voice.

She thought quickly and said that photography wasn't such an astonishing interest for Roy to have, when you thought that really it was a wonderful way of combining his present interest in drawing with his old interest in printing.

Mr. Bassart reflected upon what she had said.

So did she, reddening. "I think that's true, in a manner of speaking, Mr. Bassart."

"It's clever," he said without smiling, "but whether it's true is something I'll have to think about. What about your own plans? What are your own personal educational goals?"

Perspiring away under the brand-new peasant blouse that she had purchased for the party, she told him . . . Develop a logical mind . . . self-discipline . . . increase her general fund of knowledge . . . learn more about the world we live in . . . learn more about herself . . .

It was difficult to tell when to stop (exactly as it had been in the scholarship application), but when Mr. Bassart finally said, during a paragraph break, "Those are all good goals," she believed she had won approval enough for the time being, and shut up.

And—she later realized—he had asked not a single question about her background. He did not appear to be any more interested in the subject than Julian Sowerby; men like that judged you not on family history, but on the kind of person you were. Only Mrs. Bassart (who seemed to have fallen instantly under her sister's influence) and Irene Sowerby seemed to hold against her things she wasn't even responsible for. The others, to their credit, weren't interested in gossip and ancient history—Roy included.

Since the beginning of summer Roy had taken to picking her up at the house after dinner each night. She was always ready when he arrived, giving him little encouragement, she hoped, to linger and make conversation. On the one occasion when he seemed to be trying to draw her into revealing something, she answered so sharply that he had never brought up the subject again. It was after his first meeting with her family, all of whom were gathered in the living room after dinner. The young man arrived, was quickly introduced and led by Lucy straight back out the door.

Driving over to the movie, Roy said, "Wow, your mother's a real looker, you know that?"

"Yes."

"You know who she reminds me of?"

"No."

"Jennifer Jones." No answer. "Listen, did you see *Song of Bernadette*?"

She had, with Kitty Egan, three times; but her conversion was her own business too. It hadn't even taken place.

"Of course, your mother's older than Jennifer Jones . . ." Roy said. "And your grandfather is Mr. Carroll from the post office. Now, I didn't even know that. Ellie never mentioned it."

"He's retired," she said. Why on earth had she given in when he said it was time he was introduced to her "folks"?

They were crossing the Winnisaw Bridge. "Well, your father seems like a nice guy."

"I don't talk about him, Roy! I never want to talk about him!"

"Gee, sure, okay," he said, raising one hand over his chest. "Just making conversation."

"Well, don't."

"Well, okay, I won't."

"That subject does not interest me *at all*."

"Okay, okay," he said, smiling, "you're the boss," and after a silent minute during which she contemplated asking him to pull the car over to the side so that she could get out, he switched on the radio and began to sing.

From then on, neither Bassart nor Sowerby asked any question about her home life. Ellie couldn't have cared less, and so it was only in the company of Irene Sowerby, or Roy's mother, that Lucy became unduly conscious of what ordinarily she was able, after all these years of practice, to drive clear out of her mind. Of late she hardly ever had cause (outside the house) to think of herself as the kid who had done this or the kid whose father had done that. To the many people she met socially at the Sowerbys' for the first time on that Saturday night— among them, the principal, Mr. Brunn and his wife—she was, very simply, Roy Bassart's girl. "So," said Mr. Brunn, "this is the young lady I hear is keeping our old alum in line these days."

"Oh, it's a matter of opinion, Mr. Brunn, who's keeping who in line," said Roy.

"And are you off to school in September, dear?" asked Mrs. Brunn. Dear. Just like Mrs. Sowerby.

"Yes," said Lucy. "Fort Kean College for Women."

"They've got themselves quite a little setup down there," said Mr Brunn. "Very nice. Very nice."

"Lucy graduated twenty-ninth in the senior class this year, Mr. Brunn, before she tells you herself."

"Oh, I recognized Lucy—I knew she was up there. Good luck to you, Lucy. Keep up our reputation. We've sent them some fine girls down there and I'm sure you're going to turn out to be no exception."

"Thank you, Mr. Brunn. I'll try my best."

"Well, that'll do it, I'm sure. See you, Roy; see you, Lucy."

—

So, later that night, up in Passion Paradise, what could she do? It wasn't till Sunday that she was to tell him that she'd had enough, and it was still only Saturday night. And when she told him, what would happen? "I'm not going to be able to see you again. Ever." "*What?*" "Because we don't really have any business together, Roy." "But . . . what do you mean? Haven't these months meant anything at all? Look, why else am I going to Fort Kean to school—who inspired me to go there, except you?" "Well, you'll just have to go for a better reason than that." "What better reason is there but love!" "But it's not love—it's just sex." "It's *what?*" "Sex!" "Not to me . . . Look, is that what it is to you? Because to me . . . Oh, *no*," he'd weep, "this is terrible . . ." And then—she just knew it—he wouldn't go to Fort Kean at all. If she broke off with him now, he would give up Britannia, give up all his plans, probably in the end give up photography too, despite what she had said to his father in his defense. And then he *would* be right back in his swamp of ideas . . . But that was his affair, not hers . . . Or was it? He was so good to her, so kind to her, sweeter to her than anybody had ever been before in her life, and day in and day out too. How could she turn around now and be so heartless and cruel? Especially when it was only a matter of a few more weeks. It might even mean his whole career. Because he depended on her—he listened to her—he loved her. *Roy loves me.*

At least that's what he said.

"I love you, Angel," he said at the door. He kissed her nose. "You made a real hit tonight."

"On who?"

"Mr. Brunn, for one. Everybody." He kissed her yet again. "Me," he said. "Look, sleep tight." From the bottom of the steps he whispered, "*Au revoir.*"

She was very, very confused. Ten months ago she was still in the band, marching behind Leola Krapp, and now she was going steady! Going all the way practically every night!

She circled six days in July, and ten in August, and then on September first she took her crayon and circled four times around the day after Labor Day. She had started out to circle Labor Day itself, until she remembered that she and Roy and Ellie and Joe Whetstone were to go off canoeing on the river, an event that had been planned by Roy weeks before. If only everything weren't planned so far in advance! If only he didn't need her so, depend on her so, love her so! *But did he?*

When they arrived on Labor Day morning at the Sowerbys', Roy's Aunt Irene came outside to say that Ellie had been sick in the night and was still sleeping. She suggested that the three young people had better go off by themselves for the day. But even as she spoke, a very sad and wan-looking Ellie appeared in the upstairs hall window, wearing her bathrobe. She waved. "Hi."

"Ellie," said Mrs. Sowerby, "I suggested to the others that they'd better go off without you today, dear."

"Oh, no."

"Eleanor, if you're not well, you surely cannot go canoeing."

"Your mother's right," said Joe.

"But I want to go," Ellie called down in a weak voice.

"It wouldn't be safe, El," said Joe. "Really."

"Joe is right, Eleanor," said Mrs. Sowerby.

"But I *planned* to go," said Ellie, and suddenly she drew down the shade, as though she was about to weep.

It was decided that the three young people should come inside while Ellie washed and dressed and had a little breakfast of tea and toast; then if she really did seem to have recovered, perhaps the youngsters could go ahead with their plans. Ellie's troubles had begun the previous evening while Mrs. Sowerby had been away at an informal meeting of the officers of The Quilt Society. In Mrs. Sowerby's absence, Ellie and her father had sat around the TV set, eating three pounds of cherries, followed by a quart of vanilla fudge ice cream, topped off with half a chocolate nut cake left over from dinner.

Julian Sowerby, feeling fine, claimed Ellie's upset stomach had nothing to do with a little dish of ice cream and a piece of cake; Ellie simply had the heebie-jeebies about going away to school in two weeks. Roy said that maybe Ellie had inherited her father's good looks (everyone laughed, Julian loudest of all) but that perhaps she hadn't been so fortunate as to inherit his cast-iron stomach.

"That's probably true, Mr. Sowerby" was Joe's comment. Joe assured Mrs. Sowerby that if she let Ellie come along, he would be sure to see that she didn't touch anything sweet. Mrs. Bassart had prepared an immense picnic basket for them, but Roy said that he and Joe would take care of Ellie's portion without too much trouble.

In a few minutes Ellie came down the stairs in white shorts, white polo shirt and white sandals. Her tan—nurtured daily on the back lawn and down by the landing—looked dazzling, as did her hair, which over the summer had taken on a coppery sheen. But this morning her face looked small and worn, and her "Hullo" was hardly audible as she went off to the kitchen to try to put a little food into her long, shapely body . . . Her body. Her long and shapely body! Lucy's understanding of Ellie's condition was instantaneous. *My God, it's happened. To Ellie Sowerby.*

Julian Sowerby drove off with his clubs to the Winnisaw Golf Club, and the young people consented to forgo the canoeing and take Mrs. Sowerby's advice and find a nice shady spot up at the picnic grounds to have their outing. But even hidden away under a tree the temperature rose steadily; about one o'clock Ellie began to feel woozy, and so they drove back to the Sowerbys' in Roy's car. The house was very quiet. The shades were drawn in the front bedroom, where apparently Mrs. Sowerby was taking a nap; and the family car was still gone, a fact that caused Ellie some consternation. Apparently she had expected to find her father already home.

"Do you want me to wake your mother, El?" asked Joe.

"No, no. I'm all right."

Joe and Roy decided to go out to the backyard and listen to the Sox double-header on the Sowerby portable. Ellie asked Lucy to come up with her to her room. Once there she locked the door, threw herself on to her bed, and beneath the white organdy canopy, began to cry.

Lucy watched her friend weeping her heart out. On the lawn below she saw the person responsible pick up a croquet mallet and begin to knock a ball around through the wickets. In two days Joe was to report for freshman football practice at the University of Alabama. Partly it was Ellie's recollection of life in the South during the early years of the war that seemed to have influenced Joe to accept the Alabama scholarship. Joe was to leave for school the very next day—but would he still go? Or would Ellie now go with him?

Roy had organized the day's outing, and had his mother prepare the lunch as his own farewell party to Joe Whetstone, whom he had come to consider his closest buddy. Lucy herself had always thought of Joe as one big blah. Sure, he was a great athlete, she supposed, and you had to admit he was handsome and rugged-looking, if you liked that type, but he had not a single opinion of his own on any subject. Whatever you said, Joe agreed with. There were times when she felt like reciting the Declaration of Independence just to watch his head go up and down and to hear him say, after every famous sentence, "You bet, that sure is true, that sure does make a lot of sense, boy, that's just what my Mom says . . ." The temptation to reveal him for the imbecile that he was came over her most strongly when Roy was purposely acting for Joe's benefit, telling some funny story about what had happened to him up in the Aleutians, or discussing some college football team he and Joe called "The Crimson Tide" and which normally he didn't seem to be interested in at all. But she had never given in to the temptation; she hadn't even told Ellie her real opinion of Joe Whetstone. And now it was too late. Now Joe had gotten Ellie into trouble, the worst kind of trouble there could possibly be for a girl. And Joe didn't even appear to know it.

Roy called to Joe. "Appling's up. Two on. No score."

"*Go*, Luke," said Joe, knocking the wooden ball clear through a wicket at the other end of the lawn. "Hey, Joe the Arm," he said.

"Oh, boy," Roy said sourly, "swing and a miss. Strike one."

"Come *on*, Lukey babe," said Joe, posing with his mallet like a batter all coiled up to swing. "Hey," said Joe, "Stan the Man," and he changed his batting stance and swung at an imaginary ball. "Gooing, going—"

"Foul!" said Roy.

"Shucks," said Joe, "pulled it too hard."

"Shhh," said Roy, looking quickly up at the house as Joe fell to the lawn laughing.

. . . What about college now? What about the Sowerbys? What about Ellie's future, if she had to marry Joe Whetstone? And what if he already knew and didn't care? Maybe he wanted to marry Ellie, but she was crying because she didn't want to marry him!

"I have—I have to tell somebody," Ellie said, turning to Lucy and clutching the pillow to her chest.

"What?" said Lucy softly. "Tell what, Ellie?"

Ellie pushed her head back into the pillow and again began to weep. She had done a stupid thing. A terrible, stupid thing. Her whole life would never be the same.

". . . Why? What is it?"

She had listened in on someone else's telephone conversation. "And it's not the first time, either," said Ellie, sobbing.

Then she's not pregnant.

Down below Roy said, "Base hit!"

"Go, Sox," said Joe. "Pour it on, baby."

"And the run scores!" cried Roy. "And another! Two nothing!"

Petulantly Lucy said, "What do you mean? Ellie, I can't understand you."

"I listened in on someone else's telephone conversation . . . and it was awful."

"Whose?"

"Oh, Lucy, I don't want my mother to know. Never!"

"Know *what*?"

"Is the door locked?" asked Ellie.

"You locked it," said Lucy impatiently.

"Then . . . Sit over here. On the bed. I don't want to shout. Oh, I don't know what to do. This is so awful . . . I've been trying to tell you for so long. I needed somebody's advice that I could talk it over with . . . But I just couldn't. And I shouldn't. Oh, but I just have to—but, Lucy, you have to promise me. You can't repeat it to anyone. Not even Roy. *Especially* not Roy."

"Ellie, I don't even understand what you're—"

"My father!" said Ellie. "Lucy, don't tell ever—do you promise? You have to promise me, Lucy. Please, so I can tell you."

"I promise."

"My father has women!" Ellie burst out. "On the side!"

Lucy received these words with equanimity: it was as though a truth she had known in her heart all along had finally been confessed by Eleanor.

"And that's not all," said Ellie. "Lucy . . . he gives them money."

"Are you sure?"

"*Yes.*"

"How do you know he does?"

"That's what I heard on the phone." She closed her eyes. "Actual money," she said, and the tears rolled off her cheeks onto her white polo shirt.

Just then they heard the door to Mrs. Sowerby's room open, down the hall.

"Dear, are you in there?" she asked.

"Yes. Lucy too. We're only talking, Mother."

"Are you all right?"

"It got too hot, Mother," said Ellie, frantically wiping her eyes. "But I'm fine. I promise. It was practically a hundred, though. And buggy. And crowded. All kinds of people from Winnisaw."

For a moment they heard nothing; then the sound of Mrs. Sowerby descending the stairs. Neither of them spoke until the screen door opened down below and Joe was saying, "Sox are out in front, Mrs. Sowerby, four to nothing."

"Sure," said Roy, "she's the right one to tell, all right. Hey, Aunt Irene, tell Joe which team Luke Appling plays for. No, no, tell him what a bunt is. Come on, give him your great definition of a bunt."

Roy and Joe could be heard down on the back lawn, teasing Mrs. Sowerby about sports, and Mrs. Sowerby could be heard obligingly making them laugh . . . while upstairs Eleanor began to tell Lucy the whole story.

It had begun about a year ago, on a summer night when she and her father had been home alone. It was after eleven and she was in bed, when suddenly she remembered she had forgotten to tell Judy Rollins not to say anything to anyone about something Ellie had told her, and so she reached over and picked up her bedside telephone. Of course, the instant she heard her father talking on the downstairs line she knew she should hang up. Only, the voice on the other end she recognized as belonging to nobody but Mrs. Mayerhofer, the manager of Daddy's laundromat in Selkirk, about whom he was always complaining to her mother. Mrs. Mayerhofer was, as he put it, a little slow on the pickup; there actually wasn't a single thing that he didn't have to explain to her ten times before she got it right. He kept her on almost solely out of pity—abandoned by her husband, she had an infant child to support—and because, unlike her predecessor, the illustrious Mrs. Jarvis, it didn't appear that Mrs. Mayerhofer was going to steal him deaf, dumb and blind.

On the phone her father was saying that he just couldn't get up to Selkirk until the end of the week because he was so tied up right here in Liberty Center, and Mrs. Mayerhofer said that she didn't think she could wait until the end of the week, and Ellie still remembered thinking, "Boy, what a moron," until she heard her father laugh and say that in the meantime then she was just going to have to make do with the old hot-water bottle. Mrs. Mayerhofer laughed, and Ellie said it was as though her bones and her blood and everything inside her had turned to stone. She pushed the receiver down into her pillow and held it there for what seemed like ages; when at last she raised it to her ear again, the line was free—and so she called Rollins. What else could she do?

This was just before she and Lucy had first gotten to know each other, Ellie said. Actually, she had been dying back then to tell Lucy what she had overheard, only she'd felt so ashamed and embarrassed—and very shortly so uncertain as to whether what she had heard meant what she had taken it to mean— that she decided to stop seeing Lucy entirely for the time being, rather than risk ruining their friendship and making a terrible fool of herself and her family.

For the moment Ellie's words confused Lucy, and not simply because of the disordered way in which her friend offered her explanation. She had to work out in her head the significance of all that Ellie had just said—that is, the significance to herself.

She would lie awake, Ellie was saying, just lie awake after that for hours on end, in dread of ever overhearing such a conversation again . . . and then silently lift the phone off the receiver. It was a nightmare; she didn't want to catch him, and she couldn't stop trying to. Then that winter her father came home one evening and said that Mrs. Mayerhofer ("my mental giant" was his expression) had flown the coop; just disappeared from her apartment in Selkirk—baby, baggage and all. The very next day he drove up to interview and hire somebody else for the job. The woman selected was named Edna Spatz.

And that was all that had happened. She never heard him with Mrs. Mayerhofer on the phone a second time, nor was there any reason for her to suspect Edna Spatz. Yet every time her father went off to the Selkirk store, Ellie knew it was to carry on behind her mother's back—even though she knew too that Edna Spatz had a husband in Selkirk and two small children. This was about the time she and Lucy had started seeing each other again, and on more occasions than she could even count, Ellie had wanted to blurt out to her the whole horrible story about Mrs. Mayerhofer. Only Mrs. Mayerhofer was so terribly dumb and uneducated. So he couldn't with her, he simply couldn't. He simply wouldn't even want to.

Or so she had gotten herself to believe, until last night. She had been on the stairs when the phone rang, and so she raced up to her room thinking that it was Joe, who had said he would call around nine. In the meantime her father had picked up the downstairs phone; "It's okay, Princess," he had called up to her, "it's just for me." She had called back, "Okay, Daddy," and gone ahead into her room, closed the door, and without any knowledge that she was even going to do it, gently lifted the phone off the hook. At first she couldn't even hear the words being spoken. It was as though she had a heart beating in her head, and another in her throat, and the rest of her simply didn't exist. On the other end a woman was speaking. Whether it was Edna Spatz, she didn't know. She had come to imagine Mrs. Spatz as no less a dimwit than Mrs. Mayerhofer, and the trouble with the voice on the other end was that it sounded smart . . . and young. The woman was saying that if she couldn't cover her check she didn't know what would happen to her. Her father said this was something he would have to take care of later—*and not by telephone.* He was whispering into the phone, but he was angry. The woman began to cry. She said that the agency had threatened to take her to court. She called him Julian, Julian, and she wept. She said she was sorry, she knew she shouldn't call, she had dialed and hung up half a dozen times over the weekend, but who else did she have to turn to but Julian, Julian?

It was at that point that Ellie felt she could not bear to hear another word. The woman sounded so unhappy—and so young! So she buried the phone in the pillow again, and just sat there, not knowing what to do. Only a minute or so later her father called up the stairs to her. She replaced the phone as quietly as she could and came quickly down to him, chattering gaily all the while. She knew he was watching her every expression to see whether she had been listening, but Ellie was sure that she had not given herself away in anything she had said or done. She kept talking about Joe this and Joe that, and instantly sat next to him on the couch when invited to—"Keep me company, Daisy Mae"—and even let him hold her hand while the two of them watched TV together and ate all those cherries. That's why she had consumed so much junk; she was afraid to stop for fear he would think something was bothering her. And all the time they were sitting on the couch she had the most absurd thought: that she had an older sister, whom she knew nothing about, and that it was she who had been on the phone asking her father to send money. Of course she was only making up the idea of a sister, and knew it—and so then she began to think that maybe she was making up the whole incident.

"Lucy, I'm so confused—and miserable! Because I just don't know. Do you think it's true?"

"What's true?"

"What I heard."

"Well, you heard it, didn't you?"

"I don't know. Yes! But who is it? Who could it possibly be? And my poor mother," she said, weeping profusely once again, "she doesn't even know. Nobody knows. Nobody but you and me—and him . . . and her!"

—

All the youngsters were invited to stay for supper on the Sowerby lawn: roast beef sandwiches, corn on the cob, apple pie and ice cream—except for Ellie, who had consommé, half of which she left in the bowl. Mr. Sowerby offered each of the boys a bottle of beer, against Mrs. Sowerby's better judgment. "Come on, they'll all be in college in a week. Roy here is responsible for us winning the war against the North Pole. A little beer'll do him good, put some hair on his chest."

Joe took a sip and laid the glass aside; Roy drank his right out of the bottle. Then he opened the top button of his shirt and looked inside. "Nothing," he said.

They sat out on the lawn till long after dark. Ellie was stretched out in a beach chair with an afghan thrown over her, and just her head sticking out. It looked very, very small. Roy sat on the grass, holding his beer bottle in one hand; his head swung back against Lucy's legs whenever he took a swig from the bottle. Joe Whetstone was stretched out on his stomach, his chin resting on his two fists. He was looking up at the sky, and every once in a while he said, "Boy, oh, boy. Look at them all."

Roy said he'd known a guy in the service who believed in the stars. Joe said, "No kidding."

"Absolutely," said Roy, "to some people it's practically a religion in itself."

"No kidding," said Joe. "I wonder how many there really are."

Julian Sowerby asked how his Princess was.

"Better," she answered after a moment.

"I believe you were just missing home," said Julian Sowerby, "before you even went away from it."

"Boy, I'll bet that can happen," said Joe.

"Sure, sure. Homesick, plus all that vanilla fudge ice cream with, I understand from reliable sources, a little butterscotch sauce, *and* walnuts—"

"*Roy!*" cried Ellie weakly.

Roy and Joe laughed.

"Roy, don't tease her," said Mrs. Sowerby.

"Sorry, Ellie-o," said Roy.

Julian lit a cigar. "How about it, Joe?"

"Oh, no, sir," Joe said. "Got to stay in shape."

"Won't affect your toe, boy," Julian said.

"No, thank you just the same, Mr. Sowerby. Didn't mean to waste the beer either."

"Take it off my taxes," said Julian, to Joe's amusement. "How about you, General?" he asked Roy.

"Sure," said Roy, "if it's a good one. Toss."

Julian threw a cigar his way. "Fourteen-fifty a box, it ain't what I could call a stinkweed, wise guy."

The smoke from Roy's cigar rose around his head. "Not too bad," he said, holding it off at arm's length and muffling a cough.

"A real pro," said Uncle Julian.

Ordinarily Lucy couldn't stand to watch Roy smoke a cigar or drink a beer; he really cared very little for either. But this evening there were matters more grave to brood upon than Roy's showing off for his uncle. There was the uncle himself, whose secret had finally been revealed; there was Ellie, who knew the secret; there was Mrs. Sowerby, who did not; and there was herself. All these months she had been believing that Ellie was indifferent to her past, and suddenly it was clear that nothing but that past had caused Ellie to befriend her in September, and to resume that "friendship" again in February. It was a startling discovery. All this time, so stupidly, so innocently, so dreamily, she had been thinking that to Ellie Sowerby she was not the kid whose father hung out at Earl's Dugout, not the kid who had gained notoriety by calling the police to come take him away, when that was precisely who she was. It had caused her much pain that afternoon to understand that all of her attraction for Ellie lay in that past which she herself wanted never to think about again so long as she lived.

And it had made her angry too. Her temptation earlier in the afternoon had been to rise in indignation and tell Ellie exactly what she thought of her. "You mean that's what I am to you, Ellie? That's why you wanted me to be a friend? To my face, you actually have the nerve to admit that when you dropped me, it was because you believed you didn't *need* me any more? And what exactly did you think I was going to do for you, anyway, in return for letting me wear your precious sweater?"

On and on and on, but in her head only. At first she restrained her anger so as to hear the story of Julian Sowerby's deception to its conclusion, but even before Ellie had finished, she began to understand Eleanor's attraction to her as something else entirely. Ellie actually *admired* her. Her courage. Her pride. Her strength. Wasn't that a deeper way, a truer way, to see it? Ellie Sowerby, with all her clothes, and boys, and beauty, and money, had turned for help and advice—to her.

Well, what should Ellie do, then? *What?* Her mind began to examine the possibilities.

"Hey, what happened to Blondie tonight?" Julian was asking. "Cat got Cutie-Pie's tongue?"

"Oh, no."

"Thinking about college, aren't you, Lucy?" said Mrs. Sowerby.

"Yes."

"It's going to be a wonderful experience for all of you," said Irene Sowerby. "These will be the four most beautiful years of your life."

"That's what my Mom says too, Mrs. Sowerby," said Joe.

"Yes, it's going to do all of you a world of good," said Mrs. Sowerby, "to be away from home."

Poor Mrs. Sowerby. Poor woman. How mortifying. How wrong. How unjust . . . It was the first time that her heart had opened fully to Ellie's mother. She saw at last that she was something more than her own potential enemy. To understand that Mrs. Sowerby suffered was somehow to understand that she existed, had a life, had motives and reasons having nothing to do with frustrating and opposing Lucy Nelson. The fact was that she had never opposed her. The decision Ellie had made to stop seeing Lucy back in September had, by her own admission, nothing at all to do with any instructions she had received from her mother. Only now could Lucy see that during these past months Mrs. Sowerby had never been anything but kind to her. Her ways might be somewhat old-fashioned and her manner a little remote, but was that so bad? What harm had she ever done Lucy? My God, it wasn't Mrs. Sowerby who had been small-minded, it had been Lucy herself! She should be ashamed of herself for her suspicions. Even when she had appeared wearing one of Ellie's cashmere sweaters, Mrs. Sowerby's exasperation probably had to do entirely with Eleanor's barely disguised condescension, and nothing to do with disapproval of Lucy for being covetous of her daughter's clothes. She was a patient, gentle and sympathetic person—look at her treatment not only of Lucy, but of Roy. She alone, of his entire family, seemed to take his problems and dilemmas seriously; she alone accorded him genuine respect. Who had the dignity, the self-possession of Mrs. Sowerby? She could think of no one.

And was this the reward to be paid that dignity? Was this how Julian Sowerby chose to express his respect and gratitude to a woman of such refinement and generosity? Because she happened to have to wear special elasticized stockings; because in her middle age she was tending toward heaviness; because her hair had begun to turn to gray, was that sufficient cause for such a person to be deceived, disgraced, discarded by a philandering loud-mouthed little pig of a man? Blondie! Cutie-Pie! What a person! What a disgusting cheat of a person!

Yet in her heart she had always known. That was the amazing part.

What should Ellie do? Tell her mother? Tell her Uncle Lloyd? Or should she speak directly to her father, so as to spare her mother from ever knowing? Yes, go to him; and if he promises to end his associations with his women, promises never to resume with them again . . . Or perhaps first she ought to find out who the woman was. And then go to *her*. Yes, and tell her that she must break off relations with her father instantly, or risk exposure—even incarceration, if it turned out (as it might) that she was a prostitute who sold her services to men like Julian Sowerby. Or perhaps Ellie should keep her secret, bide her time, wait for the phone to ring again—and then lift the extension and instead of burying the truth in her pillow, instead of simply sitting like a ninny enduring his treachery, put an end to it once and for all: "This is Eleanor Sowerby. I am Julian Sowerby's daughter. I should like to know your name, please."

All at once, air colder and fresher than any they had felt in months seemed to descend on the Sowerbys and their young guests.

"Wow," said Joe softly. In his excitement he sat straight up. "It's fall. It's really fall."

"Hey, let's get this Princess in the house," said Julian Sowerby. He stood and stretched, so that his cigar went waving over his head like some signal.

"Good idea," said Joe. He and Roy told Mrs. Sowerby that since it was the maid's night off, the two of them would carry in all the dirty dishes. They made a big fuss about not letting her touch anything, and shooed her directly into the house.

Mr. Sowerby began to fold up the chairs, and Roy began to whistle "Autumn Leaves" as he went around collecting the silverware. Joe, piling plates, was saying to him, "Do you realize, Big Roy-boy, that tomorrow at this time—"

Suddenly Ellie was at Lucy's side, whispering into her ear.

"What?" said Lucy.

". . . forget everything."

"What do you mean?"

"I mean—*never mind!*"

"But . . . didn't it really happen?"

"Hey, my two colleens," Julian called, using an Irish accent. "Enough giggling now and into the house with you."

They started quickly across the lawn. Ellie shivered, pulled the afghan up over her hair, and started to run for the open door.

Lucy hissed, "But, Ellie, what are you going to do?"

Ellie stopped. "I'll—I'll—"

"What?"

"Oh, I'll just go to Northwestern."

"But," whispered Lucy, taking hold of her arm, "your mother?"

But now Roy and Joe rushed up from behind—"Coming through! Hot stuff! Watch it, ladies!"—and anything further she said would have been overheard. And then Julian Sowerby suddenly had each of them by the arm, and, laughing, ran them into the house.

The next day Joe left for Alabama, and then Ellie herself became desperately busy with shopping and packing, and was almost perpetually in the company of her mother—who still seemed to be innocent of what was happening behind her back. The few times they were together for more than a minute, Lucy hardly had a chance to open her mouth, before Ellie said, "Shhh, later," or "Lucy, I think never mind, really," and finally, "Look, I was all wrong."

"You *were*?"

"I misunderstood, I'm sure, yes."

"But—"

"*Please*, let me just get to college!"

By the time they parted they seemed hardly even to be friends any longer, if they ever had been. Ellie and her family drove off to Evanston on the second weekend in September, and on the Monday following, on a day that Lucy had encircled with five black rings on her calendar, she and Roy drove down with a carful of luggage to begin their schooling in Fort Kean.

3

SHE passed out twice in the second week of November, first in a booth in The Old Campus Coffee Shop, and the afternoon following, upon rising from her seat at the end of English class. At the student health center, a barracks building that had been converted into the infirmary, she told the doctor that she believed she might be suffering from anemia. Her skin had always been on the pale side, and in winter the tips of her toes and fingers went white and icy when it got very cold.

After the examination she dressed and sat in a chair the doctor had pulled back for her in his office. He said that he did not believe the problem was with the circulation in her extremities. Looking out the window, he asked if she had been having any trouble lately with her periods. She said no, then she said yes, and then, clutching her coat and her books in her arms, she rushed out the door. In the narrow corridor she felt herself spinning, but this time the sensation lasted only a second.

As soon as she pulled shut the door of the phone booth in the coffee shop she realized that Roy would be in class. His landlady, Mrs. Blodgett, answered, and Lucy hung up without even speaking. She thought of dialing the school and having him called to a phone; but what would she say to him? The strange sensation she began to have—as the first wave of confusion gave way to a second, even more severe—was that it did not have anything to do with him anyway. She found herself thinking like a child who does not know the facts of life, who thinks that pregnancy is something that a woman does to herself, or that simply happens to her if she wishes hard enough.

In her room she looked at all the ridiculous markings on her calendar. Just the previous Saturday, after Roy had driven her back to the dormitory from the movies, she had drawn a thick black ring around Thanksgiving Day. Suddenly she felt dreadful; she went and stood with her mouth open over the toilet, but all she could cough up were some brownish strands of liquid. The dread remained.

That evening she did not answer when the on-duty girl rapped on the door to her room and said that a Roy was on the phone.

At eight in the morning, the other girls drifting down to the dining hall or running off to class, Lucy rushed back to the infirmary. She had to wait on a bench in the corridor until ten, when the doctor finally arrived.

"I was here yesterday," she said. "Lucy Nelson."

"Come in. Sit down."

Before she began to speak he came around to the door and pushed it shut all the way. When he returned to his desk, she told him that she did not want a baby.

He pushed his chair back a little and crossed one leg over the other. That was all he did.

"Doctor, I'm a freshman. A first-semester freshman."

He said nothing.

"I've been working for years to go to college. At night. In a soda fountain. Up in Liberty Center. That's where I'm from . . . And summers too—three whole summers. And I have a Living Aid Scholarship. If I hadn't gotten in here I might not even have been able to go to school at all—because of money." But she did not want to plead poverty, or even helplessness. What he had to know was that she was not weak, she was strong, she had undergone many hardships, and much suffering —she wasn't just another eighteen-year-old girl. It wasn't merely that she needed his help; she *deserved* it. "This is my first real experience away from home, Doctor. I've been waiting for it all my life. Saving for it. It's all I've had to look forward to for years."

He continued to listen.

"Doctor, I'm not promiscuous, I swear it. I'm just eighteen! You've got to believe me!"

Until then the doctor had sat there with his glasses pushed up on his forehead. Now he adjusted the spectacles down onto the bridge of his nose.

"I don't know what to do," she said, trying to regain her self-control.

His face remained immobile. He had soft gray hair and kind eyes, but he only scratched the side of his nose.

"I don't know what to do," she said again. "I really don't."

He crossed his arms. He rocked a little in his chair.

"Doctor, I never had a boy friend before. He was my first one. That's the truth—it really is."

The doctor swung the chair around and looked out the window, toward "The Bastille," as the girls called the main building. He had pushed his glasses up again, and now he began rubbing at his eyes. Maybe he had been out on an emergency all night and was tired. Maybe he was thinking of what to say. Maybe he wasn't even listening. He came out to the school four mornings a week for two hours, so what did he care? He had a practice of his own to worry about; this was just so much extra cash. Maybe he was only letting time pass before he sent her away to deal with her own mess.

He turned back to her. "And where is the young man?" he asked.

". . . Here."

"Speak up, Lucy. Where?"

She felt herself becoming meek. Or was it protective? "In Fort Kean."

"And now that he's had his fun, that's it, I suppose."

"What?" she whispered.

He was rubbing at his temples with the tips of his fingers. He *was* thinking. He was going to help! "Don't you girls know what they're up to?" he asked in a soft and unhappy voice. "Can't you imagine what they'll be like when something like this happens? A bright and pretty little girl like you, Lucy. What were you thinking about?"

Her eyes welled with tears at the sound of her name. It might have been the first time she had ever heard it spoken. *I'm Lucy. I'm bright. I'm pretty.* Oh, her life was just beginning! So very much had happened to her in the last year alone—in the last month. Already there was a girl on her floor who knew a boy she wanted to fix Lucy up with. Only there had never once been an opportunity to meet him, what with Roy coming around every single night, if only to stop off and say hello. She was away from home at long long last—and starting to be pretty! Why, why had she gotten involved with him to begin with? Because he called her Angel? Because he took those pictures? Because he sang all those stupid songs into her ear? That big goon hadn't the faintest idea what she was all about. All summer long he'd acted as though she were some kind of girl she wasn't—as though she were some sort of Monkey Littlefield. And she had let him. She had let him have his stupid way! And now this! Only, *this* was what happened to farm girls, to girls who didn't study, who quit school, who ran away from home. To Babs Egan, but not to her. Hadn't enough happened to her already?

"Doctor, I don't *know* what I was thinking about." She began to cry, despite herself. "All I mean is, lately I don't even know what I'm doing sometimes." She covered her face with her fingers.

"And what about the boy?"

"The boy?" she said helplessly, rubbing her tears away.

"What does he plan to do about all this? Run off to the South Seas?"

"Oh no," she moaned, sadder than ever, "no, he'd marry me tomorrow," and an instant too late she realized that she had said the wrong thing. It was the truth, but it was the wrong thing to have said.

"But you don't want to." The doctor was speaking to her.

She looked up from her lap, partly. "I didn't say that."

"I have to have it straight, Lucy. Just as it is. He wants to, but you don't want to."

She rose from her seat. "But I'm not even here three whole months! I'm a first-semester freshman!"

He was moving his glasses up again. He had such a big, wrinkled, friendly face—you just knew he had a family he loved, and a nice house, and a calm and pleasant life. "If the young man wants to marry you—"

"What of it? What if he does?"

"Well, I think that's something that must at least be taken into consideration. Don't you?"

Blankly she said, "I don't understand." And she didn't.

"His feelings are something that have to be taken into consideration. His love for you."

Dumbly she sat there shaking her head. He didn't love her. He just sang those stupid songs into her ear.

"—what he wants," the doctor was saying, "what he expects, too."

"But he doesn't *know* what he wants."

"You say he wants to marry you."

"Oh, that isn't what I mean. He says things, but he doesn't even know what! Doctor—please, you're right, I don't want to marry him. I don't want to lie to you. I hate liars and I don't lie, and that's the truth! Please, hundreds and hundreds of girls do what I did. And they do it with all different people!"

"Perhaps they shouldn't."

"But I'm not bad!" She couldn't help herself, it was the truth: "I'm good!"

"Please, you must calm down. I didn't say that you were bad. I'm sure you're not. You mustn't jump at everything I say before I finish saying it."

"I'm sorry. It's a habit. I'm terribly sorry."

"They shouldn't," he began again, "because most of them aren't old enough to pay the price if they lose. If they get into trouble."

"But—"

"But," his voice rose over hers, "they're old enough to want the love. I know."

The tears moved again into her eyes. "You do understand. Because that's what happened to me, just what you said. That's exactly it."

"Lucy, listen to me—"

"I am, Doctor. Because that *is* what happened—"

"Lucy, you're not alone in this."

At first she thought he meant that there were other girls in school in the same fix—perhaps even in the infirmary rooms along the corridor beyond his office.

"There is a young man," the doctor said.

"But—"

"Listen to me, Lucy. There is a young man, and there is your family. Have you spoken to your family about this yet?"

She looked into her plaid skirt, where her fingers were clutched at the big safety pin.

"You do have a family?"

"Yes. I suppose."

"I think you have to forget your embarrassment and take this problem to your family."

"I can't."

"Why not?"

"I have a terrible family."

"Lucy, you're not the first eighteen-year-old girl to think her family is terrible. Surely you've discovered that since you've been at school."

"But my family *is* terrible. I don't think it—it's true!"

He said nothing.

"I ignore them. I have nothing to do with them. They're inferior, Doctor," she added when he still didn't seem to believe her.

"In what way?"

"My father drinks." She looked him straight in the eye. "He's a drunkard."

"I see," he said. "And your mother?"

Helplessly she was weeping again. "She's too good for him."

"That doesn't sound inferior," the doctor said quietly.

"Yes, but she should have left him years and years ago, if she had any sense. Any self-respect. She should have found a man who would be good to her and respect her." Like you, she thought. If you had met my mother, if she had married you . . . She heard herself saying, "Some people think, someone said once, she looks like Jennifer Jones. The actress."

He handed her a tissue and she blew her nose. She mustn't ask to be pitied; she mustn't whimper; she mustn't fall to pieces. That's what her mother would do.

"Lucy, I think you should go home. Today. Maybe she understands more than you imagine. Maybe she won't be angry. I would think from what you say that she wouldn't be."

She did not respond. He was trying to get out of it. That's exactly what he was beginning to do.

"You seem to love her. Probably she loves you too."

"But she can't help, Doctor. Love has nothing to do with it. Love is what's *wrong* with her. She's so weak. She's so insipid!"

"My dear, because you're upset now—"

"But, Doctor, *they can't help!* Only you can help," she said, standing. "You must!"

He shook his head. "But I can't, I'm afraid."

"*But you have to!*"

"I'm terribly sorry."

Could he mean it? Could he understand the situation as he did, and then turn around and say he wasn't going to help? "But this isn't *fair!*" she cried.

The doctor nodded his head. "It isn't."

"So then what are you going to *do* about it? Sit there pushing your glasses up and down? Sit there being wise to me? Call me 'my dear'!" Instantly she sat back down in her chair.

"Oh, I'm sorry. I didn't mean that. But why are you . . . I mean, you see what happened. You understand." She felt now that she had to plead with him, to convince him that he was right. "You *do* understand, Doctor. Please, you're an intelligent person!"

"But there are limits. On all of us. People may want things, that doesn't mean that we can give them."

"Please," she said angrily, "don't tell me what I know in that tone. I am not a child."

A moment passed. He stood.

"But what's going to happen to me? If you don't help . . ."

He came around to the side of his desk.

"Don't you care?" she asked. "What about my whole life!"

For the first time she sensed his impatience. Then he spoke. "You cannot expect me, young lady, to save your life."

She rose; she faced him where he was standing at the door. "Please do not lecture me in that superior tone! I refuse to be lectured to by a perfect stranger who doesn't know the first thing about all I have had to put up with in my life. I am not just another eighteen-year-old girl, and I won't take your lectures!"

"And what will you take instead?" he said sourly.

"What?"

"I'm asking what you expect, Lucy. You're interesting," he said, "in your expectations. You're perfectly right—you are not just another eighteen-year-old girl." He opened the door.

"But what about my life? How can you be so cruel to me!"

"I hope you come upon someone you can listen to" was his answer.

"Well, I won't," she said in a low, fierce tone.

"That would be too bad."

"Oh," she said, buttoning her coat, "oh, I hope—I hope you're happy, Doctor, when you go home to your nice house. I hope you're happy with all your wisdom and your glasses and your doctor's degree—and being a coward!"

"Goodbye," he said, blinking only once. "Good luck."

"Oh, I won't rely on luck, Doctor. Or on people either."

"On what, then?"

"Myself!" she said, and marched through the open door.

"Good luck," he said softly as she brushed by him, and then shut the door behind her.

"You coward," she moaned as she went rushing off to the coffee shop; "you weakling," she wept as she carried the phone book into the booth at the back of the store; "you selfish, heartless, cruel—" as she drew her finger down the list of physicians in the yellow pages of the directory, imagining them one after another saying to her, "You cannot expect me, young lady, to save your life," and seeing herself dragging from one office to another, humiliated, ignored and abused.

—

On Thanksgiving Day they all sat down to the turkey and she told her family that she and Roy Bassart had decided to get married. "What?" her father said. She repeated herself. "Why?" he demanded to know, and slammed down the carving instruments.

"*Because we want to.*"

Within five minutes the only one still at the table was her grandmother. She alone ate right through to the mince pie while overhead various members of the family, in various ways, tried to get Lucy to unlock her door. Berta, however, said she was sick and tired of disorder and tragedy, and refused to allow every single pleasant moment to be destroyed by one person or another, year in and year out.

Roy phoned at four in the afternoon. She came out of her bedroom to take the call, but would not speak until the kitchen was cleared of adults. Roy said that he couldn't get away to see her before nine. But what had they said when he told them? Nothing. He hadn't told them yet.

At nine-thirty he telephoned from the Sowerbys', saying that he had decided to wait until he was back in his own house, alone with his parents, before he broke the news. "Well, when will that be, Roy?" "I don't know exactly. Well, how can I know exactly? Later." But he was the one who had wanted to call them a week ago from Fort Kean; he was the one, she said, who had thought there was nothing that wrong with having to get married, so long as you were a couple who was going to marry anyway, probably, sooner or later. He was the one—

"Here," he said, "Ellie wants to talk to you."

"Roy!"

"Hi," Ellie said. "Hi, Lucy. Sorry about not writing."

"Hello, Eleanor."

"It's just been work, work, work. You can imagine. I'm going crazy in this science course. Hey, we're all rolling on the floor listening to Roy's adventures in that Britannia school. What a place! And I'm actually drinking. Hey, come over."

"I have to stay home."

"I hope it's not hard feelings, or anything, about not writing . . . Is it?"

"No."

"Well, I'll see you tomorrow. Have I got things to tell you. I've met somebody *marvelous*," Ellie whispered. "I almost sent you his picture. I mean, he's perfect."

At midnight she came out of her bedroom to call Roy at his home. "Did you tell them?"

"Listen, what are you doing? Everybody's sleeping."

"Didn't you *tell* them?"

"It was too late."

"But I told mine!"

"Look, my father's shouting down the stairs asking who it is."

"Well, tell him!"

"Will you please stop instructing me on what to do every minute?" he said. "I'll do it when I'm—" Suddenly he hung up.

She dialed again. Mr. Bassart picked up the phone. "Just who is this?" he asked.

She didn't breathe.

"Look, no pranks at this hour, whoever you are. If it's one of you boys in my fifth-period class, don't think I'm not going to find out who."

In the morning she telephoned again.

"I was going to call *you*," Roy said.

"Roy, when are you going to tell them?"

"It's only eight in the morning. We haven't had breakfast, even. My Aunt Irene's coming over."

"Then you *did* tell them."

"Who said that?"

"That's why your aunt's coming to your house!"

"How can you say that? How do you know that's even true?"

"Roy, what are you hiding from me?"

"*Nothing.* Can't you just let things settle for a few hours? My God."

"Why is your aunt coming over at eight o'clock in the morning? Who even called her?"

"Oh, look, okay," he said suddenly, "if you have to know—"

"I do! Know what!"

"Well, my father wants me to wait till June."

"Then you did tell them!"

". . . When we came home."

"Then why didn't you say that last night!"

"Because it just so happened that I wanted to give you good news, Lucy, not bad. I was trying to spare you, Lucy, *but you won't stop pushing me against my own timetable!*"

"Timetable? Roy, what are you talking about? How can we wait until June!"

"But he doesn't *know* about that!"

"And don't you tell him either, Roy!"

"I have to hang up. She's here."

At noon he called to say that he wasn't driving back to Fort Kean until Monday, so perhaps she had better plan to take the bus down on Sunday night.

"I'm calling from a booth, Lucy. I'm on my way to Mr. Brunn's to pick up something for my father. I have to hurry—"

"Roy, please explain instantly what this means."

"I'm trying to take care of some things and iron them out, all *right? Do you mind?*"

"Roy! You can't do this! I have to see you, right now!"

"I'm hanging up, Lucy."

"No!"

"Well, I am. I'm sorry. So get ready."

"If you hang up, I'm coming over to your house this minute. Hello? Do you hear me?"

But the line had been disconnected.

She called Eleanor's house.

"Ellie, it's Lucy. I have to talk to you."

"Why?"

"Oh, not you too?"

". . . Me too, what?"

"Ellie, you had to talk to me once—now I have to talk to

you. I have to know what's going on, Ellie. I'll come right over."

"Now? Lucy, you better not—right now, I mean."

"Is anybody home?"

"No. But they're all—going crazy."

"Why?"

"Well, Roy says you want to marry him."

"He wants to marry *me*! Didn't he say that?"

"Well, yes . . . Well, sort of. He says he's thinking about it . . . But, Lucy, they think you're making him— Uh-oh, somebody's pulling into the driveway. Everybody's been driving back and forth all morning . . . Lucy?"

"Yes."

". . . Are you?"

"What?"

"Well, making him."

"No!"

"Then—why?"

"Because we want to!"

"You do?"

"Yes!"

"But—"

"But what, Eleanor!"

"Well . . . you're so young. We all are. I mean, it's a surprise. I guess I just don't know what I mean, really."

"Because you're a dope, Ellie! Because you're a stupid, insipid, self-centered, selfish dope!"

In the early evening she took a bus back to Fort Kean. The doors to The Bastille were chained shut, and she had to walk all around the cold campus before she found the watchman. He led her over to the Buildings and Grounds Office in Barracks Number Three, sat her down in a chair, and took out his spectacles to look for her name in the student directory.

And all those names printed in the register made her think: *Run away*. Who would ever find her?

In her room she beat her fists on the pillow, on the headboard, on the wall. It was awful. It was horrible. Every other college girl in America was home right now, having a good time with her friends and her family. Yet her mother had begged, her grandfather had begged, even her father had asked her to stay. They said that it was just that they were stunned by the news. Wouldn't she agree, they reasoned through the door, that it was a little unexpected? They would try to get used to it, if only she wouldn't run off like this on a holiday weekend. They were shocked at first, and had maybe lost their heads. It was, after all, only the first semester of that college life she had been dreaming about for so long. But probably she knew what she was doing, if her mind was made up the way it sounded that it was. So wouldn't she stay through Monday? When she was fifteen years old and on her own decided on Catholic as her religious preference, had they stood in her way? No, she had insisted that it was what she wanted, and they had decided to let her go ahead. And later, when she had changed her mind, and turned back to Presbyterian again, well, that too had been her own decision, made on her own, without interference from any person in the family. And the same with the snare drum. Another decision made on her own, that they had honored and respected, until finally she decided to give that up too.

Of course they weren't meaning to draw any comparison between taking up the snare drum and taking a husband for life; but their attitude had been that if she preferred beating the drums to resuming piano (which, they reminded her, she had dropped at ten, her own decision once again), or beginning something like accordion, which had been Daddy Will's compromise suggestion, they had no choice but to let her have her way. Their house was not a dictatorship; it was a democracy, in which every person had his ideas—and was respected for them too. "I may not believe what you say," said Daddy Will through the door, "but I will fight for your right to say it." So wouldn't she reconsider and not rush off now to some lonely, empty school? Why didn't she stay and talk it over? After all, Grandma had been baking all week, and for her. "For Thanksgiving," said Lucy. "Well, honey, that's not much different, when you think about it. It's your first big weekend home from college, there isn't one of us doesn't realize . . . Lucy? Are you listening to me?"

But what about her father acting as though the whole thing was a monumental tragedy? Since when did anything having to do with her sacrifices, her suffering, bring tears to his eyes? She could not bear the pretense. And who said she was quitting college? He kept wandering around the house, crying, "I wanted her to go to college," but who had said she wasn't? All she had said was that she was getting married to Roy . . . Or did they know why without her explaining further? Were they content to accept what she told them, simply to avoid the humiliation of confronting the truth? She picked up her French grammar and threw it clear across the room. "They don't even *know*," she said aloud, "and still they're letting me do it!"

If only they'd say *no*. NO, LUCY, YOU CANNOT. NO, LUCY, WE FORBID IT. But it seemed that none of them had the conviction any longer, or the endurance, to go against a choice of hers. In order to survive, she had set her will against theirs long ago—it was the battle of her adolescence, but it was over now. And she had won. She could do whatever in the world she wanted—even marry someone she secretly despised.

—

When Roy returned to Fort Kean on Monday evening, and switched on the light in his room, he found Lucy sitting in a chair by the window.

"What are you doing here?" he cried, dropping his suitcase. "The shades are up!"

"Then pull them down, Roy."

Instantly he did. "How did you get inside?"

"How do I always get inside, Roy? On all fours."

"Is she home?"

"Who?"

"My landlady!" he whispered, and without another word, slipped out the door and into the hallway. She heard him whistling his way up the stairs and into the bathroom. *You sigh, the song begins, you speak and I hear* . . . Overhead she even heard him flush the toilet. Then he was sliding into the room again. "She's out," he said, shutting the door. "We better turn off the lights."

"So you won't have to look at me?"

"So she doesn't *find* you here, if she comes home. Well, she just might come home. Well, what's the matter with you?"

She rose and clutched her stomach. "Take a guess!"

"*Shhhh.*"

"But she's out."

"But she'll be back! We *always* have the lights out, Lucy."

"But I want to talk to you, and face to face, not on a phone, Roy, where you can—"

"Well, I'm sorry, but the lights are going off. So get ready."

"But are we getting married or aren't we? Tell me, so I know what to do next, or where to go, or God knows what."

"Well, at least let me take my coat off, will you, please?"

"Roy, yes or no."

"Well, how can I give you a yes or no answer when it's not a yes or no question?"

"But that's exactly what it *is*."

"Will you calm down? I've been driving for two hours."

While he was hanging his coat in the closet, she came up behind him and stood on her toes. "*Yes or no, Roy!*" up toward his ear, which was still a foot above her.

He ducked away from her. "Now, first, I'm turning the lights off. Just to be safe. Well, look, Lucy, I agreed when I rented here not to have girls in my room."

"But you had me, Roy, and plenty."

"But *she* doesn't know about it! Oh, darn it. Here go the lights," and without pausing to hear an objection, he turned them off.

"Okay, now you don't have to look at me, Roy. Tell me what happened over your long Thanksgiving holiday. While I was down here in an empty dormitory all by myself for two whole days."

"First off, I didn't tell you to go back to any empty dorm. Second, I'm going to sit down, if you don't mind. And why don't you sit, too?"

"I'll stand, thank you."

"In the dark?"

"Yes!"

"Shhhh!"

"Begin," she said.

"Well, let me get settled . . . Okay."

"What?"

"I've got them to come around part way."

"Continue."

"Oh, sit *down*, will you?"

"What's the difference? You can't see me."

"I do too see you! Hanging over me. Sit down, *please*."

She had been waiting for over an hour. It wasn't sitting she wanted, it was sleep. She lowered herself onto the edge of the bed and closed her eyes. *Go to Mr. Valerio. Run away.* But neither idea made sense. If she should see anyone, it was Father Damrosch. But what would he do? That was precisely his trouble: he couldn't *do* anything. He was about as much help as Saint Teresa, or Jesus Christ. He looked so strong, and listened to everything she said, and said such beautiful things himself . . . but it wasn't beautiful things she needed to hear. Something had to be *done*.

"First off," he was saying, "don't think it was easy for me. It was hell, actually."

"What was?"

"Pretending you weren't pregnant, Lucy, when everybody kept asking me over and over again *why?*"

"And did you tell them?"

"No."

"Are you sure?"

"Yes! *Shhhhh!*"

"You're the one who's shouting."

"Well, you make me."

"You might be shouting because you're lying, Roy."

"I did not tell them, Lucy! Will you stop accusing? Actually, I keep wondering why I don't. Why can't I just speak the simple truth? If we're going to be married anyway."

"Are we?"

"Well, we would be . . . if I told them, I mean."

"You mean if you don't, we're *not?*"

"Well, that's the point. That's what's so confused. I mean, they had so many arguments for why we should at least wait until June."

"And?"

"And, well, they're all good arguments. I mean, it's just hard to argue against a good argument, that's all."

"So you said you'd wait."

"I said I'd *think* about it."

"But how *can* we?"

"Look, I had to get out of the house, didn't I? I've missed a whole day of school already."

"You have a car, you can drive—"

"*But I couldn't leave it the way it was!* Don't you understand anything!"

"Why couldn't you? Why didn't you?"

"Why should they all be furious at me, Lucy, and so confused about everything? I'm not doing anything wrong. The opposite, in fact, the very opposite! Why don't we just tell *the truth*? I don't have to lie to my parents, you know."

"I don't have to lie to mine either, Roy, if that's what you mean."

"But you are."

"Because I want to!"

"*Why?*"

"Oh, why won't you be a man about this! Why are you acting this way!"

"But you're the one who's hiding the simple fact that would make them all understand the whole thing!"

"Roy, do you honestly believe they will all love and adore me when they hear that I'm going to have a baby?"

"They'd *understand* is all I'm saying."

"But only two people have to understand—you and me."

"Well, maybe that's all you think . . . with your family."

"And what's wrong with my family that isn't with yours, Roy? Look, you, if you don't want to marry me," she said, "because someone has begun to tell you that I'm not good enough for you, well, believe me, you don't have to."

A moment passed. And another.

"But I do want to," he said at last.

"Roy, I think you really don't." She buried her head in her hands. "That's the truth, isn't it? 'Trust me, trust me'—and that's the real truth."

"Well . . . no . . . Well, you certainly haven't been acting these last few days like the kind of person someone would like living in the same house with particularly. I'll tell you that . . . Suddenly you're so—"

"So what? Lower class?"

"No," he said. "No. Cold."

"Oh, am I?"

"Well, sort of, recently, yes, as a matter of fact."

"And what else am I?"

"Well, all kidding aside, Lucy, you're just acting so angry."

"You might be a little angry too, if you had agreed before-hand with someone—"

"But I don't mean normal angry!"

"What?"

"Well—practically crazy!"

"You honestly think because I'm angry I'm *insane*?"

"I didn't say *I* did. I didn't say insane."

"Who did say it then?"

"No one."

"Who?"

"*No one!*"

"Maybe," she said after a moment, "you *make* me insane, Roy Bassart."

"Then why do you want to marry me so much?"

"I *don't* want to!"

"Oh, then don't do me the favor, you know."

"I don't think I will," she said. "Because that's really what it would be."

"Oh, sure. And what will you do instead? Marry somebody else?"

"Do you know something, you? I've been getting rid of you since July, Roy. Since the day you took this room because it had a long bed in it, you—you baby!"

"Well, you sure are a slow worker, I'll say that for you."

"I'm not slow! I have sympathy for you! I felt *sorry* for you."

"Oh, sure."

"I was afraid you'd give up photography if I hurt your little feelings. But I was going to do it, Roy—on Thanksgiving Day of all days, and I would have, too, if I didn't have to marry you instead."

"Oh, don't feel you have to, you know."

"I thought when you collapsed, at least you'd be in Liberty Center, where you could go eat your Hydrox cookies."

"Well, don't worry about my crying, if I can put in my two cents. I don't cry that easy, for one thing. And as for Hydrox cookies, that's irrelevant to anything. I don't even know what it's supposed to mean, in fact. Besides," he said, "if you wanted to drop somebody, don't worry, you'd drop him. You wouldn't bother too much about their crying either."

"No?"

". . . Because you don't have emotions like other people."

"Don't I? And who said that?"

"Lucy? Are you crying?"

"Oh, no. I don't have emotions like other people. I'm a piece of pure stone."

"You *are* crying." He came over to the bed, where she was stretched out, her face still in her hands. "Don't. Please, I didn't mean it. Really."

"Roy," she said, "who said I was insane to you? Who said I didn't have emotions?"

"Ordinary emotions. Nobody."

"Who was it, Roy? Your Uncle Julian?"

"No. Nobody."

"And you believed him."

"I didn't. He didn't say it!"

"But I could tell you about him too! Tell you plenty. The way your Uncle Julian looks at me! How he kissed me at your party!"

"This summer, you mean? But that was a joke. You kissed him back. Lucy, what are you even saying?"

"I'm saying that you're blind! You're blind to how awful people are! How rotten and hateful they are! They tell you I'm lower class and don't have ordinary emotions, and you believe them!"

"I don't!"

"And all on the basis of what? Why, Roy? Say it!"

"Say *what*?"

"My father! But I didn't put him in jail, Roy!"

"I didn't say you did."

"He put himself there! That was years ago, and it's over, and I am not beneath you or them, or anyone!"

The door opened; the light went on over their heads.

In the doorway stood the widow from whom Roy rented his room: Mrs. Blodgett, a thin, nervous and alert woman with a little coin-slot mouth and a great capacity for expressing disapproval by merely reducing the thing in size. She did not speak right off; she did not have to.

"Well, just how did you get in here?" Roy asked, as though he were the one who was outraged. He had moved instantly between Lucy and the landlady. "Well, how, Mrs. Blodgett?"

"With a key, Mr. Bassart. How did *she* is a better question. Stand up, you hussy."

"Roy," whispered Lucy. But he continued to hide her behind him.

"I said get up from that bed," said Mrs. Blodgett. "And get out."

But Roy was intent upon making his point. "You're not supposed to use a key in another person's door, for one thing, you know."

"Don't tell me the things I'm not supposed to do, Mr. Bassart. I thought *you* were an Army veteran, or so you said."

"But—"

"But what, sir? But you don't know the rules of this house, is that what you're going to have the gall to tell me?"

"You don't under*stand*," said Roy.

"Understand what?"

"Well, if you'd calm down, I'll tell you."

"You just tell me, whether I'm calmed down or not, which I happen to be anyway. I've had others like you, Mr. Bassart. One in 1937, and another right on his heels in 1938. They look all right, but the looks is about the whole of it. Underneath they're all the same." Her mouth became invisible. "Crooked," she said.

"But this is different," said Roy. "She's my fiancée."

"Who is? You just let her out, so I can see her."

"Roy," Lucy pleaded. "*Move.*"

At last he did, smiling all the while. "This is Mrs. Blodgett, my landlady, who I mentioned to you. Mrs. Blodgett"—he rubbed his hands together, as though he had been awaiting this pleasure for a long time—"this is my fiancée. Lucy."

"Lucy what?"

Lucy stood, her skirt finally covering her knees.

"Why were the lights off and all that shouting?" asked Mrs. Blodgett.

"Shouting?" said Roy, looking around. "We were listening to music. You know I love music, Mrs. Blodgett."

Mrs. Blodgett looked at him in such a way as to openly admit to skepticism.

"The radio," he said. "We just turned it off. That was the noise, I guess. We just drove down from home. We were resting. Our eyes. That's how come the lights were dim."

"Off," said the tiny mouth, disappearing.

"Anyway," said Roy, "there's my suitcase. We did just get back."

"Who gave you permission, young man, to bring girls into my house against the rules? This is a dwelling place. I told you that when you first arrived, did I not?"

"Well, as I said, we just drove down. And I thought since she was my fiancée, you wouldn't mind if we rested." He smiled. "Against the rules." No answer. "Since we're getting married."

"When?"

"Christmas," he announced.

"Is that so?"

Lucy was the one being asked.

"It's the truth, Mrs. Blodgett," said Roy. "That's why we came down late from home. Making plans," he said with another big smile; then he turned somber and penitent. "I may have broken a rule about bringing Lucy in here, and if I did, I'm sorry."

"There are no ifs about it," said Mrs. Blodgett. "Not that I can see."

"Well then, I'm sorry then."

"Lucy what?" asked the landlady. "What's your last name, you?"

"Nelson."

"And where are you from?"

"The women's college."

"And is this true? Are you marrying him, or are you just some girl?"

"I'm marrying him."

Roy raised his hands. "See?"

"Well," said Mrs. Blodgett, "she could be lying. That's not unheard of."

"Does she look like a liar?" asked Roy, putting his hands in his pockets and shuffling over toward Lucy. "With this face?

Come on, Mrs. Blodgett," he said winningly. "She's the girl
next door. Actually, she practically is, you know."

The landlady did not smile back. "I had a boy in 1945 who
had a fiancée. But *he* came to me, Mr. Bassart—"

"Yes?"

"—and told me his plans. And then brought the young lady
around on a Sunday to be properly introduced."

"A Sunday. Well, that's a good idea, all right."

"Let me finish, please. We then arranged that she might
come here to visit until ten in the evening. I did not even have
to make it clear that the door to the room was to be left open.
He understood that much."

"I see," said Roy with considerable interest.

"Miss Nelson, I am not a close-minded person, but where I
have my rules I am strict. This happens to be my dwelling
place, and not some fly-by-night person's hotel. Without rules
it would go to rack and ruin inside of a month. Maybe you'll
understand how that happens when you're older. I certainly
hope you do, for your sake."

"Oh, we understand now," said Roy.

"Don't ever try to trick me again, Mr. Bassart."

"Oh, now that I know the ten o'clock setup—"

"And I know your name, young lady. Lucy Nelson. S-o-n or
s-e-n?"

"S-o-n."

"And I know the dean over at your school. Miss Pardee,
correct? Dean of Students?"

"Yes."

"Then don't you ever try to trick me either."

She started for the door.

"So then," said Roy, following her, "at least we're all
squared away, anyway."

When Mrs. Blodgett turned to show him what she thought
of that last remark, Roy smiled. "I mean, we're all forgiven and
everything, right? I know innocence of the law is no—"

"You are not innocent, Mr. Bassart. My back was turned.
You are guilty as sin."

"Well, I suppose in a manner of speaking . . ." And he
shrugged. "Now the rules, Mrs. Blodgett—just so I'm sure
I've got them straight."

"So long, sir, as the door is left open—"

"Oh, absolutely, wide open."

"So long as she is out of here at ten o'clock—"

"Oh, out she'll be," said Roy, laughing.

"So long as there is no shouting—"

"That was music, Mrs. Blodgett, really—"

"And so long, Mr. Bassart, as there is a marriage, Christmas Day."

For a moment he looked dumbfounded. Marriage? "Oh, sure. Good day, don't you think? Christmas?"

Mrs. Blodgett went out, leaving the door ajar.

"Bye," said Roy, and waited until he heard the door to the back parlor being closed before he fell into a chair. "Wow."

"Then we *are* getting married," said Lucy.

"Shhhhh!"—rising up out of the chair. "Will you—*yes*," he said all at once, for the parlor door had opened, and Mrs. Blodgett was headed back to the stairs. "Mom and Dad feel—oh, hi, Mrs. Blodgett." He tipped an imaginary hat. "Have a nice sleep now."

"It is nine forty-eight, Mr. Bassart."

Roy looked at his watch. "Right you are, Mrs. Blodgett. Thanks for reminding me. Just finishing up talking over our plans. Night, now."

She started up the stairs, her anger not much abated, it seemed.

"Roy—" Lucy began, but in two steps he was at her side; one hand he pressed to the back of her head, the other to her mouth.

"So," she said loudly, "Mom and Dad felt that for the most part your suggestion—"

Her eyes stared wildly at him, until the bedroom door could be heard closing overhead. He took his wet hand from her lips.

"Don't you ever—ever—" she said, so enraged that she could hardly speak, "do that again!"

"Oh, golly," he said, and threw himself backward onto his bed. "I'm actually going off my *rocker* with you! What do you expect, when she was on the *stairs*, Lucy?"

"I expect—!"

"Shhhhh!" He shot up on the bed. "We're getting married!" he whispered hoarsely. "*So shut up.*"

She was suddenly and completely baffled. She was getting married. "When?"

"Christmas! *Okay?* Now will you *stop?*"

"And your family?"

"Well, what about them?"

"You have to tell them."

"I will, I will. But just lay *off* for a while."

"Roy . . . it has to be now."

"*Now?*" he said.

"Yes!"

"But my mother is in bed, *and quiet down!*" After a moment he said, "Well, she is. I'm not lying. She goes to bed at nine and gets up at five-thirty. Don't ask me why. That's how she does it, Lucy, and how she's always done it, and there's nothing I can do to change her at this stage of the game. Well, that's the truth. And furthermore, Lucy, I have had it for tonight, really."

"But you must make this official. You just can't keep me living this way. It's a nightmare!"

"But I'll make it official when I think it should be!"

"Roy, suppose she calls Dean Pardee! I don't want to be thrown out of school! I don't need that in my one life, too."

"Well," he said, smacking the sides of his head, "I don't want to be thrown out either, you know. Why else do you think I told her what I did?"

"Then it is a lie and you don't mean it *again!*"

"It's not! I *do!* I always have!"

"Roy Bassart, call your parents, or I'll do something!"

He jumped out of the bed. "No!"

"Keep your hands away from my mouth, Roy!"

"Don't scream, for God's sakes! That's *stupid!*"

"But I am pregnant with a human baby!" she cried. "I'm going to have your baby, Roy! And you won't even do your duty!"

"I will! I am!"

"*When?*"

"Now! Okay? *Now!* But don't scream, Lucy, don't throw a stupid fit!"

"Then call!"

"But," he said, "what I told Mrs. Blodgett—I had to."

"Roy!"

"*Okay*," and he ran from the room.

In a few minutes he returned, paler than she had ever seen him. Where the hair was clipped short at his neck, she could see his white skin. "I did it," he said.

And she believed him. Even his wrists and hands were white.

"I did it," he mumbled. "And I told you, didn't I? I told you she'd be sleeping. I told you he'd have to wake her up and get her out of bed. Well, didn't I? *I wasn't lying!* And I wouldn't be thrown out of school. Why did I say *that*! I'd only be thrown out of this room—and what difference does that make anyway? Nobody else cares about my self-respect anyway, so why should I worry about it? *He* doesn't worry about it! *She* doesn't worry about it! And you—you were going to *scream*! My self-respect, oh, the heck with that, all you want to do is scream and confuse people. That's your way, Lucy—to confuse people. Everybody's way. Confuse Roy—why not? Who's he, anyway? But that's over! Because I'm not confused, Lucy, and from here on out that's the way things are going to be. We're getting married, you hear me—on Christmas Day. And if that doesn't suit people, then the day after—but that's it!"

The door opened upstairs. "Mr. Bassart, there is that shouting again! That is not music, that is clear shouting, and it will not be tolerated!"

Roy stuck his head out into the hallway. "No, no, just saying good night to Lucy here, Mrs. Blodgett—finishing up the old wedding plans."

"Say it then! Don't shout it! This is a dwelling place!" She slammed her door shut.

Lucy was crying.

"*Now* what are the tears for?" he asked. "Huh? *Now* what hundred thousand things did I do wrong? Really, you know, maybe I've had just about enough complaining and criticizing of me, you know—from you included, too. So maybe you ought to stop, you know. Maybe you ought to have a little consideration for all I've been through, *and just stop, damn it!*"

"Oh," she said, "I'll stop, Roy. Until you change your mind again—!"

"Oh, brother, I'll make that bargain. *Gladly*."

Whereupon, to his surprise, she threw open the window, and out of anger, or spite, or habit left the room as she had entered it. Roy rushed into the hallway to the front door. Noisily he opened it—"Good night," he called. "Good night, Lucy"—and noisily he closed it, so that upstairs Mrs. Blodgett would continue to believe that everything was really on the up-and-up, even if a little too loud.

—

Tuesday, Aunt Irene for lunch at the Hotel Thomas Kean.

Wednesday, his mother and father for dinner at The Song of Norway.

Thursday, Uncle Julian, a drink in the taproom of the Kean, lasting from five in the afternoon until nine in the evening.

At nine-thirty Roy dropped into a sofa in the downstairs living room of The Bastille. The corner in which Lucy had chosen to wait for him was the darkest in the room.

"And I haven't eaten," he said. "I haven't even eaten!"

"I have some crackers in my room," she whispered.

"They're not going to treat me like this," he said, glaring down his legs at the tips of his Army shoes. "I won't sit by and listen to threats, I'll tell you that."

". . . Do you want me to get the crackers?"

"That isn't the point, Lucy! The point is, pushing me around! Thinking he could make me sit there! Just *make* me, you know? Well, I don't need them that bad, I'll tell you that. And I don't want them either, not if they're going to take this kind of attitude. What an attitude to take—to me! To somebody they're supposed to care about!"

He got up and walked to the window. Looking out at the quiet street, he banged a fist into his palm. "Boy!" she heard him say.

She remained curled up on the sofa, her legs back under her skirt. It was a posture she had seen the other girls take while talking to their boy friends in the dormitory living room. If the house mother came into the living room, it would seem as though nothing were going on. So far no one in the dorm knew anything; no one was going to, either. In her two and a half months at school Roy hadn't left her alone enough to make any close friends, and even those few girls she had begun to be friendly with on the floor, she had drawn away from now.

"Look," said Roy, coming back to the sofa, "I've got the G.I. Bill, haven't I?"

"Yes."

"And I've got savings still, right? Other guys played cards, other guys shot crap—but I didn't. I was waiting to get out. So I saved! Purposely. And they should know that! I told them, in fact—but they don't even *listen*. And if worst ever came to worst, I'd sell the Hudson, too, even with all the work I put in it. Do you believe me, Lucy? Because it's true!"

"Yes."

Was this Roy? Was this Lucy? Was this them together?

"But they think money is everything. Do you know what he is, my Uncle Julian? Maybe I'm just finding out—but *he's* a materialist. And what a vocabulary! It's worse than you even think it is. What respect for somebody else!"

"What did he say? Roy, what kind of threats?"

"Oh, who cares. *Money* threats. And my father—him too. You know, by and large, whether he knew it or not, I used to respect him. But do you think he has any emotional respect for me, either? He's trying to treat me like I'm in his printing class again. But I just got out of serving my time in the Army. Sixteen months in the Aleutian Islands—the backside of the whole goddamn world. But my uncle says—you know what he says? 'But the war was over, buster, in 1945. Don't act like you fought it.' See, *he* fought it. He won a medal. And what's that have to do with anything anyway? Nothing! Oh—up his."

"Roy," warned Lucy, as some senior girls came into the living room.

"Well," he said, plopping down next to her, "they're always telling me I should speak up for myself, right? 'Make a decision and stick to it, Roy.' Isn't that all I heard since the day I got home? Isn't my Uncle Julian always shooting off about how you have to be a go-getter in this world? That's his big defense of capitalism, you know. It makes a man out of you, instead of just hanging around waiting for things to come your way. But what does he know about Socialism anyway? You think the man has ever read a book about it in his life? He thinks Socialism is Communism, and what you say doesn't make any difference at all. None! Well, I'm young. And I've got my health. And I sure don't care one way or the other about ever being in the El-ene washing-machine business, I'll tell you that much. Big threat that is. I'm going to photography school anyway. And you know something else? He doesn't know right from wrong. That's the real pay-off. That in this country, where people are still struggling, or unemployed, or don't have the ordinary necessities that they give the people in just about any Scandinavian country you can name—that a man like that, without the slightest code of decency, can just bully his way, and the hell with right and wrong or somebody's feelings. Well, I'm through being somebody he can toss his favors to. Let him keep his big fourteen-dollar cigars. Up his, Lucy—really."

The next morning, when the alarm rang at six-thirty, she went off to the bathroom to stick a finger down her throat before the other girls started coming in to brush their teeth. This made her feel herself again, provided she skipped breakfast afterward, and avoided the corridor back of the dining hall, and forced soda crackers down herself from time to time during the morning. Then she could get through the day's classes pretending that she was the same girl in the same body, and in the same way too—alone.

But what about last night? And the night before that? The fainting spells had stopped two weeks back, and the nausea she could starve to death every morning, but now that Roy's body seemed to be inhabited by some new person, the truth came in upon her as it never had before: *a new person was inhabiting hers as well.*

She was stunned. Her predicament was *real.* It was no plot she had invented to bring them all to their senses. It was no scheme to force them to treat her like flesh and blood, like a human being, like a girl. And it was not going to disappear either, just because somebody besides herself was at long last taking it seriously. It was real! Something was happening which she was helpless to stop! Something was growing inside her body, and without her permission!

And I don't want to marry him.

The sun wasn't even above the trees as she ran across Pendleton Park to downtown Fort Kean.

She had to wait an hour in the station for the first bus to the north. Her books were in her lap; she had some idea that she could study on the way up and be back for her two-thirty, but then she had not yet a clear idea of why she was suddenly rushing up to Liberty Center, or what would happen there. On the bench in the empty station she tried to calm herself by reading the English assignment she had planned to do in her free hour before lunch, and during lunch, which she didn't eat anyway. "Here you will have a chance to examine, and then practice, several skills used in writing effective sentences. The skills presented are those—"

She didn't want to marry him! He was the last person in the world she would ever want to marry!

She began gagging only a little way beyond Fort Kean. When he heard the sounds of her distress, the driver pulled to the side of the road. She dropped out the back door and threw her soiled handkerchief into a puddle. Aboard again, she sat in the rear corner praying that she would not be ill, or faint, or begin to sob. She must not think of food, she must not even think of the crackers she had forgotten in her flight from the dorm; she must not think of what she was going to say, or to whom.

What *was* she going to say?

"Here you will have a chance to examine, and then practice, several skills used in writing effective sentences. The skills presented are those used by writers of the models in the Description Section—" Years ago there was a farm girl at L.C. High who took so large a dose of castor oil to try to make the baby come out that she blew a hole in her stomach. She contracted a terrible case of peritonitis, and lost the baby, but afterward, because she had come so close to dying, everyone forgave her, and kids who hadn't even noticed her before— "Here you will have a chance to examine, and then practice, several skills used in writing—" Curt Bonham, the basketball star. He had been a year ahead of her. In March of his last term he and a friend had tried to walk home across the river one night while the ice was breaking up, and Curt had drowned. His whole class voted unanimously to dedicate the yearbook to him, and his graduation photograph appeared all by itself on the opening page of *The Liberty Bell*. And beneath the black-bordered picture was written—

Smart lad, to slip betimes away
From fields where glory does not stay . . .
ELLIOT CURTIS BONHAM
1930–1948
—

"What is it?" her mother asked when she came through the front door. "Lucy, what are you doing here? What's the matter?"

"I got here by bus, Mother. That's how people get from Fort Kean to Liberty Center. Bus."

"But what is it? Lucy, you're so pale."

"Is anyone else home?" she asked.

Her mother shook her head. She had come running from the kitchen, carrying a small bowl in her hand; now she had it thrust up to her chest. "Dear, your coloring—"

"Where is everyone?"

"Daddy Will took Grandma over to the market in Winnisaw."

"And he went to work? Your husband?"

"Lucy, what is it? Why aren't you in school?"

"I'm getting married Christmas Day," she said, moving into the parlor.

Sadly her mother spoke. "We heard. We know."

"How did you hear?"

"Lucy, weren't you going to tell us?"

"We only decided Monday night."

"But, dear," said her mother, "today is Friday."

"How did you hear, Mother?"

". . . Lloyd Bassart spoke to Daddy."

"Daddy Will?"

"To your father."

"Oh? And what came of that, may I ask?"

"Well, he took your side. Well, that's what came of it. Lucy, I'm answering your question. He took your side and without a moment's hesitation. Despite our not having been properly told by our own daughter, the day of her own wedding—"

"What did he say, Mother? Exactly."

"He told Mr. Bassart he couldn't speak for Roy, of course . . . He told Mr. Bassart we feel you are mature enough to know your own mind."

"Well—maybe I'm not!"

"Lucy, you can't think everything he does is wrong just because he does it. He *believes* in you."

"Tell him not to, then!"

"Dear—"

"I'm going to have a baby, Mother! So please tell him not to!"

"Lucy—you are?"

"Of course I am! I'm going to have a baby and I hate Roy and I never want to marry him or see him again!"

She ran off to the kitchen just in time to be sick in the sink.

She was put to bed in her room. "Here you will have a chance . . ." The book slid off the bed onto the floor. What was there to do now but wait?

The mail fell through the slot in the hallway and onto the welcome mat. The vacuum cleaner started up. The car pulled into the driveway. She heard her grandmother's voice down on the front porch. She slept.

Her mother brought her tea and toast. "I told Grandma it was the grippe," she whispered to her daughter. "Is that all right?"

Would her grandmother believe that she had come home because of the grippe? Where was Daddy Will? What had she told him?

"He didn't even come inside, Lucy. He'll be back this afternoon."

"Does he know I'm home?"

"Not yet."

Home. But why not? For years they had complained that she acted contemptuous of everything they said or did, for years they complained that she refused to let them give her a single word of advice; she lived among them like a stranger, like an enemy even, unfriendly, uncommunicative, nearly unapproachable. Well, could they say she was behaving like their enemy today? She had come home. So what were they going to do?

Alone, she drank some of the tea. She sank back into the pillow her mother had fluffed up for her and drew one finger lightly round and round her lips. Lemon. It smelled so nice. Forget everything else. Just wait. Time will pass. Eventually something will have to be done.

She fell asleep with her face on her fingers.

Her grandmother came up the stairs carrying a wet mustard plaster. The patient let her nightgown be unbuttoned. "That'll loosen it up," said Grandma Berta, pressing it down. "The two important things, rest and heat. Plenty of heat. Much as you can possible stand," and she piled two blankets more onto the patient.

Lucy closed her eyes. Why hadn't she done this at the start? Just gotten into bed and left it all to them. Wasn't that what they were always wanting to be, her family?

She was awakened by the piano. The students had begun to arrive for their lessons. She thought, "*But I don't have the grippe!*" But then she drove the thought, and the panic that accompanied it, right from her mind.

It must have begun snowing while she was asleep. She pulled a blanket off the bed, wrapped it around her, and at the window, put her mouth on the cold glass and watched the cars sliding down the street. The window began to grow warm where her mouth was pressed against it. Breathing in and out, she could make the circle of steam on the glass expand and contract. She watched the snow fall.

What would happen when her grandmother found out what really was wrong with her? And her grandfather, when he got home? And her father!

She had forgotten to tell her mother not to tell him. Maybe she wouldn't. But then would anything happen?

She scuffed with her slippers across the old worn rug and got back into her bed. She thought about picking up her English book from the floor to work a little on those sentences; instead she got way down under the blankets and with her faintly lemony fingers under her nose, slept for the sixth or seventh time.

—

Beyond the window it was dark, though from where she sat propped up in the bed the snow could be seen floating down through the light of the street lamp across the street. Her father knocked on her door. He asked if he could come in.

". . . It's not locked" was her response.

"Well," he said, stepping into the room, "so this is how the rich spend their days. Not bad."

She could tell that his words had been prepared. She did not look up from the blanket, but began to smooth it out with her hand. "I have the grippe."

"Smells to me," he said, "like you've been eating hot dogs."

She did not smile or speak.

"I tell you what it smells like. Smells like Comiskey Park, down in Chicago."

"Mustard plaster," she finally said.

"Well," he said, giving the door a push so that it closed, "that's one of your grandmother's real pleasures in life. That's one," he said, lowering his voice, "and the other is . . . No, I think that about covers it."

She only shrugged, as though she had no opinions on people's habits, one way or the other. Was he clowning because he knew, or because he didn't know? She saw from the corner of her eye that the pale hairs on the back of his hands were wet. He had washed before coming into her room.

The smell of dinner cooking down below caused her to begin to feel ill.

"Mind if I sit at the foot here?" he said.

"If you want to."

She mustn't be sick, not again. She mustn't arouse in him a single suspicion. No, she did not want him to know, ever!

"Let's see," he was saying. "Do I want to or don't I want to? I want to."

She yawned as he sat.

"Well," he said, "nice and cozy up here."

She stared straight ahead into the snowy evening.

"Winter's coming in with a rush this time," he said.

She glanced quickly over at him. "I suppose."

By looking instantly out the window, she was able to collect herself; she could not remember the last time she had looked directly into his eyes.

"Did I ever tell you," he said, "about the time I sprained my ankle when I was working over at McConnell's? It swelled way up and I came home, and your grandmother just lit up all over. Hot compresses, she said. So I sat down in the kitchen and rolled up my trouser leg. You should have seen her boiling up the water on the stove. Somehow it reminded me of all those cannibals over in Africa. She can't see how it can be good for you unless it hurts or smells bad."

Suppose she just blurted out the truth, to him?

"A lot of people like that," he said . . . "So," and gave her foot a squeeze where it stuck up at the end of the bed, "how's school going, Goosie?"

"All right."

"I hear you're learning French. Parlez-vous?"

"French is one of my subjects, yes."

"And, let's see . . . what else? You and me haven't had a good conversation in a long time now, have we?"

She did not answer.

"Oh, and how's Roy doing?"

Instantly she said, "Fine."

Her father took his hand off her foot at last. "Well," he said, "we heard, you know, about the wedding."

"Where's Daddy Will?" she asked.

"I'm talking to you right now, Lucy. What do you want him for while I'm talking to you?"

"I didn't say I wanted him. I only asked where he was."

"Out," her father said.

"Isn't he even going to have dinner?"

"He went out!" He rose from the bed. "I don't ask where he goes, or when he eats. How do I know where he is? He's out!" And he left the room.

In a matter of seconds her mother appeared.

"What happened now?"

"I asked where Daddy Will is, that's all," Lucy answered. "What's wrong with that?"

"But is Daddy Will your father or is your father your father?"

"*But you told him!*" she burst out.

"Lucy, your voice," said her mother, shutting the door.

"But you did. You told him! And I didn't say you should!"

"Lucy, you came home, dear; you said—"

"I don't want him to know! It's not his business!"

"Now stop, Lucy—unless you want others to know too."

"But I don't care who knows! I'm not ashamed! And don't start crying, Mother!"

"Then let him talk to you, *please*. He wants to."

"Oh, does he?"

"Lucy, you have to listen to him. You have to give him a chance."

She turned and hid her face in the pillow. "I didn't want him to *know*, Mother."

Her mother sat on the bed, and put her hand to the girl's hair.

"And," said Lucy, moving back, "what was he going to say, anyway? Why didn't he just say it out, if he had anything to say?"

"Because," her mother pleaded, "you didn't give him the chance."

"Well, I'm giving *you* a chance, Mother." There was a silence. "Tell me!"

"Lucy . . . dear . . . what would you think . . . What would you say . . . what would you think, I mean . . . of going for a visit—"

"Oh, no."

"*Please* let me finish. Of going to visit your father's cousin Vera. In Florida."

"And is that his idea of what to do with me?"

"Lucy, till this is over. For the little while it will take."

"Nine months is no little while, Mother—"

"But it would be warm there, it would be pleasant—"

"Oh," she said, beginning to cry into the pillow, "very pleasant. Why doesn't he ship me off to a home for wayward girls, wouldn't that be even easier?"

"Don't say that. He doesn't want to send you anywhere, you know that."

"He wishes I'd never been born, Mother. He thinks I'm why everything is so wrong with *him*."

"That's not *so*."

"Then," she said, sobbing, "he'd have one less responsibility to feel guilty about. If he even felt guilty to begin with."

"But he does, terribly."

"Well, he should!" she said. "He is!"

Some twenty minutes after her mother had run from the

room, Daddy Will knocked. He was wearing his lumber jacket and held his cap in his hands. The brim was dark where the snow had dampened it.

"Hey. I hear somebody's been asking for me."

"Hullo."

"You sound like death warmed over, my friend. You ought to be outside and feel that wind. Then you'd really appreciate being sick in bed."

She did not answer.

"Stomach settle down?" he asked.

"Yes."

He pulled a chair over to the side of the bed. "How's about another mustard plaster? Berta called me at the Erwins' and on the way home I stopped and bought a whole fresh packet. So just say when."

She turned and looked at the wall.

"What is it, Lucy? Maybe you want Dr. Eglund. That's what I told Myra . . ." He pulled the chair right up close. "Lucy, I never saw anything like the change in him this time," she said softly. "Not a drop—not a single solitary drop, honey. He is taking this whole decision of yours right in his stride. You set a date and it was just fine with him. Fine with all of us—whatever you think is going to make you and Roy happy."

"I want my mother."

"Don't you feel good again? Maybe the doctor—"

"I want my mother! My mother—and not him!"

She was still looking at the wall when her door was opened.

"Myra," her father said, "sit over there. Sit, I said."

"Yes."

"All right, Lucy. Turn over." He was standing by the side of the bed. "Roll over, I said."

"Lucy," her mother begged, "look at us, please."

"I don't have to see that his shoes are shined and his jaw is set and what a new man he is. I don't have to see his tie, or him!"

"Lucy—"

"Myra, be *quiet*. If she wants to act like a two-year-old at a time like this, let her."

She whispered, "Look who's talking about two-year-olds."

"Listen, young lady. Your backtalk doesn't faze me one way or the other. There have always been smart-aleck teen-agers and there always will be, especially this generation. You just listen to me, that's all, and if you're too ashamed to look me right in the eye—"

"Ashamed!" she cried, but she did not move.

"Are you or are you not going to visit Cousin Vera?"

"I don't even *know* Cousin Vera."

"That isn't what I'm asking."

"I can't go off alone to someone I don't even know—and what? Make up filthy lies for the neighbors—?"

"But they wouldn't be lies," said her mother.

"What would they be, Mother? The truth?"

"They would be *stories*," her father said. "That you have a husband overseas, say, in the Army."

"Oh, you know all about stories, I'm sure. But I tell the truth!"

"Then," he said, "just what do you intend to do about getting in trouble with somebody who you say you can't even stand?"

She turned violently from the wall, as though she intended to hurl herself at him. "Don't you take such a tone with me. Don't you dare!"

"I am not taking a tone!"

"Because I am not ashamed—not in front of you I'm not."

"Now watch it, you, just watch it. Because I can still give you a licking, smart as you think you are."

"Oh," she said bitterly, "can you?"

"Yes!"

"Go ahead, then."

"Oh, wonderful," he said, and walked to the window where he stood as though looking outside. "Just wonderful."

"Lucy," said her mother, "if you don't want to go to Cousin Vera's, then what do you want to do? Just tell us."

"You're the parents. You were always dying to be the parents—"

"Now look," said her father, turning to face her once again. "First, Myra, you sit down. And stay down. And you," he said, waving a finger at his daughter, "you give me your attention, do you hear? Now there is a crisis here, do you understand that? There is a crisis here involving my daughter, and I am going to deal with it, and it's going to be dealt with."

"Fine," said Lucy. "Deal."

"Then be still," her mother pleaded, "and let him talk, Lucy." But when she made a move to sit on the bed, her husband looked at her and she retreated.

"Now either I'm going to do it," he said to his wife, speaking between his teeth, "or I'm not. Now which is it?"

She lowered her eyes.

"Unless of course you want to call your Daddy in," he said.

"I'm sorry."

"Now," said her father, "if you wanted to marry that Roy Bassart—such as we understood you did, Lucy, till just today, and backed you up on all the way—that would be one thing. But this is something else entirely. Who he is I see pretty clear now, and the less said about him the better. I understand the whole picture, so there is just no need for raising voices. He was older, back from service, and just thought to himself he could come back here and take advantage of a young seventeen-year-old high school girl. And that's what he did. But he is his father's business, Lucy, and we will have to leave it to his high and mighty father, the big schoolteacher, to teach something into that boy's hide. Oh, his father thinks he is very superior and all in his ways, but I guess he is going to have another guess coming now. But my concern is with you, Lucy, and what is uppermost to you. Do you understand that? My concern is your going to college, which has always been your dream, right? Now, the question is this, do you still want your dream, or don't you?"

She did not favor him with a reply.

"Okay," he said, "I am going to go ahead on my assumption that you do, just as you always did. Now, next—to give you your dream I am going to do anything I can . . . Are you listening to me? Anything that is going to give it to you, do you follow me? Because what that so-called ex-G.I. has done to you, which I would like to put my hands around his throat for, well, that is not going to just take away your dream, lock, stock and barrel . . . Now, anything," he went on. "Even something that isn't usual and ordinary, and that might to some folks seem very—out of the question." He came closer to the bed so that he could speak without being heard outside the room. "Now do you know what *anything* means, before I go to the next step?"

"Giving up whiskey?"

"I want you to go to college, it means! I have given up whiskey, for your information!"

"Really?" she asked. "Again?"

"Lucy, since Thanksgiving," her mother began.

"Myra, you be still."

"I was only telling her—"

"But *I* will tell her," he said. "*I* will do the telling."

"Yes," his wife said softly.

"Now," he said, turning back to Lucy. "Drink is neither here nor there. Drink is not the issue."

"Oh no?"

"No! A baby is!"

And that made her look away.

"An illegitimate baby is," he said again. "And if you don't *want* that illegitimate baby"—his voice had fallen almost to a whisper now—"then maybe we will have to arrange that you don't have it. If Cousin Vera's is still something you are going to consider out of the question—"

"It absolutely is. I will not spend nine months lying. I will not get big and pregnant and lie!"

"Shhh!"

"Well, I won't," she muttered.

"Okay." He wiped his mouth with his hand. "Okay." She could see where the perspiration had formed above his lip and on his forehead. "Then let's do this in order. And without voice-raising, as there are other people who live in this house."

"We're the other people who live here."

"Be still!" he said. "Everybody knows that without your backtalk!"

"Then just what are you proposing to me? Say it!"

Her mother rushed to the bed at last. "Lucy," she said, taking hold of her hand, "Lucy, it's only to help *you*—"

And then her father took hold of the other hand, and it was as though some current were about to pass through the three of them. She closed her eyes, waited—and her father spoke. And she let him. And she saw the future. She saw herself seated between her two parents as her father drove them across the bridge to Winnisaw. It would be early morning. The doctor would only just have finished his breakfast. He would come to the door to greet them; her father would shake his hand. In his office the doctor would seat himself behind a big dark desk, and she would sit in a chair, and her parents would be together on a sofa, while the doctor explained to them exactly what he was going to do. He would have all his medical degrees right up on the wall, in frames. When she went off with him into the little white operating room, her mother and father would smile at her from the sofa. And they would wait right there until it was time to bundle her up and take her home.

When her father had finished, she said, "It must cost a fortune."

"The object isn't money, honey," he said.

"The object is you," said her mother.

How nice that sounded. Like a poem. She was just beginning to study poetry, too. Her last English composition had been an interpretation of "Ozymandias." She had only received the paper back on Monday morning—a B-plus for the first interpretation she had ever written of a poem in college. Only on Monday she had thought it was going to be her last. Before Roy had finally returned to Fort Kean that night, her recurring thought had been to run away. And now she didn't have to, and she didn't have to marry him either. Now she could concentrate on one thing and one thing only—on school, on her French, her history, her poetry . . .

> The object isn't money,
> The object is you.

"But where," she asked softly, "will you get it all?"

"Let me do the worrying about that," her father said. "Okay?"

"Will you work?"

"Wow," he said to Myra. "She sure don't pull her punches, your daughter here." The red that had risen into his cheeks remained, even as he tried to maintain a soft and joking tone. "Come on, Goosie, what do you say? Give me a break, huh? Where do you think I've been all day today, anyway. Taking a stroll on the boulevard? Playing a tennis game? What do you think I've been doing all my life since I was eighteen years old, and part-time before that? Work, Lucy, just plain old work, day in and day out."

"Not at one job," she said.

"Well . . . I move around . . . that's true . . ."

She was going to cry: they were talking!

"Look," he said, "why don't you think of it this way. You have a father who is a jack of all trades. You should be proud. Come on, Goosie-Pie, how about a smile like I used to get back in prehistoric times? Back when you used to take those 'yumps.' Huh, little Goose?"

She felt her mother squeeze her hand.

"Look," he said, "why do you think people always hire Duane Nelson, no matter what? Because he sits around twid dling his thumbs, or because he knows every kind of machine there is, inside and out? Now which? That's not a hard question, is it, for a smart college girl?"

. . . Afterward she would read in bed. She would have her assignments mailed up to her while she recuperated in her bed. Yes, a college girl. And without Roy. He wasn't so bad; he wasn't for her, that was all. He would just disappear, and she could begin to make friends at school, friends to bring home with her when she came to visit on the weekend. For things would have changed.

Could that be? At long last those terrible days of hatred and solitude, over? To think, she could begin again to talk to her family, to tell them about all the things she was studying, to show them the books she used in her courses, to show them her papers. Stuck into her English book, right there on the floor, was the essay she had written on "Ozymandias." B-plus and across the front the professor had written, "Excellent paragraph development; good understanding of meaning; good use of quotations; but please don't stuff your sentences so." And maybe she *had* overdone the main topic sentence somewhat, but her intention had been to state at the outset all those ideas that she would later take up in the body of the essay. "Even a great king," her paper began, "such as Ozymandias apparently had been, could not predict or control what the future, or Fate, held in store for him and his kingdom; that, I think, is the message that Percy Bysshe Shelley, the poet, means for us to come away with from his romantic poem 'Ozyman-dias,' which not only reveals the theme of the vanity of human wishes—even a king's—but deals also with the concept of the immensity of 'boundless and bare' life and the inevitability of the 'colossal wreck' of everything, as compared to the 'sneer of cold command,' which is all many mere mortals have at their command, unfortunately."

"But is he clean?" she asked.

"A hundred percent," her father said. "Spotless, Lucy. Like a hospital."

"And how old?" she asked. "How old is he?"

"Oh," her father said, "middle-aged, I'd say."

A moment passed. Then, "That's the catch, isn't it?"

"What kind of catch?"

"He's too old."

"Now what do you mean 'too old'? If anything, he's real experienced."

"But is this all he does?"

"Lucy, he's a regular doctor . . . who does this as a special favor, that's all."

"But he charges, you said."

"Well, sure he charges."

"Then it's not a special favor. He does it for money."

"Well, everybody has got bills to meet. Everybody has got to be paid for what they do."

But she saw herself dead. The doctor would be no good, and she would die.

"How do you know about him?"

"Because—" and here he stood, and hitched up his trousers. "Through a friend," he finally said.

"Who?"

"Lucy, I'm afraid maybe that's got to be a secret."

"But where did you hear about him?" Where *would* he hear about such a doctor? "At Earl's famous Dugout of Buddies?"

"Lucy, that's not necessary," said her mother.

Her father walked to the window again. He cleared a pane with the palm of his hand. "Well," he said, "it's stopped snowing. It's stopped snowing, if anybody cares."

"All I meant—" Lucy began.

"Is *what*?" He had turned back to her.

"—is . . . do you know anybody who he's ever done it to, that's all."

"Yes, I happen to, for your information."

"And they're alive?"

"For your information, yes!"

"Well, it's my life. I have a right to know."

"Why don't you just trust me! I'm not going to kill you!"

"Oh, Duane," her mother said, "she *does*."

"Don't speak for me, Mother!"

"Hear that?" he cried to his wife.

"Well, he might just be some quack drinking friend who says he's a doctor or something. Well, how do I know, Mother? Maybe it's even Earl himself in his red suspenders!"

"Yeah, that's who it is," her father shouted. "Earl DuVal! sure! What's the *matter* with you? You think I don't mean it when I say I want you to finish college?"

"Dear, he does. You're his daughter."

"That doesn't mean he knows whether a doctor is good or not, Mother. Suppose I die!"

"But I told you," he cried, shaking a fist at her, "you won't!"

"But how do *you* know?"

"Because she didn't, did she!"

"Who?"

No one had to speak for her to understand.

"Oh, no." She dropped slowly back against the headboard.

Her mother, at the side of the bed, covered her face with her hands.

"When?" said Lucy.

"But she's alive, isn't she?" He was pulling at his shirt with his hands. "Answer the point I'm making! I am speaking! She did not die! She did not get hurt in any way at all!"

"Mother," she said, turning to her, "when?"

But her mother only shook her head. Lucy got up out of the bed. "Mother, when did he make you do that?"

"He didn't make me."

"Oh, Mother," she said, standing before her. "You're my mother."

"Lucy, it was the Depression times. You were a little girl. It was so long ago. Oh, Lucy, it's all forgotten. Daddy Will,

Grandma, they don't know," she whispered, "—don't have to—"

"But the Depression was over when I was three, when I was four."

"What?" her father cried. "Are you kidding?" To his wife he said, "Is she kidding?"

"Lucy," her mother said, "we did it for you."

"Oh yes," she said, moving backward onto her bed, "for me, everything was for me."

"Lucy, we couldn't have another baby," said her mother. "Not when we were so behind, trying so to fight back—"

"But if only he did his job! If he only stopped being a coward!"

"Look," he said, coming angrily at her, "you don't even know when the Depression was, or what it was, either—*so watch what you say!*"

"I do too know!"

"The whole country was behind the eightball. Not just me! If you want to call names, you, call the whole United States of America names!"

"Sure, the whole *world*."

"Don't you know history?" he cried. "Don't you know anything?" he demanded.

"I know what you made her do, you!"

"But," her mother cried, "I *wanted* to."

"Did you hear that?" he shouted. "Did you hear what your mother just said to you?"

"But you're the man!"

"I am also a human being!"

"*That's no excuse!*"

"Oh, what am I arguing with *you* for? You don't know *a* from *z* as far as life is concerned, and you never will! You wouldn't know a man's job if I did it!"

Silence.

"Hear, Mother? Hear your husband?" said Lucy. "Did you hear what he just said, right out in the open?"

"Oh, hear what I *mean*," he cried.

"But what you *said*—"

"I don't care! Stop trapping me! I came in here to solve a

crisis, but how can I do it when nobody lets me even begin? Or end! You'd rather trap me—throw me in jail! That's what you'd rather do. You'd rather humiliate me in this whole town, and make me looked down on as the town joke."

"Town *drunk!*"

"Town drunk?" he said. "Town *drunk?* You ought to *see* the town drunk. You think *I'm* the town drunk? Well, you ought to just see a town drunk, and then think what you're saying twice before you say it. You don't know what a town drunk is. You don't know what anything is! You—you just want me behind bars—that's your big wish in life, and always has been!"

"It's not."

"It is!"

"But that's *over*," cried Myra.

"Oh, sure it's over," said Whitey. "Sure, people just forget how a daughter threw her own father in jail. Sure, people don't talk about that behind your back. People don't like to tell stories on a person, oh no. People are always giving other people a chance to change and get their strength back. Sure, that's what this little scene is all about too. You bet it is. Oh, she's got me fixed, boy—and that's the way it's going to be. That's how brilliant she is, your so-called college girl scholarship daughter. Well, go ahead, so-called daughter who knows all the answers—solve your own life. Because I'm not good enough for a person like you, and never have been. What am I anyway? The town drunk to her."

He pulled open the door and went loudly down the stairs. They could hear him bellowing in the parlor. "Go ahead, Mr. Carroll. You're the only one can solve things around here. Go ahead, it's Daddy Will everyone wants around here anyway. I'm just extra anyway. I'm just along for the ride, we all know that."

"Shouting won't help anything, Duane—"

"Right, right you are, Berta. Nothing will help anything around here."

"Willard," said Berta, "tell this man—"

"What's the trouble, Duane? What's the fuss?"

"Oh, nothing you can't fix, Willard. Because you're the Big Daddy, and me, I'm just along for the ride."

"Willard, where is he going? Dinner is all ready."

"Duane, where are you going?"

"I don't know. Maybe I'll go down and see old Tom Whipper."

"Who's he?"

"The town drunk, Willard! That's who the town drunk is, damn it—Tom Whipper!"

The door slammed, and then the house was silent except for the whispering that began downstairs.

Lucy lay without moving on the bed.

Her mother was crying.

"Mother, why, *why* did you let him make you do that?"

"I did what I had to," said her mother mournfully.

"You didn't! You let him trample on your dignity, Mother! You were his doormat! His slave!"

"Lucy, I did what was necessary," she said, sobbing.

"That's not always right, though. You have to do what's *right*!"

"It was." She spoke as in a trance. "It was, it was—"

"It wasn't! Not for you! He degrades you, Mother, and you let him! Always! All our lives!"

"Oh, Lucy, whatever we say, our suggestions, you refuse."

"I refuse—I refuse to live your life again, Mother, that's what I refuse!"

—

Roy's best man was Joe Whetstone, home from the University of Alabama, where he had kicked nine field goals and twenty-three consecutive extra points for the freshman football team. The maid of honor was Eleanor Sowerby. Unbeknownst to Joe, Ellie had fallen in love at Northwestern. She simply had to tell Lucy, though she made her promise to speak of it to no one, not even Roy. She would shortly be having to write Joe a letter, and she would just as soon not have to think about that during her vacation; it would be difficult enough at the time.

Either Ellie had forgiven Lucy for calling her a dope at Thanksgiving, or else she was willing to forget it during the wedding. All through the ceremony tears coursed down her lovely face, and her own lips moved when Lucy said, "I do."

After the ceremony Daddy Will told Lucy that she was the most beautiful bride he had seen since her mother. "A real bride," he kept saying, "isn't that so, Berta?" "Congratulations," her grandmother said. "You were a real bride." That was as far as she would go; she knew now that it was not the grippe that had caused Lucy to be sick in the kitchen sink.

Julian Sowerby kissed her again. "Well," he said, "I suppose now I get to do this all the time." "Now *I* do," said Roy. Julian said, "Lucky you, boy, she's a cutie-pie, all right," in no way indicating that he had once lectured Roy for four solid hours in the taproom of the Hotel Kean on the evils of becoming her husband.

Nor did Irene Sowerby indicate that secretly she believed Lucy had unusual emotions. "Good luck to you," she said to the bride, and touched her lips to Lucy's cheek. She took Roy's hand and held it a very long time before she was ready to speak. And then she was unable to.

Then her own parents. "Daughter," was all she heard in her ear; so stiff was she in his embrace that perhaps it was all he said. "Oh, Lucy," her mother said, her wet lashes against Lucy's face, "be happy. You can be if only you'll try. You were the happiest little girl . . ."

Then both Roy's parents stepped forward, and after a moment in which each seemed to be deferring to the other, the two Bassarts lunged at the bride simultaneously. The mix-up of arms and faces that ensued at long last gave everyone present something to laugh about.

Lloyd Bassart was the adult who had finally gotten behind the young couple and supported them in their desire to be married at Christmas—sooner than Christmas if it could be managed. This sharp change of attitude had occurred one night early in December when Roy broke down over the phone and in tears told *his* parents—who had been pouring it on, once again—to stop. "I can't take any more!" he had cried. "Stop! Stop! Lucy's pregnant!"

Well. Well. It had required only the two "wells." If what Roy had just confessed was the actual situation as it existed, then his father did not see that Roy had any choice but to take the responsibility for what he had done. Between a man doing the right thing and a man doing the wrong thing, there was really no choice, as far as Mr. Bassart could see. Weeping, Roy said it was more or less what he had been thinking to himself all along. "I should certainly hope so," said his father, and so that, finally, was that.

III

S HE moved into his room at Mrs. Blodgett's. Mrs. Blodgett, who had called her a hussy. Mrs. Blodgett, who had called Roy crooked. Mrs. Blodgett, with her thousand little rules and regulations.

But Lucy said nothing. In the weeks and months following the wedding she found herself trying with all her might to do what she was told. You could not question someone's every word and deed and expect to be happy with them, or expect them to be happy either. They were married. She must trust him; what kind of life would it be otherwise?

Mrs. Blodgett and Roy had worked out the arrangement beforehand: only another five dollars a month for the room. Surely Lucy had to admit that was a bargain, especially since Roy had gotten Mrs. Blodgett to throw in kitchen privileges for the hour between seven and eight in the evening. Of course, they would have to leave the kitchen exactly as they had found it. It was not, after all, the kitchen of a hotel, it was the kitchen of a dwelling place; but apparently Roy had assured Mrs. Blodgett that Lucy was neat as a pin, and knew her way around a kitchen, having worked for three years after school and summers in the Dairy Bar up in Liberty Center. "But that, Mr. Bassart, is my very point, it is not some dairy bar, it is not some—" He assured her then that he would work in the kitchen right along with Lucy. How would that be? In fact, if Mrs. Blodgett had any dishes left over from her own dinner, they could easily wash hers while washing up their own. In the Army he had once had to wash pots and pans for seventeen hours straight on K.P.; as a result, one dish more or less wouldn't faze him too much, she could be sure.

Mrs. Blodgett said she would extend them the privilege, on a trial basis, and only for so long as they didn't abuse it.

During the next few months Roy several times went out after dinner and knocked on the parlor door to ask the landlady if she would like to join them in the kitchen for dessert. Privately he said to Lucy that the extra chocolate pudding or fruit cup cost no more than a few pennies, and with someone of Mrs. Blodgett's changeable disposition, it was worth building up points on your side. Their getting married had more or less restored Mrs. Blodgett's faith in him, but still and all, where three people were living together under one roof, there was no sense looking for trouble, especially if you could just as easily avoid it by using your head in advance.

She said nothing. They must not squabble over issues that were of no real consequence. She must not criticize him for what—she told herself—was really nothing more than a desire to please. Some people did things one way, and Roy did them another. Weren't they married? Hadn't he acted as she had wanted?

TRUST HIM.

To her surprise, hardly a Sunday passed when they did not travel up to Liberty Center to visit his family. Roy said that under ordinary circumstances it wouldn't be necessary, but what with all the strain of the past months and the hard feelings that had developed, it seemed to him a good idea to try to smooth things over before the baby was born and life *really* began to get hectic. The fact was that she was a stranger to his family, as he was a stranger to hers. Now that they were married, what sense did that make? They would all be seeing a lot of one another in the years to come, and it seemed to him ridiculous to start off on the wrong foot. It was an easy two-hour ride up, and aside from the gas, what would it cost them?

So she went—to Sunday dinner at the Bassarts', and on the way out of town, over to say hello to her own family. Silently she sat in the parlor she had hoped never to set foot in again, while Roy engaged her family in fifteen minutes of small talk, most of it for the benefit of her father and Daddy Will. They talked a lot about prefab houses. Her father was supposed to be thinking about building a prefab house, and Daddy Will was supposed to be thinking that it was something her father was capable of doing. Roy said he had buddies down at Britannia who could probably help them draw up plans, when they got to that stage. Contractors were throwing up whole communities of prefabs overnight, Roy said. Oh, it's a real building revolution, her father said. It sure is, Mr. Nelson. Yep, looks like the coming thing, said Daddy Will. It sure does, Mr. Carroll, they're throwing up whole communities overnight.

One Sunday evening, while driving back down to Fort Kean, Roy said, "Well, it looks as though your old man is really on the wagon this time."

"I hate him, Roy. And I will always hate him. I told you long ago, and I meant it: *I don't want to talk about him, ever!*"

"Okay," said Roy lightly, "okay," and so no quarrel resulted. He seemed willing to forget that he had even brought up the subject—as willing as he was to forget that hatred of which Lucy had sought to remind him.

So they set off, Sunday after Sunday, like any young married couple visiting the in-laws. Buy why? *Why?*

Because that's what they were: she was his wife. And her mother his mother-in-law. And her father, with the thick new mustache and the bright new plans, was Roy's father-in-law. "But I'd really rather not, Roy, not today." "Come on, we're up here, aren't we? I mean, how would it look if we went away without even saying hello? What's the big deal? Come on, honey, don't act like a kid, get in the car—careful, watch the old belly."

And she did not argue. Could it be that she had actually argued her last? She had fought and fought to get him to do his duty, but in the end he had done it. So what more was there to fight about? She simply could not find the strength to raise her voice.

And she must respect him anyway. She must not pick at what he said, or challenge his opinions, or take issue with him, especially on matters where his knowledge was superior to her own. Or was supposed to be. She was his wife; she must be sympathetic to his point of view, even if she didn't always agree with it, as she surely didn't when he began to tell her how much more he knew than the teachers at Britannia.

Unfortunately, Britannia hadn't turned out to be the place it was cracked up to be in all those fancy brochures. For one

thing, it hadn't been established in 1910, at least not as a photography school. They had only decided to branch out into
photography after the war, so as to catch a bigger hunk of the
G.I. Bill trade. For the first thirty-five years of its existence it
had been a drafting school called the Britannia Technical Institute, and two thirds of the students still were guys interested in
getting into the building business—which was how Roy came
to know so much about the prefab boom. The drafting students, as a matter of fact, weren't too bad; it was the photography students who were a scandal. Though you had to fill out
a long entrance application, and with it send samples of your
work, it turned out that there weren't any real entrance requirements at all. The procedure for photography applicants
was just a ruse to make you think that the new department
had some sort of standards. And the quality of the faculty, he
said, was even more appalling than the quality of the students
—particularly one H. Harold LaVoy, who somewhere along
the line had got the idea that he was some sort of expert on
photographic technique. Some expert. There was more to be
learned about composition by flipping through an issue of
Look than spending a lifetime listening to a pompous idiot like
LaVoy (who some of the guys said might be a fairy, besides. A
real queer. For Lucy's edification, he imitated LaVoy walking
down the halls. A bit la-dee-da, didn't she agree? But even a
homo could teach you something if he knew something. But a
dumb homo—well, that was just about the end).

LaVoy's class was at eight in the morning, Roy's first of
the day. He got up and went off to it faithfully every single
morning of the first month of the second semester, every
morning went off to listen to that nasal-voiced know-it-all
going on and on about absolutely nothing that a ten-year-old
kid couldn't figure out if he had a pair of twenty-twenty eyes.
"Shadows are produced, gentlemen, by placing object A between the sun and object B." Bro*ther*. One stormy morning
they got as far as the front porch, when Roy turned around,
came back into the room, and Army boots, field jacket and all,
threw himself back on the bed, moaning, "Oh, I don't mind a
homo, really, but a *dumb* homo!" He said he could find better
uses to make of that hour right here in their room, he was

sure. And since his next class wasn't until eleven, by staying home he would be saving not only the hour LaVoy shot for him, but the two hours following, which he usually spent down in the lounge, watching one of the endless blackjack games that was always in session. It was so smoky and noisy down there that that's about all you could do. Having a conversation about photography was practically impossible—not that any of his fellow students seemed to be disposed in that direction anyway. Sometimes with those guys it actually seemed to him that he was back in the day room up in the Aleutians.

And what did Lucy do? She went down to the corner and caught the crosstown bus to school for her eight o'clock. Roy said he would drive her over if she wanted; now that she was getting bigger he didn't like the idea of her taking public transportation, or walking around on slippery streets. But she declined that first morning, and on those snowy mornings thereafter. It was all right, she said, there was nothing to worry about, she preferred not to inconvenience him by taking him away from his studying *if that's what studying was to him, sitting up in bed with a scissors and the magazines his mother saved for him every week, eating handfuls of those Hydrox cookies!* But maybe he knew what he was doing. Maybe the school *was* a fraud. Maybe his colleagues *were* dopes. Maybe LaVoy *was* pompous and an idiot, and a homosexual too. Maybe everything he said was true and everything he did was right.

That was what she told herself, walking through the snow to the bus, and then in class, and in the library, and in the coffee shop, where she went by herself for her lunch, after one-thirty. Most of the girls ate in the cafeteria at noon, as she had when she lived in the dorm, and she preferred now to avoid them whenever she could manage it. Eventually one of them would take a sidelong glance at her belly, and why did she have to put up with that? There was no reason for any of those little freshman twerps to look down their noses at her. To them she might only be the kid who'd had to get married over Christmas, somebody to whisper about and make fun of, but to herself she was Mrs. Roy Bassart, and she didn't intend to go around feeling ashamed of herself all day long. She had nothing whatsoever to be ashamed of or to regret. So she ate her lunch, alone, at two-thirty, in the last booth of The Old Campus Coffee Shop.

On the first Sunday of June, while they were driving up to Liberty Center, Roy decided he wasn't going to take his finals the following week. Frankly, he could go in and pass things like camera repair and negative retouching without too much sweat, to use an Army expression. So it wasn't a matter of chickening out, or of being too lazy to do the studying. There really wasn't very much studying that he could see to do. What made it senseless to go in and take the final exams—which, by the way, no one had flunked in the history of the photography department, except in LaVoy's class, where it wasn't a matter of whether you knew the material anyway but whether you agreed with Hot Shot LaVoy and his big ideas—but what made it senseless was that he had decided not to return to Britannia in the fall. At least that, at any rate, was what he wanted to talk over with her.

But they had already talked it over. To support her and the baby, he was going to have to give up school during the day; but the plan had been for him to enroll in the night program. It would take two years more that way instead of only one, but this was the solution they had agreed upon months before.

Well, that's why he was bringing it up again. He didn't see any sense hanging on at that place days *or* nights. What good did she think that Master of Photographic Arts degree was going to do him anyway? Anybody who knew anything about photography knew that a Britannia degree wasn't worth the paper it was printed on. "And given the day teachers, you can just imagine the geniuses they have teaching there at night. You know who the head of the whole night program is, don't you?"

"Who?"

"H. Pansy LaVoy. So you can imagine."

Then he told her his surprise. Yesterday morning he and Mrs. Blodgett had got into a conversation, and the upshot was that he was on the brink of his first commercial job. So who needed Peaches LaVoy? On Monday morning he was to do a portrait sitting of Mrs. Blodgett for a week's rent, provided she liked the pictures when they came out.

Up in Liberty Center, Alice Bassart took Roy aside early in the afternoon and told him about Lucy's father blackening her mother's eye. After dinner Roy got Lucy alone upstairs and as gently as he could broke the news. She immediately put on her coat and scarf and boots, and against Roy's wishes, went over to the house to see the black eye for herself. And it was not vicious gossip; it was real.

For three days Whitey had been off doing penance for his misdeed—the afternoon he chose to return was the afternoon of his daughter's visit. He never got through the door.

The baby was born four days later. The labor began in the middle of her English exam, and continued for twelve long, arduous hours. She was awake throughout, swearing to herself every minute of the time that if she survived, her child would never know what life was like in a fatherless house. She would not repeat her mother's life, nor would her offspring repeat her own.

And so for Roy (and, in a sense, for Whitey Nelson too, who after that Sunday had simply disappeared from the town), the honeymoon came to an end.

—

His first suggestion to be met with opposition was the one he made while she was still in the hospital. Why didn't they move back to Liberty Center for the summer? His family would sleep on the screened-in back porch, which they liked to do anyway in the hot weather, and the two of them and Baby Edward could have the upstairs all to themselves. It seemed to him that it would really be a wonderful change for Lucy. As for himself, he could endure living with his parents for a few months, what with all it would mean for Lucy to be able to relax and take it easy for a while. And think what it would mean to the baby, who would surely feel the heat less up in Liberty Center. All in all, it sounded like such a good idea that the previous night, when his parents came to visit at the hospital, he had taken them aside and broached it to them. He hadn't wanted to tell Lucy beforehand for fear that she would be disappointed if his family had any objections. But actually it had suited them just fine; his mother was absolutely tickled pink by the idea. It was a long while since she had been able to go full steam ahead with her specialty—Pampering with a

capital P. Furthermore, the presence of Edward would probably mean the end of that last little bit of tension still existing
between themselves and his parents—the unfortunate result
of the particular circumstances of the wedding. Moreover,
they'd now had six months of marriage, and a really harmo-
nious marriage at that. Roy said he couldn't get over how
compatible they had turned out to be, once all that premarital
uncertainty had ended; had he known it was going to be like
this, he said, taking her hand in his, he would have proposed
from the car that first night he followed her down Broadway.
He had to admit that it would give him a certain secret pleasure to go back for a while to Liberty Center and show his
doubting Thomas of a father just how fantastically compatible
his son's marriage had turned out to be.

And how, Lucy asked, would Roy support them when they
were living in his father's house?

He assured her that if ever there was a place he could pick
up jobs as a free-lance photographer, it was in his own hometown.

No.

No? What did she mean, no?

No.

He couldn't believe his ears. Why not?

No!

How could he argue with somebody in a hospital bed? For a
while he tried, but all he got was no.

Fortunately, in the month after Edward's birth, Mrs. Blodgett let them bring into the room the crib the Sowerbys had
given them, and allowed them even more expanded use of the
kitchen facilities, all for only another dollar a week. Moreover,
she had accepted the portrait Roy had done of her in exchange
for a week's rent. She thought it made her features look too
small, particularly her eyes and mouth, but she said herself that
if she expected a professional job she should have gone to a
professional; she was an honest person and would not welsh
on her end of the bargain. Certainly, said Roy, Lucy had to
agree that the landlady was doing the best she could to be considerate. A man and his wife and a tiny infant wasn't at all what
she had bargained for the year before, and so he wished that
Lucy would be a little more cordial—or else just say okay, and

even if only half the summer was left, agree to go up to his parents' for a month or so, and live for a while in an environment more suited to their present needs . . .Well, would she?

Would she what? Which question did he want answered?

Would she go up to Liberty Center?

No.

Just for the month of August?

No.

Well then, at least would she be more pleasant to Mrs. Blodgett when she passed her in the corridor? What did it cost to smile?

She was being as pleasant as was necessary.

But the woman was surely going out of her way—

The woman was being paid the money she asked for her room and her kitchen. If she didn't like the arrangement, or them, she could ask them to move.

Move? *Where?*

To an apartment of their own.

But how could they afford an apartment of their own?

How did he think?

"Well, I'm *looking* for a job. Every day! It's summer, Lucy! And that's the truth! The bosses are all on vacation. Every place I go—sorry, the boss is on vacation! And our savings are dwindling like crazy too. If we were up in Liberty Center, we wouldn't have had to spend a penny all summer long. Instead we're down here, accomplishing nothing, and the baby is hot, and our money is just dribbling away, and all I do is waste time sitting in offices waiting and waiting for people who aren't even there. We could all of us have had a little vacation—a vacation all of us need, too, whether you know it or not. Because now do you see what's happening? We're arguing. Right this minute we're having an argument. And why? We're just as compatible now as we were six months ago, Lucy, but we're arguing because of living in this one room in all this hot weather, while up in Liberty Center that whole upstairs is just sitting there going to waste."

No.

Just before Labor Day, Lucy said that since there did not seem to be any jobs for a photographer available, perhaps he should start to look for some other kind of work, but Roy said he was not going to get stuck in a job he hated, because the job he liked and was equipped to do hadn't yet come along.

But their savings *were* rapidly dwindling, and this money, she reminded him, consisted not only of what he had saved in the Army, but what she had saved during all those years at the Dairy Bar.

Well, he happened to know that. That's what he had been telling her all summer long. That was exactly what could have been avoided—and then he slammed the door and left the house before she could deliver the speech he saw coming, or before Mrs. Blodgett, who had already hammered on the floor above them with her shoe, could make it down the stairs to deliver hers.

Only an hour later there was a phone call for Roy from Mr. H. Harold LaVoy of the Britannia Institute. He said he understood that Mr. Bassart was looking for a job. He wished to inform him that Wendell Hopkins was in need of an assistant, his previous assistant having just enrolled as a full-time student in Britannia's television department, which would be getting under way in the fall.

When Roy came home at lunchtime he was flabbergasted at the message. From *LaVoy*? Hopkins, the society photographer? He was shaved and dressed and out of the house in a matter of minutes; within the hour he had called Lucy to say that he wanted her to put Edward on.

Put Edward on? Edward was sleeping. What was he even saying?

Well then, she had better tell the baby herself: his father was now the assistant to Wendell Hopkins in his studio in the Platt Building in downtown Fort Kean. Well, was it or was it not worth waiting for?

What he couldn't get over that night at dinner was that LaVoy had thought to call *him*—even after those disagreements they used to have almost daily in class, during the month that Roy had even bothered to show up. Apparently, however, LaVoy wasn't really as touchy as he had appeared to be in the classroom. True, the old fruitcake couldn't take criticism in public, but privately it appeared that he had developed a certain grudging respect for Roy's knowledge of composition, and light and shadow. Well, you had to give him credit, he was a bigger man than Roy had thought. Who knows, maybe he wasn't even a fruit; maybe that just happened, unfortunately for him, to be the way he walked and the way he talked. Who knows, if they had ever gotten beyond the arguing stage, LaVoy might even have turned out to be a pretty sharp guy. They might even have become friends. Anyway, what difference did it make now? At the age of twenty-two he was the sole assistant to Wendell Hopkins, who, it turned out, only a few years back had done a portrait of the whole Donald Brunn family of Liberty Center. Oh, what a pleasure it would be to telephone his father directly after dinner and tell him about his new job—not to mention the fact that Mr. Hopkins was the family photographer for his father's well-known boss.

Before the month was over they had found their first apartment; it was on the top floor of an old house at the north end of Pendleton Park, practically on the outskirts of Fort Kean. The rent was reasonable, the furniture wasn't bad, and the big trees and quiet street reminded Roy of Liberty Center. There was a bedroom for the baby, and a large living room in which they could also sleep, and a kitchen and bath of their very own. There was also a dank and musty cellar back of the furnace that the renting agent said Roy was welcome to turn into a darkroom, so long as he realized that he would have to leave behind him any improvements he made in the building. The apartment was a twenty-minute drive to downtown, but the prospect of the darkroom clinched the deal.

The thirtieth of September was a Saturday, brisk and cloudy. They spent the morning driving their belongings over to their new home. Late in the day, when the moving was over and they had washed the last of the plates used for their last meal, Roy sat tapping lightly and sporadically on the horn of the car, while Lucy stood up on the porch, the baby in her arms, and told Mrs. Blodgett what she thought of her.

—

In the next year Roy drove in his car all over Kean County, photographing church socials, Rotary dinners, ladies'-club meetings, Little League games—and, most frequently, grade and high school graduation classes; the biggest share of the Hopkins' business, it turned out, was not out of the Fort Kean social register, but from the Board of Education, of which his brother was a member. Hopkins himself stayed in the studio all day to do the serious sittings—the brides, the babies and the businessmen. His first week Roy had carried around a small spiral notebook in which he had planned to jot down the tips and advice that might pass from the lips of the seasoned old professional during a day's work. Shortly he came to use it to record the cost of the gas pumped each day into the car.

Edward. A pale little baby with blue eyes and white hair, who for so very long had the sweetest, mildest, most serene disposition. He smiled benevolently up at everyone who looked admiringly down into his carriage when Lucy wheeled him through the park; he slept and ate when he was supposed to, and in between times just smiled away. The elderly couple who lived in the apartment below said they had never known a baby to be so quiet and well behaved; they had been prepared for the worst when they heard that a child was going to be living over their heads, but they had to tell young Mr. and Mrs. Bassart that they had no complaint so far.

Just before Edward's first birthday, Uncle Julian hired Roy to come up to the house to take the pictures at Ellie's pinning party. The next day Roy began to talk about leaving his job and opening a studio of his own. How much longer could he go on doing the D.A.R. in the afternoon and the high school prom at night? How much longer could he go on getting peanuts for doing the dreary dirty work, the weekend work, the night work, while Hopkins raked in the money and did all the creative jobs besides (if you could call anything Hopkins did "creative")? Exactly how long was he supposed to let Hopkins get away with paying only for the gas, while Roy himself absorbed the depreciation on the automobile?

"LaVoy!" said Roy one night, after a gruesome afternoon photographing the boys and girls of the 4H Club. "I really ought to go down to the Britannia and punch that pansy one right in the mouth. Because, you know something, *he* knew what this job was all along. A glorified errand boy. The photographic technique involved—well, Eddie could do it, for God's sake. And I'm telling you something, LaVoy knew it. Well, just think about it. Remember how surprised I was? Well, it was actually a piece of vengeance against me—can you imagine?—and I'm so dumb it never dawned on me till today, right in the midst of shooting all those kids going 'cheese, cheese.' Well, I'll show him, and I'll show Hopkins too. If I started my own place, I'd have half of Hopkins' portrait trade within a year. And that's a fact. That I know for a *fact*. All he needs is a little competition, then he'd be crying Mamma, all right."

"But where would you run this studio, Roy?"

"Where would I run it? To begin with? Where would I *have* it? Is that what you mean?"

"Where would you run it? How much will it cost? What will you do to support us until the customers begin to leave Hopkins and come running to you?"

"Oh, damn," he said, banging a fist on the table, "*damn* that LaVoy. He really couldn't take criticism, not the slightest bit of it. And the thing is, I knew it all the time. But that he'd stoop to this—"

"Roy, where do you intend to start a studio?"

"Well—if you want to talk seriously about it . . ."

"*Where*, Roy?"

"Well—to start off, there'd have to be another rent, see."

"*Another* rent?"

"But that's what we can rule out. Because we have to, I know. We couldn't afford it. So, to start off, well . . . I thought, here."

"*Here?*"

"Well, the darkroom I'd have in the basement, of course."

"And your studio itself would be in our living room?"

"Just during the day, of course."

"And Edward and myself during the day?"

"Well, as I say, Lucy, it's open to question, needless to say. I'm certainly willing to talk over the pros and cons, and peacefully too—"

"And the customers?"

"I *told* you, that would take time."

"And what darkroom are you even talking about? You haven't even begun a darkroom. You've talked about beginning a darkroom; oh, you've talked about it, all right—"

"Well, I work all day long, it so happens, you know. I come home at night bushed, frankly. And half the time on weekends he's got me going out to some wedding somewhere out in the sticks—oh, forget it. You can't understand anything about my career. Or my ambitions! I have a kid growing up, Lucy. And I happen to have ambitions that I haven't given up, you know, just because I'm married. I'm sure not going to be the victim of that LaVoy's vengeance for the rest of my life, I'll tell you that. He tricked me right into this job, which is really for a grind, you know—and Hopkins pays me peanuts, compared to what photographers *can* make, and because I say I want a studio of my own to you, to my own *wife*—oh, you won't understand anything! You won't even try!" And he ran out the door.

It was nearly midnight when he returned.

"Where have you been, Roy? I have been sitting here waiting up for you, not knowing where you were. Where have you been? To some bar?"

"Some what?" he said sourly. "I went to a movie, Lucy, if you have to know. I went into town and saw a movie."

He went off to the bathroom to brush his teeth.

When the lights were off he said, "Well, I tell you one thing. I don't know about all the suckers before me, but as far as I'm concerned, Old Tightwad is at least going to split the car insurance starting when it gets renewed. I'm not working my you-know-what off to make him the richest guy in town."

The months passed. No further mention was made of the studio, though from time to time Roy would mutter about LaVoy. "I wonder if the administration of that so-called school knows about that guy. A real honest to God homemade fruitcake, just like you hear about. Old la-dee-da LaVoy. H. Harold. Boy, would I love to run into him downtown some day, would I love to confront him some day face to face."

One Sunday in the spring when they were visiting Liberty Center, Lucy overheard Roy's mother saying that a package had arrived for him and was up in his bedroom on the dresser. Driving home that night she asked him what was in the package.

"What package?" said Roy.

The next day, after cleaning up from breakfast and making Edward's bed, she began to search the apartment. Not until after lunch, when Edward was napping, did she find a small box jammed down into the top of one of Roy's old Army boots, way at the back of the hall closet. The box was from a printing firm in Cleveland, Ohio; inside were hundreds and hundreds of business cards reading

BASSART PHOTOGRAPHIC STUDIO
Finest Photographic Portraiture
in all Fort Kean

When Roy came home in the evenings, he usually played this game with his little boy (bushed as he might be). "Ed?" Roy would say as he came through the door. "Hey, has anybody here seen Edward Bassart?" whereupon Edward would pop up from behind the sofa, and aiming himself for the front door, go running full tilt into his father's arms. Roy would sweep him up off the floor and twirl him around overhead, crying out in mock amazement, "Well, I'll be darned. I will be absolutely be darned. It's the original Edward Q. Bassart himself."

The evening of the day Lucy had discovered his secret, Roy came through the door, Edward ran wildly to him, Roy swung him up over his head, and Lucy thought, "No! No!" for suppose the tiny, innocent, laughing child were to take his father for a man, and grow up in his image?

She controlled herself throughout the dinner and while Edward was read to by Roy, but after he had put his son to bed she was waiting for him in the living room with the package from Cleveland, Ohio, sitting on the coffee table. "When are you going to grow up? When are you going to do the job you have without looking for every single way there is to get out of it? *When?*"

His eyes filled with tears and he rushed out of the apartment.

Again it was midnight before he returned. He'd had a hamburger, and gone to another movie. He took off his coat and hung it in the closet. He went into Edward's room; when he came out—still refusing to engage her eye—he said, "Did he wake up?"

"When?"

He picked up a magazine and spoke while flipping through it. "While I was gone."

"Fortunately, no."

"Look," he said.

"Look what?"

"Oh," he said, plunging into a chair, "I'm sorry. Well, I am," he said, throwing up his arms. "Well, look, am I forgiven or what?"

He explained that he had seen the ad for the business cards in the back of a trade magazine down at Hopkins. A thousand cards—

"Why not ten thousand, Roy? Why not a hundred thousand?"

"Let me finish, *will you*?" he cried.

A thousand cards was the smallest amount you could order. That was the bargain, a thousand for five ninety-eight. Okay, he was sorry he had done it without talking first to her; that way they could have argued out the sense of ordering the cards before some of the other things were planned. He knew that as far as she was concerned it wasn't the money but the principle of the thing.

"It's both, Roy."

Well, maybe both, according to her, but really and truly he didn't know how much longer he could stand the way Hopkins was exploiting him for sixty-five lousy dollars a week. At this point the resale value on the Hudson was practically nil. If she was so concerned about five ninety-eight for business cards, what about that, the depreciation on the car? And what about a little thing called his career? Last week, two whole evenings photographing practically every single Brownie and Cub Scout in the county! By now he would have been a graduate of Britannia, if he hadn't had to go out and get a stupid job like this one so as to support a family.

"But you didn't *want* to graduate from Britannia."

"I'm talking about the time that's passed, Lucy, while I do Hopkins' dirty work!"

Well, if he wanted to talk about time, she would have been a junior now, and a senior in the fall; in a year she would be graduating from college. Well, said Roy, don't act as though it's my fault. But it *was* his fault, she said; whose idea was that "interruption" business but his? Look, he said, they'd been over all that a hundred times already. Over what, Roy? Over that the interruption had worked all summer, for one—and for another, she had let him do it. She had let him do it, she said, because he had forced it on her, because he had insisted and insisted— *Okay!* he cried. Then you have to take the consequences, she told him, you have to pay the price for what you do! All my *life?* he asked. A whole life long pay the price for *that?* God damn it, just because he'd had to marry her didn't mean that he had to be the slave of Hopkins for the rest of his life, or the patsy of some no-good rotten pansy fruit!

"LaVoy has nothing to do with this!" she cried.

"Oh, and I suppose Hopkins doesn't either, according to you?"

"He doesn't!"

"Oh, no? Oh, you don't happen to think so, do you? Who does then, Lucy, just me? Just me and no one else?"

The tears flowed from his eyes, and once again he ran for the door. He drove straight up to Liberty Center and did not return until the following afternoon.

Looking very determined. He wanted to have a serious talk, he said, like adults. About what? she asked. She happened to have a two-year-old child to take care of while he went off downtown to a movie, or running home to his Mommy. She happened to have a bright, alert little boy, who got up in the morning and found his father missing and didn't know what to make of it at all.

Roy followed her around the living room, trying to make himself heard over the sounds of the vacuum cleaner. Finally he pulled out the plug and refused to surrender it until she heard him out. What he wanted to talk about was a separation.

A what? Please, she told him, Edward was in his bedroom taking his nap. "What are you even saying, Roy?"

"Well, a sort of temporary separation. So we can both sort of calm down. So we can think things through, and probably afterward be all the better for it . . . An armistice, sort of."

"Who have you been talking to, Roy, about our private life?"

"No one," he said. "I just did some thinking. Is that unheard of, that a person should do some thinking about his own private life?"

"You are repeating someone else's idea. Well, is that or is that not true?"

He threw the plug to the floor and once again was out of the house.

Edward, it turned out, had not been napping; at the start of the argument he had run from his bedroom to the bathroom and fastened the little hook that locked the door. Lucy knocked and knocked. She promised him all kinds of treats if only he would just lift the little hook out of the eye of the little screw. She said Daddy was upset about something that had happened at his work, but that nobody was angry at anybody. Daddy had gone off to work, and would be home for dinner, just like every other night. Didn't he want to play his game with Daddy? She begged him to open up. Meanwhile she pressed and pressed against the door, thinking that the screw might ease free of the old boards of the house. In the end she had to bang the door sharply with her shoulder for the thing to pull out of the wall.

Edward was sitting under the washbasin, holding a washcloth over his face. He sobbed hysterically when he heard her approaching, and only after half an hour of holding and rocking him in her arms was she able to persuade him that everything was all right.

She was in bed when Roy came home that night and began to undress in the dark. She turned on the light and as softly as she could, fearing for Edward's sleep, she asked him to sit down and listen to her. They had to talk. He had to be made to understand what his behavior was doing to Edward's peace of mind. She told him about Edward's locking himself in the bathroom—a two-year-old child, Roy. She told him what it had been like to see him sitting there under the basin, hiding behind a washcloth. She told him that he could not keep running off and expect that their child, tiny as he was, was not going to understand that something was going on between his mother and his father. She told him that he could not come home from work and be all lovey-dovey to a little two-year-old, and play with him, and read to him, and kiss him good night, and then just not be there in the morning. Because the child was able to put two and two together, whether Roy knew it or not.

Several times Roy tried to speak in his defense, but she went right on, refusing to be interrupted until the truth was heard, and after a while Roy just sat there on the edge of the sofa bed, his head in his hands, saying he was sorry. Had Eddie really locked himself in the bathroom?

She told him how she'd had to force herself inside.

Oh God. He felt awful. He didn't know what was happening to him. He was just so emotionally wrought up. Nothing like this had ever happened to him in his life. How could she possibly think that he wanted to harm Edward? He loved him. He adored him. All afternoon long he looked forward to that moment when he would throw open the door and Edward would come racing at him from across the living room. He loved him so. And he loved her, he really did, even if he hadn't been acting like it. That's what made it all so confusing. She was the most important person in his life, now as always. She was so strong, so good. She was probably one of the most incredible girls for her age there had ever been. Look at Ellie— at twenty she had already dumped Joe Whetstone to get pinned to this guy Clark, and within six months was already depinned from Clark and going steady with this guy Roger. Look at the average twenty-year-old girl, then look at Lucy, and all she'd had to suffer. He knew what her father had put her family through. He knew all the things she'd had to do to save her family from him when they wouldn't save themselves. He knew what it must be like for her, to have to remember that it was she who finally had to lock the door on him, to send him away so that he never came back to ruin her mother's life.

She said that she never thought about it. Where he was, was not her concern.

Well, *he* thought about it. He knew she did not like to talk about her father, but the point was, he wanted her to know that it was her courage in the face of her father's behavior that he had always admired, and always would. She had courage. She had strength. She knew right from wrong. There was no one in the world like her. He felt privileged and honored to be her husband, did she know that? Oh, why was he crying? He didn't seem able to help it. He hadn't meant to do little Eddie any harm, she must know that. He didn't mean to do her any harm, to cause anybody in the world the least little harm or hardship. Didn't she know that? Because it was the truth. He wanted to be good, really he did. Oh, please, oh, please, she had to understand.

He was kneeling on the floor, his head in her lap, weeping uncontrollably. Oh, God, my God, he said. Oh, he had something to tell her. And she had to hear him out, she had to understand and to forgive. She had to let it be over, once he told her, and never bring it up again, but she had to know the truth.

What truth?

It was just that he had been so mixed up. He hadn't even known what he was thinking about or what he was doing. She had to understand that.

Understand what?

Well, in Liberty Center he had not gone to stay with his family; he had stayed with the Sowerbys. He admitted that the idea of a separation was not his but his uncle's.

—

Not even a week passed. At dinner one evening he began to grumble again about being shoved around by Hopkins. Before she even had a chance to reply, Edward had gotten up off the kitchen floor, where he had been playing, and rushed away.

She threw down her napkin. "Must you whine! Must you complain! Must you be a baby in front of your own child!"

"But what did I *say?*"

This time he stayed away two full days. On the second morning Hopkins telephoned to inform her that he didn't know how much longer he could put up with this disappearing act of young Roy's. She said that there was illness again in Liberty Center. Hopkins said he sympathized, if that was the truth, but he had a business to run. Lucy said she understood that, and so did Roy; she was expecting him back momentarily. Hopkins said so was he. And he hoped that when he did return he'd be better able to keep his mind on his work. Apparently two weeks back Roy had shot the Kiwanis luncheon down in Butler without any film in the camera.

That afternoon Julian Sowerby's lawyer telephoned from Winnisaw. He said that he was representing Roy. He wanted to suggest to her that she have her own lawyer get in touch with him. "Please," she replied, "I haven't time for nonsense."

He said that either she should get somebody to represent her or else they would serve the divorce papers on her personally.

"Oh, you will? And on what grounds, may I ask? Is it me who runs off? Is it me who doesn't show up for his job, who doesn't concentrate on it even when he's there? Is it me who breaks into tears and tantrums in front of a little tiny child? Is it me who dreams up business cards for a business I couldn't even begin to run? Don't tell me to get a lawyer, sir. Tell your client Mr. Sowerby to tell his nephew to grow up. I have an apartment to look after, and a confused little boy whose father keeps running out the door to get the advice of a disreputable and irresponsible person. Good*bye*!"

Roy returned a new man. All that crying business was over, finished, couldn't even understand it. Must have been off his nut, honestly. He had sat down with his father and talked the whole thing out. Till then Lloyd Bassart had known nothing about his son's secret visits up to Liberty Center. Roy had asked the Sowerbys not to speak of it, and though the first time they had agreed, when it happened again Irene Sowerby said she felt she had no choice but to tell her own sister what was going on.

The experience with his father hadn't been any picnic either. They had sat up together in the kitchen one whole night, clear through to dawn, hammering out their differences of opinion. Don't think voices weren't raised and tempers short. But they had stuck with it anyway, till daylight actually began to come through the back windows of the house. He by no means, even now, agreed with everything his father had said; and he could hardly bear the thought of the way he said it. Half of it was out of Bartlett's quotation book, to begin with. Nevertheless, arguing out all he had been brooding over for a long time —some of which she herself didn't even know about—well, it had given him the chance he needed to get a lot off his chest. It hadn't been easy, she could imagine, but he had gotten his father to admit that Hopkins was most definitely exploiting him, and exploiting the Hudson too. Secondly, he had gotten him to agree that if Roy had the financial backing (so that it wouldn't be a slap-dash operation right off the bat) a studio of his own was certainly not beyond his capabilities. If it hadn't been beyond Hopkins all these years, it surely wasn't beyond him, that Roy could guarantee. In the end he had made it clear to his father that it was a sacrifice, and a hard one too, but that he was willing temporarily to give up his professional ambitions for the welfare of his wife and child. He had only wanted his father to recognize that sacrifice was exactly the word to describe what it was.

And once his father would—around five in the morning—
everything else sort of fell into place. The decision to come
back to Lucy was Roy's own, however, and he wanted her to
know that. All the pissing and moaning of the previous weeks
(if she could pardon him using a crude but accurate old Army
phrase), well, it was as much a mystery to him as it must be to
her. But it was over, that was for damn sure. God damn sure.
There was a decision to face and he had faced it. He had come
back. And why? Because that's what he wanted to do. And if
there was anything he ought to be forgiven, then he wanted to
ask to be forgiven, too. Not down on bended knee either, but
standing up and looking her right in the eye. He wanted her to
know that he was a big enough person to admit to a mistake, if
he had made one. And in a way he supposed he had—though
it was actually more complicated than that.

But enough explaining. Because explaining was just a way of
begging, and he wasn't begging for anything. No pity, no
sympathy, no nothing. He was willing to let bygones be bygones, and to start in clean and fresh, and be a lot better off
for the experience—if she was.

She said she would not forgive him unless he promised
never to speak to Julian Sowerby again as long as he lived.

As long as he lived?

Yes, as long as they *all* lived.

But the thing was, he had really sort of led Julian down the
wrong path, in terms of what he wanted.

She did not care.

"But as long as I live—well, that's sort of ridiculous, Lucy. I
mean, that might be a very long time."

"Oh, Roy—!"

"I only mean I don't want to start off making a promise I'm
not going to *keep*, that's all. I mean, a year from now, who
knows? Well, look, either bygones *are* bygones, or they're not.
A year from now—heck, a month from now, it's all going to
be so much water under the bridge. Well, I sure hope it will
be. It will be at my end, I know that. I mean, it is now, really."

She had no choice. How else prevent him from ever again
seeking the counsel of that man? It was wrong to break a confidence, but if she failed now to tell him the truth, what would
prevent him from rushing back to Julian Sowerby the very

next time he wanted to find the easy way out of his responsibilities and obligations? How else could she make him see that the uncle who pretended to be so nice and kind and easygoing, all jokes and laughs and free cigars, was at bottom a cruel, corrupt, deceitful human being?

And so she told Roy what Ellie had overheard on the telephone. At first he was unbelieving, and then he was appalled, he said.

—

By the fourth summer of their marriage Roy found he had to tune the car up practically every month. It was now seven years old and you couldn't expect it to hold up forever without an awful lot of care. Not that he was complaining, just stating a fact. More than one Sunday morning a month Lucy looked down into the driveway to see Roy's feet sticking out from under the car, as she used to see them from Ellie's bedroom window. And once she saw him holding Edward up over the hood, explaining to him how the engine worked.

If Roy didn't have a wedding to photograph on Sundays, the three of them would go out for a ride, or else up to Liberty Center to visit Roy's family. To make the traveling time pass more rapidly, Roy would often amuse Edward by telling him about his Army days up near the North Pole. They were simple little stories about how Daddy had done this and Daddy had done that—stories involving penguins and igloos and dogs that pulled sleds over the snow—and what sometimes made her anger rise was not so much that the child naturally took them for the truth, but that Roy seemed to want him to.

She might no longer even have consented to those Sunday trips if it hadn't been for Edward, who loved so the idea that he had grandparents he had to travel to see. They kissed him, they hugged him, they gave him presents, they made him laugh, they told him what a beautiful, brilliant little boy was he . . . And why shouldn't he enjoy that? Why should he be denied anything that came as a matter of course to other children in other families? Visiting grandparents was a part of childhood, and whatever was a part of childhood he was going to have.

It pleased her far less to see how willingly her husband made the trip. He pretended, of course, that it was more or less a bore to him at this point, that he did it out of filial obligation, a sense of duty and decency, but then he had been pretending that from the start.

She saw him pretending now nearly all the time, so as to avoid the clashes that had taken place almost weekly after the first six months of the marriage. Every time he opened his mouth she could hear that he did not mean a single word, but was trying only to disarm her by saying what he thought she wanted him to say. He would do anything now to avoid a battle, anything but really change.

He pretended, for instance, that he was more or less happy working for Hopkins. Wendell had his limitations, but-then-who-didn't? he quickly added. Yeah, good old Wendell, when all the time she knew that secretly he hated Hopkins' guts.

And he pretended that he believed she had been right to discourage him from opening a studio of his own. There was still an awful lot he had to learn, and he was only twenty-four, so what was the hurry? Meanwhile, at least once a month she would find lettered in the margin of the newspaper, or doodled on the scratch pad by the phone, the words "Bassart Portrait Studio," or "Portraits by Bassart."

Worst of all, he pretended to continue to feel outrage toward Julian Sowerby. After her disclosure of Julian's secret, Roy had agreed that henceforth they must have nothing whatsoever to do with such a person. Yet as the months passed, he began to wonder if they weren't being somewhat unfair to his aunt. *She* might care to see Edward once in a while . . .

Lucy said that if Irene Sowerby wanted to see Edward badly enough she could come to visit any Sunday afternoon they were at the Bassarts'. Roy said that was true, of course, only his understanding was that Aunt Irene believed that they were as angry at her for interfering in their marriage as they were with Uncle Julian. The deeper cause of the split with Julian was something she didn't know about, and that they couldn't reveal to her, or to his family either. It was horrible to think of Aunt Irene living in ignorance of her husband's real nature, but they had problems enough of their own, Roy had decided, without trying to extricate Aunt Irene from hers. Furthermore, wasn't she better off *not* knowing? And that wasn't the issue anyway. The issue was this: Irene believed Lucy and Roy to be angry with *her*—

Lucy wished to inform Roy that Irene Sowerby wasn't altogether wrong.

What? *Were* they as angry with her? Really? A year later?

Lucy went on. She knew what his mother whispered to him on Sundays. Perhaps next time Roy should take the opportunity to whisper back to his mother that her sister Irene might have considered the welfare of this little nephew she so missed seeing when Julian Sowerby started arranging for Roy's divorce!

What?

Unless, of course, Roy didn't see in Julian's scheme anything that might endanger Edward's development as a healthy, happy child. Maybe Roy even agreed with his uncle that the well-being of one's family did not matter nearly so much as the satisfaction of one's own selfish desires.

Well, no. Well, of course not. Look, was she kidding? He had been appalled, hadn't he, practically sickened to hear about Uncle Julian and his women? And didn't she think he still was? Sometimes when he began to think about Julian's playing around like that all those years, it made him so disgusted and angry he didn't even know what to do. Was she kidding, to associate him with Julian Sowerby? Had he not said no to the whole idea of a divorce, once he gave it five minutes' thought? Look, marriage isn't something you just throw out of the window, like an old shoe. Marriage isn't something that you enter into idly, or that you dissolve idly either. The more he thought about it the more he realized that marriage was probably the most serious thing you did in your whole life. After all, the family was the backbone of society. Take away the family, and what do you have? People just running around, that's all. Total anarchy. Just try to imagine the world with no families. You actually can't do it. Oh, sure, some people of course run off to a divorce lawyer at the drop of a hat. First sign of anything that doesn't sit right with them, boom, off to the divorce court—and the heck with the children, the heck with the other person. However, if a couple has any maturity at all they sit down and talk out their differences, they voice their grievances, and then when everybody has had a chance to make his accusations—and also to admit where he might have been in the wrong (because it's never so simple as one being in the right, of course, and the other all in the wrong)—then, instead of running off to Reno, Nevada, two people who have any maturity stop being kids, buckle down and really decide to *work* at the marriage. Because that's the key word, all right—work—which you don't know, of course, when you go waltzing merrily into holy matrimony, thinking it is going to be more or less a continuation of your easygoing pre-marital good times. No, marriage is work, and hard work too, and pretty darn important work when there happens to be a little child involved, who needs you the way nobody has ever needed you before in your life.

She could not stand the pretense; so she tried with all her might to believe that it was not pretense, that he actually believed what he was saying, and found she could not stand that either.

—

After dinner and a visit with the Bassarts, they would drive Edward around to Daddy Will's house. First Great-Grandmother brought out the cookies that had been baked especially for him; then Great-Grandfather did tricks that he said he had used to do for Edward's mother when she was a little girl. He would make Edward close his eyes while he wrapped his fist and two projecting fingers into a white handkerchief. Then, well, well, he'd say, open your eyes, Edward Bassart, there's a little bunny here that would like to make your acquaintance. And there was a bunny, with two long ears and a little mouth, and an endless number of questions about Edward and his Mommy and Daddy. At the end of the conversation, Edward was allowed to whisper a wish into the bunny's ear. Once, to the delight of all assembled—except Daddy Will, who believed he had some small ability to throw his voice—Edward announced that what he wished most was that the bunny was real.

"What do you mean, real?" asked the great-grandfather.

"Real. Not a hankie."

Best of all Edward liked to climb up onto the piano bench, either beside Grandma Myra, while she played for him, or right in her lap so that he could "play." She would take his fingers in hers, and haltingly out of the piano would come "Frère Jacques" and "Mary Had a Little Lamb," and a song called "Michael Finnegan," to which Daddy Will had taught him the words. At every visit Edward and Grandma Myra and Daddy Will would sing it together, while the child's great-grandmother sat with the cookie plate in her lap, and his father, his long frame stretched out in a chair, kept time by tapping the toe of one shoe against the toe of the other.

> I know a man named Michael Finnegan,
> He grew whiskers on his chin-negan,
> Along came the wind and blew them in-negan,
> Poor old Michael Finnegan—begin-negan.

And so again they would begin, while silently Lucy watched. These were all the songs, said Grandma Myra, that Edward's mother used to like to sing when she was a little child no older than he was. Lucy saw that her son did not understand what that meant at all. His mother had been a little child? He couldn't believe it, no more than she could.

Then there was the famous story of her "yumping" from the window seat in the dining room, of which she had no recollection either. The first day that Daddy Will introduced Edward to the sport, Grandma Myra disappeared into the bathroom and did not come out until the visitors had left for home.

In the years since the disappearance of her husband, Myra had come to look her age, and more; there were Sundays when she seemed less a woman in her early forties than a woman into her sixties. Deep creases ran to the corners of her mouth, a purple hue had seeped into the skin beneath her eyes, the lovely throat had lost its smoothness and its glow. Yet the coarsening, the darkening, the wearing away, did nothing to diminish her air of delicacy. Certainly it was easier, even for those who believed they had known her intimately, to understand how deeply rooted in her nature was that characteristic softness of appearance. The years passed, the woman aged, and soon it became more and more difficult, even for her daughter, to remember that the reason Myra Nelson had suffered such abuse in her marriage was because essentially she was no more than her Daddy's little girl. Time passed, and very slowly, sitting silently in that living room, observing now as she had never been able to while the battle raged, while she herself raged—very slowly it began to dawn on Lucy that her aging mother actually had a character. "Weak" and "insipid" no longer seemed adequate to an understanding of the whole person. It began to dawn on her that why the mouth had always looked so gentle, and the eyes so merciful, and the body so yielding was not simply because her mother had been born dumb and beautiful.

Time passed, and men began to appear in the parlor on Sundays. They were invited for dinner, and to spend the afternoon. At first it was young Hank Wirges, who wasn't exactly what you could call a man, of course. He was a nice-looking, dark-haired boy who had taken journalism at Northwestern, where he had used to date a girl who was a sorority sister of Ellie Sowerby. Hank had come to Winnisaw to work as a cub reporter on the *Leader*, and had looked up the Carrolls because his grandmother and Berta had been childhood friends years and years ago.

Once a week Hank took Myra to the movie, Dutch treat, and every Sunday he was invited to the house for dinner. It pleased them all to be kind to him and make him feel that he had a home away from home, but of course no one was surprised when after a year the movie dates became less frequent. Eventually he asked if he might bring to Sunday dinner a girl named Carol-Jean, whom it turned out he had been seeing on the side.

It was actually just as well that Hank got himself involved with this Carol-Jean, said Willard, for it had begun to seem that he was developing a full-scale crush on Myra; though he never called her anything but Mrs. Nelson, he looked up to her like some sort of goddess. He came twice to dinner with his young lady friend, and then Myra went through a bad siege of migraines and Hank sort of passed out of their lives. But at least he had been a kind of gradual start back into the world for her, as Daddy Will phrased it, in that year after "Whitey's picking up, going off, and finally showing his true colors." That was a time when Myra hardly had it in her to be seen on Broadway; if she hadn't had young Hank's homesickness to pay attention to, she might have done nothing but give her lessons in the afternoon, and then retire back to her bed to weep for all those years thrown away on somebody who had "turned out to be hardly the person we all originally expected of him."

Lucy herself never gave her father a moment's thought, not if she could help it; when his name was mentioned, she simply tuned out. His welfare was of no more concern to her than hers had been to him; where he was now, what he was now, that was his business—and his doing too. She might have been the one to lock that door, but what had sent him running was his own shame and cowardice. When Edward was still an infant and they had just moved into the new apartment, the phone had rung one night while she was home alone, and to her "Hello," the other party had made no response. "Hello?" she had said again, and then she knew it was her father, that he was in Fort Kean, that he was planning to take his vengeance against her, through Edward. "Listen, you, if this is you, I advise you very strongly—" and then she had hung up. What could *he* possibly do to her? She had nothing to fear, nor to regret, either. She had locked him out—what of it? It was not *she* who had robbed *him* of a proper home and a proper family; hardly. There was a debt that would never fully be paid, but it was not hers to him; hardly . . . Then one afternoon she was pushing Edward through Pendleton Park in his stroller, when a bum rose up off a bench and came lurching toward them. Quickly she had turned the stroller around and walked away, only to realize again in a matter of minutes that even if it was her father lying in wait for her, she had nothing to fear, nothing to regret. If he was a bum, begging and sleeping in the streets, it was not she who had put him there. He was not worth a moment of her thought, or of her pity.

In the summer after Edward's third birthday Blanshard Muller began to become a regular caller at the house. Mullers had lived over on Hardy Terrace, back of the Bassarts', in fact, for as long as Willard could remember. Blanshard lived alone there now, for his wife had died a tragic death three years back—Parkinson's disease—and his children were all grown and away. The older son, Blanshard, Jr., was married and had a family of his own in Des Moines, Iowa, where he was already a junior executive in the purchasing department of the Rock Island Railroad; and Connie Muller, whom Lucy remembered as a big, beefy boy two years behind her in school, was finishing up in veterinary medicine at Michigan State.

Thirty years back Blanshard Muller had started out in business with a kit of tools and his two strong legs—Daddy Will's description—and had gone around to offices all over the county, repairing typewriters. Today he rented, sold and serviced just about every kind of office machine in existence, and was sole owner of the Alpha Business Machine Company, located right back of the courthouse in Winnisaw. In his early fifties, he was a tall man with iron-gray hair that he combed very flat, a ski nose and a manly jaw. When he removed his square rimless spectacles, which he did whenever he sat down to eat, he bore a strong resemblance to none other than Bob Hope. Which was a little ironical, Daddy Will said, because Mr. Muller himself did not have much of a sense of humor. But there was no doubt that he was a respectable, dependable and hard-working person; you only had to look at the record to know that. Berta had taken to him immediately, and even Willard was heard to say, as the months went by, that there was certainly a lot to admire in a fellow who didn't just ramble on or talk your ear off, but said what he had to say and left it at that. Certainly when he did express himself on a subject—such as the modernization of mail-sorting through automation, which Willard had brought into the conversation one Sunday after dinner—his thinking was clear and to the point.

Christmas Eve, with Whitey gone now more than three years, Blanshard Muller asked Myra to divorce her husband on the grounds of desertion, and become his wife.

—

Lucy learned of the proposal the next morning when Roy called his family, and then hers, to say that they would not be able to get up to Liberty Center for Christmas. That morning Edward had awakened with a high fever and a bad cough; that he was too sick to go up and celebrate the holiday with his adoring grandparents caused the child to cry and cry with disappointment—and this saddened her. But it was all that saddened her. She had every reason to suspect that on that day someone would have suggested that they all go on over to the Sowerbys' after dinner, or that the Sowerbys come to the

Bassarts'; and given the spirit of the holiday, what could she have said or done to prevent the reunion? Of course she knew that she could not keep Roy from his aunt and uncle forever, but she also knew that once such a meeting took place, he would once again be open to the most pernicious kinds of advice, and she and Edward would again be in danger of being abused, or even abandoned. If only she could arm him against his uncle's influence once and for all! But how?

When they finally got up to Liberty Center late in January—Edward's bronchitis had lingered nearly three weeks—they found that Lucy's mother hadn't yet given Mr. Muller a definite answer to his proposal. By the New Year, Berta had about lost patience with her daughter, but Daddy Will had made it clear to her that Myra was forty-three years old and in no way to be pushed or pressured into an important decision such as remarriage. She would make it official when she was ready to. Anybody who had eyes could see she was edging up on saying yes with every day that passed. Twice a week now she drove over to Winnisaw to have lunch with Blanshard at the inn; and even on weekday nights she either went off with him to a movie, or to a social evening among his own circle of friends. In the middle of the month she had even helped him pick out new linoleum for his kitchen floor. The kitchen and bathroom had begun to be modernized years ago, but the job had never been completed because of Mrs. Muller's illness and death. Myra told her family that helping him choose his linoleum was a favor she would have done for anyone who asked; they were not to interpret it as any kind of decision on her part to become his wife.

However, the very next night, when Blanshard had to be at home interviewing a new salesman, she had paced and paced the living room, and after an hour of anguish, gone off into the kitchen and telephoned his house. It was really none of her business, she did not want him to think that she was in any way criticizing the woman who had been his wife, but she could not keep it inside her any more. She had to tell him how much she disapproved of the color scheme that had been chosen for the upstairs bathroom; if it was not too late to cancel the cabinets and fixtures he had gone ahead and ordered, she hoped very much that he would. She would understand, of course, if he didn't wish to, for reasons of sentiment, but of course that wasn't what he said.

So the cat appeared to be in the bag, so to speak. Except that if Berta kept on endlessly chronicling Blanshard's accomplishments and virtues, she might find that single-handed she had gained just the opposite effect of what she had intended. Maybe the best thing was to let Blanshard Muller argue his own case, and let Myra herself decide whether she wanted to start out on a new life with such a man. It was surely no solution to anything to hold a shotgun to someone's head until the person said "I do"; you cannot force people to be what it simply is not within their power to be, or to feel feelings that they just do not have in their repertoire of tricks. "Ain't that so, Lucy?" he asked, figuring probably that she would ally herself with him as against Berta, but she pretended not to have been following the discussion.

It was a most dismal afternoon. Not only because she had to listen to her grandfather spouting the weak-kneed philosophy that had brought them practically to the point of ruin— the philosophy that encouraged people to believe that they couldn't be more than they were, no matter how inferior and inadequate that happened to be; it was dismal not only because what her grandfather seemed to want was to keep his daughter living in his house as long as he possibly could, and what her grandmother seemed to want was to shove her out into the street, man or no man, within the hour; it was dismal because she discovered that she herself did not really seem to care whether her mother married Blanshard Muller or not. And yet it was what she had prayed for all her life—that a man stern, serious, strong and prudent would be the husband of her mother, and the father to herself.

They drove to Fort Kean through a blizzard that evening. Roy was silent as he navigated slowly along the highway, and Edward fell asleep against her. Bundled in her coat, she watched the snow blowing across the hood and thought, yes, her mother was on the brink of marrying that good man her daughter had always dreamed of, and her own husband had stopped trying to evade his every duty and obligation. He had settled at last into the daily business, whether he liked it or not, of being a father and a husband and a man: her child had two parents to protect him, two parents each doing his job, and it was she alone who had made all this come about. This battle, too, she had fought and this battle, too, she had won, and yet it seemed that she had never in her life been miserable in the way that she was miserable now. Yes, all that she had wanted had come to be, but the illusion she had, as they drove home through the storm, was that she was never going to die—she was going to live forever in this new world she had made, and never die, and never have the chance not just to be right, but to be happy.

—

It snowed and snowed that winter, but almost always after dark. The days were sharp with cold and brilliant with white light. Edward had a blue snowsuit with a hood, and little red mittens, and new red galoshes, and when she had finished straightening up the apartment, she would dress him in his bright winter clothes and take him with her as she pulled the shopping cart to the market. He would walk along beside her, planting each red galosh into the fresh snow and then pulling it out, always with great care and concentration. After lunch and his nap, they would go around to Pendleton Park with his sled. She would draw him around the paths and down a gentle little slope on the empty golf course. More and more they took the long way home, around by the pond where the school-children were dashing about on skates, and out of the park by the women's college.

Her classmates had graduated the previous June. Probably that explained why she could now walk casually around by the campus that she had purposely avoided all these years. As for her teachers, she doubted if any of them would even remember her; she had come and gone too fast. Oh, but it was strange, very strange, to be pulling Edward on his sled past The Bastille. She wanted to tell him about the months that she had lived there. She wanted to tell him that he had lived there too. "The two of us—in that building. And no one would help, no one at all."

Since her student days, the barracks had been torn down and replaced by a long modernistic brick building that housed the classrooms, and now a new library was being built back of

The Bastille. She wondered where the student health service was located these days; she wondered if that same cowardly doctor was still employed by the college. She would not have minded if he were to cross her path some afternoon and recognize her with her child. She believed there might be some satisfaction for her in that.

Some afternoons she and Edward warmed themselves over a hot chocolate in the very same booth at the back of The Old Campus Coffee Shop where she had used to eat her lunch during the last months of her pregnancy. In the mirror beside the booth she saw the two of them, their noses red, their pale strawlike hair hanging into their eyes, and the eyes themselves, exactly the same. How far the two of them had come since those horrible days in The Bastille! Here, at her side, was the little boy she had refused to destroy—the little boy she now refused to see deprived! "Thank you, Mamma," he said, as he solemnly watched her spoon the marshmallow from the top of her hot chocolate onto his, and she thought, "Here he is. I saved his life. I did it—all alone. Oh, why should I feel such misery? Why is my life like this?"

The icicles they had passed when they had come out into the sunshine earlier on had lengthened by dusk. Every day Edward broke off the longest icicle he could find and held it carefully in his mittens until, at home, he would put it into the refrigerator for his Daddy to see when he returned from work. He was truly an adorable child, and he was hers, indisputably hers, brought into the world by her and protected in it by her too: nevertheless she felt herself doomed forever to a cruel and miserable life.

For Valentine's Day, Roy brought home two heart-shaped boxes of candy, a big one from him, a small one "from Edward." After the little boy's bath, Roy took a picture of him, with his hair combed, and in his bathrobe and slippers, presenting Lucy with her gift a second time.

"Smile, kiddies."

"Take the picture, Roy, please."

"But if you're not even smiling—"

"Roy, I'm tired. Please take it."

After Edward was in bed, Roy sat down at the kitchen table

with a glass of milk and some Hydrox cookies and one of his manila folders. He began to look through all the pictures he had taken of Edward since he was born. "You want to hear an idea I had today?" He came into the living room, wiping his mouth. "It's just an idea, you know. I mean I'm not serious about it, really."

"About what?"

"Well, sort of getting all the pictures of Eddie, putting them in chronological order according to his age, and giving it a name. You know, it's probably just a silly idea, but I've got the pictures for it, I can tell you that much."

"What is *it*, Roy?"

"Well, a book. Kind of a story in photographs. Don't you think that could be a good idea, if somebody wanted to do it? Call it 'The Growth of a Child.' Or 'The Miracle of a Child.' I wrote out a whole list of possible titles."

"Did you?"

"Well, during lunch. They sort of started coming at me . . . so I wrote them down. Want to hear?"

She got up and went into the bathroom. Into the mirror she said, "Twenty-two. I am only twenty-two."

When she came back into the living room the radio was playing.

"How you feeling?" he asked.

"Fine."

"Aren't you all right, Lucy?"

"I'm feeling *fine*."

"Look, I don't mean I'm going to *publish* a book even if I could."

"If you want to publish a book, Roy, publish a book!"

"Well, I won't! I was just having some fun. Jee—*zuz*." He picked up one of his family's old copies of *Life* and began leafing through it. He slumped into his chair, threw back his head and said, "Wow."

"What?"

"The radio. Hear that? 'It Might As Well Be Spring.' You know who that was my song with? Bev Collison. Boy. Skinny Bev. I wonder whatever happened to her?"

"How would I know?"

"Who said you'd know? I was only reminded of her by the song. Well, what's wrong with that?" he asked. "Boy, this is really some Valentine's Day night!"

A little later he pulled open the sofa, and they laid out the blanket and pillows. When the lights were off and they were in bed, he said that she had been looking tired, and probably she would feel better in the morning. He said he understood.

Understood what? Feel better why?

From the bed they could see the snow falling past the street lamp outside. Roy lay with his hands behind his head. After a while he asked if she was awake too. It was so calm and beautiful outside that he couldn't even sleep. Was she all right? Yes. Was she feeling better? Yes. Was there anything the matter? *No.*

He got up and stood for a while looking outside. He carefully drew a big letter B in the frost on the window. Then he came and stood over the bed.

"Feel," he said, putting his fingertips on her forehead. "What a winter. I'm telling you, this is just what it was like up there."

"Where?"

"The Aleutians. But at four in the afternoon. Can you imagine?"

He sat beside her and put one hand on her hair. "You're not angry at me about the book, are you?"

"No."

"Because of course I'm not even going to do it, Lucy. I mean, how could I?"

He got back under the blankets. Half an hour must have passed. "I can't sleep. Can you?"

"What?"

"Can you sleep?"

"Apparently not."

"Well, is anything the matter?"

She did not answer.

"You want something? You want a glass of milk?"

"No."

He made his way across the dark living room into the kitchen.

When he returned he sat in the chair near the bed. "Want a Hydrox?" he asked.

"No."

A car went ticking through the snowy street.

"Wow," he said.

She said nothing.

He asked if she was still awake.

She did not answer. "Twenty-two," she was thinking, "and this will be my whole life. This. This. This. This."

He went into Edward's room. When he came back, he said that Edward was sleeping like a charm. That was the great thing about kids. Lights out, and they're off in dreamland before you can count to three.

Silence.

Boy, wouldn't it be something if some day they had a little girl of their own.

A what?

"A little girl," he said.

He got up and went into the kitchen and came back with the milk carton in his hand. He poured all that remained into his glass and drank it down.

As long as he could remember, he said, he had dreamed of having a little daughter. Did she know that? And he had always known what he would call her, too. Linda. He assured Lucy that he had come upon the name long before the song "Linda" had gotten popular. Still, whenever he used to hear Buddy Clark singing it on the jukebox, back in the PX up in the Aleutians, he used to think about being married and having a family, and about this little daughter he would have some day who would be called Linda Bassart. Linda Sue. "Isn't that pretty? I mean, forget the song. Isn't it, just for itself? And it goes with Bassart. Try it . . . You awake?"

"Yes."

"Linda—Sue—Bassart," he said. "I mean, it's not too fancy, on the one hand, and yet it's not too plain either. Edward, too, is sort of right in the middle there, which is what I like."

Another car. Silence.

He got up and looked out of the window. "Miss Linda . . . Sue . . . Bassart. Pretty good, 'eh what?"

. . . Till that moment, to make him a proper father to his little boy had been so great a struggle that she had never once thought of a second child. But in that deep winter silence, listening to what he had said, and to the tone in which he said it, she thought that maybe at long last he wasn't mouthing words for the sole purpose of pleasing her. He seemed not to be pretending; she could hear it in his voice, that he was expressing a real feeling, a real desire. Maybe he really did want a daughter. Maybe he always had.

The whole next day she could not put out of her mind what Roy had said to her the previous night. It was all she could think of.

When he came home in the evening, when, as usual, he swung Edward up over his head, she thought, "He wants a daughter. He wants a second child. Can it be? Has he actually changed? Has he finally turned into a man?"

And so it was that in the early hours of the following morning, when Roy came rolling over on top of her, Lucy decided it was no longer necessary to continue to use protection. After Edward was born, the obstetrician had suggested that she might want to be fitted for a contraceptive device, if she did not already have one. Instantly she had said yes, when she understood that henceforth their fate would no longer be in Roy's hands; never again would she be the victim of his incompetence and stupidity. But now he had told her that to have a daughter was one of his oldest desires. And though it had not sounded as though he had simply been trying to please her with his words, how would she ever know unless she gave him the chance to prove himself sincere and truthful?

In the next few weeks Roy did not mention Linda Sue again, nor did she. In the dead of the night, however, she would be awakened by a hand or a leg falling upon her; and then his long body working against her small frame—or, if he was not wholly conscious, against her nightgown. This was how their love was made that February, and there was nothing extraordinary about it; it was how it had been made for years. Only now, while he pushed and thrust against her in the dark, she looked beyond his shoulder at the snow steadily blowing down, knowing that very shortly she was going to be pregnant for the second time in her life. And it would be different this time; there would be no one they would have to plead with, or argue with, nor would they have to argue with each other. They were married now, and there were no families upon whom either of them was dependent in any way. This time it would be something that Roy himself had said he wanted. And this time, she just knew, the child would be a girl.

Suddenly her illusion of an endlessly unhappy life just disappeared. All the heaviness and sadness and melancholy seemed to have been drawn out of her overnight. Could it be? A new Lucy? A new Roy? A new life? One afternoon, walking home with Edward's mittened hand in hers, and the sled rasping behind them over the cleared walks, she began to sing the silly song that Daddy Will had taught her little boy.

"'Poor old Michael Finnegan,'" he said cautiously, as though nonplused she should even know it.

"But Daddy Will told you, I used to sing when I was a child. I was a child once too. You know that."

"Yes?"

"Of course. Everyone was a child once. Even Daddy Will!"

He shrugged.

> "He grew whiskers on his chin-negan . . ."

He looked at her out of the corner of his eye, and then he began to smirk, and by the time they got to the house, he was singing with his Mamma—

> "Along came the wind and blew them in-negan,
> Poor old Michael Finnegan—begin-negan."

Really, she could not remember ever having been as happy as this in her entire life. The sensation she began to have was that the awful past had finally fallen away, and that she was living suddenly in her own future. It seemed to her that great spans of time were passing as the month wore down to Washington's Birthday, and then to that final Sunday when they drove Edward up to visit the grandparents and great-grandparents in Liberty Center.

———

After dinner Roy went outside to take pictures of Edward helping his grandfather break up a slick patch of ice in front of the garage doors. Lucy could see the three of them in the driveway, Roy telling Lloyd where to stand so that the light and the shadows fell right, and Lloyd telling Roy that he was standing where he had to in order to get the job done, and

Edward plunging his red galoshes into the drifts at the side of the drive. She stood at the sink watching the scene outside and intermittently listening to Alice Bassart's stream of chatter; they were finishing the dinner dishes, Alice washing and Lucy drying.

Ellie Sowerby was home for the weekend, and all Alice could seem to talk about was the trouble Irene was having with her daughter. Lucy wondered if the conversation was primarily intended to irritate her. She and her mother-in-law hardly had what could be called a warm and loving relationship; no girl who had taken Alice Bassart's big boy out of the house could have been her pal to begin with, but recently there had come to be another grievance. Whatever the resentment felt toward Lucy because of the marriage itself, her refusal to have anything to do with Alice's sister and brother-in-law had only made things worse. Not that Alice ever came right out with it; that was not her little way.

But what difference did Alice Bassart make to her today? Or even the Sowerbys? They were all a part of that past that seemed to have dissolved away to nothing. That past and these people had no power over her any longer. She had made it through the month without her period. There was only the future to think about now.

So, with no real discomfort and even with a certain remote curiosity, she listened to the Eleanor Sowerby story, bits and pieces of which she had been hearing since Ellie had graduated from Northwestern in June. With three friends Ellie had spent the summer at a dude ranch in Wyoming, where one of the girls' families lived. Now she was down in Chicago, with the same three girls, crammed into what was, according to Ellie, a "crazy" apartment on the Near North Side—just off Rush Street, or "Lush" Street, as Skippy Skelton, a roommate of Ellie's, called it. Of course Lucy already knew that "this Roger" (the second young man at Northwestern to give Ellie a fraternity pin) "this Roger," to whom she was to have been engaged following their graduation, had suddenly decided in the last semester of their senior year that he really didn't like Ellie as much as he thought he had. One day, out of the blue, he dropped her; and so unexpectedly, so cruelly, that Irene had had to rush all the way down to Evanston and stay for a whole week while Ellie got her bearings again. The family had only given their consent to the idea of a dude ranch way off in Wyoming in the hope that it would help get her mind off what had happened. As for this Roger, said Alice Bassart, he must have been quite a person. Do you know when he asked to have his precious pin back? A week to the day after having spent a perfectly lovely Easter vacation in Liberty Center as Ellie's house guest!

But despite his cruelty toward her, Ellie was beginning to bounce back at last; beginning to understand how much better off she was with a person such as this Roger out of her life entirely. And she wasn't having the crying sieges any more, which was a relief to them all. It was the crying that had almost made it necessary for Irene to get on a plane and fly out to Wyoming. But Skippy Skelton had apparently turned out to be a very strong young lady, and had given Ellie some kind of talking-to that made her stop feeling so sorry for herself; and now Ellie was so busy down in Chicago that she just didn't have the time any longer to spend whole days on her bed, weeping into her pillow. She was working as a receptionist at some kind of advertising research firm; and the people there were "fabulous"—she had never met so many "brainy" men before in her life. She hadn't even known that they existed. What she meant by that, they weren't quite sure as yet. Irene, frankly, was nervous, knowing how important it was for Ellie to get through the coming year without any kind of shock that would cause her another emotional setback. And Julian didn't at all like the sound of who it was she might be hanging around with down there. As he understood it, they had a university down there full of so-called brainy men, half of them Commies.

And to make matters even worse, Ellie just kept blooming and blossoming: each time you saw her she was more beautiful than the last. She had filled out so very nicely, and though she now saw some reason to wear her hair down into her face so that you could hardly even see those wonderful dimples, she was still the kind of girl who unfortunately attracted boys to her just by walking down a street minding her own business. But boys wouldn't be so bad; it was these brainy men they were worried about. She was even more of a fashion plate than she had been as a child—to walk around in Chicago a person apparently needed twenty-four pairs of shoes, said Alice—and what worried the Sowerbys was that a man without scruples would see her, make up to her, and then take advantage of her, with no regard for her feelings whatsoever. Ellie was still on the rebound from this Roger, and what with her sweet, generous, trusting nature, she might easily fall head over heels in love with somebody who would break her heart a second time in a row. The Sowerbys were particularly upset now because it turned out that Skippy, who had seemed to be such a good influence on Ellie, was going out with a thirty-seven-year-old man who wasn't living with his wife—and who was thinking of taking Skippy (age twenty-two) and going off with her to hide away in Spain for about ten years; maybe even forever. Why Ellie was home for the weekend was to talk over with her parents the kind of a girl this Skippy Skelton had turned out to be.

A few minutes later they were all in the living room when Ellie drove up in her mother's car.

Lucy didn't even have time to turn to Roy to ask if this visit had been planned: her old friend was up the walk, up the steps, and into the house.

In the first instant Ellie seemed somehow taller than Lucy remembered her. But that was an illusion, created partly by her hair—she had let it grow long and thick, like a kind of mane —and partly by her coat, which was made of some honey-colored fur and had a belt pulled tight around the middle. How dramatic. She stepped into the living room as onto a stage. Nothing Lucy could see indicated that Eleanor was a person recovering from a disaster; she did not look as though she even lived in a world where disaster was possible.

Lloyd Bassart had opened the door and so was the first to be embraced. "Uncle Lloyd! Hi!" and Ellie got him directly on the lips. Lucy could not recall ever having seen anyone kiss Lloyd Bassart on the lips before. Then Ellie's hair, cold and crackling, was against her own cheek. "Hi!" and then, Ellie was looking down at Edward: "Hey! Hi! Remember me? No? I'm your cousin Eleanor, and you're my second cousin Edward. Hi, second cousin!"

The child stood by Roy's chair, his head pressed against his father's knee. In only a few minutes, however, she had coaxed him onto her lap, where she let him cuddle up on the fur coat—which Ellie said was only otter, though the collar was mink. Edward slid his hands into her fur-lined leather gloves and everybody laughed; they fit him clear up to the elbow.

When Lucy reminded Roy that it was time to visit her family, he said that Ellie wanted to know if they would all come over to her house first. He had followed Lucy into the kitchen, to which she had retreated, offering the excuse that she wanted a glass of water. If she had to hear the name Skippy Skelton one more time, she would go out of her mind. Skippy was somebody you didn't have to worry about. Skippy had been on the Dean's List every semester but her last at Northwestern, and then she had just stopped caring about grades. Skippy had no intention of running off to Spain with the kind of phony Greg had turned out to be. Spain, in fact, had been a slight exaggeration of Eleanor's. She didn't know why she had said it, except that speaking to your mother long distance once a week, you finally ran out of things to say. Greg was back now with his wife and children, so there was nothing to fret about, at least where Skippy was concerned. You didn't have to worry about Skippy, she could just joke herself out of a tight situation, that's the kind of person Skippy was. It was Skippy herself who had told Greg that he should scoot on back to his family, once she had found out there were three little kiddies involved. Now Skippy was dating a really "hip" guy who thought that Ellie was a jerk to be wasting her talents behind a receptionist's desk for fifty dollars a week . . . Which was why Ellie was home for the weekend. Her parents might think she had made the trip up to explain about Skippy, but actually why she was here was to tell them that through Skippy's friend she had gotten an introduction to Martita. They didn't know who Martita was? Well, she just happened to have been the most important model in America before the war. Now she was retired and ran the only *real* agency in Chicago. Ellie's news was that in a matter of a few weeks she would be leaving the receptionist job to plunge headlong into a new career. "Fashion model!" she said. "Me!"

"Well," said Lloyd; "Great!" said Roy—"Don't forget who took your picture first, Ellie-o"; and Alice said, "Your parents didn't know this till today?" And here Lucy had gone off for her glass of water. She had closed the kitchen door behind her. When it opened, it was Roy, to say that Ellie's parents hoped they would all come over for coffee.

"Roy, was this all planned—and when?"

"What do you mean 'planned'?"

"Did you know Ellie was coming here?"

"Well, no, not really. Well, I knew she was in town. Look, they want to see Eddie, that's all. And they want to see us too, I think."

"Oh, they do?"

"That's what Ellie says. Well, obviously she's not lying. Lucy, look, we've been the ones who have been boycotting them— and with good reason too, I know, don't worry. But it hasn't been that they haven't wanted to see us, not that I know. And anyway, it's over. Well, it is. The mistake they made was a bad mistake, and the mistake I made was a bad mistake, but it's over. Isn't it?"

"Is it?"

"Well . . . sure. You know, another thing is that maybe this really isn't that fair to Edward any more—if you want to talk about his welfare in this thing."

"It was his welfare in this thing, Roy, that I had to bring to your attention—"

"Okay, *okay*—and you did! And so now I'm doing it to you, that's all. Whatever you think about Uncle Julian, or even Aunt Irene, whatever the two of us may think, well, they're still Eddie's aunt and uncle too, and he doesn't know anything about this, needless to say . . . Oh, come on, Lucy, Ellie's waiting."

"She can wait."

"Lucy, very honestly—" he began.

"What?"

"Do you want me to talk very honestly with you?"

"Please do, Roy."

"Why are you being so sar*cas*tic all of a sudden?"

"I'm not being 'sar*cas*tic.' If I am, I can't help it. Talk to me honestly. *Do*."

"Well, honestly, I really think that at this point, given all that's happened, and all that hasn't happened too, and this isn't a criticism, to begin with, but I think that at this point you might actually be being a little silly about this. I mean, without knowing it. Well, that's what I think, and I said it. And to be honest, it's sort of what I think my parents think too. It's over a year already that everything happened, about the way I behaved and so on, and now it's over, and maybe where the Sowerbys are concerned enough is enough, and we just sort of all ought to go on, and so forth . . . Well, what do *you* think?"

"The opinion of your parents is important to you? That's a surprise."

"I'm not saying *opinion*! I'm not saying *important*! Stop being so *sarcastic*! I'm just saying about what it looks like to a neutral party. Don't confuse me, will you, please? This is important. It's just not sensible any more, Lucy. Well, I'm sorry if that sounds like a criticism of my own wife, but it's not."

"What's not?"

"To keep up with a war, when the war is over, when nobody is even fighting any more, at least that I can see."

Ellie called from the living room. "You coming? Roy?"

"Roy," said Lucy, "if you want to go and take Edward, you go ahead."

". . . You mean it?"

"Yes."

His smile dimmed. "But what about you?"

"I'll stay here. I'll walk over to Daddy Will's."

"But I don't want you just walking around, Lucy." He reached out and flipped her bangs with his fingers. "Hey, Lucy." He spoke softly. "Come on. Why not? It's over. Let's make it really over. Lucy, come on, you look so pretty lately. Did you know that? I mean, you always look pretty to me, but lately, even more. So come on, huh, what do you say?"

She felt herself weakening. *Let's make it really over.* "Maybe I ought to go down to Chicago and be introduced to Martita, the most famous model in the history of America. Martita and Skippy Skelton—"

"Oh, come on, Lucy, you *are* pretty. To me you are, and plenty prettier than Ellie, too. Because you have character and you're you. You don't have to be a glamour puss, you don't have to have mink coats, believe me, to be pretty. That's just a material thing, you know that. You're the best person there is, Lucy. You are. Please, you come too. Why not?"

"Roy, if you want to go, you can."

"Well, I know I *can*," he said sourly.

"Pick me up at Daddy Will's at four."

"Oh, damn," he said, pushing one of the kitchen chairs into the table. "You're going to be angry later. I know it."

"What do you mean?"

". . . If I go."

"Why should I be? Are you planning to do something there that I might disapprove of?"

"I'm not planning *anything*! I'm going for a visit to a house! I'm going to have a cup of coffee!"

"All right, then."

"So just don't get angry when we get home . . . that's all I mean."

"Roy, you assured me a minute ago that the past is over, that I can rely on you. You have to admit that hasn't always been something I could do."

"*Okay.*"

"For six months now you have been assuring me that you no longer hold certain childish ideas—"

"I *don't.*"

"That you have decided to be responsible to me and to Edward."

"Yes!"

"Well, if that is really the case, if it's true that I have nothing to worry about when you are in the company of that man—if you haven't been fooling me, Roy, and just pretending—"

"I haven't been fooling anybody about anything!"

"Hey!" Ellie was calling them again. "Lovers! You coming out of hiding, or what's going on in there?"

In the living room, Alice was sitting in a chair, already in her coat and galoshes. Whenever Roy and Lucy quarreled, it was Alice's assumption that the fault lay solely with her daughter-in-law; it was something Lucy had had to accustom herself to long ago. She ignored the face that Alice turned to her, the compressed lips and the clenched jowls.

Ellie was kneeling down in front of Edward, zipping up his snowsuit; her skirt and coat had ridden up above her knee.

"Hey, let's go," said Ellie, "before we all catch puh-neu-monia."

"Lucy can't," said Roy.

—while Lucy was thinking, "Don't you dare dress him to go without my permission. It is up to me whether he sets foot in that house of yours, and sees those parents of yours, and not up to you at all. *I* am his mother."

She should never have weakened in the kitchen and said yes to Roy. The war over? The war was never over with people you could not trust or depend upon. Why, why had she relaxed her vigilance? Because this ninny was up for the weekend from Chicago? Because this *fashion model* was kneeling beside her child, playing Mommy while showing everybody her legs?

"Can't you?" said Ellie sadly. "Just for an *hour*? I haven't seen you in decades. And all I've done so far is talk about *me*. Oh, Lucy, come with us. I envy you so, married and out of the rat race. It's what I ought to do." Instantly her eyes became heavy with melancholy. "Please, Lucy, I'd actually like to talk to you. I'd just love to hear all about married life with that one."

"Oh, yeah?" said Roy, pulling on his coat. He smiled knowingly. "I'll bet you would."

"Wow," said Ellie, "how we used to sit up in that room."

"Sorry," said Lucy. She called Edward to her and hiked his snowsuit around. "You go with Daddy. I'm going to visit Grandma Myra." She kissed him.

He ran to his father, took his hand, and commenced staring at Ellie again as she pulled on her gloves. Roy laughed.

"He thinks they're his," he explained to Lucy. "The gloves."

"Gurrr," said Ellie, making one of her gloved hands into a claw. "Gurrr, Edward, here I come." The child broke into giggles, and when Ellie took a step toward him, drove his head into his father's side.

Roy looked at Lucy, then to Ellie. "Hey, El, Lucy's mother's getting married. Did you know?"

"Hey, that's terrific," said Ellie. "That's fabulous, Lucy."

Lucy took the enthusiasm coolly. "It's not definite yet."

"Well, I hope it comes off. That would be great."

Lucy neither agreed nor disagreed.

"Hey," said Ellie, "how's Daddy Will?"

"Fine."

"I really love him. I remember him at your wedding. Telling those stories about the north woods. They were really great."

No response.

To Edward, who was still staring, Ellie said, "Don't you, little Edward? Love Daddy Will?"

He nodded his head to whatever it was he thought Eleanor was asking him.

"I think it's Edward who has fallen in l-o-v-e with somebody," said Alice Bassart.

Ellie said to Lucy, "Give him a hug for me, will you? You do just want to hug him, don't you, when he starts telling those stories? He is really absolutely old-fashioned. He's just perfect. And that's what you miss in Chicago, all the fun aside— that kind of genuine person, who really cares about people and isn't just a fake and a phony. When we were on this ranch down in Horse Creek, there was a man there, and he was the foreman, and he was just so polite and old-fashioned and easygoing, and you kept thinking that's probably exactly the way America used to be. But Skippy says that's all dying out, even out there, which is sort of the last outpost. Isn't that a shame? When you think about it, it's really awful. It sure has died out in Chicago, I'll tell you that much. Sometimes I wake up in the morning, and I hear all those cars starting up outside, and I wish I were right back here in Liberty Center, where at least you don't get all that hatred and violence. Here you leave your house unlocked, and your car unlocked, and you could go away for a week, for a month even, and not worry. But you ought to see the locks we have on our door alone. Three," she said, turning to Alice.

"My goodness," said Alice. "Lloyd, did you hear that? Ellie has to have three locks because of the violence."

"*And* a chain," said Ellie.

"Eleanor, I don't know why you want to live in such a place," said Alice. "What about muggers? I certainly hope you don't walk on the streets."

"Sure, Mom," said Roy, "she walks on the air instead. What do you expect her to walk on, Mother?"

"It certainly doesn't seem to me," his mother answered, "that she should be out after dark in a place where you need three locks and a chain, Roy."

"Well," said Lloyd, "they've got a big colored problem down there, and I don't envy them."

"It isn't Negroes, Uncle Lloyd. You people think everything is Negroes—and how many Negroes do you actually know? Really know, to talk to?"

"Wait a minute," said Roy. "I knew one who I used to talk to a lot, Ellie, down at Britannia. He was a darn smart guy too. I had a lot of respect for him."

"Well," said Ellie, "I know a girl who dates a Negro."

"You do?" said Alice.

"Yes, I do, Aunt Alice. But you know what my father said? She's probably a Red. Well, the laugh is on him, actually. Because as a matter of fact she happened to have voted for President Eisenhower, which isn't exactly very communistic of her, do you think?"

"She goes out on dates with him, Eleanor? In public?" said Alice.

"Well, actually she met him at a party—and he took her home. But right on the street, and in a perfectly ordinary way, and color didn't make a bit of difference . . . That's what she said. And I believe her."

"But did she kiss him?" Roy asked.

"Roy!" said his mother.

"What are you getting excited about? I'm just asking a question. I'm just making a point."

"Well, that is some point," his mother said.

Roy went right on. "I'm only saying it's one thing to be friends and so on, which I am completely in favor of and have done myself, as I just mentioned. But to be very frank, Ellie, about this girl, well, I think very frankly intersex and so on is a whole other issue."

Ellie turned haughty. "Well, I didn't ask her about sex, Roy. That's her business, really."

"I believe," said Alice Bassart sternly, "that there is a child standing here with two very clean e-a-r-s."

"Well, all I'm saying is that every time something terrible happens everybody blames the Negroes," said Ellie, "and I refuse to listen to that kind of prejudice any more. That's all. From anyone."

"But what about all that violence, Eleanor?" Lloyd Bassart asked. "There's an awful lot of violence down there, you said so yourself."

"But that's not the fault of the Negroes!"

"Who then?" asked Alice. "They do most of it, don't they?"

"Actually," said Ellie, "more than anyone else, it's actually the dope addicts—who are really very sick people who need help. Jail is not the answer, I'll tell you that much."

"Dope addicts?" said Lloyd. "You mean dope fiends, Eleanor?"

"—are on the *streets*?" asked Alice.

"Dopey!" Edward was grinning. "Dopey, Mommy!" he said to Lucy.

Ellie threw her head back, and the mane of her hair shimmered. "Dopey! Wait'll I tell Skip. Oh, how delicious. *Dopey!*" she said, rushing to Edward and lifting him up. "And Grumpy. Right?"

"Uh-huh," he said. He put a hand out to touch the collar of her coat.

"And who else?" asked Ellie, jiggling him in her arms. "Sneezy?"

"Sneezy!" he cried.

"Lucy," said Ellie, "he's wonderful. He's fab, really. Hey, let's go!" She lowered Edward to the floor, but he kept hold of one of her hands.

"Let's go," the child said.

Roy said, "You want to come later, Lucy? After you see them? I could pick you up."

She said, "I'll be at my grandparents."

Alice said, "You're coming later, Lloyd?"

"Right, right."

Out the door they went, Edward tugging on the coat of his newly discovered relative. "And Bashful."

"Bashful! Little Bashful! How could I forget Little Bashful? He's just like you."

"And Doc too."

"Doc too!" said Ellie. "Oh, Edward what a little fellow you are. I can't even believe you exist, and here you are!"

"And the bad stepmother."

"Oh, yes, her. 'Mirror, mirror, on the wall'—" and the door closed.

Lucy watched through the window as her husband and his cousin decided which car to use, the Hudson or the new Plymouth convertible that belonged to Ellie's mother. While the debate went on, Alice Bassart stood on the front walk, holding Edward's hand and stepping first in one direction, then in the other. Roy said, "You want to get there alive, Mother, or not?" Ellie pointed at the Hudson and said something Lucy couldn't hear, but that made Roy laugh. "Oh, yeah? That's what you think," he called. "Come on, Roy," said Ellie, standing with the door of the Plymouth ajar, "live a little." "Live? In a product of Chrysler Motors?" cried Roy. "Are you kidding?" "Come on, Aunt Alice, come on, Ed," called Ellie, and Roy said, "Hey, it's not just your life, Mother—that there is the heir to my estate," and Alice said, "Roy, now stop this minute being silly!" "Well, okay," he said, "here goes nothing," and all finally piled into the Sowerby car. Edward climbed in back with his grandmother, and Roy slid in beside Ellie.

Lucy was about to move from the window when the front curb-side door opened and Roy ran around back of the car to the driver's door. At the rear of the car he slipped and fell. "Ow!" He got up, and was brushing the snow from his trouser cuffs, when he looked up and saw Lucy in the window. He waved a hand at her; she did not wave back. He cupped both hands to his mouth: "Want to come . . . in half an hour?"

Inside the car Ellie was sliding away from the steering wheel. "Lucy? Want me to—?"

She shook her head.

Then he did not seem to know what to do. She did not move. Would he decide not to go, after all? Would he remember what his uncle was? Would he take Edward from the car and come back with him into the house—of his own free will?

Ellie's window rolled down. "Roy! We're all freezing to death in here."

Roy shrugged his shoulders—then suddenly he threw Lucy a kiss and climbed in behind the wheel.

Instantly the horn went off. Ellie put her hands up over her ears. Two tries, and the motor turned over; puff after puff of fumes blackened the snow back of the car. Alice Bassart rolled the window up on her side, then rolled it down so that Edward could shove his little mitten through. Lucy raised her hand. The horn went off again, and then the car jerked away from the curb and started up toward The Grove. The last thing she saw was a red flash as Roy, for some reason of his own, hit the brakes.

—

Ellie apparently was pleading with her father to give her the car to take back to Chicago; it was supposedly her mother's, only Irene had driven it less than two hundred miles in four months, which Ellie said was ridiculous. "And he'll probably give it to her, too," said Lloyd, as Lucy came away from the window. "Not that I begrudge him that he can. I didn't go into education so as to own a fleet of automobiles in my old age. I went in for the satisfactions of training young people to meet the challenges of life, and I think you will understand, Lucy, that cars have nothing whatsoever to do with it. However, very frankly, my opinion is that Julian ought not to indulge that girl any more than he has already. I have nothing against any race, creed or color, but between the two of us, I'll tell you who I think it was who was out with a Negro. I think it was Eleanor."

"I thought it was her friend," she said, pulling on her galoshes; Ellie had shown up in heels, as though it were July.

"Well, that may well be, Lucy. I don't like the sound of that person, for such a young person. Not at all. But it was one of them who that colored boy walked home, you can be sure of that. I know young people when they talk. I have been around them all my life. It is always 'a friend of mine' when the one they are speaking of is themselves. Eleanor was always over-pampered because of her beauty, and now Julian is going to have to reap the harvest of that beautiful daughter he was always going on about. Letting a girl of twenty-two live off in the middle of a city like Chicago, without proper supervision, with wild influences all around her, that is something of which I am heartily skeptical, to say the least. Especially someone as boy-crazy as Eleanor has always been. I will tell you my personal opinion, Lucy, for whatever it is worth. Eleanor is riding for a fall, and a bad one too, given the kind of things I heard her saying here this afternoon. *But*," he said, showing her the palms of his hands, "I am keeping my nose out of it, and I have advised Alice—"

She was no longer listening. She had done a stupid thing; she saw that now. To let Roy go off by himself, to let him confront his uncle this first time without her at his side—how foolish, how dangerous!

It occurred to her to tell her father-in-law, then and there, that she was pregnant.

No, tell them all.

So the solution came to her, and it was perfect: *she would tell them all*. She would join them at the Sowerbys', and to Julian, Irene, Ellie, Alice, Lloyd, Roy and Edward, she would make her announcement. To the news of a new child, the family, all gathered together, would have no choice but to be enthusiastic . . .Yes, yes. She could see Eleanor, clapping her hands together, calling for champagne. And everyone raising his glass in a toast, as everyone had four years before at the party for Roy's future—"To Linda Sue!" and so, whatever uncertainty Roy might feel if she were to make the announcement to him alone, whatever his defiance if it seemed to him that she and his father were ganging up—well, any such response would be swept away in the general mood of celebration.

Yes, yes, this was what she would have to do:

First she would go to Daddy Will's. Wait fifteen minutes, then telephone the Sowerbys—and, yes, ask Ellie to pick her up. In the car, oh, of course, confide first in Ellie. "Ellie?" "What?" "Roy and I are going to have another baby. You're the first to know." "Oh, Lucy, fab!" Then she would tell them all—with Ellie at her side saying all the while, "Isn't that marvelous? Isn't that just divine?" In honor of the occasion, Irene Sowerby would doubtless ask them all to stay on for supper. Then she would telephone Daddy Will. She would ask her mother and Mr. Muller, and her grandparents too, to come to the Sowerbys' after supper; she had wonderful news to tell them. And then everyone would know. There would be chatter and high spirits, fun and noise, and Roy's anxiety upon hearing that he was to be a father again would be nothing to the sense he would have of pride and hope and expectation.

And she would tell them, too, that they were hoping for a girl—that that was Roy's preference—that he himself had already settled on a name—that it was the name he had always wanted, for the little girl he had always wanted. If all toasted Linda Sue together, then there would be no confusion afterward as to whose idea it was to have the little girl in the first

place. Afterward there could be no accusations, no recriminations . . . The Sowerbys had a tape recorder in their new
stereo unit; if only she could somehow get them to turn it
on—to tape-record the festivities. Then it would forever be on
record, how everyone had been absolutely thrilled by the
prospect of Linda Sue. "To our daughter, I hope," Roy would
say, *and it would be on record.*

But maybe that was going too far . . . though maybe it
wasn't at all. Had she not seen the limits to which people would
go to deny the truth? Had she not seen how people would tell
lies, make accusations, do *anything* to avoid their duties and
obligations? If only she'd had a tape recorder with her the night
Roy spoke of his desire to have a little girl . . . But surely he
would not deny *that*? How could he? Why should he? He was
perhaps slower than she in coming to maturity, but he really
wasn't a liar by nature. Nor was he a cheat, or a scoundrel, or
a gambler, or a philanderer, or a drunk. He was, under everything, a sweet and kind soul . . . and she loved him.

She loved Roy? She could not deceive herself into thinking
that she always had—or ever had, really. But that Sunday afternoon, with four harrowing years of marriage behind them, she
believed that she might actually be in love. Not with the Roy
he had been, of course, but with the new Roy he had become.
Because that was who had been addressing her in the kitchen:
a Roy no longer childish and irresponsible, a Roy no longer
pretending. Could that be? Had he changed? Had he become
a good man?

Her husband was a good man?

She was married to a good man?

The father of Edward, the father-to-be of Linda Sue, was a
good man?

Oh, she could love him, at last: she had made him a good
man.

—

It was over! He was no longer fighting the marriage, and no
one else was fighting it either. That was the meaning of Ellie's
visit—the Sowerbys had capitulated! Sending Ellie around to
invite everybody to the house was nothing less than their admission that Lucy had been right, and they had been wrong.
Julian Sowerby was admitting to defeat. With all his money

and lawyers and treacherous, deceitful ways, Julian was waving the white flag!

The misery she had undergone that previous spring, the misery she had undergone when she had been pregnant with Edward, all the heartache and humiliation—it was over. This time she would be pregnant as a woman is supposed to be. Her belly would grow round, and her breasts full, and her skin would become smooth and shiny, and none of this would cause her to feel fear and disgust and dismay. She would delight this time in what was happening. It would be spring, then summer . . . and the picture she had was of a woman in a white lace nightgown, and long hair—it was herself—and she is in bed, and her little daughter is in the bed beside her, and a man sits in a chair, smiling at the two of them. He holds in his one hand flowers he has brought for the infant, and in the other, flowers he has brought for her. The man is Roy. He watches the child feeding, and it fills him with tenderness and pride. He is a good man.

Such were her thoughts as she left the Bassarts' and walked toward Daddy Will's. Her husband was a good man . . . and Julian Sowerby had been defeated . . . and when she was in the hospital there would be flowers . . . and she would let her hair grow to her waist . . . and if in her life she had been stone, if in her life she had been iron, well, that was all over. She could now become—herself!

> Along came the wind and blew them in-negan,
> Poor poor Michael Finnegan . . .

Herself! But what would that be like? What was she even like?—that real Lucy, who had never had a chance to be—

Singing, smiling, wondering to herself—who would she be? what ever would she be like?—she climbed the stairs to her grandfather's house, and without even ringing the bell, pushed open the door upon disaster.

—

"Sit back down, Blanshard." Daddy Will was speaking. "Please, Blanshard."

Mr. Muller shook his head. He finished buttoning his coat and reached for the hat Willard was holding.

Upright, her arms crossed on her chest, Grandma Berta was

sitting in the armchair by the fireplace. Lucy looked at her angry face, then back to the two men.

Daddy Will said, "Blanshard, tomorrow is another day," but he relinquished the visitor's hat.

Mr. Muller touched the older man's shoulder, and then he walked out of the house.

Lucy said, "What is it?"

Daddy Will shook his head.

"Daddy Will, what's happened?"

"Probably nothing, honey." He made a smile. "How are you? Where's Roy and Eddie?"

Grandma Berta began slowly to draw her fingers down the loose flesh of her upper arm. "Probably nothing," she said.

"All right, Berta," said Willard.

"Probably nothing. Just that she has decided she doesn't feel like seeing him any more." In her fury, she rose and walked to the window. "And that's nothing!"

"Why won't she see him?" asked Lucy.

Her grandmother was silent now. She was watching Blanshard Muller's figure heading away from the house.

"Daddy Will, why did he go out like that? What's happening?"

"Well, tell her," said Grandma Berta.

"Nothing to tell," said Daddy Will. Berta snorted and went off to the kitchen.

"Daddy Will—"

"*There is nothing to tell!*" he said.

She moved after him, "Look," but he was up the stairs and into her mother's room; the door closed behind him.

She went into the kitchen. Now her grandmother was looking out the back window.

"I don't understand," said Lucy.

Grandma Berta did not speak.

"I said I don't understand what has happened. What is going *on* here?"

"He's back in jail," said her grandmother bitterly.

She sat alone in the parlor until Daddy Will came down the stairs. She said she wanted to know the whole story.

He said, "What story?"

She said again she wished to know the whole story. And from him, *now*, not later from some stranger.

She had her own life to worry about, Daddy Will said. "There is no story."

As he paced the room, she explained to him something that just possibly she had thought he might know by now: he could not spare people from the truth; he could not protect people from the ugliness of life by glossing over . . . She stopped. She wished to hear whatever there was to hear. If her father was in jail—

"Now who said that?"

"If he is, I want to hear it from *you*, Daddy Will. I don't want to have to piece the truth together from whispering and gossip—"

There wasn't going to be any gossip, not this time, he said. No one had been told, not even Blanshard, which was what had made it all so damn painful. Willard and Berta had decided last night that nothing was to be gained by advertising around what had happened, since, yes, something *had* happened. At dinner the previous evening Myra had lowered her head to the table and blurted out what she had been carrying around inside her for nearly a whole month. But why Lucy now had to be a party to it, he did not see. She had a life of her own to occupy her mind.

"What was it?"

"Lucy, what's the sense?"

"Daddy Will, where he is concerned I have no illusions. I took the realistic approach to him a long time ago, if you remember. Even before others did, Daddy Will—if they ever did."

"Well, sure they did—"

"Tell me the story."

"Well, it's a long one, Lucy. And I don't even know why you want to hear it."

"He is my father."

The remark seemed to confound him.

"He is my *father*! Tell the *story*."

"You're going to start yourself crying now, Lucy."

"Don't worry about me, *please*."

He walked to the foot of the stairs, then back. He would have to begin at the beginning, he said.

"Fine," she said, having brought herself under control. "Begin."

Well, first off, it seemed that Myra had more or less been in communication with him all this time. Almost since the day he left nearly four years before, he had been carrying on a kind of correspondence with her through a post-office box. Unfortunately, not one of Willard's old friends down at the post office had ever thought to tell him about Myra coming around sometimes to pick up her mail. On the other hand, he didn't know what he would have done himself in such a situation, given the rules of privacy that go hand in glove with postal work. Anyway, maybe they didn't even notice. Because it wasn't a matter of every day, or every week, or even every month—or so Myra had said, while weeping out her confession. He just sort of kept her aware of his whereabouts and progress, particularly when something important happened to him. And from time to time, depending upon her mood, how blue she was, or how nostalgic she might get for the long ago and far way, she answered.

. . . Well, to go on, if that's what Lucy wanted—in the first months after his disappearance, he was living downstate a ways, in Butler, working for an old chum of his who owned a filling station there. But around the time that Edward was born—

"He knows I have Edward."

"About most of the big things, such as Edward would be, Lucy, he more or less knows, yes."

"Why?"

"Why? Well, I don't know why, Lucy. She thought certain things, I guess, no matter what all had happened before, since he after all was still a human being we all knew once, you know . . . well, that certain things he should know."

"Of course."

Anyway, sometime after Edward's birth, he got to Florida. And down there it seems he tried to enlist in the Navy again. For a while he was actually working for them in Pensacola, and trying to get himself commissioned as a petty officer in electricity.

"An officer?"

"Lucy, I am just reporting what was reported to me. If you want me to stop, I will, gladly."

"And after Pensacola? After he didn't get to be an officer?"

After Pensacola, he went to Orlando.

"And what did he dream about there?"

He stayed for a while with his cousin Vera and her family. It seems he got real close then to a lady in Winter Park. Even got engaged. At least she believed they were engaged, until finally he told her the truth about himself.

"Oh, did he?"

"That he was married still," said Daddy Will.

"Oh, that truth."

"Lucy, I am not defending him to you. I am only telling a story that you have demanded to hear. I am telling you a story, actually, against my own better judgment. And I think, actually, that I am going to stop. 'Cause what good is the little details to you? It's done. It's over. So let's just forget it."

"Go on, please."

"Honey, you sure you got to hear all this? Because, you know, you may not be so strong on this subject—"

"Please! I am totally *indifferent* to this subject! This subject has nothing to do with me, outside of the fact that through some accident of nature that man impregnated my mother and I was the result! He is someone to whom I do not give a single moment's thought, if I can manage it. And I can. And I do! I am well aware this story has nothing to do with me, and that what has happened to him has nothing to do with me. Consequently, you have absolutely nothing to fear by telling me this story, in all its stupid little details too. I want the facts, no more and no less."

"But why?"

"So he told his fiancée 'the truth about himself.' And then how did he follow up a miracle like that, may I ask? Please go on, Daddy Will. Surely it is evident to you that I take no responsibility whatsoever for whatever idiotic things he has done since he decided to leave Liberty Center. I am not whoever it was in the Navy who told him that he was not exactly officer material—"

"Petty officer, honey."

"Petty officer. Fine. Nor did I tell him to get engaged and then unengaged."

"No one said you did, Lucy."

"Fine. So then where did he go?"

"Well, he wound up in Clearwater. That's where he stayed the longest, too. Got work in the maintenance department of The Clearwater Beach Arms, which is one of the biggest and swankiest hotels down there, apparently. And about four months back he was made chief engineer of the entire establishment."

"Really?"

"For the night shift."

"And then what happened?"

Well, apparently he had gotten on top of his drinking problem. What happened had nothing to do with that. He wouldn't touch a drop, and as he had always been a real workhorse when he was in control of himself, he most likely impressed the management with his abilities. They surely made no mistake when it came to estimating his knowledge of how to keep an establishment operating at full steam, day or night. Their mistake was to overestimate his strength of character, what with being so new to the job. Their mistake was to give him a key to just about every door in the place. But he was even managing the keys all right, or so it seemed; he was flourishing, responsibility and all, or so it seemed, until right after Christmas. It was then that Myra had sat down and written him a letter saying that she wanted him to know that after serious consideration she had decided to divorce him and marry Blanshard Muller.

Willard sank into the armchair, and with his eyes closed, rested his head in his hands. "And didn't tell any of us. All on her own, just made up her mind, all the way back then, to marry him . . . I guess she thought it was her duty to tell Whitey first . . . She didn't want him, see, to get the news first by one of his old cronies down at Earl's Dugout . . . Oh, I don't know what she thought, more or less—but what's done is done . . . And that's what she done."

"She was being a good wife, Daddy Will. She was being considerate of Whitey's feelings. She was being proper and respectable. She was being a good, subservient wife. Still!"

"Lucy, she was being herself, that's all she was being."

"And then he was *him*self, right? And what did himself do? *What?* Believe me, I can take it."

Well, when he received the news, it shook him up pretty bad. You might think that with his health back, and holding down a decent job, and living where he said he always wanted to live—you might think that having himself been more or less engaged to another person for practically a year, having stayed away for practically four years—you might think he would have been somewhat prepared for a shock such as this, and that after a day or two of getting used to the idea, he would go on with his new life and new job and new friends, and more or less adjust himself to something that was happening two thousand miles away to someone he hadn't seen in years and years. What he did do instead was absolutely stupid. And who knows, maybe he would have done it one day anyway, irregardless of Myra's letter. Maybe it had nothing at all to do with Myra, and was something he had been planning for a long time. Anyway, New Year's Eve he was in one of the offices of the hotel management, checking on some kind of trouble they were having with a window fan. Unfortunately, in that particular office some secretary had been sloppy or in a hurry or something, and had gone home for the night, leaving a whole bag of valuables sitting out on top of a filing cabinet next to the safe. "You know," said Willard, "what the guests check. Mostly jewels. Wristwatches. And some cash, too."

"So he was himself, and he took it."

"Well, a part of it."

"A part of it," she repeated, lowering her eyes.

"About a handful," said Willard sadly. "And then by the time he realized what all he had done—"

"It was too late."

"It was too late," said Daddy Will. "That's right."

"He drank it up."

"No, oh no," he said. "As for the drinking, that wasn't it. No, down there in Orlando he joined the AA again, like over in Winnisaw. But this time he stuck to it, see. That is even where he met the lady from Winter Park. No, what he did is, he took it with him to where he lived, and then, well, he couldn't even sleep, you see, realizing what he had done, as

any damn fool would. But by this time it was the next day
already, and there was already somebody had come down to
check out in the morning, and had asked for this lady's wrist-
watch, and well, it just wasn't there. And so then the checking
around started, and even before he could even get back to the
hotel, the scandal was all over the place. And then he didn't
know what to do. He knew he couldn't return it right then,
not with the mood that his boss was in and the detectives
swarming all around. So he figured for the time being it was
smartest to say nothing and just go home. He figured he
would just sort of slip the stuff all back somehow, maybe that
night. But it was only a few hours, and the finger of suspicion
had already pointed around to him, and they came to this
room where he lived, and he didn't see where there was any
choice, and since it seemed the right thing to do anyway, and
what he had planned on doing practically an hour after he had
done it to begin with, he made a clean breast of it; turned over
every single item; said he would pay out of earnings any dam-
ages. But by this time the boss had already fired the secretary
who had left the stuff out, and since he had to reassure his
guests and all, there was somebody had to be made a strong
example of. Every single thing was insured, and returned to
boot, but he didn't show no mercy. I suppose he figured he
had his interests to watch out for, too. So instead of just firing
Whitey, like he did the girl, he turned on him and hard. And
so did the judge. That's big hotel country down there, and I
guess they all know which side their bread is buttered on, and
so they really slapped it on him. As an example for others.
That's what it seems, anyway. Eighteen months. In the Florida
State Prison."

He was finished. She said, "And you believe that story. You
actually believe it."

He shrugged his shoulders. "Lucy, he is in the State Prison
in Raiford, Florida."

She was on her feet. "But it's not his responsibility, right?"

"No, I didn't say—"

"You never say! Never!"

"Honey, never say *what*?"

"He was forced to steal from being so sad, right? He didn't
know what he was doing, even! He didn't *mean* what he was

doing! He wanted to take it back once he did it! But he was framed!"

"Lucy—"

"But that's what you *believe*! The sloppy secretary! The bad boss! And people can't help it! They just have their faults and weaknesses that they were born with— Oh, you!" She was on the stairs before he could stop her.

Her mother was lying with her face in the pillow.

"Mother," she began, "Mr. Muller has just left the house. Do you know that, Mother? Do you hear me, Mother? You have just sent out of the house your one chance of having a decent human life. And why? Mother, I am asking you why."

"Leave me . . ." The voice was barely audible.

"Why? To throw twenty more years away? To be humiliated again? Abused again? To be deprived? Mother, what do you think you are doing? Who do you think you are saving? Mother, what does it possibly do or mean to tell Mr. Muller to go, when that idiot, that moron, that useless, hopeless—"

"But you should be happy!"

"What?" Suddenly she was without force.

Her mother was sitting up in the bed. Her face was swollen, her eyes sunk deep in black. She shrieked, "Because he's where you always wanted him to be!"

"I . . . No!"

"Yes! Where he never, never . . ." The rest was lost in her sobbing as she rolled back on the bed.

—

An hour later she was down the stairs and out the door before Roy could even step from the car. Her mother had a migraine and it would be too much for her to have Edward, or any of them, visiting; even Mr. Muller had gone home early. And heavy snow was predicted by the radio for the evening. They must go.

Daddy Will had followed her onto the porch. Earlier he had knocked lightly on the door of her old room, but she forbid him to enter. "I can manage alone, thank you," she had said.

"Lucy, you are acting like I'm in favor of all this. You act like I want it."

"What did you do to prevent it? What have you ever done?"

"Lucy, I am not God—"

"Leave me to myself, please! I am not the one who needs you. Go to your darling daughter!"

Now Daddy Will followed her down the driveway. She was already seated in the car, Edward beside her, when her grandfather leaned his elbows on the door.

"How's Prince Edward here doing?" He reached into the car to pull the child's hood down over his eyes.

"Don't," said Edward, giggling.

"How you, Roy?" asked Daddy Will.

"Oh, surviving," Roy said. "Tell Mom I hope she's better."

Mom was what he called Lucy's mother. *Mom!* That weak, stupid, blind . . . It was the police who had put him there. It was he himself who put him there!

"Take care, Lucy," Daddy Will said. He patted her arm.

"Yes," she said, busily adjusting Edward's hood.

"Well," said Daddy Will, as Roy started up the motor, "see you next month—"

"Yeah, see you, Willard," said Roy.

"Bye," called Edward. "Bye, Daddy-Grandpa."

Oh, no, she thought, oh no you don't . . . *I will not be accused, I will not be held responsible* . . .

Dusk. Snow. Night. As they drove, Edward made little popping noises with the saliva in his mouth, and Roy chattered away. Guess who Ellie had seen down in Chicago at Christmastime? Joe the Toe. Bumped into him down there in the Loop. Turns out he's a med student now, still down in Alabama. But the same old Joe the Toe, Ellie said. Hey, guess what Eddie said. Out of nowhere, he asked Ellie if Skippy was the name of her dog. Oh, the Sowerbys asked after her, of course. Julian had some business over at the golf club, so he'd only had a chance really to say hello. That's all he'd said to him, practically. Oh, and the big news—Ellie had invited them to spend a weekend with her this spring. They could leave Eddie with the family . . .

She closed her eyes and pretended to be asleep . . . Perhaps she did sleep, because for a while she was able to drive out of her mind any recollection of what had been said to her that afternoon.

They went almost into Fort Kean. To Edward, who had remained awake all the way down, watching the wipers beat the heavy snow off the window, Roy was saying, ". . . so the captain came in and asked, 'Who here is willing to go off and help this Eskimo find his dog?' And so I thought to myself, 'Sounds like there might be some fun in it—'" and it was here that Lucy screamed.

Roy maneuvered the car over to the side of the road. When he leaned across Edward to touch her, she pulled her shoulder away and huddled against the door.

"Lucy!"

She pressed her mouth into the cold window. *The whole thing is not worth a moment's consideration.*

"Lucy—"

And she screamed again.

Bewildered, Roy said, "Lucy, is it a pain? Where? Lucy, did I say something—?"

He sat a moment longer, waiting to hear if it was something he had said or done. Then he edged the car back onto the road and headed into the city. "Lucy, you all right now? You better? . . . Honey, I'll go fast as I can. It's slippery, you'll just have to hang on . . ."

Edward sat frozen between them. From time to time Roy reached over and patted the little boy's leg. "Everything's okay, Eddie. Mommy just has a little pain."

At the house the child followed behind, clutching to the back of his father's trousers, as Roy helped her up the three flights of stairs and into the apartment.

In the living room, Roy turned on a lamp. She dropped onto the sofa. Edward stood in the doorway in his snowsuit and red galoshes. His nose was running. When she extended a hand toward him, he ran past her into his room.

Roy's hands dangled at his side. His hair was wet and hanging onto his forehead. "Do you want a doctor?" he asked softly. "Or are you all right now? Lucy, did you hear me? Do you feel better?"

"Oh, you," she said. "You hero."

"Do you want me to open it out?" he asked, pointing to the sofa. "Do you want to rest? Just tell me."

She pulled the cushion from behind her and threw it wildly at him. "You big war hero!"

The cushion struck his leg. He picked it up. "I was only keeping him entertained. Look, I always tell him—"

"I *know* you always tell him! Oh, I know, Roy—every Sunday of our lives you tell him! Because that's all you can do! God knows you can't *show* him!"

"Lucy, what did I do wrong now?"

"You idiot! You dolt! All *you* can show him is the carburetor in the car—and probably you get that wrong too! I saw you, Roy, in that brand-new Plymouth. To drive a new Plymouth— that was your biggest thrill of the year!"

"Well, no!"

"To sit behind the wheel of a new Sowerby car!"

"Jee–*zuz*, Lucy, Ellie asked if I wanted to drive, so I said yes. I mean, that's no reason . . . Look, if you're angry because I went over there . . . Look, we talked that over, Lucy—"

"You worm! Don't you have any guts at all? Can't you stand on your own two feet, *ever*? You sponge! You leech! You weak, hopeless, spineless, coward! You'll never change—you don't even *want* to change! You don't even know what I *mean* by change! You stand there with your dumb mouth open! Because you have no backbone! None!" She grabbed the other cushion from behind her and heaved it toward his head. "Since the day we met!"

He batted down the cushion with his hands. "Look, now look—Eddie is right be—"

She charged off the sofa. "And no courage!" she cried. "And no determination! And no will of your own! If I didn't tell you what to do, if I were to turn my back—if I didn't every single rotten day of this rotten life . . . Oh, you're not a man, and you never will be, and you don't even *care*!" She was trying to hammer at his chest; first he pushed her hands down, then he protected himself with his forearms and elbows; then he just moved back, a step at a time.

"Lucy, come on, now, please. We're not alone—"

But she pursued him. "You're nothing! Less than nothing! Worse than nothing!"

He grabbed her two fists. "Lucy. Get control. Stop, please."

"Get your hands off of me, Roy! Release me, Roy! Don't you dare try to use your strength against me! Don't you dare attempt violence!"

"I'm not attempting *anything*!"

"*I am a woman! Release my hands!*"

He did. He was crying.

"Oh," she said, breathing hard, "how I despise you, Roy. Every word you speak, everything you do, or try to do, it's awful. You're nothing, and I will never forgive you—"

He put his hands over his eyes and wept.

"Never, never," she said, "because you are beyond hope. Beyond endurance. You are beyond everything. You can't be saved. You don't even want to be."

"Lucy, Lucy, no, that's not true."

"LaVoy," she said disgustedly.

"—What?"

"LaVoy's not the pansy, Roy. You are."

"No, oh no."

"Yes! You! Oh, go!" She dropped back onto the sofa. "Disappear. Leave me, leave me, just get out of my sight!"

She cried then, with such intensity that she felt her organs would be torn loose. Sounds that seemed to originate not in her body but in the corners of her skull emerged from her nostrils and her mouth. She pressed her eyes so tightly shut that between her cheekbones and her brow there was just a thin slit through which the hot tears ran. It began to seem she would be unable to stop crying. And she didn't care. What else was there to do?

—

When she awoke the apartment was without light. She turned on the lamp. Who had turned it off?

"Roy?"

He had gone out.

She rushed to Edward's room.

In the next moment she lost all sense of where she was. She could not get her mind to give her any information. *I am a freshman.*

No!

"Edward!"

She ran to the kitchen and turned on the light; then she was in his bedroom again. She opened the closet, but he was not hiding there. She opened his dresser to see . . . to see what? *He has taken him to a movie.* But it was nine o'clock at night. *He has taken him for something to eat.*

Back in the living room, she ran her hand over every surface: no note, no nothing. In Edward's bedroom she dropped to her knees. "Boo!" But he was not beneath the bed.

Of course! In the kitchen she dialed Hopkins' studio. *He is showing him where he works, showing him what a big strong man he is. Showing him the kind of studio he could have in his own house if only Mommy wasn't such a terrible person.* Well, she hoped—while the phone rang and rang—she hoped that he was also showing him where they were all supposed to live while their living and bed room became a business office, showing him what they were supposed to live on, too, while he waited for the customers to—

There was no one at the studio.

She searched the apartment again. *What am I looking for?* Then she telephoned Liberty Center. But the Bassarts were still at the Sowerbys'. The operator asked if she wished to place the call later, but she hung up without giving the Sowerbys' number. Suppose it was a false alarm? Suppose he had only taken Edward for a hamburger, and the two of them returned just as Julian Sowerby picked up the phone?

She would just wait for him to come back and explain himself. To disappear without leaving a note! To take an exhausted little child out into a snowstorm at nine o'clock at night! There were cold things in the refrigerator; there was soup on the shelves. Don't tell me it was to get him something to eat, Roy. It was to frighten me. It was to . . .

At ten-thirty Roy phoned to say that he had just arrived back in Liberty Center. She did not even wait for him to finish. She told him what he was to do. He said that Edward was fine—fine now, at any rate, but it had been one ghastly, horrible experience for him, and she ought to know it. She had to raise her voice to interrupt; once again, she made clear to him what he was to do, and instantly. But he just said she shouldn't worry. He'd take care of everything at his end; maybe she ought to just worry about getting everything under control at her own. It was necessary now to shout at him to make him understand. He was to do what she told him. He said he knew all about that, but the point was what she had done in the car, and what she had done afterward, what she had screamed at him, all in earshot of a small defenseless child. When she shouted again, he said that it would take the U.S. Marines to get him to return any child to a place where, to be honest about it, he really couldn't stand it one day longer, as long as she kept on being the way she was. He was, to repeat, not returning any three-and-a-half-year-old to live one day more with a person who—he was sorry, but he was going to have to say it—

"Say what!"

"Who he hates like poison, that's what!"

"Who hates who like poison, Roy?"

No answer.

"*Who* hates *who* like poison, Roy? You will not get away with that insinuation, I don't care where you're hiding! I demand you clarify what you just had the audacity to say to me—what you would never dare to say to my face, you crybaby! You coward! *Who* hates—"

"Hates *you!*"

"What? He loves me, you liar! You are lying! He loves me, and you return that child! Roy, do you hear me? *Return my child!*"

"I told you, Lucy, what he told me—*and I will not!*"

"I don't believe you! Not for a single second do I believe—"

"Well, you better! All the way up here, he cried his little heart out—"

"I don't believe you!"

"'I hate Mommy, her face was all black.' That's how he cried to me, Lucy!"

"*You're lying, Roy!*"

"Then why does he lock himself in the toilet? Why does he run away from his dinner every other night—"

"*He doesn't!*"

"He did!"

"Because of you!" she shouted. "Not doing your job!"

"No, Lucy, because of *you*! Because of your screaming, hateful, bossy, hateful, heartless guts! Because he never wants to see your ugly, heartless face again, and neither do I! Never!"

"Roy, you are my husband! You have responsibilities! You get into that car this instant—you start out right *now*—and whether you drive all night—"

But at the other end, there was a click; the connection was broken. Either Roy had hung up, or someone had taken the phone away and hung up for him.

2

THE last bus out of Fort Kean got her to Liberty Center just before one in the morning. The snow was barely drifting down, and there was no one to be seen on Broadway. She had to wait at the back of Van Harn's for a taxi to take her up to The Grove.

She used the time as she had used the hour of the dark trip north: rehearsing once again what she would say. What was demanded of her was now clear enough; the scene to be enacted became vague only when she had to imagine what she would do if Roy refused to drive her and Edward back to Fort Kean. To stay at Daddy Will's till morning was out of the question. That assistance she could live without. When hadn't she? Nor would she stay overnight with the Bassarts, though the chance that she would even be invited to was very slight indeed. Had her in-laws had even a grain of loyalty to her, the instant Roy arrived back in town they would have demanded some explanation of him; they were at the Sowerbys', they could have gotten on the phone with her themselves, they could have intervened in behalf of a mother and a child, even if the husband happened in this instance to be a son. There were principles to be honored, values to respect, that went beyond blood relationships; but apparently they had no more knowledge of what it meant to be human than did her own family. None of them had so much as raised a finger to stop Roy in this reckless, ridiculous adventure, not even the high-minded high school teacher himself. No, she could not be innocent, not where people like this were concerned: she knew perfectly well that when Roy pronounced himself unable to undertake a second trip to Fort Kean at one in the morning, his parents would join with the Sowerbys in supporting him. And she knew too, that if she allowed him to stay behind while she and Edward returned alone to Fort Kean, then he would never return to live with them again.

And how she wished that she could permit that to be. Had he not proved to her that his soul was an abyss, not just of selfishness, of mindlessness, but of heartless cruelty too? Try as she would to believe him capable of a deeper devotion, deceive herself as she might by believing him to be "sweet" and "kind," a good and gentle man, the truth about his character was now glaringly apparent. There was a point beyond which one could not go in believing in the potential for good in another human being, and after four nightmarish years she had finally reached it. With all her heart she wished that she and Edward might return to Fort Kean, leaving Roy behind. Let him return to Mommy and Daddy and Auntie and Uncle, to his milk and his cookies and his endless, hopeless, childish dreaming. If only it were a month ago—if only there were just herself and Edward, then Roy, for all she cared, could disappear forever. She was young and strong; she knew what work was, she knew the meaning of sacrifice and struggle, and was not afraid of either. In only a few months Edward could begin nursery school; she could get work then, in a store, in a restaurant, in a factory— wherever the pay was highest, it did not matter to her how strenuous was the labor itself. She would support herself and Edward, and Roy could go off and live in his parents' house, sleeping till noon, opening "a studio" in the garage, clipping pictures from magazines, pasting them up in scrapbooks—he could flounder and fail however he liked, but without her and Edward suffering the ugly consequences. Yes, she would get work, she would earn what they needed, and cut that monster —for who but a monster could have said on the phone those terrible things he had said to her?—cut him out of their lives, forever.

All this she would have done, and gladly too, had he revealed the depths of his viciousness as briefly as a month ago. But now such a severing was out of the question—for very shortly her job would be not to earn a living for a family, but to be a mother to a second child. There was not just herself and Edward to protect: there was a third life to consider too. Whatever her own feelings and desires, she saw no gain, but only endless hardship, in permitting this man to run out on a child in its infancy . . . So, though she had now been given every cause to loathe him; though she understood now the horrid extremes to which he would go to defend himself and humiliate her; though she would as soon open the door of the Sowerby house to learn that he was dead, for him to desert his family was out of the question. He had duties and obligations, and he was going to perform them, whether he liked them or not. He was not staying behind in that house, or anywhere in this town, and thereby unburdening himself of the pain there just happened to be in life. Who, after all, was Roy Bassart that he should feel no pain? Who was Roy Bassart that he should live a privileged existence? Who was Roy Bassart to be without responsibilities? This was not heaven. This was the world!

There were no lights on in any of the houses at The Grove. The plow had been through already, and the taxi was able to make its way easily up the street. When they stopped in front of the Sowerbys', she thought of telling the driver to wait; in a moment she would be out with her child . . . But that could not be. Hateful as he was to her, there were facts and circumstances she must not be blind to: she would never, never save herself at the expense of an unborn child.

But there was no sign of the Hudson. Either he had pulled it in the Sowerby garage—or he was no longer there. He had fled further north! To Canada! Beyond the reaches of the law! He had stolen Edward! He had abandoned her!

No! She closed her eyes to shut out the worst until the worst was known; she pressed the doorbell, heard its ring, and saw her father sitting in a cell in the Florida State Prison. He is sitting on a three-legged stool wearing a striped uniform. There is a number on his chest. His mouth is open and on his teeth, in lipstick, is written INNOCENT.

The door was opened by Julian Sowerby.

Instantly she remembered where she was and what exactly had to be done.

"Julian, I am here for Roy and Edward. Where are they?"

He was wearing a shiny blue robe over his pajamas. "Well. Lucy. Long time no see."

"I am here for a purpose, Julian. Is Roy hiding out with you or not? If he is with his parents, tell me please, and—"

He placed a finger over his lips. "Shhh," he whispered. "People are sleeping."

"I want to know, Julian—"

"Shhh, shhh; it's after one. Come on in, why don't you?" He motioned for her to hurry through the door. "Brrrr. Must be ten below."

Was she to be let in without resistance? On the bus coming north she had prepared herself for the possibility of a scene right out on the doorstep. Instead she was following Julian quietly through the hall and into the living room. And why? Of course—because what Roy had done was so obviously outrageous that even the Sowerbys' could no longer take his side. In her isolation she had exaggerated—not the seriousness of Roy's act, but the seriousness with which even her enemies would accept his story. The person who had slammed down the phone earlier was only Roy himself; the chances were he hadn't even had the nerve to make the call in the presence of a rational human being.

To understand this came as a tremendous relief. In her entire life she had never retreated from a struggle that had to be, and she would not have retreated here; she would, if necessary, actually have hurled herself against Julian Sowerby in order to enter his house and reclaim her husband and her child. But how grateful she was to be able to follow calmly and quietly behind. It was the scene with her family earlier in the day that had caused her imagination to become so extreme, that had led her to prepare herself for the fiercest struggle of her life. But as it turned out, Roy had now been revealed in such a way that even the most hard-hearted and unthinking of his supporters had lost all sympathy.

And was that not bound to happen? Eventually, must not the truth prevail? Oh, it had not been in vain then that she had sacrificed and struggled! Oh yes, of course! If you know you are in the right, if you do not weaken or falter, if despite everything thrown up against you, despite every hardship, every pain, you oppose what you know in your heart is wrong; if you harden yourself against the opinions of others, if you are willing to endure the loneliness of pursuing what is good in a world indifferent to good; if you struggle with every fiber of your body, even as others scorn you, hate you and fear you; if you push on and on and on, no matter how great the agony, how terrible the strain—then one day the truth will finally be known—

"Sit down," said Julian.

"Julian," she said evenly, "I don't think I will. I think, without delay, really—"

"Sit down, Lucy." He was smiling, and pointing to a chair.

"I'd rather not." She spoke firmly.

"But I don't care what you would rather do. I am telling you what you are going to do. First thing is sit."

"I don't need to rest, thank you."

"But you do, Cutie-Pie. You need a long, long rest."

She felt anger shoot through her. "I don't know what you think you're saying, Julian, and I don't care. I did not come here at this hour, at the end of a grueling day, to sit—"

"Oh, no?"

"—and talk with you."

She stopped. Of what use *was* talk? How she had deluded herself only the second before—how pathetic, how foolish, how innocent of her, to have a generous thought about a person such as this. They were no better than she'd thought; they were worse.

"I've been sitting up for you, Lucy," said Julian. "What do you think of that? I've been looking forward to this, actually, for a long time. I figured you'd be on that bus."

"There is no reason why you shouldn't have expected me," she said. "It's what any mother would have done."

"Yes, sir, that's you, all right. Well, sit down, Any Mother."

She did not move.

"Well," he said, "then I'll sit." He settled into a chair, all the time keeping an eye on her.

She was suddenly confused. There were the stairs—why didn't she just walk up them, and wake Roy? "Julian," she said, "I would appreciate it if you would go upstairs and tell my husband that I am here and I want to see him. I have come all the way from Fort Kean, Julian, in the middle of the night, because of what he has done. But I am willing to be reasonable about this, if you are."

Julian took a loose cigarette out of the pocket of his robe and straightened it between two fingers. "You are, huh?" he said, and lit it.

What a disgusting little man! Why did she say "if you are"— what had he to do with it? And why *was* he waiting up for her in his pajamas and robe? Was this all preparatory to making some indecent offer? Was he going to try to seduce her while his own wife, his own daughter—?

But at the top of the stairs Irene appeared—and it was then that Lucy understood fully the monstrousness of what these people were planning to do.

"Irene—" She had the sensation that she might fall backward. "Irene," she said, and had to take a deep breath to go on, "will you please, since you are up there, awaken Roy? Please tell him I have come all the way from Fort Kean. That I am here, please, for him and for Edward."

She did not have to look over at Julian to know his gaze was fixed upon her. "The snow has stopped," she said, still to the woman at the top of the stairs, who was wearing a quilted robe over her nightgown. "So we will drive home. If he is too tired, then we will take a room somewhere for the night. But he is not staying here. Nor is Edward."

Instead of heading back along the corridor to awaken Roy, Irene started down the stairs. Her hair had gone nearly white in the last few years, and she seemed heavier; or else, without a corset the thickness of her body was more easily discernible. Altogether her appearance was that of an elderly matron, thoroughly composed, and of all things, sympathetic.

"Irene, I want to tell you that your letting Roy think he could get away with this—"

"Yes?" said Julian, from where he sat, smoking.

"—will make it altogether impossible for us ever to see you again. And that means all of us, including Edward. And I hope you will all realize, once again, that this is something you have absolutely brought upon yourselves."

"We realize everything, kiddo," said Julian.

Irene moved toward her, with one hand extended. "Lucy,

why don't you sit down? Why don't we try to talk and see what's happened?"

"Look," she said, stepping back, "I do not choose to stay in this house, or even in this town, one second longer than is necessary. You are not my friend, Irene, and don't suddenly pretend that you are. I am not that stupid, and you should know that. From the very first day that Roy began to take me out, you have behaved as though I were some kind of inferior thing. As though *I* weren't worthy of *him*. I know what your true feelings are, so don't think you can trick me by taking hold of my hand. You may deceive yourself however you like, but your actions have spoken louder than your words. This is plain idiocy on Roy's part, and he and Edward are to leave here this instant, and return with me—"

"I think," said Julian, standing now, "that, first thing, you better calm yourself down."

"Don't tell me what to do, Julian!" She turned to face him, to look right into those dishonest eyes. Oh, she would wipe that little smirk off his face. How superior they thought they were, these people with the morals of animals! "You have no authority over me whatsoever. I think you had better be re-minded of that, Julian. I don't happen to be one of the people dependent upon your millions."

"Billions," he said, grinning.

Irene said, "Lucy, if I make some coffee—"

"I don't want coffee! I want my child! And my husband—such as he is! They are to be returned to me immediately. This instant."

"But, Lucy dear—" Irene began.

"Don't you 'dear' me! I do not trust you, Mrs. Sowerby—any more than I do him!"

Julian's figure had suddenly moved between Lucy and his wife. "Now," he said, "rule number one—either you calm down with that bossy little voice, missy, or you get out."

"But suppose I will *not* get out."

"Then you are a trespasser, and I will heave you out—on your butt."

"Don't you *dare* speak to me—" And she broke for the stairs. An arm, however, fell instantly upon her back; she pulled away, but he had caught hold of her coat.

"No! Let *me*—"

But his other hand fell upon her shoulder, and she was driven down so forcefully that she felt herself become ill. He had seated her; and was over her, his face purple with fury. His bathrobe had fallen open, and she had a glimpse of his stomach between the buttons of his pajamas.

She did not move or speak. He straightened up and pulled his robe closed, but remained directly before her.

Precise and exact in her diction, Lucy began. "You have no right—"

"Don't you tell me rights, you little twenty-year-old twerp. It is you who is going to learn rights."

"Well," said Lucy, her mind racing, "well, Irene"—trying to look past him to his wife—"you must be very proud of having as a husband a brute, who beats someone half his—"

"Who you are dealing with, Lucy, is me. So it's me you talk to. Not Irene."

Now Ellie came out onto the landing. She stood there in her white wrapper, both hands on the banister, looking down.

Lucy turned her face up to Julian's, and spoke so only he could hear. "I know about you, Julian. So just you be careful."

"Oh, do you?" He pushed right up against her knees. She drew her head back from his belly. "And what is it you know?" he asked, his voice gruff and low. "You trying to threaten me? Speak up!"

She could not see beyond his bulk. She could not even think now, *and she must*. "Since I did not come here to discuss your character," she began, addressing the belt of his robe, "I'm not going to, Julian."

"Good idea," he said, and stepped back.

Eleanor had disappeared.

Lucy folded her hands in the lap of her coat; she had to wait until she was sure that her voice would not falter. "So long as I can do what I came here to do, and then leave, there is no need to enter into any kind of discussion . . . That is fine with me." Then she looked up at Irene. "Now will someone please awaken my husband—*please*."

"Maybe he is sleeping," said Julian. "Ever think of that? Maybe he has had one hell of a day from you, sister."

He remained standing so that she could not get up out of

her chair; she hammered on the arms. "We have all had one hell of a day, Julian! I have had a *horror* of a day. Now, I demand that he be told—"

"But your demanding days are over. That, twerp, is the point of all this."

"Please . . ." she said, breathing deeply, "I would much prefer to deal with your wife, who has a civil tongue at least, if you don't mind."

"But my civil wife isn't dealing with you."

"Excuse me," said Lucy, "perhaps she has a mind of her own, sir—"

"My wife *dealt* with you, kiddo. Back when she told me there was still some evidence you were a human being. But it turns out that I should never have taken her advice four years ago, back when you started *out* sinking your fangs into that boy."

"That boy seduced me, Julian! It became that boy's duty to me—"

He turned away and looked at his wife. "Duty," he said, snorting.

She jumped up from the chair. "You may not like the word, Julian, but I repeat—it was his duty to me—"

"Oh," he said, shaking his head, "everybody has got that there duty to you. But who is it you got the sacred duty to, Lucy? Seems to me I forget."

"To my child!" she answered. "To the offspring of my husband and myself! To someone starting out in life, that's who! To see that he is given a home and a family and proper upbringing! To see he is not misused by all the beasts in this filthy world!"

"Oh," said Julian, "you are a real saint, you are."

"Compared to you, I most certainly am. Yes!"

"Well, Saint Lucy," he said, running a hand over his stubble, "don't worry so much about your offspring any more. Because he hates your guts."

She brought her hands up over her face. "That's not true. That's Roy's terrible, terrible lie. That's . . . no. No, that isn't—"

She felt Irene's hand on her arm.

"No, no," she wept, and fell back again into the chair.

"What . . . what are you planning to do to me? You can't steal my child. This is kidnapping, Irene. Irene, this is against every law there is."

Julian spoke. "Leave her alone."

Irene answered something that Lucy could not hear.

"We are settling something here, Irene. Get away from her. Let her alone. She has done her last—"

Suddenly Lucy came charging up at him, shaking her fists. "You won't get away with this! Whatever it is you think you are going to do to me!"

Julian only jammed his hands down into the pockets of his robe.

"This is kidnapping, Julian, if that's what you have on your mind! Kidnapping—and abandonment! He can't run out on me and take my child! There are laws, Julian, laws against people like you!"

"Fine. You go out and get yourself a lawyer. Nothing would make me happier."

"But I don't *need* a lawyer! Because I intend to solve this right here and now!"

"Oh, but you do need one, Lucy. Let me tell you something. You are going to need the best damn lawyer money can buy."

Irene said, "Julian, the child is in no condition—"

He shook off his wife's hand. "Neither is Roy, Irene! Neither is Eddie! Neither is any of us! We have all taken enough orders and insults from this little bitch here—"

"Julian—"

But here he turned angrily back to Lucy. "Because that's all you are, you know. A little ball-breaker of a bitch. That's the saint you are, kiddo—Saint Ball-Breaker. And the world is going to know it, too, before I'm through with you."

"Don't," said Irene.

"Irene, enough don't! I already have heard your don'ts a long time ago."

Lucy was shaking her head. "Let him go on, Irene. I don't care. He is only showing himself for what he is."

"Right you are, Saintie. That's what I am. And that is how come the busting of the balls stops with these. That's right, you smile through your tears, you smile how smart you are and what a terrible mouth old Julian has. Oh, I have got a terrible mouth. I am an old no-good beast, besides. But I'm going to tell you something, Lucy—you busted his balls, and you were starting in on little Eddie's, but that is *all* over. And if that strikes you funny now, let us see how funny it is going to strike you in the courtroom, because that is where I am dragging your ass, little girl. Little twerp. Little nothing. You are going to be one bloody little mess when I get through with you, Saint Lucy."

"*You're* taking *me* to a courtroom?"

"Dirty language and all. Uh-huh."

"You?" she asked, still with a strange smile on her face.

"That's right. Me."

"Well, that's marvelous." In her purse she found a handkerchief. She blew her nose. "That's wonderful, really. Because you, Julian, are a wicked man, and to get you in a courtroom—" At the top of the stairs, at last, Roy appeared. Eleanor behind him. So here they all were, those who only a few hours earlier had conspired against her . . . Well, she would not weep, she would not plead; she did not have to. She would speak the truth.

She looked from one to the other of them, and with that unshakable knowledge that she was right and they were wrong, a great calm came over her. It was not necessary to raise her voice, or to shake a fist; only to speak the truth.

"You are a wicked man, Julian. And you know it."

"Know *what*?" His shoulders seemed to have thickened as he hunched forward to hear her words. "Know what, did you say?"

"We won't need lawyers, Julian. We won't have to go any further than this living room. Because it is not for you to tell me, or to tell anyone here, what is right and what is wrong. And you know that, I'm sure. Shall I go on, Julian? Or do you wish to apologize now before your family?"

"Listen, little loudmouth," he said, and started for her.

"You are a whoremonger," she said—and it stopped him. "You pay women to sleep with you. You have had a series of mistresses. You cheat on your wife."

"Lucy!" Ellie cried.

"But isn't it the truth, Eleanor?"

"No!"

She turned to Irene Sowerby. "I would rather not have had to say what I just did—"

Irene dropped onto the couch. "You didn't have to."

"But I did," said Lucy. "You saw how he was treating me. You heard his intentions. Have I any choice, Irene, but to speak the truth?"

Irene was shaking her head.

"He had a sexual affair with the woman who was the manager of the laundromat in Selkirk. I have forgotten her name. I'm sure he can tell you, however."

The glare Julian had fastened on her was murderous. Well, let him try. Let him lay one finger on her, just let him try, and then he'll see who it is who will be appearing before a judge. Then his marvelous dream would come true all right—only the defendant would not be her, but himself.

"And," she said, returning his gaze directly, "there was another woman, who he was either supporting, or keeping, or paying for her services. I would imagine there is now someone else, somewhere. Am I wrong, 'Uncle' Julian?"

It was Irene who spoke. "Be still."

"I am only giving you the truth."

The woman stood. "You have spoken enough."

"But it is *the truth*!" said Lucy. "And it will not go away, Irene, because you refuse to believe it. He is a whoremonger! A philanderer! And adulterer! He schemes behind your back! He degrades you! He despises you, Irene! Don't you realize that? That is what it means when a man does what he is doing to you!"

Ellie was holding the banister with her two hands, her hair half covering her face. Whatever she was sobbing, Lucy could not understand.

"I'm sorry, Eleanor. This is not my idea of how to behave either. But there is only so much bullying, so much filth and treachery and hatred I can willingly stand here and take. I did not come here, I assure you, for the purpose of attacking your father. What I said I said in self-defense. He is a heartless man—"

"But she knows," wept Ellie. "She knew, she always knew."

"Eleanor!" said Irene Sowerby.

"You know?" cried Lucy. "You mean," she said to Irene, "you *know* what he is—" She was incredulous. "All of you in this room *know* what he is and what he has done and still you were going to allow . . ." Momentarily she could not even speak. "I don't believe it," she said at last. "That you can be so utterly unscrupulous and deceitful, so thoroughly corrupt and—"

"Oh, Roy," said Ellie, turning to her cousin. "She's crazy." And she put her face into his chest and wept.

Roy was wearing a plaid robe of Julian's that was sizes too small for him. With one arm he began to pat Ellie's back.

"Oh," said Lucy, looking up at the two of them, "is that the story, Roy? Not that your uncle is crazy, not that your aunt is crazy—but that I am? And what else, Roy? I'm crazy, and what else? Oh, yes, Edward hates me. And what else? Surely there must be more? What other lies have you invented to justify what you have done to me?"

"But what has he done to you!" Ellie screamed. "You are crazy, you *are*! You're insane!"

She waited until Ellie had regained enough control over herself to listen. Irene Sowerby was now standing by her husband, preventing him from making any move toward Lucy; she had her face half hidden in his chest—in the chest of that man who cared nothing at all for her honor.

To Eleanor, Lucy said, "I am not Skippy Skelton, Ellie, if that's what you mean. Nor am I you. Nor am I your mother, though probably that is clear by now."

"Nothing is clear! Nothing you *say* is clear!" cried Ellie, even as her mother raised a hand to tell her to be quiet.

But Ellie cried, "I want to know what she even means!"

Lucy said, "I mean, Eleanor, that I am not promiscuous—I don't run around with married men. I mean that I am not a vain and idiotic child. I don't spend half my waking hours, and probably more, thinking about my hair and my clothes and my shoes—"

"What are you?" wailed Ellie. "The Virgin Mary?"

Julian stepped forward, freeing himself from his wife, who had begun to cry now too. "Enough, Eleanor."

"Daddy," Ellie wept.

"Daddy," repeated Lucy. "Wonderful Daddy."

"You get on the phone, Lucy," said Julian, breathing thickly. "You call your grandfather. You tell him to get over here and take you home . . . Now either you do it, or I will."

"But my home happens not to be here, Julian. My home is in Fort Kean, with my husband and my child." She looked up toward her husband. "Roy, we are going home. I want you to get ready."

All that moved were his eyes; they darted from one to the other of the people in the living room.

"Roy, did you hear me? We're returning to our own home."

He remained motionless and silent.

"Of course," she said, "the choice is yours, Roy. You can either be a man about it, and return with me and Edward, or you can follow the advice of this most worthy—"

"Lucy!" Roy threw his hands over his head. "For God's sake, cut it out!"

"But I can't, Roy!" Cut it out, indeed! "Nor can you! Oh, you can cut out, all of you, the fact that this uncle, this Daddy, this husband here, happens to be a filthy beast. You can fool yourselves about this cheat, and tell yourselves I'm insane oh, live with him, sleep with him, who cares! But cut it *out*? Oh, no, Roy—because there happens to be one more important fact to consider. I'll tell you why it so happens you can't take your uncle's advice, Roy—and I'll tell your uncle too. It so happens, Roy, and Julian, and Eleanor, and Irene, it so happens that I am pregnant."

"You are what?" whispered Julian.

Roy said, "Lucy . . . what do you mean?"

There was no need to raise her voice now to be heard. "I am going to have a baby."

Roy said, "I don't understand you."

"The daughter that you wanted, Roy, is alive inside me. Alive and growing."

Julian was saying, "What daughter? *Now* what in hell are you—?"

"Roy is going to be the father of a second child. It is our hope that it will be a girl."

Julian was looking up at Roy.

"Roy," she said, "go ahead. Tell them."

"Tell them *what*?"

"What you told me. Roy, tell them what you told me you wanted."

"Lucy," he answered, "I don't under*stand* you."

"Roy, are you actually now going to deny—"

"Pregnant?" said Julian. "Oh, not that old song and dance—"

"Ahh, but I *am*, Julian! I know you yourself happen not to like them, but facts are facts! I am pregnant with Roy Bassart's child. The child he wanted. The child he has been dreaming of all his life. Linda, Roy. Well, tell them!"

"Oh, no," Roy said.

"Roy, you *tell* them."

"But, Lucy—"

"Roy Bassart, that snowy night—did you or did you not—I can't believe you will actually lie about this now too! Did you or did you not get out of bed—? Did you or did you not tell me—? Linda, Roy—Linda Sue!"

"But, Lucy; oh my God—we were just talking."

"*Talking!*"

He sank onto a step at the top of the landing, his head cradled in his hands. "Yes," he moaned.

"Just *talking*! Roy, do you seriously mean—"

"Daddy," cried Eleanor, "*do* something!"

But Julian had already started after Lucy, who was advancing toward the stairs.

Swiftly she turned on him. "Don't you dare lay a finger on me. Not if you know what is good for you, you whoremonger."

"You get your ass down here," he said fiercely.

"I am a woman, Mr. Sowerby. You may think I'm a twerp like your daughter, but I am not! You will not treat me like nothing. No one will! I am pregnant, whether it suits you or not. I have a family to protect, whether that pleases you or not. Now, Roy," she said, turning once again and making for the stairs.

"Oh, no," said her husband, still with his head in his hands. "I can't take any more. I really can't."

"Oh, but you can, Roy. Because you have made me pregnant again, Roy!"

"Roy," called Julian as Lucy broke for upstairs, "stop her!"

"Roy," she cried, "we are getting Edward! We are going!"

He raised his face, which was wet with tears. "But he's *asleep.*"

"Roy—move—" Then Julian's hand fell upon her once again. She kicked backward—the hand grasped and caught her ankle. Meanwhile Roy's face was moving up—to block her way! Her husband, who should be protecting her! defending her! shielding her! guarding her! instead stood between herself and her child, herself and her home, between herself and the life of a woman!

"Get her!" said Julian. "*Roy!*"

"No!" cried Lucy, and with no choice left, brought her hand up from behind her, and closing her eyes, swung it with all her might.

And had the vision once again.

INNOCENT

When she opened her eyes, she saw Roy standing over her; he was holding his mouth. She herself was stretched across the stairway.

Then above her on the landing, in his undershorts and shirt, a blanket dragging in one hand, she saw little Edward looking down.

He began to shriek, either at the blood on his mother's hand or the blood on his father's face. Eleanor, who had been hovering over Lucy, swept up the stairs, lifted the screaming child and carried him away.

They could not get her to let go of the banister, so she remained across the stairs while Julian stood on the step below her, holding firmly to the back of her coat, and Irene telephoned to Daddy Will.

He came, and moved her down the stairway, and through the hall to the door. Every light was on in the Sowerby house when Willard backed the car out of the driveway and drove her home from The Grove.

—

Father Damrosch.

Where was a window? Where was a wall? She was under a blanket. She reached out into the dark. *I am only a freshman.*

She was in a bed. In her own bedroom. She was in Liberty Center.

How long had she been sleeping?

She had let him lead her up the stairs and cover her with a blanket . . . She had been crying . . . He had been sitting in the chair beside the bed . . . And then she must have slept.

But every minute that passed was a minute lost to those who would destroy her. She must act!

Father Damrosch!

But what can he do? Father Damrosch, why can't you *do* something? She could see him—black hair that he combed with his fingers, and a great swinging jaw, and that long beautiful stride that even the Protestant girls swooned over when they spotted him in his collar rounding a corner downtown. "Father *Dam*rosch!" calls one of the girls who knows him. "Father *Dam*rosch!" He waves—"Hi"—and disappears, while they all fall moaning into one another's arms . . .

And there, bouncing, swaying, soaring from her seat, there is Lucy, off to her first retreat. And Father Damrosch, swaying too, over the enormous wheel of the bus. And the other girls, rising in their seats, then crashing down, and gazing off at the black and flashing woods like condemned prisoners being driven to the place of execution; as though shackled together, they hang together arm in arm. Someone in the back begins the singing—"Pack up your troubles in your old kit bag—" but only a voice or two joins in, and then there is just the racket again of the old parish bus. It leaps forward and lands hard, and with winter overhead, aching to move down, and the horizon pushing up a last crust of light, the mood is of a race against disaster. A bird shoots past the window, its underside illumined red; it is swinging away, behind her head, and as she twists in her seat to follow its flight, the words go plunging through her, the words of Saint Teresa: God! Lamb! Astray!

"Whoa!" bellows Father Damrosch, his Army boots pumping down on the brake pedal. "Whoa," and they swerve, so that legs spring up and skulls go rocking together. "Whoa there, Nelly," and the girls giggle.

Clinging tightly to the belt of Kitty's coat, she shuffles in her unclasped galoshes down the dark aisle of the bus. As though falling from a cliff, she drops through the open door onto the convent grounds, expecting to see fires burning.

She waits alone by the side of the bus, holding tight to Daddy Will's hunting satchel. She hears Kitty calling for her and ducks around to the back. No one can see her there. She bites into the cold dark air—to hear it snap like a hard apple, to take between her teeth a pure hard clear thing, to devour . . . Oh, she cannot wait for her first Communion! Only, she must not bite down. No, no, it will melt down into the grooves of her mouth, and stream into her body, His body, His blood . . . *and then something will happen.*

But suppose it was what secretly she prayed for? "No!" She stands alone behind the bus, her two watering eyes taking in the dark shapes, the looming figures—the priests, the nuns, the girls lining up and marching into the dark; the pickup trucks, the buses, the cars, flashing lights and rumbling away . . . She hears the tires crackling over the gravel—what would it sound like, bone beneath wheels? Inside, that is all they are, just skeletons; inside, all of them are the same. She has learned the names of every human bone in her biology class—the tibia, the scapula, the femur . . . Oh, why can't people be good? Inside, they are only bones and strings and blood, kidneys and brains and glands and teeth and arteries and veins. Why, why can't they just be good?

"Father Damrosch!"

"Who is it back there?"

". . . Lucy."

He makes his way along the side of the bus. "You all right? Lucy Nelson?"

"Yes."

"What's the trouble? You bus-sick, Lucy? You go up there and get your room. Well, what's the matter?"

Her hand reaches out and finds a motionless tire.

"Father Damrosch . . ." But can she tell him? She has not even told Kitty. She has not even told Saint Teresa. No one knows the horrible thing she really wants. "Father Damrosch . . ." She wedges her mitten down between the ridges of the tire, and into the side of her mackinaw hood, mumbles what she can no longer keep a secret— ". . . to kill my father."

"Speak up, Lucy, so I can hear you. *You* want to—"

"No! No! I want Jesus to! In a car crash! In a fall! When he's drunk and stinks and is drunk!" She is weeping. "Oh, Father Damrosch," she says, "I think I'm committing a terrible sin. I *know* I am, but I can't help it."

She presses her face against him. She feels him waiting. "Oh, Father, tell me, tell me, is it a sin? He's so bad. He's so wicked."

"Lucy, you know not of what spirit you are."

". . . No? Please, then, please—what spirit am I?"

Then she is with the sisters. Between the swishing cloaks she moves to the chapel. The candles waver all around—and above, the suffering Lord. O God! Lamb! Astray! O Jesus, who does not kill! Who comforts! Who saves! Who redeemeth us all! O Holy Glorious Gleaming Loving Healing Jesus who does not kill—*make my father a father!*

By Sunday night she is so run-down from praying that she hardly has the strength to speak. The other girls are jabbering on the side steps of St. Mary's, waiting to be picked up and taken home; in her pocket she clutches the black veil given her by Sister Angelica of the Passion. "Patience. Faith. Suffering. The little way, remember," said Sister Angelica. "I know, I will," said Lucy. "To destroy takes no patience," said Sister Angelica. "I know," said Lucy, "I know that." "Anybody can destroy. A hoodlum can destroy." "I know, I know." "To save—" "Yes, yes. Oh, thank you, Sister . . ."

"Hey, Lucy Nelson." Her father is waving at her from the car. All around her the other girls are running and shouting —horns are blowing, car doors opening and slamming shut. Everyone seems so proud! so happy! so alive! It is cold and black, clear and glittery, a Sunday night, and they are all stepping into warm cars to be driven to warm houses, to warm baths, to warm milk, to warm beds. "Please!" she prays. And so, with the others, like the others, she rushes to the door her father has pushed open.

Father Damrosch looks like something black burning as he stands directing traffic in the headlights of the cars. "Good night, Lucy."

"Yes, good night."

Her father tips his cap to the priest. Father Damrosch waves. "Hi, there. Good evening."

Lucy pulls shut the door. To Father Damrosch she calls out the window, "Bye," and out the drive they go.

"Welcome back to civilization," he says.

Let him be redeemed! Make him good! O Jesus, he is only someone gone astray! That's all!

"That's not funny," she says.

"Well, I just can't be funny right off the bat, you know." Silence. "How'd the revival meeting go?"

"Retreat."

They drive. "You didn't catch cold, I hope. You sound like you caught cold."

"They took very good care of us, Father. It's a convent. It's very beautiful, and they have plenty of heat, thank you."

But she does not want to fight. O Jesus, I don't want to be sarcastic ever again. *Help me!* "Daddy—Sunday, come with me."

"Come with you where, Goosie?"

"Please. You must. To Mass."

He cannot help himself; he smiles.

"Don't laugh at me," she cries. "It's serious."

"Well, Lucy, I am just an old-fashioned Lutheran—"

"But you don't *go.*"

"Well, when I was a boy I did. When I was your age I surely did go."

"Daddy, you know not of what spirit you are!"

He takes his eyes from the road. "And who said that, Goosie? Your priest friend?"

"Jesus!"

"Well," he says, shrugging, "nobody knows everything, of course." But he is smiling again.

"But tomorrow—don't joke with me! Don't tease! Tomorrow you'll be sick again, you know you will."

"You let me worry about tomorrow."

"You'll be drunk again."

"Hold it now, young lady—"

"But you won't be saved! You will not be redeemed!"

"Now listen, you, you may be a big religious person over in that church, but to me, you know, you are who you are."

"You're a sinner!"

"Now *enough*!" he says. "You hear me? That is enough," and he pulls the car into the driveway. "And I'll tell you something else too. If this is how you come home after going away on your so-called religious weekend, then maybe going away is something we are going to have to think twice about giving permission for, freedom of religion or not."

"But if you don't change, I swear to you, I'll become a nun."

"You will, will you?"

"Yes!"

"Well, one, I never heard of them having nuns who were only in their first year of high school—"

"When I'm eighteen I can do anything! And legally too!"

"When you are eighteen, my little friend, and if you still want to dress up like Halloween, and have a prune face, and be afraid of regular life, which is what a nun happens to be, in my estimation—"

"But you don't know! Sister Angelica is not afraid of regular life! None of the sisters are! I'll become a nun, and there is nothing you can do to stop me!"

He pulls the key from the ignition. "Well, they have sure wasted no time turning you into a real Catholic, I'll say that for them. You have got all the answers in about a month's time, don't you? You have got your own way of believing, and that's the only way anybody else in the world can believe. And that's your idea of religious freedom, that you said you were entitled to. Brother," he said, and opened the door.

"I'll become a nun. I swear it."

"Well, if you want to run away from life, you go right ahead."

She watches as he cuts across the lawn, and up the porch stairs. He pounds the snow from his boots, and enters the house.

"Jesus! Saint Teresa! Somebody!"

One month of winter passes; then another. She tells Father Damrosch everything. "The world is imperfect," he says. "But why?" "We cannot expect it to be other than it is." "But—why not?" "Because we are weak, we are corrupt. Because we are sinners. Evil is the nature of mankind." "Everyone? Every person in mankind?" "Everyone does evil, yes." "But, Father Damrosch—you don't." "I sin. Of course I sin." What does he do? How can she ask? "But when will it stop being evil?" she asks; "when will the world be not evil?" "When Our Lord comes again." "But by then . . ." "What, Lucy?" "Well, I don't mean to sound selfish, Father . . . but not just me, but every-body alive now . . . well, they'll all be dead. Won't they?" "This is not our life, Lucy. This is the prelude to our life." "I know that, Father, it's not that I don't believe that . . ." But she cannot go on. She lives too much in the here and now. Sister Angelica is right. That is her sin.

Sunday after Sunday she stays with Kitty through Mass, twice. And prays: *Make him a father!* then home to see what has happened. But Sunday after Sunday there is waiting for her only leg of lamb, lima beans, baked potato, mint jelly, Parker House rolls, pie and milk. Nothing changes, nothing ever changes. When, *when* will it happen? And what will it look like? His Spirit will enter . . . But who? and how?

Then the Friday night. She is at the dining table with her homework; her mother is in the parlor, reading a magazine and soaking her feet; the door opens. He pulls at the shade and it slips down off its fixture. She jumps to her feet, but her mother sits without moving. And her father is saying such terrible, horrible things! What should she *do*? She lives too much in the here and the now as it is. This is only the prelude to our life. The nature of mankind is evil. Christ will come again, she thinks, as her father pulls the pan from beneath her mother's feet and pours the water out onto the rug. *The nature of mankind is evil. Christ will come again*—but she can't wait! In the meantime this man is ruining their life! In the meantime they are being destroyed! Oh, Jesus, come! Now! You must! Saint Teresa! Then she rushes to the phone. "I want the police. At my house." And within minutes they arrive. I want the police, she says, and they come. Wearing pistols, it turns out. She watches while they take him away to a place where he can no longer do them any harm.

—

As she dialed the Bassarts', Daddy Will stepped into the kitchen.

"Lucy," he said. "Honey, it is three-thirty in the morning. Why are you up? What are you doing?"

"Leave me alone."

"Lucy, you cannot telephone people—"

"I know what I am doing."

At the other end her father-in-law said, "Hello?"

"Lloyd, this is Lucy."

Willard sat down at the kitchen table. "Lucy," he pleaded.

"Lloyd, your son Roy has kidnaped Edward and abandoned me. He is hiding out at the Sowerbys'. He has refused to return to Fort Kean. He has put himself into the hands of Julian Sowerby, and something must be done to stop that man immediately. They have constructed a network of lies, and they are planning to go into a courtroom with it. They are planning to go to a judge and tell him that I am an incompetent mother and Roy is a wonderful father—and he is going to try to divorce me, your son, and get custody of my child. They have made all this perfectly clear, and they must be stopped before they take a single step. They have already begun to lie to Edward, that is perfectly clear—and unless someone intervenes over there, and instantly, they are going to brainwash and brainwash that little defenseless three-and-a-half-year-old child until they can get him, a baby, to go before a judge and say he hates his own mother. But you know, Lloyd, even if they don't—you know full well that if it weren't for me he would never have been allowed into this world in the first place. Everybody else would have scraped him down a sewer, or put him into an orphanage, or given him away, or left him to roam the world alone, I suppose, without a family, without a name, and now they are going to try to establish in the courtroom that my own child would rather live with his father than with me, and that is absurd and ridiculous, and it can't be, and it isn't true, and you must step into this, Lloyd, and immediately. You are Roy's father—"

Daddy Will's hand was on her back. "Leave me alone!" she said. "*Lloyd?*"

He had hung up.

"Please," she said to her grandfather, "*please do not interfere*. You are not capable of understanding what is going on. You are an impotent and helpless man. You always were and you still are, and if it weren't for you, none of this might have begun in the first place. So please, leave this to *me*!"

She was dialing the Bassarts' once again as her grandmother came to the kitchen door. "What is that child doing, Willard? It is the middle of the night."

He looked at her, unable to speak.

"Lloyd," said Lucy into the phone, "this is Lucy again. We were cut off."

"Look," said her father-in-law, "go to sleep."

"Didn't you hear a word of what I have been telling you?"

"I heard it, Lucy. You better go to sleep."

"Don't tell me to go to sleep, Lloyd! Sleep is not the issue at a time like this! Tell me what you intend to do about your son, and your brother-in-law Julian, and their plan!"

"I am telling you nothing," Lloyd Bassart said. "I believe it is you who is going to have to do the telling, Lucy. I am not very happy about what I have heard, Lucy. Not one bit," he said ominously.

"Tell what? Tell who? I am pregnant! Do you know that? That's what I have to tell—I am pregnant!"

"I am afraid I am not going to choose to talk to you any longer in this condition."

"But have you heard what I just said? My condition is that I am pregnant with a second child!"

"As I said, I have heard an earful. I have heard plenty."

"Lies! If it's from them it is lies! I am speaking the truth, Lloyd, the only truth. I am pregnant! He cannot leave me at a time like this!"

"Good night, Lucy."

"Lloyd, you can't hang up! You're supposed to be so good, so honest—so respectable! You better not hang up on me! Lloyd, four years ago—it is exactly what he wanted to do then. I was eighteen years old, and he wanted to run then too. Exactly what you would not let him do *yourself.* Lloyd, it is the same thing—exactly the same as then!"

"Oh, is it?" he said.

"Yes!"

"Yes is right!" It was Alice Bassart.

"Alice, get off," said Lloyd.

"You cheat, you no-good cheat—you tricked our son! And now again!"

"Alice, I will take care of this."

"I tricked *him?*" said Lucy.

"Took our son, with a scheming trick! Miss Tomboy! Miss Sarcastic! Miss Sneerface!"

"Alice!"

"But he tricked *me*, Alice! Tricked me to think he was a man, when he's a mouse, a monster! A moron! He's a pansy, that's what your son is, the worst and weakest pansy there ever was!"

"Willard!" said Berta.

Daddy Will was standing over the phone, right behind her. "Don't you—" she said over her shoulder, "—dare—"

But he brought his hand down upon the phone and held it there, breaking the connection.

"What do you think you are doing?" she cried. "The world is caving in! The world is on fire!"

"Honey, Lucy, it is four A.M."

"But haven't you heard a word I've said? Don't you hear what they are trying to do to me? Don't you understand what all these good, respectable people really are? I am pregnant! Does that mean nothing to anyone? *I am pregnant and my husband refuses to be responsible!*"

"Lucy," he said softly, "in the morning, honey, if that is really so—"

"I am not waiting for any morning. By morning—" She tried to yank the phone from his hands.

"No, honey, no. That's got to be enough right now."

"But the lies are growing *every minute*! They are saying I tricked him into marrying me. When *he* seduced *me*! He made me do it in the back of that car, insisted and insisted and insisted, and wouldn't stop, ever, and finally against my will, to show him—to let him—I was seventeen years old—and now they're saying *I* tricked *him*! As though I wanted him. Wanted a *him* like that, ever! I wish he were dead, that's what I wish. I wish he had never been born." She glared at Willard. "Give me that phone."

"No."

"If you do not give me that phone, Daddy Will, then I shall have to take measures of my own. Either you give me that phone and let me call his father . . . because I want to tell that Lloyd Bassart that he is not going to be such a pillar in the community, if he doesn't stop this thing, and stop it now. Either you give me that phone—"

"No, Lucy."

"But *he* seduced *me*! Don't you see that? And now they are saying that I seduced him! Because there is nothing they won't say against me. Nothing they won't stoop to, to destroy me. Julian Sowerby will stop at nothing—don't you understand? He hates women! He hates me! He's trying to crush my life because I know the truth! And I will not let that happen!"

"Call the doctor, Willard. Dial the doctor," Berta said.

"Call a *what?*" cried Lucy.

"Berta, in the morning."

"Willard, now."

"Oh yes, oh sure," said Lucy to her grandmother. "Oh, wouldn't you like that? You've been waiting all these years to do me in—because I see through you too, you—you selfish-hearted bitch. Call a *doctor?*" She shook her fists at the two of them. "*I am pregnant!* I need a husband, not a doctor—a husband for myself and a father for my child—"

"Dial the doctor," said Berta.

But he continued to hold the phone. "Lucy," he said, "won't you just go to bed now?"

"But can you not get it into your *head*—Julian Sowerby is stealing Edward! A man who is a whoremonger! And they all know it. And they don't care! He buys women with money, and nobody cares! Do you understand what I am *saying* to you?"

"Yes, honey."

"Then what are you going to do about it? The world is full of fiends and monsters, and you do absolutely nothing, and you never did! You listen to *her*," she said, pointing to her grandmother. "But I don't! And I won't!"

She started from the kitchen, but Berta stood in the doorway.

"Let me through, please."

Her grandmother said, "Where are you going?"

"To the police station."

"No," said Daddy Will. "No, Lucy."

"Let me by, Grandmother dear. Daddy Will, tell her to let me by, if you have any power over your own wife. I am going upstairs to get my coat and my shoes, and then I am going to the police station. Because they are not getting away with this, none of them. And if they have to come and arrest them all, Roy and Julian and that famous good man, Lloyd Bassart, then that is what they will have to do. Because you cannot steal a child! You cannot ruin a life! You cannot walk out on a marriage and a family! Let me through, please, Grandmother, I am going upstairs for my coat."

"Berta," said Daddy Will, "let her go."

"And if you call a doctor once I turn my back, Daddy Will, then you are as bad as they are. I want you to know that."

"Let her go, Berta."

"Willard—"

"I'll call," he said, nodding.

"Well," said Lucy, "the truth will out, won't it, Daddy Will? I always held out some hope for you, if you care to know. But I was sadly mistaken. Too bad," she said as she stepped through the doorway and proceeded up the stairs. The door to her mother's room was closed; she must be awake in there, but as always, too timid and frightened to confront what was happening in her own family.

When she was dressed for the outdoors she came into the hall, and before heading down the stairs and off to the police station, she stopped at her mother's door. Should she leave this instant and let the words spoken by her mother that afternoon be the last ever to pass between them? Because once Edward had been returned and disaster averted, she would never again set foot in this house.

In the parlor below she could hear her grandparents talking, but what they were saying she could not make out. Did it matter? It was clear enough which side they had chosen. She had wept the whole story to Daddy Will as he drove her through the dark town to the house—and he had comforted her. In her exhaustion he had helped her onto the bed, covered her to the chin with a blanket, told her she must rest now, told her that in the morning he would take care of everything—and like one who did not understand what she had understood so long ago, like a fool, like an innocent, she had let his words and her despair drag her down into dreams of another world, another here, another now, dreams of sweet Jesus and Father Damrosch and Sister Angelica of the Passion. And now she had awakened to discover that he too had turned against her.

Oh, how absurd this all was! How unnecessary! Why must they force her always to the extreme? Why must they bring this down upon themselves when the simple and honorable solution was always and forever at hand? If only they did their duty! If only they would be men!

A doctor. That was who they were waiting for down in the parlor. Dr. Eglund! To give her a pill to make life rosy by morning! To give her a good old-fashioned talking-to! Or was Dr. Eglund a blind? At long last was she to be the bene-factor of an abortion designed to get everybody else off the hook? Yes, anything, *anything*, no matter how it might debase and mortify her—so long as it spared all those respectable peo-ple from personal burden and public shame. Oh, but shame was surely going to fall upon them all, once it became known that she had had to be driven up to The Grove in a squad car, in order to recover what they would steal, and shatter, and destroy.

For that was the choice they had left her. Surely she was not going to return alone to Fort Kean, and leave Edward behind to be assaulted with lies, to be readied by her enemies and his to be a witness against his own mother. She was certainly not going to oblige them by being idiot enough to step into a court of law with Mr. Sowerby and his lawyer, either—to op-pose her pennies to Julian's millions, oppose her scruples to the unprincipled techniques of his attorney, as they pressed their case from one court to another, and the costs mounted, and the lies were piled one atop the other. Oh, just imagine them telling the court how she—a seventeen-year-old high school girl, hopelessly innocent of all sexual experience—had seduced and deceived into marriage a man who happened to have been three years her senior and a veteran of the United States Army. Oh no, she was not about to wait patiently for that—or to wait for Ellie Sowerby, that noted authority on mental illness, to break into tears and testify in a courtroom that in her professional opinion Lucy Bassart was insane, and always had been. Nor did she intend to be a silent witness to that pathetic moment when her own grandfather was called to the stand, and proceeded to tell the judge how he himself fig-ured that maybe the best thing for Lucy was a heart-to-heart chat with the family doctor . . . No, she did not intend to be frightened of what they themselves had given her no choice now but to do to save the lives of herself, and her children, born and unborn.

—

She opened her mother's door. It was almost dawn.

"I am going now, Mother."

The form beneath the blanket did not move. Her mother lay huddled on the half of the bed nearest the window, her face hidden behind one hand. Lucy pulled on her gloves. On the back of her left hand there was a scratch, where Roy's tooth had dragged over her flesh.

"I know you're awake, Mother. I know you heard what was going on downstairs."

She remained motionless under the blanket.

"I came in here to say something to you, Mother. I'm going to speak whether you respond or not. It would be easier if you could bring yourself to sit up and face me. It would certainly be more dignified, Mother."

But there was to be no dignity; that was her mother's decision, again and again and again. She only turned her face into the pillow, showing her daughter the back of her head.

"Mother, what I heard earlier in the day—yesterday, it was —about my father—I allowed it to upset me. That's what I want to tell you. After we left here I thought about what you had said to me. You said, if you remember, Mother, that he was where I always wanted him. You said you hoped that I was happy now. And so I went back to Fort Kean, thinking, 'Oh, what a terrible person I am.' I began to think, if it weren't for me, he could have been spared whatever he is now going through. I thought, 'He has stayed away almost four years now—and why? He has been afraid even to show his face here. He has had to write to her through a post-office box—all because of me.' Then I tried to tell myself, no, no, I wasn't the reason . . . But do you know something, Mother? I am! Because of his fear of me he is not here—that's true. Because he is terrified of my judgment. And do you know? That is the only human response that man has ever had, Mother. Staying away—that is the only thing he has been able to do successfully in his entire life."

She heard her mother weeping. All at once the sunlight came into the room, and she saw a letter on the blanket. It was cradled in a fold where it must have fallen from her mother's hand. She had taken it with her into her bed. *My God, there is no limit, there is no end.*

As she charged toward the bed, her mother turned to see what was about to happen. And the fright in the woman's eyes, the grief in her face—oh, her utter hopelessness! "Mother, *he* is who destroyed our lives." She grabbed the letter from the bed. "*Him!*" she cried, shaking it over her head. "*This!*"

And then she ran. For Daddy Will burst into the doorway of the bedroom, dressed now in trousers and a shirt.

"Lucy—" He caught her by the coat, and she heard a tearing sound as she broke away from him and ran wildly down the stairs. Now Grandma Berta was moving toward her through the parlor, but she screamed, "No! You selfish, selfish—" and when her grandmother jumped back, she was able to fling open the door and rush out onto the porch.

"You stop," Berta called. "Stop her!"

But there was no one on the street, no one between herself and downtown.

Then her legs were shooting out from under her. Her elbows struck the icy ground a second before her chin; a sick sensation went through her, but she was instantly to her feet and across the street, heading toward Broadway. There was an inch of fresh snow over the cleared walks, and patches of ice underfoot, and she knew that if she fell again she would be overtaken, but she ran as fast as she was able to in coat and galoshes, for she had to get to the police station before they could stop her. Daddy Will was already out on the porch; she saw him there in the moment she took to look back. Then a car was pulling up before the house, and Daddy Will was headed down the stairs in his shirtsleeves. Dr. Eglund! They were going to come after her in the car! The car would be alongside her in seconds! Then people would be at their windows, doors would fly open, others would come running out of their houses to give aid to the two old men—to prevent her from getting justice done!

Quickly she turned up a driveway, slid between a car and a house, and plunged across the thick white crust of someone's yard. A dog barked, and she went sprawling, her foot caught upon a low wire fence buried in a drift. Then she was up, running again. There was a bluish light over everything, and the only noise was the packing sound that rose as her galoshes hammered into the snow and she ran, ran for the ravine.

But they would be waiting when she arrived! Once they had lost sight of her, they would go directly to the station house. Two old men, thoroughly confused about what actually was going on, without the slightest sense of all that was at stake, would tell the police that she was on her way. And what would the police do? Telephone Roy! By the time she had made her way across town to the ravine, and then up to Broadway by way of the river, her husband would be at the station house, waiting. And Julian! And Lloyd Bassart! And she would arrive last, her coat thick with snow, her face red and wet, breathless and exhausted, looking like some runaway child—*which was how she would be treated*. Of course! They would have so distorted the facts that instead of the police instantly coming to her aid, they would turn her over to her grandfather, to the doctor . . .

But would those others settle for that now? A man like Julian Sowerby knew only one thing—to have his ugly way. His own wife knew, his daughter knew, what he was *everybody* knew, but as long as he continued to pay everybody off, what did they care? She could hear him, hear them all, promising this, promising that, begging forgiveness, and then going right on being just what they always had been. Because they simply will not reform! They simply will not change! All they will do is get worse and worse! Why were they against a mother and a child? Why were they against a family, and a home, and love? Why were they against a beautiful life, and for an ugly one? Why did they fight her and mistreat her and deny her, when all she wanted was what was right!

But where to now? Because she knew what it would mean to continue on to the police station, she knew what Julian Sowerby would try to do; she knew the use to which such a man would put this opportunity, how he would seize it to destroy her, once and for all. Yes, because she knew right from wrong, because she saw her duty and did it, because she knew the truth and spoke it, because she would not sit by and endure treachery and betrayal, because she would not let them steal her little boy, and coddle a grown-up man, and scrape out of her body the new life beginning to grow there—they would try to make it seem that *she* was the guilty party, that *she* was the criminal!

. . . Where then? To turn back made no sense at all; there was no *back*. But to run straight into the arms of her enemies—straight into their lies and treachery! She turned and rushed back up the driveway from which she had emerged; she turned this way, the other way, toward Broadway, away from Broadway, and back out to the street again. She scuttled around corners; she withdrew against walls; she stepped deep into drifts. Powder came down into her face. She pressed her head to a drainpipe encased in ice. She fell. Her skin burned. A window flew up; she ran. The blue light became gray. She began to come upon the footprints she had left in the snow min utes earlier.

Then she was looking up into the kitchen window at the rear of Blanshard Muller's house. With one shoulder she pushed open the garage door, slipped and closed the door behind her. Gripping her side, she leaned across the trunk of the car, lowered her head and closed her eyes. Colors swam. She tried not to think. *Why should he hate me like poison? He doesn't! He can't! That's Roy's lie!*

With tremulous breaths she filled her lungs, and the sensation that all sound was being pushed outward from the inside of her head diminished. She began to be swept with chills, then grew strangely calm at the sight of the objects arranged against the side wall of the garage: a coil of garden hose, a shovel, half a bag of cement, a deflated tire tube, a pair of hip boots.

She tried the door of the car. If she could just have a moment to rest, to think; no, not to think . . .

The noise was sharp and clattering. She jumped around; there was nothing. Through the garage window she could see into the kitchen; she was able to discern on the walls the cabinets her mother had chosen for Mr. Muller. Again she heard a crash, and this time saw the ice sliding down off the roof into the yard. She stepped into the car.

And now what? Morning had come . . . If a light went on in the kitchen, how quickly could she be out of the garage? Suppose he had seen her already and was sneaking around by way of the front door? How could she explain herself? What story would he believe? What would she be able to tell him, other than the truth?

And then? She would tell him everything, what they had already done, what they planned to do; and then? He would push open the garage door, back the car out the driveway, he would take her to The Grove himself. He would ring the Sowerby bell and wait beside her on the front porch, and then he would make it clear to Irene Sowerby why he and Lucy were there . . . But if he were to come upon her unexpectedly, discover her kneeling, hiding, in the back seat of his car—he would jump to the conclusion that she was in the wrong! She must go immediately around to the back door then—no, the front door—and ring, say that she was sorry to be bothering him so early in the morning, that she understood this was totally out of the ordinary, but that she was in desperate need of . . . But would he even believe her? It was so monstrous, what they were doing, would he even believe that it could be? Might he not listen, thinking to himself all the while, "Of course, that's only her side of the story." Or suppose he listened, and then telephoned her mother to check on the story. What was Lucy Bassart to him, anyway? Nothing! Her mother and her father had seen to that. "Sorry," he would say, "but don't see that it's my affair." Of course! Why would he come to her aid, when even those closest to her had turned against her? No, there was only one person she would rely upon; it was now as it had always been—the one to save her was herself.

She must hide; she must find some hideaway nearby, and then when the moment was right, she would swoop down, make off with Edward, and the two of them would disappear.

To *where*? Oh, to some place where they would never be found! Some place where she would have her second child, and where the three of them could begin a new life. And then never again would she be so foolish and gullible and dreamy as to place the welfare of herself or of her offspring in any hands but her own. She would be mother and father to them both, and so the three of them—herself, her little boy, and soon her little girl too—would live without cruelty, without treachery, without betrayal; yes, without men.

But if Edward would not come? If she called and he ran the other way? "*Your face is all black! Go away!*"

In her glove she was still carrying the letter she had taken from her mother's bed. She had sunk to her waist in drifts of snow; she had tripped and fallen over backyard fences; she had pushed open the door of the garage, climbed into the back seat of the car—and still the letter addressed to her mother was clutched in her glove.

She should be on her way now. The moment was right. By now they were all at the police station. Soon they would disperse and begin to search. There was not a second to waste, not on something so ridiculous as a letter from him. She had barely permitted him to enter her thoughts since the day of Edward's birth; she had driven him from their lives, then from her mind. There was clearly nothing to do with this letter but destroy it. And how appropriate that would be. To burn this letter, to scatter the ashes to the wind—that would be a most fitting ceremony indeed. Yes, goodbye, goodbye, brave and stalwart men. Goodbye, protectors and defenders, heroes and saviors. You are no longer needed, you are no longer wanted— alas, you have been revealed for what you are. Farewell, farewell, philanderers and frauds, cowards and weaklings, cheaters and liars. Fathers and husbands, farewell!

The letter consisted of one long sheet of writing paper. There were spaces to be filled out at the top, and then his message below. The page was closely covered with writing on both sides, and lined in blue, so that the prisoner's handwriting ran evenly from one end to the other.

She forced it back into its envelope. At any minute Blanshard Muller would be out of bed, down the stairs, out of the house—she would be discovered! And turned over to them— her enemies! So go!

But where? To a place where no one will think to look . . . to some place close enough for her to descend quickly upon the Sowerby house . . . in the afternoon, when he is at play in the yard . . . no, at night, when they are asleep . . . yes, in the night, while he sleeps too, bundle him off—"*Your face is poison! Your face is black! Put me down!*"

No! No! She must not weaken now. She must not weaken before their filthy lies. Whatever strength was required, she must find. Whatever daring, whatever boldness . . .

She removed the letter from the envelope once again. She

would read it, and destroy it—and then be off. Of course, she would read what he had written, and in his words find that which would harden her against the trials to come . . . the lying in wait . . . the kidnap . . . the flight . . . Oh, she did not know *what* was to come, but she must not be afraid! Against the cold and the dark, in her solitude, while she waited to free her child from his captors—"*Mamma, where have you been?*"—while she waited to rescue him—"*Oh, Mamma, take me away!*"—to flee with him to a better world, to a better life, all she would have to sustain her would be the power of her hatred, her loathing, her abhorrence of those monsters who so cruelly destroy the lives of innocent women and innocent children. Oh yes, read then, and remember the horror inflicted upon you and yours, the cruelty and the meanness inflicted willingly and without end. Yes, read what he has written, and in the face of hardship you will have the courage. Whatever the wretchedness, the desolation, you will be implacable. Because you must be! Because there is only you to save your son from just such men as this—to save your helpless, innocent daughter-to-be. Oh, yes, draw them down, these words of his, inscribe them on your heart, and then fearlessly set forth. Fearlessly, Lucy! Against all odds, but fearlessly nonetheless! For they are wrong, and you are right, and there is no choice: the good must triumph in the end! The good and the just and the true *must*—

NAME: D. Nelson   NO. 70561   DATE: Feb. 14.
TO WHOM: Mrs. Myra Nelson (WIFE)

Dearest Myra:

I guess I read your letter over about twenty times. There is no question about all the things you say. I was all that and probably more. As I've said before, I am so sorry and will be as long as I live that I have caused you so much embarrassment and pain. But now there is no doubt you are really forever free of trouble from me again. I presume the State of Florida will see to that. For me, it doesn't matter. All my life has been a more or less rough deal. No plans, no matter how good they were, ever seemed to work out. But it shouldn't be arranged to hurt the one who is closer to you than anything in the world. That is what is wrong.

One thing I feel better about is that you say there is no one else. That was more than I could stand to hear. I just couldn't stand to hear it. Remember just one thing, that I had nineteen years of happiness. That the only fly in the ointment was the inability to give you the things I wanted you to have. Maybe when I get out, if I last, I will be able to be some help to you financially, even if from a distance, if that's the way you still want it. But you must have a sponsor and a job to get out of here on your minimum and though I shouldn't be bothering you I wonder if you can think of anyone at all.

Of course it will depend upon how vindictive the "alleged Justice" is inclined to be anyway. There is a point where punishment becomes corrective. Beyond that, it becomes destructive. I've seen cases just since I have been here where Justice depended upon how you spelled it. Whether as Webster spelled and defined it or by spelling it with either a dollar sign or influence. Many times already I have seen cases where Justice was not "served" but purchased. I see how fellows become hard and bitter who there was a chance of helping.

But I will not dwell on these issues. Especially not today. Myra, Myra, the growing years seem to make the memories of the past more and more poignant. I miss you so much that it is worse than hunger. I said years ago that without you I would slide to hell in a hurry. I guess it was a prediction that came all too true. There are some names I could mention who I could have lived without all right, but Myra, Myra, Myra, never you.

O Myra, I had always hoped by this time in my life I could express this wish to you much more materially, but if you can forgive me, this will have to do until the State of Florida decrees otherwise:

> As years go by—with accelerated speed,
> We find with us, an ever growing need
> To recall to mind, and a wish to live,
> In that glorious past—to re-have and re-give.
>
> We bring to mind—the mistakes we made,
> The aches and hurts—that we've caused, I'm afraid
> Are brought in distinctly—with increasing pain
> Till we wish, with all heart—to re-do it again.
>
> Only to do it better—so that the pain is gone,
> And make them all the good things, all along.
> At least the great wish that would be really mine,
> That I could just once more—be your Valentine.

Your Faithful,
Duane

—

On the third night after Lucy's disappearance two kids from the high school drove out to Passion Paradise to be alone. Near midnight, at which hour the girl had to be home, they tried to start back to town and found that the tires of the car had sunk into the snow. At first the boy pushed from behind while his companion sat at the wheel pumping on the accelerator. Then he took a shovel from the trunk, and in the dark, while the girl held her gloves against her ears and begged him to hurry, he started to dig his way out.

In this way the body was found. It was fully clothed; in fact, the undergarments were frozen to the skin. Also, a sheet of lined paper was frozen to her cheek, and her hand was frozen to the paper. An early hypothesis, that the hand might have been raised to ward off a blow, was rejected when the coroner reported that aside from a small abrasion on the knuckle of the right hand, the body bore no wounds, bruises, or punctures, no marks of violence at all. Nor was there any indication that she had been sexually molested. Of pregnancy nothing was said, either because the medical examiner found no evidence, or because the investigation included only routine laboratory tests. The cause of death was exposure.

As to how long she had been lying there undiscovered, the medical examiner could only guess; the freezing temperatures had preserved the body intact, but judging from the depths of snow above and below the body, it was surmised that the young woman had probably been dead about thirty-six hours when she was found. If that was so, she had managed to survive up in Passion Paradise through a day and a night and on, somehow, into the following morning.

—

It was some months after the funeral, during one of those cold, fresh, wet springs such as they have in the middle of America, that the letters from the prison began to come directly to the house.

PORTNOY'S COMPLAINT

Portnoy's Complaint (pôrt´-noiz kəm-plănt´) *n.* [after Alexander Portnoy (1933–   )] A disorder in which strongly-felt ethical and altruistic impulses are perpetually warring with extreme sexual longings, often of a perverse nature. Spielvogel says: 'Acts of exhibitionism, voyeurism, fetishism, auto-eroticism and oral coitus are plentiful; as a consequence of the patient's "morality," however, neither fantasy nor act issues in genuine sexual gratification, but rather in overriding feelings of shame and the dread of retribution, particularly in the form of castration.' (Spielvogel, O. "The Puzzled Penis," *Internationale Zeitschrift für Psychoanalyse*, Vol. XXIV p. 909.) It is believed by Spielvogel that many of the symptoms can be traced to the bonds obtaining in the mother-child relationship.

THE MOST UNFORGETTABLE
CHARACTER I'VE MET

S HE was so deeply imbedded in my consciousness that for the first year of school I seem to have believed that each of my teachers was my mother in disguise. As soon as the last bell had sounded, I would rush off for home, wondering as I ran if I could possibly make it to our apartment before she had succeeded in transforming herself. Invariably she was already in the kitchen by the time I arrived, and setting out my milk and cookies. Instead of causing me to give up my delusions, however, the feat merely intensified my respect for her powers. And then it was always a relief not to have caught her between incarnations anyway—even if I never stopped trying; I knew that my father and sister were innocent of my mother's real nature, and the burden of betrayal that I imagined would fall to me if I ever came upon her unawares was more than I wanted to bear at the age of five. I think I even feared that I might have to be done away with were I to catch sight of her flying in from school through the bedroom window, or making herself emerge, limb by limb, out of an invisible state and into her apron.

Of course, when she asked me to tell her all about my day at kindergarten, I did so scrupulously. I didn't pretend to understand all the implications of her ubiquity, but that it had to do with finding out the kind of little boy I was when I thought she wasn't around—that was indisputable. One consequence of this fantasy, which survived (in this particular form) into the first grade, was that seeing as I had no choice, I became honest.

Ah, and brilliant. Of my sallow, overweight older sister, my mother would say (in Hannah's presence, of course: honesty was her policy too), "The child is no genius, but then we don't ask the impossible. God bless her, she works hard, she applies herself to her limits, and so whatever she gets is all right." Of me, the heir to her long Egyptian nose and clever babbling mouth, of me my mother would say, with characteristic restraint, "This *bonditt*? He doesn't even have to open a book—'A' in everything. Albert Einstein the Second!"

And how did my father take all this? He drank—of course, not whiskey like a *goy*, but mineral oil and milk of magnesia; and chewed on Ex-Lax; and ate All-Bran morning and night; and downed mixed dried fruits by the pound bag. He suffered —did he suffer!—from constipation. Her ubiquity and his constipation, my mother flying in through the bedroom window, my father reading the evening paper with a suppository up his ass . . . these, Doctor, are the earliest impressions I have of my parents, of their attributes and secrets. He used to brew dried senna leaves in a saucepan, and that, along with the suppository melting invisibly in his rectum, comprised *his* witchcraft: brewing those veiny green leaves, stirring with a spoon the evil-smelling liquid, then carefully pouring it into a strainer, and hence into his blockaded body, through that weary and afflicted expression on his face. And then hunched silently above the empty glass, as though listening for distant thunder, he awaits the miracle . . . As a little boy I sometimes sat in the kitchen and waited with him. But the miracle never came, not at least as we imagined and prayed it would, as a lifting of the sentence, a total deliverance from the plague. I remember that when they announced over the radio the explosion of the first atom bomb, he said aloud, "Maybe that would do the job." But all catharses were in vain for that man: his *kishkas* were gripped by the iron hand of outrage and frustration. Among his other misfortunes, I was his wife's favorite.

To make life harder, he loved me himself. He too saw in me the family's opportunity to be "as good as anybody," our chance to win honor and respect—though when I was small the way he chose to talk of his ambitions for me was mostly in terms of money. "Don't be dumb like your father," he would say, joking with the little boy on his lap, "don't marry beautiful, don't marry love—marry rich." No, no, he didn't like being looked down upon one bit. Like a dog he worked— only for a future that he wasn't slated to have. Nobody ever really gave him satisfaction, return commensurate with goods delivered—not my mother, not me, not even my loving sister, whose husband he still considers a Communist (though he is a partner today in a profitable soft-drink business, and owns his own home in West Orange). And surely not that billion-dollar

Protestant outfit (or "institution," as they prefer to think of themselves) by whom he was exploited to the full. "The Most Benevolent Financial Institution in America" I remember my father announcing, when he took me for the first time to see his little square area of desk and chair in the vast offices of Boston & Northeastern Life. Yes, before his son he spoke with pride of "The Company"; no sense demeaning himself by knocking them in public—after all, they had paid him a wage during the Depression; they gave him stationery with his own name printed beneath a picture of the *Mayflower*, their insignia (and by extension his, ha ha); and every spring, in the fullness of their benevolence, they sent him and my mother for a hotsy-totsy free weekend in Atlantic City, to a fancy *goyische* hotel no less, there (along with all the other insurance agents in the Middle Atlantic states who had exceeded the A.E.S., their annual expectation of sales) to be intimidated by the desk clerk, the waiter, the bellboy, not to mention the puzzled paying guests.

Also, he believed passionately in what he was selling, yet another source of anguish and drain upon his energies. He wasn't just saving his own soul when he donned his coat and hat after dinner and went out again to resume his work—no, it was also to save some poor son of a bitch on the brink of letting his insurance policy lapse, and thus endangering his family's security "in the event of a rainy day." "Alex," he used to explain to me, "a man has got to have an umbrella for a rainy day. You don't leave a wife and a child out in the rain without an umbrella!" And though to me, at five and six years of age, what he said made perfect, even moving, sense, that apparently was not always the reception his rainy-day speech received from the callow Poles, and violent Irishmen, and illiterate Negroes who lived in the impoverished districts that had been given him to canvass by The Most Benevolent Financial Institution in America.

They laughed at him, down in the slums. They didn't listen. They heard him knock, and throwing their empties against the door, called out, "Go away, nobody home." They set their dogs to sink their teeth into his persistent Jewish ass. And still, over the years, he managed to accumulate from The Company

enough plaques and scrolls and medals honoring his salesman-
ship to cover an entire wall of the long windowless hallway
where our Passover dishes were stored in cartons and our
"Oriental" rugs lay mummified in their thick wrappings of tar
paper over the summer. If he squeezed blood from a stone,
wouldn't The Company reward him with a miracle of its own?
Might not "The President" up in "The Home Office" get
wind of his accomplishment and turn him overnight from an
agent at five thousand a year to a district manager at fifteen?
But where they had him they kept him. Who else would work
such barren territory with such incredible results? Moreover,
there had not been a Jewish manager in the entire history of
Boston & Northeastern (Not Quite Our Class, Dear, as they
used to say on the *Mayflower*), and my father, with his eighth-
grade education, wasn't exactly suited to be the Jackie Robin-
son of the insurance business.

N. Everett Lindabury, Boston & Northeastern's president,
had his picture hanging in our hallway. The framed photograph had been awarded to my father after he had sold his
first million dollars' worth of insurance, or maybe that's what
came after you hit the ten-million mark. "Mr. Lindabury,"
"The Home Office" . . . my father made it sound to me like
Roosevelt in the White House in Washington . . . and all the
while how he hated their guts, Lindabury's particularly, with
his corn-silk hair and his crisp New England speech, the sons
in Harvard College and the daughters in finishing school, oh
the whole pack of them up there in Massachusetts, *shkotzim*
fox-hunting! playing polo! (so I heard him one night, bellowing behind his bedroom door)—and thus keeping him,
you see, from being a hero in the eyes of his wife and children.
What wrath! What fury! And there was really no one to unleash it on—except himself. "Why can't I move my bowels
—I'm up to my ass in prunes! Why do I have these headaches!
Where are my glasses! Who took my hat!"

In that ferocious and self-annihilating way in which so many
Jewish men of his generation served their families, my father
served my mother, my sister Hannah, but particularly me.
Where he had been imprisoned, I would fly: that was his
dream. Mine was its corollary: in my liberation would be his—
from ignorance, from exploitation, from anonymity. To this

day our destinies remain scrambled together in my imagination, and there are still too many times when, upon reading in
some book a passage that impresses me with its logic or its
wisdom, instantly, involuntarily, I think, "If only he could read
this. Yes! Read, and understand—!" Still hoping, you see, still
if-onlying, at the age of thirty-three . . . Back in my freshman
year of college, when I was even more the son struggling to
make the father understand—back when it seemed that it was
either his understanding or his life—I remember that I tore
the subscription blank out of one of those intellectual journals
I had myself just begun to discover in the college library, filled
in his name and our home address, and sent off an anonymous
gift subscription. But when I came sullenly home at Christmastime to visit and condemn, the *Partisan Review* was
nowhere to be found. *Collier's Hygeia, Look*, but where was his
Partisan Review? Thrown out unopened—I thought in my ar-
rogance and heartbreak—discarded unread, considered *junk*-
mail by this schmuck, this moron, this Philistine father of
mine!

I remember—to go back even further in this history of dis-
enchantment—I remember one Sunday morning pitching a
baseball at my father, and then waiting in vain to see it go
flying off, high above my head. I am eight, and for my birthday have received my first mitt and hardball, and a regulation bat that I haven't even the strength to swing all the way
around. My father has been out since early morning in his hat,
coat, bow tie, and black shoes, carrying under his arm the massive black collection book that tells who owes Mr. Lindabury
how much. He descends into the colored neighborhood each
and every Sunday morning because, as he tells me, that is the
best time to catch those unwilling to fork over the ten or fifteen measly cents necessary to meet their weekly premium pay-
ments. He lurks about where the husbands sit out in the
sunshine, trying to extract a few thin dimes from them before
they have drunk themselves senseless on their bottles of "Mor-
gan Davis" wine: he emerges from alleyways like a shot to
catch between home and church the pious cleaning ladies,
who are off in other people's houses during the daylight hours
of the week, and in hiding from him on weekday nights. "Uh
—oh," someone cries, "Mr. Insurance Man here!" and even

the children run for cover—the *children*, he says in disgust, so tell me, what hope is there for these niggers' ever improving their lot? How will they ever lift themselves if they ain't even able to grasp the importance of life insurance? Don't they give a single crap for the loved ones they leave behind? Because "they's all" going to die too, you know—"oh," he says angrily, "'they sho' is!'" Please, what kind of man is it, who can think to leave children out in the rain without even a decent umbrella for protection!

We are on the big dirt field back of my school. He sets his collection book on the ground, and steps up to the plate in his coat and his brown fedora. He wears square steel-rimmed spectacles, and his hair (which now I wear) is a wild bush the color and texture of steel wool; and those teeth, which sit all night long in a glass in the bathroom smiling at the toilet bowl, now smile out at me, his beloved, his flesh and his blood, the little boy upon whose head no rain shall ever fall. "Okay, Big Shot Ballplayer," he says, and grasps my new regulation bat somewhere near the middle—and to my astonishment, with his left hand where his right hand should be. I am suddenly overcome with such sadness: I want to tell him, *Hey, your hands are wrong*, but am unable to, for fear I might begin to cry—or he might! "Come on, Big Shot, throw the ball," he calls, and so I do—and of course discover that on top of all the other things I am just beginning to suspect about my father, he isn't "King Kong" Charlie Keller either.

Some umbrella.

—

It was my mother who could accomplish anything, who herself had to admit that it might even be that she was actually too good. And could a small child with my intelligence, with my powers of observation, doubt that this was so? She could make jello, for instance, with sliced peaches *hanging* in it, peaches just *suspended* there, in defiance of the law of gravity. She could bake a cake that tasted like a banana. Weeping, suffering, she grated her own horseradish rather than buy the *pishachs* they sold in a bottle at the delicatessen. She watched the butcher, as she put it, "like a hawk," to be certain that he did not forget to put her chopped meat through the kosher grinder. She would telephone all the other women in the building drying clothes on the back lines—called even the divorced *goy* on the top floor one magnanimous day—to tell them rush, take in the laundry, a drop of rain had fallen on our windowpane. What radar on that woman! And this is *before* radar! The energy on her! The thoroughness! For mistakes she checked my sums; for holes, my socks; for dirt, my nails, my neck, every seam and crease of my body. She even dredges the furthest recesses of my ears by pouring cold peroxide into my head. It tingles and pops like an earful of ginger ale, and brings to the surface, in bits and pieces, the hidden stores of yellow wax, which can apparently endanger a person's hearing. A medical procedure like this (crackpot though it may be) takes time, of course; it takes effort, to be sure—but where health and cleanliness are concerned, germs and bodily secretions, she will not spare herself and sacrifice others. She lights candles for the dead—others invariably forget, she religiously remembers, and without even the aid of a notation on the calendar. Devotion is just in her blood. She seems to be the only one, she says, who when she goes to the cemetery has "the common sense," "the ordinary common decency," to clear the weeds from the graves of our relatives. The first bright day of spring, and she has mothproofed everything wool in the house, rolled and bound the rugs, and dragged them off to my father's trophy room. She is never ashamed of her house: a stranger could walk in and open any closet, any drawer, and she would have nothing to be ashamed of. You could even eat off her bathroom floor, if that should ever become necessary. When she loses at mah-jongg she takes it like a sport, not-like-the-others-whose-names-she-could-mention-but-she-won't-not-even-Tilly-Hochman-it's-too-petty-to-even-talk-about-let's-just-forget-she-even-brought-it-up. She sews, she knits, she darns—she irons better even than the *schvartze*, to whom, of all her friends who each possess a piece of this grinning childish black old lady's hide, she alone is good. "I'm the only one who's good to her. I'm the only one who gives her a whole can of tuna for lunch, and I'm not talking *dreck*, either. I'm talking Chicken of the Sea, Alex. I'm sorry, I can't be a stingy person. Excuse me, but I can't live like that, even if it is 2 for 49. Esther Wasserberg leaves twenty-five cents in nickels around the house when Dorothy comes, and counts up afterwards to see it's all there.

Maybe I'm too good," she whispers to me, meanwhile running scalding water over the dish from which the cleaning lady has just eaten her lunch, alone like a leper, "but I couldn't do a thing like that." Once Dorothy chanced to come back into the kitchen while my mother was still standing over the faucet marked H, sending torrents down upon the knife and fork that had passed between the *schvartze*'s thick pink lips. "Oh, you know how hard it is to get mayonnaise off silverware these days, Dorothy," says my nimble-tongued mother—and thus, she tells me later, by her quick thinking, has managed to spare the colored woman's feelings.

When I am bad I am locked out of the apartment. I stand at the door hammering and hammering until I swear I will turn over a new leaf. But what is it I have done? I shine my shoes every evening on a sheet of last night's newspaper laid carefully over the linoleum; afterward I never fail to turn securely the lid on the tin of polish, and to return all the equipment to where it belongs. I roll the toothpaste tube from the bottom, I brush my teeth in circles and never up and down, I say "Thank you," I say "You're welcome," I say "I beg your pardon," and "May I." When Hannah is ill or out before supper with her blue tin can collecting for the Jewish National Fund, I voluntarily and out of my turn set the table, remembering always knife and spoon on the right, fork on the left, and napkin to the left of the fork and folded into a triangle. I would never eat *milchiks* off a *flaishedigeh* dish, never, never, never. Nonetheless, there is a year or so in my life when not a month goes by that I don't do something so inexcusable that I am told to pack a bag and leave. But what could it possibly be? Mother, it's me, the little boy who spends whole nights before school begins beautifully lettering in Old English script the names of his subjects on his colored course dividers, who patiently fastens reinforcements to a term's worth of three-ringed paper, lined and unlined both. I carry a comb and a clean hankie; never do my knicker stockings drag at my shoes, I see to that; my homework is completed weeks in advance of the assignment—let's face it, Ma, I am the smartest and neatest little boy in the history of my school! Teachers (as you know, as they have *told* you) go home happy to their husbands because of me. So what is it I have done? Will someone with the answer to that question please stand up! I am so awful she will not have me in her house *a minute longer*. When I once called my sister a cocky-doody, my mouth was immediately washed with a cake of brown laundry soap; this I understand. But banishment? What can I possibly have done!

Because she is good she will pack a lunch for me to take along, but then out I go, in my coat and my galoshes, and what happens is not her business.

Okay, I say, if that's how you feel! (For I have the taste for melodrama too—I am not in this family for nothing.) I don't need a bag of lunch! I don't need anything!

I don't love you any more, not a little boy who behaves like you do. I'll live alone here with Daddy and Hannah, says my mother (a master really at phrasing things just the right way to kill you). Hannah can set up the mah-jongg tiles for the ladies on Tuesday night. We won't be needing you any more.

Who cares! And out the door I go, into the long dim hall way. Who cares! I will sell newspapers on the streets in my bare feet. I will ride where I want on freight cars and sleep in open fields, I think—and then it is enough for me to see the empty milk bottles standing by our welcome mat, for the immensity of all I have lost to come breaking over my head. "I hate you!" I holler, kicking a galosh at the door; "you stink!" To this filth, to this heresy booming through the corridors of the apartment building where she is vying with twenty other Jewish women to be the patron saint of self-sacrifice, my mother has no choice but to throw the double-lock on our door. This is when I start to hammer to be let in. I drop to the doormat to beg forgiveness for my sin (which is what again?) and promise her nothing but perfection for the rest of our lives, which at that time I believe will be endless.

Then there are the nights I will not eat. My sister, who is four years my senior, assures me that what I remember is fact: I would refuse to eat, and my mother would find herself unable to submit to such willfulness—and such idiocy. And unable to for my own good. She is only asking me to do something *for my own good*—and still I say *no*? Wouldn't she give me the food out of her own mouth, don't I know that by now?

But I don't want the food from her mouth. I don't even want the food from my plate—that's the point.

Please! a child with my potential! my accomplishments! my future!—all the gifts God has lavished upon me, of beauty, of brains, am I to be allowed to think I can just starve myself to death for no good reason in the world?

Do I want people to look down on a skinny little boy all my life, or to look up to a man?

Do I want to be pushed around and made fun of, do I want to be skin and bones that people can knock over with a sneeze, or do I want to command respect?

Which do I want to be when I grow up, weak or strong, a success or a failure, a man or a mouse?

I just don't want to eat, I answer.

So my mother sits down in a chair beside me with a long bread knife in her hand. It is made of stainless steel, and has little sawlike teeth. Which do I want to be, weak or strong, a man or a mouse?

Doctor, *why*, why oh why oh why oh why does a mother pull a knife on her own son? I am six, seven years old, how do I know she really wouldn't use it? What am I supposed to do, try bluffing her out, at seven? I have no complicated sense of strategy, for Christ's sake—I probably don't even weigh sixty pounds yet! Someone waves a knife in my direction. I believe there is an intention lurking somewhere to draw my blood! Only *why*? What can she possibly be thinking *in her brain*? How crazy can she possibly be? Suppose she had let me win— what would have been lost? Why a *knife*, why the threat of *murder*, why is such total and annihilating victory necessary— when only the day before she set down her iron on the ironing board and *applauded* as I stormed around the kitchen rehearsing my role as Christopher Columbus in the third-grade production of *Land Ho!* I am the star actor of my class, they cannot put a play on without me. Oh, once they tried, when I had my bronchitis, but my teacher later confided in my mother that it had been decidedly second-rate. Oh *how*, how can she spend such glorious afternoons in the kitchen, polishing silver, chopping liver, threading new elastic in the waistband of my little jockey shorts—and feeding me all the while my cues from the mimeographed script, playing Queen Isabella to my Columbus, Betsy Ross to my Washington, Mrs. Pasteur to my Louis—how can she rise with me on the crest of my genius during those dusky beautiful hours after school, and then at night, because I will not eat some string beans and a baked potato, point a bread knife at my heart?

And why doesn't my father stop her?

WHACKING OFF

Then came adolescence—half my waking life spent locked behind the bathroom door, firing my wad down the toilet bowl, or into the soiled clothes in the laundry hamper, or *splat*, up against the medicine-chest mirror, before which I stood in my dropped drawers so I could see how it looked coming out. Or else I was doubled over my flying fist, eyes pressed closed but mouth wide open, to take that sticky sauce of buttermilk and Clorox on my own tongue and teeth—though not infrequently, in my blindness and ecstasy, I got it all in the pompadour, like a blast of Wildroot Cream Oil. Through a world of matted handkerchiefs and crumpled Kleenex and stained pajamas, I moved my raw and swollen penis, perpetually in dread that my loathsomeness would be discovered by someone stealing upon me just as I was in the frenzy of dropping my load. Nevertheless, I was wholly incapable of keeping my paws from my dong once it started the climb up my belly. In the middle of a class I would raise a hand to be excused, rush down the corridor to the lavatory, and with ten or fifteen savage strokes, beat off standing up into a urinal. At the Saturday afternoon movie I would leave my friends to go off to the candy machine—and wind up in a distant balcony seat, squirting my seed into the empty wrapper from a Mounds bar. On an outing of our family association, I once cored an apple, saw to my astonishment (and with the aid of my obsession) what it looked like, and ran off into the woods to fall upon the orifice of the fruit, pretending that the cool and mealy hole was actually between the legs of that mythical being who always called me Big Boy when she pleaded for what no girl in all recorded history had ever had. "Oh shove it in me, Big Boy," cried the cored apple that I banged silly on that picnic. "Big Boy, Big Boy, oh give me all you've got," begged the empty milk bottle that I kept hidden in our storage bin in the basement, to drive wild after school with my vaselined upright. "Come, Big Boy, come," screamed the maddened piece of liver that, in my own insanity, I bought one afternoon at a butcher shop and, believe it or not, violated behind a billboard on the way to a bar mitzvah lesson.

It was at the end of my freshman year of high school—and freshman year of masturbating—that I discovered on the underside of my penis, just where the shaft meets the head, a little discolored dot that has since been diagnosed as a freckle. Cancer. I had given myself *cancer*. All that pulling and tugging at my own flesh, all that friction, had given me an incurable disease. And not yet fourteen! In bed at night the tears rolled from my eyes. "No!" I sobbed. "I don't want to die! Please—no!" But then, because I would very shortly be a corpse anyway, I went ahead as usual and jerked off into my sock. I had taken to carrying the dirty socks into bed with me at night so as to be able to use one as a receptacle upon retiring, and the other upon awakening.

If only I could cut down to one hand-job a day, or hold the line at two, or even three! But with the prospect of oblivion before me, I actually began to set new records for myself. Before meals. After meals. *During* meals. Jumping up from the dinner table, I tragically clutch at my belly—diarrhea! I cry, I have been stricken with diarrhea!—and once behind the locked bathroom door, slip over my head a pair of underpants that I have stolen from my sister's dresser and carry rolled in a handkerchief in my pocket. So galvanic is the effect of cotton panties against my mouth—so galvanic is the *word* "panties"—that the trajectory of my ejaculation reaches startling new heights: leaving my joint like a rocket it makes right for the light bulb overhead, where to my wonderment and horror, it hits and it hangs. Wildly in the first moment I cover my head, expecting an explosion of glass, a burst of flames—disaster, you see, is never far from my mind. Then quietly as I can I climb the radiator and remove the sizzling gob with a wad of toilet paper. I begin a scrupulous search of the shower curtain, the tub, the tile floor, the four toothbrushes—God forbid!—and just as I am about to unlock the door, imagining I have covered my tracks, my heart lurches at the sight of what is hanging like snot to the toe of my shoe. I am the Raskolnikov of jerking off—the sticky evidence is everywhere! Is it on my cuffs too? in my *hair*? my *ear*? All this I wonder even as I come back to the kitchen table, scowling and cranky, to grumble self-righteously at my father when he opens his mouth full of red jello and says, "I don't understand what you have to lock the door about. That to me is beyond comprehension. What is this, a home or a Grand Central station?" ". . . privacy . . . a human being . . . around here *never*," I reply, then push aside my dessert to scream, "I don't feel well—*will everybody leave me alone?*"

After dessert—which I finish because I happen to like jello, even if I detest them—after dessert I am back in the bathroom again. I burrow through the week's laundry until I uncover one of my sister's soiled brassieres. I string one shoulder strap over the knob of the bathroom door and the other on the knob of the linen closet: a scarecrow to bring on more dreams. "Oh, beat it, Big Boy, beat it to a red-hot pulp—" so I am being urged by the little cups of Hannah's brassiere, when a rolled-up newspaper smacks at the door. And sends me and my handful an inch off the toilet seat. "—Come on, give somebody else a crack at that bowl, will you?" my father says. "I haven't moved my bowels in a week."

I recover my equilibrium, as is my talent, with a burst of hurt feelings. "I have a terrible case of diarrhea! Doesn't that mean anything to anyone in this house?"—in the meantime resuming the stroke, indeed quickening the tempo as my cancerous organ miraculously begins to quiver again from the inside out.

Then Hannah's brassiere *begins to move*. To swing to and fro! I veil my eyes, and behold!—Lenore Lapidus! who has the biggest pair in my class, running for the bus after school, her great untouchable load shifting weightily inside her blouse, oh I urge them up from their cups, and over, LENORE LAPIDUS'S ACTUAL TITS, and realize in the same split second that my mother is vigorously shaking the doorknob. Of the door I have finally forgotten to lock! I knew it would happen one day! *Caught!* As good as *dead*!

"Open up, Alex. I want you to open up this instant."

It's locked, I'm *not* caught! And I see from what's alive in my hand that I'm not quite dead yet either. Beat on then! beat on! "Lick me, Big Boy—lick me a good hot lick! I'm Lenore Lapidus's big fat red-hot brassiere!"

"Alex, I want an answer from you. Did you eat French fries after school? Is that why you're sick like this?"

"Nuhhh, nuhhh."

"Alex, are you in pain? Do you want me to call the doctor? Are you in pain, or aren't you? I want to know exactly where it hurts. *Answer me.*"

"Yuhh, yuhhh—"

"Alex, I don't want you to flush the toilet," says my mother sternly. "I want to see what you've done in there. I don't like the sound of this at all."

"And me," says my father, touched as he always was by my accomplishments—as much awe as envy—"I haven't moved my bowels in a week," just as I lurch from my perch on the toilet seat, and with the whimper of a whipped animal, deliver three drops of something barely viscous into the tiny piece of cloth where my flat-chested eighteen-year-old sister has laid her nipples, such as they are. It is my fourth orgasm of the day. When will I begin to come blood?

"Get in here, please, you," says my mother. "Why did you flush the toilet when I told you not to?"

"I forgot."

"What was in there that you were so fast to flush it?"

"Diarrhea."

"Was it mostly liquid or was it mostly poopie?"

"I don't look! I didn't look! Stop saying poopie to me—I'm in high school!"

"Oh, don't you shout at *me*, Alex. I'm not the one who gave you diarrhea, I assure you. If all you ate was what you were fed at home, you wouldn't be running to the bathroom fifty times a day. Hannah tells me what you're doing, so don't think I don't know."

She's missed the underpants! *I've been caught!* Oh, *let* me be dead! I'd just as soon!

"Yeah, what do I do . . . ?"

"You go to Harold's Hot Dog and *Chazerai* Palace after school and you eat French fries with Melvin Weiner. Don't you? Don't lie to me either. Do you or do you not stuff yourself with French fries and ketchup on Hawthorne Avenue after school? Jack, come in here, I want you to hear this," she calls to my father, now occupying the bathroom.

"Look, I'm trying to move my bowels," he replies. "Don't I have enough trouble as it is without people screaming at me when I'm trying to move my bowels?"

"You know what your son does after school, the *A* student, who his own mother can't say poopie to any more, he's such a *grown-up*? What do you think your grown-up son does when nobody is watching him?"

"Can I please be left alone, please?" cries my father. "Can I have a little peace, please, so I can get something accomplished in here?"

"Just wait till your father hears what you do, in defiance of every health habit there could possibly be. Alex, answer me something. You're so smart, you know all the answers now, answer me this: how do you think Melvin Weiner gave himself colitis? Why has that child spent half his life in hospitals?"

"Because he eats *chazerai*."

"Don't you dare make fun of me!"

"All right," I scream, "how *did* he get colitis?"

"Because he eats *chazerai*! But it's not a joke! Because to him a meal is an O Henry bar washed down by a bottle of Pepsi. Because his breakfast consists of, do you know what? The most important meal of the day—not according just to your mother, Alex, but according to the highest nutritionist—and do you know what that child eats?"

"A doughnut."

"A doughnut is right, Mr. Smart Guy, Mr. Adult. And *coffee*. Coffee and a doughnut, and on this a thirteen-year-old *pisher* with half a stomach is supposed to start a day. But you, thank God, have been brought up differently. You don't have a mother who gallavants all over town like some names I could name, from Bam's to Hahne's to Kresge's all day long. Alex, tell me, so it's not a mystery, or maybe I'm just stupid— only tell me, what are you trying to do, what are you trying to prove, that you should stuff yourself with such junk when you come home to a poppyseed cookie and a nice glass of milk? I want the truth from you. I wouldn't tell your father," she says, her voice dropping significantly, "but I *must* have the truth from you." Pause. Also significant. "Is it just French fries, darling, or is it more? . . . Tell me, please, what other kind of garbage you're putting into your mouth so we can get to the bottom of this diarrhea! I want a straight answer from you, Alex. Are you eating hamburgers out? Answer me, please, is that why you flushed the toilet—was there hamburger in it?"

"I told you—I don't look in the bowl when I flush it! I'm not interested like you are in other people's poopie!"

"Oh, oh, oh—thirteen years old and the mouth on him! To someone who is asking a question about *his* health, *his* welfare!" The utter incomprehensibility of the situation causes her eyes to become heavy with tears. "Alex, why are you getting like this, give me some clue? Tell me please what horrible things we have done to you all our lives that this should be our reward?" I believe the question strikes her as original. I believe she considers the question unanswerable. And worst of all, so do I. What *have* they done for me all their lives, but sacrifice? Yet that this is precisely the horrible thing is beyond my understanding—and still, Doctor! To this day!

I brace myself now for the whispering. I can spot the whispering coming a mile away. We are about to discuss my father's headaches.

"Alex, he didn't have a headache on him today that he could hardly see straight from it?" She checks, is he out of earshot? God forbid he should hear how critical his condition is, he might claim exaggeration. "He's not going next week for a test for a tumor?"

"He is?"

" 'Bring him in,' the doctor said, 'I'm going to give him a test for a tumor.' "

Success. I am crying. There is no good reason for me to be crying, but in this household everybody tries to get a good cry in at least once a day. My father, you must understand—as doubtless you do: blackmailers account for a substantial part of the human community, and, I would imagine, of your clientele —my father has been "going" for this tumor test for nearly as long as I can remember. Why his head aches him all the time is, of course, because he is constipated all the time—why he is constipated is because ownership of his intestinal tract is in the hands of the firm of Worry, Fear & Frustration. It is true that a doctor once said to my mother that he would give her husband a test for a tumor—if that would make her happy, is I believe the way that he worded it; he suggested that it would be cheaper, however, and probably more effective for the man to invest in an enema bag. Yet, that I know all this to be so, does not make it any less heartbreaking to imagine my father's skull splitting open from a malignancy.

Yes, she has me where she wants me, and she knows it. I clean forget my own cancer in the grief that comes—comes now as it came then—when I think how much of life has always been (as he himself very accurately puts it) beyond his comprehension. And his grasp. No money, no schooling, no language, no learning, curiosity without culture, drive without opportunity, experience without wisdom . . . How easily his inadequacies can move me to tears. As easily as they move me to anger!

A person my father often held up to me as someone to emulate in life was the theatrical producer Billy Rose. Walter Winchell said that Billy Rose's knowledge of shorthand had led Bernard Baruch to hire him as a secretary—consequently my father plagued me throughout high school to enroll in the shorthand course. "Alex, where would Billy Rose be today without his shorthand? Nowhere! So why do you *fight* me?" Earlier it was the piano we battled over. For a man whose house was without a phonograph or a record, he was passionate on the subject of a musical instrument. "I don't understand why you won't take a musical instrument, this is beyond comprehension. Your little cousin Toby can sit down at the piano and play whatever song you can name. All she has to do is sit at the piano and play 'Tea for Two' and everybody in the room is her friend. She'll never lack for companionship, Alex, she'll never lack for popularity. Only tell me you'll take up the piano, and I'll have one in here tomorrow morning. Alex, are you listening to me? I am offering you something that could change the rest of your life!"

But what he had to offer I didn't want—and what I wanted he didn't have to offer. Yet how unusual is that? Why must it continue to cause such pain? At this late date! Doctor, what should I rid myself of, tell me, the hatred . . . or the love? Because I haven't even begun to mention everything I remember with pleasure—I mean with a rapturous, biting sense of loss! All those memories that seem somehow to be bound up with the weather and the time of day, and that flash into mind with such poignancy, that momentarily I am not down in the subway, or at my office, or at dinner with a pretty girl, but back in my childhood, *with them*. Memories of practically nothing—and yet they seem moments of history as crucial to my being as the moment of my conception; I might be remembering his sperm nosing into her ovum, so piercing is my gratitude—yes, *my* gratitude!—so sweeping and unqualified is my love. Yes, me, with sweeping and unqualified love! I am standing in the kitchen (standing maybe for the first time in my life), my mother points, "Look outside, baby," and I look; she says, "See? how purple? a real fall sky." The first line of poetry I ever hear! And I remember it! *A real fall sky* . . . It is an iron-cold January day, dusk—oh, these memories of dusk are going to kill me yet, of chicken fat on rye bread to tide me over to dinner, and the moon already outside the kitchen window—I have just come in with hot red cheeks and a dollar I have earned shoveling snow: "You know what you're going to have for dinner," my mother coos so lovingly to me, "for being such a hard-working boy? Your favorite winter meal. Lamb stew." It is night: after a Sunday in New York City, at Radio City and Chinatown, we are driving home across the George Washington Bridge—the Holland Tunnel is the direct route between Pell Street and Jersey City, but I beg for the bridge, and because my mother says it's "educational," my father drives some ten miles out of his way to get us home. Up front my sister counts aloud the number of supports upon which the marvelous educational cables rest, while in the back I fall asleep with my face against my mother's black sealskin coat. At Lakewood, where we go one winter for a weekend vacation with my parents' Sunday night Gin Rummy Club, I sleep in one twin bed with my father, and my mother and Hannah curl up together in the other. At dawn my father awakens me and like convicts escaping, we noiselessly dress and slip out of the room. "Come," he whispers, motioning for me to don my earmuffs and coat, "I want to show you something. Did you know I was a waiter in Lakewood when I was sixteen years old?" Outside the hotel he points across to the beautiful silent woods. "How's that?" he says. We walk together—"at a brisk pace"—around a silver lake. "Take good deep breaths. Take in the piney air all the way. This is the best air in the world, good winter piney air." *Good winter piney air*—another poet for a parent! I couldn't be more thrilled if I were Wordsworth's kid! . . . In summer he remains in the city while the three of us go off to live in a furnished room at the seashore for a month. He will join us for the last two weeks, when he gets his vacation . . . there are times, however, when Jersey City is so thick with humidity, so alive with the mosquitoes that come dive-bombing in from the marshes, that at the end of his day's work he drives sixty-five miles, taking the old Cheesequake Highway —the Cheesequake! My God! the stuff you uncover here!— drives sixty-five miles to spend the night with us in our breezy room at Bradley Beach.

He arrives after we have already eaten, but his own dinner waits while he unpeels the soggy city clothes in which he has been making the rounds of his debit all day, and changes into his swimsuit. I carry his towel for him as he clops down the street to the beach in his unlaced shoes. I am dressed in clean short pants and a spotless polo shirt, the salt is showered off me, and my hair—still my little boy's pre-steel wool hair, soft and combable—is beautifully parted and slicked down. There is a weathered iron rail that runs the length of the boardwalk, and I seat myself upon it; below me, in his shoes, my father crosses the empty beach. I watch him neatly set down his towel near the shore. He places his watch in one shoe, his eye-glasses in the other, and then he is ready to make his entrance into the sea. To this day I go into the water as he advised: plunge the wrists in first, then splash the underarms, then a handful to the temples and the back of the neck . . . ah, but slowly, always slowly. This way you get to refresh yourself, while avoiding a shock to the system. Refreshed, unshocked, he turns to face me, comically waves farewell up to where he thinks I'm standing, and drops backward to float with his arms outstretched. Oh he floats so still—he works, he works so hard, and for whom if not for me?—and then at last, after turning on his belly and making a few choppy strokes that carry him nowhere, he comes wading back to shore, his streaming compact torso glowing from the last pure spikes of light driving in, over my shoulder, out of stifling inland New Jersey, from which I am being spared.

And there are more memories like this one, Doctor. A lot more. This is my mother and father I'm talking about.

—

But—but—but—let me pull myself together—there is also this vision of him emerging from the bathroom, savagely kneading the back of his neck and sourly swallowing a belch. "All right, what is it that was so urgent you couldn't wait till I came out to tell me?"

"Nothing," says my mother. "It's settled."

He looks at me, so disappointed. I'm what he lives for, and I know it. "What did he do?"

"What he did is over and done with, God willing. You, did you move your bowels?" she asks him.

"Of course I didn't move my bowels."

"Jack, what is it going to be with you, with those bowels?"

"They're turning into concrete, that's what it's going to be."

"Because you eat too fast."

"I don't eat too fast."

"How then, slow?"

"I eat regular."

"You eat like a pig, and somebody should tell you."

"Oh, you got a wonderful way of expressing yourself sometimes, do you know that?"

"I'm only speaking the truth," she says. "I stand on my feet all day in this kitchen, and you eat like there's a fire somewhere, and this one—this one has decided that the food I cook isn't good enough for him. He'd rather be sick and scare the living daylights out of me."

"What did he do?"

"I don't want to upset you," she says. "Let's just forget the whole thing." But she can't, so now *she* begins to cry. Look, she is probably not the happiest person in the world either. She was once a tall stringbean of a girl whom the boys called "Red" in high school. When I was nine and ten years old I had an absolute passion for her high school yearbook. For a while I kept it in the same drawer with that other volume of exotica, my stamp collection.

Sophie Ginsky the boys call "Red,"
She'll go far with her big brown eyes and her clever head.

And that was my mother!

Also, she had been secretary to the soccer coach, an office pretty much without laurels in our own time, but apparently *the* post for a young girl to hold in Jersey City during the First World War. So I thought, at any rate, when I turned the pages of her yearbook, and she pointed out to me her dark-haired beau, who had been captain of the team, and today, to quote Sophie, "the biggest manufacturer of mustard in New York." "And I could have married him instead of your father," she confided in me, and more than once. I used to wonder sometimes what that would have been like for my momma and me, invariably on the occasions when my father took us to dine out at the corner delicatessen. I look around the place and think, "We would have manufactured all this mustard." I suppose she must have had thoughts like that herself.

"He eats French fries," she says, and sinks into a kitchen chair to Weep Her Heart Out once and for all. "He goes after school with Melvin Weiner and stuffs himself with French-fried potatoes. Jack, you tell him, I'm only his mother. Tell him what the end is going to be. Alex," she says passionately, looking to where I am edging out of the room, "*tateleh*, it begins with diarrhea, but do you know how it ends? With a sensitive stomach like yours, do you know how it finally ends? *Wearing a plastic bag to do your business in!*"

Who in the history of the world has been least able to deal with a woman's tears? My father. I am second. He says to me, "You heard your mother. Don't eat French fries with Melvin Weiner after school."

"Or ever," she pleads.

"Or ever," my father says.

"Or hamburgers out," she pleads.

"Or hamburgers out," he says.

"*Hamburgers*," she says bitterly, just as she might say *Hitler*, "where they can put anything in the world in that they want—and *he* eats them. Jack, make him promise, before he gives himself a terrible *tsura*, and it's too late."

"I *promise!*" I scream. "I *promise!*" and race from the kitchen —to where? Where else.

I tear off my pants, furiously I grab that battered battering ram to freedom, my adolescent cock, even as my mother begins to call from the other side of the bathroom door. "Now this time don't flush. Do you hear me, Alex? I have to see what's in that bowl!"

Doctor, do you understand what I was up against? My wang was all I really had that I could call my own. You should have watched her at work during polio season! She should have gotten medals from the March of Dimes! Open your mouth. Why is your throat red? Do you have a headache you're not telling me about? You're not going to any baseball game, Alex, until I see you move your neck. Is your neck stiff? Then why are you moving it that way? You ate like you were nauseous, are you nauseous? Well, you ate like you were nauseous. I don't want you drinking from the drinking fountain in that playground. If you're thirsty wait until you're home. Your throat is sore, isn't it? I can tell how you're swallowing. I think maybe what you are going to do, Mr. Joe Di Maggio, is put that glove away and lie down. I am not going to allow you to go outside in this heat and run around, not with that sore throat, I'm not. I want to take your temperature. I don't like the sound of this throat business one bit. To be very frank, I am actually beside myself that you have been walking around all day with a sore throat and not telling your mother. Why did you keep this a secret? Alex, polio doesn't know from baseball games. It only knows from iron lungs and crippled forever! I don't want you running around, and that's final. Or eating hamburgers out. Or mayonnaise. Or chopped liver. Or tuna. Not everybody is careful the way your mother is about spoilage. You're used to a spotless house, you don't begin to know what goes on in restaurants. Do you know why your mother when we go to the Chink's will never sit facing the kitchen? Because I don't want to see what goes on back there. Alex, you must wash everything, is that clear? Everything! God only knows who touched it before you did.

Look, am I exaggerating to think it's practically miraculous that I'm ambulatory? The hysteria and the superstition! The watch-its and the be-carefuls! You mustn't do this, you can't do that—hold it! don't! you're breaking an important law! *What* law? *Whose* law? They might as well have had plates in their lips and rings through their noses and painted themselves blue for all the human sense they made! Oh, and the *milchiks* and the *flaishiks* besides, all those *meshuggeneh* rules and regulations on top of their own private craziness! It's a family joke that when I was a tiny child I turned from the window out of which I was watching a snowstorm, and hopefully asked, "Momma, do we believe in winter?" Do you get what I'm *saying*? I was raised by Hottentots and Zulus! I couldn't even contemplate drinking a glass of milk with my salami sandwich without giving serious offense to God Almighty. Imagine then what my conscience gave me for all that jerking off! The guilt, the fears—the terror bred into my bones! What in their world was not charged with danger, dripping with germs, fraught with peril? Oh, where was the gusto, where was the boldness and courage? Who filled these parents of mine with such a fearful sense of life? My father, in his retirement now, has really only one subject into which he can sink his teeth, the New Jersey Turnpike. "I wouldn't go on that thing if you paid me. You have to be out of your mind to travel on that thing—it's Murder Incorporated, it's a legalized way for people to go out and get themselves killed—" Listen, you know what he says to me three times a week on the telephone—and I'm only counting when I pick it up, not the total number of rings I get between six and ten every night. "Sell that car, will you? Will you do me a favor and sell that car so I can get a good night's sleep? Why you have to have a car in that city is beyond my comprehension. Why you want to pay for insurance and garage and upkeep, I don't even begin to understand. But then I don't understand yet why you even want to live by yourself over in that jungle. What do you pay those robbers again for that two-by-four apartment? A penny over fifty dollars a month and you're out of your mind. Why you don't move back to North Jersey is a mystery to me—why you prefer the noise and the crime and the fumes—"

And my mother, she just keeps whispering. *Sophie whispers on!* I go for dinner once a month, it is a struggle requiring all my guile and cunning and strength, but I have been able over all these years, and against imponderable odds, to hold it down to once a month: I ring the bell, she opens the door, the whispering promptly begins! "Don't ask what kind of day I had with him yesterday." So I don't. "Alex," *sotto voce* still, "when he has a day like that you don't know what a difference a call from you would make." I nod. "And, Alex"—and I'm nodding away, you know—it doesn't cost anything, and it may even get me through—"next week is his birthday. That Mother's Day came and went without a card, *plus* my birthday, those things don't bother me. But he'll be sixty-six, Alex. That's not a baby, Alex—that's a landmark in a life. So you'll send a card. It wouldn't kill you."

Doctor, these people are incredible! These people are unbelievable! These two are the outstanding producers and packagers of guilt in our time! They render it from me like fat from a chicken! "Call, Alex. Visit, Alex. Alex, keep us informed. Don't go away without telling us, please, not again. Last time you went away you didn't tell us, your father was ready to phone the police. You know how many times a day he called and got no answer? Take a guess, how many?" "Mother," I inform her, from between my teeth, "if I'm dead they'll smell the body in seventy-two hours, I assure you!" "Don't *talk* like that! God *forbid*!" she cries. Oh, and now she's got the beauty, the one guaranteed to do the job. Yet how could I expect otherwise? Can I ask the impossible of my own mother? "Alex, to pick up a phone is such a simple thing—how much longer will we be around to bother you anyway?"

Doctor Spielvogel, this is my life, my only life, and I'm living it in the middle of a Jewish joke! I am the son in the Jewish joke—*only it ain't no joke!* Please, who crippled us like this? Who made us so morbid and hysterical and weak? Why, why are they screaming still, "Watch out! Don't do it! Alex— *no!*" and why, alone on my bed in New York, why am I still hopelessly beating my meat? Doctor, what do you call this sickness I have? Is this the Jewish suffering I used to hear so much about? Is this what has come down to me from the pogroms and the persecution? from the mockery and abuse bestowed by the *goyim* over these two thousand lovely years? Oh my secrets, my shame, my palpitations, my flushes, my sweats! The way I respond to the simple vicissitudes of human life! Doctor, I can't stand any more being frightened like this over nothing! Bless me with manhood! Make me brave! Make me strong! Make me *whole*! Enough being a nice Jewish boy, publicly pleasing my parents while privately pulling my putz! Enough!

THE JEWISH BLUES

Sometime during my ninth year one of my testicles apparently decided it had had enough of life down in the scrotum and began to make its way north. At the beginning I could feel it bobbing uncertainly just at the rim of the pelvis—and then, as though its moment of indecision had passed, entering the cavity of my body, like a survivor being dragged up out of the sea and over the hull of a lifeboat. And there it nestled, secure at last behind the fortress of my bones, leaving its foolhardy mate to chance it alone in that boy's world of football cleats and picket fences, sticks and stones and pocketknives, all those dangers that drove my mother wild with foreboding, and about which I was warned and warned and warned. And warned again. And again.

And again.

So my left testicle took up residence in the vicinity of my inguinal canal. By pressing a finger in the crease between my groin and my thigh, I could still, in the early weeks of its disappearance, feel the curve of its jellied roundness; but then came nights of terror, when I searched my guts in vain, searched all the way up to my rib cage—alas, the voyager had struck off for regions uncharted and unknown. Where was it gone to! How high and how far before the journey would come to an end! Would I one day open my mouth to speak in class, only to discover my left nut out on the end of my tongue? In school we chanted, along with our teacher, *I am the Captain of my fate, I am the Master of my soul*, and meanwhile, within my own body, an anarchic insurrection had been launched by one of my privates—which I was helpless to put down!

For some six months, until its absence was observed by the family doctor during my annual physical examination, I pondered my mystery, more than once wondering—for there was no possibility that did not enter my head, *none*—if the testicle could have taken a dive backwards toward the bowel and there begun to convert itself into just such an egg as I had observed my mother yank in a moist yellow cluster from the dark interior of a chicken whose guts she was emptying into the garbage. What if breasts began to grow on me, too? What if my penis went dry and brittle, and one day, while I was urinating, snapped off in my hand? Was I being transformed into a girl? Or worse, into a boy such as I understood (from the playground grapevine) that Robert Ripley of *Believe It or Not* would pay "a reward" of a hundred thousand dollars for? Believe it or not, there is a nine-year-old boy in New Jersey who is a boy in every way, *except he can have babies.*

Who gets the reward? Me, or the person who turns me in?

Doctor Izzie rolled the scrotal sack between his fingers as though it were the material of a suit he was considering buying, and then told my father that I would have to be given a series of male hormone shots. One of my testicles had never fully descended—unusual, not unheard of . . . But if the shots don't work, asks my father in alarm. What then—! Here I am sent out into the waiting room to look at a magazine.

The shots work. I am spared the knife. (Once again!)

———

Oh, this father! this kindly, anxious, uncomprehending, constipated father! Doomed to be obstructed by this Holy Protestant Empire! The self-confidence and the cunning, the imperiousness and the contacts, all that enabled the blond and blue-eyed of his generation to lead, to inspire, to command, if need be to oppress—he could not summon a hundredth part of it. How could he oppress?—he *was* the oppressed. How could he wield power?—he *was* the powerless. How could he enjoy triumph, when he so despised the triumphant—and probably the very idea. "They worship a Jew, do you know that, Alex? Their whole big-deal religion is based on worshiping someone who was an established Jew at that time. Now how do you like that for stupidity? How do you like that for pulling the wool over the eyes of the public? Jesus Christ, who they go around telling everybody was God, was actually a Jew! And this fact, that absolutely kills me when I have to think about it, *nobody else pays any attention to.* That he was a

Jew, like you and me, and that they took a Jew and turned him into some kind of God after he is already dead, and then—and this is what can make you absolutely crazy—then the dirty bastards turn around afterwards, and who is the first one on their list to persecute? who haven't they left their hands off of to murder and to hate for two thousand years? The Jews! who gave them their beloved Jesus to begin with! I assure you, Alex, you are never going to hear such a *mishegoss* of mixed-up crap and disgusting nonsense as the Christian religion in your entire life. And that's what these big shots, so-called, believe!"

Unfortunately, on the home front contempt for the powerful enemy was not so readily available as a defensive strategy—for as time went on, the enemy was more and more *his* own beloved son. Indeed, during that extended period of rage that goes by the name of my adolescence, what terrified me most about my father was not the violence I expected him momentarily to unleash upon me, but the violence I wished every night at the dinner table to commit upon his ignorant, barbaric carcass. How I wanted to send him howling from the land of the living when he ate from the serving bowl with his own fork, or sucked the soup from his spoon instead of politely waiting for it to cool, or attempted, God forbid, to express an opinion on any subject whatsoever . . . And what was especially terrifying about the murderous wish was this: if I tried, chances were I'd succeed! *Chances were he would help me along!* I would have only to leap across the dinner dishes, my fingers aimed at his windpipe, for him instantaneously to sink down beneath the table with his tongue hanging out. Shout he could shout, squabble he could squabble, and oh *nudjh*, could he *nudjh*! But defend himself? against *me*? "Alex, keep this back talk up," my mother warns, as I depart from the roaring kitchen like Attila the Hun, run screaming from yet another half-eaten dinner, "continue with this disrespect and you will give that man a heart attack!" "Good!" I cry, slamming in her face the door to my room. "Fine!" I scream, extracting from my closet the zylon jacket I wear only with my collar up (a style she abhors as much as the filthy garment itself). "Wonderful!" I shout, and with streaming eyes run to the corner to vent my fury on the pinball machine.

Christ, in the face of my defiance—if my father had only been my mother! and my mother my father! But what a mix-up of the sexes in our house! Who should by rights be advancing on me, retreating—and who should be retreating, advancing! Who should be scolding, collapsing in helplessness, enfeebled totally by a tender heart! And who should be collapsing, instead scolding, correcting, reproving, criticizing, faultfinding without end! Filling the patriarchal vacuum! Oh, thank God! thank God! at least *he* had the cock and the balls! Pregnable (putting it mildly) as his masculinity was in this world of *goyim* with golden hair and silver tongues, between his legs (God bless my father!) he was constructed like a man of consequence, two big healthy balls such as a king would be proud to put on display, and a *shlong* of magisterial length and girth. And they were *his*: yes, of this I am absolutely certain, they hung down off of, they were connected on to, they could not be taken away from, *him*!

—

Of course, around the house I saw less of his sexual apparatus than I did of her erogenous zones. And once I saw her menstrual blood . . . saw it shining darkly up at me from the worn linoleum in front of the kitchen sink. Just two red drops over a quarter of a century ago, but they glow still in that icon of her that hangs, perpetually illuminated, in my Modern Museum of Gripes and Grievances (along with the box of Kotex and the nylon stockings, which I want to come to in a moment). Also in this icon is an endless dripping of blood down through a drainboard into a dishpan. It is the blood she is draining from the meat so as to make it kosher and fit for consumption. Probably I am confusing things—I sound like a son of the House of Atreus with all this talk of blood—but I see her standing at the sink salting the meat so as to rid it of its blood, when the attack of "woman's troubles" sends her, with a most alarming moan, rushing off to her bedroom. I was no more than four or five, and yet those two drops of blood that I beheld on the floor of her kitchen are visible to me still . . . as is the box of Kotex . . . as are the stockings sliding up her legs . . . as is—need I even say it?—the bread knife with which my own blood would be threatened when I refuse to eat my dinner. That knife! *That knife!* What gets me is that she herself did not even consider the use of it anything to be ashamed of, or particularly reticent about. From my bed I hear her babbling about her problems to the women around the mah-jongg game: *My Alex is suddenly such a bad eater I have to stand over him with a knife.* And none of them apparently finds this tactic of hers at all excessive. I have to stand over him with a knife! And not one of those women gets up from the mah-jongg table and walks out of her house! Because in their world, that is the way it is with bad eaters—you have to stand over them *with a knife!*

It was years later that she called from the bathroom, Run to the drugstore! bring a box of Kotex! immediately! And the panic in her voice. Did I run! And then at home again, breathlessly handed the box to the white fingers that extended themselves at me through a narrow crack in the bathroom door . . . Though her menstrual troubles eventually had to be resolved by surgery, it is difficult nevertheless to forgive her for having sent me on that mission of mercy. Better she should have bled herself out on our cold bathroom floor, better *that*, than to have sent an eleven-year-old boy in hot pursuit of sanitary napkins! Where was my sister, for Christ's sake? Where was her own emergency supply? Why was this woman so grossly insensitive to the vulnerability of her own little boy—on the one hand so insensitive to my shame, and yet on the other, so attuned to my deepest desires!

. . . I am so small I hardly know what sex I am, or so you would imagine. It is early in the afternoon, spring of the year Four. Flowers are standing up in purple stalks in the patch of dirt outside our building. With the windows flung open the air in the apartment is fragrant, soft with the season—and yet electric too with my mother's vitality: she has finished the week's wash and hung it on the line; she has baked a marble cake for our dessert tonight, beautifully bleeding—there's that blood again! there's that knife again!—anyway expertly bleeding the chocolate in and out of the vanilla, an accomplishment that seems to me as much of a miracle as getting those peaches to hang there suspended in the shimmering mold of jello. She has done the laundry and baked the cake; she has scrubbed the kitchen and bathroom floors and laid them with newspapers; she has of course dusted; needless to say, she has vacuumed; she has cleared and washed our luncheon dishes and (with my

cute little assistance) returned them to their place in the
milchiks cabinet in the pantry—and whistling like a canary all
the morning through, a tuneless melody of health and joy, of
heedlessness and self-sufficiency. While I crayon a picture for
her, she showers—and now in the sunshine of her bedroom,
she is dressing to take me downtown. She sits on the edge of
the bed in her padded bra and her girdle, rolling on her
stockings and chattering away. Who is Mommy's good little
boy? Who is the best little boy a mommy ever had? Who does
Mommy love more than anything in the whole wide world? I
am absolutely punchy with delight, and meanwhile follow in
their tight, slow, agonizingly delicious journey up her legs the
transparent stockings that give her flesh a hue of stirring di-
mensions. I sidle close enough to smell the bath powder on
her throat—also to appreciate better the elastic intricacies of
the dangling straps to which the stockings will presently be
hooked (undoubtedly with a flourish of trumpets). I smell the
oil with which she has polished the four gleaming posts of the
mahogany bedstead, where she sleeps with a man who lives
with us at night and on Sunday afternoons. My father they say
he is. On my fingertips, even though she has washed each one
of those little piggies with a warm wet cloth, I smell my lunch,
my tuna fish salad. Ah, it might be cunt I'm sniffing. Maybe it
is! Oh, I want to growl with pleasure. Four years old, and yet
I sense in my blood—uh-huh, again with the blood—how
rich with passion is the moment, how dense with possibility.
This fat person with the long hair whom they call my sister is
away at school. This man, my father, is off somewhere making
money, as best he is able. These two are gone, and who knows,
maybe I'll be lucky, maybe they'll never come back . . . In the
meantime, it is afternoon, it is spring, and for me and me alone
a woman is rolling on her stockings and singing a song of love.
Who is going to stay with Mommy forever and ever? *Me.* Who
is it who goes with Mommy wherever in the whole wide world
Mommy goes? *Why me, of course. What a silly question—but
don't get me wrong. I'll play the game!* Who had a nice lunch
with Mommy, who goes downtown like a good boy on the
bus with Mommy, who goes into the big store with Mommy
. . . and on and on and on . . . so that only a week or so ago,
upon my safe return from Europe, Mommy had this to say—

"Feel."

"*What?*"—even as she takes my hand in hers and draws it toward her body—"Mother—"

"I haven't gained five pounds," she says, "since you were born. Feel," she says, and holds my stiff fingers against the swell of her hips, which aren't bad . . .

And the stockings. More than twenty-five years have passed (the game is supposed to be over!), but Mommy still hitches up the stockings in front of her little boy. Now, however, he takes it upon himself to look the other way when the flag goes fluttering up the pole—and out of concern not just for his own mental health. That's the truth, I look away not for me but for the sake of that poor man, my father! Yet what preference does Father really have? If there in the living room their grown up little boy were to tumble all at once onto the rug with his mommy, what would Daddy do? Pour a bucket of boiling water on the raging, maddened couple? Would he draw *his* knife—or would he go off to the other room and watch television until they were finished? "What are you looking away—?" asks my mother, amused in the midst of straightening her seams. "You'd think I was a twenty-one-year-old girl; you'd think I hadn't wiped your backside and kissed your little tushy for you all those years. Look at him"— this is my father, in case he hasn't been giving a hundred percent of his attention to the little floor show now being performed—"look, acting like his own mother is some sixty-year-old beauty queen."

—

Once a month my father took me with him down to the *shvitz* bath, there to endeavor to demolish—with the steam, and a rubdown, and a long deep sleep—the pyramid of aggravation he has built himself into during the previous weeks of work. Our street clothes we lock away in the dormitory on the top floor. On rows of iron cots running perpendicular to the lockers, the men who have already been through the ringer down below are flung out beneath white sheets like the fatalities of a violent catastrophe. If it were not for the abrupt thunderclap of a fart, or the snores sporadically shooting up around me like machine-gun fire, I would believe we were in a morgue, and for some strange reason undressing in front of the dead. I do not look at the bodies, but like a mouse hop frantically about on my toes, trying to clear my feet of my undershorts before anybody can peek inside, where, to my chagrin, to my bafflement, to my mortification, I always discover in the bottommost seam a pale and wispy brushstroke of my shit. Oh, Doctor, I wipe and I wipe and I wipe, I spend as much time wiping as I do crapping, maybe even more. I use toilet paper like it grew on trees—so says my envious father—I wipe until that little orifice of mine is red as a raspberry; but still, much as I would like to please my mother by dropping into her laundry hamper at the end of each day jockey shorts such as might have encased the asshole of an angel, I deliver forth instead (deliberately, Herr Doctor?—or just inevitably?) the fetid little drawers of a boy.

But here in a Turkish bath, why am I dancing around? There are no women here. No women—and no *goyim*. Can it be? There is nothing to worry about!

Following the folds at the base of his white buttocks, I proceed out of the dormitory and down the metal stairs to the purgatory wherein the agonies that come of being an insurance agent, a family man, and a Jew will be steamed and beaten from my father's body. At the bottom landing we sidestep a pile of white sheets and a mound of sopping towels, my father pushes a shoulder against a heavy windowless door, and we enter a dark quiet region redolent of wintergreen. The sounds are of a tiny, unenthusiastic audience applauding the death scene in some tragedy: it is the two masseurs walloping and potching at the flesh of their victims, men half-clad in sheets and stretched out across marble slabs. They smack them and knead them and push them around, they slowly twist their limbs as though to remove them in a piece from their sockets —I am hypnotized, but continue to follow after my father as we pass alongside the pool, a small green cube of heart-stopping ice water, and come at last to the steam room.

The moment he pushes open the door the place speaks to me of prehistoric times, earlier even than the era of the cavemen and lake dwellers that I have studied in school, a time when above the oozing bog that was the earth, swirling white gasses choked out the sunlight, and aeons passed while the planet was drained for Man. I lose touch instantaneously with that ass-licking little boy who runs home after school with his

A's in his hand, the little over-earnest innocent endlessly in search of the key to that unfathomable mystery, his mother's approbation, and am back in some sloppy watery time, before there were families such as we know them, before there were toilets and tragedies such as we know them, a time of amphibious creatures, plunging brainless hulking things, with wet meaty flanks and steaming torsos. It is as though all the Jewish men ducking beneath the cold dribble of shower off in the corner of the steam room, then lumbering back for more of the thick dense suffocating vapors, it is as though they have ridden the time-machine back to an age when they existed as some herd of Jewish animals, whose only utterance is *oy, oy* . . . for this is the sound they make as they drag themselves from the shower into the heavy gush of fumes. They appear, at long last, my father and his fellow sufferers, to have returned to the habitat in which they can be natural. A place without *goyim* and women.

I stand at attention between his legs as he coats me from head to toe with a thick lather of soap— and eye with admiration the baggy substantiality of what overhangs the marble bench upon which he is seated. His scrotum is like the long wrinkled face of some old man with an egg tucked into each of his sagging jowls—while mine might hang from the wrist of some little girl's dolly like a teeny pink purse. And as for his *shlong*, to me, with that fingertip of a prick that my mother likes to refer to in public (once, okay, but that once will last a lifetime) as my "little thing," his *shlong* brings to mind the fire hoses coiled along the corridors at school. *Shlong*: the word somehow catches exactly the brutishness, the *meatishness*, that I admire so, the sheer mindless, weighty, and unselfconscious dangle of that living piece of hose through which he passes streams of water as thick and strong as rope—while I deliver forth slender yellow threads that my euphemistic mother calls "a sis." A sis, I think, is undoubtedly what my sister makes, little yellow threads that you can sew with . . . "Do you want to make a nice sis?" she asks me—when I want to make a torrent, I want to make a flood: I want like he does to shift the tides of the toilet bowl! "Jack," my mother calls to him, "would you close that door, please? Some example you're setting for you know who." But if only that had been so, Mother! If only you-know-who could have found some inspiration in what's-his-name's coarseness! If only I could have nourished myself upon the depths of his vulgarity, instead of that too becoming a source of shame. Shame and shame and shame and shame—every place I turn something else to be ashamed of.

—

We are in my Uncle Nate's clothing store on Springfield Avenue in Newark. I want a bathing suit with a built-in athletic support. I am eleven years old and that is my secret: I want a jock. I know not to say anything, I just know to keep my mouth shut, but then how do you get it if you don't ask for it? Uncle Nate, a spiffy dresser with a mustache, removes from his showcase a pair of little boy's trunks, the exact style I have always worn. He indicates that this is the best suit for me, fast-drying and won't chafe. "What's your favorite color?" Uncle Nate asks—"maybe you want it in your school color, huh?" I turn scarlet, though that is not my answer. "I don't want that kind of suit any more," and oh, I can smell humiliation in the wind, hear it rumbling in the distance—any minute now it is going to crash upon my prepubescent head. "Why not?" my father asks. "Didn't you hear your uncle, this is the best—" "I want one with a jockstrap in it!" Yes, sir, this just breaks my mother up. "For *your* little thing?" she asks, with an amused smile.

Yes, Mother, imagine: for my little thing.

—

The potent man in the family—successful in business, tyrannical at home—was my father's oldest brother, Hymie, the only one of my aunts and uncles to have been born on the other side and to talk with an accent. Uncle Hymie was in the "soda-vater" business, bottler and distributor of a sweet carbonated drink called Squeeze, the *vin ordinaire* of our dinner table. With his neurasthenic wife Clara, his son Harold, and his daughter Marcia, my uncle lived in a densely Jewish section of Newark, on the second floor of a two-family house that he owned, and into whose bottom floor we moved in 1941, when my father transferred to the Essex County office of Boston & Northeastern.

We moved from Jersey City because of the anti-Semitism. Just before the war, when the Bund was feeling its oats, the

Nazis used to hold their picnics in a beer garden only blocks from our house. When we drove by in the car on Sundays, my father would curse them, loud enough for me to hear, not quite loud enough for them to hear. Then one night a swastika was painted on the front of our building. Then a swastika was found carved into the desk of one of the Jewish children in Hannah's class. And Hannah herself was chased home from school one afternoon by a gang of boys, who it was assumed were anti-Semites on a rampage. My parents were beside themselves. But when Uncle Hymie heard the stories, he had to laugh: "This surprises you? Living surrounded on four sides by *goyim*, and this surprises you?" The only place for a Jew to live is among Jews, *especially*, he said with an emphasis whose significance did not entirely escape me, especially when children are growing up with people from the other sex. Uncle Hymie liked to lord it over my father, and took a certain pleasure in pointing out that in Jersey City only the building we lived in was exclusively Jewish, whereas in Newark, where *he* still lived, that was the case with the entire Weequahic neighborhood. In my cousin Marcia's graduating class from Weequahic High, out of the two hundred and fifty students, there were only eleven *goyim* and one colored. Go beat that, said Uncle Hymie . . . So my father, after much deliberation, put in for a transfer back to his native village, and although his immediate boss was reluctant to lose such a dedicated worker (and naturally shelved the request), my mother eventually made a long-distance phone call on her own, to the Home Office up in Boston, and following a mix-up that I don't even want to begin to go into, the request was granted: in 1941 we moved to Newark.

Harold, my cousin, was short and bullish in build—like all the men in our family, except me—and bore a strong resemblance to the actor John Garfield. My mother adored him and was always making him blush (a talent the lady possesses) by saying in his presence, "If a girl had Heshele's dark lashes, believe me, she'd be in Hollywood with a million-dollar contract." In a corner of the cellar, across from where Uncle Hymie had cases of Squeeze piled to the ceiling, Heshie kept a set of York weights with which he worked out every afternoon before the opening of the track season. He was one of the stars of the team, and held a city record in the javelin throw; his events were discus, shot, and javelin, though once during a meet at School Stadium, he was put in by the coach to run the low hurdles, as a substitute for a sick teammate, and in a spill at the last jump, fell and broke his wrist. My Aunt Clara at that time—or was it all the time?— was going through one of her "nervous seizures"—in comparison to Aunt Clara, my own vivid momma is a Gary Cooper—and when Heshie came home at the end of the day with his arm in a cast, she dropped in a faint to the kitchen floor. Heshie's cast was later referred to as "the straw that broke the camel's back," whatever that meant.

To me, Heshie was everything—that is, for the little time I knew him. I used to dream that I too would someday be a member of the track team and wear scant white shorts with a slit cut up either side to accommodate the taut and bulging muscles of my thighs.

Just before he was drafted into the Army in 1943, Heshie decided to become engaged to a girl named Alice Dembosky, the head drum majorette of the high school band. It was Alice's genius to be able to twirl not just one but two silver batons simultaneously—to pass them over her shoulders, glide them snakily between her legs, and then toss them fifteen and twenty feet into the air, catching one, then the other, behind her back. Only rarely did she drop a baton to the turf, and then she had a habit of shaking her head petulantly and crying out in a little voice, "Oh, Alice!" that only could have made Heshie love her the more; it surely had that effect upon me. Oh-Alice, with that long blond hair leaping up her back and about her face! cavorting with such exuberance half the length of the playing field! Oh-Alice, in her tiny white skirt with the white satin bloomers, and the white boots that came midway up the muscle of her lean, strong calves! Oh Jesus, "Legs" Dembosky, in all her dumb, blond *goyische* beauty! Another icon!

That Alice was so blatantly a *shikse* caused no end of grief in Heshie's household, and even in my own; as for the community at large, I believe there was actually a kind of civic pride taken in the fact that a gentile could have assumed a position of such high visibility in our high school, whose faculty and student body were about ninety-five percent Jewish. On the other hand, when Alice performed what the loudspeaker de-

scribed as her "piece de resistance"—twirling a baton that had
been wrapped at either end in oil-soaked rags and then set afire
—despite all the solemn applause delivered by the Weequahic
fans in tribute to the girl's daring and concentration, despite
the grave *boom boom boom* of our bass drum and the gasps and
shrieks that went up when she seemed about to set ablaze her
two adorable breasts—despite this genuine display of admiration and concern, I think there was still a certain comic detachment experienced on our side of the field, grounded in the
belief that this was precisely the kind of talent that only a *goy*
would think to develop in the first place.

Which was more or less the prevailing attitude toward athletics in general, and football in particular, among the parents
in the neighborhood: it was for the *goyim*. Let them knock
their heads together for "glory," for victory in a ball game! As
my Aunt Clara put it, in that taut, violin-string voice of hers,
"Heshie! Please! I do not need *goyische naches*!" Didn't need,
didn't want such ridiculous pleasures and satisfactions as made
the gentiles happy . . . At football our Jewish high school was
notoriously hopeless (though the band, may I say, was always
winning prizes and commendations); our pathetic record was
of course a disappointment to the young, no matter what the
parents might feel, and yet even as a child one was able to understand that for us to lose at football was not exactly the ultimate catastrophe. Here, in fact, was a cheer that my cousin
and his buddies used to send up from the stands at the end of
a game in which Weequahic had once again met with seeming
disaster. I used to chant it with them.

> Ikey, Mikey, Jake and Sam,
> We're the boys who eat no ham,
> We play football, we play soccer—
> And we keep matzohs in our locker!
> Aye, aye, aye, Weequahic High!

So what if we had lost? It turned out we had other things to
be proud of. We ate no ham. We kept matzohs in our lockers.
Not really, of course, but if we wanted to *we could, and we
weren't ashamed to say that we actually did!* We were Jews—
and we weren't ashamed to say it! We were Jews—and not
only were we not inferior to the *goyim* who beat us at football,

but the chances were that because we could not commit our
hearts to victory in such a thuggish game, we were superior!
We were Jews—*and we were superior!*

> White bread, rye bread,
> Pumpernickel, challah,
> All those for Weequahic,
> Stand up and hollah!

Another cheer I learned from Cousin Hesh, four more lines
of poetry to deepen my understanding of the injustices we
suffered . . . The outrage, the disgust inspired in my parents
by the gentiles, was beginning to make some sense: the *goyim*
pretended to be something special, while *we* were actually
their moral superiors. And what made us superior was precisely the hatred and the disrespect they lavished so willingly
upon us!

Only what about the hatred we lavished upon them?

And what about Heshie and Alice? What did *that* mean?

When all else failed, Rabbi Warshaw was asked to join with
the family one Sunday afternoon, to urge our Heshie not to
take his young life and turn it over to his own worst enemy. I
watched from behind a shade in the living room, as the rabbi
strode impressively up the front stoop in his big black coat. He
had given Heshie his bar mitzvah lessons, and I trembled to
think that one day he would give me mine. He remained in
consultation with the defiant boy and the blighted family for
over an hour. "Over an hour of his time," they all said later, as
though that alone should have changed Heshie's mind. But no
sooner did the rabbi depart than the flakes of plaster began
falling once again from the ceiling overhead. A door flew open
—and I ran for the back of the house, to crouch down behind
the shade in my parents' bedroom. There was Heshie into the
yard, pulling at his own black hair. Then came bald Uncle
Hymie, one fist shaking violently in the air—like Lenin he
looked! And then the mob of aunts and uncles and elder
cousins, swarming between the two so as to keep them from
grinding one another into a little heap of Jewish dust.

One Saturday early in May, after competing all day in a
statewide track meet in New Brunswick, Heshie got back to
the high school around dusk, and went immediately across to

the local hangout to telephone Alice and tell her that he had placed third in the state in the javelin throw. She told him that she could never see him again as long as he lived, and hung up.

At home Uncle Hymie was ready and waiting: what he had done, he said, Heshie had forced him to do; what his father had had to do that day, Harold had brought down himself upon his own stubborn, stupid head. It was as though a block-buster had finally fallen upon Newark, so terrifying was the sound that broke on the stairway: Hesh came charging out of his parents' apartment, down the stairs, past our door, and into the cellar, and one long *boom* rolled after him. We saw later that he had ripped the cellar door from its topmost hinge with the force of a shoulder that surely seemed from that piece of evidence to be *at least* the third most powerful shoulder in the state. Beneath our floorboards the breaking of glass began almost immediately, as he hurled bottle after bottle of Squeeze from one dark end of the whitewashed cellar to the other.

When my uncle appeared at the top of the cellar steps, Heshie raised a bottle over his head and threatened to throw it in his father's face if he advanced so much as a step down the stairway. Uncle Hymie ignored the warning and started after him. Heshie now began to race in and out between the fur-naces, to circle and circle the washing machines—still wielding the bottle of Squeeze. But my uncle stalked him into a corner, wrestled him to the floor, and held him there until Heshie had screamed his last obscenity—held him there (so Portnoy leg-end has it) *fifteen minutes*, until the tears of surrender at last appeared on his Heshie's long dark Hollywood lashes. We are not a family that takes defection lightly.

That morning Uncle Hymie had telephoned Alice Dem-bosky (in the basement flat of an apartment building on Gold-smith Avenue, where her father was the janitor) and told her that he wanted to meet her by the lake in Weequahic Park at noon; it was a very urgent matter involving Harold's health—he could not talk at length on the phone, as even Mrs. Portnoy didn't know all the facts. At the park, he drew the skinny blonde wearing the babushka into the front seat of the car, and with the windows rolled up, told her that his son had an incur-able blood disease, a disease about which the poor boy himself did not even know. That was his story, bad blood, make of it what you will . . . It was the doctor's orders that he should not marry anyone, ever. How much longer Harold had to live no one really knew, but as far as Mr. Portnoy was concerned, he did not want to inflict the suffering that was to come, upon an innocent young person like herself. To soften the blow he wanted to offer the girl a gift, a little something that she could use however she wished, maybe even to help her find somebody new. He drew from his pocket an envelope containing five twenty-dollar bills. And dumb, frightened Alice Dembosky took it. Thus proving something that everybody but Heshie (and I) had surmised about the Polack from the beginning: that her plan was to take Heshie for all his father's money, and then ruin his life.

When Heshie was killed in the war, the only thing people could think to say to my Aunt Clara and my Uncle Hymie, to somehow mitigate the horror, to somehow console them in their grief, was, "At least he didn't leave you with a *shikse* wife. At least he didn't leave you with *goyische* children."

End of Heshie and his story.

———

Even if I consider myself too much of a big shot to set foot inside a synagogue for fifteen minutes—which is all he is asking—at least I should have respect enough to change into decent clothes for the day and not make a mockery of myself, my family, and my religion.

"I'm sorry," I mumble, my back (as is usual) all I will offer him to look at while I speak, "but just because it's your religion doesn't mean it's mine."

"What did you say? Turn around, mister, I want the courtesy of a reply from your mouth."

"I don't have a religion," I say, and obligingly turn in his direction, about a fraction of a degree.

"You don't, eh?"

"I can't."

"And why not? You're something special? Look at me! You're somebody too special?"

"I don't believe in God."

"Get out of those dungarees, Alex, and put on some decent clothes."

"They're not dungarees, they're Levis."

"It's Rosh Hashanah, Alex, and to me you're wearing overalls! Get in there and put a tie on and a jacket on and a pair of trousers and a clean shirt, and come out looking like a human being. And shoes, Mister, hard shoes."

"My shirt *is* clean—"

"Oh, you're riding for a fall, Mr. Big. You're fourteen years old, and believe me, you don't know everything there is to know. Get out of those moccasins! What the hell are you supposed to be, some kind of Indian?"

"Look, I don't believe in God and I don't believe in the Jewish religion—or in any religion. They're all lies."

"Oh, they are, are they?"

"I'm not going to act like these holidays mean anything when they don't! And that's all I'm saying!"

"Maybe they don't mean anything because you don't know anything about them, Mr. Big Shot. What do you know about the history of Rosh Hashanah? One fact? Two facts maybe? What do you know about the history of the Jewish people, that you have the right to call their religion, that's been good enough for people a lot smarter than you and a lot older than you for two thousand years—that you can call all that suffering and heartache a lie!"

"There is no such thing as God, and there never was, and I'm sorry, but in my vocabulary that's a lie."

"Then who created the world, Alex?" he asks contemptuously. "It just happened, I suppose, according to you."

"Alex," says my sister, "all Daddy means is even if you don't want to go with him, if you would just change your clothes—"

"But for what?" I scream. "For something that never existed? Why don't you tell me to go outside and change my clothes for some alley cat or some tree—*because at least they exist!*"

"But you haven't answered me, Mr. Educated Wise Guy," my father says. "Don't try to change the issue. Who created the world and the people in it? Nobody?"

"Right! Nobody!"

"Oh, sure," says my father. "That's brilliant. I'm glad I didn't get to high school if that's how brilliant it makes you."

"Alex," my sister says, and softly—as is her way—softly, because she is already broken a little bit too—"maybe if you just put on a pair of shoes—"

"But you're as bad as he is, Hannah! If there's no God, what do shoes have to do with it!"

"One day a year you ask him to do something for you, and he's too big for it. And that's the whole story, Hannah, of your brother, of his respect and love . . ."

"Daddy, he's a good boy. He does respect you, he does love you—"

"And what about the Jewish people?" He is shouting now and waving his arms, hoping that this will prevent him from breaking into tears—because the word love has only to be whispered in our house for all eyes immediately to begin to overflow. "Does he respect them? Just as much as he respects me, just about as much . . ." Suddenly he is sizzling—he turns on me with another new and brilliant thought. "Tell me something, do you know Talmud, my educated son? Do you know history? One-two-three you were bar mitzvah, and that for you was the end of your religious education. Do you know men study their whole lives in the Jewish religion, and when they die they still haven't finished? Tell me, now that you are all finished at fourteen being a Jew, do you know a single thing about the wonderful history and heritage of the saga of your people?"

But there are already tears on his cheeks, and more are on the way from his eyes. "*A*'s in school," he says, "but in life he's as ignorant as the day he was born."

Well, it looks as though the time has come at last—so I say it. It's something I've known for a little while now. "You're the ignorant one! You!"

"Alex!" cries my sister, grabbing for my hand, as though fearful I may actually raise it against him.

"*But he is! With all that stupid saga shit!*"

"Quiet! Still! Enough!" cries Hannah. "Go to your room—"

—While my father carries himself to the kitchen table, his head sunk forward and his body doubled over, as though he has just taken a hand grenade in his stomach. Which he has. Which I know. "You can wear rags for all I care, you can dress like a peddler, you can shame and embarrass me all you want, curse me, Alexander, defy me, hit me, hate me—"

The way it usually works, my mother cries in the kitchen, my father cries in the living room—hiding his eyes behind the *Newark News*—Hannah cries in the bathroom, and I cry on the run between our house and the pinball machine at the corner. But on this particular Rosh Hashanah everything is disarranged, and why my father is crying in the kitchen instead of my mother—why he sobs without protection of the newspaper, and with such pitiful fury—is because my mother is in a hospital bed recovering from surgery: this indeed accounts for his excruciating loneliness on this Rosh Hashanah, and his particular need of my affection and obedience. But at this moment in the history of our family, if he needs it, you can safely bet money that he is not going to get it from me. Because my need is not to give it to him! Oh, yes, we'll turn the tables on him, all right, won't we, Alex you little prick! Yes, Alex the little prick finds that his father's ordinary day-to-day vulnerability is somewhat aggravated by the fact that the man's wife (or so they tell me) has very nearly expired, and so Alex the little prick takes the opportunity to drive the dagger of his resentment just a few inches deeper into what is already a bleeding heart. Alexander the Great!

No! There's more here than just adolescent resentment and Oedipal rage—there's my integrity! I will not do what Heshie did! For I go through childhood *convinced* that had he only wanted to, my powerful cousin Heshie, the third best javelin thrower in all New Jersey (an honor, I would think, rich in symbolism for this growing boy, with visions of jockstraps dancing in his head), could easily have flipped my fifty-year-old uncle over onto his back, and pinned him to the cellar door. So then (I conclude) he must have lost on purpose. But why? For he knew—*I* surely knew it, even as a child—that his father had done something dishonorable. Was he then *afraid* to win? But why, when his own father had acted so vilely, and in Heshie's behalf! Was it cowardice? fear?—or perhaps was it Heshie's wisdom? Whenever the story is told of what my uncle was forced to do to make my dead cousin see the light, or whenever I have cause to reflect upon the event myself, I sense some enigma at its center, a profound moral truth, which if only I could grasp, might save me and my own father from some ultimate, but unimaginable, confrontation. *Why did Heshie capitulate? And should I?* But how can I, and still remain "true to myself"! Oh, but why don't I just try! Give it a little try, you little prick! So *don't* be so true to yourself for half an hour!

Yes, I must give in, I *must*, particularly as I know all my father has been through, what minute by minute misery there has been for him during these tens of thousands of minutes it has taken the doctors to determine, first, that there was something growing in my mother's uterus, and second, whether the growth they finally located was malignant . . . whether what she had was . . . oh, that word we cannot even speak in one another's presence! the word we cannot even spell out in all its horrible entirety! the word we allude to only by the euphemistic abbreviation that she herself supplied us with before entering the hospital for her tests: C-A. And *genug*! The *n*, the *c*, the *e*, the *r*, we don't need to hear to frighten us to Kingdom Come! How brave she is, all our relatives agree, just to utter those two letters! And aren't there enough whole words as it is to whisper at each other behind closed doors? There are! There are! Ugly and cold little words reeking of the ether and alcohol of hospital corridors, words with all the appeal of sterilized surgical instruments, words like *smear* and *biopsy* . . . And then there are the words that furtively, at home alone, I used to look up in the dictionary just to *see* them there in print, the hard evidence of that most remote of all realities, words like *vulva* and *vagina* and *cervix*, words whose definitions will never again serve me as a source of illicit pleasure . . . And then there is that word we wait and wait and wait to hear, the word whose utterance will restore to our family what now seems to have been the most wonderful and satisfying of lives, that word that sounds to my ear like Hebrew, like *b'nai* or *boruch*—benign! *Benign!* Boruch atoh Adonai, *let it be benign!* Blessed art thou O Lord Our God, *let it be benign!* Hear O Israel, and shine down thy countenance, and the Lord is One, and honor thy father, and honor thy mother, and I will I will I promise I will—*only let it be benign!*

And it was. A copy of *Dragon Seed* by Pearl S. Buck is open on the table beside the bed, where there is also a half-empty glass of flat ginger ale. It's hot and I'm thirsty and my mother, my mind reader, says I should go ahead and drink what's left in her glass, I need it more than she does. But dry as I am, I don't want to drink from any glass to which she has put her lips—for the first time in my life the idea fills me with revulsion! "Take." "I'm not thirsty." "Look how you're perspiring." "I'm not thirsty." "Don't be polite all of a sudden." "But I don't *like* ginger ale." "You? Don't like ginger ale?" "*No.*" "Since when?" Oh, God! She's alive, and so we are at it again —she's alive, and right off the bat we're starting in!

She tells me how Rabbi Warshaw came and sat and talked with her for a whole half hour before—as she now so graphically puts it—she went under the knife. Wasn't that nice? Wasn't that thoughtful? (Only twenty-four hours out of anesthetic, and she knows, you see, that I refused to change out of my Levis for the holiday!) The woman who is sharing the room with her, whose loving, devouring gaze I am trying to edge out of, and whose opinion, as I remember it, nobody asked for, takes it upon herself to announce that Rabbi Warshaw is one of the most revered men in all of Newark. Re-ver-ed. Three syllables, as the rabbi himself would enunciate it, in his mighty Anglo-oracular style. I begin to lightly pound at the pocket of my baseball mitt, a signal that I am about ready to go, if only someone will let me. "He loves baseball, he could play baseball twelve months a year," my mother tells Mrs. Re-ver-ed. I mumble that I have "a league game." "It's the finals. For the championship." "Okay," says my mother, and lovingly, "you came, you did your duty, now run—run to your league game." I can hear in her voice how happy and relieved she is to find herself alive on this beautiful September afternoon . . . And isn't it a relief for me, too? Isn't this what I prayed for, to a God I do not even believe is there? Wasn't the unthinkable thing life without her to cook for us, to clean for us, to . . . to *everything* for us! This is what I prayed and wept for: that she should come out at the other end of her operation, and be alive. And then come home, to be once again our one and only mother. "Run, my baby-boy," my mother croons to me, and sweetly—oh, she can be so sweet and good to me, so motherly! she will spend hour after hour playing canasta with me, when I am sick and in bed as she is now: imagine, the ginger ale the nurse has brought for her because she has had a serious operation, she offers to *me*, because I'm overheated! Yes, she *will* give me the food out of her mouth, that's a proven fact! And still I will not stay five full minutes at her bedside. "Run," says my mother, while Mrs. Re-ver-ed, who in no time at all has managed to make herself my enemy, and for the rest of my life, Mrs. Re-ver-ed says, "Soon Mother will be home, soon everything will be just like ordinary . . . Sure, run, run, they all run these days," says the kind and understanding lady—oh, they are all so kind and understanding, I want to strangle them!—"walking they never heard of, God bless them."

So I run. Do I run! Having spent maybe two fretful minutes with her—two minutes of my precious time, even though just the day before, the doctors stuck right up her dress (so I imagined it, before my mother reminded me of "the knife," our knife) some kind of horrible shovel with which to scoop out what had gone rotten inside her body. They reached up and pulled down out of her just what she used to reach up and pull down out of the dead chicken. And threw it in the garbage can. Where I was conceived and carried, there now is *nothing*. A void! Poor Mother! How can I rush to leave her like this, after what she has just gone through? After all she has given me—my very life!—how can I be so cruel? "Will you leave me, my baby-boy, will you ever leave Mommy?" Never, I would answer, never, never, never . . . And yet now that she is hollowed out, I cannot even look her in the eye! And have avoided doing so ever since! Oh, there is her pale red hair, spread across the pillow in long strands of springy ringlets *that I might never have seen again*. There are the faint moons of freckles that she says used to cover her entire face when she was a small child, *and that I would never have seen again*. And there are those eyes of reddish brown, eyes the color of the crust of honey cake, *and still open, still loving me!* There was her ginger ale—and thirsty as I was, I could not have *forced* myself to drink it!

So I ran all right, out of the hospital and up to the playground and right out to center field, the position I play for a softball team that wears silky blue-and-gold jackets with the name of the club scrawled in big white felt letters from one shoulder to the other: S E A B E E S, A.C. Thank God for the Seabees A.C.! Thank God for center field! Doctor, you can't imagine how truly glorious it is out there, so alone in all that space . . . Do you know baseball at all? Because center field is like some observation post, a kind of control tower, where you are able to see everything and everyone, to understand what's happening the instant it happens, not only by the sound of the struck bat, but by the spark of movement that goes through the infielders in the first second that the ball comes flying at them; and once it gets beyond them, "It's mine," you call, "it's mine," and then after it you go. For in center field, if you can get it, it *is* yours. Oh, how unlike my home it is to be in center field, where no one will appropriate unto himself anything that I say is *mine!*

Unfortunately, I was too anxious a hitter to make the high school team—I swung and missed at bad pitches so often during the tryouts for the freshman squad that eventually the ironical coach took me aside and said, "Sonny, are you sure you don't wear glasses?" and then sent me on my way. But did I have form! did I have style! And in my playground softball league, where the ball came in just a little slower and a little bigger, I am the star I dreamed I might become for the whole school. Of course, still in my ardent desire to excel I too frequently swing and miss, but when I connect, it goes great distances, Doctor, it flies over fences and is called a home run. Oh, and there is really nothing in life, nothing at all, that quite compares with that pleasure of rounding second base at a nice slow clip, because there's just no hurry any more, because that ball you've hit has just gone sailing out of sight . . . And I could field, too, and the farther I had to run, the better. "I got it! I got it!" and tear in toward second, to trap in the webbing of my glove—and barely an inch off the ground—a ball driven hard and low and right down the middle, a base hit, someone thought . . . Or back I go, "*I* got it, *I* got it—" back easily and gracefully toward that wire fence, moving practically in slow motion, and then that delicious Di Maggio sensation of grabbing it like something heaven-sent over one shoulder . . . Or running! turning! leaping! like little Al Gionfriddo—a baseball player, Doctor, who once did a very great thing . . . Or just standing nice and calm—nothing trembling, everything serene—standing there in the sunshine (as though in the middle of an empty field, or passing the time on the street corner), standing without a care in the world in the sunshine, like my king of kings, the Lord my God, The Duke Himself (Snider, Doctor, the name may come up again), standing there as loose and as easy, as happy as I will ever be, just waiting by myself under a high fly ball (*a towering fly ball*, I hear Red Barber say, as he watches from behind his microphone—hit out toward Portnoy; *Alex under it, under it*), just waiting there for the ball to fall into the glove I raise to it, and yup, there it is, *plock*, the third out of the inning (*and Alex gathers it in for out number three, and, folks, here's old C.D. for P. Lorillard and Company*), and then in one motion, while old Connie brings us a message from Old Golds, I start in toward the bench, holding the ball now with the five fingers of my bare left hand, and when I get to the infield—having come down hard with one foot on the bag at second base—I shoot it gently, with just a flick of the wrist, at the opposing team's shortstop as he comes trotting out onto the field, and still without breaking stride, go loping in all the way, shoulders shifting, head hanging, a touch pigeon-toed, my knees coming slowly up and down in an altogether brilliant imitation of The Duke. Oh, the unruffled nonchalance of that game! There's not a movement that I don't know still down in the tissue of my muscles and the joints between my bones. How to bend over to pick up my glove and how to toss it away, how to test the weight of the bat, how to hold it and carry it and swing it around in the on-deck circle, how to raise that bat above my head and flex and loosen my shoulders and my neck before stepping in and planting my two feet exactly where my two feet belong in the batter's box—and how, when I take a called strike (which I have a tendency to do, it balances off nicely swinging at bad pitches), to step out and express, if only through a slight poking with the bat at the ground, just the right amount of exasperation with the powers that be . . . yes, every little detail so thoroughly studied and mastered, that it is simply beyond the realm of possibility for any situation to arise in which I do not know how to move, or where to move, or what to say or leave unsaid . . . And it's true, is it not?— incredible, but apparently true—there are people who feel in life the ease, the self-assurance, the simple and essential affiliation with what is going on, that I used to feel as the center fielder for the Seabees? Because it wasn't, you see, that one was the best center fielder imaginable, only that one knew exactly, and down to the smallest particular, how a center fielder should conduct himself. And there are people like that walking the streets of the U.S. of A.? I ask you, why can't I be one! Why can't I exist now as I existed for the Seabees out there in center field! Oh, to be a center fielder, a center fielder—and nothing more!

—

But I am something more, or so they tell me. A Jew. No! No! An *atheist*, I cry. I am a nothing where religion is concerned, and I will not pretend to be anything that I am not! I don't care how lonely and needy my father is, the truth about me is the truth about me, and I'm sorry but he'll just have to swallow my apostasy whole! And I don't care how close we came to sitting *shiva* for my mother either—actually, I wonder now if maybe the whole hysterectomy has not been dramatized into C-A and out of it again solely for the sake of scaring the S-H out of me! Solely for the sake of humbling and frightening me into being once again an obedient and helpless little boy! And I find no argument for the existence of God, or for the benevolence and virtue of the Jews, in the fact that the most re-ver-ed man in all of Newark came to sit for "a whole half hour" beside my mother's bed. If he emptied her bedpan, if he fed her her meals, that might be the beginning of something, but to come for half an hour and sit beside a bed? What else has he got to do, Mother? To him, uttering beautiful banalities to people scared out of their wits—that is to him what playing baseball is to me! He loves it! And who wouldn't? Mother, Rabbi Warshaw is a fat, pompous, impatient fraud, with an absolutely grotesque superiority complex, a character out of Dickens is what he is, someone who if you stood next to him on the bus and didn't know he was so revered, you would say, "That man stinks to high heaven of cigarettes," and that is *all* you would say. This is a man who somewhere along the line got the idea that the basic unit of meaning in the English language is the syllable. So no word he pronounces has less than three of them, not even the word *God*. You should hear the song and dance he makes out of *Israel*. For him it's as long as refrigerator! And do you remember him at my bar mitzvah, what a field day he had with Alexander Portnoy? Why, Mother, did he keep calling me by my whole name? Why, except to impress all you idiots in the audience with all those syllables! And it worked! It actually worked! Don't you understand, the synagogue is how he earns his living, *and that's all there is to it*. Coming to the hospital to be brilliant about life (syllable by syllable) to people who are shaking in their pajamas about death is his business, just as it is my father's business to sell life insurance! It is what they each do to earn a living, and if you want to feel pious about somebody, feel pious about my father, God damn it, and bow down to him the way you bow down to that big fat comical son of a bitch, because my father *really* works his balls off and doesn't happen to think that he is God's special assistant into the bargain. And doesn't speak in those fucking *syllables*! "I-a wan-tt to-a wel-come-a you-ew tooo thee sy-no-gawg-a." Oh God, oh Guh-ah-duh, if you're up there shining down your countenance, why not spare us from here on out the enunciation of the rabbis! Why not spare us the rabbis themselves! Look, why not spare us religion, if only in the name of our human dignity! Good Christ, Mother, the whole world knows already, *so why don't you? Religion is the opiate of the people!* And if believing that makes me a fourteen-year-old Communist, then that's what I am, *and I'm proud of it!* I would rather be a Communist in Russia than a Jew in a synagogue any day—so I tell my father right to his face, too. Another grenade to the gut is what it turns out to be (I suspected as much), but I'm sorry, I happen to believe in the rights of man, rights such as are extended in the Soviet Union to *all* people, regardless of race, religion, or color. My communism, in fact, is why I now insist on eating with the cleaning lady when I come home for my lunch on Mondays and see that she is there—I will eat with her, Mother, at the same table, *and the same food*. Is that clear? If I get leftover pot roast warmed-up, then she gets leftover pot roast warmed-up, and not creamy Muenster or tuna either, served on a special glass plate that doesn't absorb her germs! But no, no, Mother doesn't get the idea, apparently. Too bizarre, apparently. Eat with the *shvartze*? What could I be talking about? She whispers to me in the hallway, the instant I come in from school, "Wait, the girl will be finished in a few minutes . . ." *But I will not treat any human being* (outside my family) *as inferior!* Can't you grasp something of the principle of equality, God damn it! And I tell you, if he ever uses the word nigger in my presence again, I will drive a real dagger into his fucking bigoted heart! *Is that clear to everyone?* I don't care that his clothes stink so bad after he comes home from collecting the colored debit that they have to be hung in the cellar to air out. I don't care that they drive him nearly crazy letting their insurance lapse. That is only another reason to be compassionate, God damn it, to be sympathetic and understanding and to stop treating the cleaning lady as though she were some kind of mule, without the same passion for dignity that other people have! And that goes for the *goyim*, too! We all haven't been lucky enough to have been born Jews, you know. So a little *rachmones* on the less fortunate, okay? Because I am sick and tired of *goyische* this and *goyische* that! If it's bad it's the *goyim*, if it's good it's the Jews! Can't you see, my dear parents, from whose loins I somehow leaped, that such thinking is a trifle barbaric? That all you are expressing is your *fear?* The very first distinction I learned from you, I'm sure, was not night and day, or hot and cold, but *goyische* and Jewish! But now it turns out, my dear parents, relatives, and assembled friends who have gathered here to celebrate the occasion of my bar mitzvah, it turns out, you schmucks! you narrow-minded schmucks! —oh, how I hate you for your Jewish narrow-minded minds! including you, Rabbi Syllable, who have for the last time in your life sent me out to the corner for another pack of Pall Mall cigarettes, from which you *reek* in case nobody has ever told you—it turns out that there is just a little bit more to existence than what can be contained in those disgusting and useless categories! And instead of crying over he-who refuses at the age of fourteen ever to set foot inside a synagogue again, instead of wailing for he-who has turned his back on the saga of *his people*, weep for your own pathetic selves, why don't you, sucking and sucking on that sour grape of a religion! Jew Jew Jew Jew Jew Jew! It is coming out of my ears already, the saga of the suffering Jews! Do me a favor, my people, and stick your suffering heritage up your suffering ass—*I happen also to be a human being!*

—

But you *are* a Jew, my sister says. You are a Jewish boy, more than you know, and all you're doing is making yourself miserable, all you're doing is hollering into the wind . . . Through my tears I see her patiently explaining my predicament to me from the end of my bed. If I am fourteen, she is eighteen, and in her first year at Newark State Teacher's College, a big sallow-faced girl, oozing melancholy at every pore. Sometimes with another big, homely girl named Edna Tepper (who has, however, to recommend her, tits the size of my head), she goes to a folk dance at the Newark Y. This summer she is going to be crafts counselor in the Jewish Community Center day camp. I have seen her reading a paperback book with a greenish cover called *A Portrait of the Artist as a Young Man.* All I seem to know about her are these few facts, and of course the size and smell of her brassiere and panties. What years of confusion! And when will they be over? Can you give me a tentative date, please? When will I be cured of what I've got!

Do you know, she asks me, where you would be now if you had been born in Europe instead of America?

That isn't the issue, Hannah.

Dead, she says.

That isn't the issue!

Dead. Gassed, or shot, or incinerated, or butchered, or burned alive. Do you know that? And you could have screamed all you wanted that you were not a Jew, that you were a human being and had nothing whatever to do with their stupid suffering heritage, and still you would have been taken away to be disposed of. You would be dead, and I would be dead, and

But that isn't what I'm talking about!

And your mother and father would be dead.

But why are you taking their side!

I'm not taking anybody's side, she says. I'm only telling you he's not such an ignorant person as you think.

And she isn't either, I suppose! I suppose the Nazis make everything she says and does smart and brilliant too! I suppose the Nazis are an excuse for everything that happens in this house!

Oh, I don't know, says my sister, maybe, maybe they are, and now she begins to cry too, and how monstrous I feel, for she sheds her tears for six million, or so I think, while I shed mine only for myself. Or so I think.

CUNT CRAZY

Did I mention that when I was fifteen I took it out of my pants and whacked off on the 107 bus from New York?

I had been treated to a perfect day by my sister and Morty Feibish, her fiancé—a doubleheader at Ebbets Field, followed afterward by a seafood dinner at Sheepshead Bay. An exquisite day. Hannah and Morty were to stay overnight in Flatbush with Morty's family, and so I was put on a subway to Manhattan about ten o'clock—and there boarded the bus for New Jersey, upon which I took not just my cock in my hands but my whole life, when you think about it. The passengers were mostly drowsing off before we had even emerged from the Lincoln Tunnel—including the girl in the seat beside me, whose tartan skirt folds I had begun to press up against with the corduroy of my trouser legs—and I had it out and in my fist by the time we were climbing onto the Pulaski Skyway.

You might have thought that given the rich satisfactions of the day, I'd have had my fill of excitement and my dick would have been the last thing on my mind heading home that night. Bruce Edwards, a new catcher up from the minors—and just what we needed (we being Morty, myself, and Burt Shotton, the Dodger manager)—had gone something like six for eight in his first two games in the majors (or was it Furillo? at any rate, how insane whipping out my joint like that! imagine what would have been had I been caught red-handed! imagine if I had gone ahead and come all over that sleeping *shikse*'s golden arm!) and then for dinner Morty had ordered me a lobster, the first of my life.

Now, maybe the lobster is what did it. That taboo so easily and simply broken, confidence may have been given to the whole slimy, suicidal Dionysian side of my nature; the lesson may have been learned that to break the law, all you have to do is—just go ahead and break it! All you have to do is stop trembling and quaking and finding it unimaginable and beyond you: all you have to do, *is do it!* What else, I ask you, were all those prohibitive dietary rules and regulations all about to begin with, what else but to give us little Jewish children practice in being repressed? Practice, darling, practice, practice, practice. Inhibition doesn't grow on trees, you know—takes patience, takes concentration, takes a dedicated and self-sacrificing parent and a hard-working attentive little child to create in only a few years' time a really constrained and tight-ass human being. Why else the two sets of dishes? Why else the kosher soap and salt? Why else, I ask you, but to remind us three times a day that life is boundaries and restrictions if it's anything, hundreds of thousands of little rules laid down by none other than None Other, rules which either you obey without question, regardless of how idiotic they may appear (and thus remain, by obeying, in His good graces), or you transgress, most likely in the name of outraged common sense —which you transgress because even a child doesn't like to go around feeling like an absolute moron and schmuck—yes, you transgress, only with the strong likelihood (my father assures me) that comes next Yom Kippur and the names are written in the big book where He writes the names of those who are going to get to live until the following September (a scene which manages somehow to engrave itself upon my imagination), and lo, your own precious name ain't among them. Now who's the schmuck, huh? And it doesn't make any difference either (this I understand from the outset, about the way this God, Who runs things, reasons) how big or how small the rule is that you break: it's the breaking alone that gets His goat—it's the simple fact of waywardness, and that alone, that He absolutely cannot stand, and which He does not forget either, when He sits angrily down (fuming probably, and surely with a smashing miserable headache, like my father at the height of his constipation) and begins to leave the names out of that book.

When duty, discipline, and obedience give way—ah, here, *here* is the message I take in each Passover with my mother's *matzoh brei*—what follows, there is no predicting. Renunciation is all, cries the koshered and bloodless piece of steak my family and I sit down to eat at dinner time. Self-control, sobriety, sanctions—this is the key to a human life, saith all those

endless dietary laws. Let the *goyim* sink *their* teeth into whatever lowly creature crawls and grunts across the face of the
dirty earth, we will not contaminate our humanity thus. Let
them (if you know who I mean) gorge themselves upon anything and everything that moves, no matter how odious and
abject the animal, no matter how grotesque or *shmutzig* or
dumb the creature in question happens to be. Let them eat
eels and frogs and pigs and crabs and lobsters; let them eat vul-
ture, let them eat ape-meat and skunk if they like—a diet of
abominable creatures well befits a breed of mankind so hopelessly shallow and empty-headed as to drink, to divorce, and to
fight with their fists. All they know, these imbecilic eaters of
the execrable, is to swagger, to insult, to sneer, and sooner or
later to hit. Oh, also they know how to go out into the woods
with a gun, these geniuses, and kill innocent wild deer, deer
who themselves *nosh* quietly on berries and grasses and then
go on their way, bothering no one. You stupid *goyim*! Reeking
of beer and empty of ammunition, home you head, a dead animal (formerly *alive*) strapped to each fender, so that all the
motorists along the way can see how strong and manly you
are; and then, in your houses, you take these deer—who have
done you, who have done nothing in all of nature, not the
least bit of harm—you take these deer, cut them up into
pieces, and cook them in a pot. There isn't enough to eat in
this world, they have to eat up the *deer* as well! They will eat
anything, anything they can get their big *goy* hands on! And
the terrifying corollary, *they will do anything as well*. Deer eat
what deer eat, and Jews eat what Jews eat, but not these
goyim. Crawling animals, wallowing animals, leaping and angelic animals—it makes no difference to them—what they
want they take, and to hell with the other thing's feelings (let
alone kindness and compassion). Yes, it's all written down in
history, what they have done, our illustrious neighbors who
own the world and know absolutely nothing of human boundaries and limits.
    . . . Thus saith the kosher laws, at least to the child I was,
growing up under the tutelage of Sophie and Jack P., and in a
school district of Newark where in my entire class there are
only two little Christian children, and they live in houses I do
not enter, on the far fringes of our neighborhood . . . thus

saith the kosher laws, and who am I to argue that they're wrong? For look at Alex himself, the subject of *our* every syllable—age fifteen, he sucks one night on a lobster's claw and within the hour his cock is out and aimed at a *shikse* on a Public Service bus. And his superior Jewish brain might as well be *made* of *matzoh brei*!

—

Such a creature, needless to say, has never been boiled alive in our house—the lobster, I refer to. A *shikse* has never been in our house period, and so it's a matter of conjecture in what condition she might emerge from my mother's kitchen. The cleaning lady is obviously a *shikse*, but she doesn't count because she's black.

Ha ha. A *shikse* has never been in our house because *I* have brought her there, is what I mean to say. I do recall one that my own father brought home with him for dinner one night when I was still a boy: a thin, tense, shy, deferential, soft-spoken, aging cashier from his office named Anne McCaffery.

Doctor, could he have been slipping it to her? I can't believe it! Only it suddenly occurs to me. Could my father have been slipping it to this lady on the side? I can still remember how she sat down beside me on the sofa, and in her nervousness made a lengthy to-do of spelling her first name, and of pointing out to me how it ended with an E, which wasn't always the case with someone called Anne—and so on and so forth . . . and meanwhile, though her arms were long and white and skinny and freckled (Irish arms, I thought) inside her smooth white blouse, I could see she had breasts that were nice and substantial—and I kept taking peeks at her legs, too. I was only eight or nine, but she really did have such a terrific pair of legs that I couldn't keep my eyes away from them, the kind of legs that every once in a while it surprises you to find some pale spinster with a pinched face walking around on top of . . . With those legs—why, *of course* he was *shtupping* her . . . *Wasn't* he?

Why he brought her home, *he* said, was "for a real Jewish meal." For weeks he had been jabbering about the new *goyische* cashier ("a very plain drab person," he said, "who dresses in *shmattas*") who had been pestering him—so went the story he couldn't stop telling us—for a real Jewish meal from

the day she had come to work in the Boston & Northeastern office. Finally my mother couldn't take any more. "All
right, bring her already—she needs it so bad, so I'll give her
one." Was he caught a little by surprise? Who will ever know.

At any rate, a Jewish meal is what she got all right. I don't
think I have ever heard the word "Jewish" spoken so many
times in one evening in my life, and let me tell you, I am a person who has heard the word "Jewish" spoken.

"This is your real Jewish chopped liver, Anne. Have you
ever had real Jewish chopped liver before? Well, my wife makes
the real thing, you can bet your life on that. Here, you eat it
with a piece of bread This is real Jewish rye bread, with seeds.
That's it, Anne, you're doing very good, ain't she doing good,
Sophie, for her first time? That's it, take a nice piece of real
Jewish rye, now take a big fork full of the real Jewish chopped
liver"—and on and on, right down to the jello—"that's right,
Anne, the jello is kosher too, sure, of course, has to be—oh
no, oh no, no cream in your coffee, not after meat, ha ha, hear
what Anne wanted, Alex—?"

But babble-babble all you want, Dad dear, a question has
just occurred to me, twenty-five years later (not that I have a
single shred of evidence, not that until this moment I have
ever imagined my father capable of even the slightest infraction of domestic law . . . but since infraction seems to hold
for me a certain fascination), a question has arisen in the audience: why *did* you bring a *shikse*, of all things, into our home?
Because you couldn't bear that a gentile woman should go
through life without the experience of eating a dish of Jewish
jello? Or because you could no longer live your own life without making Jewish confession? Without confronting your wife
with your crime, so she might accuse, castigate, humiliate,
punish, and thus bleed you forever of your forbidden lusts!
Yes, a regular Jewish desperado, my father. I recognize the syn-
drome perfectly. Come, someone, anyone, find me out and
condemn me—I did the most terrible thing you can think of: I
took what I am not supposed to have! Chose pleasure for myself over duty to my loved ones! Please, catch me, incarcerate
me, before God forbid I get away with it completely—and go
out and do again something I actually like!

And did my mother oblige? Did Sophie put together the

two tits and the two legs and come up with four? Me it seems to have taken two and a half decades to do such steep calculation. Oh, I must be making this up, really. My father . . . and a *shikse*? Can't be. Was beyond his ken. My own father— fucked *shikses*? I'll admit under duress that he fucked my mother . . . but *shikses*? I can no more imagine him knocking over a gas station.

But then why is she shouting at him so, what is this scene of accusation and denial, of castigation and threat and unending tears . . . what is this all about except that he has done something that is very bad and maybe even unforgivable? The scene itself is like some piece of heavy furniture that sits in my mind and will not budge—which leads me to believe that, yes, it actually did happen. My sister, I see, is hiding behind my mother: Hannah is clutching her around the middle and whimpering, while my mother's own tears are tremendous and fall from her face all the way to the linoleum floor. Simultaneously with the tears she is screaming so loud at him that her veins stand out—and screaming at me, too, because, looking further into this thing, I find that while Hannah hides behind my mother, *I take refuge behind the culprit himself*. Oh, this is pure fantasy, this is right out of the casebook, is it not? No, no, that is nobody else's father but my own who now brings his fist down on the kitchen table and shouts back at her, "I did no such thing! That is a lie and wrong!" Only wait a minute—it's *me* who is screaming "I didn't do it!" *The culprit is me!* And why my mother weeps so is because my father refuses to *potch* my behind, which she promised would be *potched*, "and good," when he found out the terrible thing *I* had done.

When I am bad and rotten in small ways she can manage me herself: she has, you recall—I know *I* recall!—only to put me in my coat and galoshes—oh, nice touch, Mom, those galoshes! —lock me out of the house (*lock me out of the house!*) and announce through the door that she is never going to let me in again, so I might as well be off and into my new life; she has only to take that simple and swift course of action to get instantaneously a confession, a self-scorification, and, if she should want it, a signed warranty that I will be one hundred percent pure and good for the rest of my life—all this if only I am allowed back inside that door, where they happen to have my bed and my clothes and *the refrigerator*. But when I am really wicked, so evil that she can only raise her arms to God Almighty to ask Him what she has done to deserve such a child, at such times my father is called in to mete out justice; my mother is herself too sensitive, too fine a creature, it turns out, to administer corporal punishment: "It hurts me," I hear her explain to my Aunt Clara, "more than it hurts him. That's the kind of person I am. I can't do it, and that's that." Oh, poor Mother.

But look, what is going on here after all? Surely, Doctor, we can figure this thing out, two smart Jewish boys like ourselves . . . A terrible act has been committed, and it has been committed by either my father or me. The wrongdoer, in other words, is one of the two members of the family who owns a penis. Okay. So far so good. Now: did he fuck between those luscious legs the gentile cashier from the office, or have I eaten my sister's chocolate pudding? You see, she *didn't* want it at dinner, but apparently *did* want it saved so she could have it before she went to bed. Well, good Christ, how was I supposed to know all that, Hannah? Who looks into the fine points when he's hungry? I'm eight years old and chocolate pudding happens to get me hot. All I have to do is see that deep chocolatey surface gleaming out at me from the refrigerator, and my life isn't my own. Furthermore, I *thought* it was *left over*! And that's the truth! Jesus Christ, is that what this screaming and *shrying* is all about, that I ate that sad sack's chocolate pudding? Even if I did, I didn't mean it! I thought it was something else! I swear, I swear, I didn't mean to do it! . . . But *is* that me—or my father hollering out his defense before the jury? Sure, that's him—he did it, okay, okay, Sophie, leave me alone already, I did it, *but I didn't mean it!* Shit, the next thing he'll tell her is why he should be forgiven is because he didn't *like* it either. What do you mean, you didn't *mean* it, schmuck—you stuck it in there, didn't you? Then stick up for yourself now, like a man! Tell her, tell her: "That's right, Sophie, I slipped it to the *shikse*, and what you think and don't think on the subject don't mean shit to me. Because the way it works, in case you ain't heard, is that I am the man around here, *and I call the shots!*" And slug her if you have to! Deck her, Jake! Surely that's what a *goy* would do, would he not?

Do you think one of those big-shot deer hunters with a gun collapses in a chair when he gets caught committing the seventh and starts weeping and begging his wife to be *forgiven?*— forgiven for *what?* What after all does it consist of? You put your dick some place and moved it back and forth and stuff came out the front. So, Jake, what's the big deal? How long did the whole thing last that you should suffer such damnation from her mouth—such guilt, such recrimination and self-loathing! Poppa, why do we have to have such guilty deference to women, you and me—when we don't! We mustn't! Who should run the show, Poppa, is *us!* "Daddy has done a terrible terrible thing," cries my mother—or is that my imagination? Isn't what she is saying more like, "Oh, little Alex has done a terrible thing again, Daddy—" Whatever, she lifts Hannah (of all people, Hannah!), who until that moment I had never really taken seriously as a genuine object of anybody's love, takes her up into her arms and starts kissing her all over her sad and unloved face, saying that her little girl is the only one in the whole wide world she can really trust . . . But if I am eight, Hannah is twelve, and nobody is picking her up, I assure you, because the poor kid's problem is that she is overweight, "and how," my mother says. She's not even supposed to *eat* chocolate pudding. Yeah, *that's* why I took it! Tough shit, Hannah, it's what the *doctor* ordered, not me. I can't help it if you're fat and "sluggish" and I'm skinny and brilliant. I can't help it that I'm so beautiful they stop Mother when she is wheeling me in my carriage so as to get a good look at my gorgeous *punim*—you hear her tell that story, it's something I myself had nothing to do with, it's a simple fact of nature, that I was born beautiful and you were born, if not ugly, certainly not something people wanted to take special looks at. And is that my fault, too? How you were born, four whole years before I even entered the world? Apparently this is the way God wants it to be, Hannah! In the big book!

But the fact of the matter is, she doesn't seem to hold me responsible for anything: she just goes on being good to her darling little baby brother, and never once strikes me or calls me a dirty name. I take her chocolate pudding, and she takes my shit, and never says a word in protest. Just kisses me before I go to bed, and carefully crosses me going to school, and then stands back and obligingly allows herself to be swallowed up by the wall (I guess that's where she is) when I am imitating for my beaming parents all the voices on "Allen's Alley," or being heralded to relatives from one end of North Jersey to the other for my perfect report card. Because when I am not being punished, Doctor, I am being carried around that house like the Pope through the streets of Rome . . .

You know, I can really come up with no more than a dozen memories involving my sister from those early years of my childhood. Mostly, until she emerges in my adolescence as the only sane person in that lunatic asylum whom I can talk to, it is as though she is someone we see maybe once or twice a year —for a night or two she visits with us, eating at our table, sleeping in one of our beds, and then, poor fat thing, she just blessedly disappears.

—

Even in the Chinese restaurant, where the Lord has lifted the ban on pork dishes for the obedient children of Israel, the eating of lobster Cantonese is considered by God (Whose mouthpiece on earth, in matters pertaining to food, is my Mom) to be totally out of the question. Why we can eat pig on Pell Street and not at home is because . . . frankly I still haven't got the whole thing figured out, but at the time I believe it has largely to do with the fact that the elderly man who owns the place, and whom amongst ourselves we call "*Shmendrick*," isn't somebody whose opinion of us we have cause to worry about. Yes, the only people in the world whom it seems to me the Jews are not afraid of are the Chinese. Because, one, the way they speak English makes my father sound like Lord Chesterfield; two, the insides of their heads are just so much fried rice anyway; and three, to them we are not Jews but *white* —and maybe even Anglo-Saxon. Imagine! No wonder the waiters can't intimidate us. To them we're just some big-nosed variety of WASP! Boy, do we eat! Suddenly even the pig is no threat—though, to be sure, it comes to us so chopped and shredded, and is then set afloat on our plates in such oceans of soy sauce, as to bear no resemblance at all to a pork chop, or a hambone, or, most disgusting of all, a *sausage* (ucchh!) . . . But why then can't we eat a lobster, too, disguised as something else? Allow my mother a logical explanation. The syllogism, Doctor, as used by Sophie Portnoy. Ready? Why we can't eat lobster. "Because it can kill you! Because I ate it once, and I nearly died!"

Yes, she too has committed her transgressions, and has been duly punished. In her wild youth (which all took place before I got to know her) she had allowed herself to be bamboozled (which is to say, flattered and shamed simultaneously) into eating lobster Newburg by a mischievous, attractive insurance agent who worked with my father for Boston & Northeastern, a lush named (could it be better?) Doyle.

It was at a convention held by the company in Atlantic City, at a noisy farewell banquet, that Doyle led my mother to believe that even though that wasn't what it smelled like, the plate the waiter had shoved in front of her corsage contained nothing but chicken à la king. To be sure, she sensed that something was up even then, suspected even as the handsome drunken Doyle tried to feed her with her own fork that tragedy, as she calls it, was lurking in the wings. But high herself on the fruit of two whiskey sours, she rashly turned up her long Jewish nose to a very genuine premonition of foul play, and— oh, hotheaded bitch! wanton hussy! improvident adventuress! —surrendered herself wholly to the spirit of reckless abandon that apparently had taken possession of this hall full of insurance agents and their wives. Not until the sherbet arrived did Doyle—who my mother also describes as "in looks a second Errol Flynn, and not just in looks"—did Doyle reveal to her what it was she had actually ingested.

Subsequently she was over the toilet all night throwing up. "My *kishkas* came out from that thing! Some practical joker! That's why to this day I tell you, Alex, never to commit a practical joke—because the consequences can be tragic! I was so sick, Alex," she used to love to remind herself and me, and my father too, five, ten, fifteen years after the cataclysm itself, "that your father, Mr. Brave One here, had to call the hotel doctor out of a sound sleep to come to the room. See how I'm holding my fingers? I was throwing up so hard, they got stiff just like this, like I was *paralyzed*, and *ask* your father—Jack, tell him, tell him what you thought when you saw what happened to my fingers from the lobster Newburg." "What lobster Newburg?" "That your friend Doyle forced down my throat." "Doyle? What Doyle?" "Doyle, the *Shicker Goy* Who They Had To Transfer To The Wilds of South Jersey He Was Such A Run-Around. Doyle! Who Looked Like Errol Flynn! Tell Alex what happened to my fingers, that you *thought* happened—" "Look, I don't even know what you're talking about," which is probably the case: not everybody quite senses my mother's life to be the high drama she herself experiences —also, there is always a possibility that this story has more to do with imagination than reality (more to do, needless to say, with the dangerous Doyle than the forbidden lobster). And then, of course, my father is a man who has a certain amount of worrying to do each day, and sometimes he just has to forgo listening to the conversations going on around him in order to fulfill his anxiety requirement. It can well be that he hasn't really heard a word she's been saying.

But on it goes, my mother's monologue. As other children hear the story of Scrooge every year, or are read to nightly from some favorite book, I am continually *shtupped* full of the suspense-filled chapters of her perilous life. This in fact is the literature of my childhood, these stories of my mother's— the only bound books in the house, aside from schoolbooks, are those that have been given as presents to my parents when one or the other was recuperating in the hospital. One third of our library consists of *Dragon Seed* (her hysterectomy) (moral: nothing is never ironic, there's always a laugh lurking somewhere) and the other two thirds are *Argentine Diary* by William L. Shirer and (same moral) *The Memoirs of Casanova* (his appendectomy). Otherwise our books are written by Sophie Portnoy, each an addition to that famous series of hers entitled, *You Know Me, I'll Try Anything Once*. For the idea that seems to generate and inform her works is that she is some sort of daredevil who goes exuberantly out into life in search of the new and the thrilling, only to be slapped down for her pioneering spirit. She actually seems to think of herself as a woman at the very frontiers of experience, some doomed dazzling combination of Marie Curie, Anna Karenina, and Amelia Earhart. At any rate, that is the sort of romantic image of her which this little boy goes to bed with, after she has buttoned him into his pajamas and tucked him between the sheets with the story of how she learned to drive a car when she was pregnant with my sister, and the very first day that she had her license—"the very first *hour*, Alex"—"some maniac" slammed into her rear bumper, and consequently she has never driven a car from that moment on. Or the story of how she was searching for the goldfish in a pond at Saratoga Springs, New York, where she had been taken at the age of ten to visit an old sick aunt, and accidentally fell in, right to the bottom of the filthy pond, and has not gone into the water since, not even down the shore, when it's low tide and a lifeguard is on duty. And then there is the lobster, which even in her drunkenness she knew it wasn't chicken à la king, but only "to shut up the mouth on that Doyle" had forced down her throat, and subsequently the near-tragedy happened, and she has not of course eaten anything even faintly resembling lobster since. And does not want me to either. Ever. Not, she says, if I know what is good for me. "There are plenty of good things to eat in the world, Alex, without eating a thing like a lobster and running the risk of having paralyzed hands for the rest of your life."

—

Whew! Have I got grievances! Do I harbor hatreds I didn't even know were there! Is it the process, Doctor, or is it what we call "the material"? All I do is complain, the repugnance seems bottomless, and I'm beginning to wonder if maybe enough isn't enough. I hear myself indulging in the kind of ritualized bellyaching that is just what gives psychoanalytic patients such a bad name with the general public. Could I really have detested this childhood and resented these poor parents of mine to the same degree then as I seem to now, looking backward upon what I was from the vantage point of what I am—and am not? Is this truth I'm delivering up, or is it just plain *kvetching*? Or is *kvetching* for people like me a *form* of truth? Regardless, my conscience wishes to make it known, before the beefing begins anew, that *at the time* my boyhood was not this thing I feel so estranged from and resentful of now. Vast as my confusion was, deep as my inner turmoil seems to appear in retrospect, I don't remember that I was one of those kids who went around wishing he lived in another house with other people, whatever my unconscious yearnings may have been in that direction. After all, where else would I find an audience like those two for my imitations? I used to leave them in the aisles at mealtime—my mother once actually wet her pants, Doctor, and had to go running in hysterical laughter to the bathroom from my impression of Mister Kitzel on "The Jack Benny Show." What else? Walks, walks with my father in Weequahic Park on Sundays that I still haven't forgotten. You know, I can't go off to the country and find an acorn on the ground without thinking of him and those walks. And that's nothing, nearly thirty years later.

And have I mentioned, vis-à-vis my mother, the running conversation we two had in those years before I was even old enough to go off by myself to a school? During those five years when we had each other alone all day long, I do believe we covered just about every subject known to man. "Talking to Alex," she used to tell my father when he walked in exhausted at night, "I can do a whole afternoon of ironing, and never even notice the time go by." And mind you, I am only *four*.

And as for the hollering, the cowering, the crying, even that had vividness and excitement to recommend it; moreover, that nothing was ever simply nothing but always SOMETHING, that the most ordinary kind of occurrence could explode without warning into A TERRIBLE CRISIS, this was to me *the way life is*. The novelist, what's his name, Markfield, has written in a story somewhere that until he was fourteen he believed "aggravation" to be a Jewish word. Well, this was what I thought about "tumult" and "bedlam," two favorite nouns of my mother's. Also "spatula." I was already the darling of the first grade, and in every schoolroom competition, expected to win hands down, when I was asked by the teacher one day to identify a picture of what I knew perfectly well my mother referred to as a "spatula." But for the life of me I could not think of the word in English. Stammering and flushing, I sank defeated into my seat, not nearly so stunned as my teacher but badly shaken up just the same . . . and that's how far back my fate goes, how early in the game it was "normal" for me to be in a state resembling torment—in this particular instance over something as monumental as a kitchen utensil.

> Oh, all that conflict over a spatula, Momma,
> Imagine how I feel about you!

—

I am reminded at this joyous little juncture of when we lived in Jersey City, back when I was still very much my mother's papoose, still very much a sniffer of her body perfumes and a total slave to her *kugel* and *grieben* and *ruggelech*—there was a suicide in our building. A fifteen-year-old boy named Ronald Nimkin, who had been crowned by the women in the building "José Iturbi the Second," hanged himself from the shower head in his bathroom. "With those golden hands!" the women wailed, referring of course to his piano playing—"With that talent!" Followed by, "You couldn't look for a boy more in love with his mother than Ronald!"

I swear to you, this is not bullshit or a screen memory, these are the very words these women use. The great dark operatic themes of human suffering and passion come rolling out of those mouths like the prices of Oxydol and Del Monte canned corn! My own mother, let me remind you, when I returned this past summer from my adventure in Europe, greets me over the phone with the following salutation: "Well, how's my lover?" Her *lover* she calls me, while her husband is listening on the other extension! And it never occurs to her, if I'm her lover, who is he, the *schmegeggy* she lives with? No, you don't have to go digging where these people are concerned—they wear the old unconscious on their *sleeves*!

Mrs. Nimkin, weeping in our kitchen: "Why? Why? Why did he do this to us?" Hear? Not what might *we* have done to *him*, oh no, never that—why did he do this *to us*? To us! Who would have given our arms and legs to make him happy and a famous concert pianist into the bargain! Really, can they be this blind? Can people be so abysmally stupid and live? Do you *believe* it? Can they actually be equipped with all the machinery, a brain, a spinal cord, and the four apertures for the ears and eyes—equipment, Mrs. Nimkin, nearly as impressive as color TV—and still go through life without a single clue about the feelings and yearnings of anyone other than themselves? Mrs. Nimkin, you shit, I remember you, I was only six, but I remember you, and what killed your Ronald, the concert-pianist-to-be is obvious: YOUR FUCKING SELFISHNESS AND STUPIDITY! "All the lessons we gave him," weeps Mrs. Nimkin . . . Oh look, look, why do I carry on like this? Maybe she means well, surely she must—at a time of grief, what can I expect of these simple people? It's only because in her misery she doesn't know what else to say that she says that God-awful thing about all the lessons they gave to somebody who is now a corpse. What are they, after all, these Jewish women who raised us up as children? In Calabria you see their suffering counterparts sitting like stones in the churches, swallowing all that hideous Catholic bullshit; in Calcutta they beg in the streets, or if they are lucky, are off somewhere in a dusty field hitched up to a plow . . . Only in America, Rabbi Golden, do these peasants, our mothers, get their hair dyed platinum at the age of sixty, and walk up and down Collins Avenue in Florida in pedalpushers and mink stoles—and with opinions on every subject under the sun. It isn't their fault they were given a gift like speech—look, if cows could talk, they would say things just as idiotic. Yes, yes, maybe that's the solution then: think of them as cows, who have been given the twin miracles of speech and mah-jongg. Why not be charitable in one's thinking, right, Doctor?

My favorite detail from the Ronald Nimkin suicide: even as he is swinging from the shower head, there is a note pinned to the dead young pianist's short-sleeved shirt—which is what I remember most about Ronald: this tall emaciated teen-age catatonic, swimming around all by himself in those oversized short-sleeved sport shirts, and with their lapels starched and ironed back so fiercely they looked to have been bulletproofed . . . And Ronald himself, every limb strung so tight to his backbone that if you touched him, he would probably have begun to hum . . . and the fingers, of course, those long white grotesqueries, seven knuckles at least before you got down to the nicely gnawed nail, those Bela Lugosi hands that my mother would tell me—and tell me—*and tell me*—because nothing is ever said once—nothing!—were "the hands of a born pianist."

Pianist! Oh, that's one of the words they just love, almost as much as *doctor*, Doctor. And *residency*. And best of all, *his own office. He opened his own office in Livingston.* "Do you remember Seymour Schmuck, Alex?" she asks me, or Aaron Putz or Howard Shlong, or some yo-yo I am supposed to have known in grade school twenty-five years ago, and of whom I have no recollection whatsoever. "Well, I met his mother on the street today, and she told me that Seymour is now the biggest brain surgeon in the entire Western Hemisphere. He owns six different split-level ranch-type houses made all of fieldstone in Livingston, and belongs to the boards of eleven synagogues, all brand-new and designed by Marc Kugel, and last year with his wife and his two little daughters, who are so beautiful that they are already under contract to Metro, and so brilliant that they should be in college—he took them all to Europe for an eighty-million-dollar tour of seven thousand countries, some of them you never even heard of, that they made them just to honor Seymour, and on top of that, he's so important, Seymour, that in every single city in Europe that they visited he was asked by the mayor himself to stop and do an impossible operation on a brain in hospitals that they also built for him right on the spot, and—listen to this—where they pumped into the operating room during the operation the theme song from *Exodus* so everybody should know what religion he is— and that's how big your friend Seymour is today! *And how happy he makes his parents!*"

And you, the implication is, when are *you* going to get married already? In Newark and the surrounding suburbs this apparently is the question on everybody's lips: WHEN IS ALEXANDER PORTNOY GOING TO STOP BEING SELFISH AND GIVE HIS PARENTS, WHO ARE SUCH WONDERFUL PEOPLE, GRANDCHILDREN? "Well," says my father, the tears brimming up in his eyes, "well," he asks, *every single time I see him,* "is there a serious girl in the picture, Big Shot? Excuse me for asking, I'm only your father, but since I'm not going to be alive forever, and you in case you forgot carry the family name, I wonder if maybe you could let me in on the secret."

Yes, shame, shame, on Alex P., the only member of his graduating class who hasn't made grandparents of his Mommy and his Daddy. While everybody else has been marrying nice Jewish girls, and having children, and buying houses, and (my father's phrase) *putting down roots,* while all the other sons have been carrying forward the family name, what he has been doing is—chasing cunt. And *shikse* cunt, to boot! Chasing it, sniffing it, lapping it, *shtupping* it, but above all, *thinking about it*. Day and night, at work and on the street—thirty-three years old and still he is roaming the streets with his eyes popping. A wonder he hasn't been ground to mush by a taxicab, given how he makes his way across the major arteries of Manhattan during the lunch hour. Thirty-three, and still ogling and daydreaming about every girl who crosses her legs opposite him in the subway! Still cursing himself for speaking not a word to the succulent pair of tits that rode twenty-five floors alone with him in an elevator! Then cursing himself for the opposite as well! For he has been known to walk up to thoroughly respectable-looking girls in the street, and despite the fact that since his appearance on Sunday morning TV his face is not entirely unknown to an enlightened segment of the public—despite the fact that he may be on his way to his current mistress' apartment for his dinner—he has been known on one or two occasions to mutter, "Look, would you like to come home with me?" *Of course* she is going to say "No." Of course she is going to scream, "Get out of here, you!" or answer curtly, "I have a nice home of my own, thank you, with a husband in it." What is he doing to himself, this fool! this idiot! this furtive *boy*! This sex maniac! He simply cannot—*will* not—control the fires in his putz, the fevers in his brain, the desire continually burning within for the new, the wild, the unthought-of and, if you can imagine such a thing, *the undreamt-of*. Where cunt is concerned he lives in a condition that has neither diminished nor in any significant way been refined from what it was when he was fifteen years old and could not get up from his seat in the classroom without hiding a hard-on beneath his three-ring notebook. Every girl he sees turns out (hold your hats) to be carrying around between her legs—a real cunt. Amazing! Astonishing! Still can't get over the fantastic idea that when you are looking at a girl, you are looking at somebody who is guaranteed to have on her—a cunt! *They all have cunts!* Right under their dresses! Cunts—for fucking! And, Doctor, Your Honor, whatever your name is—it seems to make no difference how much the poor bastard actually gets, for he is dreaming about tomorrow's pussy even while pumping away at today's!

Do I exaggerate? Am I doing myself in only as a clever way of showing off? Or boasting perhaps? Do I really experience this restlessness, this horniness, as an affliction—or as an accomplishment? Both? Could be. Or is it only a means of evasion? Look, at least I don't find myself still in my early thirties locked into a marriage with some nice person whose body has ceased to be of any genuine interest to me—at least I don't have to get into bed every night with somebody who by and large I fuck out of obligation instead of lust. I mean, the nightmarish depression some people suffer at bedtime . . . On the other hand, even I must admit that there is maybe, from a certain perspective, something a little depressing about my situation, too. Of course you can't have everything, or so I understand—but the question I am willing to face is: have I anything? How much longer do I go on conducting these experiments with women? How much longer do I go on sticking this thing into the holes that come available to it—first this hole, then when I tire of this hole, that hole over there . . . and so on. When will it end? Only *why* should it end! To please a father and mother? To conform to the norm? Why on earth should I be so defensive about being what was honorably called some years ago, a bachelor? After all, that's all this is, you know—bachelorhood. So what's the crime? Sexual freedom? In this day and age? Why should *I* bend to the bourgeoisie? Do I ask them to bend to me? Maybe I've been touched by the tarbrush of Bohemia a little—is that so awful? Whom am I harming with my lusts? I don't blackjack the ladies, I don't twist arms to get them into bed with me. I am, if I may say so, an honest and compassionate man; let me tell you, as men go I am . . . But why must I explain myself! *Excuse* myself! Why must I justify with my Honesty and Compassion my desires! So I have desires—only they're endless. Endless! And that, that may not be such a blessing, taking for the moment a psychoanalytic point of view . . . But then all the unconscious can do anyway, so Freud tells us, is *want. And* want! *And* WANT! Oh, Freud, do I know! This one has a nice ass, but she talks too much. On the other hand, this one here doesn't talk at all, at least not so that she makes any sense—but, boy, can she suck! What cock know-how! While here is a honey of a girl, with the softest, pinkest, most touching nipples I have ever drawn between my lips, only she won't go down on me. Isn't that odd? And yet—go understand people—it is her pleasure while being boffed to have one or the other of my forefingers lodged snugly up her anus. What a mysterious business it is! The endless fascination of these apertures and openings! You see, I just can't stop! Or tie myself to any *one*. I have affairs that last as long as a year, a year and a half, months and months of love, both tender and voluptuous, but in the end—it is as inevitable as death—time marches on and lust peters out. In the end, I just cannot take that step into marriage. But why should I? *Why?* Is there a law saying Alex Portnoy has to be somebody's husband and father? Doctor, they can stand on the window ledge and threaten to splatter themselves on the pavement below, they can pile the Seconal to the ceiling—I may have to live for weeks and weeks on end in terror of these marriage-bent girls throwing themselves beneath the subway train, but I simply cannot, I simply *will* not, enter into a contract to sleep with just one woman for the rest of my days. Imagine it: suppose I were to go ahead and marry A, with her sweet tits and so on, what will happen when B appears, whose are even sweeter—or, at any rate, newer? Or C, who knows how to move her ass in some special way I have never experienced; or D, or E, or F. I'm trying to be honest with you, Doctor—because with sex the human imagination runs to Z, and then beyond! Tits and cunts and legs and lips and mouths and tongues and assholes! How can I give up what I have never even had, for a girl, who delicious and provocative as once she may have been, will inevitably grow as familiar to me as a loaf of bread? For love? What love? Is that what binds all these couples we know together—the ones who even bother to let themselves be bound? Isn't it something more like weakness? Isn't it rather convenience and apathy and guilt? Isn't it rather fear and exhaustion and inertia, gutlessness plain and simple, far far more than that "love" that the marriage counselors and the songwriters and the psychotherapists are forever dreaming about? Please, let us not bullshit one another about "love" and its duration. Which is why I ask: how can I marry someone I "love" knowing full well that five, six, seven years hence I am going to be out on the streets hunting down the fresh new pussy—all the while my devoted wife, who has made me such a lovely home, et cetera, bravely suffers her loneliness and rejection? How could I face her terrible tears? I couldn't.

How could I face my adoring children? And then the divorce, right? The *child* support. The *alimony*. The *visitation* rights. Wonderful prospect, just wonderful. And as for anybody who kills herself because I prefer not to be blind to the future, well, she is her worry—she has to be! There is surely no need or justification for anybody to threaten suicide just because I am wise enough to see what frustrations and recriminations lie ahead . . . Baby, please, don't howl like that please— somebody is going to think you're being strangled to death. Oh baby (I hear myself pleading, last year, this year, every year of my life!), you're going to be all right, really, truly you are; you're going to be just fine and dandy and much better off, so please, you bitch, come back inside this room *and let me go!* "You! You and your filthy cock!" cries the most recently disappointed (and self-appointed) bride-to-be, my strange, lanky, and very batty friend, who used to earn as much in an hour posing for underwear ads as her illiterate father would earn in a week in the coal mines of West Virginia: "I thought you were supposed to be a superior person, you muff-diving, mother-fucking son of a bitch!" This beautiful girl, who has got me all wrong, is called The Monkey, a nickname that derives from a little perversion she once engaged in shortly before meeting me and going on to grander things. Doctor, I had never had anybody like her in my life, she was the fulfillment of my most lascivious adolescent dreams—but marry her, can she be serious? You see, for all her preening and perfumes, she has a very low opinion of herself, and simultaneously—and here is the source of much of our trouble—a ridiculously high opinion of me. And simultaneously, a very *low* opinion of me! She is one confused Monkey, and, I'm afraid, not too very bright. "An intellectual!" she screams. "An educated, spiritual person! You mean, miserable hard-on you, you care more about the niggers in Harlem that you don't even know, than you do about me, who's been sucking you off for a solid year!" Confused, heartbroken, and also out of her mind. For all this comes to me from the balcony of our hotel room in Athens, as I stand in the doorway, suitcases in hand, begging her to *please* come back inside so that I can catch a plane out of that place. Then the angry little manager, all olive oil, mustache, and outraged respectability, is running up the stairway waving his arms in the air—and so, taking a deep breath, I say, "Look, you want to jump, jump!" and out I go—and the last words I hear have to do with the fact that it was only out of love for me (*"Love!"* she screams) that she allowed herself to do the degrading things I forced quote unquote upon her.

Which is not the case, Doctor! Not the case at all! Which is an attempt on this sly bitch's part to break me on the rack of guilt—and thus get herself a husband. Because at twenty-nine that's what she wants, you see—but that does not mean, you see, that I have to oblige. "In September, you son of a bitch, I am going to be thirty years old!" Correct, Monkey, correct! Which is precisely why it is you and not me who is responsible for your expectations and your dreams! Is that clear? *You!* "I'll tell the world about you, you cold-hearted prick! I'll tell them what a filthy pervert you are, and the dirty things you made me do!"

The cunt! I'm lucky really that I came out of that affair *alive.* If I have!

—

But back to my parents, and how it seems that by remaining in my single state I bring these people, too, nothing but grief. That I happen, Mommy and Daddy, just happen to have recently been appointed by the Mayor to be Assistant Commissioner for The City of New York Commission on Human Opportunity apparently doesn't mean shit to you in terms of accomplishment and stature—though this is not exactly the case, I know, for, to be truthful, whenever my name now appears in a news story in the *Times,* they bombard every living relative with a copy of the clipping. Half my father's retirement pay goes down the drain in postage, and my mother is on the phone for days at a stretch and has to be fed intravenously, her mouth is going at such a rate about her Alex. In fact, it is exactly as it always has been: they can't get over what a success and a genius I am, my name in the paper, an associate now of the glamorous new Mayor, on the side of Truth and Justice, enemy of slumlords and bigots and rats ("to encourage equality of treatment, to prevent discrimination, to foster mutual understanding and respect—" my commission's humane purpose, as decreed by act of the City Council) . . . but still, if you know what I mean, still somehow not entirely perfect.

Now, can you beat that for a serpent's tooth? All they have sacrificed for me and done for me and how they boast about me and are the best public relations firm (they tell me) any child could have, and it turns out that I still won't be perfect. Did you ever hear of such a thing in your life? I just refuse to be perfect. What a pricky kid.

They come to visit: "Where did you get a rug like this?" my father asks, making a face. "Did you get this thing in a junk shop or did somebody give it to you?"

"I like this rug."

"What are you talking," my father says, "it's a worn-out rug."

Light-hearted. "It's worn, but not out. Okay? Enough?"

"Alex, please," my mother says, "it is a very worn rug."

"You'll trip on that thing," my father says, "and throw your knee out of whack, and then you'll really be in trouble."

"And with your knee," says my mother meaningfully, "that wouldn't be a picnic."

At this rate they are going to roll the thing up any minute now, the two of them, and push it out the window. *And then take me home!*

"The rug is fine. My *knee* is fine."

"It wasn't so fine," my mother is quick to remind me, "when you had the cast on, darling, up to your hip. How he *shlepped* that thing around! How miserable he was!"

"I was fourteen years old then, Mother."

"Yeah, and you came out of that thing," my father says, "you couldn't bend your leg, I thought you were going to be a cripple for the rest of your life. I told him, 'Bend it! Bend it!' I practically begged him morning, noon, and night, 'Do you want to be a cripple forever? Bend that leg!'"

"You scared the *daylights* out of us with that knee."

"But that was in nineteen hundred and forty-seven. And this is nineteen sixty-six. The cast has been off nearly twenty years!"

My mother's cogent reply? "You'll see, someday you'll be a parent, and you'll know what it's like. And then maybe you won't sneer at your family any more."

The legend engraved on the face of the Jewish nickel—on the body of every Jewish child!—not IN GOD WE TRUST, but SOMEDAY YOU'LL BE A PARENT AND YOU'LL KNOW WHAT IT'S LIKE.

"You think," my father the ironist asks, "it'll be in our lifetime, Alex? You think it'll happen before I go down into the grave? No—he'd rather take chances with a worn-out rug!" The ironist—and logician! "—And crack his head open! And let me ask you something else, my independent son—who would even know you were here if you were lying bleeding to death on the floor? Half the time you don't answer the phone, I see you lying here with God only knows what's wrong—and who is there to take care of you? Who is there even to bring you a bowl of soup, if God forbid something terrible should happen?"

"I can take care of myself! I don't go around like some people"—boy, still pretty tough with the old man, eh, Al?—"some people I know in continual anticipation of total catastrophe!"

"You'll see," he says, nodding miserably, "you'll get sick"— and suddenly a squeal of anger, a whine out of nowhere of absolute hatred *of me!—"you'll get old, and you won't be such an independent big shot then!"*

"Alex, Alex," begins my mother, as my father walks to my window to recover himself, and in passing, to comment contemptuously about "the neighborhood he lives in." I work *for* New York, and he still wants me to live in beautiful Newark!

"Mother, I'm thirty-three! I am the Assistant Commissioner of Human Opportunity for the City of New York! I graduated first in my law school class! Remember? I have graduated first from every class I've ever *been* in! At twenty-five I was already special counsel to a House Subcommittee—of the United States Congress, Mother! Of America! If I wanted Wall Street, Mother, I could be on Wall Street! I am a highly respected man in my profession, that should be obvious! Right this minute, Mother, I am conducting an investigation of unlawful discriminatory practices in the building trades in New York—*racial discrimination!* Trying to get the Ironworkers' Union, Mother, to tell me their little secrets! That's what I did *just today!* Look, *I* helped solve the television quiz scandal, do you *remember*—?" Oh, why go on? Why go on in my strangled high-pitched adolescent voice? Good Christ, a Jewish man with parents alive is a fifteen-year-old boy, and will remain a fifteen-year-old boy till *they die!*

Anyway, Sophie has by this time taken my hand, and with hooded eyes, waits until I sputter out the last accomplishment I can think of, the last virtuous deed I have done, then speaks: "But to us, to us you're still a baby, darling." And next comes the whisper, Sophie's famous whisper that everybody in the room can hear without even straining, she's so considerate: "Tell him you're sorry. Give him a kiss. A kiss from you would change the world."

A kiss from me *would change the world*! Doctor! Doctor! Did I say fifteen? Excuse me, I meant ten! I meant five! I meant zero! A Jewish man with his parents alive is half the time a helpless *infant*! Listen, come to my aid, will you—and quick! Spring me from this role I play of the smothered son in the Jewish joke! Because it's beginning to pall a little, at thirty-three! And also it *hoits*, you know, there is *pain* involved, a little human suffering is being felt, if I may take it upon myself to say so—only that's the part Sam Levenson leaves *out*! Sure, they sit in the casino at the Concord, the women in their minks and the men in their phosphorescent suits, and boy, do they laugh, laugh and laugh and laugh—"Help, help, my son the doctor is drowning!"—ha ha *ha*, ha ha *ha*, only what about the *pain*, Myron Cohen! What about the guy who is actually drowning! Actually sinking beneath an ocean of parental relentlessness! What about him—who happens, Myron Cohen, to be *me*! Doctor, *please*, I can't live any more in a world given its meaning and dimension by some vulgar nightclub clown. By some—some *black humorist*! Because that's who the black humorists are—of course!—the Henny Youngmans and the Milton Berles breaking them up down there in the Fountainebleau, and with what? Stories of murder and mutilation! "Help," cries the woman running along the sand at Miami Beach, "help, my son the doctor is drowning!" Ha ha ha—only it is *my son the patient*, lady! And is he drowning! Doctor, get these people off my ass, will you please? The macabre is very funny on the stage—but not to live it, thank you! So just tell me how, and I'll do it! Just tell me what, and I'll say it right to their faces! Scat, Sophie! Fuck off, Jack! Go *away* from me already!

I mean here's a joke for you, for instance. Three Jews are

walking down the street, my mother, my father, and me. It's this past summer, just before I am to leave on my vacation. We have had our dinner ("You got a piece of fish?" my father asks the waiter in the fancy French restaurant I take them to, *to show I am grown-up*—"*Oui, monsieur*, we have—" "All right, give me a piece of fish," says my father, "*and make sure it's hot*"), we have had our dinner, and afterward, chewing on my Titralac (for relief of gastric hyperacidity), I walk a ways with them before putting them in a taxi for the Port Authority Bus Terminal. Immediately my father starts in about how I haven't come to visit in five weeks (ground I thought we two had already covered in the restaurant, while my mother was whispering to the waiter to make sure her "big boy's" piece of fish—that's me, folks!—was well-done), and now I am going away for a whole month, and all in all when do they ever see their own son? They see their daughter, and their daughter's children, and not infrequently, but that is not successful either. "With that son in-law," my father says, "if you don't say the right psychological thing to his kids, if I don't talk straight psychology to my own granddaughters, he wants to put me in jail! I don't care what he calls himself, he still thinks like a Communist to me. My own grandchildren, and everything I say has to pass by him, Mr. Censor!" No, their daughter is now Mrs. Feibish, and her little daughters are Feibishes too. Where are the Portnoys he dreamed of? In my nuts. "Look," I cry in my strangulated way, "you're seeing me *now*! You're with me *right this minute*!" But he is off and running, and now that he hasn't fishbones to worry about choking on, there is no reining him in—Mr. and Mrs. Schmuck have Seymour and his beautiful wife and their seven thousand brilliant and beautiful children who come to them *every single Friday night*—"Look, I am a very busy person! I have a briefcase full of important things to do—!" "Come on," he replies, "you gotta eat, you can come for a meal once a week, because you gotta eat anyway comes six o'clock—well, don't you?" Whereupon who pipes up but Sophie, informing him that when she was a little girl her family was always telling her to do this and do that, and how unhappy and resentful it sometimes would cause her to feel, and how my father shouldn't insist with me because, she concludes, "Alexander is a big boy, Jack, he has a right to make his own decisions, that's something I always told him." You always *what*? *What* did she say?

Oh, why go on? Why be so obsessed like this? Why be so petty? Why not be a sport like Sam Levenson and laugh it all off—right?

Only let me finish. So they get into the taxi. "Kiss him," my mother whispers, "you're going all the way to Europe."

Of course my father overhears—that's why she lowers her voice, so we'll all listen—and panic sweeps over him. Every year, from September on, he is perpetually asking me what my plans are for the following August—now he realizes that he has been outfoxed: bad enough I am leaving on a midnight plane for another continent, but worse, he hasn't the slightest idea of my itinerary. I did it! I made it!

"—But where in Europe? Europe is half the whole globe—" he cries, as I begin to close the taxi door from the outside.

"I told you, I don't know."

"What do you mean? You *gotta* know! How will you get there yourself, if you 'don't know'—"

"Sorry, sorry—"

Desperately now his body comes lurching across my mother's—just as I slam shut the door—*oy*, not on his fingers, please! Jesus, this father! Whom I have had forever! Whom I used to find in the morning fast asleep on the toilet bowl, his pajamas around his knees and his chin hanging onto his chest. Up at quarter to six in the morning, so as to give himself a full uninterrupted hour on the can, in the fervent hope that if he is so kind and thoughtful as this to his bowels, they will relent, they will give in, they will say finally, "Okay, Jack, you win," and make a present to the poor bastard of five or six measly lumps of shit. "Jesus Christ!" he groans, when I awaken him so as to wash up for school, and he realizes that it is nearly seven-thirty and down in the bowl over which he has been sleeping for an hour, there is, if he's lucky, one brown angry little pellet such as you expect from the rectum of a rabbit maybe—but not from the rear-end of a man who now has to go out all clogged up to put in a twelve-hour day. "Seven-*thirty*? Why didn't you say something!" Zoom, he's dressed, and in his hat and coat, and with his big black collection book in one hand he bolts his stewed prunes and his bran flakes standing up, and fills a pocket with a handful of dried fruits that would bring on in an ordinary human being something resembling dysentery. "I ought to stick a hand grenade up my ass, if you want the truth," he whispers privately to me, while my mother occupies the bathroom and my sister dresses for school in her "room," the sun parlor—"I got enough All-Bran in me to launch a battleship. It's backed up to my throat, for Christ's sake." Here, because he has got me snickering, and is amusing himself too in his own mordant way, he opens his mouth and points downward inside himself with a thumb, "Take a look. See where it starts to get dark? That ain't just dark—that's all those prunes rising up where my tonsils used to be. Thank God I had those things out, otherwise there wouldn't be room."

"Very nice talk," my mother calls from the bathroom. "Very nice talk to a child."

"Talk?" he cries. "It's the *truth*," and in the very next instant is thomping angrily around the house hollering, "My hat, I'm late, where's my hat? who saw my hat?" and my mother comes into the kitchen and gives me her patient, eternal, all-knowing sphinx-look . . . and waits . . . and soon he is back in the hallway, apoplectic and moaning, practically in grief, "Where is my hat? *Where is that hat!*" until softly, from the depths of her omniscient soul, she answers him, "Dummy, it's on your head." Momentarily his eyes seem to empty of all signs of human experience and understanding; he stands there, a blank, a thing, a body full of shit and no more. Then consciousness returns—yes, he will have to go out into the world after all, for his hat has been found, on his head of all places. "Oh yeah," he says, reaching up in wonderment—and then out of the house and into the Kaiser, and Superman is gone until dark.

The Kaiser, time for my story about the Kaiser: how he proudly took me with him when he went after the war to trade in the '39 Dodge for a new automobile, new make, new model, new everything—what a perfect way for an American dad to impress his American son!—and how the fast-talking salesman acted as though he just couldn't believe his ears, was simply incredulous, each time my father said "No" to one after another of the thousand little accessories the cock-sucker wanted to sell us to hang on the car. "Well, I'll tell you my opinion for whatever it's worth," says that worthless son of a bitch, "she'd look two hun-erd percent better with the whitewalls—don't you think so, young fella? Wouldn't you like your dad to get the whitewalls, at least?" At least. Ah, you slimy prick, you! Turning to me like that, to stick it into my old man—you miserable lowlife thieving son of a bitch! Just who the fuck are you, I wonder, to lord it over us—a God damn Kaiser-Fraser salesman! Where are you *now*, you intimidating bastard? "No, no whitewalls," mumbles my humbled father, and I simply shrug my shoulders in embarassment over his inability to provide me and my family with the beautiful things in life.

Anyway, anyway—off to work in the radio-less whitewall-less Kaiser, there to be let into the office by the cleaning lady. Now, I ask you, why must he be the one to raise the shades in that office in the morning? Why must he work the longest day of any insurance agent in history? For whom? *Me?* Oh, if so, if so, if that is his reason, then it is all really too fucking tragic to bear. The misunderstanding is too great! For *me?* Do me a favor *and don't do it for me!* Don't please look around for a reason for your life being what it is and come up with Alex! Because I am not the be-all and end-all of everybody's existence! I refuse to *shlep those* bags around for the rest of *my* life! Do you hear me? I refuse! Stop finding it incomprehensible that I should be flying to Europe, thousands and thousands of miles away, just when you have turned sixty-six and are all ready to keel over at any minute, like you read about first thing every morning in the *Times*. Men his age and younger, *they die*—one minute they're alive, and the next dead, and apparently what he thinks is that if I am only across the Hudson instead of the Atlantic . . . Listen, what *does* he think? That with me around it simply won't happen? That I'll race to his side, take hold of his hand, and thereby restore him to life? Does he actually believe that I somehow have the power to destroy death? That I am the resurrection and the life? My dad, a real believing Christer! And doesn't even know it!

His death. His death and his bowels: the truth is I am hardly less preoccupied with either than he is himself. I never get a telegram, never get a phone call after midnight, that I do not feel my own stomach empty out like a washbasin, and say aloud—aloud!—"He's dead." Because apparently I believe it too, believe that I can somehow save him from annihilation—can, and must! But where did we all get this ridiculous and absurd idea that I am so—powerful, so precious, so necessary to everybody's survival! What was it with these Jewish parents—because I am not in this boat alone, oh no, I am on the biggest troop ship afloat . . . only look in through the portholes and see us there, stacked to the bulkheads in our bunks, moaning and groaning with such pity for ourselves, the sad and watery-eyed sons of Jewish parents, sick to the gills from rolling through these heavy seas of guilt—so I sometimes envision us, me and my fellow wailers, melancholics, and wise guys, still in steerage, like our forebears—and oh sick, sick as dogs, we cry out intermittently, one of us or another, "Poppa, how could you?" "Momma, why did you?" and the stories we tell, as the big ship pitches and rolls, the vying we do—who had the most castrating mother, who the most benighted father, I can match you, you bastard, humiliation for humiliation, shame for shame . . . the retching in the toilets after meals, the hysterical deathbed laughter from the bunks, and the tears—here a puddle wept in contrition, here a puddle from indignation—in the blinking of an eye, the body of a man (with the brain of a boy) rises in impotent rage to flail at the mattress above, only to fall instantly back, lashing itself with reproaches. Oh, my Jewish men friends! My dirty-mouthed guilt-ridden brethren! My sweethearts! My mates! Will this fucking ship ever stop pitching? When? *When*, so that we can leave off complaining how sick we are—and go out into the air, and live!

Doctor Spielvogel, it alleviates nothing fixing the blame—blaming is still ailing, of course, of course—but nonetheless, what *was* it with these Jewish parents, *what*, that they were able to make us little Jewish boys believe ourselves to be princes on the one hand, unique as unicorns on the one hand, geniuses and brilliant like nobody has ever been brilliant and beautiful before in the history of childhood—saviors and sheer perfection on the one hand, and such bumbling, incompetent, thoughtless, helpless, selfish, evil little shits, little *ingrates*, on the other!

"But in Europe *where*—?" he calls after me, as the taxi pulls away from the curb.

"I don't *know* where," I call after him, gleefully waving farewell. I am thirty-three, and free at last of my mother and father! For a month.

"But how will we know your address?"

Joy! Sheer joy! "You won't!"

"But what if in the meantime—?"

"What if what?" I laugh. "What if what are you worried about now?"

"What if—?" And my God, does he really actually shout it out the taxi window? Is his fear, his greed, his need and belief in me so great that he actually shouts these words out into the streets of New York? "What if I die?"

Because that is what I hear, Doctor. The last words I hear before flying off to Europe—and with The Monkey, somebody whom I have kept a total secret from them. "What if I die?" and then off I go for my orgiastic holiday abroad.

. . . Now, whether the words I hear are the words spoken is something else again. And whether what I hear I hear out of compassion for him, out of my agony over the inevitability of this horrific occurrence, his death, or out of my eager anticipation of that event, is also something else again. But this of course you understand, this of course is your bread and your butter.

—

I was saying that the detail of Ronald Nimkin's suicide that most appeals to me is the note to his mother found pinned to that roomy straitjacket, his nice stiffly laundered sports shirt. Know what it said? Guess. The last message from Ronald to his momma? Guess.

> *Mrs. Blumenthal called. Please bring your mah-jongg rules to the game tonight.*
>
> > *Ronald*

Now, how's *that* for good to the last drop? How's that for a good boy, a thoughtful boy, a kind and courteous and well-behaved boy, a nice Jewish boy such as no one will ever have cause to be ashamed of? Say thank you, darling. Say you're welcome, darling. Say you're sorry, Alex. Say you're sorry! *Apologize!* Yeah, for what? What have I done now? Hey, I'm hiding under my bed, my back to the wall, refusing to say I'm sorry, refusing, too, to come out and take the consequences. *Refusing!* And she is after me with a broom, trying to sweep my rotten carcass into the open. Why, shades of Gregor Samsa! Hello Alex, goodbye Franz! "You better tell me you're sorry, you, or else! And I don't mean maybe either!" I am five, maybe six, and she is or-elsing me and not-meaning-maybe as though the firing squad is already outside, lining the street with newspaper preparatory to my execution.

And now comes the father: after a pleasant day of trying to sell life insurance to black people who aren't even exactly sure they're alive, home to a hysterical wife and a metamorphosed child—because what did I do, me, the soul of goodness? Incredible, beyond belief, but either I kicked her in the shins, or I bit her. I don't want to sound like I'm boasting, but I do believe it was *both*.

"Why?" she demands to know, kneeling on the floor to shine a flashlight in my eyes, "why do you do such a thing?" Oh, simple, why did Ronald Nimkin give up his ghost and the piano? BECAUSE WE CAN'T TAKE ANY MORE! BECAUSE YOU FUCKING JEWISH MOTHERS ARE JUST TOO FUCKING MUCH TO BEAR! I have read Freud on Leonardo, Doctor, and pardon the hubris, but my fantasies exactly: this big smothering bird beating frantic wings about my face and mouth *so that I cannot even get my breath*. What do we want, me and Ronald and Leonardo? *To be left alone!* If only for half an hour at a time! Stop already *hocking* us to be *good*! *hocking* us to be *nice*! Just leave us alone, God damn it, to pull our little dongs in peace and think our little selfish thoughts—stop already with the respectabilizing of our hands and our tushies and our mouths! Fuck the vitamins and the cod liver oil! Just give us each day our daily flesh! And forgive us our trespasses—which aren't even trespasses to begin with!

"—a little boy you want to be who kicks his own mother in the shins—?" My father speaking . . . and look at his arms, will you? I have never really noticed before the size of the forearms the man has got on him. He may not have whitewall tires or a high school education, but he has arms on him that are no joke. And, Jesus, is he angry. But why? In part, you schmuck, I kicked her for *you*!

"—a human bite is worse than a dog bite, do you know that,

you? Get out from under that bed! Do you hear me, what you did to your mother is worse than a dog could do!" And so loud is his roar, and so convincing, that my normally placid sister runs to the kitchen, great gruntfuls of fear erupting from her mouth, and in what we now call the fetal position crouches down between the refrigerator and the wall. Or so I seem to remember it—though it would make sense, I think, to ask how I know what is going on in the kitchen if I am still hiding beneath my bed.

"The bite I can live with, the shins I can live with"—her broom still relentlessly trying to poke me out from my cave— "but what am I going to do with a child who won't even say he's sorry? Who won't tell his own mother that he's sorry and will never never do such a thing again, *ever*! What are we going to do, Daddy, with such a little boy in our house!"

Is she *kidding*? Is she *serious*? Why doesn't she call the cops and get me shipped off to children's prison, if this is how incorrigible I really am? "Alexander Portnoy, aged five, you are hereby sentenced to hang by your neck until you are dead for refusing to say you are sorry to your mother." You'd think the child lapping up their milk and taking baths with his duck and his boats in their tub was the most wanted criminal in America. When actually what we are playing in that house is some farce version of *King Lear*, with me in the role of Cordelia! On the phone she is perpetually telling whosoever isn't listening on the other end about her biggest fault being that she's too good. Because *surely* they're not listening—*surely* they're not sitting there nodding and taking down on their telephone pads this kind of transparent, self-serving, insane horseshit that even a pre-school-age child can see through. "You know what my biggest fault is, Rose? I hate to say it about myself, but I'm too good." These are actual words, Doctor, tape-recorded these many years in my brain. And killing me still! These are the actual messages that these Roses and Sophies and Goldies and Pearls transmit to one another *daily*! "I give my everything to other people," she admits, sighing, "and I get kicked in the teeth in return—and my fault is that as many times as I get slapped in the face, I can't stop being good."

Shit, Sophie, just *try*, why don't you? Why don't we *all* try!

Because to be *bad*, Mother, that is the real struggle: to be bad—and to enjoy it! That is what makes men of us boys, Mother. But what my conscience, so-called, has done to my sexuality, my spontaneity, my courage! Never mind some of the things I try so hard to get away with—because the fact remains, *I don't*. I am marked like a road map from head to toe with my repressions. You can travel the length and breadth of my body over superhighways of shame and inhibition and fear. See, I am too good too, Mother, I too am moral to the bursting point—just like you! Did you ever see me try to smoke a cigarette? I look like Bette Davis. Today boys and girls not even old enough to be bar-mitzvahed are sucking on marijuana like it's peppermint candy, and I'm still all thumbs with a Lucky Strike. Yes, that's how good *I* am, Momma. Can't smoke, hardly drink, no drugs, don't borrow money or play cards, can't tell a lie without beginning to sweat as though I'm passing over the equator. Sure, I say *fuck* a lot, but I assure you, that's about the sum of my success with transgressing. Look what I have done with The Monkey—given her up, run from her in fear, the girl whose cunt I have been dreaming about lapping all my life. Why is a little turbulence so beyond my means? Why must the least deviation from respectable conventions cause me such inner hell? When I *hate* those fucking conventions! When I know *better* than the taboos! Doctor, my doctor, what do you say, LET'S PUT THE ID BACK IN YID! Liberate this nice Jewish boy's libido, will you please? Raise the prices if you have to—I'll pay anything! Only enough cowering in the face of the deep, dark pleasures! Ma, Ma, what was it you wanted to turn me into anyway, a walking zombie like Ronald Nimkin? Where did you get the idea that the most wonderful thing I could be in life was *obedient*? A little *gentleman*? Of all the aspirations for a creature of lusts and desires! "Alex," you say, as we leave the Weequahic Diner—and don't get me wrong, I eat it up: praise is praise, and I take it however it comes—"Alex," you say to me all dressed up in my clip-on tie and my two-tone "loafer" jacket, "the way you cut your meat! the way you ate that baked potato without spilling! I could kiss you, I never *saw* such a little gentleman with his little napkin in his lap like that!" *Fruitcake*, Mother. Little

fruitcake is what you saw—and exactly what the training program was designed to produce. Of course! Of course! The
mystery really is not that I'm not dead like Ronald Nimkin,
but that I'm not like all the nice young men I see strolling hand
in hand in Bloomingdale's on Saturday mornings. Mother, the
beach at Fire Island is strewn with the bodies of nice Jewish
boys, in bikinis and Bain de Soleil, also little gentlemen in
restaurants, I'm sure, also who helped mommies set up mah-
jongg tiles when the ladies came on Monday night to play.
Christ Almighty! After all those years of setting up those tiles
—one bam! two crack! mah-jongg!—how I made it into the
world of pussy at all, *that's* the mystery. I close my eyes, and
it's not so awfully hard—I see myself sharing a house at Ocean
Beach with somebody in eye make-up named Sheldon. "Oh,
fuck you, Shelly, they're *your* friends, *you* make the garlic
bread." Mother, your little gentlemen are all grown up now,
and there on lavender beach towels they lie, in all their furious
narcissism. And *oy Gut*, one is calling out—to me! "Alex?
Alexander the King? Baby, did you see where I put my tar-
ragon?" There he is, Ma, your little gentleman, kissing someone named Sheldon on the lips! Because of his herb dressing!
"Do you know what I read in *Cosmopolitan*?" says my mother
to my father. "That there are women who are homosexual
persons." "Come on," grumbles Poppa Bear, "what kind of
garbage is that, what kind of crap is that—?" "Jack, please, I'm
not making it up. I *read* it in *Cosmo*! I'll *show* you the article!"
"Come on, they print that stuff for the circulation—" Momma!
Poppa! There is worse even than that—there are people who
fuck chickens! There are men who screw stiffs! You simply cannot imagine how some people will respond to having served
fifteen- and twenty-year sentences as some crazy bastard's idea
of "good"! So if I kicked you in the shins, Ma-má, if I sunk my
teeth into your wrist clear through to the *bone*, count your
blessings! For had I kept it *all* inside me, believe me, you too
might have arrived home to find a pimply adolescent corpse
swinging over the bathtub by his father's belt. Worse yet, this
last summer, instead of sitting *shiva* over a son running off to
faraway Europe, you might have found yourself dining out on
my "deck" on Fire Island—the two of you, me, and Sheldon.
And if you remember what that *goyische* lobster did to your

kishkas, imagine what it would have been like trying to keep down Shelly's *sauce béarnaise*.

So *there*.

—

What a pantomime I had to perform to get my zylon wind-breaker off my back and into my lap so as to cover my joint that night I bared it to the elements. All for the benefit of the driver, within whose Polack power it lay merely to flip on the overhead lights and thus destroy in a single moment fifteen years of neat notebooks and good grades and teeth-cleaning twice a day and never eating a piece of fruit without thoroughly washing it beforehand . . . Is it hot in here! Whew, is it hot! Boy oh boy, I guess I just better get this jacket off and put it right down here in a neat little pile in my lap . . . Only what am I *doing*? A Polack's day, my father has suggested to me, isn't complete until he had dragged his big dumb feet across the bones of a Jew. Why am I taking this chance in front of my worst enemy? What will become of me if I'm caught!

Half the length of the tunnel it takes me to unzip my zipper silently—and there it is again, up it pops again, as always swollen, bursting with demands, like some idiot macrocephalic making his parents' life a misery with his simpleton's insatiable needs.

"Jerk me off," I am told by the silky monster. "*Here? Now?*" "Of course here and now. When would you expect an opportunity like this to present itself a second time? Don't you know what that girl is who is asleep beside you? Just look at that nose. "What nose?" "That's the point—it's hardly even there. Look at that hair, like off a spinning wheel. Remember 'flax' that you studied in school? That's human flax! Schmuck, this is the real McCoy. A *shikse*! And asleep! Or maybe she's just faking it is a strong possibility too. Faking it, but saying under her breath, 'C'mon, Big Boy, do all the different dirty things to me you ever wanted to do.'" "Could that be *so*?" "Darling," croons my cock, "let me just begin to list the many different dirty things she would like you to start off with: she wants you to take her hard little *shikse* titties in your hands, for one." "She does?" "She wants you to finger-fuck her *shikse* cunt till she faints." "Oh God. Till she faints!" "This is an opportunity such as may never occur again. So long as you live." "Ah, but that's the point, how long is that likely to be? The driver's name is all X's and Y's—if my father is right, these Polish people are direct descendants from the ox!"

But who wins an argument with a hard-on? *Ven der putz shteht, ligt der sechel in drerd.* Know that famous proverb? When the prick stands up, the brains get buried in the ground! When the prick stands up, the brains are as good as dead! And 'tis so! Up it jumps, a dog through a hoop, right into the bracelet of middle finger, index finger, and thumb that I have provided for the occasion. A three-finger hand-job with staccato half-inch strokes up from the base—this will be best for a bus, this will (hopefully) cause my zylon jacket to do a minimal amount of hopping and jumping around. To be sure, such a technique means forgoing the sensitive tip, but that much of life is sacrifice and self-control is a fact that even a sex fiend cannot afford to be blind to.

The three-finger hand-job is what I have devised for jerking off in public places—already I have employed it at the Empire Burlesque house in downtown Newark. One Sunday morning —following the example of Smolka, my Tom Sawyer—I leave the house for the schoolyard, whistling and carrying a baseball glove, and when no one is looking (obviously a state of affairs I hardly believe in) I jump aboard an empty 14 bus, and crouch in my seat the length of the journey. You can just imagine the crowd outside the burlesque house on a Sunday morning. Downtown Newark is as empty of life and movement as the Sahara, except for those outside the Empire, who look like the crew off a ship stricken with scurvy. Am I crazy to be going in there? God only knows what kind of disease I am going to pick up off those seats! "Go in anyway, fuck the disease," says the maniac who speaks into the microphone of my jockey shorts, "don't you understand what you're going to see inside there? A woman's snatch." "A *snatch*?" "The whole thing, right, all hot and dripping and ready to go." "But I'll come down with the syph from just touching the ticket. I'll pick it up on the bottom of my sneaks and track it into my own house. Some nut will go berserk and stab me to death for the Trojan in my wallet. What if the cops come? Waving pistols— and somebody runs—and they shoot *me* by mistake! Because I'm underage. What if I get killed—or even worse, arrested!

What about my parents!" "Look, do you want to see a cunt or don't you want to see a cunt?" "I want to! I want to!" "They have a whore in there, kid, who fucks the curtain with her bare twat." "Okay—I'll risk the syph! I'll risk having my brain curdle and spending the rest of my days in an insane asylum playing handball with my own shit—only what about my picture in the *Newark Evening News*! When the cops throw on the lights and cry, 'Okay, freaks, this is a raid!'—what if the flashbulbs go off! And get me—*me*, already president of the International Relations Club in my second year of high school! Me, who skipped two grades of grammar school! Why, in 1946, because they wouldn't let Marian Anderson sing in Convention Hall, I led my entire eighth-grade class in refusing to participate in the annual patriotic-essay contest sponsored by the D.A.R. I was and still am the twelve-year-old boy who, in honor of his courageous stand against bigotry and hatred, was invited to the Essex House in Newark to attend the convention of the C.I.O. Political Action Committee—to mount the platform and to shake the hand of Dr. Frank Kingdon, the renowned columnist whom I read every day in *PM*. How can I be contemplating going into a burlesque house with all these degenerates to see some sixty-year-old lady pretend to make love to a hunk of asbestos, when on the stage of the Essex House ballroom, Dr. Frank Kingdon himself took my hand, and while the whole P.A.C. rose to applaud my opposition to the D.A.R., Dr. Kingdon said to me, "Young man, you are going to see democracy in action here this morning." And with my brother-in-law-to-be, Morty Feibish, I have already attended meetings of the American Veterans Committee, I have helped Morty, who is Membership chairman, set up the bridge chairs for a chapter meeting. I have read *Citizen Tom Paine* by Howard Fast, I have read Bellamy's *Looking Backward*, and *Finnley Wren* by Philip Wylie. With my sister and Morty, I have listened to the record of marching songs by the gallant Red Army Chorus. Rankin and Bilbo and Martin Dies, Gerald L. K. Smith and Father Coughlin, all those Fascist sons of bitches are my mortal enemies. So what in God's name am I doing in a side seat at the burlesque house jerking off into the pocket of my fielder's glove? What if there's violence! What if there's germs!

Yes, only what if later, after the show, that one over there with the enormous boobies, *what if* . . . In sixty seconds I have imagined a full and wonderful life of utter degradation that we lead together on a chenille spread in a shabby hotel room, me (the enemy of America First) and Thereal McCoy, which is the name I attach to the sluttiest-looking slut in the chorus line. And what a life it is, too, under our bare bulb (HOTEL flashing just outside our window). She pushes Drake's Daredevil Cupcakes (chocolate with a white creamy center) down over my cock and then eats them off of me, flake by flake. She pours maple syrup out of the Log Cabin can and then licks it from my tender balls until they're clean again as a little baby boy's. Her favorite line of English prose is a masterpiece: "Fuck my pussy, Fuckface, till I faint." When I fart in the bathtub, she kneels naked on the tile floor, leans all the way over, and kisses the bubbles. She sits on my cock while I take a shit, plunging into my mouth a nipple the size of a tollhouse cookie, and all the while whispering every filthy word she knows viciously in my ear. She puts ice cubes in her mouth until her tongue and lips are freezing, then sucks me off— then switches to hot tea! Everything, everything I have ever thought of, she has thought of too, *and will do*. The biggest whore (rhymes in Newark with *poor*) there ever was. And she's mine! "Oh, Thereal, I'm coming, I'm coming, you fucking whore," and so become the only person ever to ejaculate into the pocket of a baseball mitt at the Empire Burlesque house in Newark. Maybe.

The big thing at the Empire is hats. Down the aisle from me a fellow-addict fifty years my senior is dropping his load in his hat. His *hat*, Doctor! *Oy*, I'm sick. I want to cry. Not into your hat, you *shvantz*, you got to put that thing on your head! You've got to put it on now and go back outside and walk around downtown Newark dripping gissum down your forehead. How will you eat your lunch in that hat!

What misery descends upon me as the last drop dribbles into my mitt. The depression is overwhelming; even my cock is ashamed and doesn't give me a single word of back talk as I start from the burlesque house, chastising myself ruthlessly, moaning aloud, "Oh, no, *no*," not unlike a man who has just felt his sole skid through a pile of dog turds—sole of his shoe, but take the pun, who cares, who cares . . . Ach! Disgusting! Into his hat, for Christ's sake. *Ven der putz shteht! Ven der putz shteht!* Into the hat that he wears on his *head*!

—

I suddenly remember how my mother taught me to piss standing up! Listen, this may well be the piece of information we've been waiting for, the key to what determined my character, what causes me to be living in this predicament, torn by desires that are repugnant to my conscience, and a conscience repugnant to my desires. Here is how I learned to pee into the bowl like a big man. Just listen to this!

I stand over the circle of water, my baby's weeny jutting cutely forth, while my momma sits beside the toilet on the rim of the bathtub, one hand controlling the tap of the tub (from which a trickle runs that I am supposed to imitate) and her other hand tickling the underside of my prick. I repeat: *tickling my prickling!* I guess she thinks that's how to get stuff to come out of the front of that thing, and let me tell you, the lady is right. "Make a nice sis, *bubulu*, make a nice little sissy for Mommy," sings Mommy to me, while in actuality what I am standing there making with her hand on my prong is in all probability my future! Imagine! The *ludicrousness!* A man's character is being forged, a destiny is being shaped . . . oh, maybe not . . . At any rate, for what the information is worth, in the presence of another man I simply cannot draw my water. To this very day. My bladder may be distended to watermelon proportions, but interrupted by another presence before the stream has begun (you want to hear everything, okay, I'm telling everything) which is that in Rome, Doctor, The Monkey and I picked up a common whore in the street and took her back to bed with us. Well, now that's out. It seems to have taken me some time.

The bus, the bus, what intervened on the bus to prevent me from coming all over the sleeping *shikse*'s arm—*I* don't know. Common sense, you think? Common decency? My right mind, as they say, coming to the fore? Well, where is this right mind on that afternoon I came home from school to find mother out of the house, and our refrigerator stocked with a big purplish piece of raw liver? I believe that I have already confessed to the piece of liver that I bought in a butcher shop and banged behind a billboard on the way to a bar mitzvah lesson. Well, I wish to make a clean breast of it, Your Holiness. That—she—it—wasn't my first piece. My first piece I had in the privacy of my own home, rolled round my cock in the bathroom at three-thirty—and then had again on the end of a fork, at five-thirty, along with the other members of that poor innocent family of mine.

So. Now you know the worst thing I have ever done. I fucked my own family's dinner.

—

Unless you share with The Monkey her contention that the most heinous crime of my career was abandoning her in Greece. Second most heinous: leading her into that triumvirate in Rome. In *her* estimation—some estimation, that!—I am solely responsible for making that *ménage*, because mine is the stronger and more moral nature. "The Great Humanitarian!" she cries. "The one whose *job* it is to protect the poor poor people against their landlords! You, who gave me that *U.S.A.* to read! *You're* why I got that application blank to Hunter! *You're* why I'm killing myself to be something more than just somebody's dumb and stupid piece of ass! And now you want to treat me like I'm nothing but just some hump, to *use*—use for every kinky weirdo thing you want to do—and like *you're* supposed to be the superior intellectual! Who goes on educational fucking *television*!"

You see, in this Monkey's estimation it was my mission to pull her up from those very abysses of frivolity and waste, of perversity and wildness and lust, into which I myself have been so vainly trying all my life successfully to sink—I am supposed to rescue her from those very temptations I have been struggling all these years to *yield* to! And it is of no consequence to her whatsoever that in bed she herself has been fantasying about this arrangement no less feverishly than I have. Doctor, I ask you, who was it that made the suggestion in the first place? Since the night we met, just who has been tempting whom with the prospect of yet another woman in our bed? Believe me, I'm not trying to slither out of my slime—I am trying to slither *into* it!—but it must be made absolutely clear, to you and me if not to her, that this hopelessly neurotic woman, this pathetic screwy hillbilly cunt, is hardly what could be called *my* victim. I simply will not bend to that *victim* shit! Now she's thirty, wants to be married and a mother, wants to be respectable and live in a house with a husband (particularly as the high-paying years of her glamorous career appear to be just about over), but it does not follow that just because she imagines herself victimized and deprived and exploited (and may even be, taking a long view of her life), that I am the one upon whom they are going to pin the rap. *I* didn't make her thirty years old and single. *I* didn't take her from the coal fields of West Virginia and make her my personal charge—and I didn't put her in bed with that streetwalker either! The fact is that it was The Monkey herself, speaking her high-fashion Italian, who leaned out of our rented car and explained to the whore what it was we wanted and how much we were willing to pay. I simply sat there behind the wheel, one foot on the gas pedal, like the getaway driver that I am . . . And, believe me, when that whore climbed into the back seat, I thought no; and at the hotel, where we managed to send her up alone to our room, by way of the bar, I thought no again. No! No! No!

She wasn't bad-looking, this whore, sort of round and dumpy, but in her early twenties and with a big pleasant open face—and just stupendous tits. Those were what we'd picked her out for, after driving slowly up and down the Via Veneto examining the merchandise on parade. The whore, whose name was Lina, took her dress off standing in the middle of the room; underneath she wore a "merry widow" corset, from which the breasts bubbled up at one end, and the more than ample thighs rippled out at the other. I was astonished by the garment and its theatricality—but then I was astonished by everything, above all, that we had gone ahead after all these months of talking, and finally done it.

The Monkey came out of the bathroom in her short chemise (ordinarily a sight that made me very hot, that cream-colored silk chemise with a beautiful Monkey in it), and I meanwhile took off all my clothes and sat naked at the foot of the bed. That Lina spoke not a word of English only intensified the feeling that began to ebb and flow between the Monkey and myself, a kind of restrained sadism: we could speak to one another, exchange secrets and plans without the whore's understanding—as she and The Monkey could whisper in

Italian without my knowledge of what they might be saying, or plotting . . . Lina spoke first and The Monkey turned to translate. "She says you have a big one." "I'll bet she says that to all the boys." Then they stood there in their underwear looking my way—*waiting*. But so was I waiting too. And was my heart pounding. It had to come to pass, two women and me . . . so now what happens? Still, you see, I'm saying to myself *No!*

"She wants to know," said The Monkey, after Lina had spoken a second time, "where the *signore* would like her to begin." "The *signore*," said I, "wishes her to begin at the beginning . . ." Oh, very witty that reply, very nonchalant indeed, only we continue to sit there motionless, me and my hard-on, all undressed and no place to go. Finally it is The Monkey who sets our lust in motion. She moves across to Lina, above whom she towers (oh God, isn't she enough? isn't she really sufficient for my needs? how many cocks have I got?), and puts her hand between the whore's legs. We had imagined it beforehand in all its possibilities, dreamed it all out loud for many many months now, and yet I am dumbstruck at the sight of The Monkey's middle finger disappearing up into Lina's cunt.

I can best describe the state I subsequently entered as one of unrelieved *busy-ness*. Boy, was I busy! I mean there was just so much to do. You go here and I'll go there—okay, now you go here and *I'll* go there—all right, now she goes down that way, while I head up this way, and you sort of half turn around on this . . . and so it went, Doctor, until I came my third and final time. The Monkey was by then the one with her back on the bed, and I the one with my ass to the chandelier (and the cameras, I fleetingly thought)—and in the middle, feeding her tits into my Monkey's mouth, was our whore. Into whose hole, into what *sort* of hole, I deposited my final load is entirely a matter for conjecture. It could be that in the end I wound up fucking some dank, odoriferous combination of sopping Italian pubic hair, greasy American buttock, and absolutely rank bedsheet. Then I got up, went into the bathroom, and, you'll all be happy to know, regurgitated my dinner. My *kishkas*, Mother—threw them right up into the toilet bowl. Isn't that a good boy?

When I came out of the bathroom, The Monkey and Lina were lying asleep in one another's arms.

The Monkey's pathetic weeping, the recriminations and the accusations, began immediately after Lina had dressed and departed. I had delivered her into evil. "*Me? You're* the one who stuck your finger up her snatch and got the ball rolling! *You* kissed her on the fucking lips—!" "Because," she screamed, "if I'm going to do something, then like I *do* it! But that doesn't mean I *want* to!" And then, Doctor, she began to berate me about Lina's tits, how I hadn't *played* with them enough. "All you ever talk about and think about is tits! *Other people's tits!* Mine are so small and everybody else's in the world you see are so *huge*—so you finally get a pair that are *tremendous*, and what do you do? *Nothing!*" "Nothing is an exaggeration, Monkey—the fact of the matter is that I couldn't always fight my way *past* you—" "I am not a lesbian! Don't you dare call me a lesbian! Because if I am, *you made me one!*" "*Oh Jesus, no—!*" "I did it for you, *yes* and now you hate me for it!" "Then we won't do it again, for *me*, all right? Not if this is the fucking ridiculous result!"

Except the next night we got each other very steamed up at dinner—as in the early days of our courtship, The Monkey retired at one point to the ladies' room at Ranieri's and returned to the table with a finger redolent of pussy, which I held my nose to sniff and kiss at till the main dish arrived—and after a couple of brandies at Doney's, accosted Lina once again at her station and took her with us to the hotel for round two. Only this time I relieved Lina of her undergarments myself and mounted her even before The Monkey had come back into the bedroom from the john. If I'm going to do it, I thought, I'm going to do it! All the way! Everything! And no vomiting, either! You're not in Weequahic High School any more! You're nowhere *near* New Jersey!

When The Monkey stepped out of the bathroom and saw that the ballgame was already under way, she wasn't entirely pleased. She sat down on the edge of the bed, her little features smaller than I had ever seen them, and declining an invitation to participate, silently watched until I had had my orgasm and Lina had finished faking hers. Obligingly then—sweetly, really—Lina made for between my mistress' long legs, but The Monkey pushed her away and went off to sit and sulk in a chair by the window. So Lina—not a person overly sensitive to interpersonal struggle—lay back on the pillow beside me and began to tell us all about herself. The bane of existence was the abortions. She was the mother of one child, a boy, with whom she lived on Monte Mario ("in a beautiful new building," The Monkey translated). Unfortunately she could not manage, in her situation, any more than one—"though she loves children" —and so was always in and out of the abortionist's office. Her only precautionary device seemed to be a spermicidal douche of no great reliability.

I couldn't believe that she had never heard of either the diaphragm or the birth-control pill. I told The Monkey to explain to her about modern means of contraception that she could surely avail herself of, probably with only a little ingenuity. I got from my mistress a very wry look. The whore listened but was skeptical. It distressed me considerably that she should be so ignorant about a matter pertaining to her own well-being (there on the bed with her fingers wandering around in the damp pubic hair): That fucking Catholic church, I thought . . .

So, when she left us that night, she had not only fifteen thousand of my lire in her handbag, but a month's supply of The Monkey's Enovid—that I had given to her.

"Oh, you are some savior!" The Monkey shouted, after Lina had left.

"What do you want her to do—get knocked up every other week? What sense does that make?"

"What do I care what happens to *her*!" said The Monkey, her voice turning rural and mean. "*She's* the *whore*! And all *you* really wanted to do was to fuck *her*! You couldn't even wait until I was out of the john to do it! And then you gave her *my* pills!"

"And what's that mean, huh? What exactly are you trying to say? You know, one of the things you don't always display, Monkey, is a talent for reason. A talent for frankness, yes—for reason, no!"

"Then leave me! You've got what you wanted! Leave!"

"Maybe I will!"

"To you I'm just another *her*, anyway! You, with all your big words and big shit holy ideals and all I am in your eyes is just a cunt—and a lesbian!—and a whore!"

Skip the fight. It's boring. Sunday: we emerge from the elevator, and who should be coming through the front door of the hotel but our Lina—and with her a child of about seven or eight, a fat little boy made out of alabaster, dressed all in ruffles and velvet and patent leather. Lina's hair is down and her dark eyes, fresh from church, have a familiarly Italian mournful expression. A nice-looking person really. A sweet person (I can't get over this!). And she has come to show off her *bambino*! Or so it looks.

Pointing to the little boy, she whispers to The Monkey, "*Molto elegante, no?*" But then she follows us out to our car, and while the child is preoccupied with the doorman's uniform, suggests that maybe we would like to come to her apartment on Monte Mario this afternoon and all of us do it with another man. She has a friend, she says—mind you, I get all this through my translator—she has a friend who she is sure, she says, would like to fuck the *signorina*. I can see the tears sliding out from beneath The Monkey's dark glasses, even as she says to me, "Well, what do I tell her, yes or no?" "No, of course. Positively not." The Monkey exchanges some words with Lina and then turns to me once again: "She says it wouldn't be for money, it would just be for—"

"No! No!"

All the way to the Villa Adriana she weeps: "I want a child too! And a home! And a husband! I am not a lesbian! I am not a whore!" She reminds me of the evening the previous spring when I took her up to the Bronx with me, to what we at the H.O. commission call "Equal Opportunity Night." "All those poor Puerto Rican people being overcharged in the supermarket! In Spanish you spoke, and oh I was so impressed! Tell me about your bad sanitation, tell me about your rats and vermin, tell me about your police protection! Because discrimination is against the law! A year in prison or a five-hundred-dollar fine! And that poor Puerto Rican man stood up and shouted, 'Both!' Oh, you fake, Alex! You hypocrite and phony! Big shit to a bunch of stupid spics, but I know the truth, Alex! *You make women sleep with whores!*"

"I don't make anybody do anything they don't want to do."

"Human opportunities! *Human!* How you love that word! But do you know what it means, you son of a bitch pimp! I'll *teach* you what it means! Pull this car over, Alex!"

"Sorry, no."

"Yes! Yes! Because I'm getting out! I'm finding a phone! I'm going to call long-distance to John Lindsay and tell him what you made me do."

"The fuck you will."

"I'll expose you, Alex—I'll call Jimmy Breslin!"

Then in Athens she threatens to jump from the balcony unless I marry her. So I leave.

—

Shikses! In winter, when the polio germs are hibernating and I can bank upon surviving outside of an iron lung until the end of the school year, I ice-skate on the lake in Irvington Park. In the last light of the weekday afternoons, then all day long on crisply shining Saturdays and Sundays, I skate round and round in circles behind the *shikses* who live in Irvington, the town across the city line from the streets and houses of my safe and friendly Jewish quarter. I know where the *shikses* live from the kinds of curtains their mothers hang in the windows. Also, the *goyim* hang a little white cloth with a star in the front window, in honor of themselves and their boys away in the service —a blue star if the son is living, a gold star if he is dead. "A Gold Star Mom," says Ralph Edwards, solemnly introducing a contestant on "Truth or Consequences," who in just two minutes is going to get a bottle of seltzer squirted at her snatch, followed by a brand-new refrigerator for her kitchen . . . A Gold Star Mom is what my Aunt Clara upstairs is too, except here is the difference—she has no gold star in her window, for a dead son doesn't leave her feeling proud or noble, or feeling anything, for that matter. It seems instead to have turned her, in my father's words, into "a nervous case" for life. Not a day has passed since Heshie was killed in the Normandy invasion that Aunt Clara has not spent most of it in bed, and sobbing so badly that Doctor Izzie has sometimes to come and give her a shot to calm her hysteria down . . . But the curtains—the curtains are embroidered with lace, or "fancy" in some other way that my mother describes derisively as "*goyische* taste." At Christmastime, when I have no school and can go off to ice-skate at night under the lights, I see the trees blinking on and off behind the gentile curtains. Not on our block—God forbid!—or on Leslie Street, or Schley Street, or even Fabian Place, but as I approach the Irvington line, here is a *goy*, and there is a *goy*, and there still another—and then I am into Irvington and it is simply awful: not only is there a tree conspicuously ablaze in every parlor, but the houses themselves are outlined with colored bulbs advertising Christianity, and phonographs are pumping "Silent Night" out into the street as though—as though?—it were the national anthem, and on the snowy lawns are set up little cut-out models of the scene in the manger—really, it's enough to make you sick. How can they possibly *believe* this shit? Not just children but grownups, too, stand around on the snowy lawns smiling down at pieces of wood six inches high that are called Mary and Joseph and little Jesus—and the little cut-out cows and horses are smiling too! God! The idiocy of the Jews all year long, and then the idiocy of the *goyim* on these holidays! What a country! Is it any wonder we're all of us half nuts?

But the *shikses*, ah, the *shikses* are something else again. Between the smell of damp sawdust and wet wool in the over-heated boathouse, and the sight of their fresh cold blond hair spilling out of their kerchiefs and caps, I am ecstatic. Amidst these flushed and giggling girls, I lace up my skates with weak, trembling fingers, and then out into the cold and after them I move, down the wooden gangplank on my toes and off onto the ice behind a fluttering covey of them—a nosegay of *shikses*, a garland of gentile girls. I am so awed that I am in a state of desire *beyond a hard-on*. My circumcised little dong is simply shriveled up with veneration. Maybe it's dread. How do they get so gorgeous, so healthy, so *blond*? My contempt for what they believe in is more than neutralized by my adoration of the way they look, the way they move and laugh and speak—the lives they must lead behind those *goyische* curtains! Maybe a pride of *shikses* is more like it—or is it a pride of *shkotzim*? For these are the girls whose older brothers are the engaging, good-natured, confident, clean, swift, and powerful halfbacks for the college football teams called *Northwestern* and *Texas*

Christian and *UCLA*. Their fathers are men with white hair and deep voices who never use double negatives, and their mothers the ladies with the kindly smiles and the wonderful manners who say things like, "I do believe, Mary, that we sold thirty-five cakes at the Bake Sale." "Don't be too late, dear," they sing out sweetly to their little tulips as they go bouncing off in their bouffant taffeta dresses to the Junior Prom with boys whose names are right out of the grade-school reader, not Aaron and Arnold and Marvin, but Johnny and Billy and Jimmy and Tod. Not Portnoy or Pincus, but Smith and Jones and Brown! These people are the *Americans*, Doctor—like Henry Aldrich and Homer, like the Great Gildersleeve and his nephew LeRoy, like Corliss and Veronica, like "Oogie Pringle" who gets to sing beneath Jane Powell's window in *A Date with Judy*—these are the people for whom Nat "King" Cole sings every Christmastime, "Chestnuts roasting on an open fire, Jack Frost nipping at your nose . . ." An open fire, in *my* house? No, no, theirs are the noses whereof he speaks. Not his flat black one or my long bumpy one, but those tiny bridgeless wonders whose nostrils point northward automatically at birth. And stay that way for life! These are the children from the coloring books come to life, the children they mean on the signs we pass in Union, New Jersey, that say CHILDREN AT PLAY and DRIVE CAREFULLY, WE LOVE OUR CHILDREN—these are the girls and boys who live "next door," the kids who are always asking for "the jalopy" and getting into "jams" and then out of them again in time for the final commercial—the kids whose neighbors aren't the Silversteins and the Landaus, but Fibber McGee and Molly, and Ozzie and Harriet, and Ethel and Albert, and Lorenzo Jones and his wife Belle, and Jack Armstrong! Jack Armstrong, the All-American *Goy*!—and Jack as in John, not Jack as in Jake, like my father . . . Look, we ate our meals with that radio blaring away right through to the dessert, the glow of the yellow station band is the last light I see each night before sleep—so don't tell me we're just as good as anybody else, don't tell me we're Americans just like they are. No, no, these blond-haired Christians are the legitimate residents and owners of this place, and they can pump any song they want into the streets and no one is going to stop them either. O America! America!

it may have been gold in the streets to my grandparents, it may have been a chicken in every pot to my father and mother, but to me, a child whose earliest movie memories are of Ann Rutherford and Alice Faye, America is a *shikse* nestling under your arm whispering love love love love love!

So: dusk on the frozen lake of a city park, skating behind the puffy red earmuffs and the fluttering yellow ringlets of a strange *shikse* teaches me the meaning of the word *longing*. It is almost more than an angry thirteen-year-old little Jewish Momma's Boy can bear. Forgive the luxuriating, but these are probably the most poignant hours of my life I'm talking about—I learn the meaning of the word longing, I learn the meaning of the word *pang*. There go the darling things dashing up the embankment, clattering along the shoveled walk between the evergreens—and so here I go too (if I dare!). The sun is almost all the way down, and everything is purple (including my prose) as I follow at a safe distance until they cross the street on their skates, and go giggling into the little park side candy store. By the time I get up the nerve to come through the door—every eye will surely be upon me!—they have already loosened their mufflers and unzipped their jackets, and are raising cups of hot chocolate between their smooth and burning cheeks—and those noses, mystery of mysteries! each disappears entirely into a cup full of chocolate and marshmallows and comes out at the other end unblemished by liquid! Jesus, look how guiltlessly they eat between meals! What girls! Crazily, impetuously, I order a cup of chocolate myself—and proceed to ruin my appetite for dinner, served promptly by my jumping-jack mother at five-thirty, when my father walks into the house "starved." Then I follow them back to the lake. Then I follow them around the lake. Then at last my ecstasy is over—they go home to the grammatical fathers and the composed mothers and the self-assured brothers who all live with them in harmony and bliss behind their *goyische* curtains, and I start back to Newark, to my palpitating life with my family, lived now behind the aluminum "Venetians" for which my mother has been saving out of her table-money for years.

What a rise in social class we have made with those blinds! Headlong, my mother seems to feel, we have been catapulted into high society. A good part of her life is now given over to the dusting and polishing of the slats of the blinds; she is behind them wiping away during the day, and at dusk, looks out from between her clean slats at the snow, where it has begun to fall through the light of the street lamp—and begins pumping up the worry-machine. It is usually only a matter of minutes before she is appropriately frantic. "Where *is* he already?" she moans, each time a pair of headlights comes sweeping up the street and are not his. Where, oh where, our Odysseus! Upstairs Uncle Hymie is home, across the street Landau is home, next door Silverstein is home—everybody is home by five forty-five except my father, and the radio says that a blizzard is already bearing down on Newark from the North Pole. Well, there is just no doubt about it, we might as well call Tuckerman & Farber about the funeral arrangements, and start inviting the guests. Yes, it needs only for the roads to begin to glisten with ice for the assumption to be made that my father, fifteen minutes late for dinner, is crunched up against a telegraph pole somewhere, lying dead in a pool of his own blood. My mother comes into the kitchen, her face by now a face out of El Greco. "My two starving Armenians," she says in a breaking voice, "eat, go ahead, darlings—start, there's no sense waiting—" And who wouldn't be grief-stricken? Just think of the years to come—her two babies, without a father, herself without a husband and provider, all because out of nowhere, just as that poor man was starting home, it had to begin to snow.

Meanwhile I wonder if with my father dead I will have to get a job after school and Saturdays, and consequently give up skating at Irvington Park—give up skating with my *shikses* before I have even spoken a single word to a one of them. I am afraid to open my mouth for fear that if I do no words will come out—or the *wrong* words. "Portnoy, yes, it's an old French name, a corruption of *porte noir*, meaning black door or gate. Apparently in the Middle Ages in France the door to our family manor house was painted . . ." et cetera and so forth. No, no, they will hear the *oy* at the end, and the jig will be up. Al Port then, Al Parsons! "How do you do, Miss McCoy, mind if I skate alongside, my name is Al Parsons—" but isn't Alan as Jewish and foreign as Alexander? I know there's Alan Ladd, but there's also my friend Alan Rubin, the shortstop for our softball team. And wait'll she hears I'm from Weequahic. Oh, what's the difference anyway, I can lie about my name, I can lie about my school, but how am I going to lie about this fucking nose? "You seem like a very nice person, Mr. Porte-Noir, but why do you go around covering the middle of your face like that?" Because suddenly it has taken off, the middle of my face! Because gone is the button of my childhood years, that pretty little thing that people used to look at in my carriage, and lo and behold, the middle of my face has begun to reach out toward God! Porte-Noir and Parsons my ass, kid, you have got J-E-W written right across the middle of that face—look at the shnoz on him, for God's sake! That ain't a nose, it's a hose! Screw off, Jewboy! Get off the ice and leave these girls alone!

And it's true. I lower my head to the kitchen table and on a piece of my father's office stationery outline my profile with a pencil. And it's *terrible*. How has this happened to me who was so gorgeous in that carriage, Mother! At the top it has begun to aim toward the heavens, while simultaneously, where the cartilage ends halfway down the slope, it is beginning to bend back toward my mouth. A couple of years and I won't even be able to eat, this thing will be directly in the path of the *food*! No! No! It can't be! I go into the bathroom and stand before the mirror, I press the nostrils upward with two fingers. From the side it's not too bad either, but in front, where my upper lip used to be, there is now just teeth and gum. Some *goy*. I look like Bugs Bunny! I cut pieces from the cardboard that comes back in the shirts from the laundry and Scotch-tape them to either side of my nose, thus restoring in profile the nice upward curve that I sported all through my childhood . . . but which is now gone! It actually seems that this sprouting of my beak dates exactly from the time that I discovered the *shikses* skating in Irvington Park—as though my own nose bone has taken it upon itself to act as my parents' agent! Skating with *shikses*? Just you try it, wise guy. Remember Pinocchio? Well, that is nothing compared with what is going to happen to you. They'll laugh and laugh, howl and hoot—and worse, calling you Goldberg in the bargain, send you on your way roasting with fury and resentment. Who do you think they're always giggling about as it is? You! The skinny Yid and his

shnoz following them around the ice every single afternoon—
and can't talk! "Please, will you stop playing with your nose,"
my mother says. "I'm not interested, Alex, in what's growing up
inside there, not at dinner." "But it's too *big*." "What? What's
too big?" says my father. "My *nose*!" I scream. "Please, it gives
you character," my mother says, "so leave it alone!"

But who wants character? I want Thereal McCoy! In her
blue parka and her red earmuffs and her big white mittens—
Miss America, on blades! With her mistletoe and her plum
pudding (whatever that may be), and her one-family house
with a banister and a staircase, and parents who are tranquil
and patient and *dignified*, and also a brother Billy who knows
how to take motors apart and says "Much obliged," and isn't
afraid of anything physical, and oh the way she'll cuddle next
to me on the sofa in her Angora sweater with her legs pulled
back up beneath her tartan skirt, and the way she'll turn at
the doorway and say to me, "And thank you ever so much
for a wonderful wonderful evening," and then this amazing
creature—to whom no one has ever said "*Shah!*" or "I only
hope your children will do the same to you someday!"—this
perfect, perfect-stranger, who is as smooth and shiny and cool
as custard, will kiss me—raising up one shapely calf behind
her—and my nose and my name will have become as nothing.

Look, I'm not asking for the world—I just don't see why I
should get any less out of life than some schmuck like Oogie
Pringle or Henry Aldrich. I want Jane Powell too, God damn
it! And Corliss and Veronica. I too want to be the boyfriend of
Debbie Reynolds—it's the Eddie Fisher in me coming out,
that's all, the longing in all us swarthy Jewboys for those bland
blond exotics called *shikses* . . . Only what I don't know yet
in these feverish years is that for every Eddie yearning for a
Debbie, there is a Debbie yearning for an Eddie—a Marilyn
Monroe yearning for her Arthur Miller—even an Alice Faye
yearning for Phil Harris. Even Jayne Mansfield was about to
marry one, remember, when she was suddenly killed in a car
crash? Who knew, you see, who knew back when we were
watching *National Velvet*, that this stupendous purple-eyed
girl who had the supreme *goyische* gift of all, the courage and
know-how to get up and ride around on a horse (as opposed
to having one pull your wagon, like the rag-seller for whom I

am named)—who would have believed that this girl on the horse with the riding breeches and the perfect enunciation was lusting for our kind no less than we for hers? Because you know what Mike Todd was—a cheap facsimile of my Uncle Hymie upstairs! And who in his right mind would ever have believed that Elizabeth Taylor had the hots for Uncle Hymie? Who knew that the secret to a *shikse*'s heart (and box) was not to pretend to be some hook-nosed variety of *goy*, as boring and vacuous as her own brother, but to be what one's uncle was, to be what one's father was, to be whatever one was oneself, instead of doing some pathetic little Jewish imitation of one of those half-dead, ice-cold *shaygets* pricks, Jimmy or Johnny or Tod, who look, who think, who feel, who talk like fighter-bomber pilots!

—

Look at The Monkey, my old pal and partner in crime. Doctor, just saying her name, just bringing her to mind, gives me a hard-on on the spot! But I know I shouldn't call her or see her ever again. Because the bitch is crazy! The sex-crazed bitch is out of her mind! Pure trouble!

But—what, what was I supposed to be but *her* Jewish savior? The Knight on the Big White Steed, the fellow in the Shining Armor the little girls used to dream would come to rescue them from the castles in which they were always imagining themselves to be imprisoned, well, as far as a certain school of *shikse* is concerned (of whom The Monkey is a gorgeous example), this knight turns out to be none other than a brainy, balding, beaky Jew, with a strong social conscience and black hair on his balls, who neither drinks nor gambles nor keeps show girls on the side; a man guaranteed to give them kiddies to rear and Kafka to read—a regular domestic Messiah! Sure, he may as a kind of tribute to his rebellious adolescence say *shit* and *fuck* a lot around the house—in front of the children even—but the indisputable and heartwarming fact is that *he is always around the house.* No bars, no brothels, no race tracks, no backgammon all night long at the Racquet Club (about which she knows from her stylish past) or beer till all hours down at the American Legion (which she can remember from her mean and squalid youth). No, no indeed—what we have before us, ladies and gentlemen, direct from a long record-breaking engagement with his own family, is a Jewish boy just dying in his every cell to be Good, Responsible, & Dutiful to a family of his own. The same people who brought you Harry Golden's *For 2 ¢ Plain* bring you now—The Alexander Portnoy Show! If you liked Arthur Miller as a savior of s*hikses*, you'll just love Alex! You see, my background was in every way that was crucial to The Monkey the very opposite of what she had had to endure eighteen miles south of Wheeling, in a coal town called Moundsville—while I was up in New Jersey drowning in schmaltz (lolling in Jewish "warmth," as The Monkey would have it), she was down in West Virginia virtually freezing to death, nothing but chattel really to a father who was, as she describes him, himself little more than first cousin to a mule, and some kind of incomprehensible bundle of needs to a mother who was as well-meaning as it was possible to be if you were a hillbilly one generation removed from the Alleghenies, a woman who could neither read nor write nor count all that high, and to top things off, hadn't a single molar in her head.

A story of The Monkey's which made a strong impression on me (not that all her stories didn't compel this particular neurotic's attention, with their themes of cruelty, ignorance, and exploitation): Once when she was eleven, and against her father's will had sneaked off on a Saturday to a ballet class given by the local "artiste" (called Mr. Maurice), the old man came after her with a belt, beat her with it around the ankles all the way home, and then locked her in the closet for the rest of the day—and with her feet *tied* together for good measure. "Ketch you down by that queer again, you, and won't just tie 'em up, I'll do more'n that, don't you worry!"

When she first arrived in New York, she was eighteen and hadn't any back teeth to speak of, either. They had all been extracted (for a reason she still can't fathom) by the local Moundsville practitioner, as gifted a dentist as she remembers Mr. Maurice to have been a dancer. When we two met, nearly a year ago now, The Monkey had already been through her marriage and her divorce. Her husband had been a fifty-year-old French industrialist, who had courted and married her one week in Florence, where she was modeling in a show at the Pitti Palace. Subsequent to the marriage, his sex life consisted of getting into bed with his young and beautiful bride and jerking off into a copy of a magazine called *Garter Belt*, which he had flown over to him from Forty-second Street. The Monkey has at her disposal a kind of dumb, mean, rural twang which she sometimes likes to use, and would invariably drop down into it when describing the excesses to which she was expected to be a witness as the tycoon's wife. She could be very funny about the fourteen months she had spent with him, despite the fact that it was probably a grim if not terrifying experience. But he had flown her to London after the marriage for five thousand dollars' worth of dental work, and then back in Paris, hung around her neck several hundred thousand dollars more in jewelry, and for the longest while, says The Monkey, this caused her to feel loyal to him. As she put it (before I forbade her ever again to say *like*, and *man*, and *swinger*, and *crazy*, and *a groove*): "It was, like ethics."

What caused her finally to run for her life were the little orgies he began to arrange after jerking off into *Garter Belt* (or was it *Spiked Heels?*) became a bore to both of them. A woman, preferably black, would be engaged for a very high sum to squat naked upon a glass coffee table and take a crap while the tycoon lay flat on his back, directly beneath the table, and jerked his dong off. And as the shit splattered on the glass six inches above her beloved's nose, The Monkey, our poor Monkey, was expected to sit on the red damask sofa, fully clothed, sipping cognac and watching.

It was a couple of years after her return to New York—I suppose she's about twenty-four or twenty-five by this time—that The Monkey tried to kill herself a little by making a pass at her wrists with a razor, all on account of the way she had been treated at Le Club, or El Morocco, or maybe L'Interdit, by her current boyfriend, one or another of the hundred best-dressed men in the world. Thus she found her way to the illustrious Dr. Morris Frankel, henceforth to be known in these confessions as Harpo. Off and on during these past five years The Monkey has thrashed around on Harpo's couch, waiting for him to tell her what she must do to become somebody's wife and somebody's mother. Why, cries The Monkey to Harpo, why must she always be involved with such hideous and cold-hearted shits, instead of with *men*? Why? Harpo, speak! Say something to me! *Anything!* "Oh, I know he's alive," The Monkey used to say, her little features scrunched up in anguish, "I just know it. I mean, who ever heard of a dead man with an answering service?" So, in and out of therapy (if that's what it is) The Monkey goes—in whenever some new shit has broken her heart, out whenever the next likely knight has made his appearance.

I was "a breakthrough." Harpo of course didn't say yes, but then he didn't say no, either, when she suggested that this was who I might be. He did cough, however, and this The Monkey takes as her confirmation. Sometimes he coughs, sometimes he grunts, sometimes he belches, once in a while he farts, whether voluntarily or not who knows, though I hold that a fart has to be interpreted as a negative transference reaction on his part. "Breakie, you're so *brilliant!*" "Breakie" when she is being my sex kitten and cat—and when she is fighting for her life: "You big son of a bitch Jew! I want to be married and human!"

So, I was to be her breakthrough . . . but wasn't she to be mine? Who like The Monkey had ever happened to me before —or will again? Not that I had not prayed, of course. No, you pray and you pray and you pray, you lift your impassioned prayers to God on the altar of the toilet seat, throughout your adolescence you deliver up to Him the living sacrifice of your spermatazoa by the *gallon*—and then one night, around midnight, on the corner of Lexington and Fifty-second, when you have come really to the point of losing faith in the existence of such a creature as you have been imagining for yourself even unto your thirty-second year, there she is, wearing a tan pants suit, and trying to hail a cab—lanky, with dark and abundant hair, and smallish features that give her face a kind of petulant expression, and an absolutely fantastic ass.

Why not? What's lost? What's gained, however? Go ahead, you shackled and fettered son of a bitch, *speak to her.* She has an ass on her with the swell and the cleft of the world's most perfect nectarine! *Speak!*

"Hi"—softly, and with a little surprise, as though I might have met her somewhere before . . .

"What do *you* want?"

"To buy you a drink," I said.

"A real swinger," she said, sneering.

Sneering! Two seconds—and two insults! To the Assistant Commissioner of Human Opportunity for this whole city! "To eat your pussy, baby, how's that?" My God! She's going to call a cop! Who'll turn me in to the Mayor!

"That's better," she replied.

And so a cab pulled up, and we went to her apartment, where she took off her clothes and said, "Go ahead."

My incredulity! That such a thing was happening to me! Did I eat! It was suddenly as though my life were taking place in the middle of a wet dream. There I was, going down at last on the star of all those pornographic films that I had been producing in my head since I first laid a hand upon my own joint . . . "Now me you," she said, "—one good turn deserves another," and, Doctor, this stranger then proceeded to suck me off with a mouth that might have gone to a special college to learn all the wonderful things it knew. What a find, I thought, she takes it right down to the root! What a mouth I have fallen into! Talk about opportunities! And simultaneously: *Get out! Go! Who and what can this person be!*

Later we had a long, serious, very stirring conversation about perversions. She began by asking if I had ever done it with a man. I said no. I asked (as I gathered she wanted me to) if she had ever done it with another woman.

". . . Nope."

". . . Would you like to?"

". . . Would you like me to?"

". . . Why, not, sure."

". . . Would you like to watch?"

". . . I suppose so."

". . . Then maybe it could be arranged."

". . . Yes?"

". . . Yes."

". . . Well, I might like that."

"Oh," she said, with a nice sarcastic edge, "I think you might."

She told me then that only a month before, when she had been ill with a virus, a couple she knew had come by to make dinner for her. After the meal they said they wanted her to watch them screw. So she did. She sat up on the bed with a temperature of 102, and they took off their clothes and went at it on the bedroom rug—"And you know what they wanted me to do, while they were making it?"

"No."

"I had some bananas on the counter in the kitchen, and they wanted me to eat one. While I watched."

"For the arcane symbolism, no doubt."

"The *what?*"

"Why did they want you to eat the banana?"

"Man, I don't know. I guess they wanted to know I was really *there*. They wanted to like *hear* me. Chewing. Look, do you just suck, or do you fuck, too?"

The real McCoy! My slut from the Empire Burlesque—without the tits, but so beautiful!

"I fuck too."

"Well, so do I."

"Isn't that a coincidence," I said, "us running into each other."

She laughed for the first time, and instead of that finally putting me at my ease, suddenly I *knew*—some big spade was going to leap out of the bedroom closet and spring for my heart with his knife—or she herself was going to go berserk, the laughter would erupt into wild hysterics—and God only knew what catastrophe would follow. Eddie Waitkus!

Was she a call girl? A maniac? Was she in cahoots with some Puerto Rican pusher who was about to make his entrance into my life? Enter it—and end it, for the forty dollars in my wallet and my watch from Korvette's?

"Look," I said, in my clever way, "do you do this, more or less, all the time . . . ?"

"What kind of question is that! What kind of shit-eating re-mark is that supposed to be! Are you another heartless bastard too? Don't you think I have feelings *too!*"

"I'm sorry. Excuse me."

But suddenly, where there had been fury and outrage, there were only tears. Did I need any more evidence that this girl was, to say the least, a little erratic psychologically? Any man in his right mind would surely then have gotten up, gotten dressed, and gotten the hell out in one piece. And counting his blessings. But don't you see—my right mind is just another name for my fears! My right mind is simply that inheritance of terror that I bring with me out of my ridiculous past! That tyrant, my superego, he should be strung up, that son of a bitch, hung by his fucking storm-trooper's boots till he's dead! In the street, who had been trembling, me or the girl? Me! Who had the boldness, the daring, the guts, me or the girl? The girl! The fucking *girl!*"

"Look," she said, wiping away the tears with the pillowcase, "look, I lied to you before, in case you're interested, in case you're writing this down or something."

"Yeah? About what?" And here he comes, I thought, my *shvartze*, out of the closet,—eyes, teeth, and razor blade flashing! Here comes the headline: ASST HUMAN OPP'Y COMMISH FOUND HEADLESS IN GO-GO GIRL'S APT!

"I mean like what the fuck did I lie for, to *you*?"

"I don't know what you're talking about, so I can't tell you."

"I mean *they* didn't want me to eat the banana. My friends didn't want me to eat any banana. *I* wanted to."

Thus: The Monkey.

As for why she did lie, to *me*? I think it was her way of informing herself right off—semiconsciously, I suppose—that she had somehow fallen upon a higher-type person: that pickup on the street notwithstanding, and the wholehearted suck in her bed notwithstanding—followed by that heart-stirring swallow —and the discussion of perversions that followed that . . . still, she really hadn't wanted me to think of her as given over *wholly* to sexual excess and adventurism . . . Because a glimpse of me was apparently all it took for her to leap imaginatively ahead into the life that might now be hers . . . No more narcissistic playboys in their Cardin suits; no more married, desperate advertising executives in overnight from Connecticut; no more faggots in British warmers for lunch at Serendipity, or aging lechers from the cosmetics industry drooling into their hundred-dollar dinners at Le Pavillon at night . . . No, at long last the figure who had dwelled these many years at the heart of *her* dreams (so it turned out), a man who would be good to a wife and to children . . . a Jew. And what a Jew! First he eats her, and then, immediately after, comes slithering on up and begins talking and explaining things, making judgments left and right, advising her about books to read and how to vote, telling her how life should and should not be lived. "How do you know that?" she used to ask warily. "I mean that's just your *opinion*." "What do you mean *opinion*—it's not my opinion, girlie, it's the truth." "I mean, is that like something everybody knows . . . or just you?" A Jewish man, who cared about the welfare of the poor of the City of New York, was eating her pussy! Someone who had appeared on educational TV was shooting off into her mouth! In a flash, Doctor, she must have seen it all—can that be? Are women *that* calculating? Am I actually a naïf about cunt? Saw and planned it all, did she, right out there on Lexington Avenue? . . . The gentle fire burning in the book-lined living room of our country home, the Irish nanny bathing the children before Mother puts them to bed, and the willowy ex-model, jet-setter, and sex deviant, daughter of the mines and mills of West Virginia, self-styled victim of a dozen real bastards, seen here in her Saint Laurent pajamas and her crushed-kid boots, dipping thoughtfully into a novel by Samuel Beckett . . . seen here on a fur rug with her husband, whom People Are Talking About, The Saintliest Commissioner of the City of New York . . . seen here with his pipe and his thinning kinky black Hebe hair, in all his Jewish messianic fervor and charm . . .

—

What happened finally at Irvington Park: late on a Saturday afternoon I found myself virtually alone on the frozen lake with a darling fourteen-year-old *shikseleh* whom I had been watching practicing her figure eights since after lunch, a girl who seemed to me to possess the middle-class charms of Margaret O'Brien—that quickness and cuteness around the sparkling eyes and the freckled nose—*and* the simplicity and plainness, the lower-class availability, the lank blond hair of Peggy Ann Garner. You see, what looked like movie stars to everyone else were just different kinds of *shikses* to me. Often I came out of the movies trying to figure out what high school in Newark Jeanne Crain (and her cleavage) or Kathryn Grayson (and her cleavage) would be going to if they were my age. And where would I find a *shikse* like Gene Tierney, who I used to think might even be a Jew, if she wasn't actually part Chinese. Meanwhile Peggy Ann O'Brien has made her last figure eight and is coasting lazily off for the boathouse, and I have done nothing about her, or about any of them, nothing all winter long, and now March is almost upon us—the red skating flag will come down over the park and once again we will be into polio season. I may not even live into the following winter, *so what am I waiting for*? "Now! Or never!" So after her—when she is safely out of sight—I madly begin to skate. "Excuse me," I will say, "but would you mind if I walk you home?" If I *walked*, or if I *walk*—which is more correct? Because I have to speak absolutely perfect English. Not a word of Jew in it. "Would you care perhaps to have a hot chocolate? May I have your phone number and come to call some evening? My name? I am Alton Peterson"—a name I had picked for myself out of the Montclair section of the Essex County phone book—totally *goy* I was sure, and sounds like Hans Christian Andersen into the bargain. What a coup! Secretly I have been practicing writing "Alton Peterson" all winter long, practicing on sheets of paper that I subsequently tear from my notebook after school and burn so that they won't have to be explained to anybody in my house. I am Alton Peterson, I am Alton Peterson—Alton Christian Peterson? Or is that going a little too far? Alton C. Peterson? And so preoccupied am I with not forgetting whom I would now like to be, so anxious to make it to the boathouse while she is still changing out of her skates—and wondering, too, what I'll say when she asks about the middle of my face and what happened to it (old hockey injury? Fell off my horse while playing polo after church one Sunday morning—too many sausages for breakfast, ha ha ha!) —I reach the edge of the lake with the tip of one skate a little sooner than I had planned—and so go hurtling forward onto the frostbitten ground, chipping one front tooth and smashing the bony protrusion at the top of my tibia.

My right leg is in a cast, from ankle to hip, for six weeks. I have something that the doctor calls Osgood Shlatterer's Disease. After the cast comes off, I drag the leg along behind me like a war injury—while my father cries, "Bend it! Do you want to go through life like that? Bend it! Walk natural, will you! Stop favoring that Oscar Shattered leg, Alex, or you are going to wind up a cripple for the rest of your days!"

For skating after *shikses*, under an alias, I would be a cripple for the rest of my days.

With a life like mine, Doctor, who needs dreams?

—

Bubbles Girardi, an eighteen-year-old girl who had been thrown out of Hillside High School and was subsequently found floating in the swimming pool at Olympic Park by my lascivious classmate, Smolka, the tailor's son . . .

For myself, I wouldn't go near that pool if you paid me—it is a breeding ground for polio and spinal meningitis, not to mention diseases of the skin, the scalp, and the asshole—it is even rumored that some kid from Weequahic once stepped into the footbath between the locker room and the pool and actually came out at the other end without his toenails. And yet that is where you find the girls who fuck. Wouldn't you know it? That is the place to find the kinds of *shikses* Who Will Do Anything! If only a person is willing to risk polio from the pool, gangrene from the footbath, ptomaine from the hot dogs, and elephantiasis from the soap and the towels, he might possibly get laid.

We sit in the kitchen, where Bubbles was working over the ironing board when we arrived—in her slip! Mandel and I leaf through back numbers of *Ring* magazine, while in the living room Smolka tries to talk Bubbles into taking on his two friends as a special favor to him. Bubbles' brother, who in a former life was a paratrooper, is nobody we have to worry about, Smolka assures us, because he is off in Hoboken boxing in a feature event under the name Johnny "Geronimo" Girardi. Her father drives a taxi during the day, and a car for The Mob at night—he is out somewhere chauffeuring gangsters around and doesn't get home until the early hours, and the mother we don't have to worry about because she's dead. Perfect, Smolka, perfect, I couldn't feel more secure. Now I have absolutely nothing to worry about except the Trojan I have been carrying around so long in my wallet that inside its tinfoil wrapper it has probably been half eaten away by mold. One spurt and the whole thing will go flying in pieces all over the inside of Bubbles Girardi's box—and *then* what do I do?

To be sure that these Trojans really hold up under pressure, I have been down in my cellar all week filling them with quart after quart of water—expensive as it is, I have been using them to jerk off into, to see if they will stand up under simulated fucking conditions. So far so good. Only what about the sacred one that has by now left an indelible imprint of its shape upon my wallet, the very special one I have been saving to get laid with, with the lubricated tip? How can I possibly expect no damage to have been done after sitting on it in school—crushing it in that wallet—for nearly six months? And who says Geronimo is going to be all night in Hoboken? And what if the person the gangsters are supposed to murder has already dropped dead from fright by the time they arrive, and Mr. Girardi is sent home early for a good night's rest? What if the girl has the syph! But then Smolka must have it too!—Smolka, who is always dragging drinks out of everybody else's bottle of cream soda, and grabbing with his hand at your putz! That's all I need, with my mother! I'd never hear the end of it! "Alex, what is that you're hiding under your foot?" "Nothing." "Alex, please, I heard a definite clink. What is that that fell out of your trousers that you're stepping on it with your foot? Out of your good trousers!" "Nothing! My shoe! Leave me alone!" "Young man, what are you—oh my God! Jack! Come quick! Look—look on the floor by his shoe!" With his pants around his knees, and the *Newark News* turned back to the obituary page and clutched in his hand, he rushes into the kitchen from the bathroom—"*Now* what?" She screams (that's her answer) and points beneath my chair. "What is that, Mister—some smart high-school joke?" demands my father, in a fury—"what is that black plastic thing doing on the kitchen floor?" "It's not a plastic one," I say, and break into sobs. "It's my own. I caught the syph from an eighteen-year-old Italian girl in Hillside, and now, now, I have no more p-p-p-penis!" "His little thing," screams my mother, "that I used to tickle it to make him go wee-wee—" "DON'T TOUCH IT NOBODY MOVE," cries my father, for my mother seems about to leap forward onto the floor, like a woman into her husband's grave—"call—the Humane Society—" "Like for a rabies *dog*?" she weeps. "Sophie, what else are you going to do? Save it in a drawer somewhere? To show his children? He ain't going to *have* no children!" She begins to howl pathetically, a grieving animal, while my father . . . but the scene fades quickly, for in a matter of seconds I am blind, and within the hour my brain is the consistency of hot Farina.

Tacked above the Girardi sink is a picture of Jesus Christ floating up to Heaven in a pink nightgown. How disgusting can human beings be! The Jews I despise for their narrow-mindedness, their self-righteousness, the incredibly bizarre sense that these cave men who are my parents and relatives have somehow gotten of their superiority—but when it comes to tawdriness and cheapness, to beliefs that would shame even a gorilla, you simply cannot top the *goyim*. What kind of base and brainless schmucks are these people to worship somebody who, number one, never existed, and number two, if he did, looking as he does in that picture, was without a doubt The Pansy of Palestine. In a pageboy haircut, with a Palmolive complexion—and wearing a gown that I realize today must have come from Fredericks of Hollywood! Enough of God and the rest of that garbage! Down with religion and human groveling! Up with socialism and the dignity of man! Actually, why I should be visiting the Girardi home is not so as to lay their daughter—please God!—but to evangelize for Henry Wallace and Glen Taylor. Of course! For who are the Girardis if not *the people*, on whose behalf, for whose rights and liberties and dignities, I and my brother-in-law-to-be wind up arguing every Sunday afternoon with our hopelessly ignorant elders (who vote Democratic and think Neanderthal), my father and my uncle. If we don't like it here, they tell us, why don't we go back to Russia where everything is hunky-dory? "You're going to turn that kid into a Communist," my father warns Morty, whereupon I cry out, "You don't understand! All men are brothers!" Christ, I could strangle him on the spot for being so blind to human brotherhood!

Now that he is marrying my sister, Morty drives the truck and works in the warehouse for my uncle, and in a manner of speaking, so do I: three Saturdays in a row now I have risen before dawn to go out with him delivering cases of Squeeze to general stores off in the rural wilds where New Jersey joins with the Poconos. I have written a radio play, inspired by my master, Norman Corwin, and his celebration of V-E Day, *On a Note of Triumph* (a copy of which Morty has bought me for my birthday). *So the enemy is dead in an alley back of the*

Wilhelmstrasse; take a bow, G.I., take a bow, little guy . . . Just
the rhythm alone can cause my flesh to ripple, like the beat of
the marching song of the victorious Red Army, and the song
we learned in grade school during the war, which our teachers
called "The Chinese National Anthem." "Arise, ye who refuse
to be bond-slaves, with our very flesh and blood"—oh, that
defiant cadence! I remember every single heroic word!—"we
will build a new great wall!" And then my favorite line,
commencing as it does with my favorite word in the English
language: "*In*-dig-*na*-tion fills the hearts of all of our coun-try-
men! A-*rise*! A-*rise*! A-RISE!"

I open to the first page of my play and begin to read aloud
to Morty as we start off in the truck, through Irvington, the
Oranges, on toward the West—Illinois! Indiana! Iowa! O my
America of the plains and the mountains and the valleys and
the rivers and the canyons . . . It is with just such patriotic in-
cantations as these that I have begun to put myself to sleep at
night, after jerking off into my sock. My radio play is called *Let
Freedom Ring!* It is a morality play (now I know) whose two
major characters are named Prejudice and Tolerance, and it is
written in what I call "prose-poetry." We pull into a diner in
Dover, New Jersey, just as Tolerance begins to defend Negroes
for the way they smell. The sound of my own humane, compassionate, Latinate, alliterative rhetoric, inflated almost beyond recognition by Roget's *Thesaurus* (a birthday gift from
my sister)—plus the fact of the dawn and my being out in it—
plus the tattooed counterman in the diner whom Morty calls
"Chief"—plus eating for the first time in my life home-fried
potatoes for breakfast—plus swinging back up into the cab of
the truck in my Levis and lumberjacket and moccasins (which
out on the highway no longer seem the costume that they do
in the halls of the high school)—plus the sun just beginning to
shine over the hilly farmlands of New Jersey, my state!—I am
reborn! Free, I find, of shameful secrets! So clean-feeling, so
strong and virtuous-feeling—so American! Morty pulls back
onto the highway, and right then and there I take my vow, I
swear that I will dedicate my life to the righting of wrongs, to
the elevation of the downtrodden and the underprivileged, to
the liberation of the unjustly imprisoned. With Morty as my
witness—my manly left-wing new-found older brother, the

living proof that it is possible to love mankind and baseball both (and who loves my older sister, whom I am ready to love now, too, for the escape hatch with which she has provided the two of us), who is my link through the A.V.C. to Bill Mauldin, as much my hero as Corwin or Howard Fast—to Morty, with tears of love (for him, for me) in my eyes, I vow to use "the power of the pen" to liberate from injustice and exploitation, from humiliation and poverty and ignorance, the people I now think of (giving myself gooseflesh) as *The People*.

—

I am icy with fear. Of the girl and her syph! of the father and his friends! of the brother and his fists! (even though Smolka has tried to get me to believe what strikes me as wholly incredible, even for *goyim*: that both brother and father know, and neither cares, that Bubbles is a "hoor"). And fear, too, that beneath the kitchen window, which I plan to leap out of if I should hear so much as a footstep on the stairway, is an iron picket fence upon which I will be impaled. Of course, the fence I am thinking of surrounds the Catholic orphanage on Lyons Avenue, but I am by now halfway between hallucination and coma, and somewhat woozy, as though I've gone too long without food. I see the photograph in the *Newark News*, of the fence and the dark puddle of my blood on the sidewalk, and the caption from which my family will never recover: INSURANCE MAN'S SON LEAPS TO DEATH.

While I sit freezing in my igloo, Mandel is basting in his own perspiration—and smells it. The body odor of Negroes fills me with compassion, with "prose-poetry"—Mandel I am less indulgent of: "he nauseates me" (as my mother says of him), which isn't to suggest that he is any less hypnotic a creature to me than Smolka is. Sixteen and Jewish just like me, but there all resemblance ends: he wears his hair in a duck's ass, his sideburns down to his jawbone, and sports one-button roll suits and pointy black shoes, and Billy Eckstine collars bigger than Billy Eckstine's! But Jewish. Incredible! A moralistic teacher has leaked to us that Arnold Mandel has the I.Q. of a genius yet prefers instead to take rides in stolen cars, smoke cigarettes, and get sick on bottles of beer. Can you believe it? A Jewish boy? He is also a participant in the circle-jerks held with the shades pulled down in Smolka's living room after school, while both elder Smolkas are slaving away in the tailor shop. I have heard the stories, but still (despite my own onanism, exhibitionism, and voyeurism—not to mention fetishism) I can't and won't believe it: four or five guys sit around in a circle on the floor, and at Smolka's signal, each begins to pull off—and the first one to come gets the pot, a buck a head.

What pigs.

The only explanation I have for Mandel's behavior is that his father died when Mandel was only ten. And this of course is what mesmerizes me most of all: *a boy without a father.*

How do I account for Smolka and *his* daring? He has *a mother who works.* Mine, remember, patrols the six rooms of our apartment the way a guerilla army moves across its own countryside—there's not a single closet or drawer of mine whose contents she hasn't a photographic sense of. Smolka's mother, on the other hand, sits all day by a little light in a little chair in the corner of his father's store, taking seams in and out, and by the time she gets home at night, hasn't the strength to get out her Geiger counter and start in hunting for her child's hair-raising collection of French ticklers. The Smolkas, you must understand, are not so rich as we—and therein lies the final difference. A mother who works and no Venetian blinds . . . yes, this sufficiently explains everything to me— how come he swims at Olympic Park as well as why is he always grabbing at everybody else's putz. He lives on Hostess cupcakes and his own wits. I get a hot lunch and all the inhibitions thereof. But don't get me wrong (as though that were possible): during a winter snowstorm what is more thrilling, while stamping off the slush on the back landing at lunchtime, than to hear "Aunt Jenny" coming over the kitchen radio, and to smell cream of tomato soup heating up on the stove? What beats freshly laundered and ironed pajamas any season of the year, and a bedroom fragrant with furniture polish? How would I like my underwear all gray and jumbled up in my drawer, as Smolka's always is? I wouldn't. How would I like socks without toes and nobody to bring me hot lemonade and honey when my throat is sore?

Conversely, how would I like Bubbles Girardi to come to my own house in the afternoon and blow me, as she did Smolka, on his own bed?

—

Of some ironic interest. Last spring, whom do I run in to down on Worth Street, but the old circle-jerker himself, Mr. Mandel, carrying a sample case full of trusses, braces, and supports. And do you know? That he was still living and breathing absolutely astonished me. I couldn't get over it—I haven't yet. And married too, domesticated, with a wife and two little children—and a "ranch" house in Maplewood, New Jersey. Mandel lives, owns a length of garden hose, he tells me, and a barbecue and briquets! Mandel, who, out of awe of Pupi Campo and Tito Valdez, went off to City Hall the day after quitting high school and had his first name officially changed from Arnold to Ba-ba-lu Mandel, who drank "six-packs" of beer! Miraculous. Can't be! How on earth did it happen that retribution passed him by? There he was, year in and year out, standing in idleness and ignorance on the corner of Chancellor and Leslie, perched like some greaser over his bongo drums, his duck's ass bare to the heavens—and nothing and nobody struck him down! And now he is thirty-three, like me, and a salesman for his wife's father, who has a surgical supply house on Market Street in Newark. And what about me, he asks, what do I do for a living? Really, doesn't he know? Isn't he on my parents' mailing list? Doesn't everyone know I am now the most moral man in all of New York, all pure motives and humane and compassionate ideals? Doesn't he know that what I do for a living is I'm *good*? "Civil Service," I answered, pointing across to Thirty Worth. Mister Modesty.

"You still see any of the guys?" Ba-ba-lu asked. "You married?"

"No, no."

Inside the new jowls, the old furtive Latin-American greaser comes to life. "So, uh, what do you do for pussy?"

"I have affairs, Arn, and I beat my meat."

Mistake, I think instantly. Mistake! What if he blabs to the *Daily News*? ASST HUMAN OPP'Y COMMISH FLOGS DUMMY, *Also Lives in Sin, Reports Old School Chum*.

The headlines. Always the headlines revealing my filthy secrets to a shocked and disapproving world.

"Hey," said Ba-ba-lu, "remember Rita Girardi? Bubbles? Who used to suck us all off?"

". . . What about her?" Lower your voice, Ba-ba-lu! "What about her?"

"Didn't you read in the *News*?"

"—What *News*?"

"The *Newark News.*"

"I don't see the Newark papers any more. What happened to her?"

"She got murdered. In a bar on Hawthorne Avenue, right down from The Annex. She was with some boogey and then some other boogey came in and shot them both in the head. How do you like that? Fucking for boogies."

"Wow," I said, and meant it. Then suddenly—"Listen, Ba-ba-lu, whatever happened to Smolka?"

"Don't know," says Ba-ba-lu. "Ain't he a professor? I think I heard he was a professor."

"A professor? *Smolka?*"

"I think he is some kind of college teacher."

"Oh, can't be," I say with my superior sneer.

"Yeah. That's what somebody said. Down at Princeton."

"*Princeton?*"

But can't be! Without hot tomato soup for lunch on freezing afternoons? Who slept in those putrid pajamas? The owner of all those red rubber thimbles with the angry little spiky projections that he told us drove the girls up the walls of Paris? Smolka, who swam in the pool at Olympic Park, he's alive *too*? And a professor at Princeton *noch*? In what department, classical languages or astrophysics? Ba-ba-lu, you sound like my mother. You must mean plumber, or electrician. Because I will not believe it! I mean down in my *kishkas*, in my deep emotions and my old beliefs, down beneath the me who knows very well that of course Smolka and Mandel continue to enjoy the ranch houses and the professional opportunities available to men on this planet, I simply cannot believe in the survival, let alone the middle-class success, of these two bad boys. Why, they're supposed to be in jail—or the gutter. They didn't do their homework, damn it! Smolka used to cheat off me in Spanish, and Mandel didn't even give enough of a shit to bother to do that, and as for washing their hands before eating . . . Don't you understand, these two boys are supposed to be dead! Like Bubbles. Now there at least is a career that makes some sense. There's a case of cause and effect that confirms my ideas about human consequence! Bad enough, rotten enough, and you get your cock-sucking head blown off by boogies. Now that's the way the world's *supposed* to be run!

———

Smolka comes back into the kitchen and tells us she doesn't want to do it.

"But you said we were going to get laid!" cries Mandel. "You said we were going to get blowed! Reamed, steamed, and dry-cleaned, that's what you *said*!"

"Fuck it," I say, "if she doesn't want to do it, who needs her, let's go—"

"But I've been pounding off over this for a week! I ain't going anywhere! What kind of shit *is* this, Smolka? Won't she even beat my *meat*?"

Me, with my refrain: "Ah, look, if she doesn't want to do it, let's go—"

Mandel: "Who the fuck is she that she won't even give a guy a hand-job? A measly hand-job. Is that the world to ask of her? I ain't leaving till she either sucks it or pulls it—one or the other! It's up to her, the fucking whore!"

So Smolka goes back in for a second conference, and returns nearly half an hour later with the news that the girl has changed her mind: she will jerk off one guy, but only with his pants on, and that's *all*. We flip a coin—and I win the right to get the syph! Mandel claims the coin grazed the ceiling, and is ready to murder me—he is still screaming foul play when I enter the living room to reap my reward.

She sits in her slip on the sofa at the other end of the linoleum floor, weighing a hundred and seventy pounds and growing a mustache. Anthony Peruta, that's my name for when she asks. But she doesn't. "Look," says Bubbles, "let's get it straight—you're the only one I'm doing it to. You, and that's it."

"It's entirely up to you," I say politely.

"All right, take it out of your pants, *but don't take them down*. You hear me, because I told him, I'm not doing anything to anybody's balls."

"Fine, fine. Whatever you say."

"And don't try to touch me either."

"Look, if you want me to, I'll go."

"Just take it out."

"Sure, if that's what you want, here . . . here," I say, but prematurely. "I-just-have-to-get-it—" Where *is* that thing? In the classroom I sometimes set myself consciously to thinking about DEATH and HOSPITALS and HORRIBLE AUTO-MOBILE ACCIDENTS in the hope that such grave thoughts will cause my "boner" to recede before the bell rings and I have to stand. It seems that I can't go up to the blackboard in school, or try to get off a bus, without its jumping up and saying, "Hi! Look at me!" to everyone in sight—and now it is nowhere to be found.

"Here!" I finally cry.

"Is that it?"

"Well," I answer, turning colors, "it gets bigger when it gets harder . . ."

"Well, I ain't got all night, you know."

Nicely: "Oh, I don't think it'll be all *night—*"

"Laydown!"

Bubbles, not wholly content, lowers herself into a straight chair, while I stretch out beside her on the sofa—and suddenly she has hold of it, and it's as though my poor cock has got caught in some kind of machine. Vigorously, to put it mildly, the ordeal begins. But it is like trying to jerk off a jellyfish.

"What's a matter?" she finally says. "Can't you come?"

"Usually, yes, I can."

"Then stop holding it back on me."

"I'm not. I am trying, Bubbles—"

"Cause I'm going to count to fifty, and if you don't do it by then, that ain't my fault."

Fifty? I'll be lucky if it is still attached to my body by fifty. *Take it easy*, I want to scream. *Not so rough around the edges, please!*—"eleven, twelve, thirteen"—and I think to myself, *Thank God, soon it'll be over—hang on, only another forty seconds to go*—but simultaneous with the relief comes, of course, the disappointment, and it is keen: this only happens to be what I have been dreaming about night and day since I am thirteen. At long last, not a cored apple, not an empty milk bottle greased with vaseline, but a girl in a slip, with two tits and a cunt—and a mustache, but who am I to be picky? This is what I have been imagining for myself . . .

Which is how it occurs to me what to do. I will forget that the fist tearing away at me belongs to Bubbles—I'll pretend it's my own! So, fixedly I stare at the dark ceiling, and instead of making believe that I am getting laid, as I ordinarily do while jerking off, I make believe that I am jerking off.

And it begins instantly to take effect. Unfortunately, however, I get just about where I want to be when Bubbles' workday comes to an end.

"Okay, that's it," she says, "fifty," *and stops*!

"No!" I cry. "More!"

"Look, I already ironed two hours, you know, before you guys even got here—"

"JUST ONE MORE! I BEG OF YOU! TWO MORE! PLEASE!"

"N-O!"

Whereupon, unable (as always!) to stand the frustration—the deprivation and disappointment—I reach down, I grab it, and POW!

Only right in my eye. With a single whiplike stroke of the master's own hand, the lather comes rising out of me. I ask you, who jerks me off as well as I do it myself? Only, reclining as I am, the jet leaves my joint on the horizontal, rides back the length of my torso, and lands with a thick wet burning splash right in my own eye.

"Son of a bitch kike!" Bubbles screams. "You got gissum all over the couch! And the walls! And the lamp!"

"I got it in my eye! And don't you say kike to me, you!"

"You *are* a kike, Kike! You got it all over everything, you mocky son of a bitch! Look at the doilies!"

It's just as my parents have warned me—comes the first disagreement, no matter how small, and the only thing a *shikse* knows to call you is a dirty Jew. What an awful discovery—my parents who are always wrong . . . are right! And my eye—it's as though it's been dropped in fire—and now I remember why. On Devil's Island, Smolka has told us, the guards used to have fun with the prisoners by rubbing sperm in their eyes *and making them blind*. I'm going blind! A *shikse* has touched my dick with her bare hand, and now I'll be blind forever! Doctor, my psyche, it's about as difficult to understand as a grade-school primer! Who needs dreams, I ask you? Who needs *Freud*? Rose Franzblau of the *New York Post* has enough on the ball to come up with an analysis of somebody like me!

"Sheeny!" she is screaming. "Hebe! You can't even come off unless you pull your own pudding, cheap bastard fairy Jew!"

Hey, enough is enough, where is her sympathy? "But my eye!" and rush for the kitchen, where Smolka and Mandel are rolling around the walls in ecstasy. "—right in the"—erupts Mandel, and folds in half onto the floor, beating at the linoleum with his fists—"right in the fucking—"

"Water, you shits, I'm going blind! I'm on fire!" and flying full-speed over Mandel's body, stick my head beneath the faucet. Above the sink Jesus still ascends in his pink nightie. That useless son of a bitch! I thought he was supposed to make the Christians compassionate and kind. I thought other people's suffering is what he told them to feel *sorry* for. What bullshit! If I go blind, it's his fault! Yes, somehow he strikes me as the ultimate cause for all this pain and confusion. And oh God, as the cold water runs down my face, how am I going to explain my blindness to my parents! My mother virtually spends half her life up my ass as it is, checking on the manufacture of my stool—how am I possibly going to hide the fact that I no longer have my sight? "Tap, tap, tap, it's just me, Mother—this nice big dog brought me home, with my cane." "A *dog*? In my house? Get him out of here before he makes everything filthy! Jack, there's a dog in the house and I just washed the kitchen floor!" "But, Momma, he's here to stay, he has to stay—he's a seeing-eye dog. I'm blind." "Oh my God! Jack!" she calls into the bathroom. "Jack, Alex is home with a dog—he's gone blind!" "Him, blind?" my father replies. "How could he be blind, he doesn't even know what it means to turn off a light." "How?" screams my mother. "*How? Tell us how such a thing —*"

Mother, how? How else? Consorting with Christian girls.

Mandel the next day tells me that within half an hour after my frenetic departure, Bubbles was down on her fucking dago knees sucking his cock.

The top of my head comes off: "She *was?*"

"Right on her fucking dago knees," says Mandel. "Schmuck, what'd you go home for?"

"She called me a kike!" I answer self-righteously. "I thought I was blind. Look, she's anti-Semitic, Ba-ba-lu."

"Yeah, what do I give a shit?" says Mandel. Actually I don't think he knows what anti-Semitic means. "All I know is I got laid, *twice.*"

"You *did?* With a *rubber?*"

"Fuck, I didn't use nothing."

"But she'll get pregnant!" I cry, and in anguish, as though it's me who will be held accountable.

"What do I care?" replies Mandel.

Why do *I* worry then! Why do I alone spend hours testing Trojans in my basement? Why do I alone live in mortal terror of the syph? Why do I run home with my little bloodshot eye, imagining myself blinded forever, when half an hour later Bubbles will be down eating cock on her knees! Home—to my mommy! To my Tollhouse cookie and my glass of milk, home to my nice clean bed! *Oy*, civilization and its discontents! Ba-ba-lu, speak to me, talk to me, tell me what it was like when she did it! I have to know, and with details—exact details! What about her tits? What about her nipples? What about her thighs? What does she do with her thighs, Ba-ba-lu, does she wrap them around your ass like in the hot books, or does she squeeze them tight around your cock till you want to scream, like in my dreams? And what about her hair down there? Tell me everything there is to tell about pubic hairs and the way they smell, I don't care if I heard it all before. And did she really kneel, are you shitting me? Did she actually kneel on her *knees?* And what about her teeth, where do *they* go? And does she suck on it, or does she blow on it, or somehow is it that she does *both?* Oh God, Ba-ba-lu, did you shoot in her mouth? Oh my God! And did she swallow it right down, or spit it out, or get mad—tell me! what did she do with your hot come! Did you warn her you were going to shoot, or did you just come off and let *her* worry? And who put it in—did she put it in or did you put it in, or does it just get *drawn* in by itself? And where were all your clothes?—on the couch? on the floor? exactly *where?* I want details! Details! Actual details!

Who took off her brassiere, who took off her panties—her *panties*—did *you*? did *she*? When she was down there blowing, Ba-ba-lu, did she have anything on at all? And how about the pillow under her ass, did you stick a pillow under her ass like it says to do in my parents' marriage manual? What happened when you came inside her? Did she come too? Mandel, clarify something that I have to know—*do* they come? Stuff? Or do they just moan a lot—*or what*? How does she come! What is it like! Before I go out of my head, I have to know what it's like!

THE MOST PREVALENT FORM OF
DEGRADATION IN EROTIC LIFE

I don't think I've spoken of the disproportionate effect The Monkey's handwriting used to have upon my psychic equilibrium. What hopeless calligraphy! It looked like the work of an eight-year-old—it nearly drove me crazy! Nothing capitalized, nothing punctuated—only those oversized irregular letters of hers slanting downward along the page, then dribbling off. And *printed*, as on the drawing the rest of us used to carry home in our little hands from *first grade*! And that spelling. A little word like "clean" comes out three different ways on the same sheet of paper. You know, as in "Mr. Clean"?—two out of three times it begins with the letter *k*. K! As in "Joseph K." Not to mention "dear" as in the salutation of a letter: d-e-r-e. Or d-e-i-r. And that very first time (this I love) d-i-r. On the evening we are scheduled for dinner at Gracie Mansion—D! I! R! I mean, I just have to ask myself—what am I doing having an affair with a woman nearly thirty years of age who thinks you spell "dear" with three letters!

Already two months had passed since the pickup on Lexington Avenue, and still, you see, the same currents of feeling carrying me along: desire, on the one hand, *delirious* desire (I'd never known such abandon in a woman in my life!), and something close to contempt on the other. Correction. Only a few days earlier there had been our trip to Vermont, that weekend when it had seemed that my wariness of her—the apprehension aroused by the model-y glamour, the brutish origins, above everything, the sexual recklessness—that all this fear and distrust had been displaced by a wild upward surge of tenderness and affection.

Now, I am under the influence at the moment of an essay entitled "The Most Prevalent Form of Degradation in Erotic Life"; as you may have guessed, I have bought a set of the *Collected Papers*, and since my return from Europe, have been putting myself to sleep each night in the solitary confinement of my womanless bed with a volume of Freud in my hand. Sometimes Freud in hand, sometimes Alex in hand, frequently both. Yes, there in my unbuttoned pajamas, all alone, I lie, fiddling with it like a little boy-child in a dopey reverie, tugging on it, twisting it, rubbing and kneading it, and meanwhile reading spellbound through "Contributions to the Psychology of Love," ever heedful of the sentence, the phrase, the *word* that will liberate me from what I understand are called my fantasies and fixations.

In the "Degradation" essay there is that phrase, "currents of feeling." For "a fully normal attitude in love" (deserving of semantic scrutiny, that "fully normal," but to go on—) for a fully normal attitude in love, says he, it is necessary that two currents of feeling be united: the tender, affectionate feelings, and the sensuous feelings. And in many instances this just doesn't happen, sad to say. "Where such men love they have no desire, and where they desire they cannot love."

Question: Am I to consider myself one of the fragmented multitude? In language plain and simple, are Alexander Portnoy's sensual feelings fixated to his incestuous fantasies? What do you think, Doc? Has a restriction so pathetic been laid upon my object choice? Is it true that only if the sexual object fulfills for me the condition of being degraded, that sensual feeling can have free play? Listen, does that explain the preoccupation with *shikses?*

Yes, but if so, if so, how then explain that weekend in Vermont? Because down went the dam of the incest-barrier, or so it seemed. And *swoosh*, there was sensual feeling mingling with the purest, deepest streams of tenderness I've ever known! I'm telling you, the confluence of the two currents was terrific! And in her as well! She even said as much!

Or was it only the colorful leaves, do you think, the fire

burning in the dining room of the inn at Woodstock, that softened up the two of us? Was it tenderness for one another that we experienced, or just the fall doing its work, swelling the gourd (John Keats) and lathering the tourist trade into ecstasies of nostalgia for the good and simple life? Were we just two more rootless jungle-dwelling erotomaniacs creaming in their pre-faded jeans over Historical New England, dreaming the old agrarian dream in their rent-a-car convertible—or is a fully normal attitude in love the possibility that it seemed for me during those few sunny days I spent with The Monkey in Vermont?

What exactly transpired? Well, we drove mostly. And looked: the valleys, the mountains, the light on the fields; and the leaves of course, a lot of ooing and ahhing. Once we stopped to watch somebody in the distance, high up on a ladder, hammering away at the side of a barn—and that was fun, too. Oh, and the rented car. We flew to Rutland and rented a convertible. A convertible, can you imagine? A third of a century as an American boy, and this was the first convertible I had ever driven myself. Know why? Because the son of an insurance man knows better than others the chance you take riding around in such a machine. He knows the awful actuarial details! All you have to do is hit a bump in the road, and that's it, where a convertible is concerned: up from the seat you go flying (and not to be *too* graphic), out onto the highway cranium first, and if you're *lucky*, it's a wheelchair for life. And turn over in a convertible—well, you can just kiss your life goodbye. And this is statistics (I am told by my father), not some cockamaimy story he is making up for the fun of it. Insurance companies aren't in business to lose money—when they say something, Alex, it's true! And now, on the heels of my wise father, my wise mother: "Please, so I can sleep at night for four years, promise me one thing, grant your mother this one wish and then she'll never ask anything of you again: when you get to Ohio, promise you won't ride in an open convertible. So I can shut my eyes in bed at night, Alex, promise you won't take your life in your hands in any crazy way." My father again: "Because you're a plum, Alex!" he says, baffled and tearful over my imminent departure from home. "And we don't want a plum to fall off the tree before it's ripe!"

1. Promise, Plum, that you'll never ride in a convertible. Such a small thing, what will it hurt you to promise?

2. You'll look up Howard Sugarman, Sylvia's nephew. A lovely boy—*and president of the Hillel*. He'll show you around. *Please* look him up.

3. Plum, Darling, Light of the World, you remember your cousin Heshie, the torture he gave himself and his family with that girl. What Uncle Hymie had to go through, to save that boy from his craziness. You remember? Please, do we have to say any more? Is my meaning clear, Alex? Don't give yourself away cheap. Don't throw a brilliant future away on an absolute nothing. I don't think we have to say anything more. *Do* we? You're a baby yet, sixteen years old and graduating high school. That's a baby, Alex. You don't know the hatred there is in the world. So I don't think we have to say any more, not to a boy as smart as you. ONLY YOU MUST BE CAREFUL WITH YOUR LIFE! YOU MUST NOT PLUNGE YOUR-SELF INTO A LIVING HELL! YOU MUST LISTEN TO WHAT WE ARE SAYING AND WITHOUT THE SCOWL, THANK YOU, AND THE BRILLIANT BACK TALK! WE KNOW! WE HAVE LIVED! WE HAVE SEEN! IT DOESN'T WORK, MY SON! THEY ARE ANOTHER BREED OF HUMAN BEING ENTIRELY! YOU WILL BE TORN ASUNDER! GO TO HOWARD, HE'LL INTRODUCE YOU AT THE HILLEL! DON'T RUN FIRST THING TO A BLONDIE, *PLEASE!* BECAUSE SHE'LL TAKE YOU FOR ALL YOU'RE WORTH AND THEN LEAVE YOU BLEEDING IN THE GUTTER! A BRILLIANT INNO-CENT BABY BOY LIKE YOU, SHE'LL EAT YOU UP ALIVE!

She'll eat me up alive?

Ah, but we have our revenge, we brilliant baby boys, us plums. You know the joke, of course—Milty, the G.I., tele-phones from Japan. "Momma," he says, "it's Milton, I have good news! I found a wonderful Japanese girl and we were married today. As soon as I get my discharge I want to bring her home, Momma, for you to meet each other." "So," says the mother, "bring her, of course." "Oh, wonderful, Momma," says Milty, "wonderful—only I was wondering, in your little apartment, where will me and Ming Toy sleep?" "Where?" says the mother. "Why, in the bed? Where else should you sleep with your bride?" "But then where will *you* sleep, if we sleep in the bed? Momma, are you sure there's room?" "Milty darling, please," says the mother, "everything is fine, don't you worry, there'll be all the room you want: as soon as I hang up, I'm killing myself."

What an innocent, our Milty! How stunned he must be over there in Yokohama to hear his mother come up with such a statement! Sweet, passive Milton, you wouldn't hurt a fly, would you, *tateleh*? You hate bloodshed, you wouldn't dream of *striking* another person, let alone committing a murder on him. *So you let the geisha girl do it for you!* Smart, Milty, *smart*! From the geisha girl, believe me, she won't recover so fast. From the geisha girl, Milty, she'll *plotz*! Ha ha! You did it, Miltaleh, and without even lifting a finger! Of course! Let the *shikse* do the killing for you! You, you're just an innocent bystander! Caught in the crossfire! A victim, right, Milt?

Lovely, isn't it, the business of the bed?

—

When we arrive at the inn in Dorset, I remind her to slip one of her half-dozen rings onto the appropriate finger. "In public life one must be discreet," I say, and tell her that I have reserved a room in the name of Mr. and Mrs. Arnold Mandel. "A hero out of Newark's past," I explain.

While I register, The Monkey (looking in New England erotic in the extreme) roams around the lobby examining the little Vermont gifties for sale. "Arnold," she calls. I turn: "Yes, dear." "We simply must take back with us some maple syrup for Mother Mandel. She loves it so," and smiles her mysteriously enticing Sunday *Times* underwear-ad smile at the suspicious clerk.

What a night! I don't mean there was more than the usual body-thrashing and hair-tossing and empassioned vocalizing from The Monkey—no, the drama was at the same Wagnerian pitch I was beginning to become accustomed to: it was the flow of feeling that was new and terrific. "Oh, I can't get *enough* of you!" she cried. "Am I a nymphomaniac, or is it the wedding ring?" "I was thinking maybe it was the illicitness of an 'inn.'" "Oh, it's something! I feel, I feel so crazy . . . and so tender—so wildly tender with you! Oh baby. I keep thinking I'm going to cry, and I'm so *happy*!"

Saturday we drove up to Lake Champlain, stopping along the way for The Monkey to take pictures with her Minox; late in the day we cut across and down to Woodstock, gaping, exclaiming, sighing, The Monkey snuggling. Once in the morning (in an overgrown field near the lake shore) we had sexual congress, and then that afternoon, on a dirt road somewhere in the mountains of central Vermont, she said, "Oh, Alex, pull over, now—I want you to come in my mouth," and so she blew me, and with the top down!

What am I trying to communicate? Just that we began to feel something. Feel *feeling*! And without any diminishing of sexual appetite!

"I know a poem," I said, speaking somewhat as though I were drunk, as though I could lick any man in the house, "and I'm going to recite it."

She was nestled down in my lap, eyes still closed, my softening member up against her cheek like a little chick. "Ah come on," she groaned, "not now, I don't understand poems."

"You'll understand this one. It's about fucking. A swan fucks a beautiful girl."

She looked up, batting her false eyelashes. "Oh, goody."

"But it's a serious poem."

"Well," she said, licking my prick, "it's a serious offense."

"Oh, irresistible, witty Southern belles—especially when they're *long* the way you are."

"Don't bullshit me, Portnoy. Recite the dirty poem."

"Porte-noir," I said, and began:

> "*A sudden blow: the great wings beating still*
> *Above the staggering girl, her thighs caressed*
> *By the dark webs, her nape caught in his bill,*
> *He holds her helpless breast upon his breast.*"

"Where," she asked, "did you learn something like *that*?"
"Shhh. There's more:

> "*How can those terrified vague fingers push*
> *The feathered glory from her loosening thighs?*"

"Hey!" she cried. "Thighs!"

> *"And how can body, laid in that white rush,*
> *But feel the strange heart beating where it lies?*
> *A shudder in the loins engenders there*
> *The broken wall, the burning roof and tower*
> *And Agamemnon dead.*
> *Being so caught up,*
> *So mastered by the brute blood of the air,*
> *Did she put on his knowledge with his power*
> *Before the indifferent beak could let her drop?*

"That's it," I said.

Pause. "Who wrote it?" Snide. "You?"

"William Butler Yeats wrote it," I said, realizing how tactless I had been, with what insensitivity I had drawn attention to the chasm: I am smart and you are dumb, that's what it had meant to recite to this woman one of the three poems I happen to have learned by heart in my thirty-three years. "An Irish poet," I said lamely.

"Yeah?" she said. "And where did you learn it, at his knee? I didn't know you was Irish."

"In college, baby." From a girl I knew in college. Also taught me "The Force That Through the Green Fuse Drives the Flower." But enough—why compare her to another? *Why not let her be what she is?* What an idea! *Love her as she is! In all her imperfection—which is, after all, maybe only human!*

"Well," said The Monkey, still playing Truck Driver, "I never been to college myself." Then, Dopey Southern, "And down home in Moundsville, honey, the only poem we had was 'I see London, I see France, I see Mary Jane's underpants.' 'Cept I didn't wear no underpants . . . Know what I did when I was fifteen? Sent a lock of my snatch-hair off in an envelope to Marlon Brando. Prick didn't even have the courtesy to acknowledge receipt."

Silence. While we try to figure out what two such unlikely people are doing together—in Vermont yet.

Then she says, "Okay, what's Agamemnon?"

So I explain, to the best of my ability. Zeus, Agamemnon, Clytemnestra, Helen, Paris, Troy . . . Oh, I feel like a shit—and a fake. Half of it I *know* I'm getting wrong.

But *she's* marvelous. "Okay—now say it all again."

"You serious?"

"I'm serious! Again! But, for Christ's sake, *slow*."

So I recite again, and all this time my trousers are still down around the floorboard, and it's growing darker on the path where I have parked out of sight of the road, beneath the dramatic foliage. The leaves, in fact, are falling into the car. The Monkey looks like a child trying to master a multiplication problem, but not a dumb child—no, a quick and clever little girl! Not stupid at all! *This girl is really very special. Even if I did pick her up in the street!*

When I finish, you know what she does? Takes hold of my hand, draws my fingers up between her legs. Where Mary Jane *still* wears no underpants. "Feel. It made my pussy all wet."

"Sweetheart! You understood the poem!"

"I s'pose I deed!" cries Scarlett O'Hara. Then, "Hey, I did! I understood a poem!"

"And with your cunt, no less."

"My Breakthrough-baby! You're turning this twat into a genius! Oh, Breakie, darling, eat me," she cries, thrusting a handful of fingers into my mouth—and she pulls me down upon her by my lower jaw, crying, "Oh, eat my educated cunt!"

Idyllic, no? Under the red and yellow leaves like that?

In the room at Woodstock, while I shave for dinner, she soaks herself in hot water and Sardo. What strength she has stored in that slender frame—the glorious acrobatics she can perform while dangling from the end of my dork! You'd think she'd snap a vertebra, hanging half her torso backward over the side of the bed—in ecstasy! Yi! Thank God for that gym class she goes to! What screwing I am getting! What a deal! And yet it turns out that she is also a human being—yes, she gives every indication that this may be so! *A human being! Who can be loved!*

But by *me*?

Why not?

Really?

Why not!

"You know something," she says to me from the tub, "my little hole's so sore it can hardly breathe."

"Poor hole."

"Hey, let's eat a big dinner, a lot of wine and chocolate mousse, and then come up here, and get into our two-hundred-year-old-bed—and not screw!"

"How you doin', Arn?" she asked later, when the lights were out. "This is fun, isn't it? It's like being eighty."

"Or eight," I said. "I got something I want to show you."

"No. Arnold, *no.*"

During the night I awakened, and drew her toward me.

"Please," she moaned, "I'm saving myself for my husband."

"That doesn't mean shit to a swan, lady."

"Oh please, please, do fuck off—"

"Feel my feather."

"Ahhh," she gasped, as I stuffed it in her hand. "A *Jew*-swan! Hey!" she cried, and grabbed at my nose with the other hand. "The indifferent beak! I just understood more poem! . . . *Didn't* I?"

"Christ, you *are* a marvelous girl!"

That took her breath away. "Oh, *am* I?"

"Yes!"

"*Am I?*"

"Yes! Yes! Yes! *Now* can I fuck you?"

"Oh, sweetheart, darling," cried The Monkey, "pick a hole, any hole, I'm yours!"

After breakfast we walked around Woodstock with The Monkey's painted cheek glued to the arm of my jacket. "You know something," she said, "I don't think I hate you any more."

We started for home late in the afternoon, driving all the way to New York so that the weekend would last longer. Only an hour into the trip, she found WABC and began to move in her seat to the rock music. Then all at once she said, "Ah, fuck that noise," and switched the radio off.

Wouldn't it be nice, she said, not to have to go back?

Wouldn't it be nice someday to live in the country with somebody you really liked?

Wouldn't it be nice just to get up all full of energy when it got light and go to sleep dog-tired when it got dark?

Wouldn't it be nice to have a lot of responsibilities and just go around doing them all day and not even realize they were responsibilities?

Wouldn't it be nice to just not think about yourself for whole days, whole weeks, whole months at a stretch? To wear old clothes and no make-up and not have to come on tough all the time?

Time passed. She whistled. "Wouldn't that be something?"

"What now?"

"To be grown-up. You know?"

"Amazing," I said.

"What is?"

"Almost three days, and I haven't heard the hillbilly routine, the Betty-Boop-dumb-cunt routine, the teeny-bopper bit—"

I was extending a compliment, she got insulted. "They're not 'bits,' man, they're not routines—they're *me*! And if how I act isn't good enough for you, then tough tittie, Commissioner. Don't put me down, okay, just because we're nearing that fucking city where you're so *important*."

"I was only saying you're smarter than you let on when you act like a broad, that's all."

"Bull*shit*. It's just practically humanly im*possible* for anybody to be as stupid as you think I am!" Here she leaned forward to flip on "The Good Guys." And the weekend might as well not have happened. She knew all the words to all the songs. She was sure to let me know that. "Yeah yeah yeah, yeah yeah yeah." A remarkable performance, a tribute to the cerebellum.

At dark I pulled into a Howard Johnson's. "Like let's eat," I said. "Like food. Like nourishment, man."

"Look," she said, "maybe I don't know what I am, but you don't know what you want to be, either! And don't forget that!"

"Groovy, man."

"Prick! Don't you see what my life is? You think I *like* being nobody? You think I'm crazy about my hollow life? I hate it! I hate *New York*! I don't ever want to go back to that sewer! I want to live in Vermont, Commissioner! I want to live in Vermont with you—and be an adult, whatever the hell that is! I want to be Mrs. Somebody-I-Can-Look-Up-To. And Admire! And Listen To!" She was crying. "Someone who won't try to fuck-up my head! Oh, I think I love you, Alex. I really think I do. Oh, but a lot of good that's going to do me!"

In other words: Did I think maybe I loved her? Answer: No. What I thought (this'll amuse you), what I thought wasn't Do I love her? or even Could I love her? Rather: *Should* I love her?

Inside the restaurant the best I could do was say that I wanted her to come with me to the Mayor's formal dinner party.

"Arnold, let's have an affair, okay?"

"—Meaning?"

"Oh, don't be *cautious*. Meaning what do you *think*? An *affair*. You bang just me and I bang just you."

"And that's it?"

"Well, sure, mostly. And also I telephone a lot during the day. It's a hang up—can't I say 'hang-up' *either*? Okay—it's a *compulsion*. Okay? All I mean is like I can't help it. I mean I'm going to call your office *a lot*. Because I like everybody to know I belong to somebody. That's what I've learned from the fifty thousand dollars I've handed over to that shrink. All I mean is whenever I get to a job, I like call you up—and say I love you. Is this coherent?"

"Sure."

"Because that's what I really want to be: *so* coherent. Oh, Breakie, I adore you. Now, anyway. Hey," she whispered, "want to smell something—something *staggering*?" She checked to see if the waitress was in the vicinity, then leaned forward, as though to reach beneath the table to straighten a stocking. A moment later she passed her fingertips over to me. I pressed them to my mouth. "My Sin, baby," said The Monkey, "straight from the pickle barrel . . . and for you! Only you!"

So go ahead, love her! Be brave! Here is fantasy begging you to make it real! So erotic! So wanton! So gorgeous! Glittery perhaps, but a beauty nonetheless! Where we walk together, people stare, men covet and women whisper. In a restaurant in town one night, I overhear someone say, "Isn't that what's-her-name? Who was in *La Dolce Vita*?" And when I turn to look—for whom, Anouk Aimée?—I find they are looking at us: at her who is with me! Vanity? Why not! Leave off with the blushing, bury the shame, you are no longer your mother's naughty little boy! Where appetite is concerned, a man in his thirties is responsible to no one but himself! That's what's so nice about growing up! You want to take? You take! Debauch a little bit, for Christ's sake! STOP DENYING YOURSELF! STOP DENYING THE TRUTH!

Ah, but there is (let us bow our heads), there is "my dignity" to consider, my good name. What people will think. What *I* will think. Doctor, this girl once did it *for money*. Money! Yes! I believe they call that "prostitution"! One night, to praise her (I imagined, at any rate, that that was my motive), I said, "You ought to market this, it's too much for one man," just being chivalrous, you see . . . or intuitive? Anyway, she answers, "I have." I wouldn't let her alone until she explained what she'd meant; at first she claimed she was only being clever, but in the face of my cross-examination she finally came up with this story, which struck me as the truth, or a portion thereof. Just after Paris and her divorce, she had been flown out to Hollywood (she says) to be tested for a part in a movie (which she didn't get. I pressed for the name of the movie, but she claims to have forgotten, says it was never made). On the way back to New York from California, she and the girl she was with ("Who's this other girl?" "A girl. A girl friend." "Why were you traveling with another girl?" "I just was!"), she and this other girl stopped off to see Las Vegas. There she went to bed with some guy that she met, perfectly innocently she maintains; however, to her complete surprise, in the morning he asked, "How much?" She says it just came out of her mouth—"Whatever it's worth, Sport." So he offered her three hundred-dollar bills. "And you took it?" I asked. "I was twenty years old. Sure, I took it. To see what it felt like, that's all." "And what *did* it feel like, Mary Jane?" "I don't remember. Nothing. It didn't feel like anything."

Well, what do *you* think? She claims it only happened that once, ten years ago, and even then only came about through some "accidental" joining of his misunderstanding with her whimsy. But do you buy that? Should I? Is it impossible to believe that this girl may have put in some time as a high-priced call girl? Oh Jesus! Take her, I think to myself, and I am no higher in the evolutionary scale than the mobsters and millionaires who choose their women from the line at the Copa. This is the kind of girl ordinarily seen hanging from the arm of a Mafiosa or a movie star, not the 1950 valedictorian of

Weequahic High! Not the editor of the *Columbia Law Review*! Not the high-minded civil-libertarian! Let's face it, whore or no whore, this is a clear-cut tootsie, right? Who looks at her with me knows precisely what I am after in this life. This is what my father used to call "a chippy." Of course! And can I bring home a chippy, Doctor? "Momma, Poppa, this is my wife, the chippy. Isn't she a wild piece of ass?" Take her fully for my own, you see, and the whole neighborhood will know at last the truth about my dirty little mind. The so-called genius will be revealed in all his piggish proclivities and feelthy desires. The bathroom door will swing open (unlocked!), and behold, there sits the savior of mankind, drool running down his chin, absolutely gaa-gaa in the eyes, and his prick firing salvos at the light bulb! A laughingstock, at last! A bad boy! A *shande* to his family forever! Yes, yes, I see it all: for my abominations I awake one morning to find myself chained to a toilet in Hell, me and the other chippy-mongers of the world— "*Shtarkes*," the Devil will say, as we are issued our fresh white-on-white shirts, our Sulka ties, as we are fitted in our nifty new silk suits, "*gantze k'nockers*, big shots with your long-legged women. Welcome. You really accomplished a lot in life, you fellows. You really distinguished yourselves, all right. And you in particular," he says, lifting a sardonic eyebrow in my direction, "who entered the high school at the age of *twelve*, who was an ambassador to the world from the Jewish community of Newark—" Ah-hah, I knew it. It's no Devil in the proper sense, it's Fat Warshaw, the Reb. My stout and pompous spiritual leader! He of the sumptuous enunciation and the Pall Mall breath! Rabbi Re-ver-ed! It is the occasion of my bar mitzvah, and I stand shyly at his side, sopping it up like gravy, getting quite a little kick out of being sanctified, I'll tell you. Alexander Portnoy-this and Alexander Portnoy-that, and to tell you the absolute truth, that he talks in syllables, and turns little words into big ones, and big ones into whole sentences by themselves, to be frank, it doesn't seem to bother me as much as it would ordinarily. Oh, the sunny Saturday morning meanders slowly along as he lists my virtues and accomplishments to the assembled relatives and friends, syllable by syllable. Lay it on them, Warshaw, blow my horn, don't hurry yourself on my account, please. I'm young, I can stand here

all day, if that's what has to be. ". . . devoted son, loving
brother, fantastic honor student, avid newspaper reader (up on
every current event, knows the full names of each and every
Supreme Court justice and Cabinet member, also the minority
and majority leaders of both Houses of Congress, also the
chairmen of the important Congressional committees), entered Weequahic High School this boy at the age of *twelve*, an
I.Q. on him of 158, *one hunder-ed and-a fif-a-ty eight-a*, and
now," he tells the awed and beaming multitude, whose adoration I feel palpitating upward and enveloping me there on the
altar—why, I wouldn't be at all surprised if when he's finished
they don't pick me up and carry me around the synagogue like
the Torah itself, bear me gravely up and down the aisles while
the congregants struggle to touch their lips to some part of my
new blue Ohrbach's suit, while the old men press forward to
touch their tallises to my sparkling London Character shoes.
"Let me through! Let me touch!" and when I am world-
renowned, they will say to their grandchildren, "Yes, I was
there, I was in attendance at the bar mitzvah of Chief Justice
Portnoy"—"an ambassador," says Rabbi Warshaw, "now our
ambassador extraordinary—" Only the tune has changed! And
how! "Now," he says to me, "with the mentality of a pimp!
With the human values of a race-horse jockey! What is to him
the heights of human experience? Walking into a restaurant
with a long-legged *kurveh* on his arm! An easy lay in a body
stocking!" "Oh, please, Re-ver-ed, I'm a big boy now—so you
can knock off the rabbinical righteousness. It turns out to be a
little laughable at this stage of the game. I happened to prefer
beautiful and sexy to ugly and icy, so what's the tragedy? Why
dress me up like a Las Vegas hood? Why chain me to a toilet
bowl for eternity? For loving a saucy girl?" "Loving? *You?*
Too-ey on you! *Self*-loving, boychick, that's how I spell it!
With a capital self! Your heart is an empty refrigerator! Your
blood flows in cubes! I'm surprised you don't clink when you
walk! The saucy girl, so-called—I'll bet saucy!—was a big fat
feather in your prick, *and that alone is her total meaning, Alexander Portnoy!* What *you* did with *your* promise! Disgusting!
Love? Spelled l-u-s-t! Spelled s-e-l-f!" "But I felt stirrings, in
Howard Johnson's—" "In the prick! Sure!" "No!" "Yes! That's
the only part you *ever* felt a stirring in your *life*! You whiner!

You big bundle full of resentments! Why, you have been stuck on yourself since the first grade, for Christ's sake!" "Have *not*!" "Have! Have! This is the bottom truth, friend! Suffering mankind don't mean shit to you! That's a *blind*, buddy, and don't you kid yourself otherwise! Look, you call out to your brethren, look what I'm sticking my dicky into—look who *I'm* fucking: a fifty-foot fashion model! I get free what others pay upwards of three hundred dollars for! Oh boy, ain't *that* a human triumph, huh? Don't think that three hundred bucks don't titillate you plenty—cause it does! Only how about look what I'm loving, Portnoy!" "Please, don't you read the *New York Times*? I have spent my whole adult life protecting the rights of the defenseless! Five years I was with the ACLU, fighting the good fight for practically nothing. And before that a Congressional committee! I could make twice, *three* times the money in a practice of my own, but I don't! I don't! Now I have been appointed—don't you read the papers!—I am now Assistant Commissioner of Human Opportunity! Preparing a special report on bias in the building trades—" "Bull*shit*. Commissioner of Cunt, that's who you are! Commissioner of Human Opportunists! Oh, you jerk-off artist! You case of arrested development! All is vanity, Portnoy, but you really take the cake! A hundred and fifty-eight points of I.Q. and all of it right down the drain! A lot of good it did to skip those two grades of grammar school, you dummy!" "*What?*" And spending-money your father sent yet to Antioch College—that the man could hardly afford! All the faults come from the parents, right, Alex? What's wrong, they did—what's good, you accomplished all on your own! You ignoramus! You icebox heart! Why are you chained to a toilet? I'll tell you why: poetic justice! So you can pull your peter till the end of time! Jerk your precious little dum-dum ad infinitum! Go ahead, pull off, Commissioner, that's all you ever really gave your heart to anyway—your stinking putz!"

———

I arrive in my tuxedo while she is still in the shower. The door has been left unlocked, apparently so that I can come right in without disturbing her. She lives on the top floor of a big modern building in the East Eighties, and it irritates me to think that anybody who happened through the corridor could walk in just as I have. I warn her of this through the shower curtain. She touches my cheek with her small wet face. "Why would anyone want to do that?" she says. "All my money's in the bank."

"That's not a satisfactory reply," I answer, and retreat to the living room, trying not to be vexed. I notice the slip of paper on the coffee table. Has a child been here, I wonder. No, no, I am just face to face with my first specimen of The Monkey's handwriting. A note to the cleaning lady. Though at first glance I imagine it must be a note *from* the cleaning lady.

Must? Why "must"? Because she's "mine"?

> dir willa polish the flor by bathrum *pleze* & don't
> furget the insies of windose mary jane r

Three times I read the sentence through, and as happens with certain texts, each reading reveals new subtleties of meaning and implication, each reading augurs tribulations yet to be visited upon my ass. Why allow this "affair" to gather any more momentum? What was I thinking about in Vermont! Oh that *z*, that *z* between the two *e*'s of "pleze"—this is a mind with the depths of a movie marquee! And "furget"! Exactly how a prostitute would misspell that word! But it's something about the mangling of "dear," that tender syllable of affection now collapsed into three lower-case letters, that strikes me as hopelessly pathetic. How unnatural can a relationship be! This woman is ineducable and beyond reclamation. By contrast to hers, my childhood took place in Brahmin Boston. What kind of business can the two of us have together? Monkey business! *No* business!

The phone calls, for instance, I cannot tolerate those phone calls! Charmingly girlish she was when she warned me about telephoning all the time—but surprise, she meant it! I am in my office, the indigent parents of a psychotic child are explaining to me that their offspring is being systematically starved to death in a city hospital. They have come to us bearing their complaint, rather than to the Department of Hospitals, because a brilliant lawyer in the Bronx has told them that their child is obviously the victim of discrimination. What I can gather from a call to the chief psychiatrist at the hospital is that the child refuses to ingest any food—takes it and holds it in his mouth for hours, but refuses to swallow. I have then to tell these people that neither their child nor they are being victimized in the way or for the reason they believe. My answer strikes them as duplicitous. It strikes *me* as duplicitous. I think to myself, "He'd swallow that food if he had *my* mother," and meanwhile express sympathy for their predicament. But now they refuse to leave my office until they see "the Mayor," as earlier they refused to leave the social worker's office until they had seen "the Commissioner." The father says that he will have me fired, along with all the others responsible for starving to death a defenseless little child just because he is Puerto Rican! "*Es contrario a la ley discriminar contra cualquier persona*—" reading to me out of the bilingual CCHO handbook—that *I* wrote! At which point the phone rings. The Puerto Rican is shouting at me in Spanish, my mother is waving a knife at me back in my childhood, and my secretary announces that Miss Reed would like to speak to me on the telephone. For the third time that day.

"I miss you, Arnold," The Monkey whispers.

"I'm afraid I'm busy right now."

"I do do love you."

"Yes, fine, may I speak with you later about this?"

"How I want that long sleek cock inside me—"

"Bye now!"

What else is wrong with her, while we're at it? She moves her lips when she reads. Petty? You think so? Ever sit across the dinner table from a woman with whom you are supposedly having an affair—a twenty-nine-year-old person—and watch her lips move while she looks down the movie page for a picture the two of you can see? I know what's playing before she even tells me—from reading the lips! And the books I bring her, she carries them around from job to job in her tote bag—to read? No! So as to impress some fairy photographer, to impress passers-by in the street, *strangers*, with her many-sided character! Look at that girl with that smashing ass—carrying a book! With real words in it! The day after our return from Vermont, I bought a copy of *Let Us Now Praise Famous Men*— wrote on a card, "To the staggering girl," and had it gift-wrapped for presentation that night. "Tell me books to read, okay?"—this the touching plea she made the night we returned to the city: "Because why should I be dumb, if like you say, I'm so smart?" So, here was Agee to begin with, and with the Walker Evans' photographs to help her along: a book to speak to her of her own early life, to enlarge her perspective on her origins (origins, of course, holding far more fascination for the nice left-wing Jewish boy than for the proletarian girl herself). How earnest I was compiling that reading list! Boy, was I going to improve her mind! After Agee, Adamic's *Dynamite!*, my own yellowing copy from college; I imagined her benefiting from my undergraduate underlinings, coming to understand the distinction between the relevant and the trivial, a generalization and an illustration, and so on. Furthermore, it was a book so simply written, that hopefully, without my pushing her, she might be encouraged to read not just the chapters I had suggested, those touching directly upon her own past (as I imagined it)—violence in the coal fields, beginning with the Molly Maguires; the chapter on the Wobblies— but the entire history of brutality and terror practiced by and upon the American laboring class, from which she was descended. Had she never read a book called *U.S.A.*? Mortimer Snerd: "Duh, I never read nothing, Mr. Bergen." So I bought her the Modern Library Dos Passos, a book with a hard cover. Simple, I thought, keep it simple, but educational, elevating. Ah, you get the dreamy point, I'm sure. The texts? W.E.B. Du Bois' *The Souls of Black Folk*. *The Grapes of Wrath*. *An American Tragedy*. A book of Sherwood Anderson's I like, called *Poor White* (the title, I thought, might stir her interest). Baldwin's *Notes of a Native Son*. The name of the course? Oh, I don't know—Professor Portnoy's "Humiliated Minorities, an Introduction." "The History and Function of Hatred in America." The purpose? To save the stupid *shikse*; to rid her of her race's ignorance; to make this daughter of the heartless oppressor a student of suffering and oppression; to teach her to be compassionate, to bleed a little for the world's sorrows. Get it now? The perfect couple: she puts the id back in Yid, I put the *oy* back in *goy*.

———

Where am I? Tuxedoed. All civilized-up in my evening clothes, and "dir willa" still sizzling in my hand, as The Monkey emerges wearing the frock she has bought specifically for the occasion. *What* occasion? Where does she think we're going, to shoot a dirty movie? Doctor, it barely reaches her ass! It is crocheted of some kind of gold metallic yarn and covers nothing but a body stocking the color of her skin! And to top this modest outfit off, over her real head of hair she wears a wig inspired by Little Orphan Annie, an oversized aureole of black corkscrew curls, out of whose center pokes this dumb painted face. What a mean little mouth it gives her! She really *is* from West Virginia! The miner's daughter in the neon city! "And this," I think, "is how she is going with me to the Mayor's? Looking like a stripper? 'Dear,' and *she* spells it with three letters! And hasn't read two pages of the Agee book in an entire week! Has she even looked at the pictures? Duh, I doubt it! Oh, wrong," I think, jamming her note into my pocket for a keepsake—I can have it laminated for a quarter the next day—"wrong! This is somebody whom I picked up off the street! Who sucked me off before she even knew my name! Who once peddled her ass in Las Vegas, if not elsewhere! Just look at her—a moll! The Assistant Human Opportunity Commissioner's moll! What kind of dream am I living in? Being with such a person is for me *all wrong!* Mean-ingless! A waste of everybody's energy and character and time!"

"Okay," says The Monkey in the taxi, "what's bugging you, Max?"

"Nothing."

"You hate the way I look."

"Ridiculous."

"Driver—Peck and Peck!"

"Shut up. Gracie Mansion, driver."

"I'm getting radiation poisoning, Alex, from what you're giving off."

"I'm not giving off shit! I've said *nothing.*"

"You've got those black Hebe eyes, man, they say it for you. *Tutti!*"

"Relax, Monkey."

"*You* relax!"

"I am!" But my manly resolve lasts about a minute more. "Only for Christ's sake," I tell her, "don't say cunt to Mary Lindsay!"

"*What?*"

"You heard right. When we get there don't start talking about your wet pussy to whoever opens the door! Don't make a grab for Big John's *shlong* until we've been there at least half an hour, okay?"

With this, a hiss like the sound of air brakes rises from the driver—and The Monkey heaves herself in a rage against the rear door. "I'll say and do and wear anything I want! This is a free country, you uptight Jewish prick!"

You should have seen the look given us upon disembarking by Mr. Manny Schapiro, our driver. "Rich joik-offs!" he yells. "Nazi bitch!" and burns rubber pulling away.

From where we sit on a bench in Carl Schurz Park, we can see the lights in Gracie Mansion; I watch the other members of the new administration arriving, as I stroke her arm, kiss her forehead, tell her there is no reason to cry, the fault is mine, yes, yes, I am an uptight Jewish prick, and apologize, apologize, apologize.

"—picking on me all the time—in just the way you *look* at me you pick on me, Alex! I open the door at night, I'm so *dying* to see you, thinking all day long about nothing but you, and there are those fucking orbs already picking out every single thing that's *wrong* with me! As if I'm not insecure enough, as if insecurity isn't my whole hang-up, you get that expression all over your face the minute I open my mouth—I mean I can't even give you the time of the day without *the look*: oh shit, here comes another dumb and stupid remark out of that brainless twat. I say, 'It's five to seven,' and you think, 'How fucking dumb can she be!' Well, I'm not brainless, and I'm not a twat either, just because I didn't go to fucking Harvard! And don't give me any more of your shit about behaving in front of *The Lindsays*. Just who the fuck are *The Lindsays*? A God damn mayor, and his wife! A fucking *mayor*! In case you forgot, I was married to one of the richest men in France *when I was still eighteen years old*—I was a guest at Aly Khan's for dinner, when you were still back in Newark, New Jersey, finger-fucking your little Jewish girl friends!"

Was this my idea of a love affair, she asked, sobbing miserably. To treat a woman like a leper?

I wanted to say, "Maybe then this isn't a love affair. Maybe it's what's called a mistake. Maybe we should just go our different ways, with no hard feelings." But I didn't! For fear she might commit suicide! Hadn't she five minutes earlier tried to throw herself out the rear door of the taxi? So suppose I had said, "Look, Monkey, this is it"—what was to stop her from rushing across the park, and leaping to her death in the East River? Doctor, you must believe me, this was a real possibility —this is why I said nothing; but then her arms were around my neck, and oh, *she* said plenty. "I love you, Alex! I worship and adore you! So don't put me down, please! Because I couldn't take it! Because you're the very best man, woman, or child I've ever known! In the whole animal kingdom! Oh, Breakie, you have a big brain and a big cock and I love you!"

And then on a bench no more than two hundred feet from *The Lindsays'* mansion, she buried her wig in my lap and proceeded to suck me off. "Monkey, *no*," I pleaded, "*no*," as she passionately zipped open my black trousers, "there are plainclothesmen everywhere!"—referring to the policing of Gracie Mansion and its environs. "They'll haul us in, creating a public nuisance—*Monkey, the cops*—" but turning her ambitious lips up from my open fly, she whispered, "Only in your imagination" (a not unsubtle retort, if meant subtly), and then down she burrowed, some furry little animal in search of a home. And mastered me with her mouth.

At dinner I overheard her telling the Mayor that she modeled during the day and took courses at Hunter at night. Not a word about her cunt, as far as I could tell. The next day she went off to Hunter, and that night, for a surprise, showed me the application blank she had gotten from the admissions office. Which I praised her for. And which she never filled out, of course—except for her age: 29.

—

A fantasy of The Monkey's, dating from her high school years in Moundsville. The reverie she lived in, while others learned to read and write:

Around a big conference table, at rigid attention, sit all the boys in West Virginia who are seeking admission to West Point. Underneath the table, crawling on her hands and knees, and nude, is our gawky teen-age illiterate, Mary Jane Reed. A West Point colonel with a swagger stick tap-tapping behind his back, circles and circles the perimeter of the table, scrutinizing the faces of the young men, as out of sight Mary Jane proceeds to undo their trousers and to blow each of the candidates in his turn. The boy selected for admission to the military academy will be he who is most able to maintain a stern and dignified soldierly bearing while shooting off into Mary Jane's savage and knowing little weapon of a mouth.

—

Ten months. Incredible. For in that time not a day—very likely, not an hour—passed that I did not ask myself, "Why continue with this person? This brutalized woman! This coarse, tormented, self-loathing, bewildered, lost, identityless—" and so on. The list was inexhaustible, I reviewed it interminably. And to remember the ease with which I had plucked her off the street (the sexual triumph of my life!), well, that made me groan with disgust. How can I go on and on with someone whose reason and judgment and behavior I can't possibly respect? Who sets off inside me daily explosions of disapproval, hourly thunderclaps of admonition! And the sermonizing! Oh, what a schoolmaster I became. When she bought me those Italian loafers for my birthday, for instance—such a lecture I gave in return!

"Look," I said, once we were out of the store, "a little shopping advice: when you go off to do something so very simple as exchanging money for goods, it isn't necessary to flash your snatch at everyone this side of the horizon. *Okay?*"

"Flash *what?* Who flashed anything?"

"You, Mary Jane! Your supposedly private parts!"

"I did not!"

"Please, every time you stood up, every time you sat down, I thought you were going to get yourself hooked by the pussy on the salesman's nose."

"Jee-zuz, I gotta sit, I gotta stand, don't I?"

"But not like you're climbing on and off a horse!"

"Well, I don't know what's bugging you—he was a faggot anyway."

"What's 'bugging' me is that the space between your legs has now been seen by more people than watch Huntley and Brinkley! So why not bow out while you're still champeen, *all right?*" Yet, even as I make my accusation, I am saying to myself, "Oh, lay off, Little Boy Blue—if you want a lady instead of a cunt, then get yourself one. Who's holding you here?" Because this city, as we know, is alive with girls wholly unlike Miss Mary Jane Reed, promising, unbroken, uncontaminated young women—healthy, in fact, as milkmaids. *I* know, because these were her predecessors—only they didn't satisfy, either. They were wrong, *too*. Spielvogel, believe me, I've been there, I've tried: I've eaten their casseroles and shaved in their johns, I've been given duplicate keys to their police locks and shelves of my own in the medicine chest, I have even befriended those cats of theirs—named Spinoza and Clytemnestra and Candide and Cat—yes, yes, clever and erudite girls, fresh from successful adventures in sex and scholarship at wholesome Ivy League colleges, lively, intelligent, self-respecting, self-assured, and well-behaved young women—social workers and research assistants, schoolteachers and copy readers, girls in whose company I did not feel abject or ashamed, girls I did not have to father or mother or educate or redeem. And they didn't work out, either!

—

Kay Campbell, my girl friend at Antioch—could there have been a more exemplary person? Artless, sweet-tempered, without a trace of morbidity or egoism—a thoroughly commendable and worthy human being. And where is she now, that find! Hello, Pumpkin! Making some lucky *shaygets* a wonderful wife out there in middle America? How could she do otherwise? Edited the literary magazine, walked off with all the honors in English literature, picketed with me and my outraged friends outside of that barbershop in Yellow Springs where they wouldn't cut Negro hair—a robust, genial, large-hearted, large-assed girl with a sweet baby face, yellow hair, no tits, unfortunately (essentially titless women seem to be my destiny, by the way—now, why *is* that? is there an essay somewhere I can read on that? is it of import? or shall I go on?). Ah, and those peasant legs! And the blouse always hanging loose from her skirt at the back. How moved I was by that blithesome touch! And by the fact that on high heels she looked like a cat stuck up a tree, in trouble, out of her element, all wrong. Always the first of the Antioch nymphs to go barefoot to classes in spring. "The Pumpkin," is what I called her, in commemoration of her pigmentation and the size of her can. Also her solidity: hard as a gourd on matters of moral principle, beautifully stubborn in a way I couldn't but envy and adore.

She never raised her voice in an argument. Can you imagine the impression this made on me at seventeen, fresh from my engagement with The Jack and Sophie Portnoy Debating Society? Who had ever heard of such an approach to controversy? Never ridiculed her opponent! Or seemed to hate him for his ideas! Ah-hah, so *this* is what it means to be a child of *goyim*, valedictorian of a high school in Iowa instead of New Jersey; yes, this is what the *goyim* who have got something have got! Authority without the temper. Virtue without the self-congratulation. Confidence sans swagger or condescension. Come on, let's be fair and give the *goyim* their due, Doctor: when they are impressive, they are very impressive. So *sound*! Yes, that's what hypnotized—the heartiness, the sturdiness; in a word, her pumpkinness. My wholesome, big-bottomed, lipstickless, barefooted *shikse*, where are you now, Kay-Kay? Mother to how many? Did you wind up really fat? Ah, so what! Suppose you're big as a house—you *need* a showcase for that character of yours! The very best of the Middle West, *so why did I let her go?* Oh, I'll get to that, no worry, self-laceration is never more than a memory away, we know that by now. In the meantime, let me miss her substantiality a little. That buttery skin! That unattended streaming hair! And this is back in the early fifties, before streaming hair became the style! This was just *naturalness*, Doctor. Round and ample, sun-colored Kay! I'll bet that half a dozen kiddies are clinging to that girl's abundant behind (so unlike The Monkey's hard little handful of a model's ass!). I'll bet you bake your own bread, right? (The way you did that hot spring night in my Yellow Springs apartment, in your halfslip and brassiere, with flour in your ears and your hairline damp with perspiration—remember? showing me, despite the temperature, how real bread should taste? You could have used my heart for batter, that's how soft it felt!) I'll bet you live where the air is still unpoisoned and nobody locks his door—and still don't give two shits about money or possessions. Hey, I don't either, Pumpkin, still unbesmirched myself on those and related middle-class issues! Oh, perfectly ill-proportioned girl! No mile-long mannequin you! So she had no tits, so what? Slight as a butterfly through the rib cage and neck, but planted like a bear beneath! *Rooted*, that's what I'm getting at! Joined by those lineman's legs to this American ground!

You should have heard Kay Campbell when we went around Greene County ringing doorbells for Stevenson in our sophomore year. Confronted with the most awesome Republican small-mindedness, a stinginess and bleakness of spirit that could absolutely bend the mind, The Pumpkin never was anything but ladylike. I was a barbarian. No matter how dispassionately I began (or condescendingly, because that's how it came out), I invariably wound up in a sweat and a rage, sneering, insulting, condemning, toe-to-toe with these terrible pinched people, calling their beloved Ike an illiterate, a political and moral moron—probably I am as responsible as anyone for Adlai losing as badly as he did in Ohio. The Pumpkin, however, gave such unflawed and kindly attention to the opposition point of view that I expected sometimes for her to turn and say to me, "Why, Alex, I think Mr. Yokel is right—I think maybe he *is* too soft on communism." But no, when the last idiocy had been uttered about our candidate's "socialistical" and/or "pinko" ideas, the final condemnation made of his sense of humor, The Pumpkin proceeded, ceremoniously and (awesome feat!) without a hint of sarcasm—she might have been the judge at a pie-baking contest, such a perfect blend was she of sobriety and good humor—proceeded to correct Mr. Yokel's errors of fact and logic, even to draw attention to his niggardly morality. Unencumbered by the garbled syntax of the apocalypse or the ill-mannered vocabulary of desperation, without the perspiring upper lip, the constricted and air-hungry throat, the flush of loathing on the forehead, she may even have swayed half a dozen people in the county. Christ, yes, this was one of the great *shikses*. I might have learned something spending the rest of my life with such a person. Yes, I might—if I could learn something! If I could be somehow sprung from this obsession with fellatio and fornication, from romance and fantasy and revenge—from the settling of scores! the pursuit of dreams! from this hopeless, senseless loyalty to the long ago!

—

In 1950, just seventeen, and Newark two and a half months behind me (well, not exactly "behind": in the mornings I awake in the dormitory baffled by the unfamiliar blanket in my hand, and the disappearance of one of "my" windows; oppressed and distraught for minutes on end by this unanticipated transformation given my bedroom by my mother)—I perform the most openly defiant act of my life: instead of going home for my first college vacation, I travel by train to Iowa, to spend Thanksgiving with The Pumpkin and her parents. Till September I had never been farther west than Lake Hopatcong in New Jersey—now I am off to Ioway! And with a blondie! Of the Christian religion! Who is more stunned by this desertion, my family or me? What daring! Or was I no more daring than a sleepwalker?

The white clapboard house in which The Pumpkin had grown up might have been the Taj Mahal for the emotions it released in me. Balboa, maybe, knows what I felt upon first glimpsing the swing tied up to the ceiling of the front porch. *She was raised in this house. The girl who has let me undo her brassiere and dry-hump her at the dormitory door, grew up in this white house. Behind those* goyische *curtains! Look, shutters!*

"Daddy, Mother," says The Pumpkin, when we disembark at the Davenport train station, "this is the weekend guest, this is the friend from school whom I wrote you about—"

I am something called "a weekend guest"? I am something called "a friend from school"? What tongue is she speaking? I am "the *bonditt*," "the *vantz*," I am the insurance man's son. I am Warshaw's ambassador! "How do you do, Alex?" To which of course I reply, "Thank you." Whatever anybody says to me during my first twenty-four hours in Iowa, I answer, "Thank you." Even to inanimate objects. I walk into a chair, promptly I say to it, "Excuse me, thank you." I drop my napkin on the floor, lean down, flushing, to pick it up, "Thank you," I hear myself saying to the napkin—or is it the floor I'm addressing? Would my mother be proud of her little gentleman! Polite even to the furniture!

Then there's an expression in English, "Good morning," or so I have been told; the phrase has never been of any particular use to me. Why should it have been? At breakfast at home I am in fact known to the other boarders as "Mr. Sourball," and "The Crab." But suddenly, here in Iowa, in imitation of the local inhabitants, I am transformed into a veritable geyser of good mornings. That's all anybody around that place knows how to say—they feel the sunshine on their faces, and it just sets off some sort of chemical reaction: Good *morning*! *Good* morning! Good *morning*! sung to half a dozen different tunes! Next they all start asking each other if they had "a good night's sleep." And asking me! Did I have a good night's sleep? I don't really know, I have to think—the question comes as something of a surprise. Did I Have a Good Night's Sleep? Why, yes! I think I did! Hey—did you? "Like a log," replies Mr. Campbell. And for the first time in my life I experience the full force of a simile. This man, who is a real estate broker and an alderman of the Davenport town council, says that he slept like a log, and I actually *see* a log. *I* get it! Motionless, heavy, *like a log!* "Good *morning*," he says, and now it occurs to me that the word "morning," as he uses it, refers specifically to the hours between eight A.M. and twelve noon. I'd never thought of it that way before. He wants the hours between eight and twelve to be *good*, which is to say, enjoyable, pleasurable, beneficial! We are all of us wishing each other four hours of pleasure and accomplishment. Why, that's terrific! Hey, that's very nice! Good morning! And the same applies to "Good afternoon"! And "Good evening"! And "Good night"! My God! The English language is *a form of communication*! Conversation isn't just crossfire where you shoot and get shot at! Where you've got to duck for your life and aim to kill! Words aren't only bombs and bullets—no, they're little gifts, containing *meanings*!

Wait, I'm not finished—as if the experience of being on the inside rather than the outside of these *goyische* curtains isn't overwhelming enough, as if the incredible experience of my wishing hour upon hour of pleasure to a houseful of *goyim* isn't sufficient source for bewilderment, there is, to compound the ecstasy of disorientation, the name of the street upon which the Campbell house stands, the street where *my* girl friend grew up! skipped! skated! hop-scotched! sledded! all the while I dreamed of her existence some fifteen hundred miles away, in what they tell me is the same country. The street name? Not Xanadu, no, better even than that, oh, more preposterous by far: *Elm*. Elm! It is, you see, as though I have walked right through the orange celluloid station band of our old Zenith, directly onto "One Man's Family." Elm. Where trees grow—which must be elms!

To be truthful, I must admit that I am not able to draw such a conclusion first thing upon alighting from the Campbell car on Wednesday night: after all, it has taken me seventeen years to recognize an oak, and even there I am lost without the acorns. What I see first in a landscape isn't the flora, believe me—it's the fauna, the human opposition, who is screwing and who is getting screwed. Greenery I leave to the birds and the bees, they have their worries, I have mine. At home who knows the name of what grows from the pavement at the front of our house? It's a tree—and that's it. The kind is of no consequence, who cares what kind, just as long as it doesn't fall down on your head. In the autumn (or is it the spring? Do you know this stuff? I'm pretty sure it's not the winter) there drop from its branches long crescent-shaped pods containing hard little pellets. Okay. Here's a scientific fact about our tree, comes by way of my mother, Sophie Linnaeus: If you shoot those pellets through a straw, you can take somebody's eye out and make him blind for life. (SO NEVER DO IT! NOT EVEN IN JEST! AND IF ANYBODY DOES IT TO YOU, YOU TELL ME INSTANTLY!) And this, more or less, is the sort of botanical knowledge I am equipped with, until that Sunday afternoon when we are leaving the Campbell house for the train station, and I have my Archimedean experience: Elm Street . . . . . then . . . . . elm *trees*! How simple! I mean, you don't *need* 158 points of I.Q., you don't *have* to be a genius to make sense of this world. It's really all so very simple!

A memorable weekend in my lifetime, equivalent in human history, I would say, to mankind's passage through the entire Stone Age. Every time Mr. Campbell called his wife "Mary," my body temperature shot into the hundreds. There I was, eating off dishes that had been touched by the hands of a woman named *Mary*. (Is there a clue here as to why I so resisted calling The Monkey by her name, except to chastise her? No?) Please, I pray on the train heading west, let there be no pictures of Jesus Christ in the Campbell house. Let me get through this weekend without having to see his pathetic *punim* —or deal with anyone wearing a cross! When the aunts and uncles come for the Thanksgiving dinner, please, let there be no anti-Semite among them! Because if someone starts in with "the pushy Jews," or says "kike" or "jewed him down"— Well, I'll jew them down all right, I'll jew their fucking teeth down their throat! No, no violence (as if I even had it in me), let *them* be violent, that's *their* way. No, I'll rise from my seat— and (*vuh den?*) make a speech! I will shame and humiliate them in their bigoted hearts! Quote the Declaration of Independence over their candied yams! Who the fuck are they, I'll ask, to think they own Thanksgiving!

Then at the railroad station her father says, "How do you do, young man?" and I of course answer, "Thank you." Why is *he* acting so nice? Because he has been forewarned (which I don't know whether to take as an insult or a blessing), or because he doesn't know yet? Shall I say it then, before we get into the car? Yes, I must! I can't go on living a lie! "Well, it sure is nice being here in Davenport, Mr. and Mrs. Campbell, what with my being Jewish and all." Not quite ringing enough perhaps. "Well, as a friend of Kay's, Mr. and Mrs. Campbell, and a Jew, I do want to thank you for inviting me—" Stop pussyfooting! What then? Talk Yiddish? *How?* I've got twenty-five words to my name—half of them dirty, and the rest mispronounced! Shit, just shut up and get in the car. "Thank you, thank you," I say, picking up my own bag, and we all head for the station wagon.

Kay and I climb into the back seat, *with the dog.* Kay's dog! To whom she talks as though he's human! Wow, she really *is* a *goy.* What a stupid thing, to talk to a dog—except Kay isn't stupid! In fact, I think she's smarter really than I am. And yet talks to a dog? "As far as dogs are concerned, Mr. and Mrs. Campbell, we Jews by and large—" Oh, forget it. Not necessary. You are ignoring anyway (or trying awfully hard to) that eloquent appendage called your nose. Not to mention the Afro-Jewish hairpiece. Of course they know. Sorry, but there's no escaping destiny, *bubi*, a man's cartilage is his fate. *But I don't want to escape!* Well, that's nice too—because you can't. *Oh, but yes I can—if I should want to!* But you said you don't want to. *But if I did!*

As soon as I enter the house I begin (on the sly, and somewhat to my own surprise) to sniff: what will the odor be like? Mashed potatoes? An old lady's dress? Fresh cement? I sniff and I sniff, trying to catch the scent. There! is *that* it, is that Christianity I smell, or just the dog? Everything I see, taste, touch, I think, "*Goyish!*" My first morning I squeeze half an inch of Pepsodent down the drain rather than put my brush where Kay's mother or father may have touched the bristles with which they cleanse their own *goyische* molars. True! The soap on the sink is bubbly with foam from somebody's hands. Whose? *Mary's?* Should I just take hold of it and begin to wash, or should I maybe run a little water over it first, just to be safe. But safe from *what?* Schmuck, maybe you want to get a piece of soap to wash the soap with! I tiptoe to the toilet, I peer over into the bowl: "Well, there it is, boy, a real *goyische* toilet bowl. The genuine article. Where your girl friend's father drops his gentile turds. What do you think, huh? Pretty impressive." Obsessed? Spellbound!

Next I have to decide whether or not to line the seat. It isn't a matter of hygiene, I'm sure the place is clean, spotless in its own particular antiseptic *goy* way: the question is, what if it's warm yet from a Campbell behind—from her mother! *Mary!* Mother also of Jesus Christ! If only for the sake of my family, maybe I should put a little paper around the rim; it doesn't cost anything, and who will ever know?

I will! *I* will! So down I go—and it *is* warm! Yi, seventeen years old and I am rubbing asses with the enemy! How far I have traveled since September! *By the waters of Babylon, there we sat down, yea, we wept when we remembered Zion!* And yea is right! On the can I am besieged by doubt and regret, I am suddenly languishing with all my heart for home . . . When my father drives out to buy "real apple cider" at the roadside farmer's market off in Union, I won't be with him! And how can Hannah and Morty go to the Weequahic-Hillside game Thanksgiving morning without me along to make them laugh? Jesus, I hope we win (which is to say, lose by less than 21 points). Beat Hillside, you bastards! Double U, Double E, Q U A, H I C! Bernie, Sidney, Leon, "Ushie," come on, backfield, FIGHT!

> Aye-aye ki-ike-us,
> Nobody likes us,
> We are the boys of Weequahic High—

Aye-aye ki-ucch-us,
Kish mir in tuchis,
We are the boys of Weequahic High!

Come on—hold that line, make that point, kick 'em in the
kishkas, go team go!

See, I'm missing my chance to be clever and quick-witted in
the stands! To show off my sarcastic and mocking tongue! And
after the game, missing the historical Thanksgiving meal prepared by my mother, that freckled and red-headed descendant
of Polish Jews! Oh, how the blood will flow out of their faces,
what a deathly silence will prevail, when she holds up the huge
drumstick, and cries, "Here! For guess who!" and Guess-who
is found to be AWOL! Why have I deserted my family? Maybe
around the table we don't look like a painting by Norman
Rockwell, but we have a good time, too, don't you worry! We
don't go back to the Plymouth Rock, no Indian ever brought
maize to any member of our family as far as we know—but just
smell that stuffing! And look, cylinders of cranberry sauce at
either end of the table! And the turkey's name, "Tom"! Why
then can't I believe I am eating my dinner in America, that
America is where *I* am, instead of some other place to which I
will one day travel, as my father and I must travel every November out to that hayseed and his wife in Union, New Jersey
(the *two* of them in overalls), for real Thanksgiving apple cider.

"I'm going to Iowa," I tell them from the phone booth on
my floor. "To *where?*" "To Davenport, Iowa." "On your first
college vacation?!" "—I know, but it's a great opportunity, and
I can't turn it down—" "Oppor*tunity?* To do *what?*" "Yes,
to spend Thanksgiving with this boy named Bill Campbell's
family—" "*Who?*" "Campbell. Like the soup. He lives in my
dorm—" But they are expecting me. Everybody is expecting
me. Morty has the tickets to the game. What am I talking *opportunity?* "And who is this boy all of a sudden, Campbell?"
"My friend! Bill!" "But," says my father, "the *cider.*" Oh my
God, it's happened, what I swore I wouldn't permit!—I am in
tears, and "cider" is the little word that does it. The man is a
natural—he could go on Groucho Marx and win a fortune
guessing the secret-woid. He guesses mine, every single time!
And wins my jackpot of contrition! "I can't back out, I'm

sorry, I've accepted—we're *going!*" "Going? And how, Alex—
I don't understand this plan at all," interrupts my mother—
"*how* are you going, if I may be so bold, and *where?* and in a
convertible too, *that too*—" "NO!" "And if the highways are
icy, Alex—" "We're going, Mother, *in a Sherman tank!* Okay?
Okay?" "Alex," she says sternly, "I hear it in your voice, I
know you're not telling me the whole truth, you're going to
hitchhike in a convertible or some other crazy thing—two
months away from home, seventeen years old, and he's going
wild!"

Sixteen years ago I made that phone call. A little more than
half the age I am now. November 1950—here, it's tattooed on
my wrist, the date of my Emancipation Proclamation. Children
unborn when I first telephoned my parents to say I wasn't
coming home from college are just entering college, I suppose
—only I'm still telephoning my parents to say I'm not coming
home! Fighting off my family, still! What use to skip those
two grades in grammar school and get such a jump on everybody else, when the result is to wind up so far behind? My
early promise is legend: starring in all those grade-school
plays! taking on at the age of twelve the entire DAR! Why then
do I live by myself and have no children of my own? It's no
non sequitur, that question! Professionally I'm going somewhere, granted, but *privately*—what have I got to show for
myself? Children should be playing on this earth who look like
me! *Why not?* Why should every *shtunk* with a picture window
and a carport have offspring, and not me? It don't make sense!
Think of it, half the race is over, and I still stand here at the
starting line—me, the first one out of his swaddling clothes
and into his track suit! a hundred and fifty-eight points of I.Q.,
and still arguing with the authorities about the rules and regulations! disputing the course to be run! calling into question
the legitimacy of the track commission! Yes, "crab" is correct,
Mother! "Sourball" is perfect, right on The Nose's nose! "Mr.
Conniption-Fit"—*c'est moi!*

Another of these words I went through childhood thinking
of as "Jewish." Conniption. "Go ahead, have a conniption-
fit," my mother would advise. "See if it changes anything, my
brilliant son." And how I tried! How I used to hurl myself
against the walls of her kitchen! Mr. Hot-Under-The-Collar!

Mr. Hit-The-Ceiling! Mr. Fly-Off-The-Handle! The names I earn for myself! God forbid somebody should look at you cockeyed, Alex, their life isn't worth two cents! Mr. Always-Right-And-Never-Wrong! Grumpy From The Seven Dwarfs Is Visiting Us, Daddy. Ah, Hannah, Your Brother Surly Has Honored Us With His Presence This Evening, It's A Pleasure To Have You, Surly. "Hi Ho Silver," she sighs, as I rush into my bedroom to sink my fangs into the bedspread, "The Temper Tantrum Kid Rides Again."

—

Near the end of our junior year Kay missed a period, and so we began, and with a certain eager delight—and wholly without panic, interestingly—to make plans to be married. We would offer ourselves as resident baby-sitters to a young faculty couple who were fond of us; in return they would give us their roomy attic to live in, and a shelf to use in their refrigerator. We would wear old clothes and eat spaghetti. Kay would write poetry about having a baby, and, she said, type term papers for extra money. We had our scholarships, what more did we need? (besides a mattress, some bricks and boards for bookshelves, Kay's Dylan Thomas record, and in time, a crib). We thought of ourselves as adventurers.

I said, "And you'll convert, right?"

I intended the question to be received as ironic, or thought I had. But Kay took it seriously. Not solemnly, mind you, just seriously.

Kay Campbell, Davenport, Iowa: "Why would I want to do a thing like that?"

Great girl! Marvelous, ingenuous, candid girl! Content, you see, as she was! What one *dies* for in a woman—I now realize! *Why would I want to do a thing like that?* And nothing blunt or defensive or arch or superior in her tone. Just common sense, plainly spoken.

Only it put our Portnoy into a rage, incensed The Temper Tantrum Kid. What do you mean *why* would you want to do a thing like that? Why do you think, you simpleton-*goy*! Go talk to your dog, ask *him*. Ask Spot what *he* thinks, that four-legged genius. "Want Kay-Kay to be a Jew, Spottie—huh, big fella, huh?" Just what the fuck makes you so self-satisfied, anyway? That you carry on conversations with dogs? that you know an elm when you see one? that your father drives a station wagon made out of wood? What's your hotsy-totsy accomplishment in life, baby, that Doris Day snout?

I was, fortunately, so astonished by my indignation that I couldn't begin to voice it. How could I be feeling a wound in a place where I was not even vulnerable? What did Kay and I care less about than one, money, and two, religion? Our favorite philosopher was Bertrand Russell. Our religion was Dylan Thomas' religion, Truth and Joy! Our children would be atheists. I had only been making a joke!

Nonetheless, it would seem that I never forgave her: in the weeks following our false alarm, she came to seem to me boringly predictable in conversation, and about as desirable as blubber in bed. And it surprised me that she should take it so badly when I finally had to tell her that I didn't seem to care for her any more. I was very honest, you see, as Bertrand Russell said I should be. "I just don't want to see you any more, Kay. I can't hide my feelings, I'm sorry." She wept pitifully: she carried around the campus terrible little pouches underneath her bloodshot blue eyes, she didn't show up for meals, she missed classes . . . And I was astonished. Because all along I'd thought it was I who had loved her, not she who had loved me. What a surprise to discover just the opposite to have been the case.

Ah, twenty and spurning one's mistress—that first unsullied thrill of sadism with a woman! And the dream of the women to come. I returned to New Jersey that June, buoyant with my own "strength," wondering how I could ever have been so captivated by someone so ordinary and so fat.

—

Another gentile heart broken by me belonged to The Pilgrim, Sarah Abbott Maulsby—New Canaan, Foxcroft, and Vassar (where she had as companion, stabled in Poughkeepsie, that other flaxen beauty, her palomino). A tall, gentle, decorous twenty-two-year-old, fresh from college, and working as a receptionist in the office of the Senator from Connecticut when we two met and coupled in the fall of 1959.

I was on the staff of the House subcommittee investigating the television quiz scandals. Perfect for a closet socialist like myself: commercial deceit on a national scale, exploitation of the innocent public, elaborate corporate chicanery—in short, good old capitalist greed. And then of course that extra bonus, Charlatan Van Doren. Such character, such brains and breeding, that candor and schoolboyish charm—the ur-WASP, wouldn't you say? And turns out he's a fake. Well, what do you know about that, Gentile America? Supergoy, a *gonif*! Steals money. Covets money. Wants money, will do anything for it. Goodness gracious me, almost as bad as Jews—you sanctimonious WASPs!

Yes, I was one happy yiddel down there in Washington, a little Stern gang of my own, busily exploding Charlie's honor and integrity, while simultaneously becoming lover to that aristocratic Yankee beauty whose forebears arrived on these shores in the seventeenth century. Phenomenon known as Hating Your Goy And Eating One Too.

Why didn't I marry that beautiful and adoring girl? I remember her in the gallery, pale and enchanting in a navy blue suit with gold buttons, watching with such pride, with such love, as I took on one afternoon, in my first public cross-examination, a very slippery network P.R. man . . . and I was impressive too, for my first time out: cool, lucid, persistent, just the faintest hammering of the heart—and only twenty-six years old. Oh yeah, when I am holding all the moral cards, watch out, you crooks you! I am nobody to futz around with when I know myself to be four hundred per cent in the right.

Why didn't I marry the girl? Well, there was her cutesy-wootsy boarding school argot, for one. Couldn't bear it. "Barf" for vomit, "ticked off" for angry, "a howl" for funny, "crackers" for crazy, "teeny" for tiny. Oh, and "di*vine*." (What Mary Jane Reed means by "groovy"—I'm always telling these girls how to talk right, me with my five-hundred-word New Jersey vocabulary.) Then there were the nicknames of her friends; there were the friends themselves! Poody and Pip and Pebble, Shrimp and Brute and Tug, Squeek, Bumpo, Baba—it sounded, I said, as though she had gone to Vassar with Donald Duck's nephews . . . But then my argot caused her some pain too. The first time I said fuck in her presence (and the presence of friend Pebble, in her Peter Pan collar and her cablestitch cardigan, and tanned like an Indian from so much tennis at the Chevy Chase Club), such a look of agony passed over The Pilgrim's face, you would have thought I had just branded the four letters on her flesh. Why, she asked so plaintively once we were alone, why *had* I to be so "unattractive"? What possible pleasure had it given me to be so "ill-mannered"? What on earth had I "proved"? "Why did you have to be so pus-y like that? It was so un*called*-for." Pus-y being Debutante for disagreeable.

In bed? Nothing fancy, no acrobatics or feats of daring and skill; as we screwed our first time, so we continued—I assaulted and she surrendered, and the heat generated on her mahogany fourposter (a Maulsby family heirloom) was considerable. Our one peripheral delight was the full-length mirror on the back of the bathroom door. There, standing thigh to thigh, I would whisper, "Look, Sarah, look." At first she was shy, left the looking to me, at first she was modest and submitted only because I wished her to, but in time she developed something of a passion for the looking glass, too, and followed the reflection of our joining with a certain startled intensity in her gaze. Did she see what I saw? *In the black pubic hair, ladies and gentlemen, weighing one hundred and seventy pounds, at least half of which is still undigested halvah and hot pastrami, from Newark, NJ, The Shnoz, Alexander Portnoy! And his opponent, in the fair fuzz, with her elegant polished limbs and the gentle maidenly face of a Botticelli, that ever-popular purveyor of the social amenities here in the Garden, one hundred and fourteen pounds of Republican refinement, and the pertest pair of nipples in all New England, from New Canaan, Connecticut, Sarah Abbott Maulsby!*

What I'm saying, Doctor, is that I don't seem to stick my dick up these girls, as much as I stick it up their backgrounds—as though through fucking I will discover America. *Conquer* America—maybe that's more like it. Columbus, Captain Smith, Governor Winthrop, General Washington—now Portnoy. As though my manifest destiny is to seduce a girl from each of the forty-eight states. As for Alaskan and Hawaiian women, I really have no feelings either way, no scores to settle, no coupons to cash in, no dreams to put to rest—who are they to me, a bunch of Eskimos and Orientals? No, I am a child of the forties, of network radio and World War Two, of eight teams to a league and forty-eight states to a country. I know all the words to "The Marine Hymn," and to "The Caissons Go Rolling Along"—and to "The Song of the Army Air Corps." I know the song of the *Navy* Air Corps: "Sky anchors aweigh/ We're sailors of the air/ We're sailing everywhere—" I can even sing you the song of the Seabees. Go ahead, name your branch of service, Spielvogel, I'll sing you your song! Please, allow me—it's my money. We used to sit on our coats, I remember, on the concrete floor, our backs against the sturdy walls of the basement corridors of my grade school, singing in unison to keep up our morale until the all-clear signal sounded —"Johnny Zero." "Praise the Lord and Pass the Ammunition." "The sky pilot said it/ You've got to give him credit/ For a son of a gun of a gunner was he-e-e-e!" You name it, and if it was in praise of the Stars and Stripes, I know it word for word! Yes, I am a child of air raid drills, Doctor, I remember Corregidor and "The Cavalcade of America," and that flag, fluttering on its pole, being raised at that heartbreaking angle over bloody Iwo Jima. Colin Kelly went down in flames when I was eight, and Hiroshima and Nagasaki went up in a puff, one week when I was twelve, and that was the heart of my boyhood, four years of hating Tojo, Hitler, and Mussolini, and loving this brave determined republic! Rooting my little Jewish heart out for our American democracy! Well, we won, the enemy is dead in an alley back of the Wilhelmstrasse, and dead because I *prayed* him dead—and now I want what's coming to me. *My* G.I. bill—real American ass! The cunt in country-'tis-of-thee! I pledge allegiance to the twat of the United States of America—and to the republic for which it stands: Davenport, Iowa! Dayton, Ohio! Schenectady, New York, and neighboring Troy! Fort Myers, Florida! New Canaan, Connecticut! Chicago, Illinois! Albert Lea, Minnesota! Portland, Maine! Moundsville, West Virginia! Sweet land of *shikse*-tail, of thee I sing!

From the mountains,
To the prairies,
To the oceans, white-with-my-fooaahhh-mmm!
God bless A-me-ri-cuuuuhhhh!
My home, SWEET HOOOOOHHHH-M!

—

Imagine what it meant to me to know that generations of Maulsbys were buried in the graveyard at Newburyport, Massachusetts, and generations of Abbotts in Salem. *Land where my fathers died, land of the Pilgrims' pride* . . . Exactly. Oh, and more. Here was a girl whose mother's flesh *crawled* at the sound of the words "Eleanor Roosevelt." Who herself had been dandled on the knee of Wendell Willkie at Hobe Sound, Florida, in 1942 (while my father was saying prayers for F.D.R. on the High Holidays, and my mother blessing him over the Friday night candles). The Senator from Connecticut had been a roommate of her Daddy's at Harvard, and her brother, "Paunch," a graduate of Yale, held a seat on the New York Stock Exchange and (how lucky could I be?) played polo (yes, games from on top of a horse!) on Sunday afternoons someplace in Westchester County, as he had throughout college. She could have been a Lindabury, don't you see? A daughter of my father's boss! Here was a girl who knew how to sail a boat, knew how to eat her dessert using two pieces of silverware (a piece of cake you could pick up in your hands, and you should have seen her manipulate it with that fork and that spoon—like a Chinese with his chopsticks! What skills she had learned in far-off Connecticut!). Activities that partook of the exotic and even the taboo she performed so simply, as a matter of course: and I was as wowed (though that's not the whole story) as Desdemona, hearing of the Anthropapagi. I came across a newspaper clipping in her scrapbook, a column entitled "A Deb A Day," which began, "SARAH ABBOTT MAULSBY—'Ducks and quails and pheasants better scurry' around New Canaan this fall because Sally, daughter of Mr. and Mrs. Edward H. Maulsby of Greenley Road, is getting in practice for small game season. Shooting—" with a gun, Doctor— "shooting is just one of Sally's outdoor hobbies. She loves riding too, and this summer hopes to try a rod and reel—" and get this; I think this tale would win my son too—"hopes to try a rod and reel on some of those trout that swim by 'Windview,' her family's summer home."

What Sally couldn't do was eat me. To shoot a gun at a little quack-quack is fine, to suck my cock is beyond her. She was sorry, she said, if I was going to take it so hard, but it was just something she didn't care to try. I mustn't act as though it were a personal affront, she said, because it had nothing to do with me as an individual . . . Oh, didn't it? Bullshit, girlie! Yes, what made me so irate was precisely my belief that I was being discriminated against. My father couldn't rise at Boston & Northeastern for the very same reason that Sally Maulsby wouldn't deign to go down on me! Where was the justice in this world? Where was the B'nai B'rith Anti-Defamation League—! "I do it to you," I said. The Pilgrim shrugged; kindly she said, "You don't have to, though. You know that. If you don't want to . . ." "Ah, but I *do* want to—it isn't a matter of 'have' to. *I want to.*" "Well," she answered, "I don't." "*But why not?*" "Because. I don't." "Shit, that's the way a child answers, Sarah—'because'! Give me a reason!" "I—I just don't do that, that's all." "But that brings us back to why. *Why?*" "Alex, I can't. I just can't." "Give me a single good reason!" "Please," she replied, knowing her rights, "I don't think I have to."

No, she didn't have to—because to me the answer was clear enough anyway: *Because you don't know how to hike out to windward or what a jib is, because you have never owned evening clothes or been to a cotillion* . . . Yes sir, if I were some big blond *goy* in a pink riding suit and hundred-dollar hunting boots, don't worry, she'd be down there eating me, of that I am sure!

I am wrong. Three months I spent applying pressure to the back of her skull (pressure met by a surprising counterforce, an impressive, even moving display of stubbornness from such a mild and uncontentious person), for three months I assaulted her in argument and tugged her nightly by the ears. Then one night she invited me to hear the Budapest String Quartet playing Mozart at the Library of Congress; during the final movement of the Clarinet Quartet she took hold of my hand, her cheeks began to shine, and when we got back to her apartment and into bed, Sally said, "Alex . . . I will." "Will what?" But she was gone, down beneath the covers and out of sight: blowing me! That is to say, she took my prick in her mouth and held it there for a count of sixty, held the surprised little thing there, Doctor, like a thermometer. I threw back the blankets—this I had to see! Feel, there wasn't very much to feel, but oh the sight of it! Only Sally was already finished. Having moved it by now to the side of her face, as though it were the gear shift on her Hillman-Minx. And there were tears on her face.

"I did it," she announced.

"Sally, oh, Sarah, don't cry."

"But I did do it, Alex."

". . . You mean," I said, "that's all?"

"You mean," she gasped, "more?"

"Well, to be frank, a little more—I mean to be truthful with you, it wouldn't go unappreciated—"

"But it's getting big. I'll suffocate."

JEW SMOTHERS DEB WITH COCK. *Vassar Grad Georgetown Strangulation Victim; Mocky Lawyer Held*

"Not if you breathe, you won't."

"I will, I'll choke—"

"Sarah, the best safeguard against asphyxiation is breathing. Just breathe, and that's all there is to it. More or less."

God bless her, she tried. But came up gagging. "I told you," she moaned.

"But you weren't breathing."

"I can't with that in my mouth."

"Through your nose. Pretend you're swimming."

"But I'm *not*."

"PRETEND!" I suggested, and though she gave another gallant try, surfaced only seconds later in an agony of coughing and tears. I gathered her then in my arms (that lovely willing girl! convinced by Mozart to go down on Alex! oh, sweet as Natasha in *War and Peace*! a tender young countess!). I rocked her, I teased her, I made her laugh, for the first time I said, "I love you too, my baby," but of course it couldn't have been clearer to me that despite all her many qualities and charms—her devotion, her beauty, her deerlike grace, her place in American history—there could never be any "love" in me for The Pilgrim. Intolerant of her frailties. Jealous of her accomplishments. Resentful of her family. No, not much room there for love.

No, Sally Maulsby was just something nice a son once did for his dad. A little vengeance on Mr. Lindabury for all those nights and Sundays Jack Portnoy spent collecting down in the

colored district. A little bonus extracted from Boston &
Northeastern, for all those years of service, and exploitation.

IN EXILE

On Sunday mornings, when the weather is warm enough,
twenty of the neighborhood men (this in the days of short center field) play a round of seven-inning softball games, starting
at nine in the morning and ending about one in the afternoon, the stakes for each game a dollar a head. The umpire is
our dentist, old Dr. Wolfenberg, the neighborhood college
graduate—night school on High Street, but as good as Oxford
to us. Among the players is our butcher, his twin brother our
plumber, the grocer, the owner of the service station where my
father buys his gasoline—all of them ranging in age from thirty
to fifty, though I think of them not in terms of their years, but
only as "the men." In the on-deck circle, even at the plate,
they roll their jaws on the stumps of soggy cigars. Not boys,
you see, but men. Belly! Muscle! Forearms black with hair!
Bald domes! And then the voices they have on them—cannons
you can hear go off from as far as our front stoop a block away.
I imagine vocal cords inside them thick as clotheslines! lungs
the size of zeppelins! Nobody has to tell them to stop mum-
bling and speak up, never! And the outrageous things they
say! The chatter in the infield isn't chatter, it's kibbitzing, and
(to this small boy, just beginning to learn the art of ridicule)
hilarious, particularly the insults that emanate from the man
my father has labeled "The Mad Russian," Biderman, owner
of the corner candy store (and bookie joint) who has a "hesitation" side-arm delivery, not only very funny but very effective.
"Abracadabra," he says, and pitches his backbreaking drop.
And he is always giving it to Dr. Wolfenberg: "A blind ump,
okay, but a blind dentist?" The idea causes him to smote his
forehead with his glove. "Play ball, comedian," calls Dr. Wolfenberg, very Connie Mack in his perforated two-tone shoes
and Panama hat, "start up the game, Biderman, unless you
want to get thrown out of here for insults—!" "But how do
they teach you in that dental school, Doc, by Braille?"

Meanwhile, all the way from the outfield comes the badinage of one who in appearance is more cement-mixer than Homo sapiens, the prince of the produce market, Allie Sokolow. The *pisk* he opens on him! (as my mother would put it). For half an inning the invective flows in toward home plate from his position in deep center field, and then when his team comes to bat, he stations himself in the first-base coaching box and the invective flows uninterruptedly out in the opposite direction—and none of it has anything to do with any contretemps that may actually be taking place on the field. Quite the opposite. My father, when he is not out working on Sunday mornings, comes by to sit and watch a few innings with me; he knows Allie Sokolow (as he knows many of the players), since they were all boys together in the Central Ward, before he met my mother and moved to Jersey City. He says that Allie has always been like this, "a real showman." When Allie charges in toward second base, screaming his gibberish and double-talk in the direction of home plate (where there isn't even a batter as yet—where Dr. Wolfenberg is merely dusting the plate with the whisk broom he brings to the game), the people in the stands couldn't be more delighted: they laugh, they clap, they call out, "You tell him, Allie! You give it to him, Sokolow!" And invariably Dr. Wolfenberg, who takes himself a little more seriously than your ordinary nonprofessional person (and is a German Jew to boot), holds up his palm, halting an already Sokolow-stopped game, and says to Biderman, "Will you please get that *meshuggener* back in the outfield?"

I tell you, they are an endearing lot! I sit in the wooden stands alongside first base, inhaling that sour springtime bouquet in the pocket of my fielder's mitt—sweat, leather, vaseline—and laughing my head off. I cannot imagine myself living out my life any other place but here. Why leave, why go, when there is everything here that I will ever want? The ridiculing, the joking, the acting-up, the pretending—anything for a laugh! I love it! And yet underneath it all, *they mean it, they are in dead earnest.* You should see them at the end of the seven innings when that dollar has to change hands. Don't tell *me* they don't mean it! Losing and winning is not a joke . . . and yet it is! And that's what charms me most of all. Fierce as the competition is, they cannot resist clowning and kibbitzing around. Putting on a show! How I am going to love growing up to be a Jewish man! Living forever in the Weequahic section, and playing softball on Chancellor Avenue from nine to one on Sundays, a perfect joining of clown and competitor, kibbitzing wiseguy and dangerous long-ball hitter.

I remember all this where? when? While Captain Meyerson is making his last slow turn over the Tel Aviv airport. My face is against the window. *Yes, I could disappear, I think, change my name and never be heard from again*—then Meyerson banks the wing on my side, and I look down for the first time upon the continent of Asia, I look down from two thousand feet in the air upon the Land of Israel, where the Jewish people first came into being, and am impaled upon a memory of Sunday morning softball games in Newark.

The elderly couple seated beside me (the Solomons, Edna and Felix), who have told me in an hour's flight time all about their children and grandchildren in Cincinnati (with, of course, a walletful of visual aids), now nudge each other and nod together in silent satisfaction; they even poke some friends across the aisle, a couple from Mount Vernon they've just met (the Perls, Sylvia and Bernie), and these two *kvell* also to see a tall, good-looking, young Jewish lawyer (and single! a match for somebody's daughter!) suddenly begin to weep upon making contact with a Jewish airstrip. However, what has produced these tears is not, as the Solomons and Perls would have it, a first glimpse of the national homeland, the ingathering of an exile, but the sound in my ear of my own nine-year-old little boy's voice—*my* voice, I mean, at nine. Nine-year-old me! Sure a sourpuss, a face-maker, a little back-talker and *kvetch*, sure my piping is never without its nice infuriating whiny edge of permanent disgruntlement and grievance ("as though," my mother says, "the world owes him a living—at nine years old"), but a laugher and kidder too, don't forget that, an enthusiast! a romantic! a mimic! a nine-year-old lover of life! fiery with such simple, neighborhoody dreams!—"I'm going up the field," I call into the kitchen, fibers of pink lox lodged like sour dental floss in the gaps between my teeth, "I'm going up the field, Ma," pounding my mitt with my carpy-smelling little fist, "I'll be back around one—" "*Wait* a minute. What time? Where?" "*Up the field*," I holler—I'm very high on hollering

to be heard, it's like being angry, except without the consequences, "—*to watch the men!*"

And that's the phrase that does me in as we touch down
upon *Eretz Yisroel*: to watch the men.

Because I love those men! I want to grow up to *be* one of
those men! To be going home to Sunday dinner at one o'clock,
sweat socks pungent from twenty-one innings of softball,
underwear athletically gamy, and in the muscle of my throwing
arm, a faint throbbing from the low and beautiful pegs I have
been unleashing all morning long to hold down the opposition on the base paths; yes, hair disheveled, teeth gritty, feet
beat and *kishkas* sore from laughing, in other words, feeling
great, a robust Jewish man now gloriously pooped—yes, home
I head for resuscitation . . . and to whom? To *my* wife and
my children, to a family of my own, and right there in the
Weequahic section! I shave and shower—rivulets of water
stream off my scalp a filthy brown, ah, it's good, ah yes, it's a
regular pleasure standing there nearly scalding myself to death
with hot water. It strikes me as so *manly*, converting pain to
pleasure. Then into a pair of snappy slacks and a freshly dry-
cleaned "gaucho" shirt— perfecto! I whistle a popular song, I
admire my biceps, I shoot a rag across my shoes, making it *pop*,
and meanwhile my kids are riffling through the Sunday papers
(reading with eyes the exact color of my own), giggling away
on the living-room rug; and my wife, Mrs. Alexander Portnoy,
is setting the table in the dining room—we will be having
my mother and father as guests, they will be walking over any
minute, as they do every Sunday. A future, see! A simple and
satisfying future! Exhausting, exhilarating softball in which to
spend my body's force—that for the morning—then in the
afternoon, the brimming, hearty stew of family life, and at
night three solid hours of the best line-up of radio entertain-
ment in the world: yes, as I delighted in Jack Benny's trips
down to his vault in the company of *my* father, and Fred
Allen's conversations with Mrs. Nussbaum, and Phil Harris'
with Frankie Remley, also shall my children delight in them
with me, and so unto the hundredth generation. And then
after Kenny Baker, I double-lock the front and back doors,
turn off all the lights (check and—as my father does—double-
check the pilot on the gas range so that our lives will not be

stolen from us in the night). I kiss good night my pretty sleepy daughter and my clever sleepy son, and in the arms of Mrs. A. Portnoy, that kind and gentle (and in my sugary but modest fantasy, faceless) woman, I bank the fires of my abounding pleasure. In the morning I am off to downtown Newark; to the Essex County Court House, where I spend my workdays seeking justice for the poor and the oppressed.

Our eighth-grade class visits the courthouse to observe the architecture. Home and in my room that night, I write in my fresh new graduation autograph album, under YOUR FAVORITE MOTTO, "Don't Step on the Underdog." MY FAVORITE PROFESSION? "Lawyer." MY FAVORITE HERO? "Tom Paine and Abraham Lincoln." Lincoln sits outside the courthouse (in Gutzon Borglum's bronze), looking tragic and fatherly: you just know how much he cares. A statue of Washington, standing erect and authoritarian in front of his horse, overlooks Broad Street; it is the work of J. Massey Rhind (we write this second unname-like name of a sculptor in our notebooks); our art teacher says that the two statues are "the city's pride," and we head off in pairs for the paintings at the Newark Museum. Washington, I must confess, leaves me cold. Maybe it's the horse, that he's leaning on a horse. At any rate, he is so obviously a *goy*. But Lincoln! I could cry. Look at him sitting there, so *oysgemitchet*. How he labored for the downtrodden—as will I!

A nice little Jewish boy? Please, I am the nicest little Jewish boy who ever lived! Only look at the fantasies, how sweet and savior-like they are! Gratitude to my parents, loyalty to my tribe, devotion to the cause of justice!

And? What's so wrong? Hard work in an idealistic profession; games played without fanaticism or violence, games played among like-minded people, and with laughter; and family forgiveness and love. What was so wrong with believing in all that? What happened to the good sense I had at nine, ten, eleven years of age? How have I come to be such an enemy and flayer of myself? And so alone! *Oh*, so alone! Nothing but *self*! Locked up in *me*! Yes, I have to ask myself (as the airplane carries me—I believe—away from my tormentor), what has become of my purposes, those decent and worthwhile goals? Home? I have none. Family? No! Things I could own just by snapping my fingers . . . so why not snap them then, and get on with my life? No, instead of tucking in my children and lying down beside a loyal wife (to whom I am loyal too), I have, on two different evenings, taken to bed with me— coinstantaneously, as they say in the whorehouses—a fat little Italian whore and an illiterate, unbalanced American mannequin. And that isn't even my idea of a good time, damn it! What is? I told you! And meant it—sitting at home listening to Jack Benny with my kids! Raising intelligent, loving, sturdy children! Protecting some good woman! Dignity! Health! Love! Industry! Intelligence! Trust! Decency! High Spirits! Compassion! What the hell do I care about sensational sex? How can I be floundering like this over something so simple, so *silly*, as pussy! How absurd that I should have finally come down with VD! At my age! Because I'm sure of it: I have contracted something from that Lina! It is just a matter of waiting for the chancre to appear. But I won't wait, I can't: In Tel Aviv a doctor, first thing, before the chancre *or* the blindness sets in!

Only what about the dead girl back at the hotel? For she will have accomplished it by now, I'm sure. Thrown herself off the balcony in her underpants. Walked into the sea and drowned herself, wearing the world's tiniest bikini. No, she will take hemlock in the moonlit shadows of the Acropolis—in her Balenciaga evening gown! That empty-headed, exhibitionistic, suicidal twat! Don't worry, when she does it, it'll be photographable—it'll come out looking like an ad for ladies' lingerie! There she'll be, as usual, in the Sunday magazine section—only dead! I must turn back before I have this ridiculous suicide forever on my conscience! I should have telephoned Harpo! I didn't even think of it—just ran for *my* life. Gotten her to a phone to talk to her doctor. But would he have talked? I doubt it! That mute bastard, he *has* to, before she takes her unreversible revenge! MODEL SLITS THROAT IN AMPHITHEATRE; Medea *Interrupted by Suicide* . . . and they'll publish the note they find, more than likely in a bottle stuffed up her snatch. "Alexander Portnoy is responsible. He forced me to sleep with a whore and then wouldn't make me an honest woman. Mary Jane Reed." Thank God the moron can't spell! It'll all be Greek to those Greeks! *Hope*fully.

Running away! In flight, escaping again—and from what? From someone else who would have me a saint! Which I ain't! And do not want or intend to be! No, any guilt on my part is *comical*! I will not *hear* of it! If she kills herself— But that's not what she's about to do. No, it'll be more ghastly than that: she's going to telephone the Mayor! And that's why I'm running! But she wouldn't. But she *would*. She *will*! More than likely already has. Remember? *I'll expose you, Alex. I'll call long-distance to John Lindsay. I'll telephone Jimmy Breslin.* And she is crazy enough to do it! Breslin, that cop! That precinct station genius! Oh Jesus, *let* her be dead then! Jump, you ignorant destructive bitch—better you than me! Sure, all I need is she should start telephoning around to the wire services: I can see my father going out to the corner after dinner, picking up the *Newark News*—and at long last, the word SCANDAL printed in bold type above a picture of his darling son! Or turning on the seven o'clock news to watch the CBS correspondent in Athens interviewing The Monkey from her hospital bed. "Portnoy, that's right. Capital P. Then O. Then I think R. Oh, I can't remember the rest, but I swear on my wet pussy, Mr. Rudd, he made me sleep with a whore!" No, no, I am *not* exaggerating: think a moment about the character, or absence of same. Remember Las Vegas? Remember her desperation? Then you see that this wasn't just my conscience punishing me; no, whatever revenge I might imagine, she could imagine too. And will yet! Believe me, we have not heard the last of Mary Jane Reed. I was supposed to save her life—*and didn't*. Made her sleep with whores instead! So don't think we have heard the last word from her!

And there, to cause me to kick my ass even more, there all blue below me, the Aegean Sea. The Pumpkin's Aegean! My poetic American girl! Sophocles! Long ago! Oh, Pumpkin— baby, say it again, *Why would I want to do a thing like that?* Someone who knew who she was! Psychologically so intact as not to be in need of salvation or redemption by me! Not in need of conversion to my glorious faith! The poetry she used to read to me at Antioch, the education she was giving me in literature, a whole new perspective, an understanding of art and the artistic way . . . oh, why did I ever let her go! I can't believe it—because she wouldn't be *Jewish*? "The eternal note of sadness—" "The turbid ebb and flow of human misery—"

Only, is *this* human misery? I thought it was going to be loftier! *Dignified* suffering! *Meaningful* suffering—something perhaps along the line of Abraham Lincoln. Tragedy, not farce! Something a little more Sophoclean was what I had in mind. The Great Emancipator, and so on. It surely never crossed my mind that I would wind up trying to free from bondage nothing more than my own prick. LET MY PETER GO! There, that's Portnoy's slogan. That's the story of my life, all summed up in four heroic dirty words. A travesty! My politics, descended entirely to my putz! JERK-OFF ARTISTS OF THE WORLD UNITE! YOU HAVE NOTHING TO LOSE BUT YOUR BRAINS! The *freak* I am! Lover of no one and nothing! Unloved and unloving! And on the brink of becoming John Lindsay's Profumo!

So it seemed, an hour out of Athens.

—

Tel Aviv, Jaffa, Jerusalem, Beer-She'va, the Dead Sea, Sedom, 'Ein Gedi, then north to Caesarea, Haifa, Akko, Tiberias, Safed, the upper Galilee . . . and always it is more dreamy than real. Not that I courted the sensation either. I'd had enough of the improbable with my companion in Greece and Rome. No, to make some *sense* out of the impulse that had sent me running aboard the El Al flight to begin with, to convert myself from this bewildered runaway into a man once again—in control of my will, conscious of my intentions, doing as I wished, not as I must—I set off traveling about the country as though the trip had been undertaken deliberately, with forethought, desire, and for praiseworthy, if conventional, reasons. Yes, I would have (now that I was unaccountably here) what is called an educational experience. I would improve myself, which is my way, after all. Or was, wasn't it? Isn't that why I still read with my pencil in my hand? To *learn*? To become *better*? (than whom?) So, I studied maps in my bed, bought historical and archeological texts and read them with my meals, hired guides, rented cars—doggedly in that sweltering heat, I searched out and saw everything I could: tombs, synagogues, fortresses, mosques, shrines, harbors, ruins, the new ones, the old. I visited the Carmel Caves, the

Chagall windows (me and a hundred ladies from the Detroit Hadassah), the Hebrew University, the Bet She'an excavations —toured the green kibbutzim, the baked wastelands, the rugged border outposts in the mountains; I even climbed a little ways up Masada under the full artillery fire of the sun. And everything I saw, I found I could assimilate and understand. It was history, it was nature, it was art. Even the Negev, that hallucination, I experienced as real and of this world. A desert. No, what was incredible and strange to me, more novel than the Dead Sea, or even the dramatic wilderness of Tsin, where for an eerie hour I wandered in the light of the bleaching sun, between white rocks where (I learn from my guidebook) the tribes of Israel wandered for so long (where I picked up as a souvenir—and have in fact right here in my pocket—such a stone as my guide informed me Zipporah used to circumcise the son of Moses—) what gave my entire sojourn the air of the preposterous was one simple but wholly (to me) implausible fact: I am in a Jewish country. In this country, everybody is Jewish.

—

My dream begins as soon as I disembark. *I am in an airport where I have never been before and all the people I see— passengers, stewardesses, ticket sellers, porters, pilots, taxi drivers —are Jews.* Is that so unlike the dreams that your dreaming patients recount? Is that so unlike the kind of experience one has while asleep? But awake, who ever heard of such a thing? The writing on the walls is Jewish—Jewish graffiti! The *flag* is Jewish. The faces are the faces you see on Chancellor Avenue! The faces of my neighbors, my uncles, my teachers, the parents of my boyhood friends. Faces like my own face! only moving before a backdrop of white wall and blazing sun and spikey tropical foliage. And it ain't Miami Beach, either. No, the faces of Eastern Europe, but only a stone's throw from Africa! In their short pants the men remind me of the head counselors at the Jewish summer camps I worked at during college vacations —only this isn't summer camp, either. It's home! These aren't Newark high school teachers off for two months with a clipboard and a whistle in the Hopatcong mountains of New Jersey. These are (there's no other word!) the natives. Returned! This is where it all began! Just been away on a long vacation, that's all! Hey, here *we're* the WASPs! *My taxi passes through a big square surrounded by sidewalk cafés such as one might see in Paris or Rome. Only the cafés are crowded with Jews. The taxi overtakes a bus. I look inside its windows. More Jews. Including the driver. Including the policemen up ahead directing traffic! At the hotel I ask the clerk for a room. He has a thin mustache and speaks English as though he were Ronald Colman. Yet he is Jewish too.*

And now the drama thickens:

It is after midnight. Earlier in the evening, the promenade beside the sea was a gay and lively crush of Jews—Jews eating ices, Jews drinking soda pop, Jews conversing, laughing, walking together arm-in-arm. But now as I start back to my hotel, I find myself virtually alone. At the end of the promenade, which I must pass beyond to reach my hotel, I see five youths smoking cigarettes and talking. Jewish youths, of course. As I approach them, it becomes clear to me that they have been anticipating my arrival. One of them steps forward and addresses me in English. "What time is it?" I look at my watch and realize that they are not going to permit me to pass. They are going to assault me! But how can that be? If they are Jewish and I am Jewish, what motive can there be for them to do me any harm?

I must tell them that they are making a mistake. Surely they do not really want to treat me as a gang of anti-Semites would. "Pardon me," I say, and edge my body between them, wearing a stern expression on my pale face. One of them calls, "Mister, what time—?" whereupon I quicken my pace and continue rapidly to the hotel, unable to understand why they should have wished to frighten me so, when we are all Jews.

Hardly defies interpretation, wouldn't you say?

In my room I quickly remove my trousers and shorts and under a reading lamp examine my penis. I find the organ to be unblemished and without any apparent signs of disease, and yet I am not relieved. It may be that in certain cases (perhaps those that are actually most severe) there is never any outward manifestation of infection. Rather, the debilitating effects take place within the body, unseen and unchecked, until at last the progress of the disorder is irreversible, and the patient is doomed.

In the morning I am awakened by the noise from beyond my

window. It is just seven o'clock, yet when I look outside I see the beach already swarming with people. It is a startling sight at such an early hour, particularly as the day is Saturday and I was anticipating a sabbath mood of piety and solemnity to pervade the city. But the crowd of Jews—yet again!—is gay. I examine my member in the strong morning light and am—yet again—overcome with apprehension to discover that it appears to be in a perfectly healthy condition.

I leave my room to go and splash in the sea with the happy Jews. I bathe where the crowd is more dense. I am playing in a sea full of Jews! Frolicking, gamboling Jews! Look at their Jewish limbs moving through the Jewish water! Look at the Jewish children laughing, acting as if they own the place . . . Which they do! And the lifeguard, yet another Jew! Up and down the beach, so far as I can see, Jews—and more pouring in throughout the beautiful morning, as from a cornucopia. I stretch out on the beach, I close my eyes. Overhead I hear an engine: no fear, a Jewish plane. Under me the sand is warm: Jewish sand. I buy a Jewish ice cream from a Jewish vendor. "Isn't this something?" I say to myself. "A Jewish country!" But the idea is more easily expressed than understood; I cannot really grasp hold of it. Alex in Wonderland.

In the afternoon I befriend a young woman with green eyes and tawny skin who is a lieutenant in the Jewish Army. The Lieutenant takes me at night to a bar in the harbor area. The customers, she says, are mostly longshoremen. Jewish longshoremen? Yes. I laugh, and she asks me what's so funny. I am excited by her small, voluptuous figure nipped at the middle by the wide webbing of her khaki belt. But what a determined humorless self-possessed little thing! I don't know if she would allow me to order for her even if I spoke the language. "Which do you like better?" she asks me, after each of us had downed a bottle of Jewish beer, "tractors, or bulldozers, or tanks?" I laugh again.

I ask her back to my hotel. In the room we struggle, we kiss, we begin to undress, and promptly I lose my erection. "See," says The Lieutenant, as though confirmed now in her suspicion, "you don't like me. Not at all." "Yes, oh yes," I answer, "since I saw you in the sea, I do, I do, you are sleek as a little seal—" but then, in my shame, baffled and undone by my detumescence, I burst out—"but I may have a disease, you see. It wouldn't be fair." "Do you think that is funny too?" she hisses, and angrily puts her uniform back on and leaves.

—

Dreams? If only they had been! But I don't need dreams, Doctor, that's why I hardly have them—because I have this life instead. With me it all happens in broad daylight! The disproportionate and the melodramatic, this is my daily bread! The coincidences of dreams, the symbols, the terrifyingly laughable situations, the oddly ominous banalities, the accidents and humiliations, the bizarrely appropriate strokes of luck or misfortune that other people experience with their eyes shut, I get with mine open! Who else do you know whose mother actually threatened him with the dreaded knife? Who else was so lucky as to have the threat of castration so straight-forwardly put by his momma? Who else, on top of this mother, had a testicle that wouldn't descend? A nut that had to be coaxed and coddled, *persuaded*, drugged! to get it to come down and live in the scrotum like a man! Who else do you know broke a leg chasing *shikses*? Or came in his eye first time out? Or found a real live monkey right in the streets of New York, a girl with a passion for The Banana? Doctor, maybe other patients dream —with me, *everything happens.* I have a life *without* latent content. The dream thing *happens!* Doctor: *I couldn't get it up in the State of Israel!* How's *that* for symbolism, *bubi?* Let's see somebody beat that, for acting-out! Could not maintain an erection in The Promised Land! At least not when I needed it, not when I wanted it, not when there was something more desirable than my own hand to stick it into. But, as it turns out, you can't stick tapioca pudding into anything. Tapioca pudding I am offering this girl. Wet sponge cake! A thimbleful of something melted. And all the while that self-assured little lieutenant, so proudly flying those Israeli tits, prepared to be mounted by some tank commander!

And then again, only worse. My final downfall and humiliation—Naomi, The Jewish Pumpkin. The Heroine, that hardy, red-headed, freckled, ideological hunk of a girl! I picked her up hitchhiking down to Haifa from a kibbutz near the Lebanese border, where she had been visiting her parents. She was twenty-one years old, nearly six feet tall, and gave the impression that she was still growing. Her parents were Zionists from Philadelphia who had come to Palestine just before the outbreak of World War Two. After completing her Army service, Naomi had decided not to return to the kibbutz where she had been born and raised, but instead to join a commune of young native-born Israelis clearing boulders of black volcanic rock from a barren settlement in the mountains overlooking the boundary with Syria. The work was rugged, the living conditions were primitive, and there was always the danger of Syrian infiltrators slipping into the encampment at night, with hand grenades and land mines. And she loved it. An admirable and brave girl! Yes, a Jewish Pumpkin! *I am being given a second chance.*

Interesting. I associate her instantly with my lost Pumpkin, when in physical type she is, of course, my mother. Coloring, size, even temperament, it turned out—a real fault-finder, a professional critic of me. Must have perfection in her men. But all this I am blind to: the resemblance between this girl and the picture of my mother in her high school yearbook is something I do not even see.

Here's how unhinged and hysterical I was in Israel. Within minutes of picking her up on the road, I was seriously asking myself, "Why don't I marry her and stay? Why don't I go up to that mountain and start a new life?"

Right off we began making serious talk about mankind. Her conversation was replete with passionate slogans not unlike those of my adolescence. *A just society. The common struggle. Individual freedom. A socially productive life.* But how naturally she wore her idealism, I thought. Yes, this was my kind of girl, all right—innocent, good-hearted, *zaftig*, unsophisticated and unfucked-up. Of course! I don't want movie stars and mannequins and whores, or any combination thereof. I don't want a sexual extravaganza for a life, or a continuation of this masochistic extravaganza I've been living, either. No, I want simplicity, I want health, I want her!

She spoke English perfectly, if a little bookishly—just a hint of some kind of general European accent. I kept looking at her for signs of the American girl she would have been had her parents never left Philadelphia. *This might have been my sister*, I think, another big girl with high ideals. I can even imagine

Hannah having emigrated to Israel, had she not found Morty to rescue her. But who was there to rescue me? My *shikses*? No, no, I rescue *them*. No, my salvation is clearly in this Naomi! Her hair is worn like a child's, in two long braids—a ploy, of course, a dream-technique if ever there was one, designed to keep me from remembering outright that high school picture of Sophie Ginsky, who the boys called "Red," who would go so far with her big brown eyes and her clever head. In the evening, after spending the day (at my request) showing me around the ancient Arab city of Akko, Naomi pinned her braids up in a double coil around her head, like a *grand*mother, I remember thinking. "How unlike my model friend," I think, "with the wigs and the hairpieces, and the hours spent at Kenneth's. How my life would change! A new man!—with this woman!"

Her plan for herself was to camp out at night in a sleeping bag. She was on her week's vacation away from the settlement, traveling on a few pounds that her family had been able to give her for a birthday present. The more fanatical of her fellows, she told me, would never have accepted such a gift, and would probably disapprove of her for failing to do so. She re-created for me a discussion that had raged in her parents' kibbutz when she was still a little girl, over the fact that some people owned watches and others didn't. It was settled, after several impassioned meetings of the kibbutz membership, by deciding to rotate the watches every three months.

During the day, at dinner, then as we walked along the romantic harbor wall at Akko that night, I told her about my life. I asked if she would come back with me and have a drink at my hotel in Haifa. She said she would, she had much to say about my story. I wanted to kiss her then, but thought, "What if I *do* have some kind of venereal infection?" I still hadn't been to see a doctor, partly because of a reluctance to tell some stranger that I had had contact with a whore, but largely because I had no symptoms of any kind. Clearly nothing was wrong with me, and I didn't *need* a doctor. Nevertheless, when I turned to ask her back to the hotel, I resisted an impulse to press my lips against her pure socialistical mouth.

"American society," she said, dropping her knapsack and bedroll on the floor, and continuing the lecture she had begun as we drove around the bay to Haifa, "not only sanctions gross and unfair relations among men, but it encourages them. Now, can that be denied? No. Rivalry, competition, envy, jealousy, all that is malignant in human character is nourished by the system. Possessions, money, property—on such corrupt standards as these do you people measure happiness and success. Meanwhile," she said, perching herself cross-legged upon the bed, "great segments of your population are deprived of the minimal prerequisites for a decent life. Is that not true, too? Because your system is basically exploitive, inherently debasing and unjust. Consequently, Alex"—she used my name as a stern teacher would, there was the thrust of admonition in it—"there can never be anything resembling genuine equality in such an environment. And that is indisputable, you cannot help but agree, if you are at all honest.

"For instance, what did you accomplish with your quiz-scandal hearings? Anything? Nothing, if I may say so. You exposed the corruption of certain weak individuals. But as for the system that trained them in corruption, on that you had not the slightest effect. The system was unshaken. The system was untouched. And why? Because, Alex"—uh-oh, here it comes—"you are yourself as corrupted by the system as Mr. Charles Van Horn." (By gum, still imperfect! Dang!) "You are not the enemy of the system. You are not even a challenge to the system, as you seem to think. You are only one of its policemen, a paid employee, an accomplice. Pardon me, but I must speak the truth: you think you serve justice, but you are only a lackey of the bourgeoisie. You have a system inherently exploitive and unjust, inherently cruel and inhumane, heedless of human values, and your job is to make such a system appear legitimate and moral by acting as though justice, as though human rights and human dignity could actually exist in that society—when obviously no such thing is possible.

"You know, Alex"—what now?—"you know why I don't worry about who wears a watch, or about accepting five pounds as a gift from my 'prosperous' parents? You know why such arguments are silly and I have no patience with them? Because I know that inherently—do you understand, inherently!"—yes, I understand! English happens, oddly enough, to be *my* mother tongue!—"inherently the system in which I participate (and voluntarily, that is crucial too—voluntarily!), that that system is humane and just. As long as the community owns the means of production, as long as all needs are provided by the community, as long as no man has the opportunity to accumulate wealth or to live off the surplus value of another man's labor, then the essential character of the kibbutz is being maintained. No man is without dignity. In the broadest sense, there is equality. And that is what matters most."

"Naomi, I love you."

She narrowed those wide idealistic brown eyes. "How can you 'love' me? What are you saying?"

"I want to marry you."

Boom, she jumped to her feet. Pity the Syrian terrorist who tried to take her by surprise! "What is the *matter* with you? Is this supposed to be humorous?"

"Be my wife. Mother my children. Every *shtunk* with a picture window has children. *Why not me?* I carry the family name!"

"You drank too much beer at dinner. Yes, I think I should go."

"Don't!" And again told this girl I hardly knew, and didn't even like, how deeply in love with her I was. "Love"—oh, it makes me shudder!—"loooove," as though I could summon forth the feeling with the word.

And when she tried to leave I blocked the door. I pleaded with her not to go out and lie down on a clammy beach somewhere, when there was this big comfortable Hilton bed for the two of us to share. "I'm not trying to turn you into a bourgeois, Naomi. If the bed is too luxurious, we can do it on the floor."

"Sexual intercourse?" she replied. "With *you*?"

"Yes! With me! Fresh from my inherently unjust system! Me, the accomplice! Yes! Imperfect Portnoy!"

"Mr. Portnoy, excuse me, but between your silly jokes, if that is even what they are—"

Here a little struggle took place as I rushed her at the side of the bed. I reached for a breast, and with a sharp upward snap of the skull, she butted me on the underside of the jaw.

"Where the hell did you learn that," I cried out, "in the Army?"

"Yes."

I collapsed into my chair. "That's some training to give to girls."

"Do you know," she said, and without a trace of charity, "there is something very wrong with you."

"My tongue is bleeding, for one—!"

"You are the most unhappy person I have ever known. You are like a baby."

"No! Not so," but she waved aside any explanation I may have had to offer, and began to lecture me on my shortcomings as she had observed them that day.

"The way you disapprove of your life! Why do you do that? It is of no value for a man to disapprove of his life the way that you do. You seem to take some special pleasure, some pride, in making yourself the butt of your own peculiar sense of humor. I don't believe you actually want to improve your life. Everything you say is somehow always twisted, some way or another, to come out 'funny.' All day long the same thing. In some little way or other, everything is ironical, or self-depreciating. Self depreciating?"

"Self-deprecating. Self-mocking."

"Exactly! And you are a highly intelligent man—that is what makes it even more disagreeable. The contribution you could make! Such stupid self-deprecation! How disagreeable!"

"Oh, I don't know," I said, "self-deprecation is, after all, a classic form of Jewish humor."

"Not Jewish humor! No! *Ghetto* humor."

Not much love in that remark, I'll tell you. By dawn I had been made to understand that I was the epitome of what was most shameful in "the culture of the Diaspora." Those centuries and centuries of homelessness had produced just such disagreeable men as myself—frightened, defensive, self-deprecating, unmanned and corrupted by life in the gentile world. It was Diaspora Jews just like myself who had gone by the millions to the gas chambers without ever raising a hand against their persecutors, who did not know enough to defend their lives with their blood. The Diaspora! The very word made her furious.

When she finished I said, "Wonderful. Now let's fuck."

"You *are* disgusting!"

"Right! You begin to get the point, gallant Sabra! *You* go be righteous in the mountains, okay? *You* go be a model for mankind! Fucking Hebrew saint!"

"Mr. Portnoy," she said, raising her knapsack from the floor, "you are nothing but a self-hating Jew."

"Ah, but Naomi, maybe that's the best kind."

"Coward!"

"Tomboy."

"*Shlemiel!*"

And made for the door. Only I leaped from behind, and with a flying tackle brought this big red-headed didactic dish down with me onto the floor. I'll show her who's a *shlemiel!* And baby! And if I have VD? Fine! Terrific! All the better! Let her carry it secretly back in her bloodstream to the mountains! Let it spread forth from her unto all those brave and virtuous Jewish boys and girls! A dose of clap will do them all good! This is what it's like in the Diaspora, you saintly kiddies, this is what it's like in the exile! Temptation and disgrace! Corruption and self-mockery! Self-deprecation—and self-defecation too! Whining, hysteria, compromise, confusion, disease! Yes, Naomi, I am soiled, oh, I am impure—and also pretty fucking tired, my dear, of never being quite good enough for The Chosen People!

But what a battle she gave me, this big farm cunt! this ex-G.I.! This mother-substitute! Look, can that be so? Oh please, it can't be as simplistic as that! Not *me*! Or with a case like mine, is it actually that you can't be simplistic *enough*! Because she wore red hair and freckles, this makes her, according to my unconscious one-track mind, my mother? Just because she and the lady of my past are offspring of the same pale Polish strain of Jews? This then is the culmination of the Oedipal drama, Doctor? More farce, my friend! Too much to swallow, I'm afraid! *Oedipus Rex* is a famous tragedy, schmuck, not another joke! You're a sadist, you're a quack and a lousy comedian! I mean this is maybe going too far for a laugh, Doctor Spielvogel, Doctor Freud, Doctor Kronkite! How about a little homage, you bastards, to The Dignity of Man! *Oedipus Rex* is the most horrendous and *serious* play in the history of literature—it is not a gag!

Thank God, at any rate, for Heshie's weights. They became

mine after he died. I would carry them into the backyard, and out in the sunshine I would lift and lift and lift, back when I was fourteen and fifteen years old. "You're going to give yourself a *tsura* yet with those things," my mother would warn me from her bedroom window. "You're going to get a cold out there in that bathing suit." I sent away for booklets from Charles Atlas and Joe Bonomo. I lived for the sight of my torso swelling up in my bedroom mirror. I flexed under my clothes in school. I examined my forearms on the street corner for bulge. I admired my veins on the bus. Somebody some day would take a swing at me and my deltoids, and they would live to regret it! But nobody swung, thank God.

Till Naomi! For her, then, I had done all that puffing and quivering under the disapproving gaze of my mother. That isn't to say that she still didn't have it over me in the calves and the thighs—but in the shoulders and chest I had the edge, and forced her body down beneath me—and shot my tongue into her ear, tasting there the grit of our day's journey, all that holy soil. "Oh, I am going to fuck you, Jew girl," I whispered evilly.

"You are crazy!" and heaved up against me with all her considerable strength. "You are a lunatic on the loose!"

"No, oh no," I told her, growling from my throat, "oh no, you have got a lesson to learn, Naomi," and pressed, pressed hard, to teach my lesson: O you virtuous Jewess, the tables are turned, *tsatskeleh*! *You* on the defensive now, Naomi— explaining your vaginal discharge to the entire kibbutz! You think they got worked up over those watches! Wait'll they get a whiff of this! What I wouldn't give to be at that meeting when you get arraigned on the charge of contaminating the pride and future of Zion! Then perhaps you'll come to have the proper awe for us fallen psychoneurotic Jewish men! Socialism exists, but so too do spirochetes, my love! So here's your introduction, dear, to the slimier side of things. Down, down with these patriotic khaki shorts, spread your chops, blood of my blood, unlock your fortressy thighs, open wide that messianic Jewish hole! Make ready, Naomi, I am about to poison your organs of reproduction! I am about to change the future of the race!

But of course I couldn't. Licked her earholes, sucked at her unwashed neck, sank my teeth into the coiled braids of hair . . . and then, even as resistance may actually have begun to recede under my assault, I rolled off of her and came to rest, defeated, against the wall—on my back. "It's no good," I said, "I can't get a hard-on in this place."

She stood up. Stood over me. Got her wind. Looked *down*. It occurred to me that she was going to plant the sole of her sandal on my chest. Or maybe proceed to kick the shit out of me. I remembered myself as a little schoolboy pasting all those reinforcements into my notebook. How has it come to this?

"'Im-po-tent in Is-rael, da da daaah,'" to the tune of "Lullaby in Birdland."

"Another joke?" she asked.

"And another. And another. Why disclaim my life?"

Then she said a kind thing. She could afford to, of course, way up there. "You should go home."

"Sure, that's what I need, back into the exile."

And way way up there, she grinned. That healthy, monumental Sabra! The work-molded legs, the utilitarian shorts, the battle-scarred buttonless blouse—the beneficent, victorious smile! And at her crusty, sandaled feet, this . . . this what? This *son*! This *boy*! This *baby*! Alexander Portnoise! Portnose! Portnoy-oy-oy-oy-oy!

"Look at you," I said, "way up there. How big big women are! Look at you—how patriotic! You really *like* victory, don't you, honey? Know how to take it in your stride! Wow, are you guiltless! Terrific, really—an honor to have met you. Look, take me with you, Heroine! Up to the mountain. I'll clear boulders till I drop, if that's what it takes to be good. Because why not be good, and good and good and good—right? Live only according to principle! Without compromise! Let the other guy be the villain, right? Let the *goyim* make a shambles, let the blame fall solely on them. If I was born to be austere about myself, so be it! A grueling and gratifying ethical life, opulent with self-sacrifice, voluptuous with restraint! Ah, sounds good. Ah, I can just taste those rocks! What do you say, take me back with you—into the pure Portnovian existence!"

"You should go home."

"On the contrary! I should stay. Yes, stay! Buy a pair of those khaki short pants—become a man!"

"Do as you wish," she said. "I am leaving you."

"No, Heroine, no," I cried—for I was actually beginning to like her a little. "Oh, what a waste."

She liked that. She looked at me very victoriously, as though I had finally confessed to the truth about myself. Screw her. "I mean, not being able to fuck away at a big healthy girl like you."

She shivered with loathing. "Tell me, please, *why* must you use that word all the time?"

"Don't the boys say 'fuck' up in the mountains?"

"No," she answered, condescendingly, "not the way that you do."

"Well," I said, "I suppose they're not as rich with rage as I am. With contempt." And I lunged for her leg. Because never enough. NEVER! I have TO HAVE.

But have *what*?

"No!" she screamed down at me.

"Yes!"

"*No!*"

"Then," I pleaded, as she began to drag me by her powerful leg across toward the door, "at least let me eat your pussy. I know I can still do that."

"Pig!"

And kicked. And landed! Full force with that pioneer's leg, just below the heart. The blow I had been angling for? Who knows what I was up to? Maybe I was up to nothing. Maybe I was just being myself. Maybe that's all I really am, a lapper of cunt, the slavish mouth for some woman's hole. Eat! And so be it! Maybe the wisest solution for me is to live on all fours! Crawl through life feasting on pussy, and leave the righting of wrongs and the fathering of families to the upright creatures! Who needs monuments erected in his name, when there is this banquet walking the streets?

Crawl through life then—if I have a life left! My head went spinning, the vilest juices rose in my throat. Ow, my heart! And in Israel! Where other Jews find refuge, sanctuary and peace, Portnoy now perishes! Where other Jews flourish, I now expire! And all I wanted was to give a little pleasure—and make a little for myself. Why, why can I not have some pleasure without the retribution following behind like a caboose! Pig? Who, *me*? And all at once it happens again, I am impaled again upon the long ago, what was, what will never be! The door slams, she is gone—my salvation! my kin!—and I am whimpering on the floor with MY MEMORIES! My endless childhood! Which I won't relinquish—or which won't relinquish me! Which is it! Remembering radishes—the ones I raised so lovingly in my Victory Garden. In that patch of yard beside our cellar door. *My* kibbutz. Radishes, parsley, carrots— yes, I am a patriot too, you, only in another place! (Where I *also* don't feel at home!) But the silver foil I collected, how *about* that? The newspapers I carted to school! My booklet of defense stamps, all neatly pasted in rows so as to smash the Axis! My model airplanes—my Piper Cub, my Hawker Hurricane, my Spitfire! How can this be happening to that good kid I was, with my love for the R.A.F. and the Four Freedoms! My hope for Yalta and Dumbarton Oaks! My prayers for the U.N.O.! Die? *Why?* Punishment? *For what?* Impotent? *For what good reason?*

The Monkey's Revenge. Of course.

"ALEXANDER PORTNOY, FOR DEGRADING THE HUMANITY OF MARY JANE REED TWO NIGHTS RUNNING IN ROME, AND FOR OTHER CRIMES TOO NUMEROUS TO MENTION INVOLVING THE EXPLOITATION OF HER CUNT, YOU ARE SENTENCED TO A TERRIBLE CASE OF IMPOTENCE. ENJOY YOURSELF." "But, Your Honor, she is of age, after all, a consenting adult—" "DON'T BULLSHIT ME WITH LEGALISMS, PORTNOY. YOU KNEW RIGHT FROM WRONG. YOU KNEW YOU WERE DEGRADING ANOTHER HUMAN BEING. AND FOR THAT, WHAT YOU DID AND HOW YOU DID IT, YOU ARE JUSTLY SENTENCED TO A LIMP DICK. GO FIND ANOTHER WAY TO HURT A PERSON." "But if I may, Your Honor, she was perhaps somewhat degraded before I met her. Need I say more than 'Las Vegas'?" "OH, WONDERFUL DEFENSE, JUST WONDERFUL. GUARANTEED TO SOFTEN THE COURT'S JUDGMENT. THAT'S HOW WE TREAT UNFORTUNATES, EH, COMMISSIONER? THAT'S GIVING A PERSON THE OPPORTUNITY TO BE DIGNIFIED AND HUMAN ACCORDING TO YOUR DEFINITION? SON OF A BITCH!" "Your Honor, please, if I may approach the bench—what after all was I doing but just trying to have . . . well, what? . . . a little fun, that's all." "OH, YOU *SON OF A BITCH!*" Well, why, damn it, can't I have some *fun*! Why is the smallest thing I do for pleasure immediately illicit—while the rest of the world rolls laughing in the mud! *Pig?* She ought to see the charges and complaints that are filed in my office in a single morning: what people do to one another, out of greed and hatred! For dough! For power! For spite! For *nothing*! What they put a *shvartze* through to get a mortgage on a home! A man wants what my father used to call an umbrella for a rainy day—and you ought to see those pigs go to work on him! And I mean the real pigs, the pros! Who do you think got the banks to begin to recruit Negroes and Puerto Ricans for jobs in this city, to send personnel people to interview applicants in Harlem? To do that simple thing? This *pig*, lady —Portnoy! You want to talk pigs, come down to the office, take a look through my In basket any morning of the week, I'll show you pigs! The things that other men do—and get away with! And with never a second thought! To inflict a wound upon a defenseless person makes them *smile*, for Christ's sake, gives a little *lift* to their day! The lying, the scheming, the bribing, the thieving—the larceny, Doctor, conducted without batting an eye. The indifference! The total moral indifference! They don't come down from the crimes they commit with so much as a case of indigestion! But me, I dare to steal a slightly unusual kind of a hump, and while away on my *vacation*—and now I can't get it up! I mean, God forbid I should tear the tag from my mattress that says, "Do Not Remove Under Penalty of Law"—what would they give me for that, the chair? It makes me want to *scream*, the ridiculous disproportion of the guilt! May I? Will that shake them up too much out in the waiting room? Because that's maybe what I need most of all, to howl. A pure howl, without any more words between me and it! "This is the police speaking. You're surrounded, Portnoy. You better come on out and pay your debt to society." "Up society's ass, Copper!" "Three to come out with those hands of yours up in the air, Mad Dog, or else we come in after you, guns blazing. One." "Blaze, you bastard cop, what do I give a shit? I tore the tag off my mattress—" "Two." "—But at least while I lived, *I lived big!*"

Aaaaaaaaaaaaaaaaaaaaaaaaaaaaaaaaaaaaaaaaaaaaaaaaaaaaaaaaaa-
aaaaaaaaaaaaaaaaaaaaaaaaaaaaaaaaaaaaaaaaaaaaaaaaaaaaaaaaaaaaaa-
aaaaaaaaaaaaaaaaaaaaaaaaaaaaaaaaaaaaaaaaaaaaaaaaaaaaaaaaaaaaaa-
aaaaaaaaaaaaaaaaaaaaaaaaaaaaaaaaaaaaaaaaaaaaaaaaaaaaaaaaaaaaaa-
aaaaaaaaaaaaaaaaaaaaaaaaaaaaaaaahhhh!!!!!

PUNCH LINE

So [*said the doctor*]. Now vee may perhaps to begin. Yes?

OUR GANG

(Starring Tricky and His Friends)

To MILDRED MARTIN of Bucknell University,
ROBERT MAURER now of Antioch College,
and NAPIER WILT of the University of Chicago—
three teachers to whom I remain particularly
grateful for the instruction and encouragement
they gave me

. . . And I remember frequent Discourses with my Master concerning the Nature of Manhood, in other Parts of the World; having Occasion to talk of *Lying*, and *false Representation*, it was with much Difficulty that he comprehended what I meant; although he had otherwise a most acute Judgment. For he argued thus; That the Use of Speech was to make us understand one another, and to receive Information of Facts; now if anyone *said the Thing which was not*, these Ends were defeated; because I cannot properly be said to understand him; and I am so far from receiving Information, that he leaves me worse than in Ignorance; for I am led to believe a Thing *Black* when it is *White*, and *Short* when it is *Long*. And these were all the Notions he had concerning that Faculty of Lying, so perfectly well understood, and so universally practised among human Creatures

—Jonathan Swift, *A Voyage to the Houyhnhnms*, 1726

. . . one ought to recognize that the present political chaos is connected with the decay of language, and that one can probably bring about some improvement by starting at the verbal end. . . . Political language—and with variations this is true of all political parties, from Conservatives to Anarchists—is designed to make lies sound truthful and murder respectable, and to give an appearance of solidity to pure wind.

—George Orwell, "Politics and the English Language," 1946

Contents

1. *Tricky Comforts a Troubled Citizen* 475

2. *Tricky Holds a Press Conference* 480

3. *Tricky Has Another Crisis; or, The Skull Session* 489

4. *Tricky Addresses the Nation (The Famous "Something Is Rotten in the State of Denmark" Speech)* 526

5. *The Assassination of Tricky* 555

6. *On the Comeback Trail; or Tricky in Hell* 589

FROM PERSONAL AND RELIGIOUS BELIEFS I CONSIDER ABORTIONS AN UNACCEPTABLE FORM OF POPULATION CONTROL. FURTHERMORE, UNRESTRICTED ABORTION POLICIES, OR ABORTION ON DEMAND, I CANNOT SQUARE WITH MY PERSONAL BELIEF IN THE SANCTITY OF HUMAN LIFE— INCLUDING THE LIFE OF THE YET UNBORN. FOR, SURELY, THE UNBORN HAVE RIGHTS ALSO, RECOGNIZED IN LAW, RECOGNIZED EVEN IN PRINCIPLES EXPOUNDED BY THE UNITED NATIONS.

RICHARD NIXON,
SAN CLEMENTE, APRIL 3, 1971

1

Tricky Comforts a Troubled Citizen

CITIZEN: Sir, I want to congratulate you for coming out on April 3 for the sanctity of human life, including the life of the yet unborn. That required a lot of courage, especially in light of the November election results.

TRICKY: Well, thank you. I know I could have done the popular thing, of course, and come out *against* the sanctity of human life. But frankly I'd rather be a one-term President and do what I believe is right than to be a two-term President by taking an easy position like that. After all, I have got my conscience to deal with, as well as the electorate.

CITIZEN: Your conscience, sir, is a marvel to us all.

TRICKY: Thank you.

CITIZEN: I wonder if I may ask you a question having to do with Lieutenant Calley and his conviction for killing twenty-two Vietnamese civilians at My Lai.

TRICKY: Certainly. I suppose you are bringing that up as another example of my refusal to do the popular thing.

CITIZEN: How's that, sir?

TRICKY: Well, in the wake of the public outcry against that conviction, the popular thing—the most popular thing by far—would have been for me, as Commander-in-Chief, to have convicted the twenty-two unarmed civilians of conspiracy to murder Lieutenant Calley. But if you read your papers, you'll see I refused to do that, and chose only to review the question of his guilt, and not theirs. As I said, I'd rather be a one-term President. And may I make one thing more perfectly clear, while we're on the subject of Vietnam? I am not going to interfere in the internal affairs of another country. If President Thieu has sufficient evidence and wishes to try those twenty-two My Lai villagers posthumously, according to some Vietnamese law having to do with ancestor worship, that is his business. But I assure you, I in no way intend to interfere with the workings of the Vietnamese system of justice. I think President Thieu, and the duly elected Saigon officials, can "hack" it alone in the law and order department.

CITIZEN: Sir, the question that's been troubling me is this. Inasmuch as I share your belief in the sanctity of human life—

TRICKY: Good for you. I'll bet you're quite a football fan, too.

CITIZEN: I am, sir. Thank you, sir . . . But inasmuch as I feel as you do about the unborn, I am seriously troubled by the possibility that Lieutenant Calley may have committed an abortion. I hate to say this, Mr. President, but I am seriously troubled when I think that one of those twenty-two Vietnamese civilians Lieutenant Calley killed may have been a pregnant woman.

TRICKY: Now just one minute. We have a tradition in the courts of this land that a man is innocent until he is proven guilty. There were babies in that ditch at My Lai, and we know there were women of all *ages*, but I have not seen a single document that suggests the ditch at My Lai contained a *pregnant* woman.

CITIZEN: But what *if*, sir—what *if* one of the twenty-two was a pregnant woman? Suppose that were to come to light in your judicial review of the lieutenant's conviction. In that you personally believe in the sanctity of human life, including the life of the yet unborn, couldn't such a fact seriously prejudice you against Lieutenant Calley's appeal? I have to admit that as an opponent of abortion, it would have a profound effect upon me.

TRICKY: Well, it's very honest of you to admit it. But as a trained lawyer, I think I might be able to go at the matter in a somewhat less emotional manner. First off, I would have to ask whether Lieutenant Calley was *aware* of the fact that the woman in question was pregnant *before* he killed her. Clearly, if she was not yet "showing," I think you would in all fairness have to conclude that the lieutenant could have had no knowledge of her pregnancy, and thus, in no sense of the word, would he have committed an abortion.

CITIZEN: What if she *told* him she was pregnant?

TRICKY: Good question. She might indeed have tried to tell

him. But in that Lieutenant Calley is an American who speaks only English, and the My Lai villager is a Vietnamese who speaks only Vietnamese, there could have been no possible means of verbal communication. And as for sign language, I don't believe we can hang a man for failing to understand what must surely have been the gestures of a hysterical, if not deranged, woman.

CITIZEN: No, that wouldn't be fair, would it.

TRICKY: In short then, if the woman was not "showing," Lieutenant Calley could *not* be said to have engaged in an unacceptable form of population control, and it would be possible for me to square what he did with my personal belief in the sanctity of human life, including the life of the yet unborn.

CITIZEN: But, sir, what if she *was* "showing"?

TRICKY: Well then, as good lawyers we would have to ask another question. Namely: did Lieutenant Calley believe the woman to be pregnant, or did he, mistakenly, in the heat of the moment, assume that she was just stout? It's all well and good for us to be Monday Morning My Lai Quarterbacks, you know, but there's a war going on out there, and you cannot always expect an officer rounding up unarmed civilians to be able to distinguish between an ordinary fat Vietnamese woman and one who is in the middle, or even the late, stages of pregnancy. Now if the pregnant ones would wear maternity clothes, of course, that would be a great help to our boys. But in that they don't, in that all of them seem to go around all day in their pajamas, it is almost impossible to tell the men from the women, let alone the pregnant from the nonpregnant. Inevitably then—and this is just one of those unfortunate things about a war of this kind—there is going to be confusion on this whole score of who is who out there. I understand that we are doing all we can to get into the hamlets with American-style maternity clothes for the pregnant women to wear so as to make them more distinguishable to the troops at the massacres, but, as you know, these people have their own ways and will not always consent to do even what is clearly in their own interest. And, of course, we have no intention of forcing them. That, after all, is why we are in Vietnam in the first place—to give these people the right to choose their own way of life, in accordance with *their* own beliefs and customs.

CITIZEN: In other words, sir, if Lieutenant Calley assumed the woman was simply fat, and killed her under that assumption, that would still square with your personal belief in the sanctity of human life, including the life of the yet unborn.

TRICKY: Absolutely. If I find that he assumed she was simply overweight, I give you my utmost assurance, I will in no way be prejudiced against his appeal.

CITIZEN: But, sir, suppose, just *suppose*, that he *did* know she was pregnant.

TRICKY: Well, we are down to the heart of the matter now, aren't we?

CITIZEN: I'm afraid so, sir.

TRICKY: Yes, we are down to this issue of "abortion on demand," which, admittedly, is totally unacceptable to me, on the basis of my personal and religious beliefs.

CITIZEN: Abortion on *demand*?

TRICKY: If this Vietnamese woman presented herself to Lieutenant Calley for abortion . . . let's assume, for the sake of argument, she was one of those girls who goes out and has a good time and then won't own up to the consequences; unfortunately, we have them here just as they have them over there—the misfits, the bums, the tramps, the few who give the many a bad name . . . but if this woman presented herself to Lieutenant Calley for abortion, with some kind of note, say, that somebody had written for her in English, and Lieutenant Calley, let's say, in the heat and pressure of the moment, performed the abortion, during the course of which the woman died . . .

CITIZEN: Yes. I think I follow you so far.

TRICKY: Well, I just have to wonder if the woman isn't herself equally as guilty as the lieutenant—if she is not more so. I just have to wonder if this isn't a case for the Saigon courts, after all. Let's be perfectly frank: you cannot die of an abortion, if you don't go looking for the abortion to begin with. If you have not gotten yourself in an abortion *predicament* to begin with. Surely that's perfectly clear.

CITIZEN: It is, sir.

TRICKY: Consequently, even if Lieutenant Calley did participate in a case of "abortion on demand," it would seem to me, speaking strictly as a lawyer, mind you, that there are numerous extenuating factors to consider, not the least of which is the attempt to perform a surgical operation under battlefield conditions. I would think that more than one medic has been cited for doing less.

CITIZEN: Cited for what?

TRICKY: Bravery, of course.

CITIZEN: But . . . but, Mr. President, what if it wasn't "abortion on demand"? What if Lieutenant Calley gave her an abortion without her demanding one, or even asking for one—or even wanting one?

TRICKY: As an outright form of population control, you mean?

CITIZEN: Well, I was thinking more along the lines of an outright form of murder.

TRICKY (*reflecting*): Well, of course, that is a very iffy question, isn't it? What we lawyers call a hypothetical instance—isn't it? If you will remember, we are only *supposing* there to have been a pregnant woman in that ditch at My Lai to begin with. Suppose there *wasn't* a pregnant woman in that ditch —which, in fact, seems from all evidence to have been the case. We are then involved in a totally academic discussion.

CITIZEN: Yes, sir. If so, we are.

TRICKY: Which doesn't mean it hasn't been of great value to me, nonetheless. In my review of Lieutenant Calley's case, I will now be particularly careful to inquire whether there is so much as a single shred of evidence that one of those twenty-two in that ditch at My Lai was a pregnant woman. And if there is—if I should find in the evidence against the lieutenant anything whatsoever that I cannot square with my personal belief in the sanctity of human life, including the life of the yet unborn, I will disqualify myself as a judge and pass the entire matter on to the Vice President.

CITIZEN: Thank you, Mr. President. I think we can all sleep better at night knowing that.

2

Tricky Holds a Press Conference

M R. ASSLICK: Sir, as regards your San Dementia statement
of April 3, the discussion it provoked seems now to
have centered on your unequivocal declaration that you are
a firm believer in the rights of the unborn. Many seem to
believe that you are destined to be to the unborn what
Martin Luther King was to the black people of America, and
the late Robert F. Charisma to the disadvantaged chicanos
and Puerto Ricans of the country. There are those who say
that your San Dementia statement will go down in the history books alongside Dr. King's famous "I have a dream"
address. Do you find these comparisons apt?

TRICKY: Well, of course, Mr. Asslick, Martin Luther King was a
very great man, as we all must surely recognize now that he
is dead. He was a great leader in the struggle for equal rights
for his people, and yes, I do believe he'll find a place in history. But of course we must not forget he was not the President of the United States, as I am, empowered by the
Constitution, as I am; and this is an important distinction to
bear in mind. Working *within* the Constitution I think I will
be able to accomplish far more for the unborn of this *entire*
nation than did Dr. King working *outside* the Constitution
for the born of *a single race*. This is meant to be no criticism
of Dr. King, but just a simple statement of fact.

Now, of course I am well aware that Dr. King died a
martyr's tragic death—so let me then make one thing very
clear to my enemies and the enemies of the unborn: let there
be no mistake about it, what they did to Martin Luther
King, what they did to Robert F. Charisma and to John F.
Charisma before him, great Americans all, is not for a moment going to deter me from engaging in the struggle that
lies ahead. I will not be intimidated by extremists or mili-

tants or violent fanatics from bringing justice and equality to those who live in the womb. And let me make one thing more perfectly clear: I am not just talking about the rights of the fetus. I am talking about the microscopic embryos as well. If ever there was a group in this country that was "disadvantaged," in the sense that they are utterly without representation or a voice in our national government, it is not the blacks or the Puerto Ricans or the hippies or what-have-you, all of whom have their spokesmen, but these infinitesimal creatures up there on the placenta.

You know, we all watch our TV and we see the demonstrators and we see the violence, because, unfortunately, that is the kind of thing that makes the news. But how many of us realize that throughout this great land of ours, there are millions upon millions of embryos going through the most complex and difficult changes in form and structure, and all this they accomplish without waving signs for the camera and disrupting traffic and throwing paint and using foul language and dressing in outlandish clothes. Yes, Mr. Daring.

MR. DARING: But what about those fetuses, sir, that the Vice President has labeled "troublemakers"? I believe he was referring specifically to those who start in kicking around the fifth month. Do you agree that they are "malcontents" and "ingrates"? And if so, what measures do you intend to take to control them?

TRICKY: Well, first off, Mr. Daring, I believe we are dealing here with some very fine distinctions of a legal kind. Now, fortunately (*impish endearing smile*) I happen to be a lawyer and have the kind of training that enables me to make these fine distinctions. (*Back to serious business*) I think we have to be very very careful here—and I am sure the Vice President would agree with me—to distinguish between two kinds of activity: *kicking* in the womb, to which the Vice President was specifically referring, and *moving* in the womb. You see, the Vice President did not say, despite what you may have heard on television, that *all* fetuses who are active in the womb are troublemakers. Nobody in this Administration believes that. In fact, I have just today spoken with both Attorney General Malicious and with Mr. Heehaw at the

FBI, and we are all in agreement that a certain amount of movement in the womb, after the fifth month, is not only inevitable but *desirable* in a normal pregnancy.

But as for this other matter, I assure you, this administration does not intend to sit idly by and do nothing while American women are being kicked in the stomach by a bunch of violent five-month-olds. Now by and large, and I cannot emphasize this enough, our American unborn are as wonderful a group of unborn as you can find anywhere. But there are these violent few that the Vice President has characterized, and I don't think unjustly, in his own impassioned rhetoric, as "troublemakers" and "malcontents"—and the Attorney General has been instructed by me to take the appropriate action against them.

MR. DARING: If I may, sir, what sort of action will that be? Will there be arrests made of violent fetuses? And if so, how exactly will this be carried out?

TRICKY: I think I can safely say, Mr. Daring, that we have the finest law enforcement agencies in the world. I am quite sure that Attorney General Malicious can solve whatever procedural problems may arise. Mr. Respectful.

MR. RESPECTFUL: Mr. President, with all the grave national and international problems that press continually upon you, can you tell us why you have decided to devote yourself to this previously neglected issue of fetal rights? You seem pretty fired up on this issue, sir—why is that?

TRICKY: Because, Mr. Respectful, I will not tolerate injustice in any area of our national life. Because ours is a just society, not merely for the rich and the privileged, but for the most powerless among us as well. You know, you hear a lot these days about Black Power and Female Power, Power this and Power that. But what about Prenatal Power? Don't they have rights too, membranes though they may be? I for one think they do, and I intend to fight for them. Mr. Shrewd.

MR. SHREWD: As you must know, Mr. President, there are those who contend that you are guided in this matter solely by political considerations. Can you comment on that?

TRICKY: Well, Mr. Shrewd, I suppose that is their cynical way of describing my plan to introduce a proposed constitu-

tional amendment that would extend the vote to the unborn in time for the '72 elections.

MR. SHREWD: I believe that is what they have in mind, sir.
They contend that by extending the vote to the unborn you
will neutralize the gains that may accrue to the Democratic
Party by the voting age having been lowered to eighteen.
They say your strategists have concluded that even if you
should lose the eighteen-to-twenty-one-year-old vote, you
can still win a second term if you are able to carry the South,
the state of California, and the embryos and fetuses from
coast to coast. Is there any truth to this "political" analysis
of your sudden interest in Prenatal Power?

TRICKY: Mr. Shrewd, I'd like to leave that to you—and to our
television viewers—to judge, by answering your question in
a somewhat personal manner. I assure you I am conversant
with the opinions of the experts. Many of them are men
whom I respect, and surely they have the right to say whatever they like, though of course one always hopes it will be
in the national interest . . . But let me remind you, and all
Americans, because this is a fact that seems somehow to
have been overlooked in this whole debate: I am no Johnny-
come-lately to the problem of the rights of the unborn. The
simple fact of the matter, and it is in the record for all to see,
is that I myself was once unborn, in the great state of California. Of course, you wouldn't always know this from what
you see on television or read in the papers (*impish endearing
smile*) that some of you gentlemen write for, but it happens
nonetheless to be the truth. (*Back to serious business*) I was
an unborn Quaker, as a matter of fact.

And let me remind you—since it seems necessary to do
so, in the face of the vicious and mindless attacks upon him
—Vice President What's-his-name was also unborn once, an
unborn Greek-American, and proud to have been one. We
were just talking about that this morning, how he was once
an unborn Greek-American, and all that has meant to him.
And so too was Secretary Lard unborn and so was Secretary
Codger unborn, and the Attorney General—why, I could
go right on down through my cabinet and point out to you
one fine man after another who was once unborn. Even

Secretary Fickle, with whom as you know I had my differences of opinion, was unborn when he was here with us on the team.

And if you look among the leadership of the Republican Party in the House and the Senate, you will find men who long before their election to public office were unborn in just about every region of this country, on farms, in industrial cities, in small towns the length and breadth of this great republic. My own wife was once unborn. As you may recall, my children were both unborn.

So when they say that Dixon has turned to the issue of the unborn just for the sake of the votes . . . well, I ask only that you consider this list of the previously unborn with whom I am associated in both public and private life, and decide for yourself. In fact, I think you are going to find, Mr. Shrewd, with each passing day, people around this country coming to realize that in this administration the fetuses and embryos of America have at last found their voice. Miss Charmin', I believe you had your eyebrows raised.

MISS CHARMIN': I was just going to say, sir, that of course President Lyin' B. Johnson was unborn, too, before he came to the White House—and he was a Democrat. Could you comment on that?

TRICKY: Miss Charmin', I would be the first to applaud my predecessor in this high office for having been unborn. I have no doubt that he was an outstanding fetus down there in Texas before he came into public life. I am not claiming that my administration is the first in history to be cognizant of the issue of fetal rights. I am saying that we intend to do something about them. Mr. Practical.

MR. PRACTICAL: Mr. President, I'd like to ask you to comment upon the scientific problems entailed in bringing the vote to the unborn.

TRICKY: Well, of course, Mr. Practical, you have hit the nail right on the head with the word "scientific." This is a scientific problem of staggering proportions—let's make no mistake about it. Moreover, I fully expect there are those who are going to say in tomorrow's papers that it is impossible, unfeasible, a utopian dream, and so on. But as you remember, when President Charisma came before the Congress in

1961, and announced that this country would put a man on the moon before the end of the decade, there were many who were ready to label him an impossible dreamer, too. But we did it. With American know-how and American teamwork, we did it. And so too do I have every confidence that our scientific and technological people are going to dedicate themselves to bringing the vote to the unborn—and not before the decade is out either, but before November of 1972.

MR. PRACTICAL: Can you give us some idea, sir, how much a crash program like this will cost?

TRICKY: Mr. Practical, I will be submitting a proposed budget to the Congress within the next ten days, but let me say this: you cannot achieve greatness without sacrifice. The program of research and development such as my scientific advisers have outlined cannot be bought "cheap." After all, what we are talking about here is nothing less than the fundamental principle of democracy: the vote. I cannot believe that the members of the Congress of the United States are going to play party politics when it comes to taking a step like this, which will be an advance not only for our nation, but for all mankind.

You just cannot imagine, for instance, the impact that this is going to have on the people in the underdeveloped countries. There are the Russians and the Chinese, who don't even allow adults to vote, and here we are in America, investing billions and billions of the taxpayers' dollars in a scientific project designed to extend the franchise to people who cannot see or talk or hear or even think, in the ordinary sense of the word. It would be a tragic irony indeed, and as telling a sign as I can imagine of national confusion and even hypocrisy, if we were willing to send our boys to fight and die in far-off lands so that defenseless peoples might have the right to choose the kinds of government they want in free elections, and then we were to turn around here at home and continue to deny that very same right to an entire segment of our population, just because they happen to live on the placenta or in the uterus, instead of New York City. Mr. Catch-Me-in-a-Contradiction.

MR. CATCH-ME-IN-A-CONTRADICTION: Mr. President, what startles me is that up until today you have been characterized, and not unwillingly, I think, as someone who, if he is not completely out of touch with the styles and ideas of the young, has certainly been skeptical of their wisdom. Doesn't this constitute, if I may use the word, a radical about-face, coming out now for the rights of those who are not simply "young" but actually in the gestation period?

TRICKY: Well, I am glad you raised that point, because I think it shows once and for all just how flexible I am, and how I am always willing to listen and respond to an appeal from *any* minority group, no matter how powerless, just so long as it is reasonable, and is not accompanied by violence and foul language and throwing paint. If ever there was proof that you don't have to camp on the White House lawn to get the President's attention away from a football game, I think it is in the example of these little organisms. I tell you, they have really impressed me with their silent dignity and politeness. I only hope that all Americans will come to be as proud of our unborn as I am.

MR. FASCINATED: Mr. President, I am fascinated by the technological aspect. Can you give us just an inkling of how exactly the unborn will go about casting their ballots? I'm particularly fascinated by these embryos on the placenta, who haven't even developed nervous systems yet, let alone limbs such as we use in an ordinary voting machine.

TRICKY: Well, first off, let me remind you that nothing in our Constitution denies a man the right to vote just because he is physically handicapped. That isn't the kind of country we have here. We have many wonderful handicapped people in this country, but of course, they're not "news" the way the demonstrators are.

MR. FASCINATED: I wasn't suggesting, sir, that just because these embryos don't have central nervous systems they should be denied the right to vote—I was thinking again of the fantastic *mechanics* of it. How, for instance, will the embryos be able to weigh the issues and make intelligent choices from among the candidates, if they are not able to read the newspapers or watch the news on television?

TRICKY: Well, it seems to me that you have actually touched upon the very strongest claim that the unborn have for enfranchisement, and why it is such a crime they have been denied the vote for so long. Here, at long last, we have a great bloc of voters who simply are not going to be taken in by the lopsided and distorted versions of the truth that are presented to the American public through the various media. Mr. Reasonable.

MR. REASONABLE: But how then will they make up their minds, or their yolks, or their nuclei, or whatever it is they have in there, Mr. President? It might seem to some that they are going to be absolutely innocent of whatever may be at stake in the election.

TRICKY: Innocent they will be, Mr. Reasonable—but now let me ask you, and all our television viewers, too, a question: what's *wrong* with a little innocence? We've had the foul language, we've had the cynicism, we've had the masochism and the breast-beating—maybe a big dose of innocence is just what this country needs to be great again.

MR. REASONABLE: *More* innocence, Mr. President?

TRICKY: Mr. Reasonable, if I have to choose between the rioting and the upheaval and the strife and the discontent on the one hand, and more innocence on the other, I think I will choose the innocence. Mr. Hardnose.

MR. HARDNOSE: In the event, Mr. President, that all this does come to pass by the '72 elections, what gives you reason to believe that the enfranchised embryos and fetuses will vote for you over your Democratic opponent? And what about Governor Wallow? Do you think that if he should run again, he would significantly cut into your share of the fetuses, particularly in the South?

TRICKY: Let me put it this way, Mr. Hardnose: I have the utmost respect for Governor George Wallow of Alabama, as I do for Senator Hubert Hollow of Minnesota. They are both able men, and they speak with great conviction, I am sure, in behalf of the extreme right and the extreme left. But the fact is that I have never heard either of these gentlemen, for all their extremism, raise their voices in behalf of America's most disadvantaged group of all, the unborn.

Consequently, I would be less than candid if I didn't say that when election time rolls around, of course the embryos and fetuses of this country are likely to remember just who it was that struggled in their behalf, while others were addressing themselves to the more popular and fashionable issues of the day. I think they will remember who it was that devoted himself, in the midst of a war abroad and racial crisis at home, to making this country a fit place for the unborn to dwell in pride.

My only hope is that whatever I am able to accomplish in their behalf while I hold this office will someday contribute to a world in which *everybody*, regardless of race, creed, or color, will be unborn. I guess if *I* have a dream, that is it. Thank you, ladies and gentlemen.

MR. ASSLICK: Thank you, Mr. President.

3

Tricky Has Another Crisis; or, The Skull Session

T*ricky is dressed in the football uniform he wore during his four years on the bench at Prissier College. It is still as spanking new as the day it was issued to him some forty years ago, despite the fact that when he finds himself at night so perplexed and anguished by the burdens of the Presidency as to be unable to fall off to sleep, he frequently rises from his bed and steals down through the White House to the blast-proof underground locker room (built under his direction to specifications furnished by the Baltimore Colts and the Atomic Energy Commission) and "suits up," as though for "the big game" against Prissier's "traditional rival." And invariably, as during the Cambodian incursion and the Kent State killings, simply to don shoulder guards, cleats and helmet, to draw the snug football pants up over his leather athletic supporter and then to turn his back to the mirror and catch a peek over his big shoulders at the number on his back, is enough to restore his faith in the course of action he has taken in behalf of two hundred million Americans. Indeed, even in the midst of the most incredible international blunders and domestic catastrophes, he has till now, with the aid of his football uniform, and a good war movie, been able to live up to his own description of the true leader in* Six Hundred Crises *as "cool, confident, and decisive." "What is essential in such situations," he wrote there, summarizing what he had learned about leadership from the riots inspired by his 1958 visit, as Vice President, to Caracas, "is not so much 'bravery' in the face of danger as the ability to think 'selflessly'—to blank out any thought of personal fear by concentrating completely on how to meet the danger."*

But tonight not even barking signals at the full-length mirror and pretending to fade back, arm cocked, to spot a downfield receiver (while being charged by the opposing line) has he been able to blank out thoughts of personal fear; and as for thinking "selflessly," he has not been making much headway in that department either. Having run plays before the mirror for two full hours—having completed eighty-seven out of one hundred attempted forward passes for a total of two thousand six hundred and ten yards *gained in the air in one night (a White House record)—he is nonetheless unable to concentrate on how to meet the danger before him, and so has decided to awaken his closest advisers and summon them to the underground locker room for what is known in football parlance as a "skull session."*

At the door to the White House, each has been issued a uniform by a Secret Service agent, disguised, but for a shoulder holster, as an ordinary locker room attendant in sweat pants, sneakers and T-shirt stenciled "Property of the White House." Now, seated on benches before the big blackboard, the "coaches" listen carefully as Tricky, with his helmet in his hands, describes to them the crisis he is having trouble being entirely selfless about.

TRICKY: I don't understand it. How can these youngsters be saying what they are saying about me? How can they be chanting those slogans, waving those signs—about *me*? Gentlemen, by all reports they are growing more surly and audacious by the hour. By morning we may have on our hands the most incredible upheaval in history: a revolution by the Boy Scouts of America! (*In an attempt to calm himself, and become confident and decisive, he puts on his helmet*)

Now it was one thing when those Vietnam soreheads came down here to the Capitol to turn their medals in. Everybody knew they were just a bunch of malcontents who had lost arms and legs and so on, and so had nothing better to do with their time than hobble around feeling sorry for themselves. Of course they couldn't be objective about the war—half of them were in wheelchairs because of it. But what we have now isn't just a mob of ingrates—these are *the Boy Scouts*!

And don't you think for one moment that the American people are going to sit idly by when a Boy Scout, an *Eagle Scout*, climbs to the top of the Capitol steps and calls the President of the United States "a dirty old man." Let there be no mistake about it, if we do not deal with these angry Scouts as coolly and confidently and decisively as I dealt with Khrushchev in that kitchen, by tomorrow I will be the first President in American history to be even more hated and despised than Lyin' B. Johnson. Gentlemen, you can go to war without Congressional consent, you can ruin the economy and trample on the Bill of Rights, but you do not violate the moral code of the Boy Scouts of America and expect to be reelected to the highest office in the land!

And yet when I made that speech at San Dementia, it all seemed so . . . so perfectly and, if I may say so, so brilliantly, innocuous. Five minutes later I didn't even remember what it was I'd *endorsed*. That my political opponents could now be so desperate to oust me from power—so disrespectful, not simply of me, but of the august office of the Presidency, to take those few utterly harmless and totally meaningless words that I spoke that day, and turn them into this monstrous lie!

Gentlemen, I am no newcomer to the ugly game of politics. I have seen all kinds of chicanery and deceit in my day—falsification, misquotation, distortion, embellishment, and, of course, outright suppression of the truth. Nor am I what you would call a babe-in-the-woods when it comes to the techniques of character assassination. Years ago I looked on in disgust and horror when they crucified Senator Joseph McCatastrophy just because he kept changing his mind as to the number of Communists there were in the State Department. I saw what they did only recently to Judge Carswell. I saw what they did to Judge Haynsworth. Why, just last month look what they tried to do to Secretary Lard, when he held up that phony piece of pipe before the Senate Foreign Relations Committee and said it was from Laos instead of Vietnam. Five miles away—and they're ready to hang him for it!

But I must admit, never in my long career of dealing with falsehood have I come upon a lie so treacherous and Machiavellian as this one my enemies are trying to pass off about me . . . *What did I say?* Let's look at the record. I said *nothing! Absolutely nothing!* I came out for "the rights of the unborn." I mean if ever there was a line of hokum, that was it. Sheer humbug! And as if it wasn't clear enough what I was up to, I even tacked on, "as recognized in principles

expounded by the United Nations." *By the United Nations.*
Now what more could I possibly have said to make the whole
thing any more inane? Maybe I was supposed to have told
them "as recognized in principles expounded by the American Automobile Association." Maybe I should have given
the whole speech in Pig Latin, and made funny faces while I
was at it! Maybe I should have come out to make the statement in a clown's costume! But I did not do that—because
I refuse to talk down to the American public. I refuse to pull
my punches. I refuse to believe that the people of this great
nation are incapable of recognizing the most outrageous
kind of hypocrisy or sniffing out the most blatant contradic-
tions imaginable . . . And yet this, *this* is my reward, for my
faith in America. The Boy Scouts of America screaming to
the TV cameras that Trick E. Dixon favors sexual intercourse. Favors fornication—*between people!*

POLITICAL COACH: Of course, as of now, it's still only the Boy
Scouts, Mr. President.

TRICKY: Today the Boy Scouts (*here he sinks down onto the
bench before the blackboard, barely restraining a sob*)—tomorrow the world! . . . And what about my wife—what is she
going to think? What if *she* starts to believe it? *What about
my children?* WHAT ABOUT THE VOTERS!

SPIRITUAL COACH: Here, here, Mr. President. I sympathize
with your chagrin, particularly as it relates to your fine family.
But, frankly, I do not believe that the American people who
see you on TV, any more than those who know you at firsthand, are going to be taken in by such a blatant fabrication.
If ever a man, in his every word and deed, his every movement and gesture, his glance, his sneer, his very smile, put
the lie to such a slanderous accusation as this one, it is you.

TRICKY (*visibly moved*): Reverend, I thank you for that tribute.
Surely I have tried to give no indication whatsoever to the
people of this country that I even know what sexual intercourse *is*. Furthermore, I have instructed my family that
they must under no circumstances allow it to appear that any
of us have ever in our lives been infected by desire or lust, or,
for that matter, an appetite for anything at all, outside of
political power. This may sound immodest of me, but I hap-

pen to pride myself on the fact that if it weren't for my perspiring so on television, the American people would probably have no way in the world of telling that under my
clothes I am flesh. And, of course you all know, as a result of
a decision I reached here during a lonely vigil in the locker
room only a few nights ago, this disorder will very shortly be
corrected when I enter Walter Reed Hospital to undergo a
secret operation for the surgical removal of the sweat glands
from my upper lip. You see, gentlemen, that is how dedicated I am to dissociating myself from anything remotely
resembling a human body.

But now to accuse me of *this*! As though to be for the
rights of the unborn was prima facie evidence—that is, evidence sufficient to establish a fact, or to raise a presumption
of fact . . . that's what we lawyers mean by that phrase . . .
as you know, before entering the White House I was a
lawyer, and so I know phrases like that . . . as though that
were prima facie evidence that I was also in favor of the
process by which the unborn come into existence in the first
place. To accuse me, because of a perfectly innocuous statement like that, of encouraging people to have intercourse in
order that they should have unborn, in order that those unborn should have these rights—that don't even exist! And
that I wouldn't care about, even if they did! How could I?
Here I am, President of the United States and Leader of
the Free World, working and slaving with every fiber of my
being, night and day, three hundred and sixty-five days a
year, for the sole purpose of getting myself reelected—
where would I find the time to worry about the rights of
anything? Haven't they any idea what this job is all about?
The whole thing is so patently absurd! And yet there are
those Boy Scouts, in uniform, marching in the streets of the
nation's capital—and those signs:

GO BACK TO CALIFORNIA, SENSUALIST,
WHERE YOU BELONG

POWER TO THE PENIS? NEVER!

REPRESSION—LOVE IT OR LEAVE IT!

SPIRITUAL COACH (*solemnly, taking the arm of the shaken President*): Mr. President, forgive them, they know not what their signs say.

TRICKY: Oh, Reverend, Reverend, I assure you, under ordinary circumstances I would bend over *backwards* to forgive them. I like to think that I am the kind of man who can find it in his heart to forgive his worst enemy. Why, not only have I forgiven Alger Hiss, but when I was elected President, I sent him an anonymous telegram expressing my gratitude for all he had done in my behalf. And that man was *a perjurer*! Listen, I would actually have forgiven Khrushchev himself, yes, right there in that kitchen, if it had been politically expedient to do so. Just look what I'm up to right now: I'm in the very process of forgiving Mao Tse-tung, who by my own estimate has enslaved *six hundred million people*!

But I am afraid, Reverend, that where these Boy Scouts are concerned, we are fighting for a principle so fundamental to civilized life, that even a man of my magnanimity must rise up and say "No, this time you have gone too far." Reverend, *they are trying to prevent me from winning a second term!*

SPIRITUAL COACH: I see . . . I see . . . I must confess that I had not thought of it quite that way.

TRICKY: It is not a pleasant way to *have* to think about it. All of us would prefer to look with charity and respect upon our fellow human beings, whatever their race, creed, color or age, and to treat them according to the tenets of our religious beliefs. Certainly no one in this country wishes to appear more religious than I do. But sometimes, Reverend, people just make being religious impossible, even for someone who stands to gain as much from that posture as I do.

SPIRITUAL COACH: But if such is the case, if these Boy Scouts, for some incomprehensible reason, are out to destroy your political career by casting doubt upon your Sunday school morality, perhaps it would be best for you to go on television and give the people the facts as they really are. As you did when they accused you in the 1952 election of being the recipient of an illegal political fund. The Checkers Speech.

TRICKY (*intrigued*): You mean give it again?

SPIRITUAL COACH: Well, perhaps not the *very* same speech.

TRICKY: Why not? It worked.

SPIRITUAL COACH: True. But I wonder, Mr. President, if it addresses directly the issue at hand.

TRICKY: Maybe not. But you know, Reverend, when you're dealing with wild and reckless charges like these, when you're in the midst of a crisis such as this one, that could snowball overnight into political *disaster*, then you sometimes have to do what works, and leave things like the issues themselves for later. Otherwise, I'm afraid there might not *be* any later.

SPIRITUAL COACH: Well, I'm not a politician, Mr. President, and I must admit that I may be hopelessly naive to believe that The Truth Shall Make Ye Free. But I do think that if instead of giving the Checkers Speech again, instead of itemizing your earnings over the years and telling how much money you owe your parents and so on, you were now to make a *similar* address, in which you presented to the nation an itemized account of your sexual experiences, giving exact dates from your appointment calendar—when, where, and with whom—you might well feel secure in leaving it to the American people to judge whether or not you are an advocate of fornication.

TRICKY: You mean, go on TV *with* the appointment books . . .

SPIRITUAL COACH: Yes, and leaf through them page by page, until at last you come upon an item to read aloud. I would think the long silences will in themselves be the most eloquent part of the broadcast.

TRICKY: What about charts though? What about a graph? You see, I don't know if people are going to sit around all night in front of their television sets waiting for me to say something. But if we had a graph where we measured the hours in which I have engaged in the ordinary human activities of scheming, plotting, smearing and so on, against those I've spent having intercourse—well, it could be pretty impressive.

And I could use a pointer! At the risk of seeming immodest, I think I can hold my own with any schoolmaster in the country in using a pointer and charts, though of course by training I'm a lawyer, you know . . . And I'll borrow a dog!

Well, how does it sound to the rest of you?

POLITICAL COACH: Speaking frankly, Mr. President, I think we are barking up the wrong tree with this whole idea of using the truth *or* the dog. We've used the dog, of course, and with some success, and though I don't have my file with me, I'm sure we've used the truth some time or other in the past, too. Off the top of my head I can't remember exactly when, but if you like I'll have my secretary look it up in the morning. However, right now it seems to me that, given the hysteria of those Scouts, and the kind of coverage they're getting, if you were to go on television and say that you have had intercourse only *once* in your entire life, maybe as some kind of initiation rite when you were in the Navy—crossing the equator maybe—and that the whole thing had lasted less than sixty seconds, and you had hated it from beginning to end, and that you had to be held down throughout, and so on, even that would be enough to make you appear guilty of the charges the Boy Scouts are bringing against you.

TRICKY (*reflecting*): Of course, if you're going to rule out the dog and the truth and so on, maybe the best approach is for me to go on TV and deny the whole thing. Say I've *never* had intercourse.

POLITICAL COACH (*shaking his head*): Have you seen that mob, Mr. President? They wouldn't believe you, not at this point.

TRICKY: Suppose I spoke from HEW, with the Surgeon General at my side, and he read a medical report stating that I am not now, nor have I ever been in the past, capable of performing coitus.

SPIRITUAL COACH: Mr. President, at the risk of being politically naive again, you *are* the father of two children . . . that is, if that means anything, in this context . . .

POLITICAL COACH: Politically naive, hell—that was good thinking, Reverend.

TRICKY: But why can't we just say they were adopted?

POLITICAL COACH: No, no, that doesn't really solve the problem. Even if we are able to establish you as not only sterile, but one hundred percent impotent, even if we were able to get the American public to believe that these children who resemble you so were adopted—and, mind you, I think we

could do both, if it came down to it—you are still going to
be compromised, it would seem to me, by appearing to have
taken into your home the offspring of somebody *else's* sexual
intercourse. You are still going to be locked into this fornication issue.

LEGAL COACH: Absolutely. Open-and-shut case of guilt by association. If I were the judge, I'd throw the book at you.
And another objection. If he goes on TV and says he's impotent, most of the people out there aren't even going to
know what he's talking about. I don't doubt that half of
them are going to think that he means he's queer.

POLITICAL COACH: Wait a minute! Wait *one* minute! How
about it, Mr. President?

TRICKY: How about what?

POLITICAL COACH: Going on TV and saying you're queer.
Would you do it?

TRICKY: Oh, I'll do it, all right, if you think it'll work.

SPIRITUAL COACH: Oh, but *surely*, Mr. President . . .

TRICKY: Reverend, we are talking about *my political career*!
With all due respect, we happen now to be listening to a
man whose *business* is politics, just the way yours is religion,
and if he says that in a situation like this one the truth and
the dog and so on are not going to get us anywhere, then I
must assume he knows what he is talking about. After all,
one of the signs of a great leader is his willingness to listen to
all sides of an issue without being blinded by his own preju-
dices and preconceptions. Now I am a Quaker, as you well
know, and consequently it is only natural that I should be
prejudiced in behalf of the advice given to me by a spiritual
person like yourself. But I cannot run from the facts, just so
as to be a better Quaker in your eyes and in mine. We are
dealing with a mob of youngsters whose minds have been
poisoned with a terrible lie. We are going to have to find a
way to restore them to their senses while simultaneously
restoring to the office of the Presidency its dignity and prestige. And if in order to accomplish those two important
tasks I have to go on TV and say I am a homosexual, then I
will do it. I had the courage to call Alger Hiss a Communist.
I had the courage to call Khrushchev a bully. I assure you, I
have the courage now to call myself a queer!

The problem is not my courage to say this or say that; it never has been. The problem, as always, is one of credibility. Will they believe me?

General, will they buy it over at the Pentagon? That should certainly be a good test case.

MILITARY COACH (*considering*): They might, sir. They very well might.

TRICKY: Would it help if I batted my eyes more, when I talk?

MILITARY COACH: No, no, I think they feel you bat your eyes enough already, sir. Any more and it might not go over too well with some of the old-timers.

TRICKY: I take it from what you say that you would positively rule out my wearing a dress. Something simple. A basic black, say.

MILITARY COACH: Not necessary, sir.

TRICKY: How about earrings?

MILITARY COACH: No, I think you're fine as you are, sir.

TRICKY: The point is I don't want to come off as just a sissy. Five o'clock shadow and all, I really have to watch myself in that department.

SPIRITUAL COACH: Mr. President, if I may, in your eagerness to do the right thing for the nation, I think you may be overlooking a small technical point. Homosexuals have intercourse also.

TRICKY (*stunned*): They do? . . . *How?*

(*Here the Spiritual Coach takes Tricky by the hand—much as he might comfort one in bereavement—and, leaning forward, discreetly whispers the answer into the President's ear*)

TRICKY (*recoiling*): Why, that's awful! That's disgusting! You're making that up!

SPIRITUAL COACH: Would that I were, Mr. President.

TRICKY: But—but—(*Here he leans forward to whisper into the Reverend's ear*)

SPIRITUAL COACH: I suppose they don't care about that, Mr. President.

TRICKY (*outraged*): But that's bestial! That's monstrous! This is America! And I'm the *President* of America! And—and—(*turning in bewilderment to the other coaches*) listen, do you people realize what's going *on* in this country? Do you know what he just *told* me?

POLITICAL COACH: I think we do, Mr. President.

TRICKY: But that's *grotesque!* Uccchhy! It makes my lip crawl!

POLITICAL COACH: To be sure, Mr. President. But nonetheless in terms of the problem that is facing us, it happens to be neither here nor there. The point is this: homosexuals, regardless of whatever else they may do, are in no way involved in the sort of sexual activity that produces fetuses—and that is still what these Boy Scouts are up in arms about. Consequently, if you were to go on TV and say you were a homosexual, in the minds of most Americans you would have cleared yourself of the charge the Boy Scouts are making, that you are a heterosexual activist. You'll be entirely in the clear.

TRICKY: I see . . . I see . . . Okay—I'll do it! There—*that's* the way to be in a crisis: decisive! Just as I wrote in my book, summarizing what I learned during General Poppapower's heart attacks, "Decisive action relieves the tension which builds up in a crisis. When the situation requires that an individual restrain himself from acting decisively over a long period, this can be the most wearing of all crises."

You see, it isn't even what you decide—it's *that* you decide. Otherwise there's that darn tension; too much, and, I tell you, a person could probably crack up. And I for one will not crack up while I am President of the United States. I want that to be perfectly clear. If you read my book, you'll see that my entire career has been devoted to not cracking up, as much as to anything. And I don't intend to start now. Cool, confident and decisive. I'll do it—I'll say I'm a queer!

LEGAL COACH: I wouldn't if I were you, Mr. President.

TRICKY: You *wouldn't?*

LEGAL COACH: Nope, not if I were the President of the United States. Why should you? At the time of the Checkers Speech, when you were only a candidate for the Vice Presidency, of course it was necessary to explain and apologize and be humble and tell them how much money you owed your Mommy and Daddy and that you had a doggie and so on. Look, I wouldn't have objected back then if you had gotten down on your hands and knees on television, and demeaned and debased yourself in whatever way was most natural to you, in order to come to power. But now you are *in* power. Now you *are* the President. And who are those kids in the street, leveling these outlandish charges at you? They're kids, in a street. I don't care what kind of uniforms they wear, they are still not adults in houses. And that makes all the difference in the world.

TRICKY: Your suggestion then is what?

LEGAL COACH: No less than any other citizen in this country, Mr. President, you still have recourse to the law. I say use it. I say round 'em up, put 'em in the clink, and throw the key away.

MILITARY COACH: Objection! Enough mollycoddling of the enemy. Let's get it over with once and for all. Shoot 'em!

TRICKY (*considering*): Interesting idea. I mean that is just about as decisive as you can get, isn't it? But may I ask, General, shoot 'em *after* we round 'em up, or *before*? This of course is the problem we always have, isn't it?

MILITARY COACH: *After*, sir, and we are running the same old risk.

LEGAL COACH: On the other hand, General, *before* and don't think you aren't running a risk too. *Before*, and I can tell you now, sure as we're sitting here, you are going to get those civil-rights nuts down on your neck, and I tell you they are a great big pain in the ass to everybody involved, and can tie up my staff for days at a time.

MILITARY COACH: Granted, they are a nuisance. But *after*, and you are going to get yourself mired down with these Boy Scouts just the way we are mired down in Southeast Asia. *After*, and you are sacrificing what is fundamental to the success of any attack: the element of surprise. Common sense tells us that even the enemy is not so stupid as to stand around waiting to be shot, but if he has had sufficient warning that he is about to be killed, will take some kind of cowardly and, often enough, vicious means of protecting his life, such as fighting back. Now I, of course, abhor that kind of deviousness as much as anyone; nonetheless we must face up to it: these people haven't the slightest sense of fair play, and many of them will not even stand still waiting around to be jailed, let alone killed.

And what about the *moral* issues? I have a conscience to live with, gentlemen, I have a tradition to uphold, I am responsible to something more important than dollars and cents. And I tell you, I will not mollycoddle the enemy at the risk of American lives, unless of course I am ordered to do so. Mr. President, I must speak from my heart, I would be remiss as a General of the United States Army if I did not. Mr. President, if on the day you took office we had, with your permission, lined up and shot every single Vietnamese we could find, by so doing we would have saved fifteen thousand American lives. Instead, sir, following the course of action that you have ordered as Commander-in-Chief, and shooting and blowing them up piecemeal, catch as catch can, ten here, twenty there, and so on, we have suffered severe losses of both men and materials.

Admittedly, by doggedly pursuing your strategy, we are now beginning to see some light at the end of the tunnel. And I have every hope that we will be able to help you make good on your promise to the American people, that by Election Day 1972, and according to your own secret timetable, you will have accomplished the complete withdrawal of the Vietnamese people from Vietnam.

My point, sir, is that we have ways of accomplishing such withdrawals in a matter of hours. I beg of you, Mr. President, let us not repeat the errors of Vietnam in our own backyard.

LEGAL COACH: Of course, Mr. President, I cannot fault the General on his tactical wisdom, and believe me, I am not for a moment worried about taking on these civil-rights nuts. It's just that if we shoot these Scouts in the street *before* we round 'em up and jail 'em, it is, as I said, going to create an awful lot of unnecessary busy-work for my staff, many of them first-rate young men whom I can employ at far more useful and worthwhile tasks.

However, before *or* after, Mr. President, whichever you choose, you can count on my support. But for you to go on TV and make a confession, or an apology, or any kind of explanation for yourself *whatsoever*, well, to my mind, nothing could more seriously undermine your moral and political authority, or constitute a graver threat to the cause of law and order. I will even go so far as to say that if you appear in any way to give ground on this issue—or *any* issue for that

matter—you will be opening the floodgates to anarchy, socialism, communism, welfarism, defeatism, pacifism, perversion, pornography, prostitution, mob rule, drug addiction,
free love, alcoholism, and desecration of the flag. You'll see
a rise just in jaywalking that will stagger the imagination.
Now I don't mean to throw a scare into anyone, but the fact
is a vast criminal element in this country is waiting for just a
single sign of weakness in our leader, so as to make its move.
Anything at all that might suggest to them that Trick E.
Dixon is not totally in control, of himself *and* the nation,
and I hate to tell you what would follow.

TRICKY (*interrupting*): That's exactly why I'm having my
    sweat glands removed, to show how in control I am.

LEGAL COACH (*continuing*): Now, as you know, there is bound
    to be a certain amount of blood shed, when we go ahead
    and kill these young people, whether we do it before *or*
    after. This blood is something we seem always to run into
    with the killings, one of those facts of death we have to live
    with. Reverend, I see you shaking your head. Are you sug-
    gesting that it is possible to kill people, even youngsters like
    this, without spilling blood? If so, I'd like to hear about it.

SPIRITUAL COACH (*anguished*): Well . . . what about gas . . .
    poison gas . . . Something like that? Surely enough blood
    has been shed in our century.

MILITARY COACH: The only trouble with gas, Reverend, if I
    may speak here on the basis of my own firsthand experience
    —the trouble with gas is that unfortunately we don't have
    these Scouts in a big open space. If we had them, say, smack
    in the middle of a desert somewhere, sure, spray 'em and it's
    over with.

SPIRITUAL COACH: Couldn't we *get* them to a desert then?

LEGAL COACH: How? (*Wary*) Are you suggesting bussing them
    there?

SPIRITUAL COACH: Well, yes, busses would do it, I suppose.

TRICKY: No, I'm afraid they wouldn't, Reverend. I have
    thought this matter through and I have made my decision:
    this administration will *not* bus children from Washington,
    D.C., all the way to the state of Arizona to poison them.
    That is a matter in which the federal government simply will
    not intervene. This is a free country, and certainly one of

your fundamental freedoms here is choosing the place where you want your child to be killed.

SPIRITUAL COACH: And there's simply no way you can poison them right *here?*

MILITARY COACH: Much too dangerous, Reverend. Start out gassing these kids, and next thing, you get a wind or something, and you have poisoned some perfectly innocent adult miles away.

LEGAL COACH: Of course, you're going to get some guilty adults too, you know, if you let it spread far enough.

SPIRITUAL COACH: Gentlemen, please! I stand utterly opposed to any course of action wherein the welfare of a single innocent adult is even remotely threatened. I don't care how many guilty adults you get in the process.

MILITARY COACH: All right with me, Reverend. I'd rather shoot 'em anyway. I have always maintained that it gives the individual soldier a stronger sense of participation and accomplishment to pull the trigger and see the results with his own eyes.

SPIRITUAL COACH (*to Legal Coach*): And you?

LEGAL COACH: Fine with me. So long as we all realize beforehand that there is going to be this blood, and sure as we are sitting here, the media are going to exploit it to the hilt. I don't have any doubt whatsoever, given the kind of people who pull the strings in the press and TV, that they are going to blow this whole thing out of proportion, and, for instance, are not going to have a word to say about the restraint that's been displayed by our not using poison gas, or bussing. I mean, we could subject these kids to what is virtually a cross-country bus trip, a long hot grueling drive out to Arizona, without food, water, toilet facilities and so on, prior to killing them, and yet, as we all know, with the exception of the Reverend here, not a single member of the administration has spoken in support of such a proposal. But will you hear about that on TV? I think not.

TRICKY: Oh no. They never tell *that* side of the story. It's not *sensational* enough for them, not enough *gore*. Not enough *violence* to suit their taste. No, it's never what we didn't do, it's always what we've *done*. That, unfortunately, is what these people consider newsworthy.

LEGAL COACH: Luckily, Mr. President, the people of this country are still by and large passive and indifferent enough not to get all stirred up by this kind of irresponsible sensationalism on the part of the media.

TRICKY: Oh, don't get me wrong, I've never lost my faith in the wonderful indifference of the American people. Just because they happen to see a little Boy Scout blood on TV . . . *Boy Scout blood on TV?* (*His lip is suddenly drenched with perspiration*) They'll impeach me! They'll—!

LEGAL COACH: Nothing of the sort, Mr. President, nothing of the sort. It's only another crisis, you have nothing to worry about. Come on now—cool, confident and decisive. Come on, repeat it after me, you know how to behave in a crisis: cool, confident and decisive.

TRICKY: Cool, confident and decisive. Cool, confident and decisive. Cool, confident and decisive. Cool, confident and decisive.

LEGAL COACH: Feel better now? Crisis over?

TRICKY: I think so, yes.

LEGAL COACH: You see, you mustn't be frightened of Boy Scouts, Mr. President. Of course they're going to bleed a little and there may even be this hue and cry about it on TV, but when the country sees this sign that one of them was carrying before the bleeding began (*extracts from his briefcase a sign reading* DIXON FAVORS EFFING—*The Reverend gasps*), I think our worries are going to be over. Let the newspapers run all the photos of Boy Scout corpses they want—we'll just run a photo of this sign, and of the five thousand replicas that I have asked the Government Printing Office to run off by morning. We'll see who gets the support of the nation then.

TRICKY: Look! I've stopped sweating!

LEGAL COACH: See? You've weathered another crisis, Mr. President.

TRICKY: Wow! That makes six hundred and *one*!

(*Congratulations all around, from everyone except the Highbrow Coach, who speaks now for the first time*)

HIGHBROW COACH: Gentlemen, I wonder if I may take a somewhat different approach to the problem that we have been assembled here to solve. All the while I have been listening to your suggestions, I have simultaneously been bringing to bear upon the problem all my brainpower, wisdom, academic credentials, cunning, opportunism, love of power and so on, and the result is this list that I am holding in my hand, of the names of five individuals and/or organizations upon whom I think we can safely—if I may use the vernacular for a moment—pin the rap.

LEGAL COACH (*his interest suddenly aroused, after initial suspiciousness of "the Professor"*): The rap?

HIGHBROW COACH: "The rap."

LEGAL COACH: Which rap?

HIGHBROW COACH: You name it. Inciting to riot. Tampering with the morals of minors. If you prefer, corrupting the youth of the nation.

POLITICAL COACH: "Corrupting the youth." Hey, that's got a real campaign ring to it!

HIGHBROW COACH: And a certain historical resonance, I would think.

SPIRITUAL COACH: At the risk of sounding "square," may I put in a good word for "tampering with the morals of minors"? I've always found it to have tremendous appeal. It seems there is something in the word "tampering" that particularly infuriates people.

LEGAL COACH: That may be, Reverend, but in my book you still can't beat "inciting to riot" for scaring the hell out of the public.

TRICKY: And you, General? You look distressed again.

MILITARY COACH: I *am* distressed again! I am distressed every time the Professor opens his mouth! What is this business of bringing charges? Oh, mind you, they're good charges and I don't have anything against them personally, but the last thing I remember we were talking about shooting the bastards.

HIGHBROW COACH: General, despite your low opinion of intellectuals, I happen to have the highest regard for Army officers such as yourself, particularly in their devotion to their men and to their country. I wonder if once you have heard me read my list, you won't agree that to charge any of these five self-avowed enemies of America with the crime, to fix the responsibility for the uprising of the Boy Scouts on any one of them, will simultaneously absolve the Boy Scouts themselves of any real guilt, while totally discrediting the charges they have made against the President. The Scouts will retreat in panic . . .

MILITARY COACH: But without our firing a shot!

HIGHBROW COACH: The country isn't going away, General.

TRICKY: Sounds interesting, Professor. But why only one of the five? That strikes me as highly unusual.

HIGHBROW COACH: Well, perhaps, but I was just wondering if we haven't gone the route with the conspiracy business.

TRICKY: Oh, but it's so much fun when you get to choose two or three. Each person picks his favorites—and then all the wheeling and dealing, until we come up with the conspiracy that suits everybody.

LEGAL COACH: And, of course, Mr. President, to put in a word here in behalf of the cause of justice, the more choice you're allowed, the greater the chance of catching the right culprit. My feeling is that just to stay on the safe side, each of us should choose a minimum of three.

SPIRITUAL COACH: I know I'm outside my bailiwick again, but if it *is* going to improve the chances for justice being done, why can't we choose all *five*?

MILITARY COACH: Mr. President, I am growing more and more exasperated by the moment. Here we sit, in the comfort and splendor of this fully equipped underground locker room, in full football regalia, deliberating over the niceties of justice, while, with every passing moment, those Boy Scouts are readying themselves for battle against my men. I think it is high time we reminded the Professor that he is no longer up there in his ivory tower, where you can talk yourself blue in the face about this one's rights and that one's rights and how many rights fit on the head of a pin. There is an angry mob of Boy Scouts out there, Eagle Scouts among them, and they are growing angrier and more threatening by the moment. I say shoot 'em and shoot 'em now!

TRICKY: General, you are a brave soldier and a loyal American. But, I must say, I sense in your remarks a certain disregard for fundamental constitutional liberties such as I have pledged myself to uphold in my oath of office.

MILITARY COACH: Mr. President, I have the highest regard for the Constitution. If I didn't, I wouldn't have devoted my life to fighting to defend it. But the fact of the matter is, we are playing with a time bomb. Right now it is still only the Boy Scouts. By morning, and I can guarantee you this, their ranks are going to be infiltrated by dissolute Brownies and Cub Scouts looking for adventure. Now it's one thing to ask my men to mow down Eagle Scouts; it is another for them to have to deal with little boys and girls half that size. Those kids can run like the dickens, and they're *small*. As a result, what right now would still be a routine street massacre, will be converted into dangerous house-to-house fighting, in which we are bound to sustain heavy losses by way of our soldiers shooting mistakenly at each other.

TRICKY: I think you know, General, that nobody wants to save the lives of our boys—by that I mean, of course, our men—any more than I do. But I repeat: I will not do so by trampling upon the Constitution. I campaigned for this office as a strict constructionist where the Constitution of this country is concerned, and if I were now to take the course that you suggest and acted to prevent this group from voting in open and honest elections on the Professor's list, then the American people would have every right to throw me out of office tomorrow.

And let me make one thing perfectly clear: nobody is ever going to do that again. They have thrown me out of office enough in my lifetime! I will not be cast in the role of a loser —of a war, or of *anything*. And if that means bringing the full firepower of our Armed Forces to bear upon every last Brownie and Cub Scout in America, then that is what we are going to do. Because the President of the United States and Leader of the Free World can ill-afford to be humiliated by *anyone*, let alone by third- and fourth-graders who have nothing better to do than engage the United States Army in treacherous house-to-house combat. I don't care if we have to go into the nursery schools. I don't care if our men have to fight their way through barricades constructed of lanyards and hula hoops and bubble gum, under a steady barrage of toys being grossly misused as weapons—I, as Commander-in-Chief, will not run from the battle. Not when my prestige is at stake! If I have to call in air strikes over the

playgrounds, I will do it! Let's see them try to bring down
B-52's with their bats and their balls! Let's see them try to
flee from my helicopters on those little tricycles of theirs! No,
this mighty giant of a nation of which I am, by extension, the
mighty giant of a President, will not have its nose tweaked
by a bunch of little brats who should be at home with their
homework in the first place!

(*All applaud*)

Now, as to the voting. Since I am a decisive man, as you
can see from my book *Six Hundred Crises*, I am now going
to decide how many of these five enemies of America each of
you will be allowed to choose to charge with the crime. Of
course, we still have to decide which of the three crimes that
the Professor mentioned we're going to use, but in that it is
getting on to morning, perhaps we can put that off to a
later date. In the meantime, we will come to a decision as to
who is guilty. (*Impish endearing smile*) That's the best part,
anyway!

Now (*back to serious business*), we will proceed in the following manner: the Professor will read his list, and each person present will select as many as he wants, up to three . . .
No, two . . . No, three . . . Uh-oh, my lip's sweating—
uh-oh, I think I'm having another crisis! *Two! Two! Say two!*

POLITICAL COACH: Good going, Mr. President—you've weathered it!

TRICKY: Wow! That makes six hundred and *two* crises! Wait'll I
tell the girls what Daddy did!

LEGAL COACH: Mr. President, in that we are to be allowed only
two of the candidates from the Professor's list, may I ask if
we can each add two names of our own, should we think we
have two more that warrant suspicion?

TRICKY: Well, let *me* ask *you* a question. Is this a deal you want
to make?

LEGAL COACH: Well, if you want to think of it that way, that's
okay with me.

TRICKY: I'd prefer to. Otherwise it might seem that I was
changing my mind because I'm indecisive. But if it's just a
matter of a payoff for something or other you'll deliver in
the future, I think everybody here will understand.

LEGAL COACH: Suits me.

TRICKY: There we are then. Two from the Professor's list and two of your own choice.

HIGHBROW COACH: To the list then, gentlemen. 1: Hanoi. 2: The Berrigans. 3: The Black Panthers. 4: Jane Fonda. 5: Curt Flood.

ALL: *Curt Flood?*

HIGHBROW COACH: Curt . . . Flood.

SPIRITUAL COACH: But—isn't he a *baseball* player?

TRICKY: *Was* a baseball player. Any questions about baseball players, just ask me, Reverend. *Was* the center fielder for the Washington Senators. But then he up and ran away. Skipped the country.

HIGHBROW COACH: He did indeed, Mr. President. Curt Flood, born January 18, 1938, in Houston, Texas, bats right, throws right, entered big league baseball in 1956 with Cincinnati, played from '58 to '69 with the St. Louis Cardinals, presently under contract at a salary of $110,000 a year to the Washington Senators, on the morning of April 27, 1971, with the baseball season not even a month old, boarded a Pan Am flight bound from New York to Barcelona, giving no explanation for his hasty departure other than "personal problems." Though Flood is known to have purchased a ticket for Barcelona, he apparently disembarked in Lisbon—wearing a brown leather jacket, bell-bottomed trousers and sunglasses—there to make connections with a flight for his final European destination . . . The question, gentlemen, is obvious: why, a week to the day before the uprising of the Boy Scouts in Washington, D.C., why did Mr. Curt Flood of the Washington baseball team find it necessary to leave the country in so precipitous and dramatic a fashion?

TRICKY: Oh, I think I can answer that one, Professor, knowing sports as I do inside and out. Poor Flood was in a slump, and a bad one. In his first twenty times at bat this year, he'd had only three hits, and two of those were bunts. Fact is, Williams had benched him. He'd sat out six starts in a row against right-handed pitching. Now I may be the highest elected official in the land, but I still don't think I'm going to second-guess Ted Williams when he benches a hitter. No, sirree. On the other hand, you can well imagine the effect being benched had upon a one-hundred-thousand-dollar-a-year star player like Flood.

HIGHBROW COACH: With all due respect, sir, for your knowledge of the game, which far exceeds my own, this "slump," as you call it, might it not have been just the right "cover" for a baseball player planning to leave the country in a hurry, just the right alibi?

LEGAL COACH: If I get your drift, Professor, are you suggesting that Ted Williams, the manager of the Senators, is implicated in this as well? That benching Flood was part of some overall plan?

POLITICAL COACH: Now hold on. Before we carry this any further, I want to say that I think we are skating on very thin ice here, when we are dealing with a baseball figure of Ted Williams' stature. Despised as he was by many sportswriters in his time—and I'm sure we could call upon these people for assistance, if we should want them—my gut reaction is that it is in the best interests of this administration to maintain a hands-off policy on all Hall of Famers.

TRICKY: And *what* a Hall of Famer! I wonder how many of you know Ted Williams' record. It certainly is a record for all Americans to be proud of, and I'd like to share it with you. Just listen and tell me if you don't agree. Lifetime batting average, .344. That makes him *fifth* in the history of the game. Lifetime slugging average, .634. *That* makes him second only to Babe Ruth himself! In doubles, fourteenth with 525; in home runs fifth with 521; in extra base hits seventh with 1,117; and in all-important RBI's, and I really can't say enough about RBI's and how important they are to the national pastime, in RBI's, also seventh with 1,839. And that isn't all. Led the league in hitting in 1941 with an average of—just listen to this—.406! In '42 again, with .356; in '47 with .343; in '48 with .369— (*Suddenly angry*) And they said Jack Charisma was the one who had the memory for facts! They said *Charisma* was the one who had the grasp of the issues! Oh, how they loved to downgrade Dixon! No wonder I had a crisis in that campaign! They were always picking on me! My beard! My nose! My tactics! Well, just let me say one thing as regards my so-called "tactics": if in any of the averages I have just quoted to you, I have altered Ted Williams' record by so much as one hundredth of one percentage point, I will submit my resignation to Congress tomorrow. Now that would be an unprecedented act in American history, but I would do it, if I had dared to play party politics with the American public on a matter as serious as this one.

(*All applaud*)

POLITICAL COACH: Mr. President, that was a most impressive recitation of the facts, and has only served to strengthen my conviction that it would be utterly foolhardy to bring a slugger like Williams under federal indictment.

TRICKY: Good thinking. Good sharp political thinking. Of course, with Flood himself, we have a very different situation. To be sure, he batted over .300 for the Cards in '61, '63, '64, '65, '67, and '68, but never once did he lead the league in hitting or home runs, as Williams did, and his slugging average is almost *half* what Williams' was at the end of his career.

Of course, in 1964, Flood *did* lead the National League in base hits with 211, and something like that could stir up a certain amount of sympathy. Now let me make one thing perfectly clear: I am not saying that he is anywhere near the all-time leader in that department, George Sisler, who got 257 hits in the year 1920, but a fact is a fact, and we are going to have to confront it. Those 211 base hits could mean trouble.

HIGHBROW COACH: Mr. President, under ordinary circumstances I too might be leery of bringing a charge as drastic as whichever one we come up with, against a man who, as you so wisely remind us, led the National League in total base hits with 211. But Curt Flood is something more than your run-of-the-mill hitting star of yesteryear: he is a bona fide troublemaker, and was in hot water right up to his neck even before I put him on my list. That is *why* I put him on my list: for not only has he jumped a hundred-thousand-dollar contract and skipped the country only a month into the season, but he of course is the man who in 1970 refused to be traded by the St. Louis Cardinals to the Philadelphia Phillies, claiming that the trade denied him his basic rights to negotiate a contract for his services on the open market. Subsequently, he hired as his attorney none other than Lyin' B. Johnson's appointee to the Supreme Court . . .

POLITICAL COACH (*hopefully*): Abe Fortas!

HIGHBROW COACH: No, no, but almost as good. Arthur Goldberg. G-o-l-d-b-e-r-g. And these two instituted a suit against baseball on constitutional grounds, asserting that organized baseball was in violation of the Antitrust Laws, and that the owners, by trading players from one team to another without their permission, treated them like pieces of property, which was both illegal and immoral.

Now, impugning the sacred name of baseball in this way did not go over very well with a good many loyal Americans, including the Commissioner of Baseball himself, and in the eyes of many, sportswriters and fellow players, as well as fans throughout the country, Flood, and his mouthpiece Goldberg, appeared to be out to destroy the game beloved by millions. Flood, in a book he has written on the subject, even quotes himself as saying in conversation, "Somebody needs to go up against the system. I'm ready." And, gentlemen, that is only *one* of the self-incriminating statements that is scattered throughout that manifesto. Of course, as if all that he has said and done isn't compromising enough—including hiring a Mr. *Goldberg* to represent him in this attack upon the most American of American sports—Flood is a black man.

LEGAL COACH: Where is he now, Algeria? That would sew it up for us, if he was in Algeria.

HIGHBROW COACH: To the contrary, had he fled to Algeria—which he has not—they would already be selling posters of him at bat in a beret, and ads to "Free Flood" would be appearing daily in *The New York Times*, signed by movie stars and Jean-Paul Sartre. There'd be marches and pickets and probably one of those mule trains camping on the White House lawn.

TRICKY: Oh, those mule trains! Those marches! Really, I can't *stand* those things. It never fails—every time they start marching on Washington, *I'm* the one who has to leave town. Now does that make any sense to you? *I'm* the President, I *live* here, and still *I'm* the one who has to pack his bags and get on a helicopter and go when these marchers start pouring in from all over the country! Honestly, I've got this big beautiful house, and I spend half my life living out of suitcases. Can you imagine what it's like for a President, on practically five minutes' notice, to try to pack everything he needs in his briefcase, while outside the window the propellers are going and everybody is screaming "Hurry, hurry, let's get out of here, before they go crazy and send a delegation to the door!" Oh, it's just awful. One time I forgot my jersey, one time I forgot my cleats, one time I even forgot to pack my ball—and really, the whole weekend was just *ruined*. And those marchers couldn't care less!

HIGHBROW COACH: Well, you won't have to leave town this time, Mr. President. Because this fugitive has not fled to Algeria to set himself up as some kind of ersatz revolutionary leader in exile; nor has he fled to Africa to live among his own kind, as he might have done if he were looking to build a following. No, there isn't going to be much sympathy in this country, I can assure you, for a handsome and muscular young black man like Mr. Curt Flood, who, from all indications, has decided to make his home—gentlemen, it couldn't be better—in Copenhagen.

SPIRITUAL COACH: *No!*

HIGHBROW COACH: Yes, Reverend, Copenhagen. The Mecca toward which the filth peddlers of the world go down on their knees morning and night. The pornography capital of the world.

POLITICAL COACH: Wow! (*Ecstatic*) And that's not all they've got in Denmark to compromise Mr. Flood, is it?

HIGHBROW COACH: Very fast on your feet, young man . . . The word is miscegenation. Not that we have to come right out with it, any more than we mean to say, in so many words, that he is a known smut addict.

SPIRITUAL COACH: No, please, you mustn't. Where a baseball star is involved, we are inevitably going to be dealing with young impressionable minds, boys eight, nine, ten years of age— If they were to hear such words . . .

POLITICAL COACH: I agree, Reverend. It'll be better by far to do it by "implication."

LEGAL COACH: Fine with me. What about you, Mr. President?

Think you can manage that? A hint here, a slur there, instead of coming right out with it?

TRICKY: Well, if it's a matter of making the Reverend feel at ease about the wonderful young Little Leaguers of this country, I sure am going to try.

SPIRITUAL COACH: Thank you, Mr. President. Thank you, gentlemen.

TRICKY: You see, Reverend, there's that restraint again, there's that sense of proportion and moderation that according to the newspapers I'm not supposed to have. After all, here is a black man engaging in just about the wickedest act any American can imagine, and with the women of Denmark, who are among the whitest in the entire world, and yet instead of coming right out with it, and thus exposing our Little Leaguers to a highly dangerous and tempting idea, we are going to smear him by insinuation and innuendo.

SPIRITUAL COACH: I'm deeply indebted, Mr. President.

POLITICAL COACH: We thought that went without saying, Reverend.

HIGHBROW COACH: Good enough, gentlemen. I shall now proceed to read the list one more time, so that you may decide how you wish to cast your votes. 1: Hanoi. 2: The Berrigans—

POLITICAL COACH: May I interrupt here? I wonder if I can take a moment to make a case for the innocence of the Berrigan brothers.

LEGAL COACH (*outraged*): The *innocence* of the *Berrigan brothers?*

POLITICAL COACH (*backpedaling*): Of this charge! Of this charge!

LEGAL COACH: But we haven't even decided yet upon the exact *nature* of the charge—so how can they be innocent? Where is your evidence? Where is your proof?

POLITICAL COACH: Well, I don't have any.

LEGAL COACH: Then, maybe, young man, you oughtn't to go around calling people innocent until you do!

POLITICAL COACH: I *grant* you that—but what I am fearful of is this: if we do try to pin still another crime on those priests, we are going to produce a sympathetic reaction toward them such as you ordinarily don't get until after an assassination. I should tell you that at this very moment a Hollywood movie is in the early stages of planning, in which Fathers Phil and Dan Berrigan are to be portrayed by Bing Crosby and an actor, as yet unnamed, who will be made up to resemble the late, great Barry Fitzgerald. Now these Hollywood producers, gentlemen, no matter how they may dress or wear their hair, are not hippies or left-wing fanatics by any stretch of the imagination. Underneath those anti-establishment muttonchops they are hard-headed businessmen with a product to market and an audience to exploit, and they can spot a trend developing a long way off. According to my informants, the movie being planned deals sympathetically with two priests who decide to blow up West Point, after Army defeats Notre Dame before seventy million television fans in the big football game of the year. There'll be nuns and songs and so on, and who knows but that a picture like this could turn the whole damn country Communist overnight.

MILITARY COACH: Two hundred million Reds on American soil? Not if I have anything to say about it.

POLITICAL COACH: Easier said than done, General. Shoot two hundred million Americans—if that's what you have in mind —shoot *one* hundred million Americans, and I'm afraid you're going to give the Democrats just the kind of issue they can play politics with in the '72 elections.

MILITARY COACH: The level to which political life in this country has sunk! Now if the military were running this show . . .

POLITICAL COACH: Granted. Granted. But you do not build a utopian society overnight, General. And that is why I wish to caution you, one and all, against voting for the Berrigans. I know how tempting it is, especially after what we went through to track them down, but I am afraid that this is another one of those instances when we are going to have to display our characteristic restraint and moderation. Certainly the last thing in the world we want is Bing Crosby in a collar crooning to Debbie Reynolds in her habit about b-b-b-b-lowing things up. Not even Lenin could have devised a more sure-fire method of converting the American working class into bomb-throwing revolutionaries.

HIGHBROW COACH: Ingenious analysis. Nonetheless, I think

you misread Hollywood's intentions. If the Berrigans were to get the chair, to be sure Hollywood would immediately go into full-scale production of some kind of musical about them, along the line of *Going My Way*. But that is only an argument against killing them. Keep them in jail, and you will be surprised how quickly the public *and* the movie moguls will forget they exist.

LEGAL COACH: I agree. Bury them alive. Always better.

SPIRITUAL COACH: And more merciful, too. That way, you see, it's not capital punishment.

HIGHBROW COACH: To move on then. Number two was the Berrigans.

SPIRITUAL COACH: What was one again? Harvard?

HIGHBROW COACH: Hanoi.

SPIRITUAL COACH: Ah, yes. I knew it was something beginning with an H.

MILITARY COACH (*angrily*): And what about something *else* beginning with an "H"? What about Haiphong! How can you have Hanoi without Haiphong? That's like Quemoy without Matsu!

TRICKY: Quemoy and Matsu! Does *that* bring back memories! Quemoy and Matsu! . . . What ever happened to them?

POLITICAL COACH: Oh, they're still out there, Mr. President, if we should ever need them.

TRICKY: Well, that's wonderful. Where were they again— exactly? Wait, let me guess, let's see if I can remember . . . Indonesia!

POLITICAL COACH: No, sir.

TRICKY: Am I warm? The Philippines! No? . . . Near Hawaii? . . . No? Oh, I give up.

POLITICAL COACH: In the Formosa Straits, Mr. President. Between Taiwan and Mainland China.

TRICKY: No kidding. Hey, listen, whatever happened to what's-his-name? The Chinaman.

POLITICAL COACH: Which Chinaman, Mr. President? There are six hundred million Chinamen.

TRICKY: I know, enslaved and so on. But I'm thinking of, you know, the one with the wife. Oh, it's one of those names they have . . .

HIGHBROW COACH: Chiang Kai-shek, Mr. President.

TRICKY: Right, Professor! Shek. Little Shek, with the glasses. (*Fondly*) The Old Dixon . . . (*Chuckling*) Well! Enough wandering down memory lane. Forgive me, gentlemen. Where were we? So far we have Moscow and the Berrigans.

HIGHBROW COACH: Hanoi and the Berrigans, Mr. President.

TRICKY: Of course! See what you did with that Quemoy and Matsu? I was still back there in the fifties. Look at me, my lip is covered with goose flesh.

HIGHBROW COACH: To proceed. Number 3: The Black Panthers. No dispute there. Good. Number 4: Jane Fonda, the movie actress and antiwar activist. Number 5: Curt Flood, the baseball player. Any questions, before we proceed to the vote. Reverend?

SPIRITUAL COACH: Jane Fonda. Has she ever appeared nude in a film?

HIGHBROW COACH: I can't honestly say I remember seeing her pudenda on the screen, Reverend, but I think I can vouch for her breasts.

SPIRITUAL COACH: With aureole or without?

HIGHBROW COACH: I believe with.

SPIRITUAL COACH: And her buttocks?

HIGHBROW COACH: Yes, I believe we've seen her buttocks. Indeed, they constitute a large part of her appeal.

SPIRITUAL COACH: Thank you.

HIGHBROW COACH: Any other questions?

POLITICAL COACH: Well, about the Black Panthers—do you really think that the American people will believe that the Black Panthers are behind *the Boy Scouts?* That really does require quite a bit of imagination.

TRICKY: Now I take exception there. I don't want to influence the voting, but I do want to say this: let's not underestimate the imagination of the American people. This may seem like old-fashioned patriotism such as isn't in fashion any more, but I have the highest regard for their imagination and I always have. Why, I actually think the American people can be made to believe anything. These people, after all, have their fantasies and fears and superstitions, just like anybody else, and you are not going to put anything over on them by

simply addressing yourself to the real problems and pretending that the others don't exist just because they are
imaginary.

HIGHBROW COACH: I agree wholeheartedly, Mr. President.
May we proceed to the voting?

TRICKY: By all means . . . Of course, gentlemen, these *are*
going to be free elections. I want it to be perfectly clear beforehand that I wouldn't have it otherwise, unless there
were some reason to believe that the vote might go the
wrong way. And I am proud to say I don't think that's possible here in this locker room with men of your caliber. You
may vote for any two candidates on the list, and you may, in
the interest of justice, add any two names of your own
choosing. I will write down the votes cast for each candidate
and tabulate them on this sheet of paper.

Now, you'll see that this is an ordinary sheet of lined yellow paper such as you might find on any legal pad. I was a
lawyer, you know, before I became President, so you can be
pretty sure that I know the correct manner in which to use
this kind of paper. In fact, I should like you to examine the
paper to be sure nothing has been written on it and that it
contains no code markings or secret notations other than
the usual watermark.

HIGHBROW COACH: I'm sure we all can trust your description
of the piece of paper, Mr. President.

TRICKY: I appreciate your confidence, Professor, but I would
still prefer that the four of you examine the paper thoroughly
beforehand, so that afterwards there cannot be any doubt as
to the one hundred percent honesty of this electoral procedure. (*He hands the paper around to each*) Good! Now for a
free election! Suppose we begin with you, Reverend.

SPIRITUAL COACH: Well, really, I'm in a tizzy. I mean, I know
for sure that I want to vote for Jane Fonda—but after her I
just can't make up my mind. Curt Flood is *so* tempting.

HIGHBROW COACH: Vote for both then.

TRICKY: Or suppose you think it through a little longer and
we'll come back to you. General?

MILITARY COACH (*belligerently*): Hanoi and Haiphong!

TRICKY: In other words, that's your write-in vote, Haiphong.

MILITARY COACH: Mine, and every loyal American's, Mr. President!

TRICKY: Fair enough. (*Records vote*) Next.

POLITICAL COACH: I'll take Hanoi, too.

TRICKY: With or without Haiphong?

POLITICAL COACH: I think I like it just by itself.

TRICKY: And, anything else?

POLITICAL COACH: No, thank you, Mr. President—I stick.

TRICKY: Okay, time to hear the voice of Justice.

LEGAL COACH: The Berrigans, the Panthers, Curt Flood.

TRICKY: Slowly, please, slowly. I want to be sure to get it right. The Berrigans . . . The Panthers . . . Curt Flood . . . But that's three. You're allowed only two.

LEGAL COACH: I understand that, Mr. President. But in that my predecessors have each used only one from the Professor's list of five, it did not seem to me a violation of the *spirit* of the law, if I took up some of the slack. I am a great believer, as I think you are, sir, in the spirit of the law, if not the letter.

TRICKY: Well, okay, if that's the reason. Do you want now to add any names of your own?

LEGAL COACH: As a matter of fact, Mr. President, I do.

TRICKY: One or two?

LEGAL COACH: As a matter of fact, Mr. President, five.

TRICKY: *Five?* But you were the one who made up the rule about only *two.*

LEGAL COACH: And I stand by it, Mr. President, or would, under the circumstances such as existed at the time I suggested it. But I am dealing at this moment with what I can only call "a clear and present danger." I am afraid, Mr. President, that if I were to submit only two of these five names that I have just this minute come up with, this administration would be in the most serious clear and present danger you can imagine of appearing to be out of its mind. If, on the other hand, the five names are submitted together, thus suggesting some kind of plot, a charge that might otherwise have appeared, at best, to be an opportunistic and vicious attack on two individuals we don't happen to like, will take on an air of the plausible in the mind of the nation, such as it is.

Surely, Mr. President, you will permit me at least to *read* the names of the five. This is, after all, a free country where even the man in the street can say what's on his mind, provided it isn't so provocative that it might lead somebody in another state, who doesn't even hear it, to riot. It would be a sad irony indeed, if the man who is this nation's bulwark against those very riots that such freedom of speech tends to inspire, was to be denied *his* rights under the First Amendment.

TRICKY: It would, it would. And you can rest assured that so long as I am President that particular sad irony—if I understand it correctly—is not going to happen.

LEGAL COACH: Thank you, Mr. President. Now try not to think of the five individually, but rather as a kind of secret gang, protected, as much as anything, by the seeming disparateness of individual personality and profession. 1: the folk singer, Joan Baez. 2: the Mayor of New York, John Lancelot. 3: the dead rock musician, Jimi Hendrix. 4: the TV star, Johnny Carson . . .

ALL: *Johnny Carson?*

LEGAL COACH (*smiling*): Who better to be acquitted? It's always best, you see, to have one acquitted, especially if he appears to have been unjustly accused in the first place. It provides the jury with a means of funneling all their uncertainty in one direction, makes them feel they've been fair about the whole thing. Makes the convictions themselves look better all around. And, of course, freeing Johnny Carson, you'll be freeing the most popular man in America (besides yourself, Mr. President). Why, we can even, midway through the trial, have the President step in and make a statement in Carson's behalf. Exactly as he did about Manson, only the other way around this time. Imagine, the whole country crying "Free Johnny!" and the President going on TV and casting serious doubt on the charges raised against this great entertainer.

TRICKY: And then when he's free, I could have a press conference! Wouldn't that be something? I could say, "*H-e-e-e-re's* Johnny," and he could come out from behind the curtain and do his cute little golf stroke! He could make jokes about being in jail with the other conspirators. Maybe he could even wear a ball and chain and a striped suit!

POLITICAL COACH: Fantastic! And we could do it on prime time the night before the election. While Musty is boring their pants off about how honest the pine trees are in Maine, we'll be on TV with Johnny Carson!

LEGAL COACH: And that's not all, gentlemen. You have not yet heard the name of my *fifth* conspirator.

POLITICAL COACH: Merv Griffin!

LEGAL COACH: No, not Merv Griffin . . . Jacqueline Charisma Colossus.

(*Stunned silence*)

Daring, yes. Absurd? I think not. Consider first, gentlemen, that like the other four conspirators, her Christian name too begins with a "J". Now you cannot imagine the mileage we can get out of a seemingly nonsensical fact like that. Overnight the newspapers and the TV commentators are going to begin calling them "The Five J's," thereby linking them together in the public mind as though they were the Dionne quintuplets, or the New York Knicks. Just by that ruse alone, we will have moved halfway toward a conviction. Inevitably there would be speculation—we'll see to that—about the relationship between Mrs. Colossus and Mayor Lancelot. Isn't it about time that we turned those looks of his to our advantage instead of his? Then too there is the former First Lady's bitterness toward her own country, as manifested in her decision to marry a foreigner and live in a foreign country.

POLITICAL COACH: Well, it isn't exactly as though she's living in Peking or Hanoi, you know.

LEGAL COACH: I've considered that, and I think that the wisest course to follow is not to mention the name of the country itself. We'll just keep saying foreign—suggesting intrigue and despots and shady operations—and hope that nobody will remember it's only Greece.

POLITICAL COACH: Jackie and Lancelot—I've got to admit, we're going to get the headlines on this one. But why Jimi Hendrix, if he's dead?

LEGAL COACH: Because we haven't had a rock performer yet.

And personally I think the parents of the country are ready to hang one of those bastards. We'll start cautiously, however, with a dead one. And if we don't pick up any flak there, we'll get ourselves a live one in time for the election . . . And, of course, last but not least, his name begins with a "J."

TRICKY: I must say, from the sound if it, you certainly appear to have thought this through in all its ramifications in only about five minutes. The political advantages to be gained by associating Lancelot and the Charisma name with rock singers and folk singers seem to me inestimable. And indicting and then freeing Johnny Carson is probably just about the most fantastic opportunity for self-aggrandizement I've come upon since Hiss.

LEGAL COACH: Thank you, Mr. President.

TRICKY: But—and this is a very big but—there is the rule, of your own devising, that we all agreed to earlier. Yes, I know you see this as "a clear and present danger" to the party— but I happen to see it as nothing short of a tremendous boon. Consequently, I am not going to allow you to submit these five names. But—and here is an even bigger but—*but*, because the five *are* inextricably linked by their first initial, I am going to ask you rather to submit them as though they were one. And to indicate that they are to be tabulated as one and not five, I am going to place a large bracket here in the margin, like so . . . See? I want all of you to see. I have just done exactly as I said I would. Please take a good look, so that afterwards there is no cause to question the honesty of these proceedings. (*All examine the bracket and agree it is a bracket, just as the President said*) Now then, Professor. Your vote.

HIGHBROW COACH: I cast my vote for Curt Flood and Curt Flood alone. Not only is his a fresh name to a country that is growing pretty weary of the Berrigans and the Panthers— and, with all due respect, is sick to death of Jacqueline Charisma—but on top of that he is, as I said earlier, someone we can slander and vilify without any danger of turning him into a hero or a martyr. In the argot of baseball, he is a natural.

TRICKY: Very good. (*Records the vote*) And, Reverend? Have

you reached a final decision? You can't say I haven't given you time to make a wise choice.

SPIRITUAL COACH: No, I can't. Only I'm afraid that having listened to everything that's been said, I'm really more confused now than when I began. I mean I'm still very much for Jane Fonda. She is still far and away my first choice. But once I get beyond her—well, I just can't make up my mind. And it really would be terrible to do the wrong thing, wouldn't it, given the gravity and seriousness of what we're about . . . ? (*To the General*) Excuse me, but who did you vote for again?

MILITARY COACH: Hanoi and Haiphong.

SPIRITUAL COACH (*to Political Coach*): And you?

POLITICAL COACH: Hanoi, without Haiphong.

SPIRITUAL COACH (*to Legal Coach*): And you have the five-in-one—and what were the others?

LEGAL COACH: Berrigans, Panthers and Flood.

SPIRITUAL COACH (*throwing his hands up*): Oh, this is just impossible! Each one sounds better than the one before! Oh—the heck with it! Eeny, meeny, miney, moe . . . Okay! Jane Fonda *and* Curt Flood! Done!

TRICKY (*Records the Reverend's vote*): Now that all the ballots have been cast, gentlemen, I am going once again to pass this sheet of paper among you so that you may be certain that your votes have been correctly tabulated. Even the President of the United States, you know, is capable of making a clerical error, and if he has, he certainly hopes that he can be a big enough man to admit it. (*He passes the paper among them*)

LEGAL COACH: Jimi Hendrix, Mr. President—the first name is spelled J-i-m-i, not J-i-m-m-y, as you've written it here.

TRICKY: Well, let's correct it then, because that is just the sort of error, inadvertently made, that tends to be totally misconstrued by the press. Now I never claimed to know how to spell the names of every colored person in this country, but I will tell you this much: where someone's name is concerned, colored or not, he has a constitutional right to have it spelled correctly on any indictment that is handed down on him, no matter how absurd or outrageous the charges themselves. And so long as I am President, I am going to make every effort to see that this is done. Now, J-i-m *what?*

LEGAL COACH: I.

TRICKY: J-i-m-*i*. There. And I'll initial the change, just to make clear exactly who is responsible for both the error and the correction. There!

Now I only wish that the wonderful colored people of this country could have seen the scrupulosity with which I attended to a matter seemingly so picayune as this one. Oh sure, the media would still find something to carp about, you can bank on that. But I am certain, if I know the great majority of good, hard-working colored people in this country, that the time I just took from my pressing duties as President of the United States and Leader of the Free World to correct a single letter in one of their names would not have gone unnoticed and unappreciated. Call me a dreamer; call me a believer in humanity; call me, as the song has it, a cockeyed optimist; and be sure to call me a big man too, for admitting to my error; but I am sure that they would understand just how difficult a problem this is for us to solve, given the kinds of ways they spell those names of theirs, and I think they would have that wonderful wisdom, such as comes to people who work in menial occupations, to realize that a job of these proportions is not going to be completed overnight, and that consequently we are not about to be bullied into spelling their names correctly by marches or demonstrations or mule trains parked on the White House lawn. We will spell them right but in our own sweet time, and according to our own secret timetable, on earth as it is in Heaven.

SPIRITUAL COACH: Amen.

TRICKY: And, my friends, on that sanctimonious note, I am going to call this conference to a close. At ten A.M., we shall meet to settle upon the exact nature of the crime. In the meantime, I will remain here in the locker room, in uniform . . .

SPIRITUAL COACH: Mr. President, it is nearly dawn. You must get some rest. You must take your helmet off and go to bed.

TRICKY: I couldn't sleep now, Reverend, if I tried. Not with a smear campaign of this magnitude before me.

SPIRITUAL COACH: But a man has only so much to give . . .

TRICKY: When it comes to something like this, Reverend, I have to say, immodest as it may sound, I am indefatigable. No, I will remain in uniform, helmet and all, and with the aid of the ballots you have cast here in this free election, I will hammer out, in the lonely vigil of the night, the conspiracy that seems to me most beneficial to my career. I only hope and pray that I am equal to the task. Good night, gentlemen, and thank you.

ALL: Good night, Mr. President. (*They rise to leave*)

TRICKY: And don't forget to hand in your uniforms at the door. I won't mention names, but I understand that last time one of you tried to smuggle his out, under his street clothes, in order to show off at home to his wife and children. Of course, I understand the temptation. How many times have I wanted to address the nation in my shoulder guards! I've never told this to a soul, but strictly between us, at the time of the Cambodian incursion, I did go on nationwide TV, unbeknownst to everyone, wearing my regulation National Football League athletic supporter. I just couldn't help myself. I'd seen *Patton* and I'd invaded Cambodia, and I guess the whole thing went to my head. Of course, not a word beyond these four walls: if any of my critics found out, well, you know how they like to jump on Dixon. All I have to do is wear a football player's jockstrap on TV while making a foreign policy speech and the morning papers would have me pegged as a psychopath. Down here in the street underground locker room, it's one thing—up there in the real world, banker's gray!

ALL: You can trust us with your secrets, Mr. President.

TRICKY (*moved*): I know I can . . . All right, then. It remains only for each of you, as he passes from the room, to slap me on the behind the way the pros do coming out of the huddle. And don't forget to say, "Way to go, Tricky D, way to go!"

4

Tricky Addresses the Nation

(The Famous "Something Is Rotten in the State of Denmark" Speech)

G OOD EVENING, my fellow Americans.
I come before you tonight with a message of national importance. While it is true that I do not intend to offer you false hope by minimizing the nature of the crisis confronting our nation at this hour, I do not believe there is cause for any such alarm as you may have seen or heard in the news media from those critical of the decisions I have reached in the last twenty-four hours.

Now I know there are always those who would prefer that we take a weak, cowardly and dishonorable position in the face of a crisis. They of course are entitled to their opinion. I am certain, however, that the great majority of the American people will agree that the actions I have taken in the confrontation between the United States of America and the sovereign state of Denmark are indispensable to our dignity, our honor, our moral and spiritual idealism, our credibility around the world, the soundness of the economy, our greatness, our dedication to the vision of our forefathers, the human spirit, the divinely inspired dignity of man, our treaty commitments, the principles of the United Nations, and progress and peace for all people.

Now no one is more aware than I am of the political consequences of taking bold and forthright action in behalf of our dignity, idealism and honor, to choose just three. But I would rather be a one-term President and take these noble, heroic measures against the state of Denmark, than be a two-term President by accepting humiliation at the hands of a tenth-rate military power. I want to make that perfectly clear.

Let me tell you now the measures I have ordered taken to

deal with Denmark, and the reasons for my decision. (*Picks up his pointer and turns to map of Scandinavia*)

First: despite the treacherous manner in which the Pro-Pornography government in Copenhagen has moved against the United States, I have responded swiftly and effectively to gain the military initiative. At this very moment, the American Sixth Fleet, dispatched by my order to the Baltic and the North Seas, is in complete command of the waterways to and from Denmark, as indicated on this map. (*Points to the Baltic Sea and the North Sea*) Aircraft carriers, troop ships and destroyers have been placed in a strategic ring around the Danish peninsula of Jutland (*points*) and the numerous adjacent Danish islands, all of which you see here colored in red. Taken together these territories make Denmark approximately as large (*turns to map of United States*) as the wonderful states of New Hampshire and Vermont, famous for their beautiful autumn foliage and delicious maple syrup, and colored here in white.

Now let me tell you the results of this action, ordered by me as Commander-in-Chief of the Armed Forces meeting his responsibilities.

To all intents and purposes, Denmark is at this time isolated by a blockade as impenetrable as the blockade with which President John F. Charisma in 1962 prevented Soviet nuclear missiles from entering Cuba and the Western Hemisphere, which is here (*points to map of Western Hemisphere*). And that as we all know was the finest and most courageous hour of his Presidency. This blockade, then, is exactly like that one.

Now while it is true that I have effectively isolated Denmark from the rest of the world, I have refused to take an isolationist position for America of the kind my critics would counsel me to take in this crisis. Because let there be no mistake about it: America cannot live in isolation if it expects to live in peace.

Now I hear you ask: "Mr. President, you have moved swiftly and effectively to protect our dignity, idealism and honor; but what about our national security—isn't that endangered, too?"

Well, that is a good question and one that deserves a thoughtful answer. For we are all familiar with the belligerent and expansionist policies of the state of Denmark, in particular the territorial designs that country has had upon the continental United States ever since the eleventh century. As you remember, at that time landings were made upon the North American continent by forces under the command of Eric the Red, and later under the command of his son, Leif Ericson. These landings by the Red family and their Viking hordes were of course made without warning and in direct violation of the Monroe Doctrine. Aside from these invasions of a paramilitary nature, there were also various unsuccessful attempts made by these Vikings to establish privileged sanctuaries on our eastern seaboard, right here (*points*) in the vicinity of Boston, the birthplace of Paul Revere and his world-renowned midnight ride, and the site of the famous Boston Tea Party.

So when you ask me if our national security is threatened by these Danes, with their long-standing history of open contempt for our territorial integrity, I think I have to answer in all candor, yes it is. And that is why I have made clear to the Pro-Pornography government in Copenhagen tonight that I do not intend to react to any renewed threat to our territorial integrity, to our honor, or to our idealism, with plaintive diplomatic protests. And in order that there should be no misunderstanding of my position, I have ordered the American Seventh Army, stationed in West Germany, to be mobilized in striking position here (*points*) at the fifty-fifth parallel on the border between Germany and Denmark. And I assure you, my fellow Americans, as I have assured the Pro-Pornography government in Copenhagen, and as I would have assured the Red family regime in the eleventh century had I been your President at that time, that I will not for a moment hesitate to send our brave American fighting men over the border and into Denmark tonight, if that is what is necessary to prevent our children from having to fight the descendants of Eric the Red in the streets of (*pointing with his pointer*) Portland, Boston, New York, Philadelphia, Baltimore, Washington, Norfolk, Wilmington, Charleston, Savannah, Jacksonville, Miami, Key Biscayne and, of course, points west.

Now, though Denmark is effectively isolated from the world by the Sixth Fleet, and effectively threatened with occupation by the Seventh Army, the fact is that the Danish people have yet to see a single armed American soldier on their soil.

Contrary to whatever wild rumors have been irresponsibly disseminated by the alarmists and sensationalists in the news media, the fact of the matter is that (*checks his watch*) as of this hour, we have no troops inside Denmark, serving either in a combat capacity, or as advisers in uniform to the Danish Anti-Pornography Resistance, considered by many the legitimate Danish government-in-exile.

Whatever reports you may have heard of an armed American invasion of Danish territory are categorically false, and constitute a deliberate distortion of the facts.

The truth is this: the amphibious landing by a detachment of one thousand brave American Marines that did occur only a few hours ago, at midnight Danish time, was not an invasion of Danish territory, but the liberation from Danish domination of a landmark that has been sacred for centuries to English-speaking peoples around the world, and particularly so to Americans.

I am speaking of the liberation of the town of Elsinore, the home of the fortress popularly known to tourists as "Hamlet's Castle." After centuries of occupation and touristic exploitation by the Danes, the town and the castle, which owe their fame entirely to William Shakespeare, the greatest writer of English in all recorded history, are occupied tonight by American soldiers, speaking the tongue of the immortal bard.

Let's look again at the map. Here on the coast is Elsinore, approximately thirty-five miles north of the capital city of Copenhagen. Because of its proximity to the capital, it was believed for centuries to be heavily guarded and impregnable to attack. It is surely a great tribute to both our intelligence units and our brave fighting Marines, that American forces were able to wade ashore at midnight and under cover of darkness drive the foreign invaders from the castle without firing a single shot.

I am proud to report that the guard on duty at Elsinore was so taken by surprise that when roused from his bed by a knocking at the gate, he came to the door in his pajamas and opened it so wide that our brave Marines were able to overrun and secure the grounds in a matter of minutes. The guard, who was the only foreign invader on the premises at that time, has been taken into custody, along with his tourist guidebooks, and a thorough interrogation is currently under way in the famous dungeons of the castle, in accordance with the rules laid down at the Geneva Convention, to which this country is a proud signatory.

Following the liberation of Elsinore, I have sent a communiqué to the Pro-Pornography government in Copenhagen, making it absolutely clear that our action was in no way directed to the security interests of any nation, Denmark included. Any government that chooses to use these actions as a pretext for harming relations with the United States will be doing so on its own responsibility, and we will draw the appropriate conclusions.

Incidentally, in that connection, if the Danish Army should attempt to harass or dislodge our Marines in any way whatsoever from "Hamlet's Castle," it would be interpreted by Americans of all walks of life, professors and poets as well as housewives and hardhats, as a direct affront to our national heritage. I would have no choice but to respond in kind by retaliating against the statue of Hans Christian Andersen in Copenhagen with the largest air strike ever called upon a European city.

I realize that as a result of my decision to free Elsinore from the yoke of foreign domination, the American people are going to be assailed by counsels of defeat and doubt from some of the most widely known opinion leaders of the nation. But let me say this to those defeatists and doubters: should the state of Denmark, now or in the future, attempt to occupy Mark Twain's Missouri, or the wonderful old South of *Gone with the Wind*, in the way that they have so ruthlessly occupied "Hamlet's Castle" all these centuries, I would no more hesitate to send in the Marines to free Hannibal and Atlanta and Richmond and Jackson and St. Louis, than I did tonight to free Elsinore. And I firmly believe that the great majority of the American people would stand behind me then, as I know they do now.

Fortunately, however, I now have every expectation that not only our children, but our children's children, will never have to defend with their blood the literary landmarks of their native land from the onslaught of the Danish Tourist Office, because we, their parents, failed to do our duty by them in a quaint little seaside village in a faraway land.

The next move is up to Copenhagen. They have two choices. Either they can extend to us the diplomatic courtesy we have requested of them under international law; or, in the face of that request, they can continue to display the intransigence, belligerence and contempt that originally touched off this grave confrontation.

Now if they choose within the next twelve hours to negotiate with us in good faith by conceding to us what we want, I shall immediately call off the blockade of their coast, just as John F. Charisma called off the blockade of Cuba in his finest hour. Furthermore, I will reduce at the rate of one sixteenth a year the number of troops massed at their borders. Lastly, the guard taken prisoner at Elsinore castle will be returned to Copenhagen, provided the interrogation now being conducted does not reveal him to be a Danish citizen in the employ of the Danish government.

If, however, Copenhagen should refuse to negotiate in good faith by giving us what we want, I shall immediately order 100,000 armed American troops onto Danish soil.

Now, quickly, let me make one thing very clear: this will not constitute an invasion, either. Once we have overrun the country, bombarded the major cities, devastated the countryside, destroyed the military, disarmed the citizenry, jailed the leaders of the Pro-Pornography government, and established in Copenhagen the government currently in exile so that, as Abraham Lincoln said, it shall not perish from this earth, we shall immediately withdraw our troops.

For unlike the Danes, this great country harbors no designs on foreign territory. Nor do we wish to interfere in the internal affairs of another country. Despite our very deep sympathy with the aspirations of the Danish Anti-Pornography Resistance, we have over the years maintained a scrupulous wait-and-see attitude, in the hope that these eminently decent and idealistic men of the D.A.R. would be permitted to achieve political office in Copenhagen through democratic means. Unfortunately, the Pro-Pornography Party would not permit this to come about, but repeatedly, in one so-called free election after another, chose to brainwash the Danish people into voting *against* the D.A.R. So elaborate and thoroughgoing were these brainwashing techniques, that eventually the D.A.R. did not collect a single vote and, to all intents and purposes, might just as well not have been on the ballot. In this way did the forces of filth and smut make a mockery of the democratic processes in Denmark.

My fellow Americans, it is precisely this sort of contempt for the rights of others that Copenhagen would now display toward the United States of America. Only this country is not about to be bullied and disgraced by a tenth-rate military power, and see our credibility destroyed in every area of the world where only the power of the United States deters aggression. And that is why tonight I have put the leaders in Copenhagen on notice that if they continue to refuse what we ask of them, I will bring all our military might to bear to restore to legitimate authority in Denmark a government that will respond to reason instead of force, a government that stands for decency instead of degradation, a government, as Abraham Lincoln said, of, by and for, not only the Danish people, but the American people and all good people everywhere.

What are we asking of Copenhagen, my fellow Americans? Neither more nor less than what we requested and received from the United Kingdom in 1968, when, according to the rules of international law and the custom of civilized nations, that country returned to our shores the fugitive from justice who was later convicted of the murder of Martin Luther King.

What are we asking of Copenhagen? Neither more nor less than what we would have requested of the Soviet Union in 1963, had President Charisma's murderer attempted to take refuge for a second time in that country.

What are we asking of Copenhagen? Nothing more nor less than that they surrender to the proper American authorities the fugitive from the Washington Senators of the American League of Professional Baseball Clubs, the man who fled this country on April 27, 1971, exactly one week to the day before the uprising of the Boy Scouts in Washington—the man named Charles Curtis Flood.

—

Now events have moved so rapidly during these past twenty-four hours that in the interest of clarity I should like to review for you in all its pertinent details, the case of Charles Curtis Flood, who, previous to his disappearance, played baseball right here in Washington, under the alias "Curt Flood."

As always, I want to make everything as perfectly clear to you as I can. That is why you hear me say over and over again, in my speeches and press conferences and interviews, that I want to make one thing very clear, or two things, or three things, or as many things as I have on my agenda to make very clear. To give you a little glimpse of the lighter side of the President's life (*impish endearing smile*), my wife tells me that I even say it in my dreams. (*Back to business*) My fellow Americans, I am confident that you recognize as well as I do, that any man who says he wants to make things perfectly clear as often as I do, both awake and in his sleep, obviously does not have anything to hide.

Now who is this man who calls himself "Curt Flood"? To many Americans, particularly the wonderful mothers of our land, that name is probably as strange as the name Eric Starvo Galt, which, you may remember, was the alias taken by James Earl Ray, the convicted murderer of Martin Luther King.

Who is "Curt Flood"? Well, until a year or so ago, the answer would have been simple enough. Flood was a baseball player for the St. Louis Cardinals of the National League, a center fielder with a more than respectable lifetime batting average of .294. Not a Hall of Famer, not the best baseball player in the big leagues, but far from the worst. Many even believed that his finest years lay ahead of him. I am proud to say that I, as an avid fan of baseball as well as all manly sports, was among them.

Then tragedy struck. In 1970, with no more warning than the Japanese gave at Pearl Harbor, "Curt Flood," as he then called himself, turned upon the very sport that had made him one of the highest-paid Negroes in the history of our country. In 1970, he announced—and this is an exact quotation from his own writings—"Somebody needs to go up against the system," and proceeded to bring a legal action against Organized Baseball. According to the Commissioner of Baseball himself, this action would destroy the game of baseball as we know it, if Flood were to emerge victorious.

Now no one expects ordinary citizens, who earn their liveli-
hoods outside the legal profession, to be able to wade through
the intricacies of a legal suit such as this fugitive from justice
has brought against our great national pastime for the purpose
of destroying it. That's why people hire lawyers in the first
place. I know when I was a lawyer that was why people hired
me, and I think without boasting, that I was able to help them.
When I was a young, struggling lawyer, and Pitter and I were
living on nine dollars a week out in Prissier, California, which
is right here (*points*), I would read through my lawbooks and
study long into the night in order to help my clients, most of
whom were wonderful young people just like Pitter and myself. At that time, by the way, I had the following debts outstanding:

—$1,000 on our neat little house.

—$200 to my dear parents.

—$110 to my loyal and devoted brother.

—$15 to our fine dentist, a warm-hearted Jewish man for
  whom we had the greatest respect.

—$4.35 to our kindly grocer, an old Italian who always had
  a good word for everybody. I still remember his name.
  Tony.

—75 cents to our Chinese laundryman, a slightly-built fellow who nonetheless worked long into the night over his
  shirts, just as I did over my lawbooks, so that his children might one day attend the college of their choice. I
  am sure they have grown up to be fine and outstanding
  Chinese-Americans.

—60 cents to the Polish man, or Polack, as the Vice President would affectionately call him, who delivered the ice
  for our old-fashioned icebox. He was a strong man with
  great pride in his native Poland.

We also owed moneys amounting to $2.90 to a wonderful
Irish plumber, a wonderful Japanese-American handyman and
a wonderful couple from the deep South who happened to be
of the same race as we were, and whose children played with
ours in perfect harmony, despite the fact that they were from
another region.

I am proud to say that every last dime that we owed to these
wonderful people, I paid back through long hard hours of

work in my law office. And the point I wish to make to you tonight, my fellow Americans, is that because of those long, hard hours of work, I believe myself qualified today to understand in all its cunning and clever intricacies the legal action that this fugitive has brought against the sport made famous by Babe Ruth, Lou Gehrig, Ty Cobb, Tris Speaker, Rogers Hornsby, Honus Wagner, Walter Johnson, Christy Mathewson and Ted Williams—Hall of Famers all, and men that America can well be proud of.

And let me tell you this: having studied this case in all its ramifications, I find I can only concur in the wise opinion of the Commissioner of Baseball when he says that a victory for this fugitive would inevitably lead to the death of the great game that has probably done more to make American boys into strong, decent and law-abiding men than any single institution in the land. Frankly, I do not know of a better way for our enemies to undermine the youth of this country, than to destroy this game of baseball and all it represents.

Now there is another question you may want to ask, and it is this: "Mr. President, if Curt Flood is out to undermine the youth of this country by destroying baseball, where could he possibly find a lawyer who would be willing to take his case to court?"

Now I am going to be as forthright as I know how in answering that question.

Scrupulous and honest and dedicated to the principles of justice as ninety-nine and nine-tenths of the lawyers in this country are, there is in my profession, as in any other, I'm afraid, that tiny percentage who will do and say anything if the stakes are high enough or the price is right. In law school our professors used to call them "ambulance-chasers" and "shysters." Unfortunately, these men cling not only to the bottom rungs of the profession, which would be bad enough, but on rare occasions manage to climb to the very top—yes, even to positions of great responsibility and power.

Now I needn't remind you of the scandal that took place here in Washington during the tenure of the last administration. You all remember that a lawyer appointed by my predecessor to the Supreme Court of the United States, the highest court in the entire land, had to resign as a justice of that court because of financial wrongdoing. Horrifying as that incident was to every decent American, there seems to me nothing to be gained now by reawakening the sense of moral outrage that swept the nation at that time.

As some of you will be quick to point out, there were actually *two* men who found it necessary to resign from the Supreme Court, after they had been appointed justices of that court by my predecessor. But whether there was one, two, three, four or five, I simply do not believe it is in the interests of national unity to harp upon the errors, grievous though they were, of an administration that you voters, in your wisdom, repudiated three years ago.

What is past is past; no one knows that better than I do. If I recall to you now the names of these two men who found it necessary to tender unprecedented resignations to the highest court in the land, it is only to answer, as forthrightly as I know how, your question, "What kind of lawyer would represent Curt Flood?"

The two men who resigned from the Supreme Court were Mr. Abe Fortas and Mr. Arthur Goldberg. My fellow Americans, the name of the lawyer representing Charles Curtis Flood is Arthur Goldberg. G-o-l-d-b-e-r-g.

Now, before I am accused of trying to shock or alarm the American public, let me say that I myself am not the least bit shocked or alarmed by this turn of events. Having served on the highest court of the land, Mr. Goldberg undoubtedly now knows the ins and the outs of the law as well as the most devious lawyer in the country. Moreover, none of us should be surprised to discover a man who has fallen from the pinnacle of his profession, willing to try just about anything to get back into the public eye. Before the Flood case is concluded, I would not be surprised to find Mr. Abe Fortas joining forces with Mr. Arthur Goldberg in defense of Charles Curtis Flood.

Now you may say to me, "But surely, Mr. President, any man who wishes to destroy the game of baseball, and enlists such attorneys as these is his attempt to accomplish that end, is not even *entitled* to a hearing in court. Not only is he making a mockery of our entire judicial system, but in order for him to go 'up against the system' we, the American taxpayers, have to pay for the upkeep of the very system he is working to annihilate. If we allow that, then we might as well allow self-confessed Communists to teach our children in the classrooms. We might as well throw down our arms right now in the battle for freedom, and hand over our schools and our courtrooms without a fight to the avowed enemies of democracy."

Well, let me assure you that I couldn't agree more. In fact, we are right now studying ways of restoring the dignity and majesty and sanctity of old to the courtrooms of the land. As you know, one experiment that we have tried with some success here in Washington is the "Justice in the Streets Program." This is a program whereby sentencing and punishment, for capital crimes as well as felonies and misdemeanors, is delivered on the spot at the very moment the crime is committed, or even appears to have been committed. Through J.I.T.S.P. and related methods of expediting the judicial process, we hope to be able not only to unclog the court calendars but to wind down the whole trial system by Election Day 1972.

Now, winding down the trial system will of course be a great boon to the dignity of our judges, who will no longer be forced to demean themselves by dealing with the most undesirable elements in the population. Our judges, so terribly overworked as they are today, hopefully will not have to deal with *any* elements of the population once the trial system is completely phased out. This will leave them free for the reflection and reading that is so essential to maintaining a high level of judicial wisdom.

The second benefit to be derived from replacing the archaic and slow-moving trial system by more modern judicial methods is this: the courtrooms of this land will once again be a wonderfully inspiring place for the schoolchildren of America to visit. I see a day, in fact, when parents will be able to send their children off to visit a courtroom without fear that they will have to witness anything inappropriate or unsettling to the eyes or ears of a growing youngster. I see a day in which not only schoolchildren, but mothers holding their babies, will be able to walk through the halls of justice to observe the judges in their wonderful black robes, relieved of the time-consuming burdens of the courtroom, gathering the wisdom of the ages from their thinking and their lawbooks. I see a day when schoolchildren and mothers holding their babies will be able to sit in the jury boxes, just as though a real trial were under-way, and in this way experience at firsthand the age-old grandeur of a legal tradition that has come down to us in all its glory from Anglo-Saxon times.

But of course we cannot undo overnight the judicial mess that we have inherited from the previous administration, and the thirty-five administrations before his. As a result, even as we are winding down the trial system that has caused this country so much expense and confusion, we have still to deal in the courtroom with the likes of Charles Curtis Flood and his team of attorneys.

Now fortunately two different courts have already found *against* Charles Curtis Flood in his attempt to destroy the game of baseball. These decisions made during the tenure in office of this administration, have gone a long way, I am sure, to restoring the confidence of a public only recently so disap-pointed by the verdict reached in Mayor John Lancelot's New York, to free thirteen members of the Black Panther Party.

Of course I have no more right to tell the Mayor of New York how to run his city than he has to tell me how to run the country or the world. But I must, in all honesty, say that I was as startled as the great majority of Americans, first by that ver-dict, and second, by Mayor Lancelot's decision, following the verdict, to allow these thirteen Black Panthers to resume their political activities in his city. All I can say as President is that I trust this will not become the model for the treatment of the acquitted in other cities around the country.

Now I have no doubt that if the Mayor of New York were in my place he would not hesitate to declare a hands-off policy where Charles Curtis Flood is concerned. If self-confessed Black Panthers are to be left free to stalk the streets that are no longer safe for our wives and daughters, why bother to bring to justice a man who has *not* confessed to being a Black Pan-ther? So, I am afraid, the logic would run, if another man were in my shoes.

But so long as he is not, so long as I am the duly elected President of the United States, I can assure you that there will be no mollycoddling of any fugitive who, after twice being prevented by the courts from destroying baseball and under-mining the youth of this country, decided that he, Charles

Curtis Flood, had had enough of law and order and life within the system. There will be no mollycoddling of a man who undertook to subvert and corrupt the youth of this country by the most insidious means imaginable, with a recklessness and a viciousness equaled not even by the most hardened drug pushers and the most loathsome pornographers.

No, it was not to the dissolute, unprincipled and over-indulged on our college campuses that Charles Curtis Flood turned with his plan to destroy America. Nor was this yet another call to violence to the dropouts and hippies and flag-defilers of the left.

Who then, you ask, did he seek to corrupt? The answer, my fellow Americans, is the Boy Scouts of America. Not only did Charles Curtis Flood incite them to riot, and tamper with their morals, but what is even worse, it was he and he alone who drove the Boy Scouts headlong into the tragedy that occurred here yesterday in Washington, D.C.

Surely the great majority of Americans will agree that it is a tragedy in every sense of the word when the brave fighting men of our Army are called upon to risk their lives in the streets of Washington, D.C., instead of in a foreign country. But that is what happened here in the nation's capital, when, through a long day and a long night, our brave soldiers, armed only with loaded rifles, fixed bayonets, tear-gas canisters and gas masks, faced a mob of Boy Scouts, numbering nearly ten thousand.

I am sure you all know by now the nature of the chants and the songs that these ten thousand Boy Scouts were singing in the streets of the nation's capital. I am sure you are familiar with the kind of placards they were waving before the television cameras. I do not intend to repeat to you the wording of those posters. It should suffice to say that they did justice to the language and interests of Charles Curtis Flood, whose favorite city, according to his own writings, is Copenhagen, Denmark, the pornography capital of the world.

The posters are presently in the hands of the FBI, whose laboratories have already begun the painstaking job of finger-printing each and every poster, and submitting them to blood tests so as to determine the correlation between the obscenity printed on an individual poster and the blood type of the Boy Scout bearing the poster containing those objectionable words. If such correlations can be established with a reasonable degree of accuracy—and we think they can—it will of course be of great assistance to our law enforcement agencies. Under our program of "preventive detention," we will be able to round up those with suspect blood types *before* such demonstrations as this even get under way, thus preventing them from violating community standards of decency, and the ordinary everyday rules of courtesy, decorum and good taste that are sacred to the great majority of Americans.

As you all know from the headlines, of the approximately ten thousand Boy Scouts who assembled here in Washington during the two-day uprising to threaten the lives of our brave fighting men, it was necessary to kill only three in order to maintain law and order. That breaks down to one and one-half Scouts dead per diem, while nine thousand nine hundred and ninety-eight and a half Scouts continued to live full and active lives the first day, and nine thousand, nine hundred and ninety-seven the second.

Now I would think that by anyone's standards, a mortality rate in a crisis of this kind of .0003 is a wonderful tribute to the very great restraint with which we were able to confront what could have been a terrible tragedy for our soldiers. Certainly it should give solace to all of those who detest bloodshed as much as I do, and put the lie once and for all to the vicious charge that it was the military and not the Scouts who were responsible for the violence. On the other hand, I think the fact that we did have three Scouts dead by the end of the second day is a good indication of the necessary firmness with which we always try to balance off our very great restraint.

Of course, I am sure the great majority of Americans realize that there is always going to be a small, vocal minority of cavilers and critics, who are never going to be satisfied, no matter how perfectly balanced the restraint and the firmness with which we deal with civil disruptions of this kind. Even if there should be only one person dead over a two-day period, or as little as half a person a day; even if over a two-day period there should be only one person who is slightly *maimed*—these critics will begin to talk as though the tragedy wasn't the overwhelming danger to which tens of thousands of our brave soldiers were subjected, but the maiming of one person out of only ten thousand, and what is more than likely, an out-oftowner who, unlike our brave soldiers, had only to remain at home to stay out of harm's way.

Well, to this small vocal minority, let me make one thing very clear.

I too have great sympathy for the families of the three Boy Scouts who were killed here in Washington. I am a father, and I know full well how important children can be to a man's career; and incidentally, in that connection, a wife. As a matter of fact, my wife and I and our wonderful children had condolence messages prepared for far more than the three who died here, and were prepared to dispatch them on a moment's notice. Throughout the crisis I was in continuous touch with the morgue here in Washington, as I am with the morgues around the country, by a special "hot line," and had it been necessary to wire not three, but three thousand such messages, I assure you that my family and I would have seen that those words of sympathy had left the White House before the bodies were even cold. I am proud to say that my wife and my daughters were prepared to work far into the night in order that families less fortunate than our own might have some small comfort in their hour of need. Nor do we intend to forget these people when Christmas time rolls around.

But let there be no mistake about it: quick on the trigger as I may be with compassion for the innocent families, I am equally swift in my condemnation of these three guilty Scouts. And I say "guilty" because if they were not guilty they would not be dead. That is not the kind of country we live in.

Now I know there are those apologists for the Boy Scout uprising who have attempted to arouse sympathy for the three guilty Scouts by pointing out that while one had attained the rank of Eagle Scout, the other two were "only" Tenderfoots. If pressed they will concede that an Eagle Scout is a highly trained and disciplined youngster, capable of functioning as a guerilla insurrectionist because of the various survival tactics he has had to master in order to attain his key position in the

Scout infrastructure. But what of the two Tenderfoots, they ask. How could two little Tenderfoots pose so serious a threat to our national security as to make it necessary to kill them?

Well, let me answer that question, my fellow Americans, by showing you the weapons that were found concealed, hanging from the belts, of these "two little Tenderfoot Scouts" when their bodies were searched by the FBI, the Secret Service, the CIA, the Military Police, the Shore Patrol, the Attorney General's office, the Capitol Police Force, the Police Force of the District of Columbia, as well as by law enforcement officers summoned from around the country, to guarantee the probity and thoroughness of this investigation.

Now I am sure that we all still remember with a sad and mournful heart the 6.5-millimeter Italian carbine rifle purchased for $12.78 from a Chicago mail-order house by President Charisma's assassin, Lee Harvey Oswald, whom I mentioned earlier in connection with James Earl Ray and Charles Curtis Flood. In the mail-order catalog that rifle probably did not appear to be any more sophisticated than the weapon I am about to show you now, or any more capable of changing the course of history. And yet none of us will ever forget the impact it had upon President Charisma's career and my own. I know that to many of you this object that I am holding in my right hand looks as innocent and harmless as that $12.78 mail-order rifle undoubtedly did in the mail-order catalog. But let there be no mistake about it, it is just as effective, if not more so.

Firstly: whereas the rifle that destroyed President Charisma's political career measured forty inches overall, this knife that I hold here in my hand measures, with the blades sheathed, only four and five-eighths inches. This makes it an ideal weapon to use in public places, as opposed to a forty-inch rifle which might arouse suspicion on a school bus, or in a supermarket, or any of the hundred places where you and your loved ones find yourselves in the course of an ordinary day.

Secondly: it is a far more vicious weapon than an ordinary rifle and, needless to say, does not even begin to approach in humaneness a simple thousand-pound bomb, let alone a nuclear explosive. As one who was raised as a Quaker, you know, I have a particularly strong interest in being humane. This is why, since coming to office, I have done everything I can to get Congress to appropriate money for a weapons system that would make us number one in the world in that department. Surely there is no reason why a country with our scientific and technological resources cannot develop weapons with destructive powers so total and immediate as to guarantee to every man, woman and child on this planet what until now has been reserved for those few fortunate people who die in their sleep, and that is the comfort of passing unknowingly from this life into the next. Now that is the type of death people have dreamed about for themselves since time immemorial, and let it not be recorded that Trick E. Dixon lacked the moral and spiritual idealism to address himself to that dream.

But now let me ask you this, my fellow Americans. What could be further from the kind of painless death for men everywhere that this administration is working so hard to bring about, than that which is experienced by the victim of a knife such as I am holding in my hand? Not only is it necessary to deliver as many as five to ten horrifyingly painful stab wounds in order to kill somebody with a weapon this small, but in order to accomplish this the murderer must exhibit a sustained viciousness, a cold-blooded determination to kill, that, I assure you, would shock and appall a combat-tried B-52 bomber pilot no less than it does you and me.

And let me tell you how they manage that sustained viciousness: Unlike our pilots in Vietnam, whose satisfaction consists solely in getting the job done as quickly and thoroughly as possible, and who have no interest at all in whatever cries and moans may happen to arise from those who do not die instantly in the blast, the people who use weapons like these are obviously sadists of the sort who *enjoy* watching the blood run out of their victims, and, incidentally in that connection, hearing the cries of a person in physical torment. Why else would they use a weapon that takes up to half an hour to do the sort of job our pilots accomplish in a split second, and without the groaning and the gore?

Now let's look at the knife closely. I am going to open out the blades one by one, and describe to you the purpose and function of each. You should not be misled by its four-and-five-eighths-inch exterior into imagining that it is simply an instrument designed to kill. Like so many of the weapons carried by guerrilla revolutionaries around the world, it has multiple uses, of which murder of the agonizing and sadistic variety is but one.

Let's begin here, with the smallest of the four blades. In the language of those who employ such weapons, it is known as "the bottle opener." I'll tell you how it got that name in a moment. You will observe that it is hook-shaped at the end, and measures one inch and one-eighth. It is employed during the interrogation of prisoners primarily to gouge out one or both of the eyes. It is also used on the soles of the feet, which are sliced open, like so, with the point of the hook. Last, but not least, it is sometimes inserted into the mouth of a prisoner who will not talk, in order to slit the flesh at the upper part of the larynx, between the vocal cords. That opening up there is called the glottis, the "bottle opener" is derived from "glottal opener," the pet name originally attached to the blade by its most cold-blooded practitioners.

This second largest blade, measuring one inch and three-quarters, tapers to a point and probably looks to you to be a miniature bayonet. Do not be fooled by appearances. It has nothing to do with bayonets such as those our brave soldiers found it necessary to fix to their rifles in self-defense during the two-day Boy Scout uprising. This little blade is known as "the leather punch," and far from being an instrument of self-defense, it is yet another torture device, along the lines of the bottle opener. As its name suggests, it is used to punch holes in human flesh, or "leather" as the flesh is called by revolutionaries who consider their enemies to be no more than animals. It will come as no surprise to you to learn that it is most frequently driven into the palms of the hands, much the same way that the nails were in the movie *The Greatest Story Ever Told*.

Now this third blade, an eighth of an inch longer than the leather punch, is also wider and less tapered, and has a flat rather than a pointed end. It is known as "the screwdriver." Traditionally, it is inserted into the groove between the nails and the flesh and turned in a rotary fashion, like so. However, we know from intelligence reports that the screwdriver may also on occasion be introduced into bodily apertures, of which the nostrils and the ears are the only ones I shall choose to make mention of on nationwide television. Some of my political opponents may think otherwise—and they have every right to disagree with my position—but I, for one, have never believed it necessary to use bad language to make my point, and I have no intention of resorting to those kinds of tactics in the midst of a major address to the nation.

This last blade of the four is probably the one you're most familiar with from your nightmares. Two inches and three-quarters in length, nine-sixteenths of an inch at its widest point, it has a sharp cutting edge that I shall demonstrate for you on this piece of paper.

Incidentally, it is no accident that printed on this piece of paper is the Preamble to the Constitution, the Bill of Rights and the oft-quoted and much beloved Ten Commandments, with their famous "Thou shalt nots." As you all remember, these same Ten Commandments provided the wonderful and inspiring background for another motion picture of great spiritual value that I am sure the great majority of American families enjoyed as much as our family did. I don't think I am too far afield when I say that what you see printed on this sheet of paper (*close-up of paper*) is just about everything we believe in and cherish as a people.

I want you to watch as I demonstrate what this blade can do in a matter of seconds to all that you and I hold near and dear.

(*He slices the piece of paper into one-inch strips and then holds them up for the audience to see*)

Of course you can peel apples with a blade like this, you can slice your potatoes for frying and you can cut up your cucumbers, radishes, tomatoes, onions and celery for salad. And I am sure that those who would seek to exonerate these three Scouts will maintain that it was only to prepare a delicious salad such as I described that they secreted these weapons upon their belts and carried them hundreds of miles across state lines to the nation's capital. I am afraid that whether it is knife-carrying Boy Scouts or card-carrying Communists, there will always be a handful of apologists around to come to their defense.

My fellow Americans, I want to leave it to you, and not to the apologists, to decide. I ask you to look at this knife, with all four of its blades unsheathed, blades capable of inflicting physical torment of a kind that goes all the way back to the Crucifixion and beyond. I ask you to look at this four-pronged instrument of torture. I ask you to look at what just *one* of those blades was able to do to the Preamble to the Constitution, the Bill of Rights and the beloved Ten Commandments. And now I ask you if you think there is anything at all to be said in defense of three Boy Scouts carrying such knives into the nation's capital.

And incidentally, in that connection, these were not the only three Boy Scouts in Washington bearing concealed weapons on their belts. These were only the three we happened to kill. In all, a total of eight thousand four hundred and sixty-three knives, each resembling this one in every last detail, were confiscated during the two days the Scouts were here. That means a grand total of thirty-three thousand, eight hundred and fifty-two blades, or enough blades to torture simultaneously every single resident of Chevy Chase, Maryland, including women and children.

Now you ask, how did we prevent this bloodbath from taking place in Chevy Chase? The answer is by setting up an enclosed camping site for the Scouts who were not shot. The answer is by diverting their attention from violence and law-breaking by giving them a chance to test their scouting abilities overnight in a wilderness environment without food or shelter.

And let me tell you something: it is to the very great credit of the scouting movement in this country, that once we were able to get these boys off the streets and into a rugged camping situation—and we have the police to thank for volunteering their help in getting all the boys out there— they showed themselves worthy in every way of their famous motto, "Be Prepared."

Let's take a look at just a few of their accomplishments:

First, in the absence of toilet facilities, they did a tremendous job in disposing of their waste matter and the leaves they used for personal hygiene.

Next, what little water they had in their canteens, they shared in an admirable way, or so it would seem from the fact that not a single one of the nearly ten thousand died of thirst.

Nor did they make the mistake of drinking from, or even daring to bathe in, the pond at the campsite, so familiar were they with the danger signs of sewage and stagnation.

Now anyone familiar with Boy Scout training could have expected that they would be able to use their kerchiefs as tourniquets to stop one another's bleeding, but few of us believed they could ever do the kind of near professional job they did making splints out of vines and branches and shirts torn up into rags.

As for eating, well, I'm proud to say that by morning they had discovered edible roots and berries we didn't even know were there. And as for warmth, as you could expect, they managed during the night to start several fires in the classic Boy Scout manner of rubbing two sticks together.

In all, what might have been a nightmare for the citizens of Chevy Chase, Maryland, we converted into wonderful scouting experience for the boys themselves, and one that I'm sure they'll remember for a long time to come. I know that when the police vans returned this morning to take them away, many of the boys were reluctant to leave the campsite. So anxious were some to spend another night under the stars, and away from the so-called "comforts" of civilization such as medical attention, lawyers, telephones and food, that it was necessary for police to chase after them and literally drag them off the premises and into the waiting trucks. With fewer and fewer opportunities available to our youth for "roughing it," this administration naturally takes pride in what we were able to do for these youngsters last night. Moreover, we have given them every assurance that if and when they ever come to Washington again, we will make every effort to provide them with the same facilities, or ones even more primitive, if we can find any.

Now I know that many of you out there across the country are asking yourselves why I should be making such a generous offer to the Scouts. Why do I praise them for their behavior at the campsite? Why am I willing to forgive these youngsters and give them another chance to make a decent start in life? It must seem to those of you who saw the Scouts waving their signs here in the streets of the nation's capital—signs offensive

and insulting not only to me but, what is far worse, to my innocent family—that I more than anyone have a right to harbor
a grievance against these ten thousand Boy Scouts; and particularly against the three who are now dead and will never be
able to come to me like responsible children and apologize for
trying to smear my reputation. Why, you may ask, am I so
compassionate, judicious, charitable, tolerant and wise, when
it was my very own political career that stood to be most damaged by these signs?

Well, those are good and intelligent questions. Let me try to
answer them as forthrightly as I know how.

My fellow Americans, it is as simple as this (*quickly passes a
sponge over his upper lip and slips it back into his breast pocket*): I
would rather be a one-term President than carry a grudge
against a lot of twelve- and thirteen-year-old American kids.
Oh, sure, somebody else might try to make political capital
out of a vendetta against these youngsters, calling them hoodlums and bums and rotten apples, but I am afraid I am just too
big a man for that. As far as I am concerned, these boys have
learned their lesson, as they proved at the campsite; and that
goes for the three dead Scouts as well. Even if those three dead
boys don't come and apologize, as far as I am concerned the
past is past and I for one am willing to forgive and forget. For
make no mistake about it: while it is true that I am strongly
opposed to permissiveness, I am just as opposed to vindictiveness. I no more believe in punishing a wrongdoer to excess
than I would subscribe to the liberal philosophy that allows a
criminal to go merrily on his way, after he has committed a
crime.

But of even greater importance, I just don't think we ever
cure a disease by treating one of its symptoms. Rather, we
must get to the cause of the illness. And certainly you know as
well as I do, that the cause of America's problems is not the
Boy Scouts of America. Nobody is ever going to believe that,
and that is why I don't even attempt to make a case for it.

No, the Boy Scouts of America—and I think this will come
as a relief to all of you—are no more guilty of anything than
you or I am. They are just another group of American youngsters who have fallen prey to that small dedicated band of malcontents and revolutionaries who are out to destroy our

country by destroying our most important natural resource of all, our wonderful youth. And unless we cut these sources of contagion from our society as swiftly and thoroughly as we would excise a cancer from a living body—and I know we are all united in our opposition to cancer, Democrats and Republicans alike—this disease that has spread even to the Boy Scouts will grow in virulence until it has infected every last child in the land, including your own. And so long as I am President, I am not going to stand idly by while the children of this country come down with cancer, leukemia, or, incidentally in that connection, muscular dystrophy.

No, it is not the Boy Scouts of America, but the man who incited them to this riot by tampering with their morals who must be made to take the punishment that comes to all who would corrupt the youth of our nation. And that man, my fellow Americans, is the very same fugitive for whom the Pro-Pornography government in Copenhagen is providing refuge at this moment.

Now I cannot divulge to you over nationwide television the overwhelming evidence compiled by the Justice Department and the FBI, linking Charles Curtis Flood to the uprising of the Boys Scouts. We all know, however, the tremendous influence that major league baseball players have over the minds and hearts of the young boys of this nation. I am sure that anyone who remembers how he himself idolized the great ballplayers of his youth, will not even *need* the evidence in order to imagine just how Charles Curtis Flood might misuse and mislead these boys for his own subversive ends.

I am afraid that is all I can say to you tonight about the evidence proving Flood's guilt. As one who has practiced law, I am particularly sensitive to the Constitutional rights which every defendant is entitled to. And I certainly do not intend to endanger the chances of a conviction by appearing to try this fugitive on nationwide TV. Once he is returned to America, he will be entitled to a fair trial, despite what he has done, and by a jury that has not been prejudiced against him by so august a person as the President of the United States of America.

Right now, as your President, my duty is to do everything within my power to see that this fugitive from justice is returned to our shores. Of course, we have never expected of

Flood that he would voluntarily leave his sanctuary in Denmark, given the kinds of pleasures such a man might feel free to pursue in a country with customs that are hardly those of our own. And if Flood is incapable of tearing himself away from his pleasures so as to face the consequences of his vicious actions, neither has the Pro-Pornography government in Copenhagen done anything whatsoever to force him to surrender himself to the proper authorities for extradition. On the contrary, they have rejected out of hand every legitimate request we have made of them. Even now, with the American Army massed on their borders, the American Navy blockading their coast, and the American Marines firmly in control of "Hamlet's Castle," they continue to provide him with the same protection from the law that they provide to pornographers and filth peddlers from around the globe.

I know that in the face of such profound contempt for American power and prestige, the great majority of Americans would agree that I have no choice but to order our troops onto Danish soil so as to establish the D.A.R. as the freely elected government in Copenhagen. However, I want to tell you this: because of my Quaker background, I have, only two hours ago, made one last valiant effort to bring about a peaceful resolution of our differences with Denmark. I am going to conclude my address to you tonight by recounting in some detail the nature of that effort. It is a story of bravery and devotion to country that every American will be proud of. It is a story that will convince the entire world how very far this great nation has gone in its attempt to avoid the armed confrontation that the state of Denmark seems committed to forcing upon us.

My fellow Americans, only two hours before coming on television to address you, I gave the order, as Commander-in-Chief of the Armed Forces meeting his responsibilities, for a fleet of helicopters to make a surprise landing on the large Danish island of Zealand at a spot right here (*points*), only twenty nautical miles from the capital of Copenhagen.

Now I realized how dangerous such a gallant humanitarian effort might be. So did the brave Green Berets and Rangers who volunteered to carry it out. Not only would they have to fly in at treetop level to avoid detection by the Danish radar system, but there was no precise way of telling the exact size of the arsenal that Flood had managed to assemble, with the approval, if not the outright assistance, of the Danish government. Would he resort to poison gas? Would he dare to employ tactical nuclear weapons? There was no way in which our aerial photography could penetrate this man's skull, to see just how far he would go in violating the written and unwritten rules of warfare.

But in that reconnaissance by satellite, as well as by manned and drone aircraft, had established beyond a shadow of a doubt that this was where the fugitive was in hiding; and in that I also knew that there was no way to force the Danish government to return Flood to the United States, short of the armed conflict which I am so opposed to as a Quaker, I proceeded to give the order for this raid to take place.

Designed to capture Flood, remove him by helicopter to Elsinore, and hence by military jet to America, the mission was named, by me, Operation Courage, and assigned to Joint Contingency Task Force Derring-Do.

It is with deep pride, my fellow Americans, that I can now tell you that Operation Courage has been carried out to perfection, exactly in accordance with the meticulously rehearsed schedule drawn up beforehand.

First off, the dangerous flight from Elsinore to the landing site was made in twenty-two minutes and fourteen seconds, precisely according to the plan. Next, the hazardous search of the farmhouse, the outbuildings and the tilled acreage was accomplished in thirty-four minutes and eighteen seconds; in other words, with two full seconds to spare. The ticklish evacuation proceedings required precisely the seven minutes called for in the schedule, and the daring return flight to Elsinore, at treetop level, was accomplished in twenty-two minutes flat. That is not only four seconds under the time allotted, but I am proud to say, a new record for that distance for a Danish domestic helicopter flight. Moreover, our forces returned to safety without sustaining a single casualty. As at Elsinore, the enemy was so completely taken by surprise that they did not fire a single shot.

I am proud to tell you that the intelligence on Operation Courage was equally as impressive as the split-second timing with which this perilous mission was accomplished.

First, the seven blond-haired females who were identified on the aerial photos moving in and out of the farmhouse at all hours of the day were present at the time of the landing. They were found, as expected, in beds scattered throughout the house, and taken immediately into custody for interrogation by the Green Berets, as was the couple claiming to be their "father" and "mother." The blond-haired females found in the beds in various stages of undress ranged in age from seven to eighteen.

Second, the dark round objects visible in the aerial photographs and identified positively by intelligence as watermelons, were no longer in the field, or "patch," at the time of the landing, nor was there evidence any longer of the watermelon vines themselves. This has led intelligence to conclude that only hours before the raid, the telltale watermelons were removed and replaced with the ordinary rocks and potato plants found at the time of the landing. Obviously, this constituted a desperate last-minute attempt on the part of the fugitive to avoid detection from the air.

As for the large dark object identified as Charles Curtis Flood himself, apparently at the very last minute he too was replaced with a big black Labrador dog. This was verified when the dog was found romping in the very fields where photographs, taken the previous night, revealed the fugitive exercising by moonlight.

It is to the great credit of the commander in charge of Operation Courage—and represents the highest order of dedication and professionalism—that in order to keep faithfully to the plan, the dog was taken into custody in precisely the same amount of time as had been allotted for the capture of Flood. She was then transported in the command helicopter, bound and under heavy guard, to "Hamlet's Castle" at Elsinore. However, once the helicopters touched safely down, I immediately gave the order from the White House that the interrogation of the dog was to be suspended, and that she was to be released from her bindings and allowed to roam on a leash in the grassy enclosure on the castle grounds.

My fellow Americans, I can assure you that the friendly treatment that dog is receiving now at the hands of American soldiers is in sharp contrast to the heartlessness and cynicism with which the fugitive himself forced this defenseless animal to serve as his "stand-in" while he took flight from justice yet again.

Now it had been my hope that I could come before you tonight to tell you that Flood was in the custody of American officials, and that it would not be necessary to take further measures against a recalcitrant and contemptuous Danish government in order to secure his release. And make no mistake about it. If we were not dealing with a man so vicious that he would rather risk the life of an innocent female dog than his own, I could have done just that.

However, even though they were unable to apprehend the fugitive at this time, I should still like to take this opportunity to pay a tribute to the skill, courage and devotion with which Joint Contingency Task Force Derring-Do carried out Operation Courage. The flawless fashion in which they executed this delicate secret mission was inspirational to all Americans. And surely it must be accounted the most successful single operation of its kind staged thus far in the Danish crisis. The embarrassment alone that we have caused Copenhagen by pointing up the holes of their radar system will inevitably have a profound effect upon the morale of the Danish people and their armed forces.

My fellow Americans, I am going to conclude my address with the words of a very great man. They were written by the immortal bard and renowned humanitarian, William Shakespeare. Yes, they were written with a quill pen on a piece of parchment hundreds and hundreds of years ago, but probably never have they been so true as they are tonight. This is what Shakespeare said: "Something," he said, "is rotten in the state of Denmark." Little did the immortal bard know then, how prophetic those words would be in the centuries to come.

My fellow Americans (*here Tricky rises from his chair to sit on the edge of his desk*), something *is* rotten in Denmark—let there be no mistake about it. And if it has now fallen to American boys to step in and eradicate the rottenness that Danish boys are unable to step in and eradicate, I know they will not hesitate to do so. (*Makes fist*) Because we will not watch as the once-great homeland of Hamlet slips down the drain of depravity. (*Looks down*) Instead, with all the might that we can summon in our righteous cause, we shall (*quick friendly glance at ceiling*), with God's help, purge Denmark of corruption, now and for all time. (*Looks for a moment into eternity without batting eyelashes*)

Thank you, and good night.

5

The Assassination of Tricky

THE President of the United States is dead. We repeat this bulletin. Trick E. Dixon is dead. That is all the information we have at this time.

The White House has refused to comment on an earlier bulletin announcing that the President of the United States is dead. The White House Bilge Secretary says, "There is no truth whatsoever to reports of the President's death," but adds that he will not "categorically" deny the story at this time.

Conflicting stories continue to circulate concerning the death of the President. A second White House announcement has now called attention to the President's schedule for the day, pointing out that no mention is made there of dying. Also released was the President's schedule for tomorrow, wherein there also appears to be no plan on the part of the President or his advisers for him to die. "I think it would be best," said the White House Bilge Secretary, "in the light of these schedules, to wait for a statement, one way or another, from the President himself."

Reports out of Walter Reed Army Hospital now seem to confirm the earlier bulletin that the President of the United States is dead. Though the circumstances surrounding his death remain unclear, it appears that the President was admitted to Walter Reed late yesterday for surgery. The purpose of the secret operation was to remove the sweat glands from his hip. That is all we know at this time.

The Vice President has flatly denied reports of the President's death. Here is a portion of the Vice President's remarks, made as he was on his way to address the National Yodeling Association:

"Now this is just the kind of reckless rot and rotten recklessness that you can expect from the vile vilifiers who are out to vilify vilely."

"What of the reports, Mr. Vice President, that he had secretly entered Walter Reed last night to have the sweat glands removed from his hip?"

"Hogwash and hokum. *And* hooliganism. *And* heinous. I spoke to him only five minutes ago and found him fit as a fiddle. This lachrymose lie is a lamentable lollapalooza launched by the lunatic left."

Unconfirmed reports from Walter Reed Hospital now indicate that the President was found dead at seven A.M. this morning. No word yet on the cause of death, or where he was "found." Speculation mounts that death came following surgery for the removal of sweat glands lodged in the hip.

We take you now to Republican National Headquarters, where the chairman of the national committee is meeting with reporters:

"I cannot believe that the great majority of Americans are going to keep this great American from a second term in the White House just because he is dead, no."

"Then you are admitting, sir, that he *is* dead?"

"I didn't say that at all. I said, I just don't think that his death, if it were to come about between now and the election, would affect his popularity with the great majority of Americans. After all, this isn't the first time you people were ready to call him dead, and here he is, President of the United States."

"But we meant dead politically."

"I'm not going to get into a fancy discussion of semantics with you fellas. All I'm saying is that whether these rumors are true or false is not going to affect our campaign plans by one iota. I'd even go so far as to say that if it turns out he actually is a corpse, our margin of victory in '72 will be greater by far than what it was in '68."

"How do you figure that, Mr. Chairman?"

"Well, I for one just cannot imagine the press of this country, irresponsible and vicious as it may be, going after this man dead and buried with the same kind of virulence they used to go after him alive. Furthermore, as regards the voters themselves, it would seem to me that there is a certain sympathy, a certain warmth that a dead Dixon is going to be able to arouse in the people of this country that he never really was able to summon up when he was living and breathing and so on."

"If he is dead then, you think it would be good for his image?"

"No doubt about it. I think that in terms of exposure he may have gone about as far as he can alive. This is probably just the shot in the arm we've been looking for, particularly if the Democrats run Teddy Charisma."

"Can you explain what you mean, Mr. Chairman?"

"Well, assuming for the sake of argument that Trick E. Dixon is no more, that is going to cut strongly into the source of Charisma's appeal. It's one thing, you see, for a candidate for the Presidency to have two brothers who are dead—it's something else when the incumbent *himself* is dead. I mean, if experience is any kind of criterion—and I think it is—I just don't see how you can top the President now, where this whole death issue is concerned."

"Mr. Chairman, is there any truth at all in the growing suspicion that you people are sending up a trial balloon with these rumors of the President's death? To see just how much politi cal mileage there is in it, if any? That is, on the one hand you yourself sound convinced that the President's death would give a great boost to his waning popularity, while Vice President What's-his-name asserts that the President is 'fit as a fiddle' and that these rumors have been propagated by 'the lunatic left.'"

"Look, I have no intention of criticizing the alliteration of the Vice President of the United States of America. Under the Constitution he has a right to alliterate just as much as any other American citizen. I am speaking to you boys strictly as party chairman, and all I am saying, in language plain and simple, is that the President has absolutely no intention of withdrawing from the race for any reason whatsoever, including his own death. Anybody who counts him out because of something like that, just doesn't know the kind of guy they are dealing with. This isn't a Lyin' B. Johnson, who tosses in the towel because the country hates his guts and doesn't trust him as far as they can throw him. No, you're not going to intimidate Trick E. Dixon just by hating him. Hell, he's had that all his life; he's *used* to it. And you're not going to keep him off the ballot by killing him either. We've seen him rise from the ashes before, and I have every expectation that we are going to see precisely that again. If he has to address that convention from inside an urn, he'll do it—that's the kind of dedicated American we're talking about."

The White House has now issued a statement denying—I repeat, *denying*—that the President entered Walter Reed Hospital yesterday for the removal of the sweat glands from his hip. There continues however to be a total news blackout from that source as to whether President Dixon is dead or alive.

We take you now to the National Weightlifters Convention, where Vice President What's-his-name is in the midst of an impromptu address on those who he claims have perpetrated upon the nation this "lachrymose lie":
    "—the nitwits, the namby-pambys, the neurasthenics, the neurotics, the necrophiliacs—"

We interrupt the Vice President's alliteration to take you to Walter Reed Hospital for a special report:
    "The mood here is somber, though it remains impossible to piece the story together in its entirety. It seems now that the President did enter the hospital late yesterday for a secret operation. First reports had it that the operation was to have been on his hip, for the surgical removal of sweat glands apparently lodged in that area. However, the White House, as you know, has flatly denied that story, and only a moment ago I learned the reason why. The operation was to have been not on the Chief Executive's hip, but on his lip, l-i-p. The sweat glands were, from all reports, to have been removed from the lip this morning. But now, according to the latest White House communiqué, surgery has been postponed for the time being because of, and I quote, 'an unforeseen development.' According to highly placed sources within the hospital itself,

that unforeseen development is the death of the President of the United States. Now I see that the Secretary of Defense has just emerged from the hospital and is walking this way. Secretary Lard, have you just come from the President's side?"

"Yes."

"You seem quite despondent, sir. Can you tell us if he is dead or alive?"

"I'm not at liberty to answer that question."

"Unconfirmed reports from various sources say he was found dead at seven A.M. this morning."

"No comment."

"Can you tell us then why you were visiting him?"

"To find out his secret timetable for ending the war."

"Is there anybody other than the President who knows the secret timetable?"

"Of course not."

"Then if he's dead, he's taken the secret timetable with him to the grave?"

"No comment."

"Secretary Lard, did the President have any other visitors aside from yourself?"

"Yes. The Joint Chiefs. And of course the Professor."

"And they don't know the secret timetable either?"

"I told you, nobody knows it but him. That's what makes it secret."

"Not even his wife?"

"Well, actually, she thought she had it, when we called her this morning. But it was just an old train schedule between Washington and New York. She found it in one of his suits."

"There's no other place he might have left it?"

"It doesn't seem like it."

"Cut open the mattresses, did you?"

"Oh, all of that. Ripped up floors. Tore out paneling. Turned the place inside out. No sign of anything *resembling* a secret timetable."

"Mr. Secretary, everything you say seems to confirm the rumor that the President is dead. If that is the case, what were you and the Joint Chiefs and the Professor doing sitting around a corpse, trying to find out vital information?"

"Well, we also had a medium with us."

"A *medium?*"

"Oh, don't worry. She's worked for us before. Highest security clearance. Top-flight Gypsy."

"And did she get through to the President?"

"I believe I can say she did."

"How do you know?"

"Well, she got through to a voice who kept saying he was a Quaker."

"And what about the secret timetable?"

"He says a secret is a secret, and he owes it to the American people, who have placed their confidence in him, not to betray a sacred trust. He said they can brand and skewer him in Hell, he's never going to tell a soul."

"Honest almost to a fault."

"Well, he had to be, you know, with that sweating problem. Otherwise people tended not always to believe everything he said."

"Ladies and gentlemen, that was the Secretary of Defense, speaking directly from the lawn outside of Walter Reed Hospital. As you saw, he was distraught and very near to tears throughout the interview, thus appearing to confirm the reports of the President's death. We return you to the Vice President, who is now addressing the National Sword Swallowers Association."

"—the psychotics, the sob sisters, the skin merchants, the saboteurs, the self-styled Sapphos, the self-styled Swinburnes, the swine, the satyrs, the schizos, the sodomists, the sissies, the screamers, the screwy, the scum, the self-congratulatory self-congratulators, the sensationalists, the snakes in the grass, the sex fiends, the shiftless, the shines, the shaggy, the sickly, the syphilitic—"

We go now to the headquarters of the Federal Bureau of Investigation:

"Is it the same knife that the President demonstrated on television last night, Chief?"

"No doubt about it. Here are the four blades. Count 'em. One, two, three, four. Open-and-shut case."

"But my understanding was that some eight thousand such knives—"

"We've sifted through the eight thousand, don't worry about that. And this is the one. This is the murder weapon, no doubt about it."

"Then the President has been murdered?"

"I can't tell you that right now. But I can assure you that if there has been a murder, this is what did it."

"And do you have the murderer in custody?"

"One thing at a time. You rush in and say you've got the murderer, everybody thinks you picked up the first guy you could find out on the street. Let's at least get the announcement of a murder, before we start accusing people."

"How about the kind of murder. Stabbed to death?"

"Well, there again it's like, 'Have you stopped beating your wife.' But of course I will say this much: with a knife, you may very well find that the victim has been stabbed to death, yes. Of course, there are other possibilities as well, and I can assure you we're looking into them thoroughly."

"For instance."

"Well, you've got your bludgeoning, of course. You've got your various forms of torture such as the President himself outlined on TV the other night."

"In other words, it's possible the President's famous eyes may have been gouged out."

"I wouldn't rule that out at this time, no."

"But by whom? How? When? Where?"

"Look, as we say here at the Bureau, ask me no questions and I'll tell you no lies. The important thing right now is that we want to assure the American people, not only that we are actually on top of this case even before it has broken, but that we are keeping them abreast of the facts virtually before there are any. We just don't intend to come in for the sort of criticism on this assassination of a President that we did on the last one."

"What sort of criticism do you mean?"

"Well, last time there was just some kind of cloud over the whole thing, wasn't there? Credibility gap and so on. People thinking they weren't getting the straight story. Accusing us of covering up and being caught off guard and so on. Well, this time it's going to be different, I can assure you. This time we have the weapon and a fairly good idea of who did it beforehand, and we're really only waiting for word that it actually happened, to make an arrest. After a decent interval, of course, just so it doesn't look as though we picked up the first poor slob we found in the gutter."

"Is it a Boy Scout? That is, will it be a Boy Scout, if and when?"

"Well, of course I am only a law enforcement officer. I don't decide who commits the crime, I just catch them, after that decision has been made by the proper authorities. I will say this, however. We would not have decided on a Boy Scout knife as the murder weapon, if we didn't think there was a good strong motive to go with it. That was one of the troubles with the last assassination: didn't have a good strong motive to go with it. After all, we are talking about the assassination of the highest elected officer in the land. People like a good strong motive when something like that happens, and I can't say that I blame them. That's why this time we intend to give it to them. Otherwise, you're just going to get your national disunity, your credibility gap, your doubt, and your cloud over the whole thing."

"And you honestly think that this Boy Scout knife will clear up such doubt and incredulity?"

"Why? Don't you?"

"Well, it's not for me to say. I'm just an objective reporter."

"No, no, go ahead, *say*. What do you think? Just because you're objective doesn't necessarily make you a fool. You don't find the Boy Scout knife convincing? Is that it?"

"But what I think isn't at issue—either this is or is not the murder weapon."

"In other words, you're implying that it does seem to you far-fetched. Good enough. What would you think of this, then?"

"*That?*"

"Yes, sir—a Louisville Slugger. Curt Flood's very own baseball bat. Let me show you on this model here of the President's head the kind of damage you can do with one of these things. Remember, before, when I said 'bludgeoned'? Well, watch this."

—

To the White House now, for an important announcement by the President's Bilge Secretary.

"Ladies and gentlemen, I'd like to make the following announcement concerning the President's health. At midnight last night the President entered Walter Reed Army Hospital for minor surgery involving the surgical removal of the sweat glands from his upper lip."

"Can you spell that, Blurb?"

"Lip. L-i-p."

"And the first word?"

"Upper. U-p-p-e-r . . . Now as you know, the President has always wanted to do everything he could to gain the trust and the confidence and, if it was within the realm of possibility, the affection of the American people. It was his belief that if he could stop sweating so much along his upper lip when he addressed the nation, the great majority of the American people would come to believe that he was an honest man, speaking the truth, and maybe even like him a little better. Now this is not to say that people who sweat along the upper lip are necessarily liars and/or unlikable. Many people who sweat profusely along the upper lip are outstanding citizens in their communities and sweat the way they do because of the many civic duties they are called upon to perform. Then too there are a lot of good, hard-working ordinary citizens who simply sweat along the upper lip as a matter of course . . . That is really all I have to say to you at this hour, ladies and gentlemen. I wouldn't have bothered to call you together like this, had it not been for the continuing rumors that it was the President's 'hip' that had required surgery. There is absolutely no truth to that whatsoever, and I wanted you to be the first to know. I hope by tomorrow in fact to have available for you x-ray photos of the President's hip that will make it absolutely clear that it is in perfect condition."

"Which hip will that be, Blurb?"

"The left hip."

"What about the right one?"

"We'll try to get those to you within the week. I assure you that we're working to clear this thing up just as fast as we can. We don't want the people in this country to go around thinking the President has something wrong with his hips any more than you do."

"What about the reports that he's dead, Blurb?"

"I have nothing to say about that at this time."

"But Secretary Lard was seen weeping as he left Walter Reed today. Surely that suggests that President Dixon is dead."

"Not necessarily. It could just as well mean that he's alive. I'm not going to speculate either way, gentlemen, in a matter this serious."

"What about reports that he's been murdered by a Boy Scout gone berserk?"

"We're looking into that, and if there's any truth at all to that story, I assure you, we'll be in touch with you about it."

"Can you say anything definite about his condition at all?"

"He's resting comfortably."

"Are the sweat glands out? And if so, can we see them?"

"No comment. Moreover, it would really be up to the First Lady anyway, whether she wanted the President's sweat glands to be made available for photographs and so on. I think she might want to keep something as personal as those glands just for the immediate family, and maybe eventually build a Trick E. Dixon Library at Prissier in which to house them."

"Can you tell us how big they are, Blurb?"

"Well, I would imagine that given the sheer amount of sweating he used to do, they were pretty good-sized. But I'm only guessing. I haven't seen them."

"Blurb, is there any truth to the report that while at Walter Reed he was also going to have surgery done to prevent his eyes from shifting?"

"No comment."

"Does that mean they *were* gouged out?"

"No comment."

"Will the eyes be in the Trick E. Dixon Library at Prissier too, Blurb?"

"Once again, that would be entirely up to the First Lady."

"Blurb, what about his gestures? He's been criticized for a certain unnaturalness, or falseness, in his gestures. They don't always seem tied in to what he's saying. If he's still alive, are there any plans for him to have that fixed too? And if so, how? Can they sort of get him synchronized in that department?"

"Gentlemen, I'm sure the doctors are going to do everything they can to make him appear as honest as possible."

"One last question, Blurb. If he's dead, that would make Mr. What's-his-name the President. Is there any truth to the rumor that you people are postponing the announcement of Dixon's death because you're looking for a last-minute replacement for What's-his-name? Is that why Mr. What's-his-name himself keeps denying so vehemently the reports that the President is dead—for fear of being dumped?"

"Gentlemen, I think you know as well as I do that the Vice President is not the kind of man who would want to be President of the United States if he felt there was any doubt as to his qualifications for the office. That's not even a question I will take seriously."

"Good evening. This is Erect Severehead with a cogent news analysis from the nation's capital . . . A hushed hush pervades the corridors of power. Great men whisper whispers while a stunned capital awaits. Even the cherry blossoms along the Potomac seem to sense the magnitude. And magnitude there is. Yet magnitude there has been before, and the nation has survived. A mood of cautious optimism surged forward just at dusk. Then set the age-old sun behind these edifices of reason, and gloom once more descended. Yet gloom there has been, and in the end the nation has survived. For the principles are everlasting, though the men be mortal. And it is that very mortality that the men in the corridors of power. For no one dares to play politics with the momentousness of a tragedy of such scope, or the scope of a tragedy of such momentousness. If tragedy it be. Yet tragedies there have been, and the nation founded upon hope and trust in man and the deity, has continued to survive. Still, in this worried capital tonight, men watch and men wait. So too do women and children in this worried capital tonight watch and wait. This is Erect Severehead from Washington, D.C."

"—the flag-burners, the faggots, the fairies, the filth peddlers, the Fabian Socialists of yore, the fair-weather friends, the fairies, the faithless, the flesh-show operators—"

—

We interrupt the Vice President's address to the National Primates Association to bring you the following bulletin. A troop of Boy Scouts from Boston, Massachusetts, the home state of Senator Edward Charisma, has confessed to the murder of the President of the United States. The FBI has declined to give their names until such time as the President's murder has been announced by the White House. The Boy Scouts are being held without bail, and according to the FBI the case is, quote cinched unquote. The murder weapon, which at first was believed to be the very knife that the President had exhibited on television during his famous "Something Is Rotten in Denmark" speech, is now identified as a Louisville Slugger baseball bat, formerly the property of Washington Senator center fielder Curt Flood. We return you to Vice President What's-his-name at the Primates convention:

"—the flotsam and jetsam of the universities, the fairies, the folk singers, the fairies, the freaks, the fairies, the free-loaders on welfare, the fairies, the free-speechers with their favorite four-letter word, the fairies—"

We switch you to our correspondent at Walter Reed Army Hospital.

"Ladies and gentlemen, this terrible news has just come to us from a highly reliable source within the hospital. The President of the United States was assassinated sometime in the early hours of the morning. The cause of death was drowning. He was found at seven A.M., unclothed and bent into the fetal position, inside a large transparent baggie filled with a clear fluid presumed to be water, and tied shut at the top. The baggie containing the body of the President was found on the floor of the hospital delivery room. How he was removed from his own room, where he was awaiting surgery on his upper lip, and forced or enticed into a baggie is not known at this time. There would seem to be little doubt, however, that the manner in which he has been murdered is directly related to the controversial remarks he made at San Dementia on April 3, in which he came out four-square for 'the rights of the unborn.'

"Right now, hospital officials seem to believe that the President left his bed voluntarily to accompany his assailant to the delivery room, perhaps in the belief that he was to be photographed there beside the stomach of a woman in labor. The recent Scout uprising, and yesterday's nuclear bombing of Copenhagen, seemed to those of us here in Washington to have taken something of an edge off his campaign in behalf of the unborn, and it may well be that he had decided to seize upon this fortuitous circumstance to revitalize interest in his program. Doubtless, with the destruction of Copenhagen and the occupation of Denmark successfully accomplished, he was anxious to return to what he considered our most pressing domestic problem. Rumor has it that he intended, in his next major address, to use his new upper lip to outline his belief in 'the sanctity of human life, including the life of the yet unborn.'

"But now there will be no speech on the sanctity of human life with the new lip he would have been so proud of. A cruel assassin with a macabre sense of humor has seen to that. The man who believed in the unborn is dead, his unclothed body found stuffed in the fetal position inside a water-filled baggie on the floor of the delivery room here at Walter Reed Hospital. This is Roger Rising-to-the-Occasion at Walter Reed."

Quickly now to the White House, and the latest bulletin from the Bilge Secretary.

"Ladies and gentlemen, I have a few more facts for you now about the President's hip, including the x-ray I promised earlier. This gentleman in white that you see beside me in his surgical gloves, gown and mask is probably the foremost authority on the left hip in the world. Doctor, will you comment on this x-ray of the President's left hip for the members of the press. I'll hold it for you so you don't dirty your gloves."

"Thank you, Blurb. Ladies and gentlemen, there is just no doubt about it in my mind. This is a left hip."

"Thank you, Doctor. Any questions?"

"Blurb, the report from Walter Reed is that the President has been assassinated. Stuffed naked into a baggie and drowned."

"Gentlemen, let's try to keep to the subject. The doctor here has flown in from Minnesota right in the middle of an operation on a left hip, to verify this x-ray for you. I don't think we want to keep him longer than we have to. Yes?"

"Doctor, can you be absolutely sure that the left hip is the President's?"

"Of course I can."

"How, sir?"

"Because that's what the Bilge Secretary said it was. Why would he give me a picture of a hip and say it was the President's if it wasn't?"

(*Laughter from the Press Corps*)

"—the gadflies, the go-go girls, the geldings, the gibbons, the gonadless, the gonorrhea-carriers—"

We interrupt the Vice President's address to the National Association for the Advancement of Color Slides to switch you to our correspondents around the country.

First, Morton Momentous in Chicago:

"Here in the Windy City the mood is one of incredulity, of shock, of utter disbelief. So stunned are the people of this great Middle Western metropolis that they seem totally unable to respond to the bulletins from Washington that have come to them over radio and television. And so from the Gold Coast to Skid Row, from the fashionable suburbs of the North to the squalid ghettos of the South, the scene is much the same: people going about their ordinary, everyday affairs as though nothing had happened. Not even the flags have been lowered to half-staff, but continue to flutter high in the breeze, even as they did before the news reached this grief-stricken city of the terrible fate that has befallen our leader. Trick E. Dixon is dead, cruelly and bizarrely murdered, a martyr to the unborn the world round—and it is more than the mind or spirit of Chicago can accept or understand. And so throughout this great city, life, in a manner of speaking, goes on—much as you see it directly behind me here in the world-famous Loop. Shoppers rushing to and fro. The din of traffic continuous. Restaurants jammed. Streetcars and busses packed. Yes, the frantic, mindless scurrying of a big city at the rush hour. It is almost as though the people here in Chicago are afraid to turn for a single second from the ordinary routine of an ordinary day, to face this ghastly tragedy. This is Morton Momentous from a stunned, incredulous Chicago."

We take you now to Los Angeles and correspondent Peter Pious.

"If the people in the streets of Chicago are incredulous, you can well imagine the mood of the ordinary man in the pool here in Trick E. Dixon's native state. In Chicago they are simply unable to respond; here it is even more heart-rending. The Californians I have spoken with—or tried to speak with—are like nothing so much as small children who have been confronted with an event far beyond their emotional range of response. All they can do when they learn the tragic news that Trick E. Dixon has been found stuffed in a baggie is giggle. To be sure, there are the proverbial California wisecracks, but by and large it is giggling such as one might hear from perplexed and bewildered children that remains in one's ears, long after the giggler himself has dived off the high board or driven away in his sports car. For this is Trick E. Dixon's state and these are Trick E. Dixon's people. Here he is not just the President, here he is a friend and a neighbor, one of them, a healthy child of the sunlight, of the beaches and the blue Pacific, a man who embodied all the robustness and grandeur of America's golden state. And now that golden child of the Golden West is gone; and Californians can only giggle to suppress their sobs and hide their tears. Peter Pious in Los Angeles."

Next, Ike Ironic, in New York City.

"No one ever believed that Trick E. Dixon was beloved in New York City. Yes, he lived here once, in this fashionable Fifth Avenue apartment building directly behind me. But few ever considered him a resident of this city so much as a refugee from Washington, biding his time to return to public office. Nor did New Yorkers seem much impressed when he assumed the powers of the Presidency in 1969. But now he is gone, and all at once the very deep affection, the love, if you will, for their former neighbor, is everywhere apparent. Of course, you have to know New Yorkers to be able to penetrate the outer shell of cynicism and see the love beneath. You had to look, but you saw it today, here in New York: in the seeming boredom and indifference of a bus driver; in the impatience of a salesgirl; in the anger over nothing of a taxi driver; in the weariness of the homebound workers packed into the subway; in the blank gaze of the drunks along the Bowery; in the haughtiness of a dowager refusing to curb her dog on the fashionable Upper East Side. You had to look, but there it was, love for Trick E. Dixon . . . Only now he is gone, gone before they could, with their boredom and indifference and impatience and anger and exhaustion and blankness and haughtiness, express to him all they felt so deeply in their hearts. Yes, the bitter irony is this: he had to die in a baggie, before New Yorkers could tender him that hard-won love that would have meant so much to him. But then it is a day of bitter ironies. Ike Ironic from grief-stricken and, perhaps, guilt-ridden Fifth Avenue in the city of New York, where he lived like a stranger, but has died like a long-lost son."

Reports coming in from around the nation confirm those you have just heard from our correspondents in Chicago, Los Angeles and New York, reports of people too stunned or heartbroken to be able to respond with the conventional tears or words of sorrow to the news of President Dixon's assassination. No, the ordinary signs of grief are clearly not sufficient to express the emotion that they feel at this hour, and so they pretend for the time being that it simply has not happened; or they giggle with embarrassment and disbelief; or they attempt to hide beneath a gruff exterior, the deep love for a fallen leader that smolders away within.

And what of the madman who perpetrated this deed? For that story, we return you to the headquarters of the FBI in Washington.

"That's right, we're pretty sure now it was a madman who perpetrated this deed."

"And the Scouts? The knife? The Louisville Slugger?"

"Oh, we're not ruling out any of the hard evidence. I'm talking now about the brains behind the whole thing. More accurately, the lack of brains. You see, that's really our number one clue—everything else aside, this was a pretty stupid thing to do to the President. There he is, the President, and they do a stupid thing like this. Now if this is somebody's idea of a practical joke, well, I for one don't consider it funny. You're not just stuffing *anybody* into a baggie, you're stuffing the

President of the United States. What about the dignity of his office? If you have no respect for the man, what about the office? That's what really gravels me, personally. I mean, what do you think the enemies of democracy would think if they saw the President of the United States all curled up naked like that. Well, I'll tell you what they'd think: they couldn't be happier. That's just the kind of propaganda they love to use to brainwash people and make Communists out of them."

"Do you think then that the assassin was an enemy of democracy as well as a madman?"

"I do. And as I said, a practical joker. Fortunately, we happen to have a complete file on all madmen who are enemies of democracy and practical jokers, and they're under constant surveillance. So I don't think there's going to be any trouble finding our man, or madman. And even if we don't find him, we've got the Boy Scouts from Boston who confessed to this thing in reserve, so I'd say, on the whole, we're in much better shape than we were last time, and are really just waiting a go-ahead from the White House . . ."

"We are privileged to have with us in the studio one of the most distinguished members of the House of Representatives, a leading Republican statesman, and a friend and confidant to the late President. Congressman Fraud, this is a sorrowful day in our nation's history."

"Oh, it's a day that will live in infamy, there's no doubt about that in my mind. I am, in fact, introducing a bill into Congress to have it declared a day that will live in infamy and celebrated as such in coming years. What you've got here, as Chief Heehaw at the FBI was saying, is a real lack of respect for the office of the Presidency. What you've got here in this assassin is a very disrespectful person, and, I would agree, probably a madman to boot."

"Do you have any idea, Congressman, why the White House continues at this late hour to refuse to confirm the story of the assassination?"

"I think it goes without saying that we're in a sensitive area here, and consequently they want to move cautiously on this whole thing. I think they want, first off, to gauge the public reaction here at home, and then of course there is the reaction around the world to consider. On the one hand you've got our allies who depend upon us for support, and on the other hand you've got our enemies who are always on the lookout for some chink in our armor, and if you keep all that in mind, then I think you have to agree that in the long run it is probably in the interest of our integrity and our credibility to cover this whole thing up. I would think that some such reasoning as that is going on behind the scenes at the White House right now."

"Has the First Lady been notified?"

"Oh, of course."

"What was her reaction?"

"Well, she was understandably quite overcome in the first moment. But, as you know, she is a very decorous woman, even in moments of great emotion. Consequently, her immediate reaction was to note that the manner in which the assassin went about the assassination was in extremely bad taste. The baggie aside for the moment, she thinks that at the very least the President should have been slain in a shirt and a tie and a jacket, like John F. Charisma. She says there was a suit fresh from the dry cleaners in the closet at the hospital, and that it really shows that the assassin was a person of very poor breeding to have failed to recognize how important it is for the President, of all people, to be neatly and appropriately garbed at all times. She said she just had to wonder about the upbringing of a person who would forget something like that. She said she didn't want to blame the assassin's family, until she knew all the facts, but it was clear she felt there probably could have been a wee bit more attention given to good grooming in his house when the assassin was growing up."

"Congressman Fraud, there has been some speculation that the President's assassination is a reprisal for the destruction yesterday of the city of Copenhagen. What do you think of that idea?"

"Not very much."

"Can you explain?"

"Well, it just doesn't make any sense. The President himself went on television, after all, and explained to the American people the situation in Denmark and why we might have to destroy Copenhagen. Now he didn't have to do that, you know—but he did, because he wanted the people to have all the facts. So I just don't see how you can fault him there. And, I must say, in praise of this great country, that except for a few elderly people out there in Wisconsin—and they of course turned out to be of Danish extraction, and obviously didn't have any objectivity on this matter at all—but except for those few irresponsible demonstrators out there shouting dirty words in Danish, the overwhelming majority of the people of this country have taken the destruction of Copenhagen with the wonderful equanimity and solidarity we have come to expect of them in matters like this. No, I just can't see where somebody is going to assassinate the President for a sound policy decision such as this one, and that even goes for a madman. No, he had the mandate of the people here, lunatics included."

"And the mandate of the Congress as well?"

"Well, of course, as you know, there are unfortunately a very few Congressmen and Senators—I guess you could call them headline seekers—who will go so far as to try to make political hay out of the bombing of a little God-forsaken village out in the middle of nowhere, some crossroads nobody has ever heard of before and surely after the bombing will never hear of again—so I leave it to you to imagine what such politicians are going to do with the nuclear destruction of a place like Copenhagen. In their behalf, however, let me say that even *they* would not be so reckless as to assassinate the President because of a difference of opinion over something like bombing sites. I mean, nobody's perfect. One President chooses this target, one President chooses that target, but fortunately we have in this country a political system that can accommodate itself to that kind of disagreement, without recourse to assassination. And by and large I think you can say that in the end the mistakes in judgment and so on shake themselves out, and we pretty much destroy the places that need destroying. It seems to me, in fact, that as regards the destruction of Copenhagen, you'll find that even among the President's staunchest critics in the Senate, there was a sense that a decision of that magnitude simply couldn't have been arrived at lightly or arbitrarily. I think most of the truly responsible members of the Congress feel as I do, that having made a strong show of strength such as this in Scandinavia now, we are not going to get ourselves bogged down there later the way we did in Southeast Asia."

"So you see no connection between the 'Something Is Rotten in Denmark' speech and the assassination?"

"No, no. Frankly I can't believe that the murder of the President has to do with anything he has ever said *or* done, including his courageous remarks in behalf of the unborn and the sanctity of human life. No, this is one of those wild, crazy acts, just as the FBI describes it—the work of a madman, and, as the First Lady suggests, a pretty ill-mannered madman, at that. It seems to me that any attempt to find some rational political motive in anything so bizarre and boorish as stuffing the President of the United States unclothed into a water-filled baggie in the fetal position is so much wasted effort. It's an act of violence and disrespect, utterly without rhyme or reason, and cannot but arouse the righteous indignation of reasonable and sensible men everywhere."

"—the hairy, the half-cocked if you know what I mean, the hammer-and-sickle supporters, the hard-core pornographers, the hedonists, the Hell's Angels, those whom God won't help because they won't help themselves, the hermaphrodites, the highbrows, the hijackers, the hippies, the Hisses, the homos, the hoodlums of all races, the heroin pushers, the hypocrites—"

"Yes, the tribute has begun, the tribute to the man they loved more than they knew. By trains they come, by busses, by cars, by planes, by wheelchairs, by feet. Come some on canes and crutches, and some on artificial limbs. But come undaunted they do, like pilgrims of yesteryear and yore, to honor pay to him they loved more than they knew. Reaped by the Grim Reaper before his reaping was due, he brings us together at last, as he promised he one day would do. And doing it he is. For in they come, the ordinary people, *his* people, barbers and butchers and brokers and barkers, tycoons and taxidermists and the taciturn who till the land. It is, I daresay, a demonstration the likes of which he who has been grimly reaped by the Grim Reaper did not, alas, survive to witness. No, during his brief residence on this planet Earth, and his three years in the White House, they demonstrated not to honor him but to humiliate him, not to pay him homage and respect but to shout their obscenities at, and display their disrespect toward, him. But these are not the obscenity-shouters and the disrespect-displayers gathering here tonight along the banks of the Potomac—banks as old as the Republic itself—and beneath the cherry blossoms he so loved, and in the brooding grandeur of this city which embodies that which he who has been untimely reaped would have himself willingly laid down his life for, had of him it been asked instead of cruelly being stolen in the night from him by an ill-mannered madman with a baggie. Yet madmen there have been and madmen there will be, and still this nation has endured. And, I daresay, endure it will, while the madmen pass through these corridors of power and halls of justice and closets of virtue and dumbwaiters of dignity and cellars of idealism, leaving us in the end, if not stronger, wiser; and if not wiser, stronger; and if, alas, not either, both. This is Erect Severehead with a cogent news analysis from the nation's capital."

"This is Brad Bathos. I'm down here in the streets of Washington now, and it is a moving and heart-rending sight I see. Ever since the news first broke that the President had been found dead in a baggie at Walter Reed Hospital, the people of this great country, *his* people, have been pouring into the capital from all over the nation. Thousands upon thousands simply standing here in the streets surrounding the White House, with heads bowed, visibly shaken and moved. Many are crying openly, not a few of them grown men. Here is a man seated on the curbstone holding his head in his hands and quietly sobbing. I'm going to ask him if he will tell us where he comes from."

"I come from here, I come from Washington."

"You're sitting on the curbstone quietly sobbing into your hands. Can you tell us why? Can you put it into words?"

"Guilt."

"You mean you feel a personal sense of guilt?"

"Yes."

"Why?"

"Because I did it."

"*You* did it? *You* killed the President?"

"Yes."

"Well, look, this is important—have you told the police?"

"I've told everyone. The police. The FBI. I even tried to call Pitter Dixon to tell her. But all they kept saying was that it was kind of me to think of them at a time like this and Mrs. Dixon appreciated my sympathy and thought it was in very good taste, and then they hung up. Meanwhile, I should be *arrested*. I should be in the papers—my picture, and a big headline, DIXON'S MURDERER. But nobody will believe me. Here, here's the notebooks where I've been planning it for months. Here are tape recordings of my own telephone conversations with friends. Here, look at this: a signed confession! And I wasn't even under duress when I wrote it. I was in a hammock. I was fully aware of my constitutional rights. My lawyer was with me, as a matter of fact. We were having a drink. Here— just read it, I give all my reasons and everything."

"Sir, interesting as your story is, we have to move on. We must move on through this immense crowd . . . Here's a young attractive young woman holding a sleeping infant in her arms. She is just standing on the sidewalk gazing blankly at the White House. Heaven only knows how much anguish is concealed in that gaze. Madam, will you tell the television audience what you're thinking about as you look at the White House?"

"He's dead."

"You appear to be in a state of shock."

"I know. I didn't think I could do it."

"Do what?"

"Kill. Murder. He said, 'Let me make one thing perfectly—' and before he could say 'clear,' I had him in the baggie. You should have seen the look on his face when I turned the little twister seal."

"The look on the President's face when *you*—?"

"Yes. I've never seen such rage in my life. I've never seen such anger and fury. But then he realized I was staring at him through the baggie, and suddenly he looked just the way he does on television, all seriousness and responsibility, and he opened his mouth, I guess to say 'clear,' and that was it. I think he thought the whole thing was being televised."

"And—well, was your baby with you, when you allegedly—?"

"Oh yes, yes. Of course, she's too young to remember exactly what happened. But I want her to be able to grow up to say, 'I was there when my mother murdered Dixon.' Imagine it—my little girl is going to grow up in a world where she'll never have to hear anybody say he's going to make something perfectly clear ever again! Or, 'Let's make no mistake about it!' Or, 'I'm a Quaker and that's why I hate war so much—' Never never never never. And I did it. I actually did it. I tell you, I still can't believe it. I drowned him. In cold water. *Me*."

"And you, young man, let's move on to you. You're just walking up and down here outside the White House, very much as though you've lost something. You seem confused and bewildered. Can you tell us, in a few words, what it is you're searching for?"

"A cop. A policeman."

"Why?"

"I want to turn myself in."

"This is Brad Bathos, from the streets of Washington, where the mourners have come to gather, to pray, to weep, to lament, and to hope. Back to Erect Severehead."

"Erect, we're up here on top of the Washington Monument with the Chief of the Washington Police Force. Chief Shackles, how many people would you say are down there right now?"

"Oh, just around the monument alone we've got about twenty-five or thirty thousand; and I'd say there are twice that many over by the White House. And of course more are pouring in every hour."

"Can you describe these people? Are they the usual sort of demonstrators you get here in Washington?"

"Oh no, no. These people don't want to disrupt anything. I would say they are actually bending over backwards to cooperate with the authorities. So far, at any rate."

"What do you mean by so far?"

"Well, we haven't yet had to make any arrests. We're under orders from the White House *not* to arrest anyone under any conditions. As you can imagine, this is putting something of a strain on my men, particularly as just about everybody down here seems to have come for the purpose of *getting* himself arrested. I mean I've never seen anything like it. A lot of them are down on their knees begging to be taken in, and just about every Tom, Dick and Harry seems to have documents or photographs or fingerprints, proving that he is the one who killed the President. Of course, none of it is worth the paper it's written on. Some of it's kind of laughable, in fact, it's so unprofessional and obviously a slapdash last-minute job. But still and all, you got to give them credit for their fortitude. They grab hold of my men just like they had the goods on themselves, and actually try to handcuff themselves to the officer with their *own* handcuffs and get carted off to prison that way. We can't park a squad car anywhere, without half a dozen of them jumping into the back seat, and screaming, 'Take me to J. Edgar Heehaw—and step on it.' Now you can't arrest anybody without taking the proper procedural steps, but go try to explain that to a crowd like this. We're sort of humoring them, however, the best we can, and the ones who just won't quit, we tell them to wait right where they are and we'll round them up later. What we're hoping for is a good thunderstorm during the night, that'll sort of break the back of the whole thing. Maybe if they stand around long enough in the rain they'll get the idea that nobody is going to arrest them no matter *how* much evidence they produce, and they'll go home."

"But, Chief Shackles, suppose the rain doesn't come—suppose they are still jamming the streets in the morning. What about the workers trying to get to government offices—?"

"Well, they'll just have to suffer a little inconvenience, I'm afraid. Because I am not subjecting my men to the charge of false arrest just so somebody can get to his office in time for the morning coffee break. And then there are these orders from the White House."

"Your assumption then is that all these people here are innocent, each and every one?"

"Absolutely. If they were guilty, they would be *resisting* arrest. They would be running away and so on. They would be screaming about their lawyers and their rights. I mean, that's how you can tell they're guilty in the first place. But all these people are saying is, 'I did it, take me in.' What sort of law enforcement officer is going to arrest a person for something like that?"

—

"This is Brad Bathos. Violence has erupted here on Pennsylvania Avenue, directly outside the White House gates where upwards of thirty thousand mourners have already gathered to bid farewell to a fallen leader. Even as Police Chief Shackles was praising this crowd for their obedience to authority and respect for the law, a free-for-all broke out among a group of fifteen men in business suits. Though police intervention was necessary, no arrests were made. I have here beside me one of the gentlemen who was involved in the violent episode, and by all appearances he is still rather upset. Sir, how did the violence begin?"

"Well, I was just standing here, minding my own business, trying to confess to an officer about murdering the President, when along comes this very fancy guy in a limousine and wearing a flower in his buttonhole, and he just steps in between me and the officers and he says *he* did it. And then the chauffeur gets out of the car and he starts pushing me back and saying let his boss do the talking, his boss really did it and he was a very busy man and so on and so forth and who did I think I was, acting so high and mighty. So then some colored guy comes up—and I don't have anything against colored guys, you know—but this one was real uppity and he starts saying we're both full of it, *he* did it, and the chauffeur tells him to get at the end of the line and wait his turn, and that really starts the thing going, and the next thing you know there are fifteen guys all swinging at one another, claiming *they* all did it, too. Well, if it wasn't for the officer, I'm not kidding, somebody might have gotten hurt. It could have been awful."

"So you have nothing but praise for the police?"

"Well, yes—up to a point. I mean he broke this thing up one-two-three, but then when it was all over he *still* wouldn't make any arrests. In fact, once he'd separated us, he just disappeared, like the Lone Ranger used to. I can't find him anywhere. Some of the other guys want to find him, too. See, we gave him these confessions and all this incriminating evidence, and so on—and you know what he did with it? He just tore it up, even while he was running away. Fortunately, I had my secretary Xerox all this stuff at my office, so I've got a copy at home, but a lot of these guys were foolish enough to give him the only copy of their confessions that they had. About the

only *good* thing to come out of this is the possibility that because the fifteen of us were seen all huddled together on the
pavement here, pounding each other's heads in, we might get
picked up as a conspiracy. That is, if we can find a cop. But go
try to find even a plainclothesman when you need one. Hey,
you're not authorized to make an arrest, are you, by your network or something?"

"—and so in they continue to come. And now they have
told us why. They come not as they came to Washington to
mourn the death of President Charisma. Nor do they come as
came they did to Atlanta, to follow behind the bier of the slain
Martin Luther King. Nor come do they as to the railroad
tracks they did, to wave farewell as the tragic train that bore
the body of the murdered Robert Charisma carried to its final
resting place, him. No, the crowd that cometh to Washington
tonighteth, cometh not in innocence and bewilderment, like
little children berefteth of a father. Rather, cometh they in
guilt, cometh they to confesseth, cometh they to say, 'I too am
guilty,' to the police and the FBI. It is a sight, moving and
profound, and furnishes evidence surely, if evidence there
need surely be, of a nation that has cometh of age. For what is
maturity, in men or in nations, but the willingness to bear the
burden—and the dignity—of responsibility? And surely responsible it is, mature it is, when in its darkest hour, a nation
can look deep within its troubled and anguished blah blah blah
blah blah blah blah the guilt of all. Of course, those there are
who will seek a scapegoat, as those there will always be, human
nature being what it is instead of what it should be. Those
there are who will self-righteously stand up and shout, 'Not
me, not me.' For they are not guilty, they are never guilty. It is
always the other guy who is guilty: Bundy and Kissinger, Bon-
nie and Clyde, Calley and Capone, Manson and McNamara—
yes, the list is endless of those whom they would make responsible for their own crimes. And that is what makes this demonstration here in Washington of collective guilt so blah blah
blah blah blah blah blah blah blah. The blah blah of the spirit
and the blah blah blah blah blah blah for which our sons have
died blah blah blah blah blah blah reason and dignity blah blah
blah blah blah dignity and reason. No, blame not those who

gather here in Washington to confess to the murder of the President. Rather, praise them for their courage, their blah blah blah, their blah and their blah blah blah, for blah blah blah blah as are you and I. We are all guilty. And only at the risk of blah blah blah blah blah blah blah blah blah blah forget. This is Erect Severehead from the nation's blah."

"—the masochists, the mainliners, the minorities who think they are the majorities, the mashers, the masturbators, the mental cases, the misanthropes, the momma's boys, the much-ado-about-nothingites, the milquetoasts—"

"Gentlemen, because of the developing interest around the nation in the situation here in Washington, we have decided to move somewhat faster than we had originally planned, and to release to you tonight the x-ray of the other hip. We hope that by releasing the x-rays of *both* of the President's hips, the right virtually within a few hours of the left, we will be able to re-store some perspective as regards this whole situation."

"You mean by that the assassination, Blurb?"

"I don't know if I want to use a highly inflammatory word like that at a time like this. It may not sell newspapers, but I'd just as soon, for the sake of accuracy, stick to 'the situation.'"

"In other words, you are now admitting that there is 'a situation.'"

"I don't think we ever denied that."

"What about the funeral, Blurb?"

"Let's deal with the situation first, then we'll get to the fu-neral. Any other questions?"

"Where is the President's body right now?"

"Resting comfortably."

"Comfortably *in* the baggie or *out* of the baggie?"

"Gentlemen, don't push me. He's resting comfortably. That's the important thing."

"Will he be buried in the baggie, Blurb? One report is that the First Lady has decided that given his dedication to the rights of the unborn, burial in the baggie would be fitting and proper. Like King's body being pulled by a mule train."

"Whatever the First Lady decides, I'm sure it'll be in good taste."

"Blurb, what about Mr. What's-his-name? He's still back of the podium saying it didn't happen, that it's a pack of lies. Do you have any idea what he's talking about?"

"No comment."

"Blurb, is it true that the oath of office has already been secretly administered to the Vice President between speaking engagements, and that he actually is the President at this very moment?"

"Why would we do a thing like that? Absolutely not."

"Mr. President, can you tell us now why the oath of office was administered to you secretly between speaking engagements, so that actually you were the new President even while you went around claiming that the stories of President Dixon's assassination were lies perpetrated by the enemies of this country?"

"I think the answer to that is obvious enough, gentlemen. You cannot have a country without a President any more than you would want to have a cackle-dooper without a predipitous, or, likewise, a caloodian without a pre-pregoratory predention. Of course, the dreedles, the drishakis and the dripnaps would give their eyeteeth to have it otherwise, but the sworn swaggatelle of this sirigible, and the truncation of our truthfulness will not be trampled and torn, so long as I, as President, vent such vindictiveness as the avengers varp."

"President What's-his-name, there is an admittedly ugly rumor to the effect that the reason you denied any knowledge of the President's assassination was because you were fearful that otherwise the finger of suspicion might be pointed at you. Do you have anything to say about that admittedly ugly rumor?"

"Yes, I have this to say and I propose to say it so that there is no doubt about my feelings on this matter later. If the creeps and the cowards that crucify the crelinion, crip after crip, and who furthermore—and we have proof of this—have crossbowed the cradalious ever since the first crackadoes crusaded in the cause of caliphony, if they think they can cajulate and castigate and get away with it, there will be such a cacophony of cabs, cassanings and crinoleum through the criss and cratch of this country, that the crypto-callistans and the quasi-clapperforms will quiver rather than coopt the crokes."

"Sir, while we're on the subject of admittedly ugly rumors, can you comment on one that suggests that the reason you kept saying the President was alive when you knew he was dead, was because you were fearful that either a coup on the part of the Cabinet, or an armed revolt by the people, would have prevented you from taking office, had you announced openly your intention to do so? Were you frightened that they wouldn't let you be President because you weren't qualified?"

"Far from fear, what I felt was a filarious frostification at the far-reaching fistula into which fate had feductively fastinguished me."

"Sir, will you comment on Mrs. Dixon's decision to bury the President in his baggie at Prissier? Were you consulted on this, and if so, does it mean that your administration will be as committed as was his to the rights of the unborn and the sanctity of human life and so on?"

"Well, of course, not just me, but zillions and zillions of our zircos, zaps of our zilpags and zikons of our zikenites—"

"So the blah blah blah blah of state has been passed. Blah blah blah blah blah blah blah has ended and the republic that blah blah blah blah reason blah blah blah blah. Heavy are our blah blah blah blah blah blah blah blah blah corridors blah blah blah that he loved. And the cherry blossoms. Blah blah blah blah blah. Blah blah blah blah. Blah blah blah blah blah lest we blah blah blah blah blah our civilization with it. We can ill afford that. Blah blah blah blah blah back to normal blah blah blah blah. Blah blah blah blah blah blah blah blah blah blah. Blah blah blah blah of America, from the humblest citizen to the blah blah blah blah. Blah blah 1776 blah blah? Blah. Blah blah 1812 blah blah blah? Blah blah. Blah blah 1904–1907? Blah! Blah blah blah blah blah blah blah reason and dignity. Blah blah blah blah reason. Blah blah blah blah blah dignity. Blah blah blah blah blah blah fulfillment of the Ameriblah blah blah blah blah blah. Blah blah blah one hundred years ago. Blah blah blah blah of Galilee. And yet those would surrender hope blah blah blah blah blah. Blah blah blah blah cherry blossoms. Blah blah blah blah blah blah blah blah blah blah before him. Blah blah blah the republic. Blah blah blah the people. Blah blah blah blah blah nation's capital."

The Eulogy Over the Baggie

*(As Delivered Live on Nationwide TV
by the Reverend Billy Cupcake)*

Now today I want you to turn with me to page 853 in your dictionaries. Our eulogy is from the letter "L," the twelfth letter of the alphabet, and our word is the fifth down in the left-hand column, directly below the word "leaden." Our word is "leader." Now how does Noah Webster define "leader"?

Well, Noah writes, "A leader is one who or one that which leads." One who or one that which leads. One *who* or *that which* leads.

Just the day before yesterday I read an article in a current magazine by one of the top philosophers of all time and he wrote, "Leaders are one of man's top necessities." And in a recent Gallup Poll we've been reading where more than ninety-eight percent of the people of America believe in leadership. I was in a European country last summer and one of the top young people there told me that the teenagers in his country want leadership more than anything else. President Lincoln—before he was killed—said the same thing. So did Newton—Sir Isaac Newton, the great scientist—when he was alive.

Now when Noah tells us that a leader is one *who* or one *that which* leads, he is telling us what "leader" means in the *ordinary* sense of the word. But I wonder if he who lies here before us in this baggie was a leader in the *ordinary* sense. I don't think he was. And I'll tell you why. I talked to a psychiatrist friend of mine only this morning and he said, "He was not an ordinary leader." And one of my friends, a distinguished surgeon who does heart transplants at one of our great hospitals, wrote me a letter and said the same thing: "He was not a leader in the ordinary sense of the word."

Well, you say, what was he then, if he wasn't a leader in the ordinary sense? He—and I repeat that—*he* was a leader in the *extra*ordinary sense of that word.

Now what does that mean, the *extra*ordinary sense of that word? Fortunately, Noah defines "extraordinary" for us, too.

You will find the definition on page 428 in your dictionaries, in the right-hand column, six words down, directly beneath "extraneous." *Extra*ordinary, Noah tells us, means, "beyond what is ordinary; out of the regular and established order." *Beyond* what is ordinary. *Out* of the regular and established order.

Now what does *that* mean? I read only the week before last in an Australian newspaper that I get in my home a story about a fellow who made news down there—and why did he make news down there? Why do I know about him thousands and thousands of miles away? Because he was *extra*ordinary in some way or another. He was that rare thing among men. He was himself and no one else. Himself and no one else.

And what does Noah tell us about "himself"? "Himself," Noah says, "an emphatic form of him." An *emphatic* form of him. Here then is what was so *extra*ordinary about the leader around whose baggie we are gathered today. He was emphatically *him*self and no one else.

You know. Let me repeat that. You know, I have been to funerals of ordinary leaders the world round, and I know you have too, by way of the miracle of television. We all know the wonderful things that are said on these sorrowful occasions. But I think I have only to repeat the fine words that are intoned over the graves of ordinary dead dignitaries for you to see how truly *extra*ordinary was our own dear departed President, in and of himself. In and of himself, which, you remember, Noah tells us is the *emphatic* form of him.

Now I don't mean to disparage the ordinary leaders of this great globe by this comparison. I read a letter only three weeks ago Thursday that a radical young person wrote to his girl friend disparaging and scoffing and laughing at the leaders of this world. Now he may laugh. They laughed at Jeremiah, you know. They laughed at Lot. They laughed at Amos. They laughed at the Apostles. In our own time they laughed at the Marx Brothers. They laughed at the Ritz Brothers. They laughed at the Three Stooges. Yet these people became our top entertainers and earned the love and affection of millions. There are always the laughers and the scoffers. You know there used to be a top tune in all the jukeboxes called "I'm Laughing on the Outside, Crying on the Inside." And I read an article in a news magazine only Sunday before last by one of

our top psychologists which says that eighty-five percent—
eighty-five percent!—of those who laugh on the outside cry
on the inside because of their personal unhappiness.

I am not then trying to disparage the ordinary leaders of the
world by this comparison. I want only to illustrate to you the
extraordinary leadership of the man who walked among us for
a brief while in a business suit, and now is gone. Only yesterday morning at ten A.M., I overheard a lady in an elevator of
one of our top hotels, say to a young person. "There has never
been another like him in history, there will never be another
like him again."

Now. Let me repeat that. Now, when an ordinary leader dies
—and I mean by "ordinary" just what Noah does, on page 853,
the last word down in column one: "of the usual kind" or
"such as is commonly met with"—when an *ordinary* leader
dies, there always seem to be words and phrases aplenty with
which to bury him. However, *how ever*, when an *extra*ordinary
leader dies, a man who was *him*self and no one else—what
then do we say?

Let's try a scientific experiment. Now science doesn't hold
all the answers and many of my scientific friends tell me that all
the time. Science, for instance, doesn't know what life is yet,
and in a recent Gallup Poll did you know that five percent
more Americans believe in life after death now than they did
some twenty years ago? So science doesn't have all the answers, but it has provided us with many wonderful break-
throughs.

Let's try this scientific experiment. Let's try the phrases for
an *ordinary* man on this *extra*ordinary man. And you tell me if
you don't agree that as applies to him who lies here in his baggie, they are hollow to the ear and false to the heart, and vice
versa. Let's see if when this experiment is over, you don't say
to me, "Why, Billie, you're right, they don't describe him at
all. They describe one *who* or one *that which* leads, but not him
who was emphatically *himself* and no other."

I'm going to ask that we bow our heads now. Every head
bowed and every eye closed, and listen.

They say of an *ordinary* leader, when and if he dies, of
course—he was a man of broad outlook;

Or, he was a man of great passion;

Or, he was a man of deep conviction;
Or, he was a defender of human rights;
Or, he was a soldier of humanity;
Or, he was scholarly, eloquent and wise;
Or, he was a simple, peace-loving man, brave and kind;
Or, he was a man who embodied the ideals of his people;
Or, he was a man who fired the imagination of a generation.

They say of an *ordinary* man, when and if he dies, that the loss is incalculable to the nation and the world.

They say of an *ordinary* man, when and if he dies, that all will be better for his having passed their way.

Need I go any further? There was an article in a current magazine last month by a professor who is an authority on human behavior, and he writes that you can tell when a crowd of people is in agreement with you. Well, the professor is correct. Because I know that you are all saying to yourselves, "Why, Billy, you're right—in vain do I listen for the words or word that describes he who lies here in this baggie; for these are phrases that summon up the image of an ordinary leader, not the *extraordinary* leader we have lost."

What word or words then will describe this *extraordinary* man? I was in an African country one year ago this July and I heard a top political expert there call him "The President of the United States." The President of the United States. In another African country I heard about a teenage girl who called him "The Leader of the Free World." The Leader of the Free World. And a lawyer friend of mine, a well-known judge, who lives in South America wrote me a letter not too long ago and he had an interesting thing to say. He said he heard a man in an elevator in a top hotel in Buenos Aires, Argentina, call him "Commander-in-Chief of the American Armed Forces." Commander-in-Chief of the Armed Forces.

Yet are these the words in which he lived in the hearts of his fellow countrymen? Perhaps that is what he was to the rest of the world. But to we who knew him, nothing so majestic or formal could begin to communicate the kind of man he was and the esteem in which he was held. Because to us he was not a leader in the *ordinary* sense—he was a leader in the *extra*-ordinary sense. And that is why we who knew him think of him by a name as unpretentious and unceremonious as the name you might give to your own pet, a name as homey and familiar as you might bestow upon a little puppy.

I'm going to ask that we bow our heads again. Every head bowed and every eye closed, while we all share in the remembrance of the name by which he was known to we who knew him best, the name by which we called him in our hearts, even if we were too shy or too timid to speak it with our lips while he walked among us in a business suit. And how appropriate that it is a name even a puppy could bear, for we all remember as much as anything about him, the deep reverence he had for dogs.

The name was a simple one, my friends. The name was Tricky. Yes, to you, to me, and to all Americans for generations to come, Tricky he was and Tricky he shall be.

And now, all heads bowed and every eye closed, let us pray. Oh God, who alone art ever merciful in sparing of punishment, humbly we pray Thee on behalf of Thy servant, a man called Tricky . . .

6

On the Comeback Trail; or, Tricky in Hell

Y FELLOW FALLEN:

Let me say at the outset that I of course agree with much of what Satan has said here tonight in his opening statement. I know that Satan feels as deeply as I do about what has to be done to make Wickedness all that it can and should be in the creation. For let there be no mistake about it: we are engaged in a deadly competition with the Kingdom of Righteousness. There isn't any question in my mind but that the God of Peace is out, as He Himself has said, "to crush" us "under his feet," and that He and His gang of angels will stop at nothing to accomplish this end. I could not agree more with Satan when he says that our goal is not just to keep Wickedness for ourselves, but to extend it to all creation, because that is Hell's destiny. To extend it to all creation because the aim of the Righteous is not just to hold their own, but to extend Righteousness. But we cannot be victorious over Righteousness with a strategy of simply holding the line. My disagreement with Satan then is not about the goals for Hell, but about the means to reach those goals.

Now Satan has said that we are ahead in this competition with Righteousness. I cannot agree with that appraisal of the situation. As I look at Hell today, I believe that we are following programs of an outdated leadership. I believe we are following programs many of which have not worked in the past and will not work in the future. I say that the programs and leadership that have failed under Satan's administration are not the programs and the leadership that Hell needs now. I say that the damned and the doomed do not want to go back to the policies of the Garden of Eden. I say that the Sons and Daughters of Disobedience deserve a Devil to consummate depravity, a Devil who will devote himself not to old and worn-out iniquities, but to bold new programs in Evil that will overturn God's kingdom and plunge men into eternal death. What we need down here is not just high hopes. What we need is crafty wiles and untiring zeal. In the field of executive leadership, I believe it is essential that the Devil not only set the tone, but he also must lead; he must act as he talks.

Frankly, I don't think this is the kind of leadership we have been getting. Now since my arrival I have traveled to the very edges of the outer darkness. I have been down to the bottom of the bottomless pit. I have been burned in the unquenchable fire and have joined you in the comfortless gloom. I have talked to sinners from all walks of life. I have eaten with degenerates and blasphemed with the impious. I have looked into the eyes of the depraved and the malicious. I have familiarized myself with viciousness and baseness of all kinds. And one thing I have noted as I have traveled from one end of Hell to the other is the wonderful belief our people have in Wickedness. I tell you, with great pride, that I have never seen anything to equal our corruption. And that is why I don't think we have to settle for second best. I don't think we have to settle for anything less than a Devil who is the very embodiment of malice. And I humbly submit to you, the denizens of the greatest infernal region in all creation, that if elected, I would be that kind of Devil.

I was fortunate enough to hear an awful lot of weeping and gnashing of teeth on my trip around Hell, and I think the strongest impression I came away with was this: that you lost souls out there are just as sick and tired as I am of hearing the Devil downgraded and Hell itself dismissed as "old-fashioned" and "out-of-date." Well, maybe it is "old-fashioned" in some circles, but to those of us who live here, Hell happens to be home. And dating back as it does to the beginning of time, it happens to have been home to some of the most illustrious names in history. And I think that with that kind of history and that kind of record, it is high time we put Hell back on the map, and high time the Devil was given his due.

Now I can only say, in this regard, that maybe Satan is satisfied with the fact that at least one half of the people presently on earth—and I know this, because I just came from there—at least one half of those people no longer believe in the existence of Hell, let alone its influence in world affairs. And maybe

Satan is satisfied that the Devil, the highest official in the underworld, once the very symbol of nefariousness to millions, is considered in the upper regions to have absolutely no power at all over the decisions made there by men. And maybe Satan is satisfied when at least two thirds of the children in the world go to bed at night without any fear of fire or brimstone, or an undying worm gnawing at the heart. Incidentally, in that connection, they don't even fear the pitchfork. And maybe that's all right with Satan, too. However, let me make my position very clear. It's not all right with me. Maybe Satan is satisfied with the status quo; well, I'm not. I say that when Hell is nothing more than a dirty word in the mouths of most people living today, then something is wrong, and something has to be done about it.

What has happened to "the Devil's net" we used to hear so much about? My fellow Fallen, it is full of holes.

What has happened to "the power of the Devil" that used to terrify the hearts of men? My fellow Fallen, it has run out of steam.

And when was the last time you heard the phrase "the work of Satan"? Can you even remember? Maybe that's because after all these millennia in office, Satan is satisfied with the status quo.

But I'm not. I say the Devil's work is never done. I say he has a responsibility to get up there among the living and wage war against the forces of Righteousness. I say he has a responsibility to the denizens of Hell, and to all souls everywhere who aspire to Wickedness, to oppose truth with falsehood. I say he has a responsibility to obscure light with darkness. I say he has a responsibility to entangle men's minds in error. I say he has a responsibility to stir up hatred. I say he has a responsibility to kindle contentions and combats. And I say any Devil who does less than this is not deserving of the title "Prince of Darkness," and does serious harm to the power and prestige of Hell and to the security of the Wicked everywhere.

Now you may answer, "That is all fine and dandy, Mr. President, but what qualifications do you bring with you to the job of being a responsible Devil?"

I know as well as you do the claims my opponent makes for his experience in office. I know what has been written in grudging tribute of him, by no less than our own adversaries in Heaven. "When Satan lies," they say, "he speaks according to his own nature, for he is a liar and the father of lies." And let there be no mistake about my position on this issue: I have the highest regard for his long and distinguished record as a liar. I know that I, like so many of you out there in the fires and down there in the pit, owe a deep debt of gratitude to the example of his never-say-die spirit, where lying is concerned.

To interject a personal note, you know I was born an opportunist, out in California, and during my years in public life I had the privilege of wheeling and dealing with other opportunists as well. And I think I speak for all opportunists when I say that Satan has been a constant source of inspiration to us from time immemorial, in good times and in bad. Surely I would want it understood throughout this campaign, that I respect not only the tenacity with which he lies, but his sincerity in lying. And of course I would hope that he would agree that I am just as sincere in my lying as he is in his.

But let me make one thing perfectly clear. Much as I respect and admire his lies, I don't think that lies are something to stand on. I think they are something to build on. I don't think anyone, man or demon, can ever rely upon the lies he has told in the past, bold and audacious as they may have been at the time, to distort today's realities. We live in an era of rapid and dramatic change. My own experience has shown that yesterday's lies are just not going to confuse today's problems. You cannot expect to mislead people next year the way you misled them a year ago, let alone a million years ago. And that is why, with all due respect to my opponent's experience, I say we need a new administration in Hell, an administration with new horns, new half-truths, new horrors and new hypocrisies. I say we need a new commitment to Evil, new stratagems and contrivances to make our dream of a totally fallen world a reality.

And now let me say a word to those who point to my own record as President of the United States and contend that it is less than it could have been, as regards suffering and anguish for all of the people, regardless of race, creed or color. Let me remind these critics that I happen to have held that high office for less than one term before I was assassinated. Now not even Satan, I think, with the support of all his legions, would claim that he could bring a nation with a strong democratic tradition and the highest standard of living in the world to utter ruination in only a thousand days. Indeed, despite my brief tenure in the "White" House, I firmly believe that I was able to maintain and perpetuate all that was evil in American life when I came to power. Furthermore I think I can safely say that I was able to lay the groundwork for new oppressions and injustices and to sow seeds of bitterness and hatred between the races, the generations and the social classes that hopefully will plague the American people for years to come. Surely I did nothing whatsoever to decrease the eventuality of a nuclear holocaust, but rather continued to make progress in that direction by maintaining policies of belligerence, aggression and subversion around the globe. I think I might point with particular pride to Southeast Asia, where I was able to achieve considerable growth in just the sort of human misery that the vengeful and vindictive souls here in our great inferno would wish upon the whole of mankind.

Now of course I do not claim sole responsibility for the devastation and misery visited by my country upon the Vietnamese, the Laotians and the Cambodians. In fact, I know that in the years to come you are going to have the privilege of meeting many of the men who were equally as devoted as was I, and who worked long hard hours with great dedication and self-sacrifice, as did I, to make life a nightmare in that region for those Asian human beings. I know when they get here they are going to make a great contribution to Hell, and let me say in that connection that if I am elected Devil, I will not hesitate to avail myself of their counsel and advice here, as I did there.

While it is true then that I was not the sole author, leader and architect of this great program for suffering launched by my country in Southeast Asia, I will say this: when the opportunity to take charge of our program was presented to me, I did not stand pat on the butchery and carnage of my predecessors. Because I know, as do you, that where slaughter is concerned we cannot stand pat. We cannot stand pat for the reason that we're in a race, as I've indicated. We can't stand pat because it is essential with the conflict that we have around the globe that we not just hold our own, that we not just keep suffering for ourselves, but that we extend it to every last man, woman and child. And I am confident that if you will look at the record, you will see that this is just what I was able to accomplish throughout Southeast Asia. I think you will agree that in the very brief time allotted to me I managed to seize upon the opportunity provided me by my predecessors and, with the aid of the United States Air Force, I turned that part of the globe into nothing less than Hell on earth.

Now I realize, as you do, that despite my record in Southeast Asia, there are still those who would impugn my reputation by pointing to certain so-called "humane" or "benevolent" actions that I undertook while President of the United States. Well, let me say, as regards these wholly unfounded attacks upon my bad name, that I intend, after this broadcast, to issue a black paper, showing that in every single instance where they claim I was "humane" or "benevolent," I was in actual fact motivated solely by political self-interest, and acted with utter indifference, if not outright contempt and cynicism, for the welfare of anybody other than myself. If and when any good whatsoever accrued to anything but me and my career, it was —as I am confident the black paper will make perfectly clear— wholly unintentional and inadvertent.

Now I am not saying that ignorance of benign consequences is any excuse for a demon who aspires to be your Devil. I am only admitting to you that I was not so hideous on earth as I might have been. But then I am sure that the great majority of demons in Hell weren't either, and that you share with me regrets about wasted opportunities and pangs of conscience. But let there be no mistake about it: I am no longer a man burdened by all the limitations and weaknesses of that condition, such as conscience, caution and consideration for one's reputation. And I am no longer the President of the United States, with all the barriers and obstructions that stand between the holder of that powerful office and his own capacity for evil. I am at long last a citizen of Hell, and let me tell you, that is a great challenge and a great opportunity. And that is why I can assure you, my fellow Fallen, that down here where no holds are barred and nothing is sacred, you are going to see a New Dixon, a Dixon such as I could only dream of being

while still an American human being, a Dixon who humbly
submits that he has what it takes in experience and energy to
be the kind of Devil all you lost souls deserve.

Now in order that the four demons on tonight's panel can
proceed to questioning Satan and myself—and let me say, I
welcome their questions—I shall now bring my opening statement to a close. But before I do, I want to make one last thing
particularly clear to the denizens of Hell, and that is this. In
terms of eternity, I am a relative newcomer to the Realm of
Wickedness. But I am a student of history also, and I must say
that in reading through the record of the current administration, and in particular its relations with the Kingdom of
Righteousness, I have been shocked by a blatant example of
what I can only call an attitude of appeasement—an attitude, I
am sorry to say, of outright submission and surrender. I am
talking, of course, of the famous Job case.

Now I know that in defense of his actions in that case Satan
has described to you in great detail all the sufferings that he
heaped upon this good man, Job. And I am not going to say
to you that he did not torment him in the extreme. I am not
going to try to build myself up by downgrading the job he did
on Job's sheep and his servants, and the loathsome sores with
which he afflicted him from head to foot. There is no question
but that the program of pain and punishment devised by Satan
was the right one in those circumstances.

Yet the question still remains, thousands of years after the
event, under whose auspices and in whose behalf was that program devised? Under the auspices of Hell? In behalf of the
cause of Wickedness?

My fellow Fallen, the answer is no. I am afraid that if you
read the record, as I have done, you will find that it was under
the auspices of Heaven, and in behalf of Righteousness, that
your own Devil planned and executed Job's program of P&P,
a program by the way involving a considerable expenditure of
our resources. I am afraid that if you read the record you will
find your own Devil taking his orders from none other than
the Lord God Himself. I am afraid you will find that your own
Devil did not so much as undertake one Evil act without first
obtaining the permission of God. I am afraid that you will find

that the reason he exercised the patience of Job was not to drive him from obedience and destroy him, but to serve God's justice—and, what is worse, to cause God's righteousness to shine forth.

Now Satan has indicated on several occasions during this campaign that I have been misrepresenting his role in the Job case. In order to set the record straight once and for all, I am going to use my remaining few minutes to read to you verbatim from the minutes of the meeting that took place between God and Satan at that time. And I leave it to you, the degenerate and the debauched, the dissolute and the depraved, to judge whether the charges I have made during the campaign, and that I repeat here tonight on this broadcast, constitute "a reckless distortion and deliberate misreading of history." I leave it to you to judge whether Satan was, as he claims, working "diabolically" and "fiendishly" for the cause of wickedness, or whether he was, to put it in language everyone can understand, acting in accordance with Divine Will.

This document I am holding in my claw is called the Holy Scripture. It doesn't lie. That is why it is nothing less than the Bible of our enemies. This is their number-one best seller of all time. This is the book with which they brainwash their children. Contained here are all the truths with which they intend to conquer the world. You can open it anywhere and find enough wisdom and beauty on a single page to disgust and outrage every loyal and hard-working citizen of Hell.

Let me read to you from the secret conversation between God and Satan, as documented in their Bible:

THE LORD: *Whence have you come?*

SATAN: *From going to and fro on the earth, and from walking up and down on it.*

THE LORD: *Have you considered my servant Job, that there is none like him on the earth, a blameless and upright man, who fears God and turns away from evil?*

SATAN: *Does Job fear God for naught? Hast thou not put a hedge about him and his house and all that he has, on every side? Thou has blessed the work of his hands, and his possessions have increased in the land. But* [and I am still quoting from Satan], *but put forth thy hand now, and touch all that he has, and he will curse thee to thy face.*

THE LORD: *Behold, and all that he has is in your power, only upon himself do not put forth your hand.*

That was the instruction given Satan by the Lord. And what did Satan do? Exactly as God told him to. Yes, my fellow Fallen, your own Devil became an instrument of God's wrath.

Let me read to you now from the minutes of the second secret meeting that took place in an unspecified location between the Emperor of Wickedness and the God of Peace. For the sake of brevity I will read to you only the most pertinent material.

THE LORD (*speaking of Job*): *He still holds fast to his integrity.*

SATAN: . . . *Put forth thy hand now, and touch his bone and his flesh, and he will curse thee to thy face.*

THE LORD: *Behold, he is in your power; only spare his life.*

And having received this second set of instructions, what did Satan do? Let me read it to you, just as it is written here in their Bible. "So Satan went forth from the presence of the Lord, and afflicted Job with loathsome sores from the sole of his foot to the crown of his head."

And did Satan spare Job's life, as God instructed him to? I am afraid the answer is yes, he did that too.

We all remember, I am sure, the unhappy ending to that story. Job's faith was not broken; it was strengthened and increased. And the Lord, as the record here states, "gave Job twice as much as he had before."

(*Tricky closes Bible. Quickly wipes perspiration from his scales with the back of his claw*)

My fellow Fallen, I challenge Satan to refute these charges that I have made here tonight. I challenge Satan to deny his role in the Job case. I challenge him to deny that he acted willingly and knowingly in behalf of the sworn enemies of Hell. I challenge him to deny that if this was not an outright act of treason, it was one so neglectful of the security interests of the Wicked, that Satan might just as well have been in the employ of the Righteous.

Now Satan may prefer to call these actions of his "fiendish" and "diabolical." But I call what he has done here surrender, and let me tell you something—I think that's what the leaders in Heaven are calling it, too. Because make no mistake about it—I know the other side. I have met with their representatives.

I know the kind of ruthless and fanatical people they are, and I can assure you, if you surrender to their Will, if you think it will stop them to surrender a single soul to their Righteousness, you are sadly mistaken. That will only whet their appetite for more. Because this God of Peace does not just want Job. He wants all the Jobs. And if we do not stop him each and every time, the day will come, my friends, when he will be hammering here at the Gates of Hell.

And that is why I say the time has come to stop appeasing the God of Peace. That is why I say the time has come to step up our own activities, and launch a new offensive in this battle for the minds and hearts and souls of men. For it is nothing less than an ideological battle that we are fighting; and that is why we need a Devil who is willing and able to stand on his ideals. It isn't the size or the age of a man's horns that counts —it's what he's going to do with them. It's our whole lives that you should be judging here tonight. It's what we stand for. It's what we believe. What I am trying to indicate to you tonight is that the tide of history is on our side, and that we can keep it on our side, because we're on the right side, and that's the side of Evil. And let there be no mistake about it: if I am elected Devil, I intend to see Evil triumph in the end; I intend to see that our children, and our children's children, need never know the terrible scourge of Righteousness and Peace.

Thank you.

THEN I SAW AN ANGEL COMING DOWN FROM HEAVEN, HOLDING IN HIS HAND THE KEY OF THE BOTTOMLESS PIT AND A GREAT CHAIN. AND HE SEIZED THE DRAGON, THAT ANCIENT SERPENT, WHO IS THE DEVIL . . . AND BOUND HIM FOR A THOUSAND YEARS, AND THREW HIM INTO THE PIT, AND SHUT IT AND SEALED IT OVER HIM, THAT HE SHOULD DECEIVE THE NATIONS NO MORE . . .

THE BOOK OF REVELATION

THE BREAST

The Breast

I T BEGAN oddly. But could it have begun otherwise, however it began? It has been said, of course, that everything under the sun begins oddly and ends oddly, and *is* odd. A perfect rose is "odd," so is an imperfect rose, so is the rose of ordinary rosy good looks growing in your neighbor's garden. I know about the perspective from which all that exists appears awesome and mysterious. Reflect upon eternity, consider, if you are up to it, oblivion, and everything becomes a wonder. Still, I would submit to you, in all humility, that some things are more wondrous than others, and that I am one such thing.

It began oddly—a mild, sporadic tingling in the groin. During that first week I would retire several times a day to the men's room adjacent to my office in the humanities building to take down my trousers, but upon examining myself, I saw nothing out of the ordinary, assiduous as was my search. I decided, halfheartedly, to ignore it. I had been so devout a hypochondriac all my life, so alert to every change in body temperature and systemic regularity, that the reasonable man I also was had long found it impossible to take seriously all my telltale symptoms. Despite the grim premonitions of extinction or paralysis or unendurable pain that accompanied each new ache or fever, I was, at thirty-eight, a man of stamina and appetite, six feet tall with good posture and a trim physique, most of my hair and all of my teeth, and no history of major illness. Though I might rush to identify this tingling in my groin with some neurological disease on the order of shingles —if not worse—I simultaneously understood that it was undoubtedly, as always, nothing.

I was wrong. It was something. Another week passed before I discerned a barely perceptible pinkening of the skin beneath the pubic hair, a blemish so faint, however, that I finally instructed myself to stop looking; it was no more than a minor irritation and certainly nothing to worry about. After another week—making, for the record, an incubation period of twenty-one days—I glanced down one evening while stepping into the shower and discovered that through the hectic day of teaching and conferences and commuting and dining out, the flesh at the base of my penis had turned a shade of pale red. Dye, I instantly decided, from my undershorts. (That the undershorts at my feet were light blue meant nothing in that panic-stricken burst of disbelief.) I looked *stained*, as though something—a berry of some sort—had been crushed against my pubes and the juices had run down onto my member, raggedly coloring the root.

In the shower I lathered and rinsed my penis and pubic hair three times, then coated myself carefully from thighs to navel with a thick icing of soap bubbles that I proceeded to massage into my flesh for a count of sixty; when I rinsed with hot water —burning hot this time—the stain was still there. Not a rash, not a scab, not a bruise or a sore, but a deep pigment change that I associated at once with cancer.

It was just midnight, the time when transformations routinely take place in horror stories—and a hard hour to get a doctor in New York. Nonetheless, I immediately telephoned my physician, Dr. Gordon, and despite an attempt to hide my alarm, he heard the fear easily enough and volunteered to dress and come across town to examine me. Perhaps if Claire had been with me that night instead of back at her own apartment preparing a curriculum-committee report, I would have had the courage of my terror and told the doctor to come running. Of course on the basis of my symptoms at that hour it is unlikely that Dr. Gordon would have rushed me then and there into a hospital, nor does it appear from what we now know—or continue not to know—that anything could have been done in the hospital to prevent or arrest what was under way. The agony of the next four hours I was to spend alone might perhaps have been alleviated by morphine, but nothing indicates that the course of the disaster could have been reversed by any medical procedure short of euthanasia.

With Claire at my side I might have been able to cave in completely, but alone I suddenly felt ashamed of losing control; it was no more than five minutes since I'd discovered the stain, and there I was, wet and nude on my leather sofa, trying vainly to overcome the tremolo in my voice as I looked down and described into the phone what I saw. *Take hold*, I thought —and so I took hold, as I can when I tell myself to. If it was what I feared, it could wait until morning; if it wasn't, it could also wait. I would be fine, I told the doctor. Exhausted from a hard day's work, I had just been—startled. I would see him in his office at—I thought this brave of me—about noon. Nine, he said. I agreed and, calmly as I could, said good night.

Not until I hung up and examined myself yet again under a strong light did I remember that there was a third symptom— aside from the tingling groin, and the discolored penis—that I had failed to mention to the doctor; I had taken it, until that moment, for a sign of health rather than of disease. This was the intensity of local sensation I had experienced at sex with Claire during the preceding three weeks. To me it had signaled the resurgence of my old desire for her; from where or why I did not even care to question, so thrilled—and so relieved— was I to have it back. As it was, the strong lust her physical beauty had aroused in me during the first two years of our affair had been dwindling for almost a year now. Until lately, I would make love to her no more than two or three times a month and, more often than not, at her provocation.

My cooling down—my coldness—was distressing to both of us, but as we both had endured enough emotional upheaval in our lives (she as a child with her parents, I as an adult with my wife), we were equally reluctant to take any steps toward dissolving our union. Dispiriting as it surely was for a lovely and voluptuous young woman of twenty-five to be spurned night after night, Claire displayed outwardly none of the suspicion or frustration or anger that would have seemed justified even to me, the source of her unhappiness. Yes, she pays a price for this equanimity—she is not the most expressive woman I have ever known, for all her sexual passion—but I have reached the stage in my life—that is, I *had*—where the calm harbor and its placid waters were more to my liking than the foaming drama of the high seas. Of course there were times—out in company, or sometimes just alone over our dinner—when I might have wished her livelier and more responsive, but I was far too content with her dependable sobriety to be disappointed in her for lacking color. I had had enough color, thank you, with my wife.

Indeed, during the course of three years, Claire and I had worked out a way of living together—which in part entailed living separately—that provided us the warmth and security of each other's affections, without the accompanying dependence, or the grinding boredom, or the wild, unfocused yearning, or the round-the-clock strategies of deception and placation which seemed to have soured all but a very few of the marriages we knew. A year back I had ended five years of psychoanalysis convinced that the wounds sustained in my own Grand Guignol marriage had healed as well as they ever would, and in large part because of my life with Claire. Maybe I wasn't the man I'd been, but I wasn't a bleeding buck private any longer, either, wrapped in bandages and beating the drum of self-pity as I limped tearfully into the analyst's office from that battlefield known as Hearth and Home. Life had become orderly and stable—the first time I could say that in more than a decade. We really did get on so easily and with so little strain, we liked each other so much that it seemed to me something very like a disaster (little I knew about disaster) when, out of the blue, I began to take no pleasure at all in our lovemaking. It was a depressing, bewildering development, and try as I might, I seemed unable to alter it. I was, in fact, scheduled to pay a visit to my former analyst to talk about how much this was troubling me, when, out of the blue again, I was suddenly more passionate with her than I had ever been with anyone.

But "passion" is the wrong word: an infant in the crib doesn't feel passion when it delights in being tickled playfully under the chin. I am talking about purely tactile delight—sex neither in the head nor the heart, but excruciatingly in the epidermis of the penis, sex skin-deep and ecstatic. It was a kind of pleasure that made me writhe and claw at the sheets, made me twist and turn in the bed with a helpless abandon that I had previously associated more with women than with men—and women more imaginary than real. During the final week of my incubation period, I nearly cried with *tears* from the sheer tortuous pleasure of the friction alone. When I came I took Claire's ear in my mouth and licked it like a dog. I licked her hair. I found myself panting, licking my own shoulder. I had been saved! My life with Claire had been spared! Having lain indifferently beside her for nearly a year, having begun to fear the worst about our future, I had somehow—blessed mysterious somehow!—found my way to a pure, primitive realm of erotic susceptibility where the bond between us could only be strengthened. "Is this what is meant by debauchery?" I asked my happy friend whose pale skin bore the marks of my teeth; "it's like nothing I've ever known." She only smiled, and closed her eyes to float a little more. Her hair was stringy with perspiration, like a little girl's from playing too long in the heat. Pleasured, pleasure-giving Claire. Lucky David. We couldn't have been happier.

Alas, what has happened to me is like nothing *anyone* has ever known: beyond understanding, beyond compassion, beyond comedy. To be sure, there are those who claim to be on the very brink of a conclusive scientific explanation; and those, my faithful visitors, whose compassion is seemingly limitless; and then, out in the world, those—why shouldn't there be?—who cannot help laughing. And, you know, at times I am even one with them: I understand, I have compassion, I too see the joke. Enjoying it is another matter. If only I could sustain the laughter for more than a few seconds—if only it weren't so brief and so bitter. But then maybe more laughs are what I have to look forward to, if the medical men are able to sustain life in me in this condition, and if I should continue to want them to.

I am a breast. A phenomenon that has been variously described to me as "a massive hormonal influx," an "endocrinopathic catastrophe," and/or "a hermaphroditic explosion of chromosomes" took place within my body between midnight and 4 A.M. on February 18, 1971, and converted me into a mammary gland disconnected from any human form, a mammary gland such as could only appear, one would have thought, in a dream or a Dali painting. They tell me that I am now an organism with the general shape of a football, or a dirigible; I am said to be of spongy consistency, weighing one hundred and fifty-five pounds (formerly I was one hundred and sixty-two), and measuring, still, six feet in length. Though I continue to retain, in damaged and "irregular" form, much of the cardiovascular and central nervous systems, an excretory system described as "reduced and primitive," and a respiratory system that terminates just above my mid-section in something resembling a navel with a flap, the basic architecture in which these human characteristics are disarranged and buried is that of the breast of the mammalian female.

The bulk of my weight is fatty tissue. At one end I am rounded off like a watermelon, at the other I terminate in a nipple, cylindrical in shape, projecting five inches from my "body" and perforated at the tip with seventeen openings, each about half the size of the male urethral orifice. These are the apertures of the lactiferous ducts. As I am able to understand it without the benefit of diagrams—I am sightless—the ducts branch back into lobules composed of the sort of cells that secrete the milk that is carried to the surface of the normal nipple when it is being suckled, or milked by machine.

My flesh is smooth and "youthful," and I am still a "Caucasian." The color of my nipple is rosy pink. This last is thought to be unusual because in my former incarnation I was an emphatic brunet. As I told the endocrinologist who made this observation, I find it less unusual than certain other aspects of the transformation, but then I am not the endocrinologist around here. Embittered wit, but wit at last, and it must have been observed and noted.

My nipple is rosy pink—like the stain at the base of my penis the night this all happened to me. Since the apertures in the nipple provide me with something like a mouth and vestigial ears—at least it has seemed to me that I am able to make myself heard through my nipple, and, faintly, to hear through it what is going on around me—I had assumed that it was my head that had become my nipple. But the doctors conclude otherwise, at least as of this month. For one thing, my voice, faint as it is, evidently emanates from the flap in my midsection, even if my sense of internal landscape doggedly continues to associate the higher functions of consciousness with the body's topmost point. The doctors now maintain that the wrinkled, roughened skin of the nipple—which, admittedly, is exquisitely sensitive to touch like no tissue on the face, including the mucous membrane of the lips—was formed out of the glans penis. That puckered pinkish areola encircling the nipple is said to have metamorphosed from the shaft of the penis under the assault of a volcanic secretion from the pituitary of "mammogenic" fluid. Two fine long reddish hairs extend from one of the small elevations on the rim of my areola.

"How long are they?"

"Seven inches exactly."

"My antennae." The bitterness. Then the disbelief. "Will you pull one, please?"

"If you like, David, I'll pull very gently."

Dr. Gordon wasn't lying. A hair of mine had been tugged. A familiar enough sensation—indeed, so familiar that I wanted to be dead.

Of course it was days after the change—the "change"!—before I even regained consciousness, and another week after that before they would tell me anything other than that I had been "very ill" with "an endocrine imbalance." I keened and howled so wretchedly each time I awoke to discover anew that I could not see, smell, taste, or move that I had to be kept under heavy sedation. When my "body" was touched, I didn't know what to make of it: the sensation was unexpectedly soothing, but far away, it reminded me of water lapping at a beach. One morning I awakened to feel something new happening to me at one of my extremities. Nothing like pain—rather more like pleasure—yet it felt so strange just to *feel* that I screamed, "I've been burned! I was in a fire!"

"Calm yourself, Mr. Kepesh," a woman said. "I'm only washing you. I'm only washing your face."

"My face? Where is it! Where are my arms! My legs! Where is my mouth! *What happened to me?*"

Now Dr. Gordon spoke. "You're in Lenox Hill Hospital, David. You're in a private room on the seventh floor. You've been here ten days. I've been to see you every morning and night. You are getting excellent care and all the attention you require. Right now you're just being washed with a sponge and some warm soapy water. That's all. Does that hurt you?"

"No," I whimpered, "but where is my face?"

"Just let the nurse wash you, and we'll talk a little later in the morning. You must get all the rest you can."

"What happened to me?" I could remember the pain and the terror, but no more: to me it had felt as though I were being repeatedly shot from a cannon into a brick wall, then marched over by an army of boots. In actuality it was more as though I had been a man made of taffy, stretched in opposite directions by my penis and my buttocks until I was as wide as I had once been long. The doctors tell me that I couldn't have been conscious for more than a few minutes once the "catastrophe" got going, but in retrospect, it seems to me that I had been awake to feel every last bone in my body broken in two and ground into dust.

"If only you'll relax now—"

"How am I being fed!"

"Intravenously. You mustn't worry. You're being fed all you need."

"Where are my arms!"

"Just let the nurse wash you, and then she'll rub some oil in, and you'll feel much better. Then you can sleep."

I was awakened like this every morning, but it was another week or more before I was sufficiently calm—or torpid—to associate the sensations of washing with erotic excitement. By now I had concluded that I was a quadruple amputee—that the boiler had burst beneath the bedroom of my parlor-floor apartment, and I had been blinded and mutilated in the explosion. I sobbed almost continuously, giving no credence whatsoever to the hormonal explanations that Dr. Gordon and his colleagues proposed for my "illness." Then one morning, depleted and numb from my days of tearless weeping, I felt myself becoming aroused—a mild throbbing in the vicinity of what I still took to be my face, a pleasing feeling of . . . engorgement.

"Do you like that?" The voice was a man's! A stranger's!

"*Who are you? Where am I? What is going on?*"

"I'm the nurse."

"Where's the other nurse!"

"It's Sunday. Take it easy—it's only Sunday."

The next morning the regular nurse, Miss Clark, returned to duty, accompanied by Dr. Gordon. I was washed, under Dr. Gordon's supervision, and this time, when I began to experience the sensations that accompany erotic fondling, I let them envelop me. "Oh," I whispered, "that does feel nice."

"What is it?" asked Dr. Gordon. "What are you saying, David?"

The nurse began to rub in the oil. I could feel each one of her fingers kneading that face no longer a face. Then something began to make me tingle, something that I soon realized was only the soft palm of her hand slowly moving in caressing circles on that faceless face. My whole being was seething with that exquisite sense of imminence that precedes a perfect ejaculation. "Oh, my God, this is so wonderful." And then I began to sob so uncontrollably that I had to be put back to sleep.

Shortly thereafter, Dr. Gordon came with Dr. Klinger, who for five years had been my psychoanalyst, and they told me what it is I have become.

I was washed gently but thoroughly every morning and then smeared with oil and massaged. After I heard the truth about myself—after learning that I live now in a hammock, my nipple at one end, my rounded, bellied underside at the other, and with two velvet harnesses holding my bulk in place—it was several months before I could take even the remotest pleasure in these morning ablutions. And even then it was not until Dr. Gordon consented to leave me alone in the room with the nurse that I was again able to surrender wholly to Miss Clark's ministering fingers. But when I did, the palpations were almost more than could be borne, deliciously "almost"—a frenzy akin to what I had experienced in those final weeks of lovemaking with Claire, but even more extreme, it seemed, coming to me in my state of utter helplessness, and out of nothingness, and from this source dedicated solely to kindling my excitement. When the session was over and Miss Clark had retired from my room with her basin of warm water and the vials of oil (I imagined colored vials), my hammock would sway comfortingly to and fro, until at last my heaving stopped, my nipple softened, and I slept the sleep of the sated.

I say the doctor consented to leave us alone in the room. But how do I know anyone has ever left me alone, or that this is even a room? Dr. Gordon assures me that I am under no more surveillance than any other difficult case—I am not on display in a medical amphitheater, am not being exposed to closed-circuit television . . . but what's to prevent him from lying? I doubt that in the midst of this calamity anybody is watching out for my civil liberties. That *would* be laughable. And why do I even care if I am not alone when I think I am? If I am under a soundproof glass dome on a platform in the middle of Madison Square Garden, if I am on display in Macy's window—what's the difference to me? Wherever they have put me, however many may be looking in at me, I am really quite as alone as anyone could ever wish to be. Best to stop thinking about my "dignity," regardless of all it meant to me when I was a professor of literature, a lover, a son, a friend, a neighbor, a customer, a client, and a citizen. If ever there was a time to forget about propriety, decorum, and personal pride, this is it. But as these are matters intimately connected to my idea of sanity and to my self-esteem, I am, in fact, troubled now as I wasn't at all in my former life, where the style of social constraint practiced by the educated classes came quite easily to me, and provided real satisfaction. Now the thought that my morning sessions with Miss Clark are being carried live on intra-hospital TV, that my delirious writhings are being observed by hundreds of scientists assembled in the galleries overhead . . . well, that is sometimes almost as unbearable as the rest of it. Nonetheless, when Dr. Gordon assures me that my "privacy" is being respected, I no longer contradict him. I say instead, "Thank you for that," and in this way I am able at least to pretend to them that I think I am alone even if I'm not.

You see, it is not a matter of doing what is right or seemly; I can assure you that I am not concerned with the etiquette of being a breast. Rather, it is doing what I must, to continue to be me. For if not me, who? Or what? Either I continue to be myself or I go mad—and then I die. And it seems I don't want to die. A surprise to me too, but there it is. I don't foresee a miracle either, some sort of retaliatory raid by my anti-mammogenic hormones, if such there be (and God alone knows if there are in someone made like me), that will undo the damage. I suspect it's a little late for that, and so it is not with this hope springing eternally in the human breast that the human breast continues to want to be. Human I insist I am, but not that human. Nor do I believe the worst is over. I get the feeling that the worst is yet to come. No, it is simply that having been terrified of death since the age of two, I have become entrenched in my hatred of it, have taken a personal stand *against* death from which I seem unable to retreat because of This. Horrible indeed This is; but on the other hand, I have been wanting not to die for so long now, I just can't stop doing it overnight. I need time.

That I have not died is, as you can imagine, of great interest to medical science. *That* miracle continues to be studied by microbiologists, physiologists, and biochemists working here in the hospital and, I am told, in medical institutions around the country. They are trying to figure out what makes me still tick. Dr. Klinger thinks that no matter how they put the puzzle together, in the end it could all come down to those old pulpit bromides, "strength of character" and "the will to live." And who am I not to concur in such a heroic estimate of myself?

"It appears then that my analysis has 'taken,'" I tell Dr. Klinger; "a tribute to you, sir." He laughs. "You were always stronger than you thought." "I would as soon never have had to find out. And besides it's not so. I can't live like this any longer." "Yet you have, you do." "I do *but I can't*. I was never strong. Only determined. One foot in front of the other. Good grades in all subjects. It goes back to handing homework in on time and carrying off the prizes. Dr. Klinger, *it's hideous in here*. I want to quit, I want to go crazy, to go spinning off, ranting and wild, *only I can't*. I sob. I scream. I touch bottom. I lie there on that bottom! But then I come around. I make my mordant little jokes. I listen to the radio. I listen to the phonograph. I think about what we've said. I restrain my rage and I restrain my misery—and I wait for your next visit. But this is madness, my coming around. To be putting one foot in front of the other is madness—*especially as I have no feet!* This ghastly thing has happened, and I listen to the six o'clock news! This incredible catastrophe, and I listen to the weather report!" No, no, says Dr. Klinger: strength of character, the will to live.

I tell him that I want to go mad, he tells me that it's impossible: beyond me, *beneath* me. It took This for me to find that I am a citadel of sanity.

So—I may pretend otherwise, but I know they are studying me, watching as they would from a glass-bottomed boat the private life of a porpoise or a manatee. I think of these aquatic mammals because of the overall resemblance I now bear to them in size and shape, and because the porpoise in particular is said to be an intelligent, perhaps even rational, creature. Porpoise with a Ph.D. Associate Porpoise Kepesh. Oh, really, it is the silliness, the triviality, the *meaninglessness* of life that one misses most in a life like this. For quite aside from the monstrous, ludicrous fact of me, there is the intellectual responsibility that I seem to have developed to this preposterous misfortune. WHAT DOES IT MEAN? HOW COULD IT HAVE HAPPENED? IN THE ENTIRE HISTORY OF THE HUMAN RACE, WHY PROFESSOR KEPESH? Yes, it is clever of Dr. Klinger to keep to what is ordinary and familiar, to drone on about strength of character and the will to live. Better those banalities than the grandiose or the apocalyptic; for citadel of sanity though I may be, there is really only so much that even I can take.

As far as I know, my only visitors other than the scientists, the doctors, and the hospital staff, have been Claire, my father, and Arthur Schonbrunn, formerly my department chairman and now the Dean of Arts and Sciences. My father's behavior has been staggering. I don't know how to account for it, except to say that I simply never knew the man. Nobody knew the man. Aggressive, cunning, at his work tyrannical—with us, the little family, innocent, protective, tender, and deeply in love. But this self-possession face to face with such horror? Who would have expected it from the owner of a second-class South Fallsburg hotel? A short-order cook to begin with, he rose eventually to be the innkeeper himself; retired now, he "kills time" answering the phone mornings at his brother's booming catering service in Bayside. Once a week he comes to visit and, seated in a chair that is drawn up beside my nipple, tells me all the news about our former guests. Remember Abrams the milliner? Cohen the chiropodist? Remember Rosenheim with the card tricks and the Cadillac? Yes, yes, I think so. Well, this one is near death, this one has moved, this one's son has gone and married an Egyptian. "How do you like that?" he says; "I didn't even know they would allow that over there." It is an awesome performance. Only is it performance? Is he the world's most brilliant actor, or just a simpleton, or just completely numb? Or has he no choice other than to go on being himself? *But doesn't he get what has happened? Doesn't the man understand that some things are more unusual even than a Jew marrying an Egyptian?*

One hour, and then he leaves for home—without kissing me. Something new for my father, leaving without that kiss. And that is when I realize he is no simpleton. It *is* a performance—and my father is a great and brave and noble man.

And my excitable mother? Mercifully for her she is dead; if she weren't, this would have killed her. Or am I wrong about her too? She put up with alcoholic bakers and homicidal salad men and bus boys who still wet the bed—so who knows, maybe she could have put up with me too. *Beasts*, she called them, *barnyard animals*, but always she went back to the kettles, back to the cleanser and the mops and the linens, despite the *angst* she endured from Memorial Day weekend to Yom Kippur because of the radical imperfection of our help. Isn't it from my mother that I learned determination to begin with? Isn't it from her example that I learned how one goes on from summer to winter to summer again, in spite of everything? So, still more banality: I am able to bear being a mammary gland because of my upbringing in a typically crisis-ridden Catskill hotel.

Claire, whose equanimity has from the first been such a tonic to me, a soothing antidote to the impulsiveness of my former wife, and I suppose even to my mother's palpitations and all the hotel-kitchen crises—Claire, oddly, was not nearly so good as my father at quelling her anguish right off. What was astonishing wasn't her tears, however, but the weight of her head on my midsection when she broke down and began to sob. *Her face on this flesh? How can she touch me?* I had been expecting never to be handled again by anyone other than the medical staff. I thought, "If Claire had become a penis . . ." But that was just too ridiculous to contemplate—inasmuch, that is, as it hadn't happened. Besides, what had happened to me had happened to me and no one else because it could not happen to anyone else, and even if I did not know why that was so, *it was so*, and there must be reasons to make it so, whether I was ever to know them or not. Perhaps, as Dr. Klinger observed, putting myself in Claire's shoes was somewhat beyond the call of duty. Perhaps; but if Claire *had* become a five-foot-nine-inch male member, I doubt that I would be capable of such devotion.

It was only a few days after her first visit that Claire consented to massage my nipple. Had she wept from a safe distance, I could never have been so quick to make the suggestion; I might never have made it at all. But the very moment I felt the weight of her head touch down upon me, *all* the possibilities opened up in my mind, and it was only a matter of time (and not very much of that) before I dared to ask for the ultimate act of sexual grotesquerie, in the circumstances.

I must make clear, before going further, that Claire is no vixen; though throughout our affair she had been wonderfully aroused by ordinary sexual practices, she had no taste, for instance, for intercourse *per anum*, and was even squeamish about receiving my sperm in her mouth. If she performed fellatio at all, it was only as a brief antecedent to intercourse, and never with the intention of bringing me off. I did not complain bitterly about this, but from time to time, as men who have not yet been turned into breasts are wont to do, I registered my discontent—I was not, you see, getting all I wanted out of life.

Yet it was Claire who suggested that she would play with my nipple if that was what I most desired.

This was during her fourth visit in four days. I had described to her for the first time how the nurse ministered to me in the mornings. I planned—for the time being anyway—to say this and no more.

But Claire immediately asked, "Would you like me to do what she does?"

"Would you—do that?"

"Of course, if you want me to."

Of course. Cool, imperturbable girl!

"I do!" I cried. "Please, I do!"

"You tell me what you like then," she said. "You tell me what feels best."

"Claire, is anyone else in the room?"

"No, no—just you and me."

"Is this being televised, Claire?"

"Oh, sweetheart, no, of course it isn't."

"Oh, then squeeze me, squeeze me hard!"

Once again, days later, after I made incoherent conversation about my nurse for nearly an hour, Claire said, "David dearest, what is it? Do you want my mouth?"

"Yes, yes!"

How could she? How can she? Why does she? Would *I*? I say to Dr. Klinger, "It's too much to ask. It's too awful. I have to stop this. I want her to do it all the time, every minute she's here. I don't want to talk any more. I don't want her to read to me—I don't even listen. I just want her to squeeze me and suck me and lick me. I can't get enough of it. I can't stand it when she stops. I shout, I scream, "Go on! More! Go on!" But I'll drive her away, I will, I know, if I don't stop. And then I'll have no one. Then I'll have the nurse in the morning—and that's all I'll have. My father will come and tell me who died and who got married. And you will come and tell me about my strong character and my will to live. *But I won't have a woman!* I won't have Claire or sex or love ever again! I don't want to drive her away, it's bizarre enough now—but I want her clothes off, all of them off, at her feet, on the floor. I want her to get up on me and *roll* on me. Oh, Doctor, I want to fuck her! With my nipple! But if I even say it, it will drive her away! She'll run and never return!"

Claire visits every evening after dinner. During the day she teaches fourth grade at the Bank Street School here in New York. She is a Phi Beta Kappa graduate of Cornell; her mother is principal of a school in Schenectady, divorced now from her father, an engineer with Western Electric. Her older sister is married to an economist in the Commerce Department, and lives with him and four little children in Alexandria, Virginia. They own a house on the South Beach of Martha's Vineyard, where Claire and I visited them on our way to a week's vacation in Nantucket last summer. We argued politics—the Vietnam war. That done, we played fly-catcher-up with the kids down on the beach and then went off to eat boiled lobsters in Edgartown; afterward we sat in the movies, big, hearty, hairy carnivores, reduced in the cozy dark to nothing more than wind-burned faces and buttered fingers. Delicious. We had a fine time, really, "square" as were our hosts—I know they were square because they kept telling me so. Yet we had such a good time. She is something to look at on the beach, a green-eyed blonde, tall and lean and full-breasted. Even with desire on the wane, I still liked nothing better than to lie in bed and watch her dress in the morning and undress at night. Down in the hollow of the dunes, I unclip the top of her bikini and watch it drop away. "Imagine," she says, "where they'll be at fifty, if they droop like this at twenty-five." "Can't," I say, "won't," and drawing her to her knees, I lean back on the hot sand, dig down with my heels, shut my eyes, and wait with open lips for her breast to fill my mouth. Oh, what a sensation, there with the sea booming below! As though it were the globe itself—suckable soft globe!—and I Poseidon or Zeus! Oh, nothing beats the pleasures of the anthropomorphic god. "Let's spend all next summer by the ocean," I say, as people do on the first happy day of vacation. Claire whispers, "First let's go home and make love." It's been some time—she's right. "Oh, let's just lie here," I say—"Where is that strange thing? Oh, again, again." "I don't want to cut off your air. You were turning green." "With envy," I say.

Yes, I admit openly, that is what I said. And if this were a fairy tale instead of my life, we would have the moral now: "Beware preposterous desires—you may get lucky." But as this is decidedly *not* some fairy tale—not to me, dear reader—why should a wish like that have been the one to come true? I assure you that I have wanted things far less whimsically in my life than I wanted on that beach to be breasted. Why should playful, loverly words—spoken on the first day of our idyllic vacation! —become flesh, while whatever I have wanted in deadly earnest I have been able to achieve, if at all, only by putting one foot in front of the other over the course of thirty-eight years? No, I refuse to surrender my bewilderment to the wish-fulfillment theory. Neat and fashionable and delightfully punitive though it may be, I refuse to believe that I am this thing because this is a thing that I wanted to be. No! Reality is just a little grander than that. Reality has *some* style.

There. For those who prefer a fairy tale to life, a moral: "Reality," concludes the embittered professor who for reasons unbeknown to himself became a female breast, "has style." Go, you sleek, self-satisfied Houyhnhnms to whom nothing disgusting has yet happened, go and moralize on that!

It was not to Claire that I made my "grotesque" proposal then, but to my female nurse. I said, "Do you know what I think about when you wash me like this? Can I tell you what I am thinking about right now?"

"What is that, Professor Kepesh?"

"I would like to fuck you with my nipple."

"Can't hear you, Professor."

"I get so excited I want to fuck you! I want you to sit on my nipple—with your cunt!"

"I'll be finished with you now in just a moment   "

"*Did you hear me, whore? Did you hear what I want?*"

"Just drying you down now . . ."

By the time Dr. Klinger arrived at four I was one hundred and fifty-five pounds of remorse. I even began to sob a little when I told him what I had done—against all my misgivings and despite his warning. Now, I said, it was recorded on tape; for all I knew, it would be on page one of tomorrow's tabloids. A light moment for the straphangers on their way to work. For there certainly was a humorous side to it all; what is a catastrophe without its humorous side? Miss Clark—as I had known all along—is a short, stocky spinster, fifty-six years old.

Unlike Dr. Gordon, Claire, and my father, who continually assure me that I am not being watched other than by those who announce their presence, Dr. Klinger has never even bothered to dispute the issue with me. "And? If it is on page one? What of it?"

"It's nobody's business!" Still weeping.

"But you certainly would like to do it, would you not?"

"Yes! Yes! But she ignored me! She pretended I'd asked her to hurry up and be done! I don't want her any more! I want a new nurse!"

"Have anyone in mind?"

"Someone young—someone beautiful! Why not!"

"Someone who will hear you and say yes."

"Yes! Why not! It's insane otherwise! I should have what I want! This is no ordinary life and I am not going to pretend that it is! *You* want me to be ordinary, you *expect* me to be ordinary—in this condition! I'm supposed to go on being a sensible, rational man—in this condition! But that is crazy of you, Doctor! I want her to sit on me with her cunt! And why not! I want Claire to do it! What makes that 'grotesque'? To be denied my pleasure in the midst of this—*that* is grotesque! I want to be fucked! Why shouldn't I be fucked? Tell me why that shouldn't be! Instead you torture me! Instead you prevent me from having what I want! Instead I lie here being sensible! And there's the madness, Doctor—being sensible!"

I do not know how much of what I said Dr. Klinger even understood; it is difficult enough to follow me when I am speaking deliberately, with concentration, and now I was sobbing and howling with no regard for the TV cameras or the spectators up in the stands . . . Or is that *why* I was carrying on so? Was I really so racked by the proposal I'd made that morning to Miss Clark? Or was the display largely for the benefit of my great audience, to convince them that, appearances aside, I am still very much a man—for who but a man has conscience, reason, desire, and remorse?

This crisis lasted for months. I became increasingly lewd with the stout, implacable Miss Clark, until finally one morning I offered her money. "Bend over—take it from behind! I'll give you anything you want!" How I would get the money into her hands, how I would go about borrowing if she demanded more than I had saved in my account I tried to figure out during my long, empty days. Who would help me? I couldn't very well ask my father or Claire, and they were the only two people by whom I was willing to be seen. Ridiculous perhaps, given how sure I was that my image was being mercilessly recorded by television cameras and my daily progress publicized in the *Daily News*, but then I am not arguing that since my transformation I have been a model of Mature Adult Responsible Behavior. I am only trying to describe, as best I can, the stages I have had to pass through on the way to the

present phase of melancholy equilibrium . . . Of course to
assist me—to get hold of the money, to make the financial
arrangements, either with Miss Clark, or, if need be, with some
woman whose profession is not circumscribed by a nurse's ethical outlook—I could easily have called upon a young bearded
colleague, a clever poet from Brooklyn who is no prude and
whose sexual adventurousness has made him somewhat notorious in our English Department. But then neither was I a
prude, and once upon a time I had had a taste for sexual adventure no less developed than my young friend's. You must
understand that it was not a man of narrow experience and
suffocating inhibitions who was being tormented by his desires
in that hammock. I had experimented with whores easily
enough back in my twenties, and during a year as a Fulbright
student in London, I had for several months carried on a
thrilling, overwrought affair with two young women—students
my age on leave together from university in Sweden, who
shared a basement bedroom with me—until the less stable of
the pair tried halfheartedly to pitch herself under a lorry. No,
what alarmed me wasn't the strangeness of my desires in that
hammock, but the degree to which I would be severing myself
from my own past—and kind—by surrendering to them. I was
afraid that the further I went the further I would go—that I
would reach a point of frenzy from which I would pass over
into a state of being that no longer had anything to do with
who or what I once had been. It wasn't even that I would no
longer be myself—I would no longer be anyone. I would have
become craving flesh and nothing more.

So, with Dr. Klinger's assistance, I set about to extinguish
—and if not to extinguish, at least (in Klinger's favorite word)
to *tolerate*—the desire to insert my nipple into somebody's
vagina. But with all my will power—and, like my mother's, it
can be considerable when I marshal my forces—I was helpless
once that bath began. Finally it was decided that nipple and
areola should be sprayed with a mild anesthetic before Miss
Clark started preparing me to meet the day. And this in fact
did sufficiently reduce sensation so as to give me the upper
hand in the battle against these impractical urges—a battle I
won, however, only when the doctors decided, with my consent, to change my nurse.

That did the trick. Inserting my nipple into either the mouth or the anus of Mr. Brooks, the new male nurse, is something I just can't imagine with anything like the excitement I would imagine my nipple in Claire, or even in Miss Clark, though I realize that the conjunction of male mouth and female nipple can hardly be described as a homosexual act. But such is the power of my past and its taboos, and the power over my imagination of women and their apertures, that I am able now— temporarily anesthetized and in the hands of a man—to receive my morning ablutions like any other invalid, more or less.

And there is still Claire, angelic imperturbable Claire, to "make love" to me, with her mouth if not with her vagina. And isn't that sufficient? Isn't that incredible enough? Of course I dream of MORE, dream of it all day long—but what good is MORE to me anyway, when there is no orgasmic conclusion to my excitement, but only this sustained sense of imminent ejaculation in which I writhe from the first second to the last? Actually I have come by now to settle for less rather than MORE. I think I had better if I don't want Claire to come to see herself as nothing but the female machine summoned each evening to service a preposterous organism that once was David Kepesh. Surely the less time she spends at my nipple, the greater my chances of remaining something other to her (and to myself) than that nipple. Consequently, it is only for half of her hour-long visits that we now engage in sex—the rest of the time we spend in conversation. If I can, I should like to cut the sex play by half yet again. If the excitement is always at the same pitch, neither increasing nor decreasing in intensity once it's begun, what's the difference if I experience it for fifteen rather than thirty minutes? What's the difference if it is for only *one* minute?

Mind you, I am not yet equal to such renunciation, nor am I convinced that it is desirable even from Claire's point of view. But it is something, I tell you, simply to entertain the idea after the torment I have known. Even now there are still moments, infrequent but searing, when I have all I can do not to cry out, while her lips are rhythmically palpating my nipple, "Fuck on it, Ovington! With your cunt!" But I don't, I don't. If Claire were of a mind to, she would have made the suggestion herself already. And, after all, she is still only a fourth-grade teacher at the Bank Street School, a girl brought up in Schenectady, New York, and Phi Beta Kappa at Cornell. No sense causing her to consider too carefully the grotesqueries she has already, miraculously, declared herself willing to participate in with the likes of me.

Sometime between the first and the second of the two major "crises" I have survived so far here in the hospital—if hospital it is—I was visited by Arthur Schonbrunn, Dean of Arts and Sciences at Stony Brook, and someone I have known since Palo Alto, when he was *the* young hot-shot Stanford professor and I was there getting my Ph.D. It was as the chairman of the newly formed comparative-literature department that Arthur brought me from Stanford to Stony Brook eight years ago. He is nearly fifty now, a wry and charming gentleman, and for an academic uncommonly, almost alarmingly, suave in manner and dress. It was his social expertise as much as our long-standing acquaintanceship that led me (and Dr. Klinger) to settle finally on Arthur as the best person with whom to make my social debut following the victory over the phallic cravings of my nipple. I also wanted Arthur to come so that I could talk to him—if not during this first visit, then the next—about how I might maintain my affiliation with the university. Back at Stanford I had been a "reader" for one of the enormous sophomore classes he lectured in "Masterpieces of Western Literature." I had begun to wonder if I couldn't perform some such function again. Claire could read aloud to me the student papers, I could dictate to her my comments and grades . . . Or was that a hopeless idea? It took Dr. Klinger several weeks to encourage me to believe that there would be no harm in asking.

I never got the chance. Even as I was telling him, a little "tearfully"—I couldn't help myself—how touched I was that he should be the first of my colleagues to visit, I thought I could hear giggling. "Arthur," I asked, "are we alone—?" He said, "Yes." Then giggled, quite distinctly. Sightless, I could still picture my former mentor: in his blue blazer with the paisley lining tailored in London for him by Kilgore, French; in his soft flannel trousers, in his gleaming Gucci loafers, the diplomatic

Dean with his handsome mop of salt-and-pepper hair—giggling! And I hadn't even made my suggestion about becoming a reader for the department. Giggling—not because of anything ludicrous I had proposed, but because he saw that it was true, I actually *had* turned into a breast. My graduate-school adviser, my university superior, the most courtly professor I have ever known—and yet, from the sound of it, overcome with the giggles *simply at the sight of me.*

"I'm—I—David—" But now he was laughing so, he couldn't even speak. Arthur Schonbrunn unable to speak. Talk about the incredible. Twenty, thirty seconds more of uproarious laughter, and then he was gone. The visit had lasted about three minutes.

Two days later came the apology, as elegantly done, I'd say, as anything Arthur's written since his little book on Robert Musil. And the following week, the package from Sam Goody's, with a card signed, "Debbie and Arthur S." A record album of Laurence Olivier in *Hamlet.*

Arthur had written: "Your misfortune should not have had to be compounded by my feeble, unforgivable performance. I'm at a loss to explain what came over me. It would strike us both as so much cant if I even tried."

I worked on my reply for a week. I must have dictated easily fifty letters: gracious, eloquent, forgiving, lighthearted, grave, hangdog, businesslike, arch, vicious, wild, literary—and some even sillier than the one I dispatched. "Feeble?" I wrote Arthur. "Why, if anything it is evidence of your earthly vitality that you should have laughed yourself sick. I am the feeble one, otherwise I would have joined in. If I fail to appreciate the enormous comedy of all this, it is only because I am really more of an Arthur Schonbrunn than you are, you vain, self-loving, dandified prick!" But the one I finally settled on read simply: "Dear Debbie and Arthur S.: Thanx mucho for the groovy sides. Dave 'The Breast' K." I checked twice with Claire to be sure she had spelled thanks with that *x* before she went ahead and mailed my little message. If she mailed it. If she even took it down.

The second crisis that threatened to undo me and that I appear—for the time being—to have weathered might be called a crisis of faith. As it came fully a month after Arthur's visit, it is hard to know if it was in any way precipitated by that humiliation. I am long since over hating Arthur Schonbrunn for that day—at least I continue to work at being long since over it—and so I tend now to agree with Dr. Klinger, who thinks that what I had to struggle with next was inevitable and can't be blamed on my three minutes with the Dean. Evidently nothing that has happened can be blamed on anyone, not even on me.

What happened next was that I refused to believe I had turned into a breast. Having brought myself to relinquish (more or less) my dreams of nippled intercourse with Claire, with Miss Clark—with whoever would have me—I realized that the whole thing was impossible. A man cannot turn into a breast other than in his own imagination.

It had taken me six months to figure this out.

"Look, this isn't happening—it can't!"

"Why can't it?" asked Dr. Klinger.

"You know why! Any child knows why! Because it is a physiological and biological and anatomical impossibility!"

"How then do you explain your predicament?"

"It's a dream! Six months haven't passed—that's an illusion, too. I'm dreaming! It's just a matter of waking up!"

"But you are awake, Mr. Kepesh. You know very well that you're awake."

"Stop saying that! Don't torture me like that! Let me get up! Enough! I want to wake up!"

For days and days—or what pass for days in a nightmare—I struggled to wake myself up. Claire came every evening to suck my nipple and talk, my father came on Sunday to tell me the latest news, Mr. Brooks was there every morning, rousing me from sleep with a gentle pat just at the edge of my areola. At least I imagined that he had just awakened me by touching the edge of my areola. Then I realized that I had not been awakened from a real sleep, but from the sleep that I slept within the nightmare itself. I wasn't an awakening breast—I was myself, still dreaming.

Oh, how I cursed my captors—though, to be sure, if it was a dream I was only cursing captors of my own invention. *Stop torturing me, all of you! Somebody help me get up!* I cursed the spectators in the gallery I had constructed, I cursed the technicians on the television circuit I had imagined—*Voyeurs!* I cried, *heartless, ogling, sadistic voyeurs!*—until at last, fearing that my battered system might collapse beneath the emotional strain (yes, those were the words of concern that I put into their lying mouths), they decided to place me under heavy sedation. How I howled then!—*Cold cunt of a Claire! Idiot, ignoramus of a father! Klinger you quack! Klinger you fraud!*—even as the drug enfeebled me, a sedating drug somehow administered to the dreamer by himself.

When I came around, I at last realized that I had gone mad. I was not dreaming. I was crazy. There was to be no magical awakening, no getting up out of bed, brushing my teeth, and going off to teach as though nothing more than a nightmare had interrupted my ordinary and predictable life; if there was ever to be anything at all for me, it was the long road back— becoming sane. And of course the first step toward recovering sanity was this realization that my sense of myself as a breast was the delusion of a lunatic, the realization that rather than being slung in a hammock following an endocrinopathic catastrophe unlike any the endocrinologists had ever known before, I was, more than likely, simply sitting, deluded, in a room in a mental hospital. And that is something we know can and does happen to all too many people, all the time. That I could not see, that I could not taste, that I could not smell, that I could only faintly hear, that I could not make contact with my own anatomy, that I experienced myself as speaking to others like one buried within, and very nearly strangulated by, his own adipose tissue—were these symptoms so unusual in the trance-world of psychosis?

Why I had lost my sanity I couldn't understand, however. What could have triggered such a thoroughgoing schizophrenic collapse in someone seemingly so *well*? But then whatever might have caused such a breakdown was undoubtedly so frightening that I would have *had* to obliterate all memory of it . . . Only why then was Dr. Klinger—and that it was Dr. Klinger with whom I was talking I was sure; I had to be sure of something if I was to make a start, so I clung to his mildly accented English, to his straightforward manner and his homely humor as proof that at least *this* in my experience was real— why then was Dr. Klinger telling me to *accept* my fate, when clearly the way back to sanity was to *defy* this absolutely crazy conception of myself? The answer was obvious—should have been all along! *That wasn't what Klinger was saying.* My illness was such that I was taking his words, simple and clear as they were when he spoke them, and giving them precisely the opposite meaning.

When he came that afternoon, I had to call forth all my famous strength of character in order to explain, as simply and clearly as *I* could, my incredible discovery. I sobbed when I was finished, but otherwise was as inspired in speech as I have ever been. When teaching, one sometimes hears oneself speaking in perfect cadences, developing ideas into rounded sentences, and combining them into paragraphs full to brimming, and it is hard then to believe that the fellow suddenly addressing his hushed students with a golden tongue and great decisiveness could have made such a muddle of his notes only the hour before. Well, harder still to believe that the measured tones in which I had just broken the good news to Dr. Klinger came from the vituperous madman who had to be sedated only the day before by his keepers. If I was still a lunatic—and still a breast, I was still a lunatic—I was now, at least, one of the more lucid and eloquent on my floor.

I said, "Curiously, it's Arthur Schonbrunn's visit that convinces me I'm on the right track. How could I ever have believed that Arthur would come here and *laugh*? How could I take that blatantly paranoid delusion for the truth? I've been cursing him for a month now—and Debbie too, for those idiotic records—and none of it makes any sense at all. Because if there is one person in the world who simply *couldn't* lose control like that, it's Arthur."

"He is beyond the perils of human nature, this Dean?"

"You know something? The answer to that is yes. He is beyond the perils of human nature."

"Such a shrewd operator."

"It isn't that he's so shrewd—that's going at it the wrong way round. It's that I've been so mad. To think that I actually made all that up!"

"And his note, which you answered so graciously? The note that made you so livid?"

"More paranoia."

"And the recording of *Hamlet*?"

"Ah, *that's* Mr. Reality. That is real—and right up Debbie's alley. Oh yes, I can feel the difference now, even as I talk I can sense the difference between the insane stuff and what's truly happened. Oh, I do feel the difference, *you must believe me.* I've gone mad, but now I know it!"

"And what do you think caused you, as you put it, to 'go mad'?" Dr. Klinger asked.

"I don't remember."

"Any idea at all? What could have drawn someone like you into such a fully developed and impenetrable delusion?"

"I'm telling you the truth, Doctor. I don't have the least idea. Not yet, anyway."

"Nothing comes to mind? Nothing at all?"

"Well, what comes to mind, if anything—what came to mind this morning—"

"Is what?"

"I'm grasping at straws—and I know how whimsical it seems in the circumstances. But I thought, 'I got it from fiction.' The books I've been teaching—they put the idea in my head. I'm thinking of my European Literature course. Teaching Gogol and Kafka every year—teaching 'The Nose' and 'Metamorphosis.'"

"Of course, many other literature professors teach 'The Nose' and 'Metamorphosis.'"

"But maybe," said I, the humor intentional now, "not with so much conviction."

He laughed.

"I *am* mad, though—aren't I?" I asked.

"No."

I was set back only momentarily. I realized that I had inverted his meaning as easily, and as unconsciously, as we turn right side up the images that flash upon the retina upside down.

"I want to tell you," I calmly explained, "that though you just answered yes when I asked whether I was mad, I heard you say no."

"I did say no. You are not mad. You are not suffering from a delusion—or certainly haven't been, up till now. You are a breast, of sorts. You have been heroic in your efforts to accommodate yourself to a mysterious misfortune. Of course one understands the temptation: this is all just a dream, a hallucination, a delusion—even a drug-induced state of mind. But, in fact, it is none of these things. It *is* something that has happened to you. And the best way to go mad—do you hear me, Mr. Kepesh?—*the way into madness* is to start to pretend otherwise. The comfort of that will be short-lived, I can assure you. I want you right now to disabuse yourself of the notion that you are insane. You are not insane, and to pretend to be insane will only bring you to grief. Insanity is no solution—neither imagined insanity nor the real thing."

"Again I heard everything reversed. I turned the sense of your words completely around."

"No, you did not."

"*Does* it make any sense to you to think of my delusion as somehow fueled by years of teaching those stories? I mean, regardless of the trauma that triggered the breakdown itself."

"But there was no trauma, not of a psychological nature; and as I have told you, and tell you now again, and will continue to tell you: *this is no delusion.*"

How to press on? How to break through this reversing?

With an artfulness that pleased me—and bespoke health! health!—I said, "But if it were, Dr. Klinger—since I again understood you to say just the opposite of what you said—*if* it were, would you *then* see any connection between the kind of hallucination I've embedded myself in and the power over my imagination of Kafka or Gogol? Or of Swift? I'm thinking of *Gulliver's Travels*, another book I've taught for years. Perhaps if we go on speaking hypothetically—"

"Mr. Kepesh, enough. You are fooling no one but yourself —if even yourself. There has been shock, panic, fury, despair, disorientation, profound feelings of helplessness and isolation, the darkest depression and fear, but through it all, quite miraculously, quite marvelously, no delusions. Not even when your old friend the Dean showed up and had his laughing fit. Of course that shocked you. Of course that crushed you. Why shouldn't it have? But you did not imagine Arthur Schonbrunn's unfortunate behavior. You have not made up what has happened to you, and you did not make up what happened here to him. You didn't have to. You are pretending to be a naïf, you know, when you tell me that such a reaction is simply out of the question for a man in Arthur Schonbrunn's position. You are a better student of human nature than that. You've read too much Dostoevsky for that."

"Will it help if I repeat to you what I thought I heard you say?"

"No need. What you thought you heard, you heard. That is known as sanity. Come off the lunatic kick, Mr. Kepesh—and the sooner the better. Gogol, Kafka, and so on—it is going to get you into serious trouble if you keep it up. The next thing you know you will have produced in yourself genuine and irreversible delusions exactly like those you now claim to want to be rid of. Do you follow me? I think you do. You are a highly intelligent man and you have a remarkably strong will, and I want you to stop it right now."

How exhausting to hear it all backwards! How ingenious insanity is! But at least I *knew*. "Dr. Klinger! Dr. Klinger! Listen to me—I won't let it drive me crazy any more! I will fight myself free! I will stop hearing the opposite! I will start hearing what you are all saying! Do you hear *me*, Doctor? Do you understand *my* words? I will not participate any longer in this delusion! I refuse to be a part of it! You *will* get through to me! I *will* understand what you mean! Just don't give up! Please," I pleaded, "don't give me up for lost! I will break through and be myself again! I am determined! With all my strength—with all my will to live!"

Now I spent my days trying to penetrate the words I heard so as to get through to what actually was being said to me by the doctors, and by Claire, and by Mr. Brooks. The effort this required was so total, and so depleting, that by nightfall I felt it would take no more than a puff from a child's lips to extinguish for good the wavering little flame of memory and intelligence and hope still claiming to be me.

When my father came for his Sunday visit, I told him everything, even though I was sure that Claire and Klinger would have let him know by phone the day it happened. I babbled like a boy who'd won a trophy. It was true, I told him—I no longer believed I was a breast. If I had not yet been able to throw off the physical sense of unreality, I was daily divesting myself of the preposterous psychic delusion; every day, every hour I sensed myself slowly turning back into myself, and could even begin to see through to the time when I would again be teaching Gogol and Kafka rather than experiencing vicariously the unnatural transformations they had imagined in their famous fictions. Since my father knows nothing of books, I told him how Gregor Samsa awakens in the Kafka story to discover that he has become an enormous beetle; I summarized for him "The Nose," recounting how Gogol's hero awakens one morning missing his nose, how he sets out to look for it in St. Petersburg, places an ad in the newspaper requesting its return, sees "it" walking on the street, one ridiculous encounter after another, until in the end the nose just turns up again on his face for no better reason than it disappeared. (I could imagine my father thinking, "He teaches this stuff, in a college?") I explained that I still couldn't remember the blow that had done me in; I actually became deaf, *could not hear*, when the doctor tried to get me to face it. But whatever the trauma itself may have been—however terrifying, horrifying, repellent—what I knew was that my escape route was through the fantasy of physical transformation that lay immediately at hand, the catastrophe stories by Kafka and Gogol that I had been teaching my students only the week before. Now, with Dr. Klinger's assistance, I was trying to figure out just why, of all things, I had chosen a breast. Why a big brainless bag of dumb, desirable tissue, acted upon instead of acting, unguarded, immobile, hanging, *there*, as a breast simply hangs and is *there*? Why this primitive identification with *the* object of infantile veneration? What unfulfilled appetites, what cradle confusions, what fragments out of my remotest past could have collided to spark a delusion of such classical simplicity? On and on I babbled to my father, and then, once again, joyously, I wept. No tears, but I wept. Where *were* my tears? How soon before I would feel tears again? When would I feel my teeth, my tongue, my toes?

For a long while my father said nothing. I thought that perhaps he was crying too. Then he went into the weekly news report: so-and-so's daughter is pregnant, so-and-so's son has bought himself a hundred-thousand-dollar home, my uncle is catering Richard Tucker's younger brother's son's wedding.

He hadn't even heard me. Of course. I may have broken

through the *idea* that I was a breast, but I still seemed required virtually to give a recitation, as from a stage, if I wanted to make myself understood. What I believed was a normal conversational tone tended, apparently, to come out sounding like somebody muttering across the room. But this wasn't because my voice box was buried in a hundred-and-fifty-five-pound mammary gland. My body was still a body! I had only to stop whispering! I had only to speak out! Could that be part of the madness? That when I believed I was speaking aloud, I was speaking only to myself? Speak up then!

And so I did. At the top of my lungs (my two good lungs!) repeated to my father the story of my breakthrough.

And then it was time to take the next step. One foot in front of the other. "Dad," I said, "where are we? You tell me."

"In your room," he answered.

"And tell me, have I turned into a breast?"

"Well, that's what they say."

"But that's not true. I'm a mental patient. Now tell me again—what am I?"

"Oh, Davey."

"*What am I?*"

"You're a woman's breast."

"That's not true! What I heard you say is not true! I'm a mental patient! In a hospital! And you are visiting me! Dad, if that's the truth, I just want you to say yes. Listen to me now. You must help me. I am a mental patient. I am in a mental hospital. I have had a severe mental breakdown. Yes or no. *Tell me the truth.*"

And my father answered, "Yes, son, yes. You're a mental patient."

"I heard him!" I cried to Klinger when he came later in the day. "I heard my father! I heard the truth! I heard him say I'm a mental patient!"

"He should never have told you that."

"I heard it! I'm not imagining it either! It didn't get reversed!"

"Of course you heard it. Your father loves you. He's a simple man and he loves you very much. He thought it would help if he said it. He knows now that it can't. And so do you."

But I couldn't have been happier. My father had gotten through to me. I could be gotten through to! It would follow with the others soon enough. "I heard it!" I said. "I'm not a breast! I'm mad!"

How I strain in the coming days to be my sane self again! How I dredge at the muck of my beginnings, searching for what will explain—and thus annihilate—this preposterous delusion! I have returned, I tell the doctor, to the dawn of my life, to my first thousand hours after the eons of hours of nothing—back to when all is oneself and oneself is all, back to when the concave is the convex and the convex the concave . . . oh, how I talk! How I work to outsmart my madness! If I could only remember my hungering gums at the spigot of love, my nose in the nourishing globe—! "Oh, if she were alive, if she could tell me—" "Yes? Tell you what?" asks Klinger. "Oh," I moan, "how do I know?" But where else to begin but there? Only there there is nothing. It is all too far back, back where I am. To dive to that sea bottom where I began—to find in the slime this secret! But when I rise to the surface, there is not even silt beneath my fingernails. I come up with nothing.

Perhaps, I say, perhaps, I tell him, it is all a post-analytic collapse, a year in the making—the most desperate means I could devise to cling to Klinger. "Have you ever thought what fantasies of dependence bloom in your patients merely on the basis of your name? Have you realized, Doctor, that all *our* names begin with K, yours and mine and Kafka's? And then there is Claire—and Miss Clark!" "The alphabet," he reminds me, a language teacher, "only *has* twenty-six letters. And there are four billion of us in need of initials for purposes of identification." "But!" "But what?" "But *something*! But *anything*! Please, a clue! If I can't—then *you*. Please, some clue, some lead—I have to get out!"

I go over with him again the salient moments in my psychological development, once again I turn the pages in the anthology of stories that we two had assembled as text for the course conducted by us, three times a week for five years, in "The History of David Alan Kepesh." But in fact those stories have been recounted and glossed so exhaustively so many times that they are as stale to me as the favorite literary chestnut of the most retrograde schoolteacher in America. My life's drama, as exciting in the early years of therapy as *The Brothers Karamazov*, has all the appeal now of some tenth-grade reader beginning with "The Necklace" and running through to "The Luck of Roaring Camp." Which accounts for the successful termination of analysis the year before.

And *there*, I thought, is my trauma! Success itself! There is what I couldn't take—a happy life! "What is that?" asks Dr. Klinger quizzically. "What was it you couldn't take?" "Rewards —instead of punishment! Wholeness! Comfort! Pleasure! A gratifying way of life, a life *without*—" "Wait just a minute, please. Why couldn't you take such things? Those are wonderful things. Come off it, Mr. Kepesh. As I remember, you could take happiness with the best of them." But I refuse to listen, since what I hear him saying isn't what he's saying anyway. That is just my illness, turning things around to keep me insane. On I go instead, talking next about what patients will talk about sooner or later—that imaginary friend they call My Guilt. I talk about Helen, my former wife, whose life, I have been told, is no better now than when we suffered together through five years of that marriage. I remember I couldn't help but gloat a little when I heard about Helen's continuing unhappiness from an old San Francisco friend, who had come to dinner with me and my lovely, imperturbable Claire. Good for the bitch, I thought . . . "And now," Klinger asks with amusement, "you believe you are punishing yourself in this way for such ordinary, everyday malice?" "I'm saying that my happy new life was too much for me! It's why I lost my desire for Claire—it was all too good to last! So much satisfaction seemed—seemed unjust! Compared to Helen's fate, seemed somehow iniquitous! My Guilt!" I plead. "My dear sir," he replies, "that is analysis right out of the dime store—and you know it as well as I do." "Then if not that, *what*? Help me! Tell me! *What did it?*"

"Nothing 'did it.'"

"*Then why in God's name am I mad?*"

"But you're not. And you know that too."

The next Sunday, when he comes to visit, I again ask my father if I am a mental patient—just to be sure—and this time he answers, "No."

"*But last week you said yes!*"

"I was wrong."

"*But it's the truth!*"

"It's not."

"I'm reversing again! I've lost it now with you! I'm back where I was! I'm reversing with everyone!"

"You're not at all," said Dr. Klinger.

"What are you doing here? This is Sunday! My father is here, not you! You're not even here!"

"I'm here. With your father. Right beside you, the two of us."

"This is getting all crazy again! I don't want to be crazy any more! Help me! Do you hear me? Am I being heard? Help me, please! I need your help! I cannot do this alone! Help me! Lift me! Tell me only the truth! If I am a breast, where is my milk! When Claire is sucking me, where is the milk! Tell me *that!*"

"Oh, David." It was my father, his unshaven cheek on my areola! "My son, my poor sonny."

"Oh, Daddy, what's happened? Hold me, Poppy, please. What's really happened? Tell me, please, *why did I go mad?*"

"You didn't, darling," he sobbed.

"*Then where is my milk? Answer me! If I am a breast I would make milk! Hold milk! Swell with milk! And that is too crazy for anybody to believe! Even me! THAT SIMPLY CANNOT BE!*"

But evidently it can be. Just as they are able to increase the milk yield of cows with injections of the lactogenic agent GH, the growth hormone, so it has been hypothesized that I very likely could become a milk-producing mammary gland with appropriate hormonal stimulation. If so, there must be those out in the scientific world who would jump at the chance to find out. And when I have had my fill of all this, perhaps I will give it to them. And if I am not killed in the process? If they succeed and milk begins to flow? Well, then I will know that I am indeed a wholly authentic breast—or else that I am as mad as any man has ever been.

In the meantime fifteen months have passed—by their calendar—and I live for the moment in relative equanimity. That is, things have been worse and will be again, but for now, for now Claire still comes to visit every day, does not miss a single day, and still, for the first half hour of each hour,

uncomplainingly and without repugnance attends to my pleasure. Converts a disgusting perversion into a kindly, thoughtful
act of love. And then we talk. She is helping me with my
Shakespeare studies. I have been listening of late to recordings
of the tragedies. I began with the Schonbrunns' gift, Olivier in
Hamlet. The album lay for months here in the room before I
asked Mr. Brooks one morning to break the cellophane wrapper and put a record on the phonograph. (Mr. Brooks turns
out to be a Negro; and so, in my mind's eye—a breast's mind's
eye, to be sure—I imagine him looking like the handsome
black Senator from Massachusetts. Why not, if it makes this
cozier for me?) Like so many people, I have been meaning ever
since college to sit down someday and reread Shakespeare. I
may even once have said as much to Debbie Schonbrunn, and
she bought the record album because she realized that I now
had the time. Surely no satire was ever intended, however
much I may have believed otherwise when the *Hamlet* arrived
the week after Arthur's three-minute visit. I must remember
that aside from the more obvious difficulties occasioned by my
transformation, I am no longer the easiest person in the world
to buy a present for.

For several hours every morning and again sometimes in the
afternoons when there is nothing better to do, I listen to my
Shakespeare records: Olivier playing Hamlet and Othello, Paul
Scofield as Lear, *Macbeth* as performed by the Old Vic company. Unable to follow with a text while the play is being spoken, I invariably miss the meaning of an unfamiliar word, or
lose my way in the convoluted syntax, and then my mind begins to wander, and when I tune in again, little makes sense for
lines on end. Despite the effort—oh, the effort, minute-by-
minute this effort!—to keep my attention fixed on the plight
of Shakespeare's suffering heroes, I do continue to consider
my own suffering more than can be good for me.

The Shakespeare edition I used in college—Neilson and
Hill, *The Complete Plays and Poems of William Shakespeare*,
bound in blue linen, worn at the spine by my earnest undergraduate grip, and heavily underlined by me then for wisdom
—is on the table beside the hammock. It is one of several
books I have asked Claire to bring from my apartment. I remember exactly what it looks like, which in part is why I

wanted it here. In the evenings, during the second half hour of her visit, Claire looks up for me in the footnotes words whose usage I long ago learned and forgot; or she will slowly read aloud some passage that I missed that morning when my mind departed Elsinore Castle for Lenox Hill Hospital. It seems to me important to get these passages clear in my head—my brain—before I go off to sleep. Otherwise it might begin to seem that I listen to *Hamlet* for the same reason that my father answers the phone at my Uncle Larry's catering establishment —to kill time.

Olivier is a great man, you know. I have fallen in love with him a little, like a schoolgirl with a movie star. I've never before given myself over to a genius so completely, not even while reading. As a student, as a professor, I experienced literature as something unavoidably tainted by my self-consciousness and all the responsibilities of serious discourse; either I was learning or I was teaching. But responsibilities are behind me now; at last I can just listen.

In the beginning I used to try to amuse myself when I was alone in the evenings by imitating Olivier. I worked with my records during the day to memorize the famous soliloquies, and then I performed for myself at night, trying to approximate his distinctive delivery. After some weeks it seemed to me that I had really rather mastered his Othello, and one night, after Claire had left, I did the death-scene speech with such plaintive passion that I thought I could have moved an audience to tears. Until I realized that I had an audience. It was midnight, or thereabouts, but nobody has given me a good reason yet why the TV camera should shut down at any hour of the day or night—and so I left off with my performance. Enough pathos is enough, if not, generally, too much. "Come now, David," said I to myself, "it is all too poignant and heartbreaking, a breast reciting 'And say besides, that in Aleppo once . . .' You will send the night shift home in tears." Yes, bitterness, dear reader, and of a shallow sort, but then permit my poor professorial dignity a little rest, won't you? This is not tragedy any more than it is farce. It is only life, and I am only human.

Did fiction do this to me? "How could it have?" asks Dr. Klinger. "No, hormones are hormones and art is art. You are not suffering from an overdose of the great imaginations." "Aren't I? I wonder. This might well be my way of being a Kafka, being a Gogol, being a Swift. They could envision the incredible, they had the words and those relentless fictional-izing brains. But I had neither, I had nothing—literary longings and that was it. I loved the extreme in literature, idolized those who wrote it, was virtually hypnotized by the imagery and the power—" "And? Yes? The world is full of art lovers—so?" "So I took the leap. Made the word flesh. Don't you see, I have out-Kafkaed Kafka." Klinger laughed, as though I meant to be only amusing. "After all," I said, "who is the greater artist, he who imagines the marvelous transformation, or he who mar-velously transforms himself? Why David Kepesh? Why me, of all people, endowed with such powers? Simple. Why Kafka? Why Gogol? Why Swift? Why anyone? Great art happens to people like anything else. And this is my great work of art! Ah," but I quickly added, "I must maintain my sane and reasonable perspective. I don't wish to upset you again. No delusions—delusions of grandeur least of all."

But if not grandeur, what about abasement? What about de-pravity and vice? I could be rich, you know, I could be rich, notorious, and delirious with pleasure every waking hour of the day. I think about it more and more. I could call my friend to visit me, the adventurous younger colleague I spoke of ear-lier. If I haven't dared to invite him yet, it isn't because I'm frightened that he'll laugh and run like Arthur Schonbrunn, but rather that he'll take one look at what I am—and what I could be—and be all too eager to help; that when I tell him I have had just about enough of being a heroically civilized fel-low about it all, enough of listening to Olivier and talking to my analyst and enjoying thirty minutes every day of some virtuous schoolteacher's idea of hot sex, he won't argue, the way others would. "I want to get out of here," I'll say to him, "and I need an accomplice. We can carry with us all the pumps and pipes that sustain me. And to look after my health, such as it is, we can hire the doctors and nurses to come along—money will be no problem. But I am sick and tired of worry-ing about losing Claire. Let her go and find a new lover whose sperm she will not drink, and lead with him a normal and pro-ductive life. I am tired of guarding against the loss of her angelic goodness. And between the two of us, I am a little tired of my old man too—he bores me. And, really, how much Shakespeare do you think I can take? I wonder if you realize how many of the great plays of Western literature are now available on excellent long-playing records. When I finish with Shakespeare, I can go right on to first-rate performances of Sophocles, Sheridan, Aristophanes, Shaw, Racine—but to what end? To what end! That *is* killing time. For a breast it is the bloody *murder* of time. Pal, I am going to make a pot of money. I don't think it should be difficult, either. If the Beatles can fill Shea Stadium, why can't I? We will have to think this through, you and I, but then what was all that education for, if not to learn to think things through? To read more books? To write more critical essays? Further contemplation of the higher things? How about some contemplation of the lower? I will make hundreds of thousands of dollars—and then I will have girls, twelve- and thirteen-year-old girls, three, four, and five at a time, naked and giggling, and all on my nipple at once. I want them for days on end, greedy wicked little girls, licking me and sucking me to my heart's content. And we can find them, you know that. If the Rolling Stones can find them, if Charles Manson can find them, then with all our education we can probably find a few ourselves. And women. There will also be women quite eager to open their thighs to a cock as new and thrilling as my nipple. I think we will be happily surprised by the number of respectable women who will come knocking at the dressing-room door in their respectable chinchillas just to get a peek at the tint of my soft hermaphroditic flesh. Well, we will have to be discriminating, won't we, we will have to select from among them according to beauty, good breeding, and the lewdness of their desire. And I will be deliriously happy. *And I will be deliriously happy.* Remember Gulliver among the Brobdingnags? How the maid-servants had him strolling out on their nipples for the fun of it? He didn't think it was fun, poor lost little man. But then he was a humane English physician, a child of the Age of Reason, a faithful follower of the Sense of Proportion trapped on a continent of outlandish giants; but this, my friend and accomplice, is the Land of Opportunity, this is the Age of Self-Fulfillment, and I am the Breast, and will live by my own lights!"

"Live by them or die by them?"

"It remains to be seen, Dr. Klinger."

Permit me now to conclude my lecture by quoting the poet Rilke. As a passionately well-meaning literature teacher I was always fond of ending the hour with something moving for the students to carry from the uncontaminated classroom out into the fallen world of junk food and pop stars and dope. True, Kepesh's occupation's gone—*Othello*, Act III, Scene 3— but I haven't lost entirely a teacher's good intentions. Maybe I haven't even lost my students. On the basis of my fame, I may even have acquired vast new flocks of undergraduate sheep, as innocent of calamity as of verse. I may even be a pop star now myself and have just what it takes to bring great poetry to the people.

("Your fame?" says Dr. Klinger. "Surely the world knows by now," I say, "excepting perhaps the Russians and Chinese." "In accordance with your wishes, the case has been handled with the utmost discretion." "But my friends know. The staff here knows. That's enough of a start for something like this." "True. But by the time the news filters beyond those who know and out to the man in the street, he tends by and large not to believe it." "He thinks it's a joke." "If he can take his mind off his own troubles long enough to think anything at all." "And the media? You're suggesting they've done nothing with this either?" "Nothing at all." "I don't buy that, Dr. Klinger." "Don't. I'm not going to argue. I told you long ago —there of course were inquiries in the beginning. But nothing was done to assist anyone, and after a while these people have a living to make like everybody else, and they move right along to the next promising misfortune." "Then no one knows all that's happened." "All? No one but you knows it all, Mr. Kepesh." "Well, maybe I should be the one to tell all then." "Then you *will* be famous, won't you?" "Better the truth than tabloid fantasy. Better from me than from the chattering madmen and morons." "Of course the madmen and the morons will chatter anyway, you know. You realize that you will never be taken on your own terms, regardless of what you say." "I'll still be a joke." "A joke. A freak. If you insist on being the one to tell them, a charlatan too." "You're advising me to leave well enough alone. You're advising me to keep this all to myself." "I'm advising you nothing, only reminding you of our friend with the beard who sits on the throne." "Mr. Reality." "And his principle," says Klinger.)

And now to conclude the hour with the poem by Rainer Maria Rilke entitled "Archaic Torso of Apollo" written in Paris in 1908. Perhaps my story, told here in its entirety for the first time, and with all the truthfulness that's in me, will at the very least illuminate these great lines for those of you new to the poem—particularly the poet's concluding admonition, which may not be so elevated a sentiment as appears at first glance. Morons and madmen, tough guys and skeptics, friends, students, relatives, colleagues, and all you distracted strangers, with your billion different fingerprints and faces—my fellow mammalians, let us proceed with our education, one and all.

> We did not know his legendary head,
> in which the eyeballs ripened. But
> his torso still glows like a candelabrum
> in which his gaze, only turned low,
>
> holds and gleams. Else could not the curve
> of the breast blind you, nor in the slight turn
> of the loins could a smile be running
> to that middle, which carried procreation.
>
> Else would this stone be standing maimed and short
> under the shoulders' translucent plunge
> not flimmering like the fell of beasts of prey
>
> nor breaking out of all its contours
> like a star: for there is no place
> that does not see you. You must change your life.

CHRONOLOGY

NOTE ON THE TEXTS

NOTES

Chronology

Born Philip Roth on March 19 in Newark, New Jersey, second child of Herman Roth and Bess Finkel. (Bess Finkel, the second child of five, was born in 1904 in Elizabeth, New Jersey, to Philip and Dora Finkel, Jewish immigrants from near Kiev. Herman Roth was born in 1901 in Newark, New Jersey, the middle child of seven born to Sender and Bertha Roth, Jewish immigrants from Polish Galicia. They were married in Newark on February 21, 1926, and shortly afterward opened a small family-run shoe store. Their son Sanford ["Sandy"] was born December 26, 1927. Following the bankruptcy of the shoe store and a briefly held position as city marshal, Herman Roth took a job as agent with the Newark district office of the Metropolitan Life Insurance Company, and would remain with the company until his retirement as district manager in 1966.) Family moves into second-floor flat of two-and-a-half-family house (with five-room apartments on each of the first two floors and a three-room apartment on the top floor) at 81 Summit Avenue in Newark. Summit Avenue was a lower-middle-class residential street in the Weequahic section, a twenty-minute bus ride from commercial downtown Newark and less than a block from Chancellor Avenue School and from Weequahic High School, then considered the state's best academic public high school. These were the two schools that Sandy and Philip attended. Between 1910 and 1920, Weequahic had been developed as a new city neighborhood at the southwest corner of Newark, some three miles from the edge of industrial Newark and from the international shipping facilities at Port Newark on Newark Bay. In the first half of the twentieth century Newark was a prosperous working-class city of approximately 420,000, the majority of its citizens of German, Italian, Slavic, and Irish extraction. Blacks and Jews composed two of the smallest groups in the city. From the 1930s to the 1950s, the Jews lived mainly in the predominantly Jewish Weequahic section.

1938   Philip enters kindergarten at Chancellor Avenue School in January.

1942   Roth family moves to second-floor flat of two-and-a-half-family house at 359 Leslie Street, three blocks west of Summit Avenue, still within the Weequahic neighborhood but nearer to semi-industrial boundary with Irvington.

1946   Philip graduates from elementary school in January, having skipped a year. Brother graduates from high school and chooses to enter U.S. Navy for two years rather than be drafted into the peacetime army.

1947   Family moves to first-floor flat of two-and-a-half-family house at 385 Leslie Street, just a few doors from commercial Chancellor Avenue, the neighborhood's main artery. Philip turns from reading sports fiction by John R. Tunis and adventure fiction by Howard Pease to reading the left-leaning historical novels of Howard Fast.

1948   Brother is discharged from navy and, with the aid of G.I. Bill, enrolls as commercial art student at Pratt Institute, Brooklyn. Philip takes strong interest in politics during the four-way U.S. presidential election in which the Republican Dewey loses to the Democrat Truman despite a segregationist Dixiecrat Party and a left-wing Progressive Party drawing away traditionally Democratic voters.

1950   Graduates from high school in January. Works as stock clerk at S. Klein department store in downtown Newark. Reads Thomas Wolfe; discovers Sherwood Anderson, Ring Lardner, Erskine Caldwell, and Theodore Dreiser. In September enters Newark College of Rutgers as pre-law student while continuing to live at home. (Newark Rutgers was at this time a newly formed college housed in two small converted downtown buildings, one formerly a bank, the other formerly a brewery.)

1951   Still a pre-law student, transfers in September to Bucknell University in Lewisburg, Pennsylvania. Brother graduates from Pratt Institute and moves to New York City to work for advertising agency. Parents move to Moorestown, New Jersey, approximately seventy miles southwest of Newark; father takes job as manager of Metropolitan Life's south Jersey district after having previously managed several north Jersey district offices.

1952   Roth decides to study English literature. With two friends, founds Bucknell literary magazine, *Et Cetera*, and becomes its first editor. Writes first short stories. Strongly influenced in his literary studies by English professor Mildred Martin, under whose tutelage he reads extensively, and with whom he will maintain lifelong friendship.

1954   Is elected to Phi Beta Kappa and graduates from Bucknell magna cum laude in English. Accepts scholarship to study English at the University of Chicago graduate school, beginning in September. Reads Saul Bellow's *The Adventures of Augie March*, and under its influence explores Chicago.

1955   In June receives M.A. with Honors in English. In September, rather than wait to be drafted, enlists in U.S. Army for two years. Suffers spinal injury during basic training at Fort Dix. In November, is assigned to Public Information Office at Walter Reed Army Hospital, Washington, D.C. Begins to write short stories "The Conversion of the Jews" and "Epstein." *Epoch*, a Cornell University literary quarterly, publishes "The Contest for Aaron Gold," which is reprinted in Martha Foley's *Best American Short Stories 1956*.

1956   Is hospitalized in June for complications from spinal injury. After two-month hospital stay receives honorable discharge for medical reasons and a disability pension. In September returns to University of Chicago as instructor in the liberal arts college, teaching freshman composition. Begins course work for Ph.D. but drops out after one term. Meets Ted Solotaroff, who is also a graduate student, and they become friends.

1957   Publishes in *Commentary* "You Can't Tell a Man by the Song He Sings." Writes novella "Goodbye, Columbus." Meets Saul Bellow at University of Chicago when Bellow is a classroom guest of Roth's friend and colleague, the writer Richard Stern. Begins to review movies and television for *The New Republic* after magazine publishes "Positive Thinking on Pennsylvania Avenue," a humor piece satirizing President Eisenhower's religious beliefs.

1958   Publishes "The Conversion of the Jews" and "Epstein" in *The Paris Review*; "Epstein" wins *Paris Review* Aga Khan Prize, presented to Roth in Paris in July. Spends first summer abroad, mainly in Paris. Houghton Mifflin awards Roth the Houghton Mifflin Literary Fellowship to publish the novella and five stories in one volume; George Starbuck, a poet and friend from Chicago, is his editor. Resigns from teaching position at University of Chicago. Moves to two-room basement apartment on Manhattan's Lower East Side. Becomes friendly with *Paris Review* editors George Plimpton and Robert Silvers and *Commentary* editor Martin Greenberg.

1959　　Marries Margaret Martinson Williams. Publishes "Defender of the Faith" in *The New Yorker*, causing consternation among Jewish organizations and rabbis who attack magazine and condemn author as anti-Semitic; story collected in *Goodbye, Columbus* and included in *Best American Short Stories 1960* and *Prize Stories 1960: The O. Henry Awards*, where it wins second prize. *Goodbye, Columbus* is published in May. Roth receives Guggenheim fellowship and award from the American Academy of Arts and Letters. *Goodbye, Columbus* gains highly favorable reviews from Bellow, Alfred Kazin, Leslie Fiedler, and Irving Howe; influential rabbis denounce Roth in their sermons as "a self-hating Jew." Roth and wife leave U.S. to spend seven months in Italy, where he works on his first novel, *Letting Go*; he meets William Styron, who is living in Rome and who becomes a lifelong friend. Styron introduces Roth to his publisher, Donald Klopfer of Random House; when George Starbuck leaves Houghton Mifflin, Roth moves to Random House.

1960　　*Goodbye, Columbus and Five Short Stories* wins National Book Award. The collection also wins Daroff Award of the Jewish Book Council of America. Roth returns to America to teach at the Writers' Workshop of the University of Iowa, Iowa City. Meets drama professor Howard Stein (later dean of the Columbia University Drama School), who becomes lifelong friend. Continues working on *Letting Go*. Travels in Midwest. Participates in *Esquire* magazine symposium at Stanford University; his speech "Writing American Fiction," published in *Commentary* in March 1961, is widely discussed. After a speaking engagement in Oregon, meets Bernard Malamud, whose fiction he admires.

1962   After two years at Iowa, accepts two-year position as writer-in-residence at Princeton. Separates from Margaret Roth. Moves to New York City and commutes to Princeton classes. (Lives at various Manhattan locations until 1970.) Meets Princeton sociologist Melvin Tumin, a Newark native who becomes a friend. Random House publishes *Letting Go.*

1963   Receives Ford Foundation grant to write plays in affiliation with American Place Theater in New York. Is legally separated from Margaret Roth. Becomes close friend of Aaron Asher, a University of Chicago graduate and editor at Meridian Books, original paperback publisher of *Goodbye, Columbus.* In June takes part in American Jewish Congress symposium in Tel Aviv, Israel, along with American writers Leslie Fiedler, Max Lerner, and literary critic David Boroff. Travels in Israel for a month.

1964   Teaches at State University of New York at Stony Brook, Long Island. Reviews plays by James Baldwin, LeRoi Jones, and Edward Albee for newly founded *New York Review of Books.* Spends a month at Yaddo, writers' retreat in Saratoga Springs, New York, that provides free room and board. (Will work at Yaddo for several months at a time throughout the 1960s.) Meets and establishes friendships there with novelist Alison Lurie and painter Julius Goldstein.

1965   Begins to teach comparative literature at University of Pennsylvania one semester each year more or less annually until the mid-1970s. Meets professor Joel Conarroe, who becomes a close friend. Begins work on *When She Was Good* after abandoning another novel, begun in 1962.

1966   Publishes section of *When She Was Good* in *Harper's.* Is increasingly troubled by Vietnam War and in ensuing years takes part in marches and demonstrations against it.

1967   Publishes *When She Was Good.* Begins work on *Portnoy's Complaint* of which he publishes excerpts in *Esquire, Partisan Review*, and *New American Review*, where Ted Solotaroff is editor.

1968   Margaret Roth dies in an automobile accident. Roth spends two months at Yaddo completing *Portnoy's Complaint.*

1969   *Portnoy's Complaint* published in February. Within weeks
            becomes number-one fiction best-seller and a widely dis-
            cussed cultural phenomenon. Roth makes no public ap-
            pearances and retreats for several months to Yaddo. Rents
            house in Woodstock, New York, and meets the painter
            Philip Guston, who lives nearby. They remain close
            friends and see each other regularly until Guston's death
            in 1980. Renews friendship with Bernard Malamud, who
            like Roth is serving as a member of The Corporation of
            Yaddo.

1970   Spends March traveling in Thailand, Burma, Cambodia,
            and Hong Kong. Begins work on *My Life as a Man* and
            publishes excerpt in *Modern Occasions*. Is elected to Na-
            tional Institute of Arts and Letters and is its youngest
            member. Commutes to his classes at University of Penn-
            sylvania and lives mainly in Woodstock until 1972.

1971   Excerpts of *Our Gang*, satire of the Nixon administration,
            appear in *New York Review of Books* and *Modern Occa-
            sions*; the book is published by Random House in the fall.
            Continues work on *My Life as a Man*; writes *The Breast*
            and *The Great American Novel*. Begins teaching a Kafka
            course at University of Pennsylvania.

1972   *The Breast*, first book of three featuring protagonist David
            Kepesh, published by Holt, Rinehart, Winston, where
            Aaron Asher is his editor. Roth buys old farmhouse and
            forty acres in northwest Connecticut, one hundred miles
            from New York City, and moves there from Woodstock.
            In May travels to Venice, Vienna, and, for the first time,
            Prague. Meets his translators there, Luba and Rudolph
            Pilar, and they describe to him the impact of the political
            situation on Czech writers. In U.S., arranges to meet
            exiled Czech editor Antonin Liehm in New York; attends
            Liehm's weekly classes in Czech history, literature, and
            film at College of Staten Island, City University of New
            York. Through friendship with Liehm meets numerous
            Czech exiles, including film directors Ivan Passer and Jiří
            Weiss, who become friends. Is elected to the American
            Academy of Arts and Sciences.

1973   Publishes *The Great American Novel* and the essay
            "Looking at Kafka" in *New American Review*. Returns to
            Prague and meets novelists Milan Kundera, Ivan Klíma,
            Ludvik Vaculik, the poet Miroslav Holub, and other

writers blacklisted and persecuted by the Soviet-backed
Communist regime; becomes friendly with Rita Klímová,
a blacklisted translator and academic, who will serve as
Czechoslovakia's first ambassador to U.S. following the
1989 "Velvet Revolution." (Will make annual spring trips
to Prague to visit his writer friends until he is denied an
entry visa in 1977.) Writes "Country Report" on Czechoslovakia for American PEN. Proposes paperback series,
"Writers from the Other Europe," to Penguin Books
USA; becomes general editor of the series, selecting titles,
commissioning introductions, and overseeing publication
of Eastern European writers relatively unknown to American readers. Beginning in 1974, series publishes fiction by
Polish writers Jerzy Andrzejewski, Tadeusz Borowski,
Tadeusz Konwicki, Witold Gombrowicz, and Bruno
Schulz; Hungarian writers György Konrád and Géza
Csáth; Yugoslav writer Danilo Kiš; and Czech writers Bo-
humil Hrabal, Milan Kundera, and Ludvik Vaculik; series
ends in 1989. "Watergate Edition" of *Our Gang* published,
which includes a new preface by Roth.

1974   Roth publishes *My Life as a Man*. Visits Budapest as well
as Prague and meets Budapest writers through Hungarian
PEN and the *Hungarian Quarterly*. In Prague meets Va-
clav Havel. Through friend Professor Zdenek Strybyrny,
visits and becomes friend of the niece of Franz Kafka,
Vera Saudkova, who shows him Kafka family photographs
and family belongings; subsequently becomes friendly in
London with Marianne Steiner, daughter of Kafka's sister
Valli. Also through Strybyrny meets the widow of Jiří
Weil; upon his return to America arranges for translation
and publication of Weil's novel *Life with a Star* as well as
publication of several Weil short stories in *American
Poetry Review*, for which he provides an introduction. In
Princeton meets Joanna Rostropowicz Clark, wife of
friend Blair Clark; she becomes close friend and introduces Roth to contemporary Polish writing and to Polish
writers visiting America, including Konwicki and Kazi-
mierz Brandys. Publishes "Imagining Jews" in *New York
Review of Books*; essay prompts letter from university
professor, editor, writer, and former Jesuit Jack Miles.
Correspondence ensues and the two establish a lasting intellectual friendship.

1975   Aaron Asher leaves Holt and becomes editor in chief at
        Farrar, Straus and Giroux; Roth moves to FSG with Asher
        for publication of *Reading Myself and Others*, a collection
        of interviews and critical essays. Meets British actress
        Claire Bloom.

1976   Interviews Isaac Bashevis Singer about Bruno Schulz for
        New York Times Book Review article to coincide with pub-
        lication of Schulz's *Street of Crocodiles* in "Writers from
        the Other Europe" series. Moves with Claire Bloom to
        London, where they live six to seven months a year for
        the next twelve years. Spends the remaining months in
        Connecticut, where Bloom joins him when she is not act-
        ing in films, television, or stage productions. In London
        resumes an old friendship with British critic A. Alvarez
        and, a few years later, begins a friendship with American
        writer Michael Herr (author of *Dispatches*, which Roth
        admires) and with the American painter R. B. Kitaj. Also
        meets critic and biographer Hermione Lee, who becomes
        a friend, as does novelist Edna O'Brien. Begins regular
        visits to France to see Milan Kundera and another new
        friend, French writer-critic Alain Finkielkraut. Visits Israel
        for the first time since 1963 and returns there regularly,
        keeping a journal that eventually provides ideas and ma-
        terial for novels *The Counterlife* and *Operation Shylock*.
        Meets the writer Aharon Appelfeld in Jerusalem and they
        become close friends.

1977   Publishes *The Professor of Desire*, second book of Kepesh
        trilogy. Beginning in 1977 and continuing over the next
        few years, writes series of TV dramas for Claire Bloom:
        adaptations of *The Name-Day Party*, a short story by
        Chekhov; *Journey into the Whirlwind*, the gulag autobi-
        ography of Eugenia Ginzburg; and, with David Plante,
        It Isn't Fair, Plante's memoir of Jean Rhys. At request
        of Chichester Festival director, modernizes the David
        Magarshack translation of Chekhov's *The Cherry Orchard*
        for Claire Bloom's 1981 performance at the festival as
        Madame Ranyevskaya.

1979   *The Ghost Writer*, first novel featuring novelist Nathan
        Zuckerman as protagonist, is published in its entirety in
        The New Yorker, then published by Farrar, Straus and

Giroux. Bucknell awards Roth his first honorary degree; eventually receives honorary degrees from Amherst, Brown, Columbia, Dartmouth, Harvard, Pennsylvania, and Rutgers, among others.

1980   *A Philip Roth Reader* published, edited by Martin Green. Milan and Vera Kundera visit Connecticut on first trip to U.S.; Roth introduces Kundera to friend and *New Yorker* editor Veronica Geng, who also becomes Kundera's editor at the magazine. Conversation with Milan Kundera, in London and Connecticut, published in *New York Times Book Review*.

1981   Mother dies of a sudden heart attack in Elizabeth, New Jersey. *Zuckerman Unbound* published.

1982   Corresponds with Judith Thurman after reading her biography of Isak Dinesen, and they begin a friendship.

1983   Roth's physician and Litchfield County neighbor, Dr. C. H. Huvelle, retires from his Connecticut practice and the two become close friends.

1984   *The Anatomy Lesson* published. Aaron Asher leaves FSG and David Rieff becomes Roth's editor; the two soon become close friends. Conversation with Edna O'Brien in London published in *New York Times Book Review*. With BBC director Tristram Powell, adapts *The Ghost Writer* for television drama, featuring Claire Bloom; program is aired in U.S. and U.K. Meets University of Connecticut professor Ross Miller and the two forge strong literary friendship.

1985   *Zuckerman Bound*, a compilation of *The Ghost Writer*, *Zuckerman Unbound*, *The Anatomy Lesson*, with epilogue *The Prague Orgy*, published.

1986   Spends several days in Turin with Primo Levi. Conversation with Levi published in *New York Times Book Review*, which also asks that Roth write a memoir about Bernard Malamud upon Malamud's death at age 72.

1987   *The Counterlife* published; wins National Book Critics Circle Award for fiction. Corresponds with exiled Romanian writer Norman Manea, who is living in Berlin, and encourages him to come to live in U.S; Manea arrives the next year, and the two become close friends.

1988   *The Facts* published. Travels to Jerusalem for Aharon Appelfeld interview, which is published in *New York Times Book Review*. In Jerusalem, attends daily the trial of Ivan Demjanjuk, the alleged Treblinka guard "Ivan the Terrible." Returns to America to live year-round. Becomes Distinguished Professor of Literature at Hunter College of the City University of New York, where he will teach one semester each year until 1991.

1989   Father dies of brain tumor after yearlong illness. David Reiff leaves Farrar, Straus. For the first time since 1970, acquires a literary agent, Andrew Wylie of Wylie, Aitken, and Stone. Leaves FSG for Simon and Schuster. Writes a memoir of Philip Guston which is published in *Vanity Fair* and subsequently reprinted in Guston catalogs.

1990   *Deception* published by Simon and Schuster. Roth marries Claire Bloom in New York.

1991   Travels to post-Communist Prague for conversation with Ivan Klíma, published in *New York Review of Books*.

1991   *Patrimony* published; wins National Book Critics Circle Award for biography. Renews strong friendship with Saul Bellow.

1992   Reads from *Patrimony* for nationwide reading tour, extending into 1993. Publishes brief profile of Norman Manea in *New York Times Book Review*.

1993   *Operation Shylock* published; wins PEN/Faulkner Award for fiction. Separates from Claire Bloom. Writes *Dr. Huvelle: A Biographical Sketch*, which he publishes privately as a 34-page booklet for local distribution.

1994   Divorces Claire Bloom.

1995   Returns to Houghton Mifflin, where John Sterling is his editor. *Sabbath's Theater* is published and wins National Book Award for fiction.

1997   John Sterling leaves Houghton Mifflin and Wendy Strothman becomes Roth's editor. *American Pastoral*, first book of the "American trilogy," is published and wins Pulitzer Prize for fiction.

1998   *I Married a Communist*, the second book of the trilogy, is published and wins Ambassador Book Award of the English-Speaking Union. In October Roth attends three-day international literary program honoring his work in Aix-en-Provence. In November receives National Medal of Arts at the White House.

2000　Publishes *The Human Stain*, final book of American trilogy, which wins PEN/Faulkner Award in U.S., the W. H. Smith Award for best book of the year in the U.K., and the Prix Medicis for the best foreign book of the year in France. Publishes "Rereading Saul Bellow" in *The New Yorker*.

2001　Publishes *The Dying Animal*, final book of the Kepesh trilogy, and *Shop Talk*, a collection of interviews with and essays on Primo Levi, Aharon Appelfeld, I. B. Singer, Edna O'Brien, Milan Kundera, Ivan Klíma, Philip Guston, Bernard Malamud, and Saul Bellow, and an exchange with Mary McCarthy. Receives highest award of the American Academy of Arts and Letters, the Gold Medal in fiction, given every six years "for the entire work of the recipient," previously awarded to Willa Cather, Edith Wharton, John Dos Passos, William Faulkner, Saul Bellow, and Isaac Bashevis Singer, among others.

2002　Wins the National Book Foundation's Medal for Distinguished Contribution to American Letters.

2003　Receives honorary degrees at Harvard University and University of Pennsylvania. Roth's work now appears in 31 languages.

2004　Publishes novel *The Plot Against America*, which becomes a best-seller and wins the W. H. Smith Award for best book of the year in the U.K.; Roth is the first writer in the 46-year history of the prize to win it twice.

2005　*The Plot Against America* wins the Society of American Historians' James Fenimore Cooper Prize as the outstanding historical novel on an American theme for 2003–04.

Note on the Texts

This volume contains Philip Roth's novels *When She Was Good* (1967), *Portnoy's Complaint* (1969), *Our Gang* (1971), and *The Breast* (1972, revised 1980).

When She Was Good was published in New York by Random House and in England by Jonathan Cape in 1967. Before its publication excerpts appeared in *The Atlantic* (November 1966), *Harper's* (November 1966), *The Saturday Evening Post* (February 11, 1967), and *Cosmopolitan* (September 1967). The text in this volume is taken from the 1967 Random House edition of *When She Was Good*.

Excerpts from *Portnoy's Complaint* began appearing in periodicals in 1967, when sections were published in *Esquire* (April), *Partisan Review* (Summer), and the inaugural issue of *New American Review*, which appeared in September. Other excerpts were published in *New American Review* 3 (1968) and *Sports Illustrated* (June 1969). The novel was brought out by Random House in New York and by Jonathan Cape in England in 1969; the 1969 Random House edition of *Portnoy's Complaint* contains the text printed here.

Our Gang was first excerpted in *The New York Review of Books* (May 6, 1971, and June 3, 1971) and *Modern Occasions* 2 (1971) before being published by Random House in fall 1971. Jonathan Cape brought out the novel in England that year as well. Two paperback editions of *Our Gang*, the "Watergate Edition" and the "Pre-Impeachment Edition," were published in 1973 and 1974, respectively; although Roth did not revise the novel, he added a preface for each of these editions, which are included in the Notes to the present volume. The 1971 Random House edition of *Our Gang* provides the text printed here.

Roth wrote *The Breast* in 1971, and it was published in New York by Holt, Rinehart and Winston in 1972 and in England by Jonathan Cape in 1973. He revised *The Breast* for inclusion in *A Philip Roth Reader* (New York: Farrar, Straus and Giroux, 1980); the text printed here is taken from that edition.

This volume presents the texts of the original printings chosen for inclusion here, but it does not attempt to reproduce nontextual features of their typographic design. The texts are presented without change, except for the correction of typographical errors. Spelling, punctuation, and capitalization are often expressive features and are not altered, even when inconsistent or irregular. The following is a list of typographical errors corrected, cited by page and line number:

28.27, is is; 187.8, La Voy; 261.23, rung; 370.12, triumverate; 401.10, boner"'; 418.20, Portnoy—; 436.40, The Collar; 441.34, *skikse*; 442.35, 'Windview'; 514.29, (*backpeddling*); 522.18, see as; 545.5, used; 552.36, down.; 553.24, system,; 558.20, "the; 559.38, Professors; 567.7, way; 570.19, President's; 587.31, Forces.; 636.11, This.

Notes

In the notes below, the reference numbers denote page and line of this volume (the line count includes chapter headings). No note is made for material included in standard desk references. Biblical quotations are keyed to the King James Version. Quotations from Shakespeare are keyed to *The Riverside Shakespeare*, ed. G. Blakemore Evans (Boston: Houghton Mifflin, 1974).

WHEN SHE WAS GOOD

16.1   Eastern Star] Masonic organization for women.

57.10–11   "My worthy . . . sharp."] Robert Burns, "Second Epistle To J. Lapraik" (1785), lines 43–44.

59.17   Four Freedoms] In his 1941 State of the Union address, Franklin D. Roosevelt declared, "We look forward to a world founded upon four essential human freedoms": freedom of speech and expression, freedom of every person to worship God in his own way, freedom from fear, and freedom from want.

61.21   The guy . . . enemy] Brigadier General Anthony McAuliffe (1898–1975), acting commander of the American Army's 101st Airborne Division when the Germans encircled the Belgian town of Bastogne during the Battle of the Bulge. On December 22, 1944, when given an ultimatum to surrender by the Germans and cede Bastogne, McAuliffe replied, "Nuts!" The Americans held the town until reinforcements arrived four days later. McAuliffe's remark was highly publicized.

67.21   Linda Darnell] American actress (1923–1965) who starred as Amber in *Forever Amber* (1947).

76.13   Fritz Reiner] Hungarian-born American musician (1888–1963), conductor and musical director of the Chicago Symphony Orchestra from 1953 to 1963.

83.39–40   Dick Haymes] Singer, radio personality, and movie actor (1916–1980).

84.5   Vaughn Monroe] Band leader and singer (1911–1973).

92.38   along with Margaret Whiting] Pop singer (b. 1924), singing Billy Reid's "A Tree in the Meadow."

108.16–17　　*Song of Bernadette*]　Movie adaptation (1943) starring Jennifer Jones of Franz Werfel's 1941 novel about Bernadette Soubirous (1844–1879), a French peasant girl whose visions in the town of Lourdes were widely believed to be visitations of the Virgin Mary.

152.5–6　　Smart lad . . . stay]　A. E. Housman, "To an Athlete Dying Young."

PORTNOY'S COMPLAINT

279.37　　*bonditt*]　Bandit, rogue.

282.27　　*shkotzim*]　Plural of *shegetz*, disparaging term for a non-Jewish boy or young man.

286.25–26　　I would never . . . dish]　I.e., violate kosher laws, which prohibit eating dairy products off a dish meant for meat or meat products off a dish meant for dairy.

292.38　　*Chazerai*]　Pig's feed, anything rotten, junk food.

293.30　　*pisher*]　Little squirt.

312.38　　Bund]　The German American Bund, an American Nazi group, was active in New York and New Jersey in the years before World War II.

322.14　　*genug*!]　Enough.

322.30–31　　*b'nai* or *boruch*]　Hebrew blessings.

322.31　　Boruch atoh Adonai]　"Blessed are you, Lord," the words that begin the Sabbath prayer.

329.15　　*rachmones*]　Mercy, compassion, pity.

333.6　　*shmutzig*]　Soiled, dirty.

334.38　　*shmattas*]　Rags. Worthless objects.

337.26　　*shrying*]　Crying.

338.28　　*punim*]　Face.

339.3　　"Allen's Alley,"]　Comic "alley" peopled with stock characters featured on the radio show of comedian Fred Allen (1894–1956).

339.24–25　　"*Shmendrick*,"]　An incompetent or foolish person.

341.1　　*Shicker*]　Drinker. Drunk.

343.23　　Markfield]　Wallace Markfield (1926–2002), author of *To an Early Grave* (1964).

344.7　　José Iturbi]　Spanish-born American pianist (1895–1980).

346.18   *Exodus*] Popular movie epic (1960) based on the 1957 novel by Leon Uris about the founding of the state of Israel, with a heroic "classical" score by Ernest Gold.

353.36   the television quiz scandal] In 1958, the New York District Attorney's office convened a grand jury to evaluate accusations of rigging and fraud on TV quiz shows such as *Dotto* and *Twenty-One*. More than 150 witnesses, mostly contestants, testified to the grand jury, many of whom lied under oath about the honesty and fairness of the programs. When Judge Mitchell Schweitzer took the unusual step of sealing the grand jury testimony from the public, the House Subcommittee on Legislative Oversight held hearings about the alleged fraud. The hearings revealed that some contestants had been shown questions ahead of time and had been provided with the answers. Charles Van Doren, the son of a prominent literary family who had achieved national stardom for his performance on *Twenty-One*, pleaded guilty to charges of perjury committed while giving his grand-jury testimony. Seventeen other quiz-show contestants and a television producer were also convicted. All received suspended sentences.

354.17   Sam Levenson] American humorist and author (1911–1980) known for best-sellers such as *Sex and the Single Child* (1969).

354.22   Myron Cohen] Dialect comedian (1902–1986).

367.35–36   Rankin . . . Coughlin] John Elliott Rankin (1882–1960), a 16-term congressman from Mississippi's First District, was a racial demagogue. Theodore G. Bilbo (1877–1947) served terms as Mississippi governor and U.S. senator and advocated white supremacy. Martin Dies (1901–1972), Texas congressman who served as the first chairman of the House Un-American Activities Committee from 1938 to 1945. Gerald Lyman Kenneth Smith (1898–1976), Christian fundamentalist preacher and supporter of extreme right-wing organizations. Charles Coughlin (1891–1979), a Catholic priest and popular radio broadcaster during the 1930s who made anti-Semitic and pro-fascist statements in his broadcasts.

368.5   America First] Isolationist group established in 1940 to oppose American involvement in World War II; its most visible and notorious public spokesman was Charles Lindbergh.

368.31   *shvantz*] Tail, penis. Variant of *shmuck*.

370.17   that *U.S.A.*] Trilogy of novels (1930, 1932, 1936) by John Dos Passos (1896–1970).

378.11–15   like Henry . . . *Judy*] Henry Aldrich and Homer J. Brown were characters on the Aldrich family radio show, first aired on NBC in 1939. *The Great Gildersleeve* was a radio comedy show first aired on NBC in 1941. Corliss Archer on radio and Veronica in the comics were portrayed as typical teenage girls of the 1940s. Oogie Pringle was a teenage paperboy on the radio, and also Judy's boyfriend in the 1948 film *A Date with Judy*, with Wallace Beery, Elizabeth Taylor, and Jane Powell.

379.3–4 Ann . . . Faye] Ann Rutherford (b. 1920) played Andy Hardy's girlfriend in the movies. Alice Faye (1912–1998) was a singer, film actress, and radio personality.

382.28–34 Debbie . . . Harris] Actor and singer Eddie Fisher (b. 1928) was married to actress Debbie Reynolds from 1955 to 1959; playwright Arthur Miller (1915–2005) was married to Marilyn Monroe from 1956 to 1961; Alice Faye hosted an NBC radio show with her husband, the bandleader and comic Phil Harris (1904–1995).

382.35 marry one] Samuel Brody, a lawyer serving as Mansfield's manager when both were killed in a car accident on June 30, 1967.

383.4 Mike Todd] Elizabeth Taylor's third husband, the movie producer Mike Todd (1910–1958), died in a plane crash on March 22, 1958. The following year Taylor married Eddie Fisher, Todd's close friend.

383.12 *shaygets*] See note 282.27.

384.4 Harry . . . *Plain*] Harry Golden's book, *For 2¢ Plain* (1959) is a sentimental account of Jewish life on New York's Lower East Side. "2¢ Plain" is a colloquial reference to seltzer water.

388.24 Eddie Waitkus!] Philadelphia Phillies' first baseman Eddie Waitkus was shot by a female admirer in his Chicago hotel room in 1949.

394.21 Glen Taylor] Henry Wallace's running mate in Wallace's unsuccessful campaign for president in 1948.

396.4 A.V.C.] American Veterans Committee, organized in 1945 by men and women who had served in the armed forces during World War II.

396.33 Billy Eckstine collars] Billy Eckstine (1914–1993), baritone singer of jazz ballads, started a fashion craze with his "Mr. B" custom shirts with pique collars and French cuffs.

398.9–10 Pupi . . . Valdez] Pupi Campo was an Afro-Cuban orchestra leader. Tito Valdez is a conflation of Tito Puente and Carlos "Patato" Valdez, two Latin music stars.

398.26 Thirty Worth] Thirty Worth Street in Manhattan, a New York City government building.

399.26 *noch*] Even.

405.22 Joseph K.] Tormented and persecuted protagonist of Kafka's novels *The Trial* (1917) and *The Castle* (1926).

405.25   Gracie Mansion]   Mayor's residence in New York City.

407.3–4   swelling the gourd (John Keats)]   Cf. Keats, "Ode to Autumn."

410.29   poem.]   "Leda and the Swan," by William Butler Yeats.

411.22–23   "The Force . . . Flower."]   By Dylan Thomas.

417.15   *shande*]   Disgrace, shame.

421.37–422.3   *Let Us Now* . . . photographs]   In summer 1936, writer James Agee (1909–1955) and photographer Walker Evans (1903–1975) traveled through the American South for a story on sharecropping on assignment for *Fortune* magazine. Their work was rejected by the magazine but was published as the collaborative book *Let Us Now Praise Famous Men* (1941), which Agee described as a "photographic and verbal record of the daily living and environment of an average white family of tenant farmers."

422.8   Adamic's *Dynamite!*]   Journalist and novelist Louis Adamic (1899–1951) published *Dynamite: A Century of Class Violence in America (1830–1930)* in 1934.

422.17   Molly Maguires]   Secret organization formed within the Ancient Order of Hibernians which gained power in Pennsylvania anthracite coal fields in the 1870s; it was accused of committing criminal acts against officials considered unfair to labor, and key leaders of the organization were arrested in 1876.

422.17   Wobblies]   Members of the Industrial Workers of the World, revolutionary socialist industrial union founded in 1905.

422.20–21   Mortimer Snerd . . . Bergen]   Mortimer Snerd was ventriloquist Edgar Bergen's (1903–1978) second dummy. Snerd joined Charlie McCarthy on Bergen's radio show in 1939.

424.34   Aly Khan's]   Prince Aly Khan (1911–1960) was the son of Aga Khan, spiritual leader of millions of Asian and African Muslims and self-proclaimed descendant of the Prophet Mohammed. Prince Aly married American actress Rita Hayworth in 1949.

430.25   *vantz*]   Bedbug. An insignificant person. Pest.

433.6   *vuh den?*]   What else?

434.25–26   *By the waters . . . Zion!*]   Psalm 137.1.

436.26   *shtunk*]   A stinkin' nobody.

438.37–38   House subcommittee . . . scandals]   See note 353.36.

439.7   *gonif*]   Thief.

439.12   Stern gang]   In 1940, Avraham Stern (1907–1942) organized Lehi (Fighters for the Freedom of Israel). Called the "Stern Gang," Lehi was committed to an armed struggle for the independence of British Mandate Palestine and the creation of a Jewish state. The Stern Gang was feared for its lethal attacks on British targets.

441.20   Colin Kelly]   On December 10, 1941, Captain Colin Kelly (14th Bomb Squadron, 19th Bomb Group), with his B-17C crew, destroyed the Japanese cruiser *Ashigara* deep in enemy waters. His plane was shot down while returning to Clark Field in the Philippines. On the orders of General Douglas MacArthur, Kelly was awarded posthumously the Distinguished Flying Cross for sacrificing his life to save his crew.

442.25   Desdemona . . . Anthropapagi]   See *Othello*, I.iii.494–5.

445.33–34   Connie Mack . . . Panama hat]   Dapper baseball manager Cornelius Alexander (Connie) Mack (1862–1956) managed the Philadelphia Athletics from 1901 until his retirement at the age of 88. He won nine pennants and five World Series, and holds the record for wins (3,776) by a manager.

446.4   *pisk*]   Mouth. Perjoratively, a big mouth, braggart.

447.21   *kvell*]   Delighted with happiness and pride.

449.24   *oysgemitchet*]   Tired to death from work.

451.40–452.2   "The eternal . . . misery—"]   Lines from "Dover Beach" by English poet Mathew Arnold (1822–1888).

452.16   Profumo]   John Dennis Profumo (b. 1915), Conservative member of Parliament. In 1963, Profumo resigned from Prime Minister Harold MacMillan's cabinet (in which he served as Secretary of State for War) after the public disclosure of his affair with a teenager, Christine Keeler, who was at the same time involved with a Soviet naval attaché.

453.2   Hadassah]   American Zionist women's organization.

454.7   *Ronald Colman*]   British actor (1891–1958), a leading man in many American films.

457.30   *zaftig*]   Pleasantly plump, busty.

459.16–17   quiz-scandal hearings]   See note 353.36.

462.36   Doctor Kronkite]   Dr. Kronkheit was a character of the Jewish vaudeville act Smith and Dale, featured in the dialect skit "Dr. Kronkheit and His Only Living Patient."

463.25   *tsatskeleh*]   Cute doll of a woman.

466.6   Victory Garden] To build patriotism and encourage conservation during World War II, Americans were encouraged to plant "Gardens for Victory."

466.14   Four Freedoms!] See note 59.17.

466.15   Yalta and Dumbarton Oaks!] The Yalta Conference, February 4–11, 1945, brought together Churchill, Roosevelt, and Stalin to discuss how to re-establish the nations of Europe after the inevitable German defeat. The Dumbarton Oaks Conference, named for the mansion in Washington, D.C., where it took place, was a series of meetings that led to the creation of the United Nations.

466.16   U.N.O.] United Nations Organization.

OUR GANG

The short prefaces printed below were written by Roth for two special Bantam paperback editions of *Our Gang* that appeared in 1973 and 1974. The "Watergate Edition" preface (May 9, 1973) and the preface to the "Pre-Impeachment Edition" (May 8, 1974) are in part the author's reactions to some of the negative commentary about *Our Gang* after it was first published by Random House in the fall of 1971. In an editorial, *Time* (October 25, 1971) called the novel a "manically scurrilous satire" and accused the author of being "extravagantly hostile." *The New Republic* in an unsigned review (November 6, 1971) criticized Roth's sense of "decorum" in that he made "no effort to disguise" the fact that his "target" was Richard M. Nixon, President of the United States.

The novel's scathing portrayal of the Nixon administration pre-dated the damning revelations from the Senate Select Committee on Presidential Campaign Activities that investigated Watergate (May 17–August 7, 1973), Vice President Spiro T. Agnew's resignation (October 10, 1973), and the House Judiciary Committee's presidential impeachment hearings (July 24–30, 1974). Richard M. Nixon formally resigned the presidency at noon on August 9, 1974.

PREFACE TO THE WATERGATE EDITION

My publisher has asked me if there is any statement I should like to make about my 1971 Nixon book, *Our Gang*, as a result of what I read in the press and see on television about the Watergate scandal. Yes, there is. I wish publicly to apologize to President Nixon. Only now do I realize that I had no right whatsoever to depict him back then, if only in fiction, as a moral hypocrite, a lawless opportunist, a shameless liar, and a thorough-going totalitarian at heart. What evidence did I have to support such a fantasy? My fellow Americans, what evidence did any of us have? Did we have a wire-tap on the White House phones that gave us reason to portray Nixon with such viciousness? I am afraid the answer is we did not. Did we have records and reports burglarized from White House file cabinets? I am afraid once again the answer is no. Did we have depositions taken from White House employees that cast doubt upon the President's probity? Once again, no. Did we have so much as a single unsubstantiated charge made by a White House aide to save his own neck by turning on his boss? No, we did not. We—alas, I—had nothing even faintly resembling the incriminating kind of evidence that is now to be found every morning in the daily newspaper and every night on the evening news. Nonetheless, without a single shred of the sort of evidence with which we are presently being bombarded, I went ahead and concocted out of whole cloth this fantasy in which the President of the United States of America is held up to ridicule and scorn. How I could have permitted myself to go off on this bender of cynicism and paranoia is, I fear, something only a psychiatrist can explain. I think I will break into the office of one at midnight tonight, and ask for help.

In the meantime, I announce publicly that I am sorry for any pain or embarrassment that my hostile, malicious, and, for all I may discover, pathological imaginings may have caused the President and his family. For whatever damage I may have inflicted upon the Office of the Presidency, I will of course have to answer to the American people. Let me say to them, in the President's own words: "The responsibility belongs here. I accept it." To do otherwise would be, as the President himself said, "cowardly."

Philip Roth

May 9, 1973

PREFACE TO THE PRE-IMPEACHMENT EDITION

Just a year ago, at the time of the Watergate Hearings, my publisher asked if I would contribute an introduction to a special "Watergate Edition" of *Our Gang*, my 1971 satire of the Nixon administration. Now, as a result of the release and publication of *The White House Transcripts*, Bantam Books is no longer "asking" me for introductions—they are demanding an explanation. To be sure, they have no quarrel with me about the depiction of "Tricky," the U.S. President of *Our Gang*. Apparently they have compared the candid exchanges between President Nixon and his advisers in the transcripts to those between Tricky and his friends in *Our Gang* and have concluded that I did not in any way attempt a whitewash of presidential wrongdoing, nor did I try to represent the President and his advisers as any less crooked, or any smarter, than they come off in the transcripts. What disturbs them about *Our Gang* is that in it I failed to give any indication whatsoever of the profanities that apparently punctuate President Nixon's conversation. Indeed, not only did I delete the expletives favored by the President, I even deleted the bracketed phrase "expletive deleted." In short, I stand accused by Bantam Books of taking part in a "cover-up" of the President's dirty mouth—what is worse, I allegedly did this in a book that was submitted to them as a no-holds-barred political satire. There are even those who would have me now "come clean" by inserting into the President's mouth the words that rightfully belong there.

In my defense let me first off assure the American reading public that I at no time had any prior knowledge of the President's fondness for foul language. I had no more reason than any other American to believe that the close associate of President Eisenhower, the Quaker who attends Sunday worship services in the White House conducted by Billy Graham, Tricia's father, Pat's husband, David Eisenhower's father-in-law, could possibly use language as indecent—well, to be utterly candid about it, as indecent as the language in some of my own fiction. I am, of course, willing to take full responsibility for whatever I may inadvertently have done to mislead the American people about their President. But as for inserting dirty words into the President's mouth, let me make one thing perfectly clear. I have no doubt that that might be the popular thing for me to do at this point in time. But I for one do not intend to jump on a man when he is down, renowned [expletive deleted] that he may be.

Philip Roth
May 8, 1974

475.16–17   Lieutenant Calley . . . My Lai] In March 1968, 24-year-old Lieutenant William Calley was a platoon leader in charge of Charlie Company, American Division's 11th Infantry Brigade. In the central Vietnamese village of My Lai, Calley and his men murdered between 200 and 500 unarmed civilians. For his involvement in the incident Calley was charged with four specifications of premeditated murder: the murder of at least 30 noncombatants at the south end of the village; the murder of at least 70 civilians in a ditch; the murder of a South Vietnamese man in white robes (who may have been a monk) with his hands raised; and assault with intent to murder a small child. On March 29, 1971, after the longest court-martial in American history, Calley was found guilty of the premeditated murder of at least 22 civilians at My Lai. Two days later he was sentenced to life imprisonment at hard labor; President Nixon immediately ordered that Calley be released from the stockade and placed under house arrest at Fort Benning, Georgia, while his conviction was appealed. Calley's sentence was reduced on administrative appeal to 20 years imprisonment in August 1971 and to ten years in April 1974; he was paroled on November 9, 1974. Ten other soldiers from Charlie Company were charged for crimes committed at My Lai; one was acquitted at court-martial and the charges against the other nine were dismissed. Colonel Oran Henderson, the former commander of the 11th Brigade, was court-martialed for his role in concealing the massacre and acquitted on December 17, 1971. Similar charges brought against 13 other officers, including Major General Samuel Koster, the former commander of the American Division, were dismissed.

489.14 *the Cambodian incursion*] In spring 1970, President Nixon and his national security adviser, Henry Kissinger, ordered American troops across Vietnam's border with Cambodia. On April 30, 1970, Nixon went on television to announce the "incursion" (invasion) into Cambodia and his intention to "clean out" bases that the enemy had been using for "increasing military aggression." In addition, the President sent B-52s to bomb the Ho Chi Minh Trail, the enemy's principal supply route in Cambodia and Vietnam. This was a major escalation of the Vietnam War.

489.15 *Kent State killings*] On May 4, 1970, there was a student demonstration at Kent State University in Ohio to protest the "incursion" into Cambodia and the widening war in Vietnam. Ohio governor James Rhodes ordered the National Guard to keep the peace. The guardsmen, untrained for riot duty, panicked and fired on the crowd of protestors, wounding 13 and killing four.

489.24 Six Hundred Crises] Cf. Nixon's *Six Crises* (1962).

489.24–25 *"cool, confident, and decisive."*] See the chapter on Alger Hiss in *Six Crises*: "The ability to be cool, confident, and decisive in a crisis is not an inherited characteristic but is the direct result of how well the individual has prepared himself for the battle."

489.27 *riots . . . Caracas*] On May 13, 1958, during a state visit to Caracas, Venezuela, Nixon's car was attacked by anti-American demonstrators.

490.25–26 Vietnam soreheads . . . medals in] On April 23, 1971, during an antiwar demonstration in Washington, D.C., led by Vietnam Veterans Against the War, about 700 veterans discarded their medals in front of the United States Capitol.

490.39–491.1 as coolly . . . kitchen] On July 24, 1959, Vice President Nixon visited the American National Exhibition in Moscow with Soviet premier Nikita Khrushchev. In an hour-long exchange in the kitchen of a model "American" house built for the exhibition, Nixon lectured the Soviet premier on the advantages of the American free enterprise system over Marxism. Nixon said, "We do not claim to astonish the Russian people. We hope to show our diversity and our right to choose. . . . Would it not be better to compete in the relative merits of washing machines than in the strength of rockets?"

491.23–26 Senator Joseph McCatastrophy . . . State Department] Joseph McCarthy (1908–1957), Republican senator from Wisconsin, chaired a Senate committee investigating communist influence in government. On February 9, 1950, in a speech in Wheeling, West Virginia, McCarthy attacked the State Department, calling Secretary of State Dean Acheson "a pompous diplomat in striped pants," and claiming that he (McCarthy) had the names of 57 people in the State Department who were members of the American Communist Party. On other occasions he cited different numbers of communists in the department.

491.26   Judge Carswell] In January 1970, Nixon nominated federal appeals court judge G. Harrold Carswell to the Supreme Court. Soon afterward it was revealed that Judge Carswell, in a 1948 speech given while campaigning for the Georgia legislature, had declared, "I yield to no man . . . in the firm, vigorous belief in the principles of white supremacy, and I shall always be so governed." The Senate rejected the nomination 51–45 in April 1970.

491.27   Judge Haynsworth] The Senate rejected the Supreme Court nomination of federal appeals court judge Clement F. Haynsworth 55–45 in November 1969; concerns about Haynsworth's ethics and his opposition to civil rights were largely responsible for his defeat.

491.28   what they tried . . . Lard] At a press conference in February 1971, less than a month after the beginning of a U.S.-backed South Vietnamese offensive into Laos, Defense Secretary Melvin Laird showed reporters a fragment of an oil pipeline running along the Ho Chi Minh Trail, giving the impression that the pipeline was recently cut and thus an example of the South Vietnamese new success in disrupting the North Vietnamese supply line. It was revealed the following week that the piece of pipeline had been taken in an old raid, well before the South Vietnamese offensive. Laird was criticized for fostering a misleading impression.

494.8–11   Alger Hiss . . . perjurer!] Alger Hiss (1904–1996) held several positions in the New Deal Administration of Franklin D. Roosevelt and began working for the State Department in 1936. He was part of the American delegation at Yalta and was present at the United Nations organizing meeting in 1945. As a freshman Republican congressman from California, Nixon was a member of the House Un-American Activities Committee (HUAC) in 1948 when it was investigating communist influence in the State Department. Nixon set his sights on Hiss, whom the Committee accused of spying after Whittaker Chambers, a former communist who had become a fierce anti-communist, approached the Committee voluntarily and accused Hiss of having been a communist infiltrator at the State Department. After a heated public confrontation between the two men, Hiss sued Chambers for slander; in testimony before a grand jury, Hiss denied Chambers' claim that he had given secret documents to him for transmittal to Moscow and testified that he had not seen Chambers after January 1937. He was then indicted on two counts of perjury. His first trial resulted in a hung jury; in a second, he was convicted of perjury and served 44 months of a five-year sentence. Nixon's national reputation as a relentless interrogator and staunch anti-communist was solidified; he later said that he would not have become vice president without the Hiss case. For his part, Hiss maintained that the allegations against him were false even after Soviet intelligence files made public in the 1990s appeared to confirm that he had worked for them as an operative.

494.36–37   when they accused you . . . Checkers Speech] Nixon was the vice-presidential candidate on the 1952 Republican ticket headed by Dwight D. Eisenhower. His future as a candidate was jeopardized when he was accused of using a secret campaign fund for his private use. On September 23, 1952, Nixon went on television to defend himself against the charges. In a short speech, he was able to turn his political liabilities to his advantage and convince Eisenhower to keep him as his running mate. The press called his performance the Checkers Speech after his reference to a "little cocker spaniel dog" that his six-year-old daughter, Tricia, was given as a gift. "And you know, the kids, like all kids, love the dog and I just want to say this right now, that regardless of what they say about it, we're gonna keep it." Tricia named him Checkers.

515.3   Phil and Dan Berrigan] Daniel Berrigan (b. 1921) and his younger brother Philip (1923–2002) were Roman Catholic priests and nonviolent antiwar protestors during America's involvement in Vietnam.

516.21   Quemoy and Matsu! . . . memories] In 1949, after Mao Tse Tung and his Communist army took over the Chinese mainland and deposed Nationalist president Chiang Kai-shek, Chiang fled with a million of his followers to Formosa (Taiwan) and to the islands of Quemoy and Matsu, eight miles off the coast of the mainland. The Communists and the Nationalists claimed the islands and nearly fought a war over them several times during the 1950s and 60s. In the 1960 American presidential campaign both candidates pledged to use American military force if necessary to defend Taiwan from attack by the People's Republic of China; during the presidential debate, Nixon charged that Kennedy would not defend the disputed islands of Quemoy and Matsu against the mainland Chinese in the event of an invasion.

520.31   Exactly as he did about Manson] The "family" of young followers of Charles Manson (b. 1934) committed a murder spree on August 9–10, 1969, at Manson's instigation. Among their victims were Sharon Tate, pregnant with director Roman Polanski's child, coffee heiress Abigail Folger, her boyfriend Wojciech Frykowski, and hair stylist Jay Sebring. On August 3, 1970, during the murder trial of Manson in Los Angeles, Nixon declared publicly that Manson "was guilty, directly or indirectly, of eight murders without reason." After being criticized for judging the case, he retreated from his remark with a "clarification" from his press secretary that he had meant to use the word "alleged" with regard to Manson's guilt and a formal statement claiming that the press had misunderstood him. Manson's lawyers argued unsuccessfully for a mistrial because of the President's remark; Manson himself, hoping to cause a mistrial, held up a newspaper in the courtroom with the headline "Mansion Guilty, Nixon Declares."

521.4–5   Musty . . . Maine] Former Maine governor Edmund Muskie (1914–1996) served in the U.S. Senate (1958–1980) and was the Democratic vice-presidential candidate in 1968. In 1972, he ran for the Democratic Party nomination for president.

524.17   the song] "A Cockeyed Optimist," from the Rodgers and Hammerstein musical *South Pacific* (1949): "So they called me a cockeyed optimist . . . I hear the human race / Is fallin' on its face / And hasn't very far to go, / But ev'ry whippoorwill / Is sellin' me a bill, / And tellin' me it just ain't so."

525.21   *Patton*] Heroic film biography (1970) of World War II general George S. Patton. Nixon said it was his favorite film and it was screened at the White House several times during his presidency.

535.36–38   the scandal . . . last administration] An attempt to slander the Johnson administration over the activities of Abe Fortas, associate justice of the Supreme Court and a Democratic political ally. Lyndon Johnson had nominated Fortas (1910–1982) for the Court's "Jewish seat" on July 28, 1965, after associate justice Arthur Goldberg (1908–1990), at Johnson's request, stepped down and was appointed Ambassador to the United Nations. Fortas resigned from the Court on May 14, 1969, because of charges that he had taken $20,000 from a foundation controlled by Louis Wolfson, a financier who was being investigated for violating federal securities laws.

538.17–18   verdict . . . Black Panther Party] In 1971, 13 members of the militant Black Panther Party were tried and acquitted in New York City of conspiring to bomb public places.

565.15   Erect Severehead] Eric Severeid was a veteran radio and television newsman. He first established his reputation as a young man broadcasting from London with Edward R. Murrow during the Blitz (1940).

567.21   Roger Rising-to-the-Occasion] Roger Mudd, CBS News television reporter. As in other instances cited below, the President is willfully mutilating the names of prominent reporters.

568.16   Morton Momentous] Morton Dean of CBS News.

569.25   Peter Pious] Peter Jennings of ABC News.

570.11–12   Ike Ironic] Ike Pappas of CBS News.

571.23   Congressman Fraud] Gerald R. Ford (b. 1913), 38th President of the United States, spent 25 years in Congress. From 1965 to 1973, Ford was House Minority Leader.

584.3   *Reverend Billy Cupcake*] Reverend Billy Graham (b. 1918), an evangelical minister and spiritual adviser to presidents.

585.34   Ritz Brothers] Alfred (1901–1965), Jimmy (1904–1985), and Harry (1907–1986) were the Ritz Brothers comedy team. Ritz was a theatrical name for Joachim.

592.2–3   "he speaks . . . lies."] John 8:44.

THE BREAST

634.4–5   "The Necklace" . . . "The Luck of Roaring Camp."] Stories by Guy de Maupassant and Bret Harte, respectively.

636.10–11   handsome . . . Massachusetts] Republican Edward Brooke (b. 1919), elected to the first of two terms in the U.S. Senate in 1966, was the first African-American senator elected by popular vote.

Library of Congress Cataloging-in-Publication Data

Roth, Philip.
  [Novels. Selections]
  Novels, 1967–1972 / Philip Roth.
      p. cm. — (The Library of America ; 158)
  Includes bibliographical references.
  Contents: When she was good—Portnoy's complaint—Our
gang—The breast.
  ISBN 1–931082–80–4 (alk. paper)
          I. Title: When she was good. II. Title: Portnoy's complaint.
III. Title: Our gang. IV. Title: Breast. V. Title. VI. Series.

PS3568.O855A6   2005
813'.54—dc22   2005040917

THE LIBRARY OF AMERICA SERIES

The Library of America fosters appreciation and pride in America's literary heritage by publishing, and keeping permanently in print, authoritative editions of America's best and most significant writing. An independent nonprofit organization, it was founded in 1979 with seed money from the National Endowment for the Humanities and the Ford Foundation.

1. Herman Melville, *Typee, Omoo, Mardi* (1982)
2. Nathaniel Hawthorne, *Tales and Sketches* (1982)
3. Walt Whitman, *Poetry and Prose* (1982)
4. Harriet Beecher Stowe, *Three Novels* (1982)
5. Mark Twain, *Mississippi Writings* (1982)
6. Jack London, *Novels and Stories* (1982)
7. Jack London, *Novels and Social Writings* (1982)
8. William Dean Howells, *Novels 1875–1886* (1982)
9. Herman Melville, *Redburn, White-Jacket, Moby-Dick* (1983)
10. Nathaniel Hawthorne, *Collected Novels* (1983)
11. Francis Parkman, *France and England in North America*, vol. I (1983)
12. Francis Parkman, *France and England in North America*, vol. II (1983)
13. Henry James, *Novels 1871–1880* (1983)
14. Henry Adams, *Novels, Mont Saint Michel, The Education* (1983)
15. Ralph Waldo Emerson, *Essays and Lectures* (1983)
16. Washington Irving, *History, Tales and Sketches* (1983)
17. Thomas Jefferson, *Writings* (1984)
18. Stephen Crane, *Prose and Poetry* (1984)
19. Edgar Allan Poe, *Poetry and Tales* (1984)
20. Edgar Allan Poe, *Essays and Reviews* (1984)
21. Mark Twain, *The Innocents Abroad, Roughing It* (1984)
22. Henry James, *Literary Criticism: Essays, American & English Writers* (1984)
23. Henry James, *Literary Criticism: European Writers & The Prefaces* (1984)
24. Herman Melville, *Pierre, Israel Potter, The Confidence-Man, Tales & Billy Budd* (1985)
25. William Faulkner, *Novels 1930–1935* (1985)
26. James Fenimore Cooper, *The Leatherstocking Tales*, vol. I (1985)
27. James Fenimore Cooper, *The Leatherstocking Tales*, vol. II (1985)
28. Henry David Thoreau, *A Week, Walden, The Maine Woods, Cape Cod* (1985)
29. Henry James, *Novels 1881–1886* (1985)
30. Edith Wharton, *Novels* (1986)
31. Henry Adams, *History of the U.S. during the Administrations of Jefferson* (1986)
32. Henry Adams, *History of the U.S. during the Administrations of Madison* (1986)
33. Frank Norris, *Novels and Essays* (1986)
34. W.E.B. Du Bois, *Writings* (1986)
35. Willa Cather, *Early Novels and Stories* (1987)
36. Theodore Dreiser, *Sister Carrie, Jennie Gerhardt, Twelve Men* (1987)
37. Benjamin Franklin, *Writings* (1987)
38. William James, *Writings 1902–1910* (1987)
39. Flannery O'Connor, *Collected Works* (1988)
40. Eugene O'Neill, *Complete Plays 1913–1920* (1988)
41. Eugene O'Neill, *Complete Plays 1920–1931* (1988)
42. Eugene O'Neill, *Complete Plays 1932–1943* (1988)
43. Henry James, *Novels 1886–1890* (1989)
44. William Dean Howells, *Novels 1886–1888* (1989)
45. Abraham Lincoln, *Speeches and Writings 1832–1858* (1989)
46. Abraham Lincoln, *Speeches and Writings 1859–1865* (1989)
47. Edith Wharton, *Novellas and Other Writings* (1990)
48. William Faulkner, *Novels 1936–1940* (1990)
49. Willa Cather, *Later Novels* (1990)
50. Ulysses S. Grant, *Memoirs and Selected Letters* (1990)

51. William Tecumseh Sherman, *Memoirs* (1990)
52. Washington Irving, *Bracebridge Hall, Tales of a Traveller, The Alhambra* (1991)
53. Francis Parkman, *The Oregon Trail, The Conspiracy of Pontiac* (1991)
54. James Fenimore Cooper, *Sea Tales: The Pilot, The Red Rover* (1991)
55. Richard Wright, *Early Works* (1991)
56. Richard Wright, *Later Works* (1991)
57. Willa Cather, *Stories, Poems, and Other Writings* (1992)
58. William James, *Writings 1878–1899* (1992)
59. Sinclair Lewis, *Main Street & Babbitt* (1992)
60. Mark Twain, *Collected Tales, Sketches, Speeches, & Essays 1852–1890* (1992)
61. Mark Twain, *Collected Tales, Sketches, Speeches, & Essays 1891–1910* (1992)
62. *The Debate on the Constitution: Part One* (1993)
63. *The Debate on the Constitution: Part Two* (1993)
64. Henry James, *Collected Travel Writings: Great Britain & America* (1993)
65. Henry James, *Collected Travel Writings: The Continent* (1993)
66. *American Poetry: The Nineteenth Century,* Vol. 1 (1993)
67. *American Poetry: The Nineteenth Century,* Vol. 2 (1993)
68. Frederick Douglass, *Autobiographies* (1994)
69. Sarah Orne Jewett, *Novels and Stories* (1994)
70. Ralph Waldo Emerson, *Collected Poems and Translations* (1994)
71. Mark Twain, *Historical Romances* (1994)
72. John Steinbeck, *Novels and Stories 1932–1937* (1994)
73. William Faulkner, *Novels 1942–1954* (1994)
74. Zora Neale Hurston, *Novels and Stories* (1995)
75. Zora Neale Hurston, *Folklore, Memoirs, and Other Writings* (1995)
76. Thomas Paine, *Collected Writings* (1995)
77. *Reporting World War II: American Journalism 1938–1944* (1995)
78. *Reporting World War II: American Journalism 1944–1946* (1995)
79. Raymond Chandler, *Stories and Early Novels* (1995)
80. Raymond Chandler, *Later Novels and Other Writings* (1995)
81. Robert Frost, *Collected Poems, Prose, & Plays* (1995)
82. Henry James, *Complete Stories 1892–1898* (1996)
83. Henry James, *Complete Stories 1898–1910* (1996)
84. William Bartram, *Travels and Other Writings* (1996)
85. John Dos Passos, *U.S.A.* (1996)
86. John Steinbeck, *The Grapes of Wrath and Other Writings 1936–1941* (1996)
87. Vladimir Nabokov, *Novels and Memoirs 1941–1951* (1996)
88. Vladimir Nabokov, *Novels 1955–1962* (1996)
89. Vladimir Nabokov, *Novels 1969–1974* (1996)
90. James Thurber, *Writings and Drawings* (1996)
91. George Washington, *Writings* (1997)
92. John Muir, *Nature Writings* (1997)
93. Nathanael West, *Novels and Other Writings* (1997)
94. *Crime Novels: American Noir of the 1930s and 40s* (1997)
95. *Crime Novels: American Noir of the 1950s* (1997)
96. Wallace Stevens, *Collected Poetry and Prose* (1997)
97. James Baldwin, *Early Novels and Stories* (1998)
98. James Baldwin, *Collected Essays* (1998)
99. Gertrude Stein, *Writings 1903–1932* (1998)
100. Gertrude Stein, *Writings 1932–1946* (1998)
101. Eudora Welty, *Complete Novels* (1998)
102. Eudora Welty, *Stories, Essays, & Memoir* (1998)
103. Charles Brockden Brown, *Three Gothic Novels* (1998)
104. *Reporting Vietnam: American Journalism 1959–1969* (1998)
105. *Reporting Vietnam: American Journalism 1969–1975* (1998)
106. Henry James, *Complete Stories 1874–1884* (1999)
107. Henry James, *Complete Stories 1884–1891* (1999)

108. *American Sermons: The Pilgrims to Martin Luther King Jr.* (1999)
109. James Madison, *Writings* (1999)
110. Dashiell Hammett, *Complete Novels* (1999)
111. Henry James, *Complete Stories 1864–1874* (1999)
112. William Faulkner, *Novels 1957–1962* (1999)
113. John James Audubon, *Writings & Drawings* (1999)
114. *Slave Narratives* (2000)
115. *American Poetry: The Twentieth Century,* Vol. 1 (2000)
116. *American Poetry: The Twentieth Century,* Vol. 2 (2000)
117. F. Scott Fitzgerald, *Novels and Stories 1920–1922* (2000)
118. Henry Wadsworth Longfellow, *Poems and Other Writings* (2000)
119. Tennessee Williams, *Plays 1937–1955* (2000)
120. Tennessee Williams, *Plays 1957–1980* (2000)
121. Edith Wharton, *Collected Stories 1891–1910* (2001)
122. Edith Wharton, *Collected Stories 1911–1937* (2001)
123. *The American Revolution: Writings from the War of Independence* (2001)
124. Henry David Thoreau, *Collected Essays and Poems* (2001)
125. Dashiell Hammett, *Crime Stories and Other Writings* (2001)
126. Dawn Powell, *Novels 1930–1942* (2001)
127. Dawn Powell, *Novels 1944–1962* (2001)
128. Carson McCullers, *Complete Novels* (2001)
129. Alexander Hamilton, *Writings* (2001)
130. Mark Twain, *The Gilded Age and Later Novels* (2002)
131. Charles W. Chesnutt, *Stories, Novels, and Essays* (2002)
132. John Steinbeck, *Novels 1942–1952* (2002)
133. Sinclair Lewis, *Arrowsmith, Elmer Gantry, Dodsworth* (2002)
134. Paul Bowles, *The Sheltering Sky, Let It Come Down, The Spider's House* (2002)
135. Paul Bowles, *Collected Stories & Later Writings* (2002)
136. Kate Chopin, *Complete Novels & Stories* (2002)
137. *Reporting Civil Rights: American Journalism 1941–1963* (2003)
138. *Reporting Civil Rights: American Journalism 1963–1973* (2003)
139. Henry James, *Novels 1896–1899* (2003)
140. Theodore Dreiser, *An American Tragedy* (2003)
141. Saul Bellow, *Novels 1944–1953* (2003)
142. John Dos Passos, *Novels 1920–1925* (2003)
143. John Dos Passos, *Travel Books and Other Writings* (2003)
144. Ezra Pound, *Poems and Translations* (2003)
145. James Weldon Johnson, *Writings* (2004)
146. Washington Irving, *Three Western Narratives* (2004)
147. Alexis de Tocqueville, *Democracy in America* (2004)
148. James T. Farrell, *Studs Lonigan: A Trilogy* (2004)
149. Isaac Bashevis Singer, *Collected Stories I* (2004)
150. Isaac Bashevis Singer, *Collected Stories II* (2004)
151. Isaac Bashevis Singer, *Collected Stories III* (2004)
152. Kaufman & Co., *Broadway Comedies* (2004)
153. Theodore Roosevelt, *The Rough Riders, An Autobiography* (2004)
154. Theodore Roosevelt, *Letters and Speeches* (2004)
155. H. P. Lovecraft, *Tales* (2005)
156. Louisa May Alcott, *Little Women, Little Men, Jo's Boys* (2005)
157. Philip Roth, *Novels & Stories 1959–1962* (2005)
158. Philip Roth, *Novels 1967–1972* (2005)
159. James Agee, *Let Us Now Praise Famous Men, A Death in the Family* (2005)
160. James Agee, *Film Writing & Selected Journalism* (2005)
161. Richard Henry Dana, Jr., *Two Years Before the Mast & Other Voyages* (2005)

This book is set in 10 point Linotron Galliard,
a face designed for photocomposition by Matthew Carter
and based on the sixteenth-century face Granjon. The paper
is acid-free Domtar Literary Opaque and meets the requirements
for permanence of the American National Standards Institute. The
binding material is Brillianta, a woven rayon cloth made by
Van Heek-Scholco Textielfabrieken, Holland. Compo-
sition by Dedicated Business Services. Printing by
Malloy Incorporated. Binding by Dekker Book-
binding. Designed by Bruce Campbell.